FOREVER ALTERED

N.W. Couillard

*To my sister, Patti, who encouraged me to write
my story. Without you nudging me along, it
would have stayed in my head forever.*

It was a lighthearted question
innocently asked ~
What would you do if first contact was made?
No one ever expected it to truly happen…

CONTENTS

CHAPTER 1

Andromeda Galaxy
Delician Battle Cruiser
June 2024

As Nox stood staring at the hologram of Earth, his eyes were drawn to the deep blue of the oceans, wondering what creatures inhabited its depths. Swirling clouds of white floated over the brown and green continents, lands untouched by any life from space, or so they had thought. He couldn't help but think that contacting Earth might not be such a good idea. They had limited technology, no light speed drives for space travel, and for a planet that had almost seven billion inhabitants on it, he personally felt they were not ready for first contact.

Fingering the holster at his hip, his laser gun at the ready like all soldiers in the Delician military were trained to be. Not that he was a soldier, he was a scientist, but in his line of work and especially on this mission, he needed to be able to protect himself. He'd never actually had to fire a weapon to defend himself, but he would if he had to. His home planet, Delicia, had been at peace for many millenniums. Earth, on the other hand, the last time they had been observed, had little to no technology and seemed more intent on killing one another than advancing their civilization. This was the reason why Earth had been placed on the prohibited planet list decades ago by the United Alliance of Planets, or the UAP as they were generally referred to. He knew they would be unable to fathom dealing with outside forces from space. If first contact was not done in the right way, widespread panic would lead to chaos, perhaps even war on this tiny blue and green ball.

He considered his current assignment and thought about why they were currently on the battle cruiser *Maelstrom.* The Hexians, the scourge of the galaxy, were creating problems—again. It seemed like there was little choice but to come to Earth's defense ever since finding out that the Hexians and their leader Tarquin had secretly been visiting Earth for who knows how long. The UAP had Tarquin constantly under surveillance, so it was shocking that he was even able to infiltrate Earth—right under the UAP's noses. Discovering his plan had caused quite a stir within the executive council of the UAP and so they decided to send a team to Earth to investigate the threat, eliminate it and then determine when and how first contact should be made, if at all.

Nox had worked for the UAP for a number of years as their director of scientific development. As their leading expert in determining the level of technological advancement in planets that were placed on the prohibited list, he would be required to give as much information to General Tarek as he could regarding Earth. Unfortunately for Earth, his other projects had required more of his time over the years and so it had been a long time since anyone had been monitoring the list. It was just by luck that they happened to find out Tarquin's vile plan for Earth's inhabitants.

Looking up from the hologram, Nox's gaze went to the bank of windows that lined one wall of the room. Tiny stars dotted the infinite dark abyss of space. Crossing his muscular arms, Nox took a wide stance as he stared out at the darkness. He loved exploring the thousands of planets across the galaxy. His mind yearned to discover all the knowledge and wonders that were out there. With a deep breath, he sighed, rubbing his hand across his eyes.

What to do, he thought. With the incoming threats from Hexia, he considered whether they had little choice but to let the humans know. As a scientist he had been successful in creating numerous scientific advancements, but his greatest so far was in force field technology for the UAP. He hoped that by using this new technology, he would be able to save Earth from the Hexians. He just needed to figure out how he would accomplish that but he was confident he would. He despised the Hexians and Tarquin. Wherever they went, there always seemed to be a path of misery and destruction left behind.

The door to the Captain's conference room suddenly opened—his assistant, Loris, came hurrying into the room. He glanced around, making sure he wasn't as late as he thought, and headed in the direction of his boss. His long brown hair, pulled back at the nape of his neck, swished back and forth as he tried not to look rushed.

"Still dwelling over that substratal planet?" Loris asked softly, trying not to be overheard.

Frowning, Nox checked his wrist comm, noting the time. "I'm glad to see someone is in a good mood today. Do you have everything we need for this meeting? You know the General is going to want all the specs."

"Well…yes, but first tell me again why we're wasting our time on such a boring planet."

Nox shook his head at his friend. "Loris, humans are far from boring. They just lack a sense of—"

"Sophisticated culture and auxiliary technology?"

"No, Loris. I—"

"Contributory obligations to the rest of the universe?" He beamed at Nox, his smile radiating a sense of pride at his superior.

"They don't have much to offer the UAP, Loris, but remember the purpose of our mission? To stand up…"

"…for inferior races that make up the galaxy. Yeah, I know."

"So, do you have all the information I asked for?" Nox questioned. He had told his assistant hours ago that he needed time to think about the necessary steps and precautions they needed to take. If they were really going to contact Earth, Nox wanted to be absolutely sure it was the right thing to do.

Nox moved to take a seat at the table; his fellow team members were already seated. He could tell by the stern look on General Tarek's face that he was ready to explode.

"The Hexian people should be eliminated outright!"

Nox hesitated before responding to the General's outburst.

Studying General Tarek's militant expression, Nox thought maybe he might not be the best person to be the face of this mission. But since Tarek was in charge, he had the final say on any decisions. Nox needed to stick to the science of the mission.

"Have we gotten any more information on the location of the Hexians, sir?"

"Had you been here the entire time instead of hiding in your lab, you would know," Tarek replied. "Staring at that hologram is not going to help with this decision."

Steeling himself, Nox remained calm despite the General's lack of understanding of his work process. Jagger, the captain of the ship, jumped to Nox's defense.

"Tarek, Director Nox has been studying how we can best use his force field technology on this mission. We are trying to figure out how we can somehow create a boundary between the Hexians and the humans." Jagger turned to Nox and gave him a nod of support.

The General took a long look at Nox. After a moment of tense silence, he sighed. Placing both hands on his hips, he gestured to the hologram. "Show me what you have learned so far."

Taking a steadying breath, Nox gathered his thoughts. "I'm still trying to determine how to best use the force fields. I'm not sure we can without making Earth aware of us and I'm still not sure involving the humans is a good thing. More than likely they won't even know what a force field is. Are you sure we should be considering making contact? I just don't see the reasoning behind it."

"Because now that the Hexians have secretly been visiting Earth, they need to be informed of this threat and taught how to defend themselves." Tarek blew out a breath, trying to contain his annoyance. "Taking into consideration their lack of technology, we're the only hope they have at this point. We're going to need to make them understand that we want to be their allies and that they are not alone. It's not going to be an easy task, but if you consider the alternatives, they're not going to have much of a choice. Besides, Tarquin is not going to leave this alone. Not when he sees all the profit he can make from the humans."

Tarek was commander of the entire Delician military fleet. Since Delicia was a major player in the United Alliance of Planets, the UAP always turned to Tarek whenever problems needed solving. General Tarek was a well-respected leader and had a reputation for being successful in achieving his goals. The UAP had specifically asked for his help when this threat was uncovered. He wasn't happy about this situation either, but now that the Hexians knew about Earth, other races were going to be following their lead. "Tarquin needs to be stopped!" Tarek ground out.

"Telling the humans that they're not alone in the universe is not going to be an easy thing. Just look at past instances from other planets," insisted Nox. "This has the potential to go very wrong if not done carefully."

"Well, it's better than the alternative," Tarek sighed, squeezing the bridge of his nose between his fingers.

Conceding to Tarek, Nox breathed out a heavy sigh. "Well, if this is your decision, I would suggest that we consider contacting them discreetly so we don't start a planet-wide panic."

"Agreed."

Nox turned to his assistant, who was seated next to him. "Loris, bring up the specs I asked for alongside a diagram of the planet Earth."

Loris began inputting commands into his console and immediately a hologram of Earth popped up in front of them.

"Hexians are ruthless criminals always looking for profit, anywhere, anyhow. Their planet doesn't even have indigenous beings," Tarek said as Nox started looking at the specs.

"Despite being a wasteland of a planet, it's located in the outer edge of the UAP territory," Captain Jagger inserted as he took a spot behind Nox's chair. Jagger was not only the captain of the *Maelstrom* but also best friends with General Tarek. He fiddled with a green glowing sphere, tossing it from hand to hand. "Even though technically they're not under our control, we still can't let them go around unchecked. They need to be made to pay for their actions."

"Yeah, well their leader, Tarquin, is lethal," Nox replied.

"He is that and much much more. Trust me. I've had more dealings with Tarquin than I have ever wanted. Hear me well, you never want to turn your back on him," Jagger told them, now tossing the sphere up with one hand and catching it with the other.

"So, what did the last message say regarding this plan of Tarquin's? Did it confirm what we already surmised?" Nox turned to Tarek as he asked his questions.

"Worse than we thought. The Hexian plan is to start with Earth's natural resources and then eventually do a total colonization of Earth. That we have already confirmed," replied General Tarek. Jagger held onto the sphere tightly as Nox looked back at him, a stunned silence was felt around the room.

"That is disgusting," Nox uttered furiously—the Hexians were so barbaric. Now he understood why General Tarek was quick to take violent measures.

Jagger resumed tossing his glowing orb into the air. "The fact that the Hexians even found Earth is something that is still unclear. And what are they looking for exactly?"

6

"You mean what have they found," replied Nyx, who had been sitting quietly at the end of the table, intently reading something on his comm unit. Commander Nyx was Tarek's second in command. His focus was solely on creating and implementing any battle strategies they might need. "It's still uncertain. I've contacted a few of our ships in the area, but they can't get a good read on the Hexian communications systems. They're being blocked out."

The door silently opened as a Delician female crewmember came through, heading towards Jagger. Her slender figure glided to a stop next to him. She was small in stature with fairylike features that were typical for all Delician women. Standing next to Jagger, who was spinning his sphere on one finger, the stark difference between the Delician males and females was vastly apparent.

"Well, if it isn't my favorite denizen of my team. Hello Marsel," he smiled at her. She smirked and before he could stop her, reached out, swiftly grabbing the glowing orb. Marsel was his science officer and he loved nothing more than to tease her. As serious as she was about her job, she was also an easy mark, although she could sometimes get the better of him.

"Hey, give that back!" Marsel tossed the ball delicately into the air in a U formation several times, catching it in the opposite hand. Jagger tried to interfere, but Marsel was too swift for him.

"I brought the latest reports on the Hexians and I think we may have figured out what they are after on Earth. It's all here for you to read, Captain," she stated while juggling. Tossing Jagger his orb back with a sly grin, she handed Nox the data key before exiting the room. Jagger grabbed the ball and held onto it with all his might, peering back at Marsel as if she had stolen his favorite toy.

General Tarek playfully slapped the back of Jagger's head. "Stop fooling around and pay attention."

Jagger rubbed the back of his head, shooting Tarek a

nasty glare.

Ignoring the interchange between his two commanding officers, Nox inserted the data that Marsel had given him into his comm unit in front of him. "ARI, display data and read back."

An emotionless voice began to speak, "Particles analyzed from Earth's atmosphere indicate that Hexians' ships have been landing in the Punjab region of Pakistan. Pakistan is a country located on the continent of Asia. The Khewra Mine in the Himalayan Mountains is Pakistan's largest and oldest salt mine on Earth. White salt is made up of sodium chloride. Himalayan pink salt contains 84 naturally occurring trace elements in their natural mineral form. Himalayan pink salt, although having no benefit to humans, can be used to create curative substances for many species throughout the galaxy."

"ARI, stop." Nox rubbed his face with his hand, not trusting himself to look around the room.

"That greedy skizoid!" Tarek was furious. He jumped to his feet and began pacing around the room. "This is the reason why Tarquin is so interested in Earth. Can you just imagine the impact this would have on planets in our sector of space?"

Nox's shocked face matched his fellow crewmembers. "Yes, sir, I can. From what I'm reading here, the benefits of just a small sample could change how medicines and vaccines are made, which would be a welcomed relief to some of our lesser advanced planets." He blew out a breath in disbelief. The number of lives that could be saved from the discovery of this substance was immeasurable.

"And the humans have no idea what type of natural material they are sitting on. This is unbelievable," Loris interjected.

"This changes everything." Tarek sat down heavily and looked each person at the table in the eye. "Do we even know how long they've been secretly visiting Earth?"

"ARI, is there any indication as to how long the Hexians have been visiting Earth?" Nox asked into his comm unit.

"Particle analysis shows that the Hexians have been visiting Earth for the past eight of Earth's lunar cycles."

"Well, the only good thing about this information is that because of the distance to this planet, they've only been there a limited amount of time. Let's hope they haven't caused too much damage. I'd still like to know how they've been getting onto Earth undetected," Tarek muttered looking at Jagger thoughtfully.

"I don't know," Jagger replied, adding, "We definitely need to do some investigating into this. I'll get Marsel to start doing some scans of the area." He got up and left the room to go talk to his science officer.

The room fell silent for a moment while everyone seemed to reflect on the information they had just discovered. This definitely changed everything, and now more than ever the concept of making first contact seemed all the more important.

The hologram of Earth still spinning on its axis, its colors swirling around, was prominently displayed in the middle of the table. Nyx, who had been studying the hologram with the experienced eye of a seasoned military officer, looked up in disbelief asking, "What are those objects orbiting the planet? Um—are those satellites?"

Peering intently at the hologram, Nox couldn't believe his eyes. There were multiple satellites orbiting Earth. *Why didn't I see this before? Well, because you were so sure they had no technology you never bothered to look. Not good Nox!*

Upon closer inspection, he thought he noticed some type of network array surrounding a few of the satellites. He wondered what its purpose was and who built it. This piqued his curiosity and surprised him that humans could be familiar with this type of science. Maybe this would go better than he thought. *I guess I was wrong in thinking they were still living in caves and just learning how to use fire—no not really, but close.*

"Loris, put the larger of the satellites on the hologram and display all the specs."

Loris started inputting commands and the image of Earth changed to the strange-looking satellite. Alongside the image, the specs of the satellite appeared. "Are there humans on there? If so, it would appear their technological advances are greater than we anticipated." Loris considered he may have to amend his opinion about humans. Maybe humans weren't as boring as he had originally thought.

"You're right about that, Loris. The type of technology we're looking at indicates that they have been very busy. I think we definitely need to take a closer look at exactly what the humans have been up to." Nox silently berated himself for not paying closer attention to Earth. *I better take a closer look at the Prohibited Planet List. I wonder how many other planets have progressed farther than I had originally thought.*

Reading off the display, Loris informed the room, "It looks like it's a structure orbiting about 400 kilometers above Earth. It appears to circle the planet every 90 of Earth's minutes at a speed of 27600 kilometers per hour. Long-range sensors indicate that there are six life forms on board."

The door to the conference room opened and Jagger entered, interrupting Loris. "Marsel will be working on finding out any information on how Tarquin and his gang of mercenaries have been sneaking onto Earth." Noting the serious look on Tarek's face, he asked, "What did I miss?"

Tarek looked up from his console, telling him, "Some very interesting findings."

After filling him in on what they had learned, Tarek sat back rubbing his chin, considering this new information. "How did we miss this, Director Nox? I thought you would have been more up to date on the advances of the humans.

Maybe you should revisit the planets that are on the UAP's list."

Nodding his head in agreement, Nox wondered if the General had been reading his mind.

Taking a moment to think things through, General Tarek came to a decision. "We will make first contact with the humans on board that station."

"But, sir, with all due respect, can't we just reconsider if first contact with the humans is the right choice?" Nox tried one more time to get the General to see things from his point of view.

General Tarek stared at Nox with his intense forest green eyes, "And why is that, Director Nox? Have you got any other ideas? If so, I'm listening."

Hesitating for a moment, the last thing Nox wanted was to involve the humans in a war with the Hexians. "In light of this new information regarding the humans, I would like more time to do some research on our latest findings. I would hate to bring the humans into this if they're not ready. Yes, the technology we're seeing is highly advanced, especially considering where they were a few hundred solar cycles ago. But we don't know how widespread their knowledge is within their planet. I would like to gather more data before a decision is made." Nox hoped he was making a good enough case so that the General would re-think his decision.

When he saw that the General wasn't moving on his opinion, Nox tried again—imploring him to reconsider. "How are we going to get them to listen to us when they don't even know there is life beyond their planet? You know their first inclination is to think we're here to attack them." Nox threw his hand up in the air, begging Tarek. "Please, sir, can't we protect them from afar?"

Commander Nyx, who had been intensely studying the hologram, spoke up, suggesting, "What if we rendezvous with the rest of the fleet along their outer solar system and take care of the threat without having to involve them? We can get in and out without them ever knowing."

Giving Nyx a deliberate look, Tarek responded tightly, "Because the Hexians have already been secretly visiting Earth." Sitting up in his chair, the General looked at the hologram again, tapping his fingers on the table in front of him as he considered the recommendations from his crew.

The Hexians have already infiltrated the planet, thought Nox. *Destruction, chaos, and bloodshed are clouding the General's mind.* Nox knew Tarek's past and what led him to a life in the Delician military. Tarek was big, bigger than most Delicians. Close to seven feet tall, he was selected early on by the Delician military for his size, hoping he would overshadow most males in his command. He did. Tarek had met and joined Nyx in battle for many decades making them an unstoppable duo. He and his elite team of soldiers were considered the finest in the Delician military—in the entire UAP, really. A team highly praised for their quick thinking and action in a crisis. Numerous awards and commendations had been bestowed on them, but they meant nothing to Tarek. His only concern was the outcome of a mission, not the rewards.

Nox looked down at himself and compared his 6'7" build to Tarek's. He considered himself lucky to be working under such a powerful leader, but he knew in his heart that contacting Earth was not the right move for any of them.

"They need to be informed of this threat and taught how to defend themselves," stated the General. Taking his eyes off the hologram, he looked from Nox to Nyx. "The humans will need to understand that we are their allies. Especially before the Hexians try to make contact. I'm counting on this team to aid the humans in defusing this threat before any real damage is done. It's not going to be an easy task, but if you consider the alternatives, we are their only hope."

"I see your point." Nox conceded, knowing that his protests were falling on deaf ears. Capitulating to the General, he replied, still worried about what type of reaction they were going to receive, "If that is your decision, I will do all I can to help this mission to succeed, but we need to make sure we're able to do this quietly and ease Earth into first contact."

Tarek nodded his head in agreement, adding, "All right then, it is agreed we should try to keep the panic at a minimum while we get Earth to understand that we are here to help them, not conquer them."

"All they have to do is get one look at you and they will probably run and hide," Jagger laughed out of the side of his mouth.

Maybe it would be better if my face was the first one that the humans saw, Nox thought. He had more of a leaner build and he wasn't so intimidating at first glance, whereas Tarek was all muscle and brawn.

Glaring at Jagger with his eyes flashing, Tarek's nostrils flared with aggravation. "You got a problem with how I look? I've done more first contacts than I care to remember. I happen to excel at diplomacy." All around the room, hands moved to cover mouths, trying to hide their smirks.

Tarek surprised them by laughing sharply. "I promise to keep my menacing to a minimum." The tension in the room lessened at Tarek's joke. "We will make first contact at the humans' orbiting space station. The UAP wants the Hexian threat eliminated and they want it done quickly and quietly. After we've achieved that, then we can discuss where to go from there with the humans. I understand it will take time for them to get used to the fact that they're not alone in the universe, but they don't have a choice. We don't have a lot of options right now."

"Agreed. Hopefully the Hexians aren't already on their way," Jagger put in. Everyone knew how much he hated the Hexians. It had been especially hard on him having spent years cleaning up the destruction that the Hexians had caused within the UAP territory. He leaned his well-muscled arms on the table and stared at the hologram. "I wonder how the humans are going to react to seeing beings from another planet. They better hope we get there before Tarquin and his crew. It could spell disaster for the humans. Tarquin will stop at nothing to get what he wants and doesn't care who or what gets destroyed in the process. You know that profit is their one and only goal. That's their way of life." Rubbing his hands together slowly, he added readily, "I'm looking forward to kicking some Hexian ass."

Tarek gave Jagger a knowing look, "You'll get your chance my friend. You'll get your chance."

"General," Nox interrupted, "I'll work out the specifics of what we're going to say to the humans. As you said, we'll contact the station first, but I'll stream out a message to those arrays. Just maybe they'll get it and be able to decipher it. If we don't get a message back, we'll just have to go knocking on the station's door."

"Yeah, and probably scare the shit of them," Nyx chuckled.

"Well, let's hope we don't have to witness that." Nox wrinkled his nose at that thought. "I think a holographic message should be sent introducing ourselves and that we'd like to open a dialog with them. I'll have to think on how to word it, but I also think it would be better if we brought their representatives to our ship to explain the situation. That way they can see for themselves that we're here to help them and not trying to take over their planet."

"I agree," Tarek said. "Jagger, you stay on the ship and prepare for our *guests*. Nyx, I want you to accompany me and Nox. We'll use a cloaked shuttle to take us alongside the station. If necessary, we can uncloak briefly so they can see that our transmission is real. I concur that it's imperative we are clear in our motives so they don't think we're trying to trap them or deceive them. Then once they agree, we'll transport them to the *Maelstrom*."

"Now that will probably make them shit their pants,"

laughed Jagger.

Ignoring Jagger's comments, Tarek asked him, "How long before we reach Earth's solar system?"

"In about six weeks, five if I push it."

"I think you need to push it. No telling how long before the Hexians find out we know about their plan." Standing up, Tarek continued, "Nox, compose a message to the humans and then send me a copy. I'll review it and send the plan outline to the UAP to keep them informed."

Nox turned, addressing the General with sincerity, "I won't let you down, sir."

"I know you won't." General Tarek placed his hand on Nox's shoulder. "Now go and strategize on how we can complete this mission successfully."

Turning to his assistant, Nox started giving him instructions. "Loris, when you get to the lab, have the specs on the Earth space station uploaded onto the lab's hologram and start putting together a list of talking points. Hopefully, the humans will listen to what we have to say. I also want to take a closer look at that network array that's surrounding some of their satellites."

Nodding his head to the group, Nox turned towards the door, mentally composing a message that he hoped the humans would take seriously.

Entering the elevator, Nox spoke out, "Deck 2" as the doors closed behind Loris. Considering all that had been discussed in the meeting, his hands clenched at his sides as he contemplated General Tarek's orders.

"That was a lot to take in, Nox. I mean it's hard to fathom that humans have advanced as far as they have. I guess we were wrong." Loris looked at his boss to see if he agreed.

Nox nodded at his friend, trying not to reproach himself

too badly for dismissing the humans as quickly as he had. *I know I've been busy with my own research, but it's part of my job to be on top of this.* Ever since his mother's accident, he had been in his lab consumed with his research on force field technology. Anything to hide the pain of losing his mother. However, that was no excuse. At least now he had a chance to be part of a plan to help save the human race. After that, he promised himself, he would take a closer look at that damn list.

"Loris, remind me to talk to the representative from the UAP in charge of the Prohibited Planets list. I want them to get someone else other than me to oversee it. It's apparent that I've been too busy with my own work to be the best person for the job. It's imperative that someone starts checking on these planets to see just how advanced they've become. This is my fault but I plan on rectifying this when we get back."

When the elevator doors opened onto their floor, they headed down the hall towards their lab. Nox's lab onboard the ship was located on the same deck as the medical bay and he nodded his head to one of the medics as he passed. He had been on this ship for only a few weeks and already he was known as being friendly but always too preoccupied in his work to stop for conversation.

Entering his lab, he approached his workstation located in the middle of the room. Stepping up onto the platform, he walked around the center table that housed the hologram. The entire workstation was made with transparent material that allowed him to survey the entire room with one glance. Standing at the table, he was surrounded on opposite sides by six large transparent screens separated by two openings to allow easy access to the platform.

"ARI, display one of the satellites orbiting Earth that has a network array attached to it. Loris, I want a closer look at that array. I find it fascinating that humans have advanced this much to develop such technology. I want to see how it's made and what type of material it's composed of."

"Sure thing," Loris replied taking a seat at one of the workstations located along the far wall of the lab. "Sending you the information now."

The information he requested appeared on one of the screens surrounding him. Studying it intently, Nox was impressed at the ingenuity of the humans. It appeared to be a communication satellite that had a series of nodes installed on it. *I wonder what their purpose is for doing that.*

"ARI, display all communication satellites orbiting Earth."

Nox watched as a plethora of satellites started popping up around the planet. Motioning Loris to join him on the platform, he told him, "Take a look at this. What do you think its purpose is?"

"I have no idea." Loris was unhappy that he finally had to admit he was wrong. "Okay, I concede. I guess the humans aren't as boring as I thought."

"No, definitely not boring. I can't wait to meet the person responsible for creating this array."

As he became more and more familiar with the human technology, a plan began to form in his mind. After a few hours of back and forth with Loris, Nox felt that they might just have a working model of how he could integrate his force field technology into this network array. There was no way he would be able to put a force field around the entire planet. Even though he could replicate the resources that he needed, there just wasn't enough time. If he could use the force fields to protect their communications network, then General Tarek and his elite soldiers could take care of the Hexians before they reached Earth. If any of Tarquin's ships did manage to slip by Nyx's fighters, which he highly doubted, at least the humans' communication capabilities would remain intact.

With the plan set in his mind, Nox went into his office which was tucked into the corner of his lab. He was lucky

- it was the only place in his lab that had a window. Sometimes staring out into space helped focus his mind, and with this mission he definitely needed a clear head. For some unknown reason Nox had been feeling restless on this trip, like something was coming but he just didn't know what.

Pushing those thoughts aside, he pulled out his chair and sat at his desk. Settling himself against the comfortable cushion that molded to his body, he began entering commands into his console. *I better inform the General of my plan.*

General Tarek's face appeared in front of him. He looked as tired as Nox felt.

"General, I've come up with some ideas on how we can help the humans."

Seeing Tarek nod his head for him to continue, Nox went on to outline his plan, including what he thought the message to the humans should say.

"Good work, Nox. Prepare what you need and as soon as we're in range, we'll implement your plan. I'll inform the UAP on how we're going to proceed. Keep me updated of any changes. And, Nox, I appreciate your efforts. I know I'm not always the easiest person to work for, but sometimes I have to be hard to get the required results."

"Thank you, General."

Nodding his head to Nox, the General's face disappeared.

Nox sat back in his chair and turned to stare out the window. It was quiet in here—his office door blocking out the sounds of Loris as he moved around the lab. He liked the silence. It allowed him to think and to consider all that had happened over the last six hours. *I hope we are doing the right thing by contacting the humans, but I have to agree with the General, Tarquin must be stopped at all costs.*

Closing his eyes for *just a few seconds* Nox drifted off for a much-needed nap before all hell broke loose.

CHAPTER 2

Planet Earth
Boston, Massachusetts

Emeline Cameron adjusted her glasses on her nose as she stood staring out the window of her loft at the Boston skyline. She missed seeing the stars she'd spent many a hot summer night gazing up at back home with her dad. The lights from the city always obscured them from view and especially now that they had just entered the month of August, the hot, humid weather had moisture-filled clouds hanging low over the city.

Feeling the breeze of her air conditioner blowing cool against her skin, she was glad to be inside out of the intense summer heat. She tried to push the feeling of melancholy away as she thought about her father. Growing up in the woods of New Hampshire, stargazing was a favorite pastime for her family. Her dad, Hank, had a telescope that he would set up on the deck, ready and waiting to see whatever came across the night sky. Living in the woods allowed for no light pollution, so the stars always looked bright and shiny. He used to joke that you never knew who was up there watching you.

The Perseids meteor shower would be starting up in a few weeks and she wondered if she would be able to make it back home to view it in her parents' backyard. Hank loved it when his family was out there altogether—each of them shouting out when they would see a falling star. As children, Emeline's siblings, Liam and Isabelle, would lie out on the grass staring up, waiting anxiously for any streaks of color to zoom across the sky.

These were the moments that Emeline missed most

now that her father was gone. Emeline was Hank's baby. While he loved all his children, Emeline was the one who turned him into a big old softy. Belle and Liam used to tease her that if they wanted something, they would just send Emeline in to ask Dad. Maybe it was because she was the youngest or maybe it was because Emeline would turn her big baby blues on him, making him feel like Superman. After all, when Hank walked in the door after a hard day at the office, Emeline was the first to greet him with a smile so bright he felt like a superhero.

Now when she looked out at the night sky, all she felt were bittersweet memories. Like the meteors fizzling out in the sky, Hank's heart gave out one Sunday afternoon. His family thought he was just snoozing away in his favorite chair watching a NASCAR race. Emeline's mother had constantly reminded her husband of his history of high cholesterol—that he needed to take better care of himself.

"You're going to die on me one day and leave me all alone. Is that what you want?" she would ask, exasperated with him. He would only laugh, teasing her mother that she was never getting rid of him.

Emeline thought she would have more time with her father. He was only sixty-two. Her mother had been after him for years to watch his diet and exercise, but he would only laugh at them, pat his bulging belly and blame his wife.

"It's your mother's fault for being such a good cook," he would say, his normal excuse for not cooking himself. *"Why would I cook when your mother does it so much better?"*

Of course, when Mum tried to change their diet, Hank wasn't happy and would grumble to them. *"Your mother is killing me! No more sugar or carbs. It's veggies and more veggies. Eating is no fun anymore!"*

Emeline would only hug him and remind him it was because they loved him so much. She loved the feeling of his strong, warm body surrounding her, making her feel that everything was right with the world. Boy, did she miss his hugs.

It had been two years since his death and it still haunted her from time to time. Gazing up at the stars made her hopeful that he was out there watching over her.

Shaking her head to clear her sad thoughts, Emeline checked her smart watch for the time. *Oh shit, I better get going,* she thought, especially if she was going to be ready for when her friends arrived for their potluck dinner. Lucky for her, the batch of chili she'd made last Sunday night only had to be thawed.

Going into the kitchen, she turned down the heat on the large pot she had going on the stove. The block of ice that was her chili had slowly melted and was now bubbling red —wafting smells of spicy goodness throughout her apartment.

Taking a taste, she hummed with delight. *Yup, just enough cumin.*

Checking her watch again, not realizing how late it had gotten, she rushed out of the kitchen, aware that her friends would have a lot to say about her tardiness. *Ami, Heather, and Lorelei are gonna harrass me if I'm not dressed again when they get here.*

Other than her sister and her mother, these three women meant the most to her, and not only in her personal life, but professionally as well. Having all gone to MIT at some point in their academic careers, all four women seemed to click as soon as they'd met.

Ami Jefferson was not only the lead aerospace engineer on Emeline's latest project but was also her second in command at her company, EAC Global Network Solutions. Currently, their mission was working with NASA to develop solutions to solar flares that were affecting orbiting satellites and the International Space Station. It was more than Emeline could handle alone. Plus, Ami always seemed to have the right solutions to Emeline's problems.

Then there was Lorelei Windwalker, who led the astrophysics team. Her smart wit and crazy personality were just the right mix for dealing with the mythos of the galaxy. Sometimes Emeline wondered if Lorelei had been abducted by aliens as a kid as her ideas were certainly...out there. However, she could always count on Lorelei for a comforting shoulder and a cocktail, usually one right after the other.

Finally, there was Heather Garcia. She was not only their computer whiz, but the logical-minded one of the bunch. If you needed anything hacked, tracked, or figured out, Heather was your girl. She was also good for a swift dose of reality, especially when things didn't go as planned.

Emeline loved these three women unconditionally—knew that they had her back. But lately they'd been so busy that these dinner nights were important to fit in whenever they could. Mostly it was just an excuse to eat good food, drink some fancy drinks, and chill. Girl time was important.

Looking around, making sure all her clutter was picked up and put away, Emeline couldn't help but smile. She had been so happy when she moved into one of the new highrises in the Seaport District in Boston. It was a dream come true for her. Sure, it was expensive, but then again, she'd busted her butt to build her company to where she could more than afford to live where she wanted. The One Building was close to her lab, meaning she could get to work without having to deal with Boston traffic. Her company was located in one of the warehouses along the waterfront, about a ten-minute walk from home. Walking through the door at the end of a long day allowed Emeline to find a refuge from her hectic life. On the list of all her happy places in the world, her loft was now at the top.

With just a few minutes left before her friends arrived, Emeline refilled the water pitcher in the fridge. Walking by the couch, she snagged a wine glass from behind a pillow and raced it back to the dishwasher. *Oops!* She thought. *I wondered what happened to this glass.* Though she hated a messy house, Emeline also hated to clean, putting her between a rock and hard place. Spying her laundry rack still blocking the backdoor to her apartment, she grabbed her clean clothes off it and thought to herself, *I'll just put this in my room and take care of it later.* She knew that Lorelei would be the first one to grab her clean laundry and start folding it for her, while Heather would just step over it, going to get whatever she needed from the fridge. Ami on the other hand would rib her, saying, "Isn't it time for the cleaning lady to show up?"

Heading to her bedroom to change, admiring the design on her way in, Emeline smiled happily. Out of all the rooms in her loft, she liked this room the best. Having to share a bedroom with her sister growing up, and then there was that roommate in college who stuck to her like glue, Emeline never really got to choose her style—that is, until now. She loved her cream-colored walls with splashes of different shades of reds that were accented throughout the room in pillows, her bedspread, and even the red glowing lava rock lamp on her night stand. It was a little too obvious that red was her favorite color, but she could add as much as she wanted because after all—it was all hers. She had earned every bit of it.

After a fast shower and a quick change into yoga pants and a cami, she popped in her contacts. Glancing in the mirror, *no time to wash the hair,* she thought, opting instead to put her long blond hair up into a ponytail. Her hair was so thick that it sometimes took hours for it to dry and there was just no time right now.

Shoes were another dilemma. *Barefoot or flats,* thought Emeline, *or my new black boots I just picked up at DSW?* Not that she didn't have options to choose from since she was a total shoe-aholic. Her collection of high heels alone cost more than most new cars. With her friends arriving in seconds, barefoot seemed to be the best option. She shoved her shoes into the closet, just barely managing to pull the door shut.

I may be five eight, she thought, *but I love wearing heels on dates.*

Not that she had been dating much. Between the time spent at her lab and what little time she had left for family and friends; dating had been pushed to the back of Emeline's life. Of course, there were the occasional dates that led to a hook-up here or there, but those generally left her feeling cold and unsatisfied. Lately, Emeline found more satisfaction with her favorite vibrator she kept hidden under her bed.

"Don't need anyone finding that," Emeline chuckled to herself. "I mean, a girl's gotta have some secrets."

Hearing her doorbell, she did one last look around, wondering why she really should care. These were her friends, women she loved and had come to depend on for everything.

Hurrying to the front door, Emeline grinned as she opened it, greeting her three besties.

Ami pushed past her with a smile. "I've got my newest creation of mac and cheese," she said before quickly dropping a kiss on Emeline's cheek as she headed to the kitchen.

Set in the corner of her loft, the kitchen was Emeline's favorite place to be. Cooking has always been a "thing" in her family. If they weren't cooking in the kitchen then they were planning on what was going to be cooked. When Emeline bought her loft, she made sure the kitchen was gourmet and included all the newest technology on the market.

Ami carefully put her pot on the stove, telling them, "I went with a southwestern theme tonight. Hope you all like spicy," she said with a twisted smile.

"Oh great! Let me just grab the Tums," laughed Emeline, knowing even that may not help with Ami's chili powder addiction.

Ami had been Emeline's friend since freshman year at MIT. Her father, Tom, was a Navy Seal who proudly retired last year. He met her mother while he was stationed in Korea, making Ami both African American and Korean. Being a child of mixed race could be challenging at times in America, but being a military brat helped as most of her classmates were of mixed races also. Growing up with an abundance of nationalities and cultures was normal for her. She loved her mocha skin, telling her friends that she saw it as a combination of both her parents. Emeline always loved listening to Ami when she would speak Korean on the phone when her mom would call, which was just as much as her own mother's calling habits—a lot.

Lorelei breezed into the kitchen with a shopping bag in each carefully manicured hand.

"I brought the drinks. Tonight is Fuzzy Nipples night," she told them, wagging her eyebrows. "I also brought some veggies."

Ami nudged her shoulder. "You cooked?"

"No," Lorelei told her. "You know I can't cook, but I can do the next best thing—stop at the market and grab premade. Nothing wrong with buying store-made meals. I mean, someone has to support the local economy. Besides, you know I make a mean cocktail."

Lorelei was from the Navajo Nation in northern Arizona. As a child, she was always inside studying, working on her passion of becoming an astrophysicist. She loved the stars almost as much as Emeline did. Although trying to balance the teachings her grandmother wanted to pass down to her along with her love of science could be a challenge at times. Her only focus was on finding the answers to the galaxy, which meant she had to get into MIT for graduate school. Her dreams came true, but sometimes she wondered at what cost. Maybe she'd call her grandmother next week, she said aloud as she set to work making drinks for everyone.

Heather was the last to come through the door. "I brought dessert."

"I hope it's chocolate." Emeline wagged her finger at her.

Looking at Emeline, Heather smiled. "Of course. I know what you like, woman. I know everything, remember?"

Heather grew up in New York City; however, she grew up in a rather beat-up neighborhood with rundown buildings and graffiti plastered on almost every available surface. Her parents came to New York from Puerto Rico three years before she was born, hoping, like most people, to provide a better life for their children. They named her Heather, hoping that having an Anglican name would help her be accepted easier. Unfortunately, growing up in a gang-riddled neighborhood, it didn't matter what her name was. She was a body for them to use and abuse. Brown hair cut into a pixie, she was small and cute, and stick thin with beautiful chocolate brown eyes. She could eat anything and never gain an ounce, which totally annoyed Ami and Emeline. Luckily for Heather, the Girls Club of America offered a class on computers that her father had signed her up for the day after she came home with her first gang tattoo. She credited them and her father for saving her life. A scholarship to MIT through the Girls Club set her on a path that her parents had only dreamed of for their daughter.

Walking over to the stove to give her chili one last stir, Emeline nodded when Lorelei asked, "Almost ready?" She began pouring drinks and within minutes had handed them all a shot glass.

"Cheers!" they shouted, shooting the drinks down their throats.

"Whoa, that's strong!" Ami croaked. "Maybe a little too much vodka?"

"You can never have too much vodka," Lorelei countered, licking her lips.

Rolling her eyes, Ami grabbed a plate and started piling

it high with food. "Changing Mom's wok mac and cheese to southwestern has really given it a kick."

"Ya think," Emeline winced as the spicy food slid down her throat.

As the women sat eating and drinking, their conversation morphed from dating, clothes, work, back to dating again. All four of them acknowledged that they were just too busy right now to think about men. When Lorelei joked that BOB had become her new best friend, they'd all burst out laughing.

Laughing on the outside, Emeline inwardly cringed when Lorelei mentioned her vibrator, not wanting to admit she secretly agreed.

Wiping her eyes from tears of laughter, Emeline glanced at her phone and saw another text from her mom. She and Fiona had always been close and now even more so since her dad had died. She was reminded of their last conversation. "I've got a question for you."

"About BOB?" Heather laughed. The girls' fits of laughter persisted.

Emeline nearly spewed her drink at them. "Would you stop putting that visual in my head. I may need another drink if you keep bringing that up. No, I was talking to mum today and she wanted to know if I wanted my dad's telescope. She's trying to clean out the house to get it ready to be sold, but she reminded me of a running joke her and Dad used to talk about."

"Oh, I don't want to know about your parents doing it," Heather giggled into her drink.

"Eww—please no...la la la," Ami put her fingers into her ears.

"No, no, I promise it's not that!" Emeline laughed. "It was about aliens making first contact."

"Yeah, what about it?" Ami asked. "Were they worried about their relationship becoming a threesome?"

Lorelei roared with laughter, hitting Ami on the arm.

"You are too much, girlfriend."

Grabbing her drink and shooting it back in one gulp, Emeline gave them a disgusted look—images of her parents' sex life was not something she wanted floating around in her head, ever. "So, don't think I'm crazy but... what would you do and how would you feel if aliens made first contact?"

Her friends stopped laughing. They looked at her in silence for a moment, wondering if she might know something they didn't. Given their line of work with NASA, Emeline was usually the first to know information for the team.

Heather was the first to ask, "Are you serious?"

Emeline watched, intrigued, as they stopped, each giving her question some serious consideration.

Heather mumbled softly, "Aliens, really? That's just crazy talk, *charla loca*. I think you guys have had one too many Fuzzy Nipples."

They all laughed and looked at Emeline.

"Well, it's your question. Tell us what you think." Ami raised her eyebrows asking, "What would you do?"

Pausing for a second, wondering what they would think of her theory, she said, "Well—honestly, I think it's pretty plausible. I mean, don't you think it's rather arrogant to think we're the only life forms here? Why should we be the only ones in the universe? Seriously, that doesn't make any sense."

Looking from Ami to Lorelei, she went on, "I mean, come on, think about it. You're in science. Isn't it at least possible that there is something alive out there?" They just stared at her as she continued. "Now I'm not saying whether that's good or bad but it is possible, don't you think?"

Emeline shivered thinking about how terrified she'd be if aliens really did come to Earth and her mother's question today had only served to intensify the level anxiety she'd been feeling lately. *That weird data coming through the array is making me nervous.* Her crazy imagination was working overtime and it was all because of the data she'd been reviewing that was being collected from the network arrays they had placed in their test satellites orbiting Earth. It was supposed to show what particles were coming towards Earth from solar flares being emitted from the sun, and it did, but it also showed some anomalies that shouldn't have been there. She'd planned on talking to Heather about double-checking her findings tomorrow when she got to the lab. Something was off and it was making her feel uneasy.

Lorelei nodded her head in agreement with Emeline. Deep down she loved the idea of alien life out there in the universe. Her secret vice was reading alien romance novels. Reading books by just a few of her favorite authors, Ruby and Anna, she hoped if aliens ever did come, they would at least look like some of the hot alien hunks on the covers of their books. Wide muscular chests and strong broad shoulders with sculpted abs that showed all those deliciously defined muscles running down along either side of their exquisitely toned bodies that just called for her touch. Phew! Well, a girl could dream.

Hoping her face didn't give her thoughts away, she fanned herself. "Is it hot in here? I think it is. I'll just open the patio door." Standing by the open door for a moment, the hot muggy air did nothing to cool down Lorelei's raging libido.

Giving up and closing the door, Lorelei wiped the sweat from her brow and headed into the kitchen. Standing with her head in the freezer, suddenly three bodies crowded around hers, trying to steal her cold air.

Spinning around, she shooed them away, telling them to go sit at the island. "Go—sit. I'll make you a special drink." She paused thoughtfully, "Hmm, you know, instead of making you a Fuzzy Nipple, I'm going to make you a Fuzzy Alien Dick." The women did as they were told, grinning back at Lorelei.

Laughing, she grabbed the middle of her long straight jet-black hair and pulled it up into a ponytail to get it out of her way. As much as she loved her hair, no one wanted it in their drinks. Looking through the ingredients on the counter, she mulled over an idea. "Let's see, what would be in a Fuzzy Alien Dick?"

Grabbing a cocktail shaker, she put ice in and grabbed the bottle of Blue Curaçao. "Well, most aliens are blue, aren't they?"

Snickering at her conjecture, Heather told her she'd been reading too many of those alien novels she loved so much.

Stunned, Lorelei stared wide-eyed at her.

Heather just smirked at her saying, "What? You think I don't know your little secret? I'm a hacker, remember. I know everything,"

Ignoring the howls of laughter coming from Ami and Emeline, Lorelei gave her concoction one last shake before pouring it into a tall slender glass. Grabbing a carrot from the fridge and after pretending to perform oral sex on it, she plopped it in the drink. Next, she handed it to Heather, who gave her a look of disgust but shrugged her shoulders and drank it anyway.

Emeline and Ami scrunched their faces together yelling, "GROSS."

"What? Alcohol kills everything."

Heather high-fived Lorelei before the two of them fell into fits of laughter.

After taking a moment to enjoy her drink, Emeline looked at Ami with a glint in her eye. "So, Ames—what are your thoughts on aliens?"

Mulling over how she really felt about first contact, Ami felt more practical about it, mainly because as an aerospace engineer, she was trained to think outside the box. Grinning, she reminded them, "Well, maybe I'll find out sooner than you think."

She was scheduled to go up to the International Space Station to work on the network array for her team. This was Emeline's baby and Ami was thrilled to have had a role in it. It was still hard to believe how much her life had changed since the moment she'd met Emeline Cameron. Being asked to work on her project was the chance of a lifetime. She'd spent the last eight weeks training with NASA to get ready for her first trip into space. That's why eating good food tonight had been such a treat. Going into space was hard on the human body and she had been training nonstop, preparing for this important mission.

Going into space had always been her passion, and actually being able to see Earth from the ISS was a dream come true. Emeline's brother, Liam, would be piloting the shuttle taking her up there. Ami had known him through her friendship with Emeline for a number of years. But it had been a pleasant coincidence finding out that her father had actually known Liam from his time in the service. Liam was an astronaut and a Navy pilot and had years of experience, but she was still apprehensive about going.

How would she feel if she came face to face with an alien? *Probably shit my pants! Let's just hope that if it ever happens, they are friendly.* She couldn't believe she was going into space and she wasn't going to allow anything, not even nerves, derail her dream.

Ami grinned at her friends. "Well, if aliens do show up, which I highly doubt, let's just hope they're friendly, and of course having sexy hot bods would be a plus."

Glancing at her watch, Emeline saw that it was getting late but she wanted to tell her friends about the call she had received that afternoon from their old professor from MIT, Dr. Whittemore. She had asked Emeline to speak at the Women in Science and Engineering symposium.

"That's great, Em," Lorelei said. "How is Marilyn? I've always admired her. She had to put up with a lot of crap being a woman in a male-dominated field."

Emeline shrugged her shoulders. "I told her I'd think about it. I'm not sure I want to do it. I'm really busy with the network array. Ami is going up to the ISS and it's at the same time. I need to be here so we can get the other satellites online."

"But it's only one day and it's right here in Boston. It's not like you have to travel out of town," Ami reminded her. "It will be fine. You should do it. You'll be wonderful. You've earned all of this. You've worked your ass off to get where you are. I mean, come on, girl—you built a freakin' Deflector Network Array. And don't think we overlooked those initial—D N A. What was up with that? You couldn't think up another name? Geez."

Jumping to her feet, Emeline started pacing around, collecting dirty dishes and glasses to bring to the kitchen. It was a long time ago but she could still feel that familiar clench in her stomach at the mention of their alma mater. Thinking back, she had been so excited to get accepted into one of the most prestigious schools in the country.

Between being from a small town in New Hampshire and going to a crappy high school, she never thought in a million years she would get accepted. Getting top scores on her SATs and winning the NH Science Award brought her to the attention of the acceptance committee. Her family was so proud of her. Quiet, studious and absolutely stunning to look at was both a blessing and a curse for her. Emeline was tall, blond, and leggy. She spent most of her life dancing in competitions with her sister and her body showed the years of work she had put into it. Her face was beauty itself and matched the kindness in her soul.

When she had arrived for accepted students' day, it had surprised her at the reception she'd received from some of her peers, both male and female. It was as if they took one look at Emeline and immediately decided "Dumb Blonde."

32

They couldn't have been further from the truth.

Being stereotyped for the way she looked was surprising to Emeline given the current political climate. Women were supposed to be supporting each other and instead she was shunned and pushed aside simply because of her outward appearance.

Sighing to herself, Emeline thought back to how hard she'd had to work in order to achieve her goals. Having dyslexia but never really telling anyone about her disability, she'd had to work just that much harder than everyone else. Her saving grace was that she was unmatched in the lab. That was her haven. Setting foot in her lab, surrounded by all the familiar sights of the glass hood, Bunsen burners, and the smells of the different chemicals, Emeline felt at home. Lucky for her, Dr. Whittemore looked past all the outward appearances and saw her potential underneath. She thanked her lucky stars every day that Dr. Whittemore was willing to take a chance on her since she was known for only taking on a few undergrad students in her lab. Having a contract with NASA, her lab was well funded and so everyone wanted to be picked to be one of her elite "lab rats." When Emeline was first offered the job, she couldn't believe her luck. Finally, something was going right at school. Calling her mum every day crying had started to get old. She had found her niche, which helped get her through the next five years.

But even after being picked for such a prestigious position, Emeline's peers still wouldn't cut her any slack. She heard the rumors and cruel whispers about why she had gotten the position. Dr. Whittemore being gay, even in today's "enlightened" mentality, still bothered some of her older colleagues. Oh, they would never say it to her face, but you could tell by their facial expressions what they thought, but since her lab brought in so much money, who had the last laugh! She had tenure after all and no one could touch her.

Lorelei stopped her mid pace, pulling her in for a hug.

"Em, I know you still feel the pain those bastards put you through. They made your life a living hell for so many years, but at least Marilyn was there for you. You have to do this for her."

Leaning into Lorelei's shoulder, Emeline breathed deeply, trying to calm herself. *Breathe, Center, Focus.* Those three words had been drummed into her head since she was a little girl. Mum was right. *Fiona Cameron usually was,* Emeline thought as she laughed to herself.

Straightening her shoulders, she told Lorelei she was right. Dr. Whittemore had put herself out there for her. Of course, she would do the symposium. She only hoped that things went according to plan with the arrays and that she could figure out where that funky data was coming from.

"I love you guys." Emeline grabbed her drink and held it up. "A toast—to my best friends in the whole world. Ami —may you be the first to find out if there is alien life out there."

Ami grumbled into her empty glass, "Bite your tongue, girlfriend. Are you trying to scare the crap out of me? Lorelei—I need another one of these Fuzzy Alien drink thingies. Better add more dick this time."

The four women busted out laughing as Lorelei got up to refill her glass.

CHAPTER 3

International Space Station
Five weeks later

"Ami—Ami. Come on—wake up." Liam nudged her arm, trying to wake her up.

"Fine, I'm up. I'm up." Ami looked around disoriented at where she was. *Oh yeah, I'm on the freakin' International Space Station!*

That ride up through the atmosphere strapped to a rocket still had her ears ringing. Oh sure, she'd spent months training in a simulator, but that was nothing compared to the real thing. The feeling of going from 0 to 17500 miles an hour in eight minutes was the ultimate rush. Between the shaking and the rattling of the shuttle as they pulled away from Earth's atmosphere, she wondered if she might have rattled something loose in her brain.

Feeling a heavy hand nudge her again, she slowly rolled over and glared at him.

"Ames, I know you're tired from yesterday, but we've got work to do. The equipment for the array needs our attention."

She could tell Liam was getting annoyed with her. Stretching her arms over her head, she rubbed the sleep from her eyes. "Okay, okay. I guess I'm still feeling the effects of that ride up from Earth. Although, I have to compliment you on your driving skills." Pushing herself upright, she grinned at him. "Thanks for getting us up here in one piece."

Liam's face flushed red. Geez, sometimes a ruddy complexion was a dead giveaway, especially when he was embarrassed, but getting praise for his accomplishments always made him feel he'd definitely made the right choice in becoming a Navy pilot. "You're welcome, now hurry up and get dressed. I want to get this day started." He turned to give her some privacy while he thought about the tasks that needed to be completed today.

Ami disentangled herself from her space bed, wondering how she was able to sleep last night. Sleeping in such a strange position was not her norm, but hey, she couldn't really complain too much because she was after all living her dream.

Hanging onto the walls or anything else that was available for her to latch onto, she looked around for her uniform. She was still getting used to the zero gravity— meaning you had to be careful where you put your hands. Causing any malfunctions on her first day was frowned upon, not to mention dangerous. *I know it was my dream, but seriously, there has got to be a better way of getting up here. I know one thing for sure—when I get back home, I'm going to be doing some research on getting some gravity up here. This floating around all the time is going to get old real fast.*

Managing to get into her uniform without giving herself too many bruises, she looked at her reflection in the mirror. *Oh god, look at this hair. Well, there's no helping it.* Grabbing a hair clip, she tried the best she could to get her hair under control, but trying to do simple things while floating and trying not to damage anything was difficult. After one last look, she was ready for her first full day on the Space Station. Her only wish was that her stomach would settle. It felt like it was still back on Earth.

Liam floated just outside her quarters reading off his tablet waiting for her. He had been a really great friend to her over the years and was glad he was partnering with her on this mission. His sister Emeline was counting on them to complete this phase of the process with the network array for the communication satellites and so far, things had gone according to plan.

Grabbing onto Liam's arm in an attempt to steady herself, the view from the window caught her eye. When they had first arrived, they had been too busy getting acclimated to their surroundings and meeting their fellow astronauts to pay too much attention to the view outside. Right now, Ami was mesmerized.

Liam couldn't help smiling at the look of wonderment on Ami's face. This was his third trip to the station. It wasn't that he didn't appreciate the majesty of space, he did, but he felt troubled. His sister Emeline weighed heavy on his mind, distracting him from appreciating the view. What she told him about the strange data they were picking up through the network array concerned him deeply.

"Somebody pinch me. Isn't this the most amazing thing you've ever seen?" Ami sighed.

"OUCH"

Liam grinned at her as she rubbed her arm, glaring back at him. Ami was one of his sister's best friends. She was also a highly intelligent, strong-willed woman, not to mention beautiful, but someone you didn't want to mess with. She had been known to kick some serious ass in their training classes. Her mocha skin, combined with her almond-shaped chocolate brown eyes and long soft curly brown hair gave her an unusual look. You would think that he would have been falling all over himself to get her to turn those beautiful eyes on him. Yeah, well sadly, he felt nothing. Absolutely nothing. It was weird, Liam thought, but she'd always felt more like a sister than a lover. Add to the fact that he had served in the Navy with her father, dating Ami was not in the cards for him. He grinned as she was practically jumping up and down, having a hard time containing her excitement.

"After you've been up here for a while, you get busy doing experiments and it kind of becomes second nature."

Ami shook her head in disbelief. "I don't know how you can say that. I don't think it will ever feel that way for me.

I love space. You know how I feel about this—actually getting to come here to the Space Station."

She gazed out the window, whispering softly, "I mean just look at it...all blue and green with white swirls all over it. What a wonder it is being able to see it from here."

As she turned toward Liam, her voice grew with excitement. "I mean, we're always looking up at the stars and the moon and now I'm looking down at the Earth from space. How'd we get so lucky to be able to have such fantastic jobs that we get to go into space?"

"You can thank Em for that. I swear from the time she was a little kid she was always—I can't even decide which word would be better suited—obsessed, engrossed, absorbed, fanatical with all things space realted. More times than I can count on hot summer nights we'd find her lying on the grass staring up at the sky trying to count the stars. She'd always look up at us with those shining blue eyes of hers and beg me or Dad to lie down beside her on the blanket. Seriously, how could you say no to that sweet face?" Liam grinned having forgotten that memory until just now.

"The stories she would tell, geez, I mean, what an imagination. I used to worry about her sometimes, but as usual she showed me, didn't she? She's really an incredible woman and I'm so proud of her. Dad would have been beaming about his baby girl." Turning his head, his face began to show his emotions a little too much for his liking —Liam liked to keep those thoughts to himself. He needed to focus on completing this mission and pulling up a boat load of emotions right now wouldn't help him do it. He pushed those feelings down into a place he could return to at another time.

Grinning at Ami, he said, "You and my sister watch enough sci-fi movies and read enough alien books—I don't even want to think about what unbelievable theories you've all come up with."

Sticking her tongue out at him, she laughed, "Yeah, well, when an alien comes knocking, I want to be there to see your face. I just hope they're hot and sexy looking."

She raked her eyes up and down Liam's toned muscular body thinking what a pity—Liam was a catch. Looking like he just stepped off the pages of a Scottish romance novel with his reddish-brown hair and sparkling blue eyes, she sighed. He had a spectacular body to look at, but unfortunately it was all lost on her. She only felt brotherly love for him. Too bad she wouldn't be able to check having zero gravity sex off her bucket list. "I will be so disappointed if they turn out to be little green men."

"Would you stop." Liam rolled his eyes at her. "What about sexy alien women? What—are there no gorgeous alien females? Why is it only about the men?"

"Hey, it's my fantasy, why would I want the competition?"

"Enough. Get your mind out of the gutter. We need to focus on our mission and not on sex," he laughed. He didn't need to be getting aroused with no way to take care of it. He needed to focus on the task at hand.

They were on a mission that had the potential to change history if all went as planned. Emeline and her team had developed a system that would all but eliminate any communication disruptions from the radiation given off by solar flares   This was huge. When a solar flare shoots a stream of electromagnetic energy out towards Earth, it only takes approximately eight minutes to reach here. Their network array was designed to determine the type of charge coming towards the satellite and then give off the same charge back into the particle stream. This would cause the electromagnetic radiation to be deflected away from the satellite. The arrays were about to be installed on a few dozen satellites orbiting the Earth. It had been successful in the four test satellites they had been monitoring over the last six months. Now they were going to increase the number of units, eventually hoping that all satellites will be equipped with their device. Liam couldn't be prouder of his little sister and her friends. They made a great team.

"Come on, let me show you the lab where we'll be working, unless you're still a little woozy from the ride up."

"Woozy! I'll show you woozy." Turning a little too fast, her head started to spin as her stomach began making noises.

Grabbing her by the arm and pulling her in close, her eyes widened as her head fell back against Liam's arm. "Well, I guess that ride up might have been a little more overwhelming than I thought," she said, looking up into his concerned face. Her skin felt clammy and she had the sudden urge that she was going to lose whatever was in her stomach—except that's right, she didn't have anything in there. Eating had not been forefront of her mind yesterday morning when she got ready to go into space.

OH MY GOD, I'M IN SPACE!!!!! Okay, calm down. What does Fiona always say? Oh yeah, Breathe, Center, Focus. I got this!

Liam could tell she was trying to hold things together. "Tell me you are not doing that breathing thing my mother is always going on about."

"Laugh all you want, fly boy. It works for me and don't tell me you haven't done it because I've seen you. Remember who was sitting next to you on a freakin' rocket ship yesterday!"

He looked at her sheepishly, knowing he never wanted to admit that his mother was right. It did help. "Come on. When was the last time you ate?"

"Last night—no wait, yesterday morning maybe. I'm not sure. I was so worried, excited, sick to my stomach all at the same time that eating wasn't a priority. I suppose you ate a lumberjack breakfast?"

Grinning from ear to ear, Liam replied, "You know me so well. Let's get you something to eat. Besides, I need to talk

An Space Stars don't 'Twinkle'!

to you about this weird data that Emeline found. Did she tell you about it?" Ami nodded as he continued, "Heather double-checked it and this is different from the previous data. It's almost like there is some intelligence to it because there appears to be an embedded repeatable pattern." Shaking his head, confused, he added, "It doesn't seem to make any sense. I need you to take a look at the latest results and tell me what you think?"

Nudging him with her elbow Ami replied, "Em did mention something about it but as you can appreciate, I had other things on my mind. Feed me first and then I'll take a look at it."

Holding onto Liam, Ami floated her way into the kitchen area. Eating space food wasn't something she was looking forward to, but hey, a girl's gotta eat. "So, let's see, freeze-dried breakfast or lunch?" Grabbing the breakfast pack, she opened it up, making a face. *Oh well, you wanted to go to space, so quit complaining. When I get back to Earth, I'm going to make that southwest mac and cheese again and eat the entire pan! Then I'm going to have grandma make me some grits.*

She stopped and looked out the window again at the millions of twinkling lights blinking back at her. Still trying to comprehend where she was, Ami called out in wonder, "Look Liam, the sun is setting on Earth. Isn't that the most amazing thing you've ever seen?"

Smiling back at her, Liam gazed out the window. He knew the sun set on Earth every 90 minutes, so after a while he hadn't paid too much attention to it. *Okay, I guess I might be a little jaded.* Seeing it through Ami's eyes, he took in the beauty of the scene unfolding before him. It really was a wonder to look out at the sunlight shining down on Earth, showing all the colors and textures on the surface. It was breathtaking.

Liam's tablet beeped, breaking the moment. Seeing he had a message from Emeline, he told Ami to finish up so they could go over the data that Emeline had sent.

Shoving the last bit of food into her mouth, trying to decide if she wanted another breakfast packet, Ami thought better of it. It might be a good idea to wait to see how her stomach handled the first one.

Disposing of her trash, she grumbled back to him, "Okay, okay. Just give me a minute. I'm going to attempt to use the bathroom before we get started."

Liam chuckled, remembering his first time using the Space Station bathroom facilities. "Just watch out for the vacuum. It can really do a number on your private parts."

Snorting, Ami shot back, "Don't remind me." This is the one part of this whole experience that she could do without. "Next project will be working on a solution to the gravity problem up here," she called after him.

Chuckling, he told her, "Suck it up. You'll get used to it. I'll meet you in the lab." He turned and headed back towards their work area.

Floating towards the bathroom, Ami grumbled to herself, saying, *yeah, not soon enough.*

After surviving her first bathroom experience, Ami felt a little better. With her head starting to clear and the food seeming to help settle her stomach, she headed over to the lab. She waved to a couple of the other astronauts doing experiments in one of the other labs as she attempted to stay upright as she traversed the hallway.

Making her way over to Liam, who was scrolling through the data on his tablet, she grabbed his arm in an attempt to stop her momentum. Reading over his shoulder she tried to discern the data Emeline had found. It was weird that the arrays should be picking up this strange data. The report indicated that the readings on the electromagnetic radiation were all consistent with what they expected, so she ruled out something being wrong with the arrays. It had to be something else that was being sent towards Earth that they were picking up.

Between the flashing of the monitors and the constant whirring noises in the background, it was hard for Ami to concentrate. Focusing on Liam's tablet as the data scrolled by, she started noticing the embedded pattern that Emeline had mentioned. Why did the data seem to be running in a synchronized loop? *This is weird. What could be causing this?* It appeared manmade but that was impossible, wasn't it? How is this happening?

As Ami turned to relay her findings to Liam, suddenly, a shimmer of light began to appear near the side window in the lab. She opened her mouth to get Liam's attention when a being materialized right in front of them.

Staring directly at them, the being began to speak,

"Please do not be alarmed. We are from the planet Delicia. We know that this is a first contact situation for you, but we've come with important knowledge that your planet must be made aware of. My name is Director Nox. I am the lead scientist assigned by the United Alliance of Planets to come here to speak to you. It is imperative for the future well-being of your planet that you listen to what we have to say. Our shuttle is ready to dock alongside your station and we request that you send a representative to our ship so that we may discuss this urgent matter. We understand you need to contact your superiors, therefore we will give you two of Earth hours before we attach our docking portal. Please—I cannot stress enough how important this is to your planet. Time is of the essence."

The being nodded his head to them before disappearing into thin air.

The silence in the room was only permeated by the noise of the various fans, the machines whirling and the heavy breathing coming from Liam and Ami. A look of stunned disbelief showed on their faces as they tried to comprehend what they had just witnessed. With mouths agape, they stared at one another, making sure they'd both seen the same thing.

"WHAT THE FUCK WAS THAT?"

Stunned, Ami felt Liam's hand covering her mouth as he hissed softly into her ear, "Sshh. We can't let the other guys know what just happened. I have no idea what the fuck that was. I mean, seriously, was that even real?"

Ami frantically nodded her head in agreement. "Did you see that?" Her words were muffled against Liam's hand.

"Oh, I saw it." Liam said, his voice hoarse as he looked into Ami's wide, frightened eyes.

Shaking his head trying to clear it—hoping that maybe he had been hallucinating—Liam released Ami and started floating around trying to wrap his mind around what he had just seen. They didn't really prepare you for this in astronaut training. *Damn, I wish we had gravity. I need to pace.* Okay, he definitely needed to do the *Breathe, Center, Focus* thing.

Slowly pulling in a deep breath, he just as slowly let it out. Feeling his body start to calm, he whispered to Ami, "We need to make a plan. I think we need to call Leslie Merriman on her secure line and tell her what the hell just happened. We don't have much time and if what that guy... guy, yeah right. Alien? Man, this is hard to wrap my head around."

Looking over at Ami, he saw her rigid body floating un-tethered. Her glassy eyes fixated on the window while her mouth hung open. "Ami—you okay?" She shook her head slowly, her breathing sounding labored, making it hard for her to speak.

"I can't catch my breath," she gasped.

"Come here." He floated over, pulling her gently against his chest. He could feel her body shaking—her heart thumping hard—a match to his own. Rubbing his hands up and down her back, he whispered his mother's mantra *Breathe, Center, Focus* over and over into her hair.

Ami let out a hysterical laugh before slumping in his

arms, her blood pressure lowering just a fraction as her breathing began to even out. "Thank you—again—Fiona and thanks, Liam. I don't know what the hell that was. That was some real freaky shit. I'd think I was hallucinating but I know you saw that too."

"Yeah, I feel the same way. We need to call Leslie at NASA headquarters right away. We only have a short time left before they come back. Are you going to be okay?"

"Sure. Why wouldn't I be? I mean, come on, isn't it every day that aliens send you a message telling you that your planet is in danger and they want you to go onto their spaceship? Sure, why wouldn't I be just hunky dory?" Feeling her blood pressure starting to rise again, she tried to suck in another deep breath. "I mean, come on; did you get a look at that alien? OMG—he was hot. What was he—about seven feet tall, and man, talk about muscles. I mean, shit—did you get a look at his skin? I've never seen skin like that before. It looked almost like an opal. Wow! I mean I've never seen iridescent skin before. Well at least he wasn't green." Gasping again, her voice began to edge higher as she continued her tirade. "And his hair, geez did you see the streaks of purple in it?" Ami clutched at her chest, "All right, all right, I'm babbling I know, but I mean..." Grabbing the front of Liam's uniform, she yelled in a hushed whisper, "WHAT THE FUCK!!!"

Squeezing her hands before prying them off his uniform, Liam headed to his tablet so he could put in a call to his superior. He wondered what he was going to say to her that didn't make him sound like he was suffering from a psychotic breakdown. "Unlike you, Ami, instead of looking at his body, I was listening to what he had to say about Earth. It sounds like something bad is about to go down and I think we should focus on that instead of his "smokin'" body. Look, I need you to pull it together and help me here. We don't have much time and I need you to download his message onto your tablet. I want to make sure that Leslie can see the transmission for herself."

Nodding her head, Ami grabbed her computer as she followed Liam's command. He was right, enough freaking out —time to do her job.

Opening up a file, she started downloading the recording. What was Leslie going to say when she saw this, she wondered once she had finished the download.

Stopping abruptly, Ami came to a startling realization— it was going to be her and Liam that went to the alien ship because they were the only ones available. *Shit, shit, shit!*

Breathing deeply for like the thousandth time since she'd seen her first alien, Ami mentally slapped herself. *What's that old saying? Oh yeah, be careful what you wish for because you might just get it.* This, she could have done without. Okay "Center" "Focus" The alien guy, what was his name again, oh that's right, Nox—he didn't seem like he would take no for an answer, and if she was honest with herself, she wanted to go. *Hell yes, she was going. Boy, the girls are going to be so jealous. Lorelei is going to flip out.*

Suddenly, Leslie Merriman's annoyed face appeared on the computer screen. Being the head of NASA, she was probably wondering why they were calling her instead of their mission manager. Descended from a melting pot of ancestors, she had a degree in business and biochem. Small in stature but trim and fit, she was an attractive woman who took her job very seriously.

Scowling at them, she inquired as to why they were interrupting her dinner.

Liam and Ami both started talking at once.

Holding up her hand, she gestured her head toward Liam and barked, "Explain."

"We just got a message from aliens!" Ami yelled softly.

Leslie glared at Ami. "Liam, what the devil is she talking about?"

Glancing at Ami, Liam squeezed her hand, trying to reassure her. He knew she was having a hard time comprehending the events of last few minutes. She wasn't alone in that by any means. Taking a deep breath, his voice hardened like a steel sword. He needed both women to understand just how serious this situation was. This alien —Director Nox—appeared adamant about the threat to Earth. Calmly and methodically, he told Leslie about the transmission and then played the message for her.

He finished by telling her that the alien stressed that time was important. "I think we need to take this seriously."

Leslie was stunned. Dumbfounded, she murmured, "Wow. It has finally happened." Gathering herself together, she asked in a quiet voice, "How much time before they make contact?"

"A little over an hour before we meet them at the docking bay," Liam replied.

Looking incredulously at the both of them, Leslie tried to focus her mind. "Okay, give me a minute to think."

After taking a few moments to collect her thoughts, she started giving orders. "First thing, I'll need to contact the President. We actually have a protocol in place for this, but honestly, I never thought we'd ever need it. You realize you'll be the ones going onboard the alien ship?" Seeing them nod in agreement, she continued. "Liam, I want your recorders on at all times and if possible, have the feed transmitted directly to me. I will get back to you after I talk to President Jenkins, but I don't think there will be enough time before you leave—"

Knowing she sounded snarky, Ami couldn't stop herself from interrupting, "And just what exactly are we supposed to talk about with these aliens? *Oh hey, how's it going? Want to grab some dinner or I know—would you like to take over our planet and enslave all humans?*"

"Well Ami, why don't you just sit and listen to what they have to say first before shooting your mouth off," Leslie admonished her. "This is something we've never had to deal with before and it sounds like the fate of the planet is at stake. I need you to take this seriously." Giving Ami a stern look, she added, "If you don't think you're up to this, Liam will go alone and you will stay on the station and wait for him to return."

Ami pulled back as if she had been slapped. Gritting her teeth, she tried not to bellow at Leslie, opting instead to purse her lips before grinding out, "If you think for one second I'm going to let Liam go onto an alien ship alone, think again. I know I'm not sounding particularly sane right now, but hey I—," her eyes flashed with anger, "we've just witnessed something that no one has ever, ever seen before. So, I'm sorry if I'm acting a little crazy, however, let me be clear, I will be going with Liam."

Leslie nodded; relief showed on her face. "Glad to see you've started using your brain again. I know you'd never let Liam go alone. But and this is a very big but, you are representing the planet Earth to an alien species. I need you to pull it together and start acting like the professional I know you are. Liam is counting on you and you will need a cool head going forward."

Liam, who had been watching the exchange between Ami and Leslie, knew Ami was having trouble grasping this whole turn of events. Hell, he was too. It was Ami who was the one to jump in with a joke when situations got tough —that was how she coped with stressful situations. But when it came to having someone watch your back, it was Ami Liam wanted in his corner. Not only was she smart with a logical mind, but she was quick-thinking when it came to finding solutions to problems. Not to mention she had been working with him on self-defense training for a number of years. She was strong and could be extremely tenacious when necessary. That's the Ami he needed right now.

Turning Ami towards him, he peered into her eyes. Staring back at him, he could see she was trying to wrap her head around the situation they found themselves in. He held her gaze, letting her see that he understood how she felt. "Ami," he said softly, not wanting to disrupt the control she was trying so desperately to hang onto. "I need you right now. I need the Ami that is strong and resilient. Do you remember our training sessions?"

"Yes."

"What is the first thing that I taught you?"

Swallowing hard, she answered, "Never let them see your fear."

"Can you do that for me? Can I count on you to pull it together and have my back?"

Ami gazed directly into Liam's eyes, letting him know he could count on her. Straightening her shoulders, she exhaled, telling him, "I've got this."

Giving Liam a grateful look, she turned to Leslie saying, "I apologize for my outburst, Ms. Merriman. I am going with Liam. I won't let you down." Mouthing to Liam, "I got you."

Leslie looked from Liam and Ami as she contemplated the two of them. Seeming to make a decision, she nodded in agreement. "Good. Now it's imperative that you get a good understanding of why they are here and what they want from us. You're going to be on your own once you are on their ship with only each other to rely on should things go badly." She raised her eyebrow at Ami, silently asking if she could handle this. Satisfied when Ami acknowledged the seriousness of the situation, Leslie continued, "I will be showing this recording to the President. I have no idea what his reaction is going to be, so get as much information as you can."

Liam frowned, all of a sudden remembering the other astronauts on the ISS, and asked Leslie, "What about the other crewmembers here? Do we read them in on this? It's going to be hard for them not to notice an alien ship docking alongside the station."

Leslie thought for a moment as she considered the four other astronauts onboard the Space Station. "There is no way we can keep this from them, especially once you leave the station. I'm sure their governments will be talking to them, but I will discuss this with the President. I'm assuming he'll be contacting the UN Security Council. It will be up to their individual governments to make the decision on what they want them to know. As of right now, this is a strictly need-to-know operation."

"Affirmative," Liam replied.

"Just keep your eyes and ears open. I'll want a detailed report as soon as you're able."

"We will. You can count on us," Liam told Leslie.

"I know I can." Leslie looked from one to the other, her expression showed her apprehension at the undeniably dangerous situation she was placing them in. Speaking softly, she said, "I realize this is asking a lot of you both, but just know that your country, hell, your planet, is counting on you. The fate of Earth is in your hands. Good luck. Merriman out."

The video screen went blank, the sounds of the Space Station continued around them, unaware of how the next few hours would change the course of Earth forever.

"Yeah, not too much pressure," Ami quipped. Liam smiled reassuringly at her.

Blowing out a breath, Ami grumbled to him, "Did she have to say the fate of Earth was in our hands? Okay—well, I guess we're going on an alien ship."

Checking the time, Liam saw they needed to get going if they were going to make it to the docking bay and get into their suits before the aliens would attach their portal. They needed to suit up because he was not going on board any ship without his spacesuit on. He had no idea what they were walking into and he wanted to be prepared.

Grabbing two recording devices, he floated over to Ami and helped her attach one to her uniform before attaching his own. "Come on, we better get down to the docking bay. There's not much time before they get here and I want to be ready. You going to be okay?"

Cringing slightly, embarrassed at her meltdown, she said, "Yeah. I'm sorry about that whole going crazy episode. I don't know what came over me. You know I'm not usually like that."

Squeezing her hand, he started to steer them towards the docking bay. "I don't blame you, but can you handle this? No one will fault you if you don't think you're up for this."

Letting go of his hand, she swatted him on the arm saying, "Now who's being crazy? Give up a chance to see a real live alien? Not happening. Besides, I wouldn't be able to go home again if I ditched you on this. Between my dad and the girls, I'd never live this down. Not to mention Lorelei would never forgive me. You're stuck with me." Giving him a meaningful look, she spoke from her heart. "You can count on me."

He smiled, relieved his fearless Ami was back. "I know."

Pushing ahead of him, she called softly, "Come on, fly boy, let's go meet some hunky, hot aliens."

Grinning, he followed her towards the docking bay. Glancing out the window as he floated by, he couldn't help but wonder what the next few hours of his life was going to be like. One thing for sure—life as he knew it was going to change. Good or bad, things were never going to be the same.

CHAPTER 4

Nox couldn't help wondering about the humans he was about to meet. From his current position, he watched as Nyx maneuvered the cloaked shuttle alongside the human space station. Once he was lined up with their docking hatch, a docking portal was deployed, attaching their shuttle to the Space Station's airlock. His full lips smirked as he considered what the primitive humans would think about the cloaked shuttle they were about to board. The cloaking device was a handy piece of technology that was only allowed to be used by the military. Nox had done some research on it when he was creating his force field technology and it fascinated him. The UAP was worried this type of technology would fall into the wrong hands, especially the Hexians.

Pausing, Nox wondered if it was possible Tarquin had gotten his hands on a cloaking device. That would certainly explain how he'd been getting onto Earth without being seen. Nox looked over at Tarek, making a mental note to talk to him about his theory when they got back to the ship.

He glanced down at his wrist comm, checking the time just as Commander Nyx secured the door. Considering what was about to happen, Nox felt anxious and excited all at once. As a scientist it was always thrilling to be included in a new discovery, and first contact with an indigenous species would be the centerpiece of his many accomplishments. His mother would have loved being a part of this adventure.

Ami and Liam stood waiting in their space suits on the other side of the hatch for it to open, stomachs clenched with the anticipation of what was about to happen.

"Stay behind me...I'll go through first," Liam told Ami through his headset.

Ami held tightly to the hand rails embedded onto the side of the walls. Moving around in a spacesuit with zero gravity proved difficult, so she merely nodded her head in agreement.

They had no idea what they were walking into and Liam wasn't going to let anything happen to Ami if he could possibly avoid it. He patted her arm with his gloved hand, trying to reassure her as best he could, all the while knowing that was impossible.

Without warning, the door swung open and they were motioned through, getting their first glimpse of actual beings from another planet.

"Welcome."

Stepping forward, Nox motioned them away from the door. "It is an honor to meet a species similar to ours. You will not need your suits...our atmosphere is compatible with yours."

Looking at Liam for his approval, Ami took off her helmet, her eyes scanning her surroundings. The first thing that stood out were the two enormous, well-armed aliens studying her. *Deep breaths. You got this.*

Her impression of the two males, aside from their skin-tight uniforms which left nothing to the imagination, was that it was clear they were military. It showed in how they carried themselves, especially the one who was obviously in charge. He emanated an authoritative demeanor which made her pause.

As Ami tried not to stare, she took in their appearance, noting that their features were similar to humans—two eyes, a nose, a mouth, and eyebrows. Doing a quick scan, she checked for any strange appendages or horns. Nope—no horns! *Yeah, that would be Lorelei's first question!* Their skin though—boy that was something to see. Shiny luminescent white with flecks of blues, purples and pinks with hints of pale yellows. *Like sprinkles on a vanilla ice cream cone. It's so pretty looking! I get the feeling pretty isn't what they were going for.*

The second thing that Ami noticed was the alien who had delivered the message to them. *Director Nox—okay, different, but hey, who am I to judge a person on their name or anything else for that matter, especially considering who my parents are?* He was standing closest to her and seeing him in the flesh really drove home just how real this situation was. This was a moment Ami would never forget, but putting that aside, the future of her planet was at stake. Definitely needed to focus. Centering and breathing would also be a plus. All of a sudden, it clicked in her brain that she could understand him. *Why didn't I catch that? How can we understand him?* She asked him that very question.

"Let me explain," he said. "When soldiers first enter the military, a translator chip is injected into their brain. Our ARI monitored your radio waves and created a database of your languages. It was quite fascinating to find that you had so many different ones. On Delicia we have only one."

"What's an ARI?" she asked, rubbing her head, thinking that having anything injected into her brain would be unnerving.

"Essentially it's what you would call an artificial intelligence that oversees all our ship's computers. We refer to it as ARI."

"Amazing."

Nox hid his smirk, mumbling, "You have no idea."

By this time Liam had removed his helmet and was assessing the situation. His Navy training began to kick in now that the initial shock was over. Taking in the information from Nox, he appraised the other aliens on the shuttle, noting the weapons hanging from their utility belts. The type of weapons he'd certainly never seen before and could definitely cause deadly damage to the human body.

Straightening as tall as he could, shoulders back, he addressed the three aliens. "I am Lieutenant Commander Liam Cameron of the United States of America. On behalf of the planet Earth, I welcome you." Gesturing towards Ami, he said, "This is Ami Jefferson, an aerospace engineer with EAC Global Network Solutions."

Nox pointed to himself, replying, "My name is Director Nox. As I have already told you, we are from the planet Delicia. I was the one you saw in our message." Pointing at the largest alien, he said, "This is General Tarek, head of the Delician military and leader of this mission." He nodded at the remaining male who was removing the docking portal. "This is Commander Nyx. He is our pilot and General Tarek's second in command."

Liam extended his hand to Nox in a greeting. Staring at Liam's hand, Nox looked confused. Ami grabbed Nox's hand and shook it as she told him, "This is how we greet each other. How do you greet each other?"

Nox turned to Liam and grasped him by the forearm and

nodded his head. Liam returned the greeting to each of the Delicians.

General Tarek began giving orders to Nyx before indicating where Liam and Ami should sit for the short flight back to their battle cruiser, the *Maelstrom*. Addressing the humans, he said, "I realize this is new to you, but we have important information that we need to discuss. When we arrive back onboard our ship, we will explain why we came to your planet." Giving them a rare reassuring smile, he turned back to speak to Nyx.

After taking off their spacesuits, Liam and Ami looked at each other, bewildered. The aliens had obviously solved any gravity problems since no one was floating around or strapped in as the ship moved away from the Space Station. Sitting quietly, they were at a loss as to what to say to these aliens. They had a million questions but didn't know where to start.

Swallowing his rising fear, Liam mentally berated himself to get a grip. This was a mission just like any other. Just because it was aliens and the future of the planet was at stake shouldn't change his behavior. He needed to start relying on his training and not just blindly trust anything about this situation. He was a Lt. Commander in the United States Navy. *Start acting like it.*

Ami squirmed in her seat. The aliens were staring at her, making her feel uncomfortable. Moving closer to Liam, she murmured out of the corner of her mouth so no one else could hear, "I win. No little green men."

Seeing a quick smile come and go on the general's face, Liam glared down at her as if to say now is not the time for jokes. This was a serious situation they were in. They needed to be on guard.

Nox sat down, trying to keep his gaze from straying to the humans. His analytical mind started to kick in as he began to quietly study them. He couldn't help himself. Science was his life. He wondered what they thought about all this. It had to be overwhelming for them. Nox had never been a participant in a first contact situation before, but he had been exposed to other species his whole life. He counted himself lucky that he was raised on Delicia. They had always been a member of the UAP. He tried to imagine what the humans must feel like finding out they were not the only species in the universe. *I guess it would depend on the circumstances of the contact. If it was the Hexians who made first contact, fear would be the main sentiment. That may still be the case if they're not able to stop Tarquin and his mercenaries. They had no choice but to succeed. Too many lives were at stake.*

Glancing at Lt. Commander Cameron, Nox considered him thoughtfully. Outward appearances suggested that he took care of his body and trained to stay fit. Nox couldn't wait to have a conversation with him about his training routine and his position in the military. He felt that the Lt. Commander could provide valuable insight into Earth and its inhabitants. It was important to develop a level of trust between them, which might not be such an easy task considering the circumstances. Nox glanced at Tarek knowing he was thinking the same thing. Clear communication would be key in gaining the humans' trust.

Looking over at the female human, Nox thought *she certainly is interesting to look at and she wasn't at all hesitant in speaking her mind.* Judging from the vids he had seen, her skin tone and the shape of her eyes indicated she was a product of a mixed race. She was tall and solid looking, which was the total opposite of Delician women. Her toned body attested that training was also a part of her daily routine. Her beautiful face showed the anxiety of the situation she found herself in.

Delician women were delicate, almost fragile looking...although sometimes appearances could be deceiving. There were a few Delician women he had known who may have looked gentle on the outside but their strength of will belied that belief. His mother came to mind. *No. We are not going there right now.*

He glanced at Ami and saw that she was moving around in her seat. "How you doing?" he asked her.

"Well, I could lie and tell you everything is great but I won't. I have so many questions running through my head that I can't decide which one to ask first."

"It is understandable for you to feel that way. This must all be a shock to you," Nox said, his eyes giving her a look of compassion.

"Yeah, you could say that. This was not how I thought my day would go, that's for sure," Ami replied, staring back at Nox before she turned her gaze to Liam, who was intently watching the pilot.

Liam couldn't take his eyes off Nyx—watching his every move as he piloted the shuttle. This was so different from any aircraft he'd seen before. What surprised him the most was the quiet. Every plane Liam had ever flown was noisy. From the sound of the engine or the wind rushing by or in the case of the space shuttle, the roar of the fuel burning as they ascended into the skies, pilots had to wear headsets to offset the sounds. Here on the alien shuttle, there was silence—other than the sound of Ami's breathing coming out a little too fast.

Liam squeezed Ami's hand reassuringly—satisfied when she squeezed his in return.

"We'll be docking in a moment. Once we're cleared to disembark, we'll head to my conference room to talk," General Tarek told them, his eyes focused on the viewscreen in front of them.

Liam and Ami gasped in unison as they watched a massive structure enter their line of sight. Ami held in a bubble of laughter thinking about all the sci-fi movies she and the girls loved to watch. The ship that appeared before them didn't resemble the Star Trek Enterprise in the least. For one thing it was sleek with cleaner lines—no deflector arrays or engines that stuck out from the rear of the ship. It was shaped like an arrow head with a smooth black hull made from a material she had never seen before. With the practiced eye of an engineer, Ami considered the alien ship from a design and construction point of view. *I'd love to get a look at their schematics.*

Liam looked at the ship from the standpoint of a pilot. Having watched Nyx pilot the shuttle, he had to admit to himself that he had *"pilot envy."* What he wouldn't give to be able to fly one of these babies, he thought to himself.

Nox watched the reactions of the humans when they saw the *Maelstrom* for the first time. Judging by the expressions on their faces, he couldn't help chuckling to himself. *This is probably the most exciting thing they have ever seen.* He wasn't wrong.

He started giving the humans a brief description of the

Delician battle cruiser. "The *Maelstrom* is an elite class warship, one of many in the Delician fleet, but this one is special. Even though it's equipped to carry senior members of the Delician government, it's General Tarek's personal ship. Don't be fooled by its size. It can be quite maneuverable when necessary. It carries a fleet of star fighters and has a fully equipped medical bay with several regen units onboard. It's a self-contained ship that carries a crew of up to 1500."

"We have been cleared for docking, General." Nyx's voice interrupted Nox to inform the General who was watching intently as Nyx maneuvered the shuttle through the open docking bay doors.

Ami stared mesmerized out the front viewscreen as they glided slowly into the bay. "Do you think I could have a tour of the ship while we're here?"

"I think a guided tour could be arranged," the General replied taking note of her interest in his ship. "But I think we need to discuss our reason for contacting you first."

"Sorry," Ami murmured trying to hide her blush. "This place is freaking amazing—I don't know where to look first."

"I understand completely. After our meeting, I'll arrange for you to have a tour of my ship," Tarek told her as he turned his attention to Nyx who landed the shuttle smoothly on the deck of the ship, showing just how much of an experienced pilot he was.

Once they were cleared to disembark, they were led out through the shuttle doors into an enormous hangar. Their shuttle was one of a handful—all placed side by side in a neat row. All around them were members of Tarek's crew, all Delicians. Their iridescent skin shimmered in the light. Every crew member they passed stopped what they were doing and saluted them as they walked by. Ami was impressed with the level of respect the crew had for General Tarek.

"This place is beyond amazing," she murmured. Her eyes constantly scanning the area, taking in as much as she could.

Liam took in the small ships lined up in perfect unison all along the hangar floor that were set apart from the shuttles. These were fighter ships, Liam surmised, judging from their shape. They were streamlined and looked extremely fast. He itched to get his hands on one, wishing he could spend some time down here learning all that he could. This was a chance to see something that no other human ever had, plus he would love to get a ride in one. That would be a dream come true for him.

Following General Tarek and Nox, with Nyx bringing up the rear, Ami and Liam were directed along a series of corridors through the ship. The lighting was unusual in that it appeared to radiate out from the walls—a soft bluish gray glow giving off just the right amount of light as they walked by. The walls themselves were smooth except in places where computer panels were inserted. The floors and ceilings were solid—no steel beams showing, similar to what you would see on a cruise ship only without the carpet. They passed countless doors with symbols on them that of course she couldn't understand. Ami supposed it didn't matter if she could read the words—she didn't expect that they'd give her free rein to wander around the ship by herself.

Looking around, Ami laughed inwardly. The girls would be totally freaking out right about now. She could hear Lorelei— "You bitch!" But she would be laughing as she said it. Lorelei would want Ami to experience everything she could but she would want all the details when she got home. Heather would be shocked and that was saying something because nothing much ever did. She would want to know all about how ARI worked and Ami had to agree that did sound fascinating.

It's hard to say how Emeline would feel. On the outside she would be all about the science and helping in any way she could, but on the inside, Ami felt Emeline would be more than a little bit frightened. Ever since Emeline's dad had died, she had gotten strangely quiet. Her focus on work was understandable with the deflector network array and all, but she had forgotten about a private life. On nights when she wasn't working, she was either at the gym training or home cooking...usually alone. Ami had hoped to talk to Liam about Em while they were on the ISS, but she guessed that just got pushed into the background.

Entering an elevator brought everyone into close proximity, which made Ami feel small—something she wasn't particularly used to. She was above average in height for a woman, but standing next to these guys, she actually felt petite. She thought about Heather and how tiny she was. It was going to be a hoot watching Heather's reaction to these perfect specimens of male anatomy.

Ami already knew what Lorelei would do when she saw these aliens, especially General Tarek. *"Wow, I mean just wow. Talk about a body. I mean, the guy could be a Greek statue come to life, a naked gorgeous man statue come to*

when she saw that everyone was staring at her.

Liam nudged her arm, giving her his *will you shut up* look. "Sorry," she murmured under her breath.

Nox slid into the empty seat next to Loris, catching his eye as his friend shook his head at the human female. This was the first time any of them had ever seen a human and they appeared nothing like any of them had expected.

General Tarek began the meeting with introductions. "Lt. Commander Cameron, Ami Jefferson, this is Captain Jagger. He is the captain of this ship. Next to him is Commander Ezio. He is a member of my elite team along with Lt. Ramola, who is our weapons specialist. Commander Nyx, my second in command. Next to Nox is his assistant Loris. Please, Director Nox, start the presentation you have prepared for the humans."

Nox signaled Loris to have ARI display the hologram.

"ARI, display planet Earth and its orbiting satellites." Loris spoke out loud seemingly to no one but rather quickly from the center of the table, Earth in all its glory appeared before them with the satellites orbiting around it. A look of satisfaction appeared on Loris's face as he watched the humans' reaction.

Nox was also curious to see the humans' reaction to the hologram technology as well. He wasn't disappointed, their eyes nearly bulging out of their heads as they peered at their planet being displayed before them. *This is some of our older technology. Just wait until they see some of the really advanced tech.*

"As you can see from this hologram of Earth, we were able to detect satellites orbiting Earth." Nox stood, pointing at the many satellites seen moving in their orbits. Pointing to the International Space Station, he continued, "Using our long-range sensors, we detected six life forms located here on this large satellite. Once we saw—"

"Excuse me. Sorry—but you were able to tell that people were onboard the station from how far away?" Ami interrupted incredulously. "That's incredible."

The aliens in the room smiled indulgently as Nox replied, "This is minor technology for us."

"Yeah well, I'm sure it is, but to us this is amazing stuff."

Nox gave another command. "ARI, display a map showing all planets within the UAP territory." The image of Earth morphed into a map of the universe that showed a plethora of planets that comprised the United Alliance of Planets. Earth appeared to shrink and shifted off towards the very edge of the map looking lonely—like a small blue ball discarded on an empty playground.

"As you can see by the map, these are all the planets that are under the jurisdiction of the UAP," Nox swung his arm at the different colored planets that appeared suspended in front of them.

Ami gave up trying to count how many planets there were. There had to be hundreds. "Are they all inhabited?"

When Nox nodded yes, Ami nearly fainted from the shock. "This is unbelievable. So much for being alone in the universe," she quipped under her breath.

Liam's eyes were glued to the hologram. "And the UAP is what again?"

"United Alliance of Planets, but everyone just refers to it as the UAP. It was formed several millennia ago as a way to bring unity and trade alliances to this sector of the universe. Each planet has a representative on the council where trade deals are negotiated and conflicts are resolved."

"So how does a planet get to be a member of your UAP?" Ami asked. This whole experience was bizarre, to say the least. She fully expected to see bruises on her legs tomorrow from the pinches she kept giving herself as a reminder that she wasn't dreaming.

"Any planet that has knowledge of other species can apply for membership. Now your planet—Earth," he said as his fingers moved over the console in front of him—the little blue planet appeared to grow in size. "Your planet has no awareness of life outside of its solar system, which means you were automatically placed on the prohibited planet list. This means Earth is off limits and no contact can be made unless authorized by the UAP. If this directive is not followed per the UAP decree, serious consequences are levied against offenders."

Liam contemplated Nox's words. "I can certainly understand why you would place Earth on this list, but how often do you check up on these planets to see how far they've advanced?"

Nox's voice held a hint of contriteness as he answered Liam. "It seems that we have not been doing enough of, as you say 'checking up on.' It's evident that we should have been monitoring your planet more closely. It appears that Earth has advanced far beyond what we had surmised."

"Yeah, you could say that again," Ami said, giving him a smug look.

Nox looked sharply at Ami, replying, "I understand you're upset that you have been kept unaware of life outside of your solar system, but you've got to understand we did this for your own benefit as well as ours. We have to be careful on how we go about bringing planets into the Alliance. First contact can be volatile. History has shown us that disaster and chaos often follows if not done correctly.

It's mainly for their own safety that the UAP is cautious."

He pointed to a planet near the center of the map. "This is Delicia, our home planet. We've been a member since the beginning of the Alliance." Delicia was a large planet surrounded in a pastel mist. It had two moons that orbited on either side of the planet.

As Liam sat listening to Nox, he couldn't help but wonder why if Earth was off limits, they were sitting on an alien ship. *Something bad must be happening if they've decided Earth should be contacted.* He glanced at Ami and saw that she was ready to interrupt with more questions of her own. He shook his head, indicating she should stay quiet.

Nox held up his hand, indicating they hold off with any questions until he was finished. He pointed to a section of the map at a reddish-brown planet sitting all alone off on the opposite side of the universe from Earth. "This is Hexia, a planet that is not a member of the UAP but resides inside our territory. It's a terrible place. ARI, enhance image of Hexia."

Hexia appeared before them, showing a lackluster planet that was similar in size to Earth.

Nox pointed at the reddish-brown globe that looked anything but hospitable. "This planet is a vapid hellhole that makes it a perfect location for criminals and outcasts. It has no native inhabitants, so it's become a haven for anyone who wants to remain anonymous to the UAP."

"Not a place I would choose for my next vacation then." Ami had a feeling that Nox was just about to get to the part in his story that would not be good for Earth or humans.

"No, definitely not a vacation spot. ARI, display an image of Tarquin, leader of Hexia."

Ami stared enthralled as an image of a large, muscular-looking alien male appeared before them. His skin was different than the Delicians in that his was weathered—leathery, almost reddish looking in appearance. She could tell just by looking at him he was a hard man who had seen way more of the darker side of life than any human had ever thought to. He appeared to be tall and well-built—similar to the Delician males who were sitting around the table, but that's where the similarities ended. It wasn't just that their hair was a deep brown with varying degrees of purple-colored highlights running through it; it was in how they held themselves—definitely military. Tarquin, on the other hand, looked more pirate than soldier. His head was covered with a cloth hat...his eyes dark, almost black, giving him a rather devilish appearance. But what seemed to redeem his hard features was his wide mouth that was curved into an easy smile. It made you almost want to ask what had him so amused, almost but not quite.

General Tarek stood, picking up where Nox left off. "This is Tarquin, the self-imposed leader of Hexia." Tarek voice came out rough. "Tarquin has been a thorn in the side of the UAP for many years. He's a sneaky, arrogant skizoid who thinks only of gaining profit with no regard as to who gets hurt in the process. He has a whole planet of mercenaries at his fingertips and he enjoys using them. We've been trying to capture him for many years, but he always seems to be one step ahead of us."

Not wanting to interrupt but her mouth just wouldn't stop, Ami shuddered, asking, "What's a skizoid? That sounds like an alien rat."

Jagger spoke for the first time, a look of disgust on his

face as he made a shooting motion with his hand. "Close. It's a nasty piece of vermin that will eat anything and they're hard to kill. Luckily, they're not on Delicia. They're about the only thing indigenous to Hexia. I've used them for target practice whenever I have to go to that dump of a planet."

Tarek shared a smirk with his friend. "Yes, skizoids are about a foot long with sharp nasty teeth. They have a natural armor that covers their bodies, making them hard to kill, but not impossible, right, Jagger?"

Suddenly remembering the cloaking device, Nox interrupted Tarek with his theory. "I have a theory about how he's been avoiding capture. I have a feeling he has somehow obtained a cloaking device."

Tarek's eyes hardened as he considered this new information. "I think you might be right. That has to be how he's been sneaking onto Earth and why he thinks his plan is actually going to work."

"Wait. What?" Liam jumped to his feet. "What do you mean? Are you saying this guy has been visiting Earth?"

"I wouldn't exactly use the word 'visiting,'" Tarek replied back to him. "It is more like skulking around for any new opportunities that will increase his wealth and power is how I'd put it. The whole purpose of us contacting you is because of this worthless piece of scum and his plan for your planet."

"Go on," urged Liam as he sat back down in his seat, stress beginning to show on his face. "I get the feeling his plans for us are not going to be all sunshine and rainbows."

Frowning, Tarek wasn't sure what Liam just said but he got the gist.

"No, his plans for Earth and its inhabitants will not bode well for anyone. That's why the UAP sent us here to contact you, and now that it appears he has somehow obtained a cloaking device—it explains a lot. We're not sure how long he's been visiting Earth, but from the intelligence we have gathered, it appears to have been a while. Judging from the topography surrounding the location of the curative substance he's after, and if you add in the fact that he has a cloaked ship, it seems he plans to use Earth as his personal playground."

"What substance are you talking about?" Ami could feel her blood pressure beginning to rise as a feeling of anger began to consume her. *How dare he!*

"A substance called salt mined from the Himalayan Mountain region," Nox interjected. "ARI, display the Himalayan Mountain region on planet Earth."

Liam and Ami looked at each other in disbelief. "Did you just say salt?" Liam was stunned as he looked at the image that had appeared before him. "As in the stuff we use in cooking? You can't be serious? I mean, why would someone go through all this trouble just for salt?"

Loris, who had been reading his notes, looked up, telling them, "What may be a common substance on your world has far more important, far more reaching benefits for other species. This particular salt has elements in it that can be used in vaccines and medicines for cures on a multitude of planets throughout our universe."

Nox took up the narrative, explaining what they thought the Hexians' plan was. "Tarquin planned to quietly slip onto Earth and start an initial takeover of the salt mines. We don't have all the details but we have received enough information from our informants that Tarquin and the Hexians plan to strip Earth of this natural resource and any other resources that could bring them profit. They don't care who gets hurt in the process. That's why we have been sent here. The UAP can't allow Earth's natural progression of evolution to be changed by the Hexians." Nox's tone was serious as he tried to get across to the humans just how important this mission was.

Ami stood and began pacing back and forth...the information that ran through her mind was just too unbelievable to comprehend.

Stopping mid pace to gaze out the bank of windows that lined the walls of the room, the multitude of stars staring back at her made her realize just how small her world really was.

Turning, her outrage was palpable. "You've got to be kidding me. Salt. Seriously? I mean sure over the last few years pink Himalayan salt has been the "fad" with some websites touting its healing properties. But anyone with any scientific background knows that's just hype used to get people to buy it. You're saying that someone actually wants to destroy our planet for something as simple as salt!"

"A "fad" to you is something that could stop an outbreak of a sickness to someone else," Nox said gently. He could see that the humans were beginning to comprehend the seriousness of the situation.

Glancing at Liam, Nox noted the human male looked ready to take some action.

And Nox was right—Liam was ready to take action, but since he was on an alien ship, he could only do so much. With a fierce look of determination, he asked the General,

"So, what's the plan? How do we stop this asshole from thinking it's perfectly okay for him to come to our planet and do whatever the hell he wants? I assume you have a plan in place, otherwise you wouldn't be here."

It was Nox who answered him and what he had to say next caused Liam to look up sharply. "When we first got this mission, we weren't sure what we were going to do. We were all under the assumption that Earth was still living without much technology but once we started to scan your planet, we discovered that you have become more advanced than we initially thought."

"Great, just great. Still thought we were Neanderthals, I suppose," grumbled Ami as she sat back down in her seat.

"No, not quite...well, okay, maybe I did think you might still be discovering fire," he said sheepishly, "but once we started doing long-range scans on your planet, we discovered we were mistaken." Nox smiled at her, hoping to ease some of the hurt he saw showing on her face. "When our scans discovered your orbiting space station, a decision was made to contact the life forms inhabiting the station. We were particularly interested in the deflector array installed on a few of the orbiting satellites."

Sharing a look of unease with Liam, Ami choked out, " Deflector array? Why do you need that?"

"Before we discuss that," Tarek interrupted, "I think it's more important to discuss how to go about informing your government about this situation. Determining how to make first contact without creating a planet-wide panic is the first thing we should consider."

Liam understood the seriousness of the General's words. Looking down at his recorder, Liam saw that it had stopped working. Taking if off his uniform, he started to run through the checklist for rebooting the recorder.

"Your recorder has been deactivated."

Liam looked up sharply at the General. "What do you mean?"

"We automatically disabled your devices as soon as you boarded the shuttle. We can't take any chances with unauthorized devices recording anything confidential." Holding up his hand for silence when Ami and Liam started talking at once, Tarek's tone overrode any of their objections. "It's understandable you would want to have a recording of these proceedings, but you have to see it from our point of view. We know practically nothing about you and what we thought we did was wrong."

Liam fingered his recorder, not at all happy, but he got it. "I appreciate your understanding, but from where I stand, we need a record to present to our governments to help them understand what's happening. After receiving Director Nox's message, we immediately contacted our superior. It's standard procedure for us to wear a recording device when we go on missions. This way we have an accurate account of the events."

Taking her recorder off and seeing no telltale red light indicating it was recording, Ami interjected, "That way if things go sideways, we know who to blame." Pursing her lips together, she put it in her pocket. "We're from a country called the United States of America."

Pointing to the planet Earth, Ami used her finger to pinpoint the US on the hologram. "I won't go into detail about how our country is governed, but let's just say it's one of many countries who are going to want answers. We're not sure what's going on back on Earth right now. Our superior's name is Leslie Merriman. She said there was a protocol in place for just this scenario. Although between you and me, I don't think anyone really thought it would ever be used."

Sharing a smile with Ami, Liam filled Tarek and his team in on his conversation with Leslie. "Ms. Merriman told us she would contact our President and we were to keep her informed if at all possible—hence the recorders,"

Liam watched Tarek consult with his team. They were speaking in Delician so they obviously didn't want them to hear their discussion. The General listened as each crewmember gave their input into the discussion. This gave Liam a chance to quietly observe the aliens in the room.

Leaning in close to Ami, he spoke low so that only she could hear. "What are you thinking? So far, I'm not getting any negative vibe. They appear to genuinely want to help us."

Ami whispered back that she agreed but she wasn't letting her guard down. "Let's just see how this all plays out. It looks like they've come to some decision." She shut her mouth when the General started speaking.

"I'd like to talk to your superior. Can you give me her contact information?" Tarek asked.

Liam nodded, rattling off the information and ARI immediately began initiating contact. Voice-activated computers weren't anything new to Liam, but he had a feeling this computer ARI was something on a completely different level. *Damn, I wish I had my recorder. This ship is incredible.*

ARI indicated that contact had been established as a

screen appeared on the wall at the end of the table. Leslie Merriman's stern face appeared on the screen. Her dark eyes scanned the room, looking first at Liam and Ami and then her eyes widened when she took in the Delician delegation. When she locked eyes with General Tarek, she visibly swallowed.

Clearing her throat, she managed not to sound too squeaky saying, "I'm Leslie Merriman, Director of National Aeronautical Space Agency."

"Hello Leslie Merriman. I am General Tarek from the planet Delicia. I am a representative of the United Alliance of Planets." He went around the room introducing his team.

"Thank you, General. I send greetings from Gregory Jenkins, President of the United States and also from the United Nations Security Council." Leslie spoke directly to General Tarek. "President Jenkins and the Council are anxious to hear what brought you to our planet." Seeing Liam and Ami sitting together, Leslie addressed them asking, "Are you two all right?"

"As all right as we can be considering we're sitting with a bunch of aliens who are telling us someone wants to attack Earth for our salt," Ami talked over Liam, who had started to answer Leslie at the same time she did.

"What? Salt? Ami, if you can't be serious, please let Liam speak." Turning to Liam, Leslie nodded her head to indicate he should start talking.

Sitting back in her chair, Ami clamped her lips together trying to hide her embarrassment. *When am I going to learn there are thinking things and speaking things?* Glancing around, she was relieved when she saw everyone was focused on the video screen and not her.

Relaying all the information that they had just learned, Liam ended with the question that Tarek had just posed to them about first contact.

Stunned, Leslie let out a low whistle. "Wow! This is so unbelievable. Salt, huh? Who would have thought?"

Clearing her throat, she took a moment to collect her thoughts before she addressed the room. "I have spoken with the President and shown him the recording that you sent to the Space Station. To say he was concerned is an understatement. He has conferred with the UN Security Council and I have been authorized to work with you in eliminating any threat to Earth. He explicitly expressed great concern about any possible damage to our planet and its people."

Nodding his head, Tarek acknowledged the concerns of Earth's leaders. "I assure you that our mission from the UAP is to mitigate this threat as quickly and as quietly as possible. When and if first contact is considered acceptable, we will meet with Earth's representatives as to how this should be done."

Turning to Nox, Tarek asked him to outline the plan to them.

Nox drew their attention back to the hologram. "We noticed that you had some type of deflector array installed on some of your orbiting satellites. I propose we use that equipment in combination with my force field technology. At the very least it will protect your communication network in the event we engage the Hexians in battle."

"Wait, do you honestly think there will be a battle, like as in a real shoot 'em up space battle only with lasers and blasters and spaceships?" Ami was worried. "I know, I'm sorry. Shut up right, okay shutting up, but do you honestly think it will come to that?"

"Anything is possible when it comes to the Hexians." It was Captain Jagger who spoke. His amethyst eyes flashed with an underlying anger he tried to hide. "I've had more experience with the Hexians than I care to think about, but one thing I can tell you is they are not to be taken lightly. So, to answer your question, yes—I do feel we will be having a battle. Now, that said, we will try to draw them away from Earth before any action is taken."

Nox continued when Jagger stopped talking. "ARI, display a close-up of Earth's orbiting satellites."

As ARI complied, Nox stood pointing at one of the orbiting arrays. "As I was saying, my plan is to integrate my technology into each of these arrays which will encircle the satellite with a force field. These fields are designed to withstand any type of known blast. We have been using them on our ships for some time. It won't protect your entire planet, but it will protect your communications network from being destroyed.

Once we have this threat neutralized, we can discuss possibly putting a force field around all your satellites. Time won't permit us to do that right now. I will need to work with the human who developed this technology. I find it fascinating you have advanced your technology to such a degree. I'm looking forward to talking to this human scientist. Can you tell me the purpose of the deflector array?"

Leslie, Ami and Liam all looked at each other. Liam was especially concerned because it was his sister Nox was referring to. This meant that she would have to be brought into this situation, which was something he had been hoping to avoid.

Leslie cleared her throat to speak when Liam cut her off saying to the room, "Is there any way you can do this without having to bring the scientist into this situation? Can't Ami be the one you work with? I mean, she is after all the engineer working on the team that created this."

"Is there a problem with this human scientist?" General Tarek asked, concerned.

Ami turned to Liam, touching his arm. "Liam, I know you don't want to involve Em, but we have no choice. Sure, I can help install the equipment on the other satellites, but we can't do this without her. This is her project and she deserves to be involved if we're going to make any changes to it. She would be very angry if we excluded her from this. You know how pissed she'd be." Waving her hand to the room before continuing, she added, "Besides, she set up security measures using her retinal scan so that she's the only person who can activate the program."

When Leslie sighed in frustration, Ami pushed back, telling her heatedly, "Hey, it was you who ordered her to set it up this way. I told you at the time this was a bad idea. Although knowing Em she probably had Heather put in a backdoor to gain access to the program but she would have kept that to herself."

Nox and Tarek look at each other as if to say, *what seems to be the issue here?*

Sighing, Liam told them that the scientist who developed this technology was his sister and it was her company that Ami worked for. "The EAC in EAC Global Network

Solutions stands for Emeline Agnes Cameron and she's my baby sister. She'll be able to explain the science behind her network array."

Stunned, Nox leaned back in his chair as he stroked his chin. *A female and a young one at that.* Not that Delician women didn't work in the science field. *I mean, my mother was a scientist and a brilliant one, but a human female? I have to meet her.* He looked from Liam to Ami, waiting for them to continue.

Liam informed the room that Emeline was a brilliant scientist. When she started her company, she asked her friends to join her. Leslie interjected that Emeline had been working off and on with NASA since her university days and that she was sure Emeline would jump at the chance to help in any way she could.

Speaking to the room, she continued pressing an important point, "The only problem is getting Director Nox to Earth without being seen and creating a frenzy if the media got wind of any of this. Any ideas on how to get Director Nox to Earth?" Leslie looked at the Delicians, waiting for their answer.

As they continued to discuss a plan for getting Nox to Emeline's lab, Jagger's wrist comm beeped. He excused himself and left the room, signaling they should continue without him.

After a few minutes, he returned, informing them, "Our sensors have detected Tarquin and his forces heading towards Earth."

"How long do we have before they enter Earth's solar system?" Tarek asked.

"They should reach the outer edge in about ten Earth

days.

General Tarek immediately began giving orders. "Nox, you now have less time to get your force fields installed and initiated. I want to make sure that if it comes to a battle, it's not visible from Earth. If it does come close, at least their communication network will be protected. Ezio, you and Ramola coordinate a squadron to intercept the Hexians and engage them before they can get past the outer edge of the solar system." Turning to Nyx, he told him he wanted him to work with the humans.

Nox understood Liam's concerns about his sister, but they needed her help if they were to give Earth some protection. "I understand your apprehension, but we need to get to work. We can use the cloaked shuttle to take us to Earth."

Liam knew he was going to lose this one, especially with what was at stake. Besides, if Emeline found out he had made a decision like this without consulting her, there would be hell to pay. He didn't have the energy for that right now. "Fine. I think it would be better to work from Emeline's lab in Boston. We can have the Delicians drop us on the roof after dark...that way no one should see us."

"You realize she is going to wonder how the hell we ended up in her lab when we're supposed to be on the ISS." Ami smiled to herself thinking of the look on her friend's face when she came face to face with an honest-to-god alien. Knowing Emeline like she did, she would put on her geeky science face and jump right in. It would be later on that she would sneak out to have a quiet nervous breakdown in peace.

Leslie concurred with the Delicians' plan, telling them

she would inform President Jenkins and the Council. Talking directly to Liam, she said, "I can't stress enough to you that this whole situation be kept as quiet and as confidential as possible. The President wants regular updates, so keep me informed every step of the way."

To General Tarek she said, "Thank you for coming to Earth to help us. I can't imagine what we would have done without your assistance. Our defenses would have been no match for these Hexians. We will speak again, I'm sure, over the next ten days." Giving one last look to Liam, she said, "You have ten days to get these force fields up and running. Don't let me down. Merriman out."

The screen on the wall faded to black, leaving only silence in the room, each one of them reflecting on what the next ten days would bring to Earth and its population.

Tarek stood, the seriousness of the situation showing on his face. He ordered Nyx to prepare a shuttle, "I want you to leave as soon as night falls on this Boston that Liam mentioned. After you drop them off, return to the ship and we will draw up a battle plan. We don't have much time to prepare."

To the rest of the room, he said, "Get done what you have to do and then I want you back on this ship ready to activate the force fields within the next 6 days. That will give us four days before Tarquin arrives."

Ami couldn't help but be disappointed—*Bummer I guess that tour is out of the question.*

They all filed out of the room, leaving Tarek and Jagger alone. Tarek rubbed his chin in contemplation. "Well, my friend, I think that went better than I had anticipated. I like that their leaders are being cautious with the idea of first contact. We've had to deal with too many aftereffects of rushing the process."

Jagger nodded his head in agreement. He stood over by the window, lost in thought for a moment. "What did you think of the humans? I found Ami Jefferson fascinating, didn't you?"

Tarek moved over to stand next to Jagger. His arms were crossed, legs spread slightly...his usual stance as he gazed over at his friend. "She is unique. Smart, loyal. Did you notice the close relationship she has with the Lt. Commander?"

"I did. Do you think they're lovers?" Jagger always loved a good piece of gossip. He said it was the nature of his job. He had to deal with too many crewmembers not to pick up a few juicy tidbits here and there.

Tarek didn't care about stuff like that, so he ignored his friend. "She is more outspoken than I'm used to, but I find her refreshing. Maybe I have become too complacent in my life lately. The humans certainly add some excitement that's been missing around here. "

Taking a moment to study his friend, Jagger threw his head back with a laugh. "Since when do you care about excitement?"

Tarek glared at his friend. This wasn't the first time someone had made mention of his rigid nature. "All I'm saying is that I agree with you. I think the humans may surprise us. I found them both intriguing. Keep an eye on the Lt. Commander. He impressed me. I'd like to invite him to train with us. Ask him to join us at one of our sessions before they return to Earth. Also, see if Ami wants join us."

Jagger burst out with another loud laugh, catching

Tarek off-guard. "Are you trying to scare them off?"

"What's that supposed to mean?" Tarek tried not to take offense, but it was getting tiresome.

"Nothing. Nothing at all. I'll go set it up." Jagger turned towards the door, mumbling to himself, "I'll just make sure to bring along a few portable regen devices."

CHAPTER 5

Smiling happily, Emeline slid her phone into her pocket. Having just finished talking to Dr. Whittemore about the conference today, she was thrilled at how well it had gone. At first being back at school had filled her with so many memories, mostly happy but more than a few unpleasant ones. She'd considered cancelling her presentation after running into one of her particularly nasty professors from her college days in the hallway, but she was glad she didn't.

Wearing her red power suit, Emeline stood tall on the stage as she told her story to a group of women who listened to her, enthralled. The question portion of her presentation had ended with a hail of complaints coming from the audience members who still wanted to ask questions —many of them following her out into the hall. Smiling broadly at her college nemesis, she continued answering questions until Dr. Whittemore intervened, saying Emeline's time was up.

Thanking everyone, Emeline left with a bounce in her step, excited to call her mother and tell her how wonderfully it had gone. It was refreshing for Fiona to hear the excitement in her daughter's voice for once when she spoke about anything that had to do with her academic life.

Heading into her lab, she checked the time on her watch. Damn, she thought, still three hours to wait before her video call with Ami and Liam aboard the ISS. It had been over 24 hours since their last call and she was anxious to find out if they were able to interpret anything from the unusual data that had been coming from the arrays. She couldn't shake the feeling that something was going on. Ever since she had first seen the strange data, she'd felt uneasy and she was the type of person who liked to find answers to problems but this was stumping her. She just couldn't put her finger on what the data meant.

Coming out of her office bathroom, it was a relief to be back in her work clothes—jeans and a T-shirt. After replacing her contacts with her glasses, she started putting on her lab coat when she heard the door to the lab open.

Looking out to see who it was, thinking it was Lorelei wanting to hear all about her presentation, she was shocked to see Ami coming through the door with Liam behind her. *What the hell!*

"Ami? Liam?" She rushed forward to greet them, worry graced her face. "What the hell are you doing here?"

Liam was the first to reach her. He pulled her into a tight hug speaking softly into her hair, "Oh, Em. You are never going to believe what's happened." He gently pushed her away, staring into her eyes.

A feeling of panic swept through her. Something bad had happened. She could feel it. "Tell me," she whispered.

"Em, we know what the data means."

"You do? That's awesome." She felt a hint of excitement —mixed with fear.

"First contact has been made."

"What?" Emeline pushed away from him, giving him and Ami a look of disbelief before saying, "Cut it out. Be serious and tell me what's really going on."

They both stood there staring at her, not moving. You know the old saying "deer in the headlights look"? Yeah, that's what she was looking at.

Anger started to coat her tone as she yelled at them, "Why are you talking crazy? And furthermore, why aren't you up on the ISS working on our project instead of standing here saying such outrageous things to me? And you"— pointing her finger to Ami—"why are you being so quiet?" Nothing. "Would someone please start talking—don't leave me hanging here."

Ami looked from Emeline to Liam saying, "Liam, why

don't we just show her? I think it would be easier."

Emeline had had enough. She turned in a circle, hands in the air as she huffed out, "Stop stalling and just tell me what's going on? I mean, you're supposed to be on the Space Station and now you're here. How is that even possible when you only left two days ago? It isn't. I would have heard if there had been an aborted liftoff." Finally running out of breath, Emeline softly pleaded, "Please—what the hell is going on?"

Going over to the door, Ami pulled it open to reveal a person standing in the corridor. It appeared to be a man, a very tall, well-built man wearing jeans and a hoodie pulled forward hiding his face. As Ami pulled him forward into the light, his hood fell back revealing his face.

Emeline froze.

Standing before her was the handsomest man she had ever seen in her life. *Man, no, that can't be right.* He looked like a man—kind of—but his skin was all wrong for a human. He was pale, the palest skin she'd ever seen. It seemed to sparkle in the overhead light, giving off varying shades of pastel colors. Her eyes started at his feet, moving up slowly, taking in every detail of a body that just begged to be explored.

When she reached his eyes, deep amethyst that shined like a crystal, stared back so intensely...as if he could see directly into her soul. Emeline's emotions took over. Her body felt flushed while her heart, which she swore had stopped, began beating double time. She couldn't understand her reaction to this strange alien. *I can't believe I'm going to faint.* And with that last thought, Emeline crumpled slowly to the floor.

Liam jumped forward, catching her before Nox, who had moved at the same time he had. Lifting Emeline into his arms, Liam carried her into her office, placing her gently on the couch.

Locking the lab door, Ami rescued Emeline's glasses

from the floor and then sprinted after Liam. "This is all my fault. I should have known this would happen. We should have come up with a better way to explain him," Ami cried, tilting her head at Nox who was trailing behind Liam, totally focused on Emeline.

Checking his sister's pulse, Liam asked Ami to get a wet cloth from the bathroom. Looking at Nox, who was hovering too close beside him, he directed him to get a bottle of water. "Open that cabinet over on the left. There should be a box in there with bottles of water." Liam brushed back a strand of hair from Emeline's ashen face. "I wish there had been a better way to break the news to her. I'm just surprised she fainted. Em never faints. I guess this was too much of a shock for her."

Coming out of the bathroom with a wet cloth, Ami handed it to Liam.

Gently wiping her face, Liam gazed down at his baby sister. He saw how pale she was with dark smudges under her eyes. "Geez, just look at her. She's almost the same color as Nox."

Sighing heavily, Liam felt helpless. "You know I had hoped with the success of her company and being asked to speak at the Women in Science and Engineering conference, she'd snap out of this funk she's been in for the last two years. I had planned on talking to Mum about her. She's been worried about her too. I just ran out of time before the mission and now with this whole crazy aliens conquering the world thing going on—crap, life just got a whole lot crazier. Come on, Em—time to wake up."

Nox's worried expression was evident as he approached the couch just as Emeline was beginning to stir.

Trying to sit up, she asked hoarsely, "What happened?" Seeing the worried looks on Liam's and Ami's faces, she gave them an unsteady smile, trying to reassure them until she looked over Liam's shoulder at the stranger in the hoodie. She could feel her checks blush as she lowered her eyelashes. Not understanding why she felt this way, Emeline needed answers to what the hell was going on. "Who are you?" she squinted at the strange man with the beautiful eyes.

Nox handed her a bottle of water...their fingers briefly touching. Warmth wound its way around their fingers, making them both gasp in surprise. Smiling down into the bluest eyes he'd ever seen, he said, "My name is Nox."

Frowning, Liam looked from Emeline to Nox, wondering why he suddenly felt like he was interrupting a private moment. Whatever was going on, he didn't like it. Putting that thought aside, handing Emeline her glasses, he calmly told her what had happened to them. "Em, this is what we were trying to tell you. When we were up at the Space Station, we were contacted by aliens—well, Delicians actually. This is Director Nox. He's a scientist from the planet Delicia. He and other members of his planet have come to save Earth and we need your help."

Emeline tried to sit up, but dizziness caused her to flop back down. Thoughts swirled through her head, causing it to ache. Her eyes kept straying to the alien in the room. *An honest-to-god alien is staring at me. Man, his eyes are incredible—sexy. I mean, he is gorgeous; I mean SERIOUSLY gorgeous. Okay, Em, cut it out. You just fainted, for heaven's sake. Don't you think you should find out what the hell is going on before you think about jumping his bones!* But oh yeah, she could feel his eyes on her—all the way down to her toes.

Leaning over, Ami grabbed Emeline's arm, pulling her upright. "Sorry for the shock, girlfriend. There probably was a better way, but hell—we haven't had five seconds to process this. You have no idea what the last 24 hours have been like for us. Between being shot into space and then finding out we're not alone in the universe. Now that was shocking. Add to that some really bad dudes are coming to try to take over our planet just for our salt. I mean, this is some serious shit. If I had thought about it, I probably would have fainted too. We even landed on the roof in a cloaked spaceship!"

Shock appeared on Emeline's face as she listened to Ami babble. Batting the cloth away from Liam, who was still trying to wipe her face, she blurted out, "Liam, can you please tell me what's going on and wait...what about salt?"

Taking the chair across from Emeline, Nox's eyes never left her face as she twisted off the cap to the water bottle and took a long drink.

Eyeing the two of them, Liam told her, "You had better lean back and get comfortable. This is going to take a while."

Taking her brother's suggestion, Emeline settled back against the couch. As Liam began telling the most outrageous story, she briefly considered that they were punking her. Maybe she wished they were instead of having to accept the truth in what they were saying. She did her best trying to focus on Liam's words, but it was hard not to steal glances at the alien whose gaze never wavered from her.

When Liam finished, Nox took over. "Emeline." His voice was deep, soft—sending shivers throughout her body. "It is nice to finally meet you. I have been wanting to meet the person who developed the technology in your satellites."

Ami interrupted him with a pointed glare, telling Emeline, "Yeah, he was surprised to find out we weren't all running around wearing furs and throwing spears at each other."

"Wait, what?" Emeline looked between them, confused.

Nox frowned at Ami as he turned back to Emeline. "I must apologize to you. You see, Earth has been on the prohibited planet list for so long that it was just assumed that you had little to no technology.

"Well, you know what they say about assuming," Ami threw back at him.

Not understanding her meaning, Nox looked from her

to Emeline.

"Never mind," Ami grumbled to herself.

Emeline ignored her friend, instead focusing on Nox. "What do you mean 'prohibited planet list'? Who put Earth on this list and how is my array supposed to help save the planet? And why do they want our salt again?"

Nox tried to calm his racing mind. He didn't understand why he was having trouble forming thoughts. What was it about this human female? The moment he'd laid eyes on this beautiful creature, his mind and body stopped co-operating. She made him feel things—things that certainly weren't appropriate at this moment. *What is happening to me? I need to focus on this mission. Too many lives are at stake.*

Glancing at his hand he saw a light ripple of color move slowly across his skin. *What? No, no, no, no, no. Not now, not with a human!* He gazed into Emeline's worried deep blue eyes as a stunning realization came to him—*I have found my bondmate!*

Closing his eyes, he tried in vain to force these emerging feelings back inside. *Now is not the time to be losing control. We have a mission to complete. Maybe once this is over, I can think about having found my bondmate, but not now!* But he knew these feelings could not be pushed aside. There was no denying one's bondmate. It just wasn't done.

Taking a deep breath, he looked into Emeline's waiting face, hoping she wouldn't notice his rampant desire for her. *Stars, she is so beautiful.*

Swallowing hard, he began by telling her in more detail about the UAP and how it worked. He explained the purpose of the list—conceding to them, especially Ami, that yes, they had been terribly lacking in monitoring the list. He filled in more of the details about the Hexians and Tarquin's plans for the salt.

Emeline was amazed when Nox explained about the curative elements in the salt and what it could mean to species all over the UAP. "That's something we have in common—greed. I'm sure a substance like this is worth an enormous amount of money. It makes me sick."

Nox applauded her outrage. He felt the same way knowing Tarquin planned on taking all of it for himself and his planet. "My team and I have been working on force field technology for a while and it's been quite successful. There isn't enough time to put a force field around all your satellites, but we can save your major communication ones." He then went on to briefly explain how his technology could be integrated into her array to help protect orbiting satellites from the Hexian weapons. "I'm going to need your help in getting everything ready to be activated before the Hexians arrive."

He purposely left out that she was his newly discovered bondmate and that their lives were forever tied together. How could he tell her that something so innocent as handing someone a bottle of water could trigger a bondmating? He'd barely grazed her hand. That was a discussion for another time. Right now, his biggest worry was the tightness of the human clothing Liam and Ami had made him wear. Nox was not a fan of *jeans.* Especially when a certain part of his body was making itself known.

Emeline stood up shakily from the couch. Looking from face to face, she realized this was no joke. They were dead serious in what they were telling her. Taking another sip of her water, she started to pace between the couch and her desk, "I need a moment to take all this in."

"Sure, honey, you take all the time you need, only unfortunately we don't have much of that." Ami came over and rubbed her back, trying to soothe her.

Nox wished it was his hands on her body trying to reassure her. *Where did that thought come from? Pull it together, Nox. She's had enough shocks for one day. Let's not scare her before we even get to know her.* His fingers tingled just at the thought of touching her.

Squeezing Ami's arm, acknowledging her concern, Emeline moved over to her desk, straightening her clothing as she paced...thinking out loud to herself. Leaning her hip against her desk, she counted off on her fingers. "Okay, so let me see if I've got this straight. 1. Humans are not alone in the universe. 2. Aliens are coming to attack Earth and steal our salt, and 3. You need me and my array to integrate alien force field technology in our satellites in order to protect our communications network from being destroyed by the aforementioned aliens when they attack us. God, I really just said aliens are going to attack us, didn't I? Have I got all this right?"

Liam came over and squeezed her shoulder, trying to reassure her that everything was going to be okay, although he didn't really believe that himself. "Yup, Em, as unbelievable as this sounds, you got it right."

Pushing off the desk, Emeline began her pacing again as panic started to take a hold of her. She could feel fear starting to rise into her throat. "No! Wait. I've got to call Mum. And Belle—where's my phone?"

"No!" Ami, Liam and Nox all shouted at the same time.

"What do you mean 'no'? Of course, we have to tell them."

With a stricken look on her face, Emeline stopped, searching around for her cell phone, fear and then anger beginning to show on her face. "I will not let them die. I can't—I won't lose anyone else." Her eyes started to fill as she tried not to think about losing any more of her family. "Don't you understand? I will do anything I can to protect Mum and Belle. I will not let anything happen to them!"

Liam ran his hand through his hair as he tried to reason with his sister. "I get it, Em, but you can't call them. Just stop and think for one second what would happen if this got out. Can you imagine people's reactions to this? The panic, the rioting. No, I'm sorry, I can't let you call them." Liam kept his voice calm as he continued, "You think I'm not worried sick about this...probably more so since I've actually been up there on their ship. I mean seriously—I can't even believe any of this myself and I saw it with my own two eyes!"

His look of disbelief made Emeline pause.

"Em, we have to work with Director Nox to save the planet first. Then we can decide what to tell Mum and Belle, but not now. You know this secret would be too hard for Mum to keep. First, she'd have to call her sister and then her cousin Anne and before you know it, all 32 of her cousins are going to know everything. You know how it works in this family, and right now we need to focus on stopping these bastards from thinking they can just waltz onto our planet and take whatever they want. I need you to do this for me, Em. Can you—can you work with Nox to get his force field up and running?" Liam held her gaze, imploring her to make the right decision.

"Give me a second to digest all of this, okay?" Taking her bottle of water, Emeline sat at her desk going over everything that had just been dropped in her lap. *Okay, Emeline, get a hold of yourself. Earth needs you to be calm and focused.* Laughing to herself, she remembered her mum's mantra. *Well, if we ever needed those three words before, now was the time.* She glanced over at Nox, who was talking with Liam, wondering what he thought of this whole scene. *He probably thinks I'm insane with my reaction to all of this. Well too bad, I'm allowed a weak moment after hearing this crazy stuff, aren't I? Okay girl, time to show the world just what you're made of. If I was able to show those academic snobs, I can certainly do the same with aliens. God, did that really just come out of my mouth? Besides I know Dad is looking down at me watching to see what I'll do. He had so much faith in me. I will not let him down.*

Pushing to her feet, she gave herself a mental shake as Nox and Liam looked over at her. "Director Nox, my brother is right. Why don't we go into my lab and you can outline your plan for me? I'm willing to do whatever it takes to stop these—what were they called again?"

"Hexians," Ami replied.

"Yeah, right, Hexians."

Heading out into her lab, Emeline grabbed her lab coat and slipped into it before leading the group over to her whiteboard. Handing Nox a marker, she asked him to please write an outline on the board with everything that had happened while she turned on the recorder on her computer. Being dyslexic, she found if she recorded her work sessions, it helped her understand and retain information better. It was a technique she had discovered while working for Dr. Whittemore, a technique that changed her life.

Nox looked at the marker with interest. *Didn't they have an ARI that could do this for them? I guess not,* he thought to himself. *Having the use of an ARI would make this go so much faster.* He considered using his wrist comm that was equipped with a portable ARI, but thought better of it. He especially didn't want to anger Ami again. She had a tendency to get mad every time he mentioned their lack of technology.

Standing at the board, he started outlining the chain of events for Emeline.

Grabbing the marker out of his hand, Ami nudged him out of the way, saying, "Evidently your translation chip doesn't work on the written word."

Looking at what was written on the board, Nox realized that he had started writing in Delician. This was going to be much more difficult than he thought. "I guess we need ARI to translate between your language and mine. I mean the scientific theory should still be the same since math and physics are universal."

Emeline asked what ARI was and Ami told her about the ship's computer. "I have got to see that in action."

As Ami continued to write on the board, Emeline's phone rang. It was Lorelei...probably wondering why she hadn't called her yet to talk about the conference. "Let me just take this. Otherwise, she'll come banging on the door."

"You do remember that she has her own keycard, right?" Ami chimed in.

"Just don't tell her anything about this. I know she's part of your team, but we need to keep this just between us right now. You can't tell her we're here," Liam reminded her.

While Emeline talked to Lorelei on the phone, Liam and Nox discussed what their next move should be. Ami was busy writing down everything on the board so Emeline could see the timeline of the events that had already happened. She called Nox over and had him dictate to her what he needed Emeline to do from her end at the lab.

As they were finishing up, Emeline returned and told them Lorelei wanted to get together but Emeline told her that she was busy and was going to be up late waiting to talk to the two of them from the Space Station. Lorelei had wanted to wait with her, but Emeline told her that she was going to FaceTime Fiona so not to bother. "I told her I'd touch base with her tomorrow afternoon and tell her how the call went. I just hope she doesn't try to stop by anyway."

Nox contacted Tarek informing him that they were ready to start working on the array to make the necessary adjustment. Liam and Ami would be installing the equipment on the communication satellites currently in orbit. After much discussion, it was decided that Nyx would pick up Liam and Ami and take them back to the ship. Nyx would help them with the installation while Nox stayed here with Emeline to finish up what they needed to do in the lab. They would return to the ship within the week.

Liam was not happy about leaving Nox here alone with Emeline, but they really didn't have much of a choice. If he could, he would ask Lorelei or Heather to come and stay with her, but that was against orders. It was imperative they keep the number of people "in the know" as limited as possible.

Pulling her aside to get her feelings on Nox, he asked her to be candid with him. "Tell me, Em, if this makes you uncomfortable, we'll figure something else out. Maybe Ami can go with Nyx and I'll stay here with you."

Squeezing his arm lightly, Emeline tried to reassure her brother. "Liam—I've got this. I know I kind of fell apart there for a minute but you can count on me. Besides, you need to go with Ami to help her install the equipment. This Nyx, he wouldn't know anything about our equipment and you do."

"I just don't like leaving you alone here with him." Liam ran his hand down his worried face.

"Do you not trust him? Has he given you any reason why I should be worried?" Emeline saw the concern on her brother's face but she honestly didn't see what choice they had.

"No—yes—I don't know. I just have this feeling about him."

"A bad feeling, like he's a bad guy?" Emeline whispered, shooting a glance at Nox. He was talking to Ami and she seemed okay with him. He didn't look creepy.

"No, no, not a bad guy, but I'm getting some kind of vibe from him especially when he looks at you. It unnerves me a little bit that's all." Liam gave her his protective brother look.

"Oh boy, are you going all big brother on me now?"

"Maybe."

Emeline laughed, hugging him tightly. "I love you."

He returned her hug, squeezing back just as tightly. "I love you too. I'm just looking out for you."

"Well, you can just stop it and trust me. I'm a big girl and I can take care of myself. Besides, wasn't I one of your best students in class? I learned my lessons well, big bro, thanks to you."

"Yes, you did, but he's a big man-alien...fuck, can you

believe this? Anyway, he's a lot bigger than you and you've never been in a real fight before. If you get into trouble, do you remember what to do?"

"Oh yeah, but don't worry—if I can't take him down then at least he's going to be hurting in a very delicate place." Emeline winked at him. "So, what do you think, he's about 6'7"?

"At least. But you should see the other Delicians. He's kind of short compared to them. Wait until you meet General Tarek, now there's a textbook alien. I mean the guy must be over seven feet tall," Liam told her.

Flabbergasted, Emeline was beyond curious about the Delicians. "Do they all have that color skin? I mean I've never seen anything like that. Did you see the colors ripple through his hand? It was so cool."

"No, I didn't notice that when I met with them on the ship. I'll have to check it out when I get back there. Oh Em, wait until you see their ship. It's the most amazing thing I've ever seen. They have these small fighter jets that they use in battle. I want to fly one so bad." He looked like a little kid at Christmas asking Santa for his favorite toy, anticipation shining in his eyes.

Ami called over to them, asking if they were finished. She said Nox had heard from Nyx and he would be landing on the roof in about an hour. Liam said he needed to put in a call to Leslie Merriman to keep her informed of their progress.

Abruptly, Emeline slapped her forehead, crying out, "Wait, this isn't going to work."

"What are you talking about?" Liam stopped mid dial.

"We don't have enough equipment to install in all the satellites. We only have enough units completed for about a dozen arrays. Crap, what are we going to do?" Emeline chewed lightly on her bottom lip as she tried to figure out her next move.

"I can help you with that," Nox interrupted.

"Yeah, how you going to do that? I suppose you have a replicator?" Ami quipped at him.

Sighing heavily, Nox looked hesitantly at Ami, finally admitting, "Actually yes, we do."

"Of course, you do, why wouldn't you?" Ami glared at him, hating that he made her feel inferior.

"I'm sorry if this makes you angry, Ami Jefferson."

"It's fine. I'm just being cranky. It's been a really, really long day and it's Ami, just Ami. Jefferson is my last name. When you meet someone on Earth, you usually call them by their first name," Ami told him.

"Thank you, Ami." He nodded his head in respect to her. "If you give ARI the specs for your equipment, it will replicate whatever you need. Nyx will have everything loaded onto the shuttle for you to install onto the satellites. How long does it take to install each array?"

"Well, there are about 1100 satellites orbiting Earth right now and it takes a minimum of two hours to install each one, so we won't be able to do all of them. I'll ask Leslie which ones she wants done first," Ami told him. Nox nodded in understanding.

Emeline came over to stand near Nox, asking him, "You really have a replicator?" At his nod, she nearly squealed in delight, "Oh, this I've got to see." For some reason she had this strange desire to touch him, almost like a compulsion, but she held her hand back. *Stop it. You have to work with this...this...Nox, so get control of yourself. I am seriously going to need to visit my vibrator when this is all over. Oh, screw the vibrator, maybe I'll get me some alien lovin'.*

Trying to ignore her rising lust, she asked Nox, "What can it make?"

"Anything you want—well we do have some restrictions." Nox told her they were not allowed to replicate weapons without proper clearance.

Ami piped in, "Think 3D printer, only way better."

Emeline's mind reeled with the possibilities. She wondered if she could get one for the lab when this was all over. The things she could do with one. Oh boy, she'd have to look into getting the aliens to give her one.

Liam returned from his phone call with NASA. Leslie said the President and the UN Security Council approved their plan and to proceed with implementation. They were to still keep this as quiet as possible—need to know only.

Looking at his watch, Liam saw that Nyx would be there in about fifteen minutes so they had better get up to the roof. Turning to Emeline and Nox, he told them to keep in touch with him every couple of hours.

Emeline told him she would make up a cot in the lab for Nox to sleep on. She'd take the couch. She wanted to wait until tomorrow night to go home. She had enough food and drinks in the lab from when they worked long hours that they could stay here for a few days if necessary.

Nox informed Liam that Captain Jagger would assign them quarters on the ship and to get some rest tonight. They could all begin fresh after some sleep.

Liam agreed with Nox about getting some rest...he was bone tired. Looking over at his sister as she talked to Ami, he saw her shoulders had begun to droop, indicating how exhausted she was. It had been a long day for everyone, but since there was no room for them to all sleep in the lab, he supposed that going back to the *Maelstrom* was the better choice.

Studying Nox for a second, Liam motioned him over. Looking him square in the eye, Liam wanted this alien to know he was not comfortable leaving his sister alone with him. "I'm trusting you with my sister. This has been hard for all of us to accept, so I'm relying on you to keep her safe. She's been in a vulnerable place lately so be easy with her."

Nox glanced at Emeline noticing how tired she looked. "You have my word."

"Well, I know my sister, and trust me, she'll work herself ragged to get everything completed. That's just who she is.

I know we have a deadline, but make sure she gets some rest."

Nox tried to reassure Liam. He understood that this human was worried about leaving his beautiful sister alone with a strange being. If he had a sister, he would feel the same way. "We should be able to complete the necessary adjustments long before the Hexians get here. I'll make sure she takes breaks and doesn't tire herself. You can trust me, Liam."

Giving Nox a look like *you better or I will come back and beat your ass*, Liam called to Ami that it was time to head up to the roof to meet Nyx. Since it was well past midnight, he didn't worry about anyone from the building seeing them.

Pulling Emeline in for a long hug, Liam whispered into her hair, "You remember what I told you. Don't let your guard down and make sure you lock the door when we leave. I'll contact Nox when we get back to the ship to let you know we've arrived. If you run into any problems and can't get me, call Leslie. She'll do whatever she can to help you."

"Liam, I'll be fine. I promise. I've got the knife you gave me for my birthday in my desk, so if anything goes wrong, I do know how to use it. Go and get the network arrays up and running. I'll take care of things on this end."

"Okay." He rested his forehead against hers, letting out a long sigh. "I just worry, you know."

"I know you do, but I've got this." Shoving him towards the door, she grabbed Ami for a hug, saying, "You should be more worried about Ami."

"Me? What about me?" Ami looked at Emeline, confused.

"Yeah you. I know you. I want to see how long it takes you to have half the aliens on that ship falling in love with you." She wagged her eyebrows at Ami.

"Well, I never." Ami gave her an insulted look as her face began to redden.

"Oh yes you have and you will again if given half the chance," laughed Emeline. "Go, both of you. We'll be fine here, right, Nox?"

"I will take good care of Emeline. Please do not worry," Nox replied.

As the door closed behind them, Emeline and Nox turned to look at one another...really seeing each other for the first time without other people in the room. As they stood there, their eyes locked as time seemed to stop and all sounds went missing from the room. In its place was a feeling that everything was going to be okay because they were together.

Nox took a step towards Emeline but she backed up— her hand coming out to stop him. Breathless, she told him, "I'm just going to get the cot and blankets for you. It's been a really, really long day and I need to be alone right now. I'll be right back."

Taking his cue from her, he stepped back, putting hands up as if to say *it's okay.* "I agree. A good rest will do us both good."

As she opened the closet and started pulling out the cot, she told him, "If you hear the door open, come into my office right away. I can hide you in the bathroom so no one will see you."

"Yes, of course."

Finishing setting up the bed in silence, Emeline showed him where the light was and then showed him the bathroom and how everything worked. He said it was similar to how it worked on Delicia before she disappeared into her office.

Emeline didn't know what to think. Her head was pounding. *I need some Ibuprofen.* Grabbing her purse and taking two pills out, she grabbed her water bottle and downed them, hoping that would help get rid of some of the pain at least. Moving to sit on her office couch, Emeline took off her glasses and kicked off her sneakers. She stretched out *just for a minute* she told herself before she drifted off to sleep. It was the end of an extremely odd day for Emeline.

As Nox came out of the bathroom, the light from the door showed Emeline asleep on the couch. He stood there mesmerized...his eyes didn't know where to look first. She was so beautiful. *I could stand here all night and gaze at her loveliness.*

Shaking his head, he shut off the light and headed towards his cot. He needed to think and sleep, but he didn't know in which order he should do it. The long day finally getting the best of him, he lay down and gave Emeline's office one last lingering look. He knew they would dream of each other. He knew the reason for this strong connection, but Emeline had no clue as to why she was feeling the things she was. Tomorrow when they started working, he would try to explain what was happening to them. Hopefully, yeah hopefully, as he too drifted off to sleep.

CHAPTER 6

Opening her eyes slowly, Emeline rolled onto her back, pointing her toes as she raised her arms in a gentle stretch. Her shoulders and neck felt tighter than usual. It was time for a yoga class—or even better, a training session with Liam. *Maybe both.* Either one was always good for a total body workout.

Yawning, she put on her glasses and looked at the clock before noticing she was still dressed in her clothes—and sleeping in her office. *What the heck?* Hearing movement from her lab, it all came flooding back. *Aliens! Oh, crap! That wasn't a dream.*

Rising off the couch in one movement, she glided quietly towards the bathroom before Nox could see her. *Shower, definitely a shower,* she thought as she shut the door. Remembering Liam's warning, she engaged the lock, although for some reason she found it unnecessary. She wasn't the least bit afraid of Nox. In fact, it was just the opposite...her feelings had moved way past friendly and that worried her.

Turning on the shower before she took care of her personal needs, Emeline considered the events of last night. She would need to be professional. No way was she going to let her weirdly growing feelings for Nox get in the way of completing her mission. If she thought about it, this was an opportunity of a lifetime. *This is a sci-fi fan's ultimate fantasy come to life and I get to live it.*

Looking at herself in the mirror, she was more than a little taken aback at her appearance, *Oh god, I'm a mess.* Staring back at her was a face that looked like it could use a two-week vacation. *Maybe when this is all over, I'll talk the girls into a trip to Aruba. I could really use some sun.*

Large tired eyes with dark smudges underneath peered back at her. She was pale, but then again, she was always pale. Her hair hung limp along either side of her face. *Geez, this hair could use some attention.* Making a mental note to call her hairdresser, she pulled off her dirty clothes and stepped into the shower. The hot water felt heavenly cascading over her body. She positioned herself so that the water hit directly on her neck and shoulders. The heat and gentle pounding of the water slowly began to loosen her tight muscles.

As the water worked its magic, she pondered her fixation with Nox. He had invaded her dreams all night. Dreams so sensual she was surprised she didn't wake him up with her screams of passion. *Weird. I have never experienced such intense feelings for anyone, especially this quick.*

Running her hand over her body she could almost feel the way Nox touched her in her dream. She grabbed the shampoo bottle and poured a small amount into her hand. Massaging her scalp, the soap felt slick in her hands as it slid slowly down her body. *What is it about him? Oh yeah, his gorgeous body, or was it his eyes when they lingered on me.* He made her feel as if he couldn't bear to look away from her.

Bringing her soapy hands down over her neck, the scent of vanilla soothed her nerves. Circling her breasts, her fingers brushed against her nipples, causing her to gasp. That familiar feeling of arousal sent a spark to her core. Just that quick touch set her body on fire—her thoughts focused solely on the alien in her lab.

Looking around, afraid she might get caught, she laughed at herself for being silly. Besides, she'd locked the door. Only the sound of the water hitting the shower floor could be heard. Her body ached with need. If she didn't get some modicum of relief soon, she'd never make it through the day. Since her vibrator was at home, she wiggled her fingers...she'd use the next best thing.

Pouring body soap onto a loofah, she moved it slowly along her body—her mind picturing Nox's strong hands. *His long thick fingers lightly massaging her shoulders before moving down to touch her breasts.* Her nipples hardened with each brush of her hands. She gasped as her body shivered with the building tension—her skin flushed with desire.

The more she touched herself, the more her lower abdomen began to ache, pulsing all the way down to her center...loving that feeling of pleasure that radiated through her. While one hand started to roll and pull her nipples, alternating from one to the other, her other hand slowly worked its way downward. She was wet—so very wet. *She could see him leaning against the shower door watching as she pleasured herself—passion burning in his smoldering eyes.*

Her fingers moved slow and gently at first, circling the center of her desire. *She pictured his fingers touching her instead of her own—his fingers working their magic on her.* She felt her need begin to build as she coordinated her hands to give herself maximum pleasure. Faster and faster her fingers moved as she felt the heat in her core intensifying, bringing her to that point between pleasure and pain. The muscles in her body clenched as she reached for that trigger that would send her over the edge. A set of amethyst eyes flashed through her mind, causing her to come hard—harder than she ever had before. She felt like a dam burst inside her as she cried out in surprise.

Leaning her head against the shower wall, she panted, trying to catch her breath. She could feel wetness slowly seeping out from between her thighs as a wave of intense pleasure spread over her whole body. It took her a few minutes to come down from her high, but when she did, she felt amazing. *WOW. Just—WOW.*

A knock on the door startled her out of her stupor. She could hear Nox calling her name. "Emeline. Emeline. Is everything alright? I heard you cry out."

Great, just great. What's he got superhero hearing or something?

Her voice was still a bit shaky as she called back to him, "I'm good. Just dropped the soap. Be out in a minute." She knew her face would be bright red with the thought that he'd heard her—but boy, she really needed that.

Dressing quickly in jeans and a T-shirt, Emeline opened the door and stuck her head out. Seeing her office was empty, she stepped out and reached for her phone to check her messages. There were a few that she could answer later. Sending a quick text back to Lorelei and Heather, she told them she would call them later this afternoon and give them an update. She planned to tell them that the array placement was proceeding on schedule and that Liam and Ami were taking care of everything. It wasn't a lie exactly, but she still felt bad about not being able to tell them what was going on. They were her family as well as her colleagues. It didn't sit right with her. *Oh, I know why I have to keep the secret, but I still don't like keeping this from them. If it was me, I'd be pissed.*

There was a message from Liam saying that they had arrived on board the *Maelstrom* and had gotten some rest. He and Ami were getting all the equipment replicated and would be leaving this afternoon to start the installations on the satellites. *Okay that's great. We're on track with the equipment.*

Emeline looked out into her lab and saw Nox standing by the whiteboard. She had been so exhausted last night, she'd forgotten to close the blinds and lock the door between her office and the lab. She had exposed herself, allowed herself to be vulnerable to this stranger. She winced at having not thought to follow Liam's warning. He would be furious with her for being so careless. *Well, I'm still alive, so that's a check in Nox's favor.* Liam would have to trust her judgment. She was a grown woman who owned a successful, well-respected company that was making some really cool stuff and she was only 29!

Feeling her stomach start to growl, she knew it was time to face the alien. *Ha! I just invented a new game show.* Giggling, she slipped into her lab coat and headed out to face her new lab partner.

"Good morning. How did you sleep last night?" she asked, looking around for the cot he'd slept in.

"Very well and how about you?"

"Great. Perfect. Dead to the world." She could feel her face getting a little warm as she looked at him, her body still tingling from the effects of her shower. "Are you hungry? Let me check the fridge to see what we have. I can always make us a smoothie if I can't find much."

Stopping mid step, she turned and looked at him, "Oh I didn't even think to ask—what do you eat? I mean, I don't know what a...Delician?" She looked at him for confirmation that she had said it right. Getting a nod, she asked him, "What kinds of food do you eat?"

"I eat pretty much anything. Like Earth, we do grow some foods, but since food replicators are so widely available, no one goes hungry on our planet. In fact, the art of cooking is a very important part of the Delician culture. We take our cooking very seriously. Personally, I prefer to eat lots of fruits and vegetables along with protein. I live near the sea, so I tend to eat a lot of food from there."

Emeline looked in wonder at Nox. *Handsome, built like a god and he can cook! Okay, if it sounds too good to be true, is it really? Why do I hope it is true?*

"Well then you and I are going to get along just fine. My family and I love to cook and create new foods all the time. If we're not cooking and eating, we're talking about cooking and eating."

Nox smiled at her, pleased that something so important in the Delician culture was also important to his bondmate. "Maybe before we go back to my ship, we can cook a meal together."

Smiling back at him, she agreed, "Absolutely. In fact, tonight, I'm going to cook for you. We'll wait until it's dark before we leave. My loft is only a few blocks from here so it won't take long to get there. With your height, people will just assume you're a basketball player, so no one will take much notice. We just need to keep your skin covered. That would be harder to explain." Her hand wanted to reach out to feel the texture of his skin. Her fingers itched to trace the colors that rippled slowly across his face.

Clearing her throat, she told him that if he wanted to shower, he was welcome to use her bathroom. "There are some clothes in there from Liam. I'm not sure if any of his pants will fit, but there should be some shirts that might."

Nox wasn't sure what a basketball player was, making a note to ask ARI, but getting clean was something he desperately needed. As he turned and headed towards the bathroom, Emeline told him breakfast would be ready when he was finished.

She watched him as he walked away, marveling at how for such a tall man, his body seemed to fit him perfectly. With his hood off she still couldn't get over the shoulder-length brown hair with the purple highlights running through it. It looked soft and wavy and oh so touchable. *Rein it in, girl.* They had a planet to save, not an alien—no, make that a sexy Delician—to lust after.

Going into the little kitchen attached to her lab, she made them both smoothies. It was easy to make and gentle on the stomach...just in case Earth food didn't agree with him. As she cleaned up the blender, her mind wandered to the bathroom. Was he feeling what she was? Shaking her head, she was getting a little worried about herself. These feelings of lust were getting out of control.

Heading into the lab, she carried both drinks and placed them on the table. Grabbing her headphones, she headed to her computer workstation so she could listen to the events of yesterday. Enough lusting. She needed to start focusing on how she could help with retrofitting the satellites.

As Nox entered the bathroom, all he could smell was Emeline...her scent was everywhere—warm and inviting. Stepping into the shower, he hesitated as he turned the water to hot. What he really needed was a cold shower to calm his growing lust for Emeline. He couldn't count the number of times he'd wanted to grab her around the waist and pull her tight against his body. This feeling had been growing stronger ever since he'd first laid his eyes on her. Judging by the sound coming from the bathroom and the pink glow on Emeline's cheeks, she evidently felt the same way. The bondmating was pulling them both in at an alarming rate. He needed time for her to get used to him, to want him as much as he wanted her before he told her about the bond.

I can't believe I found my bondmate. I never thought this would happen. The joy I feel in my heart when I look at her fills me with so much wonder. I'm curious if this was why my mother had been sad whenever she looked at my father. She had always wanted to find her bondmate. It wasn't fair that her father made her marry Sandovar, but then she wouldn't have me she used to tell me. She would have been so happy for me and would have loved Emeline.

Grabbing the shampoo bottle, he washed his hair and his body, trying not to notice what his desire for her was doing to him. He looked down—amazed to see the colors rippling around his body. Soon others would start to notice the changes in him but he wasn't ready to address this to anyone other than Emeline just yet.

Maybe if I take the edge off, I'll be able to concentrate on our mission. Working in the lab today with Emeline was going to be long and torturous. He'd endure it—anything if it meant he could spend time with her. The problem was he wasn't used to having such intense sexual feelings...about anyone. It wasn't that he hadn't been with females over the years. He had just never encountered anyone who elicited feelings quite to this magnitude before. His focus was usually on his work. He didn't have time for a relationship, and besides, he wanted to find his bondmate. That was the excuse he'd given his father when he wouldn't agree to the arranged marriage Sandovar kept pushing on him.

Taking a hold of his erection, he moved his hand slowly—up and down...thinking of Emeline and how beautiful she was. *Her hair was the color of the Delician sand on the beach where he swam each morning. He pictured her lying on the soft golden sand. Her nude body glistening in the sun. Her eyes raking up and down his body as he stalked towards her—his skin wet from his swim, sparkling in the sun.* His breathing became labored the faster his hand moved. Leaning his forehead against the shower wall, he was filled with that wonderful scent that was purely Emeline. Closing his eyes, he reveled in the blissful feeling as his release swept through him. *Will it feel this wonderful when I have Emeline in my arms? Absolutely.*

Nox finished rinsing his body and stepped out of the shower, feeling slightly calmer than he'd been since first meeting Emeline. Looking around the bathroom for a body dryer, he spied towels hanging on a rack. Noticing that one was wet, he chuckled to himself at their lack of technology.

Grabbing a dry towel and bringing it to his face, he noticed the wonderful smell that called to him. It reminded him of Emeline—sweet with a hint of passion. A scent that would follow him throughout the day.

Opening a door that led to a closet, he pulled out a T-shirt that looked like it belonged to Liam. Although he was taller and bulkier than Liam, he pulled it over his head knowing that it would be a tight fit. He didn't care. He was happy he had a clean shirt to put on. If he was on board the *Maelstrom,* he would have replicated whatever he needed.

Nox reminded himself that even though the humans had excelled in some areas, they were still markedly lacking in others.

Looking in the mirror, he grabbed Emeline's comb and ran it through his hair. It was longer than he normally wore it, but life had been crazy lately. Studying his reflection, he again noticed the changes to his face. The darkening colors only seemed to enhance the luminosity of his skin tone.

He considered his father's reaction the next time they video commed. Sandovar would know on first glance he'd found his bondmate. *He'll be more upset at the loss of his plan he had for me. Not that I was ever going to do what he wanted. He'll be angry and won't hesitate to voice his disappointment. So what? I've been a disappointment to him my whole life anyway. What's one more thing? He'll have no choice but to accept that I've found my bondmate.*

Giving the mirror one last look at his appearance, he tried to swallow his emerging feelings for his bondmate. *Time to get started on finishing this mission. Then I can concentrate on Emeline.*

As he entered the lab, he heard Emeline on her communications device she held in her hand—"cell phone" she had called it. She looked over at him, holding her finger to her lips indicating he should keep quiet.

Nodding his head, he moved to the window. He was eager to see Earth for the first time in daylight. It had been dark last night when Nyx dropped them on the roof, so he wasn't able to see much of this city called Boston. Gazing out at the skyline, he noticed it wasn't any different from the cities back on Delicia in that people wanted to live together in a centralized space. In that moment he realized he knew next to nothing about humans. Sure, he could spout statistics down to every last atom about Earth, but when it came to understanding an entire species, he had a lot to learn.

Hearing Emeline finishing up on her call, he was determined to change his way of thinking starting right then and there. Turning towards her, Nox smiled inwardly—Emeline would be perfect to teach him about Earth and humans.

"Mum, you know I can't FaceTime when I'm working in the lab. You don't have a security clearance."

"I know, sweet girl, I just wanted to see your smiling face. I'm just a little lonely out here in the woods all by myself."

"I know." A note of sadness tinged Emeline's voice.

"Hey, it's okay. I'm fine, really. You know everyone has been great, calling and trying to get me to go out, but sometimes it's hard. I'm usually the third wheel and I hate that."

"Mum, once you get the house sold, I'd like you to consider moving into the city closer to me and Belle."

"You keep saying that, but I'm not sure. I'll think about it, but it's hard to leave behind everything you've always known and start over. I mean I'll have to find a new esthetician and you know how hard it is to find someone you like."

"True, but at least you'll be near your kids."

"You're right. Speaking of kids, have you heard from Liam? It always makes me nervous when he goes up into space."

"He's fine. I spoke to him and Ami last night and things are going according to plan." Emeline hated lying to her mother. She glanced over to Nox, who was still staring out the window. "Listen, Mum, I gotta go. I have another call coming in," she winced—adding yet another lie to her fast-growing list.

"Okay, baby girl, I'll talk to you later. Have a good day. Love you."

"Love you too, Mum."

Hanging up, Emeline turned to Nox. He looked damn fine in her brother's too tight shirt. His biceps stretched the arms almost to the breaking point while the shirt pulled tight across his chest, accentuating his well-defined muscles. Swallowing hard, she told him who she was talking to. "That was my mother. She's worried about me. I hate lying to her, and when she finds out...I can tell you there will be hell to pay." At his confused look, she told him that lying was not condoned in her family. "I swear my mother could spot a lie before it even left your mouth. It was usually easier to tell the truth. Your punishment was infinitely worse the more you lied."

Nodding in agreement, he told her that it was only until the threat from the Hexians was over. Then it would be up to Earth's governments to decide when or if at all its inhabitants would be told about the Hexians.

His stomach chose just that moment to rumble, which caused Emeline to exclaim, "Oh geez—I'm sorry. I made you a smoothie. I hope you like it. It's made with fruit and some veggies. I added some protein powder to give you a little added boost."

She reached over and handed him his drink—her hand brushing lightly against his as he took it from hers. It sounded cliché to say but she swore that a gentle spark shot through her fingers, up her arm, settling in her chest around her heart. Her eyes locked onto his and she saw that he had felt the same thing. Her eyes widened as confusion began to show on her face. She jerked her hand back, slowly bringing it to her chest, rubbing the area around her heart. *Okay, that was weird. I'm not having a heart attack, am I?* She saw that Nox was mimicking her with his own hand.

"Um, sorry about that. I must have created some static walking over here. I didn't mean to shock you like that." She laughed lightly, trying to cover her discomfort.

Nox gave her a small smile, trying to calm his own racing heart. "Maybe we should get started." Taking a sip from his smoothie, he was surprised at how delicious this human drink was. "This is my first taste of human food. It's very good. Usually I'm cautious about trying food from other species. I've had a few unpleasant experiences in the

114

past, but I like this. You'll have to show me how to make it."

"I'm glad you like it." Emeline was relieved Nox was enjoying one of her favorite drinks. "You've got me curious now. Maybe later you'll tell me more about your experiences. I'm eager to learn about your planet—and well, I guess now your whole universe."

Nox laughed wholeheartedly. "I'd be delighted to tell you anything I can."

"Great." Sitting down at her workstation, Emeline fiddled with her glasses. Giving him a quick glance, she murmured shyly, "Maybe we should get back to our mission. What's the first thing you need from me?" She knew she was blushing like a fool and wanted to get the topic back onto more important things.

"Of course. I'd like to know the purpose of your network array, but first can I ask, why do you wear those?" he asked pointing to her glasses.

Emeline's hand went to her face, pulling her glasses off. "These? Oh, I have terrible eyesight. I've worn glasses since the first grade. I usually wear my contacts, but I need to get them refilled. Why? Don't Delicians wear glasses?"

"No," Nox told her. "It's not necessary with our regen units. If you'd like, Dr. Datrem can correct your vision when we get to the ship."

Elated at never having to wear glasses again, Emeline agreed to see the doctor.

Turning back to her work, Emeline began bringing up her lab notes. "Well, I guess I should probably start by asking if you know about solar flares and how they work?"

Nox pulled up a stool and sat down near Emeline, trying to keep a safe distance between them. "Yes. It's when a sun releases energy from its surface, sending electromagnetic radiation out into space."

"Simply put, yes. However, the waves that are contained within the radiation can cause disruptions in our satellites. Over the last few years, we've been seeing an increasing number of solar flares. It was merely common sense to try to find a way to protect our satellites." Her fingers flew over her keyboard as the transparent screens around her workstation came to life. She continued inputting commands and a flowchart of how her process worked appeared on the screen directly in front of them.

Nox was impressed as she launched into her explanation on how her array worked. Her face glowed with pride. He could see she was proud of her work. It showed in how confidently she gave her presentation. *Wait until she sees how ARI works. I can't wait to show her my lab.* Nox was happy when he thought about the prospect of working alongside his bondmate.

"...so, since like charges repel, the premise is to identify the charge and then direct a like charge back into the radiation coming toward the satellite. It would then deflect the particles away from the satellite, thus almost eliminating any disruptions."

"Interesting concept." Distracted, he tried to drag his eyes away from her luscious mouth.

Misinterpreting him, Emeline gave him a skeptical look —slightly annoyed at his tone. "You're just saying that to be nice. I know what you think of us. I heard what Ami said."

Nox had the good grace to feel some remorse. "Honestly, I'm not. Yes, it is true I was surprised at how technologically advanced Earth has become. However, your research shows me how forward-thinking humans can be. I know it seems unfair to you, but to us, your planet has been on the prohibited planet list for a long time."

"Well, maybe you and your UAP should be checking up on who you have on this list of yours once in a while." She knew she sounded snarky, and in fairness, she did understand their reasoning. It still hurt, though, at being thought of as less, especially when you'd worked so hard to be the best.

Nox conceded to her point saying, "You're not the first

116

to say that to me. I promise you when I give my report to General Tarek and the UAP, I'll be clear in my assessment. I was serious when I said you are brilliant. Earth is fortunate to have someone with your dedication working for them."

Emeline was floored at the compliment that Nox had paid her. She remembered how hard she had worked to get NASA to agree to implement her plan. "I wish I could tell you it was easy to convince them to fund my idea. They said I was too *young*."

Nox completely understood what she was saying, "I was young when I began working on my force field technology. It was extremely hard to get people to take me seriously. Fortunately for me I had an ally—my mother."

Emeline's eyebrows rose in surprise when Nox mentioned his mother being a scientist like himself.

"We worked together for years. She taught me everything she knew. When her colleagues saw how much she encouraged me, I was able to work on my idea with the support of the lab. It was because of her, I was successful. My technology is now being used in more applications than I ever imagined, but it was because of my mother that I was even given the chance."

Emeline didn't miss the note of sadness that edged his voice at the mention of his mother. There was obviously a story there. Hopefully tonight she could get him to open up about his family.

"You were lucky to have her. I have to say it was a lot harder for me when I first started in this field. It's taken me years and a lot of hard work, but I have put together a team of scientists that are some of the smartest people in this industry. Lucky for me they happened to be three of my best friends." She moved to her lab desk and grabbed a framed photo off it. "You've met Ami."

Handing it to him, she pointed to each person in the photograph. "This is me and there's Ami. This is Lorelei. She's our astrophysicist. Her family is Native American, meaning that they are indigenous to the United States of America. And this little peanut here is Heather. She's our computer genius. She can hack anything—so watch out. It's amazing to watch her mind at work. You might want to be careful when talking about Earth's lack of technological advances in front of her. She will not take kindly to it. Especially considering our lab has probably the most advanced systems on Earth. Trust me, you don't want to piss her off. She's a master at finding out your secrets. She might do it just on principle alone."

Emeline laughed at Nox's look of concern. "Don't worry. I'll protect you from her. Man, I can't wait when Lorelei and Heather find out that first contact has been made." The thought of seeing their faces when they met Nox put a huge grin on hers.

"Anyway, back to what we were talking about." Putting the diagram of her array up on a secondary screen, she continued her explanation. "Here you can see the parts of the array and how it is put together. I came up with the name late one night after maybe one or two glasses of wine too many. It's called the Deflector Network Array (DNA)." She started to laugh but stopped when she noticed his confusion. "Oh, sorry—of course you wouldn't get it. You see human bodies are made up of Deoxyribonucleic acid or DNA."

Nox's eyes lit up with understanding, "Ah, I understand. Yes, there is a big difference in the meaning between the two."

"Yeah—so you can see how mixing wine and science can sometimes not work out so well," she laughed. "Now we just call it the network array except when Ami tries to be funny."

"I can see where Ami would find that amusing," he laughed with her.

What a sound it was to hear him laughing, Emeline thought. The sound seemed to resonate through her and she felt herself flushing warm all over. *What is happening to me? I swear my face has been red since he walked through the door. For some reason when I look at him, I just want to climb him like he's an ice-cream cone and lick him from the top down.* Smiling at him, she excused herself and headed to the bathroom.

Wetting a cloth, she pressed it lightly to her face. The heat from her face faded into the cloth...replaced by a feeling of relief from the cool water. Raising her head, she looked at herself in the mirror. *Okay, let's get a grip here. You have got to pull it together.*

Grabbing her makeup bag, she began pulling out what she would need to fix her face. As she worked, she reminded herself that Earth was about to be attacked by aliens and she had a job to do. If the Delicians weren't able to stop the Hexians, Earth needed their satellites to be protected. If their communication capabilities were destroyed, Earth had no way to communicate with countries around the world. This was vital to Earth and people were counting on her.

Giving herself one last look in the mirror, she was happy with how she looked. *Put these feelings you have for Nox aside at least until tonight. Focus on the job at hand.* She considered her feelings for a minute and decided right then and there she was going to get to know Nox better. She found him intriguing and wanted to know more. Tonight, she'd cook him a human meal and see where the evening went. She was making Ami's recipe for Korean beef barbecue. Hopefully his alien stomach could handle a little bit of spice. She knew she had all the ingredients in the fridge. She'd had a craving for it the last time she went shopping and luckily it was a quick and easy meal to prepare.

Happy she had a plan in place, Emeline grabbed two water bottles from her office mini fridge before heading back out into her lab.

Handing him a water bottle, she asked him to explain to

her how her array could be used as a force field.

Nox took the bottle of water from Emeline and watched her as she put the end of the bottle to her lips and swallowed. He couldn't take his eyes off of her. His tongue pulled his lower lip between his teeth as he watched her. He could feel the bonding starting to intensify the more time they spent together and he could tell she was feeling what he was. His body was becoming attuned to hers. These were new feelings for him. It felt strange having such strong feelings for someone from another species but he was happy—ecstatic actually. But they needed to focus on the mission. He'd told himself when she was in the bathroom that he needed to stop fixating on her and focus on getting this force field program adapted to Emeline's network array.

Giving Emeline a determined look, he started to explain to her how the satellites could be integrated with his force fields. They worked for several hours mapping out how they would move forward.

They were interrupted when Nox got a call from his assistant Loris on his wrist comm. Emeline was enthralled when she saw the hologram of Loris appearing to pop out of the band Nox wore on his arm.

When Nox signed off from his conversation with Loris, he showed Emeline his wrist comm, explaining how it worked. The band looked wider on the top and tapered around the wrist to meet on the other side. When he placed his finger on the center of the band, a small beam came out and scanned his right eye. When the beam disappeared, a transparent screen hovered right above his wrist about the size of a piece of copy paper and had touch screen technology.

Emeline's mouth dropped open. "Amazing." She reached her hand out but thought better of it—dropping her arm just shy of his. "Show me how this works. Is this a computer?" she asked him. The awe in her voice excited him.

Nox moved to stand next to her, the heat from his body made her temperature rise. "Not in the way that you're used to. This is an embedded artificial intelligence that runs our databases. ARI, as we call it, takes verbal commands and then searches through the multitude of databases at incredible speed. Here, let me show you. ARI, bring up a hologram showing Earth and the orbiting satellites that have the network array installed."

When Earth, with the newly installed satellites with her network array appeared to hover just above his wrist, Emeline couldn't take her eyes off it, blurting out, "This is so cool." Giving him a slight defeated look, she murmured, "Okay, I concede. Our technology is primitive compared to yours. I get it. But now you've hooked me. Now, I want to see more. Can you imagine the incredible things we could do with this technology? I mean, we could get rid of hunger, poverty, cure cancer—heart disease." She gulped thinking about her dad.

"Yes, it can do all those things but you must remember, humans don't know about us and your governments have forbidden us to say anything."

"But how can we not use it to help people?" Holding out her hand, Emeline looked into his eyes as she tried to get control of her emotions. Millions of lives could be saved with this alien technology. "I understand what you're saying. Save Earth first, then we can talk about helping my people. But know this, Nox, this conversation isn't over."

He took her hand in his, trying to give her comfort. She had a soft heart for a scientist. "I promise as soon as your government allows it, we'll talk about this again. Now, would you like to see how this works?"

"Of course." Pulling her hand back, Emeline was eager to learn everything she could.

Nox had ARI display the diagram of how his technology could merge with hers. He told her that he had already replicated the equipment that they would need to merge with hers on the satellites. Nyx was having it loaded onto the shuttle. It wasn't a large piece of equipment and would attach to her network array easily. It contained an engineered crystal that was the source of the energy needed for the force field. The force field would use her equipment to shield the satellite by emitting particles that would encompass the entire structure.

At first Emeline had trouble comprehending Nox's notes.

Noticing her headphones, Nox reached over and handed them to her as he told ARI to transmit the audio through her Bluetooth to her headphones.

She frowned until she heard a voice explaining what was displayed on the hologram. Looking at Nox, she gave him a wide smile as she read along with what she was hearing.

Nox touched her arm, startling her. "I'm sorry. I just wanted to tell you that all you have to do is say stop or repeat. I've programmed my wrist comm to accept your voice commands. It will have to scan your eye to get a reading if you're okay with that."

"Yes, that would be great. Thank you." Removing her glasses, she gave him a shy smile asking, "Does this mean I can use your comm and ask ARI to do whatever I want?"

"Yes." He laughed as he told ARI what he wanted. Shutting the screen for a moment, he took his comm and held it up to Emeline's right eye. "Now just hold still for a moment. It will only take a few seconds for ARI to scan your eye."

She nodded her head as she turned her face to his. Nox placed his hand along her left cheek to hold her still. She fought the urge to roll her head into his warm palm.

Opening her eye, trying to hold as still as possible, Emeline told Nox she was ready. A green beam appeared and scanned her eyeball; taking only moments before it disappeared. She looked up into Nox's eyes, blinking away the tears that had formed.

They stood for a moment lost in each other's gaze—each knowing they should walk away. A ringtone was heard coming from her pocket, breaking the moment. Turning away, Emeline replaced her glasses and checked her phone. Seeing that it was Lorelei, she thought to herself, *Damn. I can't put this off. They'll be banging on the door if I blow them off again.*

Telling Nox she had to take this call, she went into her office and closed the door. Looking out as she pushed accept, she saw Nox begin talking softly to ARI. Diagrams appeared in front of him as he continued to have a conversation with his comm unit. When Lorelei yelled for her to pay attention, she settled in her chair and began to tell her a story that contained half-truths, hoping to appease her friend. She was fooling herself if she thought Lorelei was buying her made-up story. Especially when she told her she couldn't do a girls' night because she was tired and planned to go to bed early—blaming her late-night call with Liam and Ami. As much as she loved her friends, sometimes their concern was a bit overwhelming. Hopeful that Lorelei would think she was dating someone and just didn't want anyone to know, she'd leave it alone. *Well, one can only hope.*

Seeing Nox continuing to work in the lab, Emeline ended the call with Lorelei and put in one to Heather. Heather wanted an update on the weird data that they had picked up. Emeline told her that it had stopped. The current data being picked up was now in line with what they had expected. Emeline told her that it must have been an anomaly. They'd probably never truly know what it was. Crossing her fingers and relaying the same story she told Lorelei, trying to stick as close to the truth as possible, she again hated herself for not being able to fill them in.

Shutting off her phone, she stuck it in her back pocket and went back out into the lab to join Nox. When she asked if she could try to use ARI, he handed her his wrist comm.

"Just tell ARI what you want to do."

"ARI display a hologram of the International Space Station, please."

"You don't have to say please. It doesn't have a personality. It's just a tool," Nox told her with a laugh.

"I'm polite. What can I say, my Mumma taught me manners," she told him sheepishly. The ISS popped up in front of her, along with its specs.

"ARI display all communication satellites orbiting the Earth." The ISS disappeared, replaced by Earth with its orbiting communication satellites. There were a lot of them. She wasn't sure if they would be able to protect all of them.

She pulled up the prioritized list of satellites that Leslie Merriman had emailed her, checking off which ones had already had the network array installed on it. "It's good they've narrowed the list. This is much more manageable. I'll make sure Liam and Ami have this updated list of satellites. Can I send them a message using ARI?"

"Yes. Just give ARI their contact information."

"Sweet." Emeline did as Nox instructed, and faster than she could have imagined, she had a reply from Liam thanking her for the list. "I've got to get me one of these."

As the day wore on, Emeline began to see the plan that Nox and the Delicians were implementing starting to take shape. It may take her a few days, but she was confident that they would succeed in protecting the satellites. *And maybe tonight I might get to know a certain Delician a little bit better. Life is looking up!*

CHAPTER 7

Looking through the final pieces of the data on how Nox's force field would integrate with her array, Emeline was encouraged at the progress they were making. Noticing that the sun was beginning to set, she rolled her neck, then stretched her arms over her head to loosen her stiff muscles. It would soon be safe enough to bring Nox over to her loft. Her stomach was beginning to protest the lack of food, figuring Nox must be hungry as well. A smoothie and a granola bar weren't enough to satisfy her for the day. She could only imagine how someone as big as Nox must be feeling.

Her eyes strayed from the data to look at him. The darkening skies outside meant that the lights in the lab became more pronounced, highlighting just how pale his skin was. The purples, blues and pink hues that reflected off his skin definitely made him look like an alien. Another dead giveaway was his eyes—she'd never met anyone with that color purple eyes before.

Judging by the look on his face, she could see he was engrossed in what he was reading. She studied him from beneath her lashes. *He looks so at home in the lab. I can definitely relate to that feeling. Being in here working is one of the few places where I can be myself and think without anyone judging me. I get the feeling he would agree with me.*

Grabbing her cup, she finished off the last of her tea —*geez how many cups have I had today?* Her eyes did another quick scan of his body. Desire for this strange alien pooled in her belly. He still wore the jeans he showed up in last night, but the shirt he'd borrowed from Liam looked like it was cutting off his circulation. It was tight, pulled taut around his upper arms. She wanted to run her fingers around the edge of the shirt, fooling herself that it was just to give him some relief from where it was cutting into his skin. If she was honest with herself, it was more of an excuse to touch him, even if for a moment.

Trailing her eyes across his broad shoulders, the play of his muscles as he moved showed the strength he possessed. Emeline wondered how it would feel to be held by him. Sighing heavily, she leaned over his arm to see what he was reading. The scent of vanilla had been playing havoc with her senses all day as she worked closely beside him. She wasn't sure if it was coming from him or her, but just thinking of him using her shampoo in the shower caused her insides to flutter.

Nox moved his gaze from what he was reading to look down into Emeline's upturned face. What he wouldn't give to just bend down and kiss her. Her lips, still glistening from the tea she'd just drank, nearly undid him. He had to fight the urge to lean for a quick taste. *Tonight*, he thought, *tonight I am going to taste those luscious lips.*

Adjusting his pants...again, he tried to get his body to relax in these strange clothes. With his feelings for Emeline increasing at an alarming rate and the tightness of these— *What were they called again? Oh yeah, jeans. How can human men bear to wear these pants all the time? They're very restricting. I can't wait to be back in my own clothes, but I get why I have to wear them. I have to blend in, I understand that, but do they have to be so tight?*

Clearing his throat, he decided he just had to touch her skin, if only for a moment. Taking her hand in his, he smiled softly at the small gasp of surprise that pushed through her delicious-looking lips. "I can't get over how the color of your skin is similar to mine," he told her. His voice had a slight husky edge to it as his fingers moved up past her wrist to caress her arm. It had been torture every time they'd inadvertently brushed against one another. He wanted more than just a few quick touches here and there.

He wanted—yeah, he just wanted her.

Her eyes softened as she looked down at their joined hands. "I don't know if I'd say similar. I mean, your skin is shiny—and it glows." Her voice gave a small hitch as he continued to stroke her hand. "Do all Delicians have this color skin?"

"Yes."

Emeline couldn't have stopped herself from touching him even if she tried—she didn't try. Instead, she ran her fingers up and down his arm, surprised at the softness of his skin. At first glance she'd thought his skin would have a harder texture—similar to marble because of the way the light reflected the colors. Rather, it felt similar to hers, soft and warm—alive.

"Your skin is smooth." Her eyes softened as she gazed, almost mesmerized by the movement of the colors. "It's beautiful." Her hand moved involuntarily up his arm, past his elbow, coming to rest with her fingers wrapped around his bicep. Well, maybe *attempted* to wrap was a better way to put it. The muscles in his upper arm were so well defined, indicating what a strong and powerful man he was. *Okay, maybe I wouldn't be able take him down in a training class, but it would sure be fun to try.*

Her fingers slipped gently under the tight edge of his shirt, pulling slightly, trying to give him some relief. Grabbing the scissors, she thought to make some cuts along the edge to give him a little more room but he stopped her with his other hand.

"I don't want you to ruin Liam's shirt. It's nice of him to let me wear it." But to himself he knew that if it was up to him, she could shred the whole thing so he could stand before her shirtless. "I don't want to damage something that doesn't belong to me." It wasn't his nature to be destructive.

"It's fine, really. You're right. I just didn't want you to be uncomfortable."

"You have a kind heart."

Blushing, Emeline was embarrassed. Stepping back from him, trying desperately to tone down her overwhelming desire for him, she told him she needed to find him better-fitting clothes. "When we get to my loft, I'll find you something else to put on. If we're going to be working together here for a few days, we can't have you being uncomfortable in your clothes. If I can't find anything at home, I'll just order something over the internet with next-day delivery."

This idea of ordering over the internet intrigued Nox. "How does this work—ordering clothes on your internet? Can you show me?"

"Sure, come sit here near me." She grabbed her laptop and logged into her Amazon account. "See—here is the main page of the website." Looking him over, she mused, "We should search for clothes in the big and tall section." Her fingers moved over the keyboard as she showed him how the webpage worked. "We'll need to get your exact measurements, but they should have something in your size. They have everything you could ever want and then some."

Grabbing a measuring tape off the shelf, she had him stand in front of her as she took a few quick measurements of his body. It was the hardest thing she had ever done, especially as she tried to control her hands from lingering too long in any particular spot. He held his body stiff, like the part of him that was very pronounced in his tight jeans as her hands roamed over him.

She knew her face was bright red as she finished up telling him, "Okay, I think I've got it. Let's see what you might like to wear." Concentrating on the screen in front of her was hard as they both tried to downplay the effects of her attempt at getting a correct size for him.

Scrolling through all the men's clothing, Nox shook his head at most of the pants shown. "How is it that your males can wear such constricting pants?" he asked her. "On my planet we have replicators that will make anything you want."

"Now see, that's another question that's on my list. I really do want to learn more about your technology, but let's get you some clothes first."

They finally settled on loose-fitting khakis and a few button-down shirts. The breadth of his chest and biceps being what they were, T-shirts were out of the question. Nox really wished he could have just replicated his own clothing, but the style and material used in Delician clothing would be a dead giveaway if he was seen by anyone here on Earth.

Nox watched Emeline as she finished completing the purchase, checking the option for next-day delivery before closing out of the website. "How do you make restitution for the clothing?" he asked. The concept of shopping online was fascinating, but then everything about this planet was. This internet that she "surfed" was intriguing to Nox. "How will you pay for the clothing? I don't have any human money to give you."

"Oh, that's okay. I charged it to my credit card. I'll pay the balance at the end of the month. No worries," she assured him.

"There is so much to learn about humans and how you live. It would be amazing to stay here and study the human way of life."

"Well, I don't think 'us' humans would appreciate being studied in such great depth by aliens, but I get what you mean. I have the same feelings about Delicia and how your culture works." She glanced at her phone, checking the time. It was getting late and she was hungry.

"I think it should be dark enough to head over to my loft. Why don't you grab your hoodie? I'll check my phone to see where Lorelei and Heather are before we head out."

Picking up her phone, she started scrolling through her

apps.

"What do you mean where they are?" Nox asked her as he looked down at her phone. It had a screen on one side and glitter on the other. He had observed that she was very attached to this device.

"See here on my phone—these are applications that you can use to do all kinds of things. I can pay my bills, contact my friends, listen to music, read. It's endless. I can even play games on it." Lowering her voice as if she is trying to hide her guilty pleasure, she added shyly, "I like to take breaks and play video games during the day sometimes.

"You play games on your phone? What kind of games?" he asked, his interest piqued.

"We could have a whole long conversation about video games, but I think we'll save that for another time. I'm hungry and I'm sure you are too. Let's head over to my loft. I have a really great dinner planned that I'm hoping you'll like."

Nox nodded his head. Food he could definitely do and having her cook for him—well, that was a bonus. It also meant he could spend more time with her. Alone.

"Perfect." Looking down at her phone again, she sighed with relief. "This is great. Lorelei and Heather have already gone home. At least we don't have to worry about running into them. There is no way we'd get out of here without doing a lot of explaining." She stuck her phone in her pocket, telling him, "We must have been drinking when we decided it was a good idea to put *Find Friends* on our phones. I personally think it can be a bit too intrusive." She laughed, adding, "Of course those are the times that I 'accidentally' happen to shut the app off on my phone. Come on, time to sneak you out of the building. Fingers crossed we don't run into anyone I know." She held up her hand, two fingers crossed. Seeing the confusion on his face, she shook her head, laughing.

Heading into her office, she grabbed her coat, turned off

the lights and walked over to Nox as he was pulling the hoodie over his head. She reached up and pulled the hood forward to hide his hair and skin. "We need to make sure your face is covered. Just keep your hands in your pockets and keep your sleeves pulled down. Your hair wouldn't be a problem in today's culture, but your skin, that would be a bit harder to explain. No point in looking for problems. I think we've got enough on our plate right now, don't you think?"

"I agree with you," he said, looking down as her hand seemed to linger on his hood. "No need to bring attention to ourselves when we have to focus on our mission," he added softly. He could have stayed there all night just looking at her.

She wanted to take her palm and cup his cheek just to feel the connection between her hand and his skin. *Do Delicians men shave their faces? I don't see any five o'clock shadow and we've been together all day. I'll have to add that to the list of things I want to ask. Well, let's at least get some food into him before I begin my 20—no, make that 100— questions.*

She fought her desire to lean into him, opting instead to breathe deeply, taking in his unique scent. There wasn't any one particular scent that stood out—well, maybe except for the vanilla from her shampoo. Instead, his smell reminded her of home...warm, comforting, maybe even a little bit spicy.

Looking up into his eyes, she saw a hint of hunger staring back and thought maybe it was time to go home. "Okay, let's do this." Sliding her laptop into her backpack, she walked to the door with him right behind her. Cracking it open, she checked the hallway, making sure no one was there. Leading him to the elevator, she checked him one last time to make sure he was covered before she pushed the button.

It felt like forever before the door opened. Stepping in warily, she chuckled at his apprehension. He moved to the back wall, watching her every move.

Pushing the button for the ground floor, she began to tell him what he should expect once they stepped out into the street. "Boston is one of the oldest cities in this country. This section where I work and live has been undergoing a revitalization. It's a really cool place to live. I love looking at the older architecture mixed in with all the new shiny high-rises. There's a ton of restaurants and shops and beautiful parks."

He watched her as she told him some of the history of her city.

"... over 250 years ago, England, a country across the Atlantic Ocean, considered this new land to be under its rule. Anyone who lived in the "colonies," as it was referred to, had to live under the laws put forth by the king. Taxes had to be paid, but of course, as with any tyrant, the taxes just kept rising higher and higher and soon the people of the colonies began to resent England. An uprising by the people occurred and the Revolutionary War was fought, freeing the people. That's how this country became known as the United States of America." She finished with a note of pride in her voice.

Nox listened intently as Emeline talked. "In my research of Earth, I have found that your planet is made up of all different countries with many languages. That's why I was glad to have a translator chip. I can understand all of your planet's languages," he said as he pointed at his head.

"That's another of the many questions on my list to ask you tonight," Emeline told him as the door opened on the ground floor. Lucky for them only a few people were milling around and no one seemed to take any notice of the tall man in the hoodie and the beautiful blond woman as they walked through the lobby door out into the night.

The first thing Nox noticed was the blast of heat that hit him full force. It was hot and humid. Delicia had two suns, so he knew all about summer heat, but this was different.

This heat was wet and Nox's human clothes felt like they were glued to his skin. Luckily, there was a warm breeze coming off the water they were walking by that gave him brief moments of relief.

The second thing he noticed was the smell—and not a very good smell at that. It was a mixture of gasoline, dirt and brine from the water—and people, lots of people. It took him a moment to control his senses as he took in the scene around him. The main street they were on was covered in a black coating with raised platforms for people to walk on. It was similar to Delicia with people milling around—all seeming to be in a rush to get where they were going. But what amazed him the most was the number of vehicles he saw people riding in. They were everywhere and they were loud and emitted a noxious gas out of the back of them. It was apparent that humans hadn't progressed enough to stop the polluting of their air.

"Why are people driving around in those vehicles that put such noxious fumes into the air?" he asked Emeline—his eyes couldn't stop taking in the sight and sound around him.

Giving him a heavy sigh, she replied, "I'm guessing on Delicia it's not like this."

"No. Well, I mean we do have vehicles that transport people, but they don't put toxins into the air."

"Well, I guess that is one major difference between our worlds. We are trying to make better vehicles. Electric cars are becoming more prevalent, but unfortunately, they're expensive. Not everyone has the same economic status and so people make do with what they can in order to survive. There are laws and regulations on how many emissions can be spewed into the air, but as you can see, it's not enough. Change is hard sometimes. I'm sure you have found this on your own planet."

"Yes, you're right," he agreed.

They continued walking as Nox tried not to turn his

head and stare at all the people he saw. Humans were fascinating. He saw humans of all different colors, shapes, sizes, hair colors. Some were walking, talking into devices—cell phones—similar to what Emeline carried, while others were in such a hurry, they nearly pushed them into the road.

Emeline grabbed his arm, steering him down another street that seemed to block out some of the noise. It was astounding how loud her city was. The sounds of engines, wheels squeaking, horns beeping, people talking and yelling. They walked by one building that was lit with colored lights with loud noise blaring through the door. He could hear people laughing, and when he looked in saw that they were dancing.

"Is that music typical of Earth?" he asked, captivated by the harsh din coming from the crowded nightclub.

Emeline grinned at his reaction to the noisy club. "That is just one particular type of music. We have all different types. Some people like classical or rock and roll or even rap, hip hop. I personally like country music."

"Fascinating. I mean it. I could spend a long time here studying your human culture."

"That must be the scientist in you," she replied. "I could say the same thing about your planet. When we get to my loft, I'll put on some music I like and you can judge for yourself."

Passing a doorway of a building that was old and had seen better days, Nox noticed an elderly man in filthy clothes lying on the ground. A dirty sign asking for help was tucked inside a container that held a few pieces of equally dirty human money.

Stopping to stare, Nox was alarmed at what he saw. "Emeline, why is that elderly human lying on the ground? Shouldn't we help him?"

Pulling on his arm to move him along the street, Emeline glanced back sorrowfully at the man sleeping on the ground. "Unfortunately, this is a sad part of our society. There are people who are sick, mentally and physical, who can't take care of themselves. These are people who can't cope with living in society and become what we call 'homeless.' It is a sad and ever-growing problem, not just in our country but globally. We try to help them by providing shelters where they can get a hot meal, a place to sleep and medical care if they want it. Unfortunately, a lot of them won't take advantage of it. It breaks my heart that we can't do more."

Letting go of Nox's arm, she fished some money out of her purse and went back and dropped it into the homeless man's cup. She only wished he would spend it on a hot meal but knew with a heavy heart he would most likely use it to buy alcohol. *This is where replicator technology could be used to help a lot of people. I need to talk to Nox about this when this threat to Earth is over.*

They continued walking until she pulled him to a stop in front of a high-rise building. "This is where I live," she told him as she opened the front door and quickly led him across the lobby to a bank of elevators. Thankfully, the lobby was relatively empty, making it easy to go unnoticed. "I live on the top floor. It was the one major splurge I made when my company became successful." She loved her loft and was always happy to come home after a long day.

The elevator ride was quiet as she thought about the ingredients she would need to put together the dinner she had planned for him. *This is crazy. I'm bringing an actual alien into my home.* The elevator dinged, shaking her from her thoughts. Looking out again to make sure her neighbors weren't in the hallway, Emeline hurried Nox down the hall to her door. Punching the code into the keypad, a security measure Liam had insisted on, she stepped through the door, motioning for Nox to follow her. She led him down the hallway that opened onto a large open living space.

Nox smiled as he looked around at her home. He could see her touches everywhere throughout the space. It was a large room with floor-to-ceiling windows that looked out onto the city skyline. One window was actually a door that led out onto a large outdoor space. The space was surrounded by a brick wall that was covered in small twinkling lights. It reminded him of his own home. There was a table and chairs and a small couch with bright colorful cushions arranged on it. He could see plants scattered all along the patio, adding just the right amount of green to make the space look cozy and inviting.

The living space itself was a long room, separated into three sections—cooking, eating and a seating area with a fireplace along the side wall. There was a door on the left before entering the room, which Nox assumed was a room used for sleeping and another one just off the living room on the right. The cream-colored walls were tall with two large metal pipes that hung down from the ceiling that ran the length of the room. It was a comfortable-looking room that made Nox want to sit down and relax.

Smiling at Emeline, he pulled off his hoodie, glad to be in a space that was cool instead of out on the hot city streets. "Your home is lovely, Emeline. Thank you for bringing me here."

Flustered, Emeline was happy that Nox liked her place. "Thanks. It's one of my happy places. It's where I can be at peace."

"I can see why you like it here." Going over to the window, he gazed out at the city. The brightness from the city lights obscured the stars from his view. He saw the lights of an airplane blinking as it moved through the hazy sky. "Just fascinating," he said under his breath for like the hundredth time since he walked out of Emeline's lab.

Moving over to a door off to the side, she motioned for him to follow her. "Come on—I'll give you a tour. This is the spare bedroom where you'll be staying. There is a bathroom through that door. Clean towels are in the closet. This is a dresser for you to store your clothes—well, the clothes that should be here tomorrow," she told him shyly.

Stepping out of the room, she moved towards the other door. "This is my bedroom. I'm just going to change out of these clothes and take a quick shower if you want to do the same. Help yourself to anything you might need. I'll be right back." She disappeared into her room, shutting the door behind her as she hurried into her bathroom for a quick shower. Remembering this morning's shower, she could feel her body start to flush. *Okay, we do not have time for that, Emeline.*

While Emeline was in her bedroom, Nox took another look at his surroundings. Humans weren't any different than Delicians in that they liked to live comfortably and all the small details in her home showed that she had a passion for decorating. He found that he enjoyed the same things she did—clean lines, comfortable furnishing and lots of light.

Breathing deeply, he could smell her; fresh, clean, and what was that smell she had said, oh yeah vanilla—whatever that was.

Pulling up his wrist comm, he said into it, "ARI, what is vanilla?" "Vanilla is a substance grown on Earth made from a bean used to flavor sweet foods." *Hmm sweet—yes, I would agree that Emeline is sweet.*

After taking a quick shower, he realized he didn't have any clean clothes to put on. Looking at the *jeans*, he shook his head, wondering again why human men subjected themselves to this type of restrictive clothing. Sighing, knowing it was his only option, he slipped the tight jeans back on and went looking for Emeline.

Walking out into the main living area, he saw she was in the kitchen pulling items out of what looked like a large box that cold air was coming out of. She was wearing a blue and white striped dress that came to just above her knees.

The top of the dress was snug at her breasts and tapered down her body, flaring out from the waist. Her hair was up in her usual ponytail that hung down her back but swished back and forth as she moved effortlessly from the counter to the box. As she leaned down to get something out of a lower drawer, he couldn't help but notice the firm muscles contouring down her long body ending at the roundness of her hips and buttocks. Adjusting his pants again, he hoped she didn't notice how much he wanted her.

Emeline turned as Nox came into view. His appearance caused her to drop the items she had in her hands. Her mouth felt as dry as the hot summer sand at the beach. With her mouth agape, she stood staring at Nox's bare chest. *My god, he's beautiful.* She couldn't look away even if she tried, but hey, why would she want to? He was standing there in a pair of tight jeans that hung low on his hips, arms crossed over his wide chest accentuating his muscles that seemed to go on forever. Seriously, *I've seen six-packs but he's got a ten-pack. Lorelei's description was right on point.*

Nox came around the island and quickly bent to pick up the items Emeline had dropped on the floor. Placing the items on the counter, he was thrilled seeing the look of desire in her eyes. His heart pounded as her hands moved almost involuntarily to caress his chest. Goosebumps followed her fingers as they moved in slow gentle circles. It took all of his willpower not to throw her on the counter and take her right then and there.

Emeline watched the colors of his skin dance in the light as her eyes followed her fingers as if trying to catch some of the colors before they moved away. Awed by the colors' movement—her mouth longing to follow her fingers—wanting desperately to see if she could catch them on her tongue. She could feel what he was feeling. All that pent-up desire—a craving that if they didn't find relief soon, they'd combust. She came back into herself as she felt his warm fingers gently stroking the back of her hands.

Emeline saw the heat in his amethyst eyes, knowing in that moment he would be hers. *What is happening to me? I haven't had these feelings in—well, never have I felt like this. Maybe I'm sick—or maybe he is doing something to me.*

Pulling away, she felt his hands fall to his side as she turned to grab a few more items from the refrigerator. Moving to the end of the island, hoping to put a little distance between them, praying this feeling of longing would stop, Emeline felt embarrassed.

"I-I'm so sorry. I don't know what came over me. I'm not usually like that. It's just you're so—so—well I don't know what you are, but I'm sorry. I'll try to keep my hands to myself." Emeline felt the heat rising in her cheeks again.

Looking away and then back at him, she blurted out, "Shirt. You need a shirt. Hang on and let me go find something for you to put on. I'm sure I've got something in my drawer that should cover your—," her hand made a circling motion towards his chest. "I mean that should fit your—grrr, that you can wear."

Disappearing into her bedroom, she rummaged through her closet trying to find something to cover that spectacular chest of his. *We're never going to eat at this rate.*

Coming back to him, she handed him one of her over-sized Live Free or Die T-shirts which he quickly pulled over his head, hiding all that magnificence from sight. Swallowing hard, she choked out, "I need a drink. Would you like a drink? I think we need some alcohol. How about a strawberry margarita?"

Opening the freezer, she rummaged around looking for a bag of frozen strawberries, muttering to herself. "What am I saying—you don't know what that is." She felt like she was talking too much—she couldn't help it; he made her nervous.

Catching the ice cream before it could hit the floor, she grinned at him, finally asking, "Would you like a drink?"

Nox reached over, rescuing the strawberry bag before

it slipped from her hand. He grinned back, leaning in to whisper in her ear, "Emeline, I'd love to try one of your drinks."

A tremor ran the length of her body as his breath caressed the side of her neck. So caught up in his closeness, she didn't realize she'd been holding her breath until a sigh escaped her lips. "Great—good. I'll make us a drink."

She turned, heading over to one of the cabinets and opened one of the doors. Reaching inside, she pulled out her blender and set it on the counter. *Focus, girl. You've done this a million times. Make Lorelei proud.* Emeline knew she had to get her feelings under control. He was here helping to save Earth. *And maybe experience a little human interaction in the process.*

"Can I do anything to help?" He stood watching her, the frozen strawberries still in his hand. He could feel her confusion as she shook her head no. He could also feel her desire—it matched his own. Her scent assaulted his senses, made all the more intense because he was wearing her shirt. He might just need to take another shower but he knew it wouldn't help. *I think it's time we had a discussion. I can see that she is having trouble dealing with the feelings the bondmating is having on her.*

Taking a sip of the cold drink to clear the roughness from his voice, he marveled at the taste. "This is really delicious. What is it exactly?" Nox thought maybe if he started slowly, he could ease into the topic that was in the forefront of his mind.

Pulling deeply through her straw, Emeline savored the cool refreshing taste as it slid down her throat before answering him. "This is what I call heaven on a hot day but is more commonly known as a frozen strawberry margarita. It's made with tequila from Mexico. It's very potent stuff. I try never to drink too many of these. It makes me crazy." She laughed, taking another sip from her drink.

Nox couldn't take his eyes away from her lovely face.

Her cheeks were flushed, but not from the alcohol. She had barely put an ounce in for both drinks. She was opening up about herself—telling him about a time when she and her girls had drunk too many shots of this tequila. Her deep blue eyes showed each emotion as her mouth moved from smile to frown to concentration as she told him how horrified they'd been when they'd woken up the next morning. They found themselves outside on her patio at six am with the music blaring and her phone blowing up from members of her condo association. It had not endeared her to her neighbors. After much apologizing and promising to never do it again, the four friends had to institute a new rule—only two shots of tequila were allowed in any one night.

Emeline laughed into her drink, telling him, "Lorelei was not happy with me at all. As our resident drink specialist, Lorelei doesn't like to be censured when it comes to making drinks." Seeing that his drink was finished, she asked if he'd like another one.

"Not right now." His voice sounded dry. "I wonder if I could have a drink of water."

"Of course. I'll show you how everything works so you can help yourself." Glad for any excuse to break the moment, Emeline showed him where the glasses were and how to use the refrigerator. "I'm going to start dinner while you get your water. Umm, before I make dinner, I know you said you eat fish, but do you eat red meat?"

"I do. I try to eat a balanced diet."

"Yes, I can tell you do," she said as her eyes raked up and down his body. *Get a grip here, girl.*

"I like to train and stay as fit as possible. Most Delician males train to keep their bodies in peak condition. Do human males train to stay fit?"

Emeline laughed, actually laughed out loud. "Oh god no."

Seeing the confused look on his face, she stopped and

looked at him seriously saying, "No, human males do not. Well, no, that's not true. There are tons of people who train and work out, but then there are those who don't for whatever reason—work, family or just have no desire. The thing about the planet Earth is that we are made up of all different kinds of people. It's what makes humans so unique."

"I see that. I am most interested in human females. The physical differences between you and Ami are unique to Delicians females."

"What do you mean?" she asked as she placed a skillet on the stove, turning the heat on low.

Nox took a moment to consider how to answer her. "Our females are small in stature—what you would call delicate. Most of our males are big like me, most even bigger. I'm considered on the small side."

"Really!" Emeline exclaimed. "Please tell me more while I cook. I'm going to make Korean beef lettuce rollups with some rice and fruit. It's Ami's mother's recipe. It's one of my favorites. I hope you like it."

"May I help you cook? I'd really like to learn this recipe."

"Only if you tell me more about Delicians. It's so interesting."

"Of course."

Emeline lined up all the ingredients on the island and after a quick explanation of how she wanted the items chopped, Nox got busy chopping vegetables while she started on the marinade for the beef. While they worked, Nox told Emeline about his people. He watched as she whisked garlic powder and fresh ginger into her mixture of sesame oil, soy sauce and brown sugar in a bowl before adding the beef. He explained that even though Delician women were small in size, they were strong in character. Being small didn't mean you couldn't contribute to society. They had equality among the sexes and in fact Delician females were actually quite competitive with the males except in instances that required anything physical.

"Interesting. As you saw earlier, human females come in all sizes and shapes." She added olive oil to the hot pan, swirling it around, making sure the whole surface was covered. "Take me for instance," she said. "I'm actually a little taller than average height, but my mother is small and petite. She's barely 5'2". And you've met Ami. She's tall for a woman. I have several female friends who are over six feet tall."

Adding the meat to the hot pan, she cooked each piece— searing it on both sides. Nox watched her every move, loving that Emeline was so at ease with cooking. He watched as she removed all the cooked beef and added the vegetables he'd just cut up. He became alarmed when he saw her grab a bottle from counter, tipping it over the vegetables, and began to twist the top. Pink salt sprinkled out all over the food.

Alarmed, Nox reached for Emeline's arm asking if she is sick.

Confused, she stared at his hand on her arm, asking him slowly, "What are you doing?"

"Are you sick?" he asked again.

"No. I'm fine. What's wrong?" She could see the panic on his face.

"Then why are you putting pink salt on your food?"

Staring at him like he was a crazy person, it took her a moment to understand what he was talking about. "Oh, the Himalayan salt? I get it. Remember it doesn't work that way on humans. As I said before, we use this to season our food. It doesn't have any curative effects on us, although it would be awesome if it did."

"You're right. I'm sorry," he said, releasing her arm. "I saw the salt and immediately was worried about you."

"Thank you, but you don't have to worry. I'm fine," she said, trying to reassure him. "Actually, I feel better than I have in a long time—lighter for some reason. You'd think with what was about to happen to Earth I'd be scared. Instead, I feel wonderful." She looked over at him bashfully.

"I feel the same way, Emeline."

Blushing, she took a sip from her drink before stirring the vegetables around in the pan. Taking a container of brown rice from the fridge, she took the cover off, placing it in the microwave to heat.

The smell of her cooking started to make his mouth water as his stomach made a noisy grumble. Rubbing it gently, he laughed, telling her he couldn't wait to try her cooking.

Once the meal was ready, she showed him how to construct his rollup. "You take a lettuce leaf and put the cooked veggies in the bottom. Then you add the beef, sprinkling chopped peanuts on the top. I have a sauce here you can dip the end in and then you just take a bite."

After they had filled their plates, they sat down at the table to eat.

Nox's first bite caused his eyes to widen—his eyebrows rising up to almost disappear into his hair. "This is delicious," he exclaimed as the flavors exploded on his tongue. "Wow, this is really good. I must have this recipe to take back to my planet."

"Sure, but I don't think you will be able to get the ingredients on your planet, but you might be able to get close."

"Actually, if I can get the molecular makeup of the ingredients, I can replicate it." Nox said.

"Okay, well I guess that could work, but do you think it will taste the same as using naturally grown foods?" she asked, taking a forkful of the nutty brown rice that perfectly complimented their meal.

"It will be exactly the same," he said confidently.

"Then why not just replicate your food instead of cooking it yourself?" she asked him. She loved how the light was making the purple highlights in his hair sparkle as he moved his head. He was eating her food and enjoying every mouthful of it. It warmed her on the inside watching him marvel at what she'd made for him. She hadn't felt this good in forever. Especially not since her dad had died.

Watching Nox eat, he smiled at her as he explained how cooking was an enjoyable pastime for Delicians—almost like an art. People were always trying new ways to cook the different foods grown on Delicia and also the countless items you could get from other planets. It brought people together, he was saying as she watched him finish up everything on his plate. Telling him to help himself to more food, Emeline smiled as Nox moved over to the counter to fix himself another plate.

Her mind wandered to Liam and Ami and their mission. "Nox, I'm worried about my brother and Ami. Have you heard from them lately?"

Sitting beside her at the table, his plate filled with a second helping, Nox replied, "Not for a few hours. I believe they were going to start installing the new equipment with Nyx. I know they wanted to get as many satellites retrofitted as they could. There is no need for concern. They're in good hands with Nyx."

Waving her hand at him to continue eating, she stared out the window. A feeling of guilt washed over her. She'd spent the last two hours enjoying her time with Nox, totally forgetting their mission. "I can't help it. This is a huge responsibility. And here I sit eating dinner, having a wonderful time, and all the while there are beings out there ready to destroy our world."

"Emeline." Nox grabbed her hand and held it firmly in his, turning her to face him. His fingers intertwined with hers, stirring up those crazy feelings again. "There is no reason for you to feel guilty because you took a few hours to yourself to laugh and be happy. Life will continue to go on around us and it's important that we take whatever time we have to experience the joy of being alive."

Staring down at their hands, she finally asked what had been plaguing her mind ever since she'd first laid eyes on him. "Why—what—I mean, is it me or do you feel the same things I do?"

Gazing lovingly into her eyes, letting her know he understood, he replied softly, "I do. It's like you've awakened something inside me. And when I touch you, a spark shoots through me, wrapping around my heart like a warm hug."

"I feel the exact same thing," she exclaimed. "Why—why do we feel this way?"

Sitting back in his chair, his plate of food momentarily forgotten, he sighed, hoping he could find the right words —words that wouldn't scare her away. "It's complicated. Maybe we should get comfortable. It might take a while to explain."

Nodding her head, Emeline stood up as Nox released her hand. "Why don't I clean up the dishes and then we can go sit on the couch."

"Can I help you?" he asked, picking up his half-full plate and following her into the kitchen.

"No. I've got it. Go get comfortable. I'll just be a few minutes. I want to freshen up anyway."

"Can I get you anything to drink?" he said, picking up his water glass.

"A glass of water would be great. I have a feeling I might need a clear head for this discussion."

After filling a glass for her and refilling his own, Nox went in to sit on the couch, his face serious, which made Emeline nervous.

Putting the dishes in the dishwasher and wiping down the counters, she headed into her bedroom to freshen up. Did she want to hear what Nox had to say? *Yes, she did. It felt right, he felt right.* Emeline looked at herself in the mirror, seeing her flushed cheeks and a sparkle in her eye. She hadn't felt this positive in a long time. She wanted to be with Nox. Earth may be headed for trouble, but she was going to grab every bit of happiness she could get before bad things happened.

Straightening her dress, she headed out, anxious to hear what Nox had to tell her about why they had such strong feelings for one another. Good or bad, she had a feeling whatever Nox had to say was going to change her life forever.

CHAPTER 8

Settling back against the couch, Nox contemplated the best approach to telling Emeline about being his bondmate. She was in a vulnerable place right now with so much being asked of her. He hated adding to her distress. Having the fate of a planet placed directly on your shoulders would be hard on anyone. He wanted to help ease her worries, not add to them. Being told you were the bondmate to someone who was not from your planet would be bizarre enough. Having to come to terms with the fact that you would be tied to this person for the rest of your life was something else altogether.

How would she feel about leaving Earth for Delicia? Would she even want to go? It would mean leaving her family and friends. Furthermore, what about her company and all the success she'd had as a scientist? If she completed the bond, how would she react to the changes in her body? Nox had even more questions than he had answers and he wasn't sure if Emeline would even want to have him be a part of her life.

Taking his glass of water, he headed out onto the patio where he could feel the summer heat starting to abate. It was still hot, but the cool breeze coming off the water filled his nose with the smells of a city shutting down for the night. He could still hear the occasional sounds of a siren mixed in with the gentle lapping of the waves against the moorings along the bridges in the harbor. And of course, there were still the sounds and smells of their motorized vehicles as they moved along the city streets as people went about their business.

Emeline. He sensed her coming toward him before he heard her as she moved out onto the patio. She had taken her hair out of its clasp and it swung silently across her shoulders as she walked toward him. A look of uncertainty graced her face as she closed the distance between them, her own water glass in her hand.

Setting her glass on the table, she moved to stand beside him, leaving a small space between them. It was as if she was afraid to stand too close because of the feelings he knew she felt flowing through her body.

Smiling up at him, she turned, looking across the skyline at the city spread out before them, her hands resting lightly on the railing. It was a beautiful sight—her, not the city. She was lovely. The moonlight played across her face as she gazed up into the cloudless night, a peaceful look settling upon her face. He wanted to kiss her and run his fingers through her long hair. His hand took on a life of its own and reached out to feel her hair. It was soft and silky, just as he knew it would be.

At his touch Emeline turned, seeing her hair threaded through his fingers. Her body leaned into his, seemingly pulled into this one perfect moment.

Gazing up at him, her eyes lingered on his lips—lips that looked perfect for kissing.

He leaned down, lightly brushing his lips against hers. That familiar spark they'd both been feeling drew them together—closer—slowly, until their bodies were touching—not even a feather could come between them. Gently, he pressed his lips to hers, tasting, touching. She tasted of want and desire.

He deepened the kiss, feeling her tongue hesitantly reach for his. Ever so slowly they savored this wondrous feeling that consumed them...a feeling of oneness. Love flowed through them as they pressed their bodies together. Time became nonexistent as they reveled in what was happening between them.

Nox was the first to pull away. Not that he wanted to but because he became aware of his surroundings when he heard the cry of a bird circling above.

Looking down at Emeline—her eyes closed, her lips swollen and moist from their kiss, her face flushed with need—a need that matched his. Trying to bring his own desire under control, he brought his hand up, cupping the side of her cheek as she turned her head slightly for a better fit. He marveled at how lucky he was to have found his bondmate in such an amazing female. It didn't matter to him that she was a human. He wanted Emeline no matter who she was.

His gaze landed on her hand that she had placed on his chest, a ripple of colors swept lightly across the top of it. *Oh stars. The bonding has started. It must have been from their kiss. And what a kiss!* Never had a kiss made him feel this much emotion, such depth of feelings, such passion— passion that could quickly burn out of control if he didn't check himself. Emeline needed to be told about the bonding. How would she feel about all of this, of him, of the changes her body would be going through? They needed to talk and they needed to do it now.

Putting his finger under her chin, he gently raised it until her eyes met his. He murmured softly to her, "Emeline, you are the most beautiful female I have ever encountered. That kiss was amazing. I find I'm having trouble coming up with the right words to tell you just how I'm feeling at this very moment. I think ARI needs to work on the database for the translator chip." His eyes crinkled as he smiled at his attempt at humor.

Emeline could only nod her head at him, her voice having suddenly vanished.

"I think we need to talk about what is happening between us." Reaching down to take her hand, he led her back inside her loft...leaving the nighttime sounds of the city behind them.

Sitting together on the couch, her hand still nestled within his large warm palm, seeming to anchor herself to him, Emeline was also feeling the effects of their kiss. Her body, still quivering from his touch, was doing things to her insides that she'd only read about in books. *Yeah—sigh —that kiss. It was something else entirely—maybe even out of this world.* She laughed internally, glad he couldn't read her thoughts—or at least she hoped he couldn't read her thoughts.

Silently trying to clear her throat, she spoke softly at first, her voice finally finding its strength, "Nox, I don't know what to say. That was the most amazing kiss I've ever had. Oh, I mean not that I've kissed a lot of men, I mean I have—not a lot but…this is coming out all wrong."

Nox gently touched her lips with his finger, "Sshh, it's okay. I know what you mean. I feel the same—and it's okay that I'm not your first kiss. You're not my first kiss either. We have both lived our lives separately until now. It's those experiences that have made us who we are today." Looking intently into her eyes, he said, "What's important is where we go from here."

Emeline smiled warily at him, shaking her head, "I'm not sure. I only know that what I feel for you is beyond anything I've ever felt for anyone. I'm not exactly sure how I'm supposed to handle this, you, me. I'm not even sure why I'm feeling this way. I mean I've only known you, what, 36 hours and already I can't seem to stay away. It's like my body isn't listening to my brain."

"And what is your brain saying to you, Emeline?"

"It's confused. It knows that we haven't known each other very long and that we come from very different… well let's just say worlds for lack of a better term. It also knows that we have a mission to save the planet and taking time for a romance is not something we should be thinking about. But—"

"But?" His expression was hopeful.

"But it also knows that this, whatever it is between us, is special and not something to be tossed aside. It's important. You're important and I know I want to see where this goes. So, tell me, why do I feel this way? Help me to understand where these feelings are coming from."

Nox pulled Emeline into his embrace. Taking her hand in his, he kissed her fingertips as he started to talk. "I think it might be better if I told you a story. It might help you to understand what's happening between us—because, Emeline, I feel the same way you do. Ever since I first laid eyes on you, you have consumed me. When I'm supposed to be focusing on force fields, all I can think of is how soft and smooth your skin looks. How I want to run my hands all over your incredible body."

Emeline turned her face away in a feeble attempt to hide her pink cheeks.

Nox couldn't take his eyes off her. She captivated him. "I want to tell you the story of my parents. I'm afraid it's not a very happy story, but I think it will help you to understand what this is between us."

Taking a deep breath, trying to focus his thoughts, Nox hoped that what he had to tell Emeline wouldn't cause her to turn away from him. She was in a vulnerable state right now with all that had happened in the last few days.

Choosing his words carefully, he started his story. "When it comes to pairings of couples on Delicia, we have within our biology the ability to find our bondmate."

At his words, Emeline turned to look at him, fascinated. She wanted to ask what he meant but didn't want to interrupt him.

"A bondmate is what on Earth you would consider as your soulmate. It's something all Delicians desire more than anything to find when looking for a life partner. It is that one person that completes you and when you meet that person, your life changes forever. You will never be able to turn away from them and once you complete the bond, your bodies will actually begin to merge until a connection so strong is created that not even death will separate you. It is something that all Delicians hope for, long for, but unfortunately finding one's bondmate has become rare over the last many decades."

Nox paused for a moment to judge Emeline's reaction to the information he had given her. He could see that her interest was piqued. She opened her mouth to ask a question but stopped herself so he could continue.

"I know what you are going to ask, 'How do people cope without a bondmate?'" Emeline nodded her head as he went on. "When bondmates became harder and harder to find, our population started to dwindle and it soon became a serious cause for alarm. Since Delician women can only have two pregnancies during their lifetime—"

"Wait—what? Only two pregnancies! Why?" Emeline's eyes widened in surprise.

"It's just the functionality of their bodies. They will only produce two eggs in their lifecycle and there are usually quite a few years in between births. We have not been able to determine why this occurs. It's just how nature works on our planet."

"How long do Delicians live?" Emeline asked, amazed at what she was hearing. What she heard next made her nearly fall off the couch.

"Roughly 600 of your Earth years."

Stunned at this, Emeline could only gape at him, her mouth moving but no sound came out.

"I know that sounds like a lot but remember the passage of time is different on our planet than it is on Earth. How long is the typical life cycle for humans?"

Finding her voice, she told him that humans generally live into their 80s and if a person was really healthy, could live well into their 90s.

"How old are you?" she asked, her curiosity getting the better of her.

"I am 147 of your Earth years."

Emeline looked at him astonished. A bubble of laughter

started in her throat and she couldn't help herself from telling him he looked fantastic for an old man.

Nox laughed with her, happy at how she seemed somewhat accepting of what she was hearing.

"So, if people haven't been able to find their bondmates then what happens?" Emeline asked, although in her mind she had a more important question she wanted to ask but wasn't sure if she was ready to hear the answer.

"Our government knew that we had to solve this crisis, so it became acceptable to have arranged marriage."

"Arranged marriages! That's barbaric."

"To you, maybe. I can see how you would feel that way, but you have to understand, we were facing a worldwide catastrophe with our population dwindling to historic lows."

"I suppose, but what about love? Is that not something that is important in your society?" Emeline looked at him, trying to see if he agreed with her about such an important topic.

"Yes, it is. Love—it's a key ingredient in forming a connection between two people and that's not to say that love didn't grow between the arranged couples. However, bringing our population back to an acceptable level was deemed more important," Nox told her. He could see that she didn't agree with the way the Delicians had decided to solve their problem.

"Do you agree with what they decided?" Emeline asked, hoping that he didn't. As a scientist she could see why they would take this path but morally she felt it was wrong. Granted, at one time on Earth it was considered a normal practice, but that was discontinued generations ago. Only few countries around the world still practiced this custom.

"It was before I was born and now it's something that is considered acceptable. But to answer your question, no, I do not believe in arranged marriages. There is a growing number of people who would agree with you and me.

Nowadays, more and more people are opting to enter into unions of their own choosing if they haven't found their bondmates. Rather than live a life alone without children, these types of marriages have become normal for Delicians."

"I can understand why your government made this decision, but it feels wrong to cast aside love." Emeline felt a level of sadness for the Delicians. She was lucky that her parents had married for love. She smiled as she thought about the loving relationship Hank and Fiona had. She saw the way they had looked at each other, like they were the only two people in the world. There were times when her siblings would tease them about how sickening it was when they would catch them making out—they did love to show affection. Always touching, kissing and when they thought no one was looking the occasional butt grab as they passed each other. That's what she wanted and she wasn't going to settle for anything less even if it meant being alone. Her track record with men showed that she wasn't willing to settle, which was why she was alone at this point in her life.

"Is that what happened to your parents, an arranged marriage?" she asked, but already knew the answer judging by the sadness on his face.

"Yes. Both my parents wanted to wait to find their bondmates, but being from prominent families, the choice was taken from them. Unfortunately for my parents, it led them to a lifetime of misery."

Before he could continue, Nox stood and walked over to the window in an attempt to get his emotions under control.

Emeline could see he struggled whenever he mentioned his mother.

Going into the kitchen, she grabbed a bottle of wine as she thought to herself, *definitely going to need more alcohol for this conversation. I'm getting the feeling his mother is gone and I can totally understand his feelings on that subject.* Even though it had only been two years since her dad had died, he was never very far from her thoughts.

Filling two wineglasses, she watched the emotions play across his face as he appeared lost in a long-forgotten memory. The reflection from the moon upon his strong handsome face intrigued her as she watched the colors ripple just under his skin.

Setting the glasses on the coffee table, she moved over to him. Her hand came up to caress his cheek, a feeling of warmth flooding through her fingers.

He turned his face into her hand as he pulled her gently against him, his large body engulfing her as a feeling of comfort settled over her. She felt his heart pounding against her breast or maybe that was hers—possibly theirs beating together as one…coming together in a moment of commonality of having suffered the same sense of loss.

Quietly she asked, "What happened to them?"

Sighing, he continued to hold her as he slowly rubbed his hand up and down her back. "My parents came from families that were prominent in our government with both their fathers being senators. My father, Sandovar, is from the mountain region and my mother—her name was Elara —from the coastal region. On Delicia, there are three regions—the coastal region, the mountain region and the polar region. Each region has four senators that are elected by the people to run our government. Their fathers thought by arranging a marriage between the two families it would give them an edge over voting on particular issues. Both men were powerful and didn't give any thought as to what their children wanted. Instead, they were used as tools to further each of their agendas.

"My father was expected to follow along in what was considered his duty to become a senator just as his father had. My mother was a scientist and wanted nothing to do with politics, which went against everything my father believed in. He was like his father in that he sought power and influence and expected his wife to be the dutiful political wife. And for a number of years, she tried. When I was born it was assumed that I would follow in my father's footsteps, but I had other plans." He smiled at that thought. His father had been furious when Nox announced he was going to study science instead of politics.

Stepping back with a feeling of reluctance, Emeline took his hand and led him over to the couch.

Handing him his wine, she took a sip of her own while she gently asked him what happened next. It was a fascinating story but one that she knew in her heart didn't end well.

"When I was younger, I saw my father a lot because we lived in the capital city. As I grew older, I spent more and more time with my mother in her lab. We would get together as a family when time permitted and of course for any senatorial functions we needed to be at, but even those had ceased towards the end."

"Your mom is—"

"Yes. She was killed several years ago in a shuttle accident." Sadness clouded his eyes as he thought of that horrible day when he got the news that his mother wasn't coming back. They had worked together for years making a very successful team, although she had trouble holding back her motherly advice. She would remind him, *Hold on, my son, let's run this experiment one more time.* He would grumble thinking she didn't believe the results that he was showing her. But it was just her way of making her point— always saying that you needed to do multiple experiments to make sure you had accurate data. A scientist is only as good as her data, she would say.

Nox told Emeline how even now, he could picture her staring at a monitor, her long brown hair pulled away from her face, purple streaks shining in the light. He missed her wit and sense of humor, along with her love of science. She was small and delicate like most Delician women, but she was tough, always working her body to stay strong unlike a lot of other females. She would look at him with her laughing amethyst eyes ready to tease him or trying to grab his arm to wrestle. Secretly, it was only to show him how toned her biceps were. But it didn't matter how hard she worked, she would always be small and delicate.

"She never should have been on that damn jungle planet. It should have been me. I was supposed to go with her but she wouldn't hear of it. No, she'd said. She needed to get the raw materials for the project she was working on. I was needed here to complete the force field changes for the UAP. She kept telling me it would be fine—she had a security team with her so she felt safe. Yeah, well, those changes could have waited. I should have protected her."

Nox could feel Emeline's hand lightly drawing circles on the back of his hand trying to comfort him. He smiled down at her, floored at how compassionate his bondmate was as he continued his story. "My mother would have loved to be here meeting the humans. They probably would have had to restrain her from asking too many questions." Laughing lightly at the memory, he smiled at Emeline, saying, "She would have been impressed with you and your work." He kept the thought of how happy Elara would have been that her son had found his bondmate to himself. No reason in scaring her at this point.

Emeline listened to Nox, aching inside for him because she also knew about the pain of losing that one person in your life who understood you—your own personal cheerleader. "What about your father after the accident? I take it your relationship didn't get any better."

Nox frowned at the mention of his father, saying, "No, although we tried for a while but I was always a disappointment to him. When he decided that I would enter into an arranged marriage he had set up, well, let's just say things became very strained between us."

Looking to see her reaction to his words, he saw that she was deep in thought. "What? Ask me what you want."

Emeline wiggled her lower lip between her teeth, trying to decide how to ask the question that had been burning in her stomach. Deciding to just go for it, she asked, "It's just I was wondering if you were married or if you had found your own bondmate. You hadn't mentioned anyone special in your life and I couldn't help wondering because of these feelings that we're both having." Emeline tried to hide the uneasiness she was feeling, not sure what to think of all that she had learned from Nox.

"No, I am not married, which is why my father is so angry with me. The last time we spoke I told him that just because he gave up his dream of finding his bondmate, I would not. I was going to wait. I didn't want to end up in a loveless, anger-filled arrangement like the one he and my mother had."

Emeline snorted, "I'm guessing that didn't go over very well."

Replying back cynically, he said, "Not in the least. We haven't spoken since then, although I'm sure he'll be in contact soon to try to persuade me once again."

"And what will you tell him when you talk to him next?" Emeline asked softly, not sure she wanted to know but the need to ask was all too consuming.

"I think you know what I will tell him," he replied carefully, watching her expression as he took her hand in his.

Gently brushing his lips across the back of her hand, he closed his eyes briefly before replying, "I have found my bondmate in the most unlikely of places."

Taking her face in both his hands, he started to kiss her forehead, her brows, down to her eyes and slowly, almost reverently, he moved across kissing her cheeks until his lips brushed hers as he looked deeply into her eyes and said with a whisper of a voice, "You, Emeline. You are my bondmate."

Emeline could have said she was surprised at his words, but deep down she knew what he said was true. She had felt it down in her soul whenever she looked at him or touched him.

Staring deeply into his soulful eyes, the truth of his confession was reflected back at her. She didn't want to look away, to break this moment that was going to define her life from this point on, but as usual the scientist in her had questions. *Well, those questions can wait for just a minute longer if you don't mind.* She gently pressed her lips to his, wanting, no, needing to feel their tender warmth against hers.

He pulled her in closer as his mouth reached for hers. This was a gentle kiss, a kiss not to be rushed but to be savored as he tasted her sweet mouth. She tasted of strawberries with a mixture of desire, yearning and dare he hope...love. They sat together entwined in each other's arms, neither of them wanting to end this moment for fear of losing it.

Finally pulling away after what seemed like an eternity, Emeline's insecurities surfaced along with the multitude of questions she had temporarily pushed to the rear of her mind. Her questions began flowing as fast as a swift-moving river. "How do you know I'm your bondmate? How would that even work when you're a Delician and I'm a human? I mean, are we even compatible? What about the future? How is this even possible? Gosh, I have so many questions."

Nox pulled her onto his lap, his arms holding her close in his embrace, trying to assuage her fears. "I will tell you anything you want, but to your first one of how did I know —I knew the moment I laid eyes on you that you were mine. There was never any doubt in my mind."

"But how did you know?" she asked again, trying desperately to calm her racing mind, all kinds of questions and emotions zipping through her head.

Letting go of her hand, he lifted his arm just as a ripple of color moved slowly up his arm, disappearing beneath the fabric of the shirt he was wearing. "Did you just see that ripple of color move across my arm?"

"Yes. I thought that was normal for Delicians."

"No, it's not normal for the colors to move as they do. Basically, our skin is what you would describe as iridescent, similar to an opal stone on Earth, but the colors are usually stationary—that is, until we meet our bondmates. Then, the colors start moving or rippling through our bodies. The moment I met you, a connection began to form between us. Our souls recognized each other and that's when my colors began to reach out to you."

As he spoke, her fingers followed a particular pattern of colors as they moved across his skin. "I saw the colors move across your body when you came into the kitchen earlier after your shower. Does it hurt? Is it all over your body?" Emeline asked hesitantly.

Nodding, he pushed her forward and stood up. Emeline's eyes were glued to his body as he slowly lifted his shirt over his head.

Inch by slow agonizing inch, his beautifully sculpted body revealed itself to her. Her eyes followed the track of colors as they moved, no, rippled across the wide expanse of muscle. His nipples were tight nubs just begging her to taste them. *Whoa.*

Turning him around, she became mesmerized by the colors as they cascaded in no discernible pattern across his broad shoulders. Emeline tried to control her trembling fingers as she traced one set of colors as they moved up from the waistband of his pants. She followed them as they meandered up his long firm back, the muscles lean and strong, all the way up as they disappeared beneath his hair—hair that brushed against her hand, feeling thick and soft.

She could feel his body tense, his breathing becoming uneven the more she touched him, or maybe that was her that was breathing hard. Her core muscles tightened, heat beginning to flood through her the more she explored his body.

As she continued to feel his warm flesh under her fingers, she noticed that the colors from his skin seemed to jump onto her fingers, moving just under her skin. As if spellbound, she watched the colors continue to move from his skin to hers as if blending their two bodies together. *Okay, this is just a little bit freaky. Does this mean I'm going to turn all shiny and colorful like him?*

Stepping back abruptly, she stared down at her hand as she watched the purples, blues and pink colors move slowly across it. "Nox," she said, fear beginning to rise in her voice. "What's happening to me?"

Speaking to her softly, trying to keep his words gentle, not wanting to add to her fear, he told her, "It's the bond-mating process."

"Can you make it stop?" she whispered, her forehead wrinkling into a frown.

"Do you want it to stop? Do you not want to bond with me?" He didn't want to hear her answer for fear it would break his heart. But he needed her to be honest with him. If she rejected him, then so be it. He would finish out the mission and return to Delicia, alone. *At least I'll have these few moments of memories of being with her.*

Looking at Nox, wondering how she should answer him, she considered his question. *Do I? I'm not sure. Okay, let's do what Dad always said when presented with a problem that needed solving. Find out more data.*

Handing him his shirt, she moved to sit in one of the armchairs near the fireplace. She definitely needed to put a little distance between them while she considered her list of questions. "Before I answer that, I need a few more facts. First let me say, there is no denying I have feelings for you. However, if as you say I'm your bondmate, what does that mean exactly? Will you be honest with me?"

"Always." He pulled the shirt over his head. Emeline's scent washed over him as he straightened the shirt before sitting back down onto the couch. He hated the distance between them, but he understood why she had put it there. She was a scientist, and if she was to make an informed decision, she had to have the correct data. *Isn't that what mother always said?*

Taking a moment to collect his thoughts, he replied with all sincerity, "I will always be honest with you, Emeline. Even if you won't like the answer, I will never lie to you. Besides, you can't lie to your bondmate."

"Wait, you can't lie to me?"

Shaking his head, he replied, "No, never."

"So that means I can't lie to you if as you say I'm your bondmate." She was floored.

"That is correct."

"Good to know, although I'm not much into lying. Dad used to always tell us that telling the truth was so much easier than lying. Besides, he never believed in it—said he was never any good at lying anyway, so why bother."

He smiled telling her he felt the same way. "What else can I tell you?"

"All right—so no lying. Awesome, I like that." She thought for a moment, asking him, "What happens when and if we do complete the bond and I'm assuming we complete the bond by physically coming together?" She felt her cheeks heat up as she asked that question. The prospect of making love to Nox was not a new thought in her mind. She had been thinking about doing just that since the moment she'd laid eyes on him. Although, now that would be put on hold until she'd made the decision about her future. There were too many variables and not enough data for her to make that big of a decision without weighing all the facts.

Nox's voice dropped an octave, his eyes closed for a moment before answering her. "Yes, that is correct. If you make that decision, when we make love, the bond will become completed. Meaning that we will be bound together —forever."

He paused, giving her a moment to absorb his words. When her eyes met his, he added, "As for the rest of it, I'm not sure. As far as I know, this is the first interspecies bonding. How your body will react is something we will need to study further. When we get back to the ship, we can go to medical and talk to the medics about this. I can guarantee you they're going to want to run all sorts of tests on the both of us. Emeline, this is as new to you as it is to me." He wanted to reassure her but wasn't sure how.

Thinking about the ramifications of bonding with Nox, Emeline stopped abruptly mid-thought. "Wait, you said Delicians live to be around 600 years old."

"Yes, that is true."

"And you are 147 years old."

"Yes."

"So, since I'm only 29, what does that mean for the bond? Won't I die well before you? I mean, I'll age and you'll still be young."

Standing up, Emeline threw her hands up as she paced around the room. Flustered, she told him, "This is never going to work? I'll be an old lady and you'll still be this gorgeous hunk of a man. No, that can't be right."

Nox stood, moving towards Emeline, but she held her hand up to hold him back. She needed a few minutes to digest this. *This is never going to work. Why would he bond with a human if we don't have the same lifespan? No, this can't be right.*

Nox was just as worried about this as she was. "Emeline, before you get upset, I think we need to do some more research. I can't believe that fate would bring us together just to tear us apart after such a short time. When we get back to my lab, we'll have ARI do some research on this before we jump to any conclusions."

Stopping dead in her tracks, Emeline pressed her fingers to her forehead, trying to get her emotions under control. Breathing deeply, she let out a deep sigh, agreeing with him. "Okay. Good idea. We'll leave that data point for now. Okay, next point, where would we live—on Earth or Delicia?"

"I'm not sure. Where would you like to live?"

Emeline flopped down into her chair, considering his question. "I don't know. I don't want to leave my family or my friends or my business, for that matter." Just the thought of leaving her family and all that she had built was too much for Emeline to wrap her mind around. "Would it be possible to come back and forth from Delicia so that I could still see my family? Do you think our governments would even allow this bond to happen?"

Picking up his glass of wine, Nox took a long drink before leveling his gaze at her. "Emeline, these are all valid points and ones I don't have any answers to just yet. If you decide to bond with me, we will figure this all out. I promise you." He tried to give her a reassuring look, but she still looked troubled.

"Well, maybe I can see if Mum will come with us," she said thoughtfully. "Is that possible, do you think? She's been through too much over the last couple of years since Dad died. I can't move to another planet and leave her behind."

"If that's what you want and she is willing to come, then I will do whatever it takes to make it happen. I know how important your family is to you and I know your work has proven vital to the well-being of Earth. I would never want to cause you any pain. Just know this, Emeline, whether we complete the bond or not, if you want to stay here on Earth, I will stay with you. Even if I can only come out at night and I have to cover up, I will do whatever it takes to be with you." The passion in his voice matched the seriousness in his eyes. "My feelings for you are too deep to ever let you go."

Nox meant every word he was saying to her. Now that he had found his mate, he wasn't going to let anything or anyone come between them. If the UAP or Delicia had a problem with him bonding with a human, well—they'd have to get over it. His feelings for Emeline were growing at an exponential rate. He had never felt such happiness in his heart before. He now understood why his mother was so angry at her father for making her marry Sandovar. He only wished she could have found the joy of a mate before she died. Even if he and Emeline never completed the bond, he would never leave her side. Just the thought of it sent a wave of pain through his body.

Emeline was astounded at Nox's words. No one had ever put her feelings first, not once. There had been relationships over the years, but never serious enough to want marriage. It wasn't that she didn't want to get married and have children—she absolutely did. It was only that none of the guys she had dated had wanted the same things she did. It had gotten to the point she decided to focus more on her career and her family and friends than wasting her time on meaningless relationships. Nox wanted more—he wanted her, just as she was. *So, what does this mean for us? I feel like there are too many roadblocks for this relationship to work. Not to mention he's an alien. Did I mention he was an alien? Seriously, Em, it's hard to deny these feelings he elicits every time he looks at you. No one has ever looked, I mean, really looked at the real me. Do I want to throw this away or do I want to try to find a way, somehow, god only knows how, to make this work?*

Noticing the indecision on her face, Nox tried again to reassure her. "I'm not trying to pressure you. I know the last few days have been life-changing for you. We can take this as slowly as you want."

Leaning forward in her chair, a pensive look on her face, Emeline voiced the question they were both thinking out loud, "I guess a more important question is what would happen if we didn't bond?" As the words came out of her mouth, her body started to tremble. Just the thought of not being near Nox made her stomach clench.

Watching her intently, Nox shrugged his shoulder. "Well, nothing as bad as dying, but honestly I've never heard of anyone who wanted to reject their bondmate. From what I've heard, it's always been a cause for celebration." Nox felt his body temperature rising. This was not going at all how he thought this conversation would go.

All at once he felt restless, unsettled at the thought of not being near Emeline.

He stood suddenly, moving swiftly over to the window...staring out into the darkness—not wanting her to see the sadness in his eyes.

Emeline's heart broke when she saw Nox's distress. "Okay, give me a minute here."

Breathing deeply, trying to stop the rising nausea, she thought about his words. *Why do I feel so sick at the thought of leaving him? Because he is what you have been searching for your whole life. Are you seriously considering letting him go?*

Seeing the defeated look in his eyes, she knew he felt the same way she did. "I guess rejecting the bonding is not something either of us wants."

Nox turned with a start. He didn't dare hope but he had to ask. "You're not rejecting the bond?"

Seeing the look of hope on Nox's face, Emeline rushed into his arms. His solid body pressed against her...her body instantly reacting to his. That nauseous feeling disappeared, replaced instead by a feeling of calm and clarity.

All of a sudden, she could breathe freely again.

Gazing up into his expectant face, she could feel his own doubts dissolving along with hers. "Nox, I don't know where this is going to take us, but I want to do it together. I'm not saying I'm going to complete the bond right away. After all, we do have a planet to save."

She smiled shyly up at him before laying her head on his chest. His beating heart calmed her soul.

With a smile so bright that it reached his eyes, Nox wrapped his arms around his bondmate's body, pulling her tight up against him. His world quickly straightened—that off-kilter feeling gone at her words. He whispered into her hair that whatever she decided, it would be fine with him. As long as they could be together, things would work out.

Squeezing him tight, she reminded him, "Well, I still have a ton of questions that I need answers to."

Pulling away, she moved into the kitchen. "But I think we need some ice cream first. Do you like sweets?" she asked him, heading towards the freezer.

"I do like sweets, maybe a little too much." Nox wagged his eyebrows at her, eliciting a giggle out of her. "What is ice cream?" he asked, following her into the kitchen and taking a seat at the island. He felt lighter, happier, like maybe things were going to work out for them.

"Oh, ice cream is awesome. It's cold and creamy and just what you need on a hot summer night. My personal favorite is chocolate. Here, try this," she said, handing him a dish of the dark brown yummy deliciousness, wondering just how it would taste if she smeared some on his tight abs and licked it off...slowly. *Okay, Em, not going there right now.*

"This is amazing." He licked his spoon trying to get every drop. "We don't have anything like this on my planet, but I'm going to program the replicator to make this. Is this the only flavor?"

"Oh no, there are tons of flavors. You can get very creative and put in whatever you want. Although, vegetable ice cream or meat ice cream is just plain disgusting. It has to be sweet," she explained as she watched him dig into his tasty treat. The cold creamy goodness sliding down her throat, giving her that happy feeling chocolate always did.

Licking her spoon slowly, Emeline gave Nox a thoughtful look. "Okay, I have a few more questions."

"Of course, you do." He gave her a silly grin as he told her to ask him anything.

"First off, are Delicians and humans even compatible, you know in a, um, mating sort of way?" Her face began to flush at the thought of them being intimate.

Loving the way her cheeks turned a pretty shade of deep red crimson, Nox playfully replied, winking at her, "Yes, we are very compatible—in a mating way."

Relieved and embarrassed at the same time, Emeline tried to stifle a giggle. "Okay, that's good. Good to know. I mean, you don't have any major differences like—" Her face heated as she thought how to ask him such a personal question, "...physically wise I mean—okay—you don't have two penises, do you?"

Startled at her question, he laughed, nearly choking on his ice cream. "No, only one." He couldn't stop laughing, which made her all the more flustered. *Oh, she's adorable.*

Mortified at how ridiculous she must sound, she ground out, "Okay—no laughing. This is serious."

Trying to wipe the grin off his face, he bit the inside of his cheek, trying to get himself under control. "Nope—no laughing. See I'm being very serious. Can I ask you a question?"

"Sure."

"Do you have two cunts?"

She nearly swallowed her spoon.

Shocked, practically yelling she told him, "Oh god, don't say that word!"

Holding her hand over his mouth, she cried emphatically, "No—no, no, no—we don't use that word. That's a bad, bad word. We only use that word when we want to be vulgar and that's not very often. Women don't like that word —at all. And please—I beg you, when you meet my mother, don't ever use that word."

He didn't think her face could turn any darker red but it did. He was happy when she'd said he would meet her mother. They were making good progress here. "Okay, no saying...that word then." He smiled innocently as she rolled her eyes at him. "So, what do you call the female genitalia then if not..."

She waited for him to continue but he didn't—thankfully. "Well, it's called lots of things. 'Vagina' is the medical term but people call it all kinds of names: pussy, beaver, box, vajayjay, snatch. *Agh*, I can't believe we're having this conversation," she said as she covered her face with her hands, her body shaking with laugher.

"So, what do you call it?" he asked, loving the expression on her face.

Stuttering, she finally spit out, "I don't call it anything, really. I generally just refer to it as my lady parts." Well, she had no one to blame but herself for how this conversation was going. Taking another spoonful of ice cream, she decided to change topics.

"Okay, moving on, tell me about where you live on Delicia? You've seen my home, what is yours like?" She was glad to get off the topic of female genitalia names before he started asking about other names for penises.

Nox began telling her about his world and his home. "As I told you, we split our time between the Capital and my mother's home on the coast. After she died, I decided to make her house my permanent residence." He told her how he spent his free time swimming or just walking along the shoreline...thinking. Whenever he had a particular problem he needed a solution to, he found taking long walks always seemed to clear his head. "It's where I do my best thinking."

Emeline knew all about that, telling him, "I get it. I do my best thinking in the shower."

She told him about Earth and its different countries and how sometimes their differences could result in violence. But that most humans really just wanted to live happy, healthy lives.

He explained that Delicia had been living in relative peace for about a millennium. They discussed the merits of advanced technology and how on his world hunger and poverty were all but eliminated. They argued a bit when she gave him a list of reasons why they needed to introduce some of the alien technology to Earth. He argued back that they needed to be cautious not to disrupt Earth's natural evolution and that ultimately it would be up to the UAP to make that decision. They decided to set this discussion aside for a later time.

"This discussion isn't over," she told him, her passion for this subject apparent.

They moved over to the couch and settled in with her tucked up underneath his arm, her head resting on his chest as she told him about her family and what it was like growing up as the youngest of three children. They laughed together as she told him what Liam was like growing up and the pranks they played on each other. He held her tightly as she told him about her dad and how devastated she'd felt when he died. How alone she'd felt since his death. He wiped her eyes as she cried over the sadness she felt knowing that her dad was gone and even though her family and friends tried to fill the void, no one ever could. He understood because he had felt the same way when his mother had died. He'd isolated himself in his work, avoiding his family and friends until finally the only real friend he had was his assistant, Loris.

For a few hours, their worlds, the Hexians, their mission, was forgotten. For just a short time, it was only the two of them getting to know each other, telling stories about their lives, finding their similarities and differences —giving no thought as to how the two of them would fit together into this new world they were creating.

As the night wore on, Emeline's eyes slowly closed. She thought maybe she should go to bed, but she was comfortable lying in Nox's embrace, his strong arms wrapped around her making her feel warm and safe. So comfortable she didn't want to move as her eyes closed, a smile splayed on her face as she drifted off into a wonderfully erotic dream.

Nox watched Emeline's face as she slept. He could feel her emotions through their bond. He shifted them so they were lying on the couch, her back to his chest, his arms cradling her gently while she slept. He drifted off into the same dream, hoping someday it would be more than a dream—a blissful reality the two of them shared.

CHAPTER 9

Emeline gazed out the window as she lay comfortable...
all sleepy and warm. The morning sky was hazy, indicating it was going to be another scorching day in the city. She
didn't want to move except that something was pressing
into her backside and it wasn't her Kindle that she usually
found in her bed.

Nox!

Just that thought should have sent her running for the
safety of her lab.

Nope.

Instead, she leaned back, snuggling down, enjoying
his big beautifully well-muscled body while his masculine
scent filled her mind. *Stop it, Em. You know where that can
lead to and we're not ready for that yet.*

Thinking that maybe a shower and breakfast should be
her first and second priorities, Emeline moved to rise when
a large, sparkly hand moved around her body, settling on
her stomach, holding her in place. All thoughts of getting
up flew from her mind as strong fingers made slow circles
up and down her abdomen, sending wave after wave of
warm tingles into the center of her core, while his other
hand came up underneath her, finding its way under the
top of her dress.

"Tell me to stop," was whispered into her ear as he stilled
his hands waiting for her answer.

Did she want him to stop? *Hell no.* She shook her head,
not trusting her voice.

His hand moved slowly down her legs until he reached
the hem of her dress...slipping underneath as her thighs
slowly opened for him. His fingers weren't soft for a man
who was used to being in a lab all day, nor were they rough,

but against her skin she could feel their firmness as he guided them up the inside of her legs. Desire flooded her senses as his name slipped out from between her soft lips.

"Nox."

The sound of her breathing quickened as he made circles along the inside of her thighs while his other hand toyed with her nipples. They were hard to the point of almost painful, but she felt only immense pleasure as she gasped out, "We shouldn't be doing this but—oh, my god—that feels so unbelievable."

Breathless, she felt – no, needed him to move his fingers…just a little higher…to that spot that was causing her to crave his touch. "Yes, right there. Oh, God, Nox, why do I feel so crazed?"

His lips caressed behind her ear, sending warm, tingly waves throughout her body as he whispered, "I could say it's the bond, but even if we weren't bondmates, I'd still want you."

Hearing his words, she smiled and closed her eyes as she let herself be taken away in this beautiful moment.

Nox knew the exact moment she gave herself to him. He was honored and humbled that this beautiful female would trust him with her heart and body. He vowed at this moment he would lay down his life for her if necessary, her happiness his number one priority. *Her beautiful body was made for me. Touching her, tasting her…loving her. She is my life now.*

She brought her hand up, cupping the back of his head as she felt his tongue wander down her neck, settling into that sweet spot just above her shoulder. When his fingers finally found their way to her secret place, she arched her back, murmuring his name over and over. She couldn't control the shiver that shot down her body.

Hearing his name spoken breathlessly from her lips, Nox was in heaven as he explored his prize. She was wet against his fingers. As he pulled on her thong, feeling it snap beneath his strong nimble fingers, she opened to him as an exotic flower did in the morning sun. His hand felt a rectangle of hair covering her sweetness, causing him to pause for a fraction of a second before Emeline's moan inspired him to continue—showing him just how much she was enjoying his exploration. He took his time, finding his way...learning what made her gasp and sigh.

"Don't stop," she panted out before leaning back against him, her legs falling farther apart.

Running his fingers through her delightful covering, it was soft and curled around his fingers. *I will enjoy exploring this.* The more he played, the more Emeline's body tensed... pushing against his hand. His fingers slipped through her moist folds...her sweet noises guiding him as he searched to give her the ultimate pleasure. He moved his fingers through her wetness, finding the small bundle of nerves at the top of her vagina. He smiled to himself at that word, remembering their conversation from the night before and how embarrassed she'd gotten. He gently rubbed back and forth and then in small circles all the while watching the intensity beginning to rise on her face, her eyes closed as he could feel her orgasm starting to build.

Taking two fingers, he entered her. She was tight...hot. Thrusting in and out, all the while using his thumb to continue his focus on that small nub that caused her to squirm in his embrace.

"Oh god, Nox—that feels so good. Oh god, yes, don't stop." Her legs started to shake as her hips moved in time with his fingers as he increased his pace. He felt her shatter before she cried out his name as her orgasm took hold of her. A feeling of satisfaction thrummed through his body as she relaxed back into his, a smile blooming across her beautiful face, a breathless giggle escaping from between her soft lips.

Turning her face to his, she reached up to pull his head down for a searing kiss, her body still throbbing from his touch. She slowly rolled towards him, trapping him between her thighs. He had never been this hard before but he would live with it—anything if he could wake up like this every morning. However, his seductive bondmate had other ideas.

Still riding the high from her explosive release, she reached her hand down to explore that part of him that had been pressing into her. Running her fingers along his jeans, she could feel his length pushing against his zipper. She could tell that his size was definitely in proportion to the rest of his body as she continued to dance her fingers up and down his length through his jeans. She felt the catch in his breath, causing her to smile as she continued to press and rub her fingers. *He is so beautiful, and man, his fingers are magic. That orgasm was one for the books. Phew!*

His hand stopped hers as he murmured that she didn't have to continue if she didn't want to. He expected nothing from her, only wanting to see to her pleasure.

"Sshh," she said against his lips.

Not one to be selfish, Emeline brushed his hand away as she carefully lowered the zipper to his pants. Not sure what an alien penis would look like or even feel like, she ran her hand up and down along his length. He felt hot and hard… smooth all at once. She ran her thumb over the rounded head of his penis—a drop of wetness warm against her skin.

His lips found hers again in a hard kiss as she continued to run her hand up and down his length, marveling at his size. He was a big man, a very big man, and so wide her fingers could barely fit around him. The more she moved her hand, the harder he kissed her, his tongue moving against hers in concert with her hand until finally his whole body shuddered as she felt all of his desire release through the bond that existed between them. A desire so strong, it caused her to orgasm for a second time.

She smiled into his lips as his breath came out in pants,

his forehead pressed against hers. A feeling unlike anything she had ever felt before settled around her heart as they both tried to catch their breathes. *That was WOW!!*

He leaned down, his lips brushing feather kisses along her forehead down to lightly touch her swollen lips. A sigh of satisfaction escaped him as he pulled her close...gently rubbed her back.

Sighing into his neck, she shut her eyes, happiness filling her for the first time in so long she could hardly remember.

Looking down, she got her first glimpse at an alien penis. It didn't look any different from a human male except for the fact that it was big, shiny white and there were colors moving up and down along its length. Did she mention it was big? *Yeah, okay, it's big, huge even. Lorelei will be more than impressed and I'm sure she'll be asking me about it the minute she gets the chance. But you know there are some things you just didn't share.*

She was surprised to see that he had no hair. As she looked over his body, her hand lightly brushed along his arm. He was smooth and warm, and definitely hairless except for what was on his head. Looking at her own arm, she thought to herself, *Interesting. I wonder what he thinks of me. I'm covered in hair.*

A ripple of color moved just under her skin, causing her to smile. She should feel shy around him, especially after what they had just shared, but she wasn't.

Looking up, she saw the reflection of her eyes in his, the same feeling of bliss stared back at her. She was happy and contented, wanting to stay nestled up against him all day.

"Are you alright?" he asked her, his voice muffled by her hair.

Nodding, her head tucked up under his chin, her eyes closed, taking in the scent of...them. She soaked in this moment...enjoying this brief respite of serenity before all hell broke loose.

Holding her close, Nox had to agree that life was about to get very complicated. Tarek would know the minute he laid eyes on him that he'd found his bondmate. He considered the general's reaction, almost groaning, knowing there would an intense session in the training room in his very near future. *So be it. Emeline is worth it. She's my bondmate and nothing or no one could change that.*

"Emeline, I think we should talk about what to expect when we return to my ship."

Rubbing her nose against his chest, she sighed, silently bemoaning that their brief moment of bliss was over.

"Are you worried about going? What am I saying—of course you are." Kissing her hair, he murmured to her, "You don't have to be. I promise to never leave your side."

Emeline leaned back, looking at him with a frown on her face. "I won't lie. It scares the crap out of me just thinking about leaving Earth. Do you know why I sent Ami up to the station instead of going myself?"

"No. Tell me."

She moved to sit on the side of the couch facing him, her skirt settling around her knees as she leaned against him, not ready to break their connection just yet. "Well, it's not because I didn't want to go to space—because I do. It's more the having to be strapped to a rocket and shot into the sky to get there. I have a major issue with that."

Nox laughed at her expression of horror, agreeing with her. If that's how he'd had to get into space, he would stay on the ground too. "Well, it's a good thing you'll be with me. We will be going up to the ship in a shuttle that uses crystals as an energy source." He gave her a teasing smile. "No rockets—I promise."

He told her how Commander Nyx would be picking them up in the shuttle. Once there, they'd be working out of his lab. He told her about the *Maelstrom* and how he'd been on the ship for about eight Earth weeks. That they had a fully equipped lab where he worked with his assistant, Loris.

When he mentioned General Tarek, Emeline's face stiffened.

"You don't have to be anxious about the General. You only need to worry when he asks you to train with him," teased Nox.

She stared at him—her eyes wide with a hint of fear. "I heard he is really big."

"He is. He's only slightly above average for Delician males. He expects a lot but he's fair minded. I think you'll like him. Are you thinking what he'll say about our bonding?" he asked caressing her cheek, concern showing on his face.

She nodded slowly, "Maybe a little bit. I mean, even though we haven't completed our bond yet, they can't do anything to us, can they?" She reached out to touch his face, her concern matching his.

"No. No one will ever come between us. Trust me, my beautiful girl."

Emeline gasped, asking, "Why did you call me that?"

Pulling her closer, he cupped her cheek in his hand. Kissing her lips, a sigh escaped from her mouth. "Because you are beautiful."

Pulling away slightly, she trailed her finger from his brow, following the curve of his face, "That's what my dad used to call me."

Smiling with his eyes, he replied, "I think I would have liked your father."

She grinned at him, saying, "He was a great guy." Kissing the end of his nose before pushing herself up, she inhaled sharply as she wrinkled her nose at herself. "Okay, I need a shower."

Heading towards her bedroom, she called over her shoulder that she was going to shower and change, only to come to a stop when her cell phone rang. Seeing that it was the front desk of her building calling, she told him, "Oh good—I think your clothes are here."

Stepping into her bedroom to take the call, she returned a few minutes later telling Nox that the doorman would be bringing his clothes up and putting them by the front door. "Why don't you go shower and I'll meet you back here when you're finished, then we can make breakfast. I'm going to make you a frittata." She leaned up and kissed his lips before disappearing into her bedroom.

"Sound delicious." Nox headed into the bathroom and turned on the hot water. He was truly happy for the first time in what felt like forever. Even if they never completed their bond, he would always have these wonderful memories to pull out and look at every now and then. Her beautiful face as she climaxed was burned into his mind forever. He would not give her up. Emeline was his. He just needed to make her understand they were meant to be together. Smiling to himself as he relived the last few moments with her, he didn't think it would take too much convincing.

It was General Tarek that he was mainly worried about. He needed to contact him as soon as breakfast was over. Tarek needed to know there had been a major development in his life. He only hoped Tarek would be happy for him. If he had the General's approval, it would go a long way toward convincing the UAP. Although there wasn't much anyone could do or say. A bondmate was chosen by the Fates. It was the other half of your soul, a bond too strong to be broken. Never had anyone rejected their bondmate... why would they? To feel that connection with another person, someone who you just knew would always be there for you. It was both terrifying and glorious, but it mainly felt perfect. He knew that Jagger and Nyx would torment him. He could already imagine they would end up beating on each other in the training room. That he could handle. He was actually looking forward to kicking some Delician butt.

Smiling, he stepped into the shower...his stomach rumbling. He was definitely looking forward to breakfast.

Half an hour later, Emeline felt clean and refreshed… content. Smiling to herself as to the reason why she felt so good, she went to her front door to get the clothes they had ordered online. Placing them on the bed in Nox's room, the bathroom door still closed, she headed into the kitchen to make some coffee. *I wonder if he even drinks coffee. We'll see.*

Getting all the ingredients out of the fridge to start the frittata, she turned on the oven to 325 degrees and started organizing her vegetables and meat on the island. She wanted Nox to see how she made the dish, so she poured herself a cup of coffee while she waited for him.

Leaning against the counter watching a plane play peek-a-boo with the high-rises across the skyline, Emeline took a few moments to reflect. Life had certainly gotten crazy—real fast.

She needed to make some decisions about her company, and that meant talking to Lorelei and Heather. She didn't want to lie to them any longer than she had to. She also had to call her mum and have a conversation with her. She would tell them she had to go to Florida for a meeting with NASA for a week. They would have expected this trip to happen eventually to check on progress with the network array. Hopefully all of this would be over by then and then she could introduce them to Nox, swear them to secrecy under penalty of death—death by lecture, which they all hated. *Yeah, threaten torture and that will keep their mouths shut!*

Seeing Nox come out of the bedroom caused her to stop and stare, yup, stop and stare. He was such a gorgeous male. He smiled at her as he came into the kitchen.

Leaning in, he pulled her up against him and kissed her until her oven beeped, telling her it was ready.

Yeah, I'm ready too.

Nipping her bottom lip, he stepped back and took a seat at the island.

Watching her chop and sauté, he loved that she looked so comfortable with herself. She poured him a cup of her favorite drink, fixing it the same way she liked it for him to try. *Not bad. I could get used to this.* She chatted on about what she was doing and how her mother was the real cook in the family. Everyone always wanted to eat at their house when they knew that Fiona was cooking. Nox loved hearing about how her family celebrated the many holidays that the humans in her country observed. He hoped that someday he could go to the Thanksgiving dinner they had with all their relatives. Cooking for 35 people was a lot, but she told him that everyone participated, making all their favorite dishes. It sounded like an intimate celebration with family and friends and he looked forward to the day when he could share that with her.

"Tell me about mealtime when you grew up." Emeline closed the oven door and set the timer for 25 minutes.

Nox groaned at her question. "It's not going to be as interesting or as fun as what you experienced."

"I don't care. I want to know." She squeezed his hand encouragingly.

"All right. Growing up, all dinners, whether just a daily dinner or a celebration, were eaten in the formal dining room where you were always dressed in your best clothing. It wasn't warm or friendly—it was cordial. Topics for discussion were centered on the latest deal or whatever the latest issues were being presented in the senate chambers. It was tedious at best and I was more than thrilled when Mother moved us to her home city closer to the sea. Those times with her were the best." Taking her hand, he kissed the inside of her wrist saying, "Now that I have you, we'll make new memories."

Emeline was caught in his gaze—interrupted only by the oven timer as it dinged, indicating their food was ready. A delectable smell of cheese and eggs had both their stomachs grumbling. Laughing together, their mood was light and happy. The promise of new beginnings gave them hope for the future.

Placing the casserole dish on the table, they sat across from one another. As they enjoyed Emeline's cooking, they continued to talk about their lives, learning more about each other.

Emeline suggested they play a game called 20 questions. Nox was eager to learn about her, but they decided to limit the game to all their favorite things. Things such as red was her favorite color; chili was her favorite food; a dog was her favorite pet; she didn't have just one favorite song, she loved too many to pick; roses were her favorite flower and vanilla was her favorite scent.

She learned that Nox didn't have a favorite color until he saw the blue of her eyes. Now that was his favorite color, which made her sigh in delight. His favorite food was anything from the sea and his favorite thing to do was to swim at the beach near his home. But most of all he loved being in his lab.

Thrilled, Emeline reached over and squeezed his hand. "I can so relate to that. I love being in my lab, any lab really. When we discovered the particle that we were able to use in our network array, it was such an exhilarating feeling." She sat back, smiling from ear to ear.

"I know how you feel." He smiled at her exuberance. "I felt the same way the first time my force field technology worked. My mother was so proud."

"And your father, how did he feel?" she asked, drawing circles on the back of his hand.

Nox squeezed her hand, grateful for her support. "Of course, he was thrilled, but not in the way you'd think. He wanted to exploit my work, but I wouldn't allow it. I brought it to the attention of the UAP before he could try to manipulate me into working with him. It was the worst fight we'd ever had, but in the long run it worked out better for him. He was able to boast that it was his son who developed the latest cutting-edge technology for the entire UAP territory. It gave him more leverage over his fellow senators. He, of course, was so proud, but honestly I could have cared less for his opinion," Nox said with distain.

Emeline thought Nox's father was a piece of work. It would be interesting to see what he thought of her and Nox's bondmating. She would bet anything that he was not going to be happy about it.

"Tell me more about the particle that you discovered— Hanthon, wasn't it? What gave you the idea?" Nox shifted the focus away from his father and back onto work. Generally, the less he thought about Sandovar, the better he felt.

Emeline couldn't help but get excited when she talked about her work. "We were able to use an element called Lazonium to create the Deflector Network Array. It was Liam's idea, really. He'd seen a few of the experiments they were doing on the ISS during one of his missions. We knew what we needed—we just didn't know how to get it. He suggested we try doing the experiments with the Lazonium on the station in a more controlled environment."

She explained that by using the temperature and pressure of space, it allowed the atoms to last longer since on Earth, the half-life of Lazonium was too short to be of any use. Results of the experiments determined that by lining the network arrays with this element, they were then able to use the light energy from the sun to create the new particle. This new particle, which they named after Emeline's dad Hank, when emitted through the array would react with the electromagnetic radiation coming from the solar flares causing the radiation to deflect away from the network array. This all but eliminated any disruptions that could affect the orbiting satellites.

Nox was impressed. "And by controlling the amount of sunlight that comes through your network array, you control how much of the particle is emitted out."

Emeline was thrilled that Nox understood her work.

"Yes! You get it. Like I said, we had the concept, but it was discovering the particle that really brought this to the success it is. It was a total team effort—I really owe a lot to them. So enough about me—I want to hear how you first started developing your force field technology."

He started to tell her, but was interrupted when his wrist comm indicated an incoming call. "It's General Tarek," he told her. "He probably wants an update on our progress." They still had some work to do before they were able to interface with the satellites. Now that he had a better understanding of the inner workings of the array, he knew it was only a matter of time before they were ready for deployment. They had spent yesterday in her lab going over the plan that Tarek and his team were developing for the Hexians, making sure that Liam and Ami had the equipment they needed to install on the satellites. Nox had Loris running a preliminary analysis on the interface program.

Giving her a reassuring look, Nox accepted the call. He swallowed hard, not wanting Emeline to know how apprehensive he truly was. The minute his face came into view, Tarek would know he had found his bondmate.

Sure enough, when the General's face appeared in front of them, his eyes widened in surprise.

Emeline held her breath as she waited for the explosion that she was sure was going to happen.

It didn't.

Instead, Tarek's face broke into a wide smile, his eyes alight with amusement. "Well, I see that coming to Earth has proven successful for you." Nodding his head towards Nox's face, he said with a wry smile, "You have found your bondmate."

Nox couldn't hide his surprised look, causing the General to laugh out loud. "Don't be so shocked. I know how rare this is. Of course, I'm happy for you." His eyes darted to Emeline. He nodded his head, acknowledging her.

Giving him a shy smile, she held onto Nox's hand—

the connection between them apparent to anyone who saw them. "Hi General," she said, trying to keep her voice steady. "I'm Emeline Cameron."

Nox jumped in before the General could speak, saying, "Forgive me. I guess I'm just surprised at your reaction. General, this is my beautiful bondmate, Emeline. Emeline, General Tarek, head of our mission and commander of the Delician military." Gazing down into Emeline's beaming face, he was pleased about Tarek's reaction to Emeline. "I can tell you it was as much of a surprise to me as it is to you. I was unsure what your reaction would be when you found out that my bondmate was a human."

Tarek smiled at the both of them, saying, "I am pleased for you both. This is a wonderful thing. However, I'm not going to lie to you and say this will not be an issue moving forward. Not only is our relationship with the humans tenuous at best, but the UAP may have a say in all of this. Of course, you and I both know that there really isn't much they can do about it."

Tarek looked at both their faces, then down at their entwined hands, noting the rippling colors. "You have not completed the bond, I see."

Nox shook his head. Looking down at Emeline's worried face, he said, "We have discussed it and decided to wait until this threat is over before taking the final step. We haven't made any decisions yet. There is much to consider." Nox gently pushed away a piece of hair that had fallen across her forehead.

Emeline turned to look at the General, telling him, "I haven't had a chance to talk to my brother about any of this. I only just found out about this whole bondmating concept last night. As you can imagine, it's been a lot to take in. I need a bit more time to process what this all means. Can I ask you to keep this between us? I want to be the one to explain it to him." Emeline could just imagine her big brother's reaction to her mating with an alien, let alone her mother and sister.

"Well unfortunately that conversation might be happening sooner rather than later," Tarek said.

"Why? What's happened?" Nox interjected.

General Tarek ran his fingers through his short chocolate brown hair, showing his aggravation. "We need to move up the timetable on your return to the ship. Tarquin and his crew are moving faster than we anticipated. I'm sending Nyx to pick you up later tonight. Can you be ready?" The general was all business now. The bondmating discussion would have to be put on hold until the threat to Earth was eliminated.

"I think we should be able to finish up on our preparations here in time. It shouldn't be a problem to continue our work in my lab on the ship." Nox looked up trying to judge her reaction to the General's news. Seeing her face pale at the change in the timetable, he smiled at her reassuringly before asking her, "Are you okay with this? Can you be ready to leave tonight?"

Looking between Nox and Tarek and seeing the concern on both their faces, Emeline gave them a small smile, nodding her head. She was already creating a mental checklist of things she needed to get done before they left. "Yes, it should be fine. I'll need to make arrangements with Lorelei and Heather to take over the existing projects we have going on right now. And I need to call my mum and my sister. I already thought up a cover story that should keep them satisfied. I'm going to tell them that I have to go to NASA for a meeting with Leslie Merriman. That should give me about a week before they start getting suspicious. Will I be able to contact them from your ship?" she asked both of them. "If I don't talk to them at least once a day, they'll wonder why. And if I don't talk to my mum, there'll be hell to pay and we can't have that."

"Certainly," the general replied. "Nox will set you up with whatever you need."

"Can I have a wrist comm?" Emeline asked hopefully. She was dying to get hands on one so she could explore more of ARI.

The General smiled indulgently at her, noting the excitement in her voice at the prospect of using Delician technology. "Of course. Nox will handle all that for you."

"Thank you, General." Emeline beamed at him, causing him to chuckle at her.

"Please call me Tarek. We will be spending a lot of time together. I have to say that your brother Liam has impressed me."

Smiling, Emeline was happy that Liam was making a good impression with the Delicians. "I'm glad. He's a great guy. What about Ami? How are you getting along with her?"

Tarek paused for a moment, a look of perplexity on his face causing Emeline to laugh as he said, "She is a unique individual."

Grinning, she agreed with him. "She definitely is. Trust me though—when things get tough, Ami is the girl you want on your side. She'll stop at nothing to defend any one of us." The pride in her voice indicated how much she regarded Ami.

"I don't doubt that in the least," Tarek replied.

"Speaking of the humans, Tarek," Nox interrupted them, "we need to talk to Dr. Datrem in medical about our bonding. I have no knowledge of interspecies bondmating. I think we should run some tests to see what the effects will be on Emeline once the bond is completed." Nox's eyes searched Emeline's face as he spoke, checking her reaction to being examined by aliens.

Emeline's eyes met his as she nodded her head in agreement. "I want as much information as possible before committing to the bond." Although she knew there was no way she was going to be separated from Nox. They would find some way to make whatever was happening between them work.

Tarek considered their situation before agreeing with them. "Nox, Emeline—I envy you both and I'm sure most of the crew will as well. How you will be received by our people on Delicia, only time will tell. We can only hope it is with the joy that it should be." Tapping his chin with his finger, Tarek pondered their situation. "Bonding with humans—this is unexpected."

Turning to address Emeline, Tarek gave her some fatherly advice. "Emeline, I urge you to take whatever time you need to consider all aspects of bondmating before you take this final step. Be cautious that this is what you truly want because once the bond is completed there is no going back. You two will be tied together for the rest of your lives. What you are choosing will not be easy, but judging from the way you two look at each other, I think you can overcome any problems that may arise. I wish you much joy and happiness."

Thanking him, Emeline took Tarek's words to heart. "I will consider carefully all my options before making my final decision. I have to tell you though that I will be telling my mother and sister about all of this once this threat is over. I can't even consider taking the final step until I talk to my family first." She could see his eyebrows slant into a frown at her words. *Too bad. I will not leave without first telling Mum and Belle.*

Tarek appeared to consider her words before nodding his head at the both of them, saying, "I see you two have a lot to talk about. I must caution you that your leaders do not want our presence known on Earth, so please be aware of this as you make your decision."

Turning to Nox, he added, "Nyx will contact you when he is set to arrive at your location. I will see you both tonight back onboard the ship."

"Thank you for your support. We will definitely heed your words," Nox replied.

Tarek's wide mouth became serious, telling him, "You are part of my team and as such I will always have your back. Especially when your father finds out about this - you're going to need all the support you can get." Tarek gave him a knowing smile as the vid call ended.

Sighing at Tarek's last words, Nox pulled Emeline in for a hug. He needed to feel her against him. With her head resting on his chest, he considered all that Tarek had said. He was right of course. They had plenty of questions and very few answers, but one thing that was apparent was that neither of them wanted to give up on their bond. They would get through this, but they needed to save Earth first. He would deal with his father later.

Since they needed to wait until dark to return to Emeline's lab, they each took some time to themselves—Nox to contact Loris and Emeline to contact her friends and family. Nox needed to inform Loris that they would be arriving back on board their ship later tonight. He wanted Loris to replicate a wrist comm using a specific design he had created. He couldn't wait to see Emeline's reaction to his gift. He also needed Loris to prepare a workstation for Emeline's use. They had a lot of work to do and he wanted them to be able to start fresh in the morning.

Listening to Emeline talking on her cellphone with Lorelei discussing her trip to NASA, she was outlining what needed to be done regarding the other projects that her company was working on. He could tell she was uncomfortable lying to her friends but it couldn't be helped. He only hoped that when Earth was saved from the Hexians, they would understand.

Touching his wrist comm, he instructed ARI to bring up the schematics of his force field. As he began to review the plans, he looked up at Emeline as she hung up from her call.

Grabbing two bottles of water out of the fridge, she moaned out loud, "I hate lying to her. She's going to be so mad at me when she finds out that she wasn't able to be a part of this mission. I hope she will forgive me. What am I saying? Of course, she will. She'll just make my life miserable," Emeline sighed.

Coming over, she wrapped her arms around his waist. It amazed her that she felt so comfortable touching him whenever she felt the need even after only knowing him for such a short time.

Rubbing her nose into his shirt, she sighed again and pulled away. *I'm going to be getting an ass kicking in our next training class, I just know it.*

She handed him one of the bottles, telling him, "I'm going to go pack a bag to take with me."

Turning to go into the bedroom, he grabbed her hand, pulling her back against his hard chest. He rubbed her back, sending shivers through both their bodies. *I just love the feel of her in my arms.*

Nox kissed the side of her cheek, saying, "It'll be okay. Once this is over, we'll sit down with her and Heather and explain why we had to keep them both out of this mission. Why cause them needless worry?"

Kissing her forehead, he reminded her that she didn't need to bring too many clothes. "You can replicate anything you might need on the ship."

"You're right. In all this excitement, I'd forgotten. There are just a few personal items I want to bring with me. Besides, I need to call my mum and then I'll make us something to eat before we head back to my lab. It should be dark in a few hours." After giving him a quick kiss, she headed into her bedroom.

"Take your time. I have a few things to work on." He turned back to his work while she disappeared into her room. *I cannot wait to get Emeline up to the ship. I have so much to show her.* Then remembering that her brother was going to be there as well, Nox wondered what reaction he would get from Liam about his bond with his sister. Judging from the way Liam had behaved before, Nox didn't think he was going to take this very well. *I should probably be prepared for Liam's reaction when we get to the ship. We might be spending a lot of time in the training room.* Shrugging, thinking he'd faced worse things, he turned back to his work. *It will be worth it.*

Emeline glanced at her phone, trying to get up the nerve to call her mother. Fiona had a way of knowing when Emeline was keeping things from her. She didn't have time to deal with that right now. Her eye caught a pattern of colors as they rippled across her hand. Checking her reflection in the mirror, the pastel colors were barely discernible but still —she couldn't chance her mother noticing. *No FaceTiming this time.*

She was still mulling over her list of pros and cons about the bond—not sure what she was going to do. One thing she knew for certain was she was not going to give Nox up. Not when she finally found her other half. *Alien or not—he's mine.*

Taking a deep breath, she hit the call button and waited for her mother to pick up. "Hi, Mum," she said as her mother's voice came over the phone.

"Hey, baby girl, what's going on? Have you heard from your brother?"

"Yeah, Mum. I talked to him last night. He and Ami are doing fine. Still driving each other crazy living in such close quarters. How's the downsizing going?"

Their conversation went on about the house and Fiona told her she was reconsidering selling. She wasn't sure if she was ready to part with their family home. Instead, she was going to visit her sister Sarah in California. Emeline was relieved—she hadn't been happy about Fiona's decision to sell in the first place. She listened to her mother go on about some of the arrangements she was making, glad to hear some optimism in her voice. *I wonder how she'll feel when she finds out about Nox. God, can you imagine the look on her face when she meets him? It's going to be priceless. Of course, first I have to deal with Liam later on tonight and Ami —crap. Ami will have lots to say.*

"Mum, I hate to cut this short, but I called to tell you that I have to go down to NASA tonight for some meetings. I'll probably be gone for about a week, maybe ten days."

"Does it have to do with the work you and Liam are doing on the ISS?"

"Yeah, it does. I'll try to call when I can, but I'm going to be tied up in meetings most of the time. I'll text you whenever I can but you know how security conscious they are."

"Don't worry about me. I'm fine. Your sister's coming to spend a few days with me, and Heather and Lorelei call me every day. They are such sweet girls."

Emeline smiled at how thoughtful her friends were. "They are, but I still worry."

"Em, I know you have a lot on your plate right now. Don't worry about me. I'm fine."

"I can't help it. Once this is all over, maybe we can do a few days down the Cape."

"That would be wonderful. You know how I love to shop in Provincetown."

"I do. I'll call Belle and give her a heads up that I'm going to be away for a while. Mum, please take care of yourself. Call me if you need anything. Love you tons."

"Love you more, beautiful girl. Take care of yourself."

As she hung up the phone, she tried to shake off the feeling that it was going to be a lot longer before she got a chance to see her mother again. *I better call Belle.* Hitting her sister's number, she got Belle's voicemail. *Crap. I really wanted to talk to her before I left.* Leaving a message that she would be gone for a week or so, she finished off by telling her that she'd call her as soon as she got the chance.

Grabbing a bag from the closet, she began to pack some of her personal items. *I might be able to replicate what I need, but a girl's gotta have some of her own stuff.*

When she had finished, Emeline changed into black

jeans with her usual blouse and a jacket before heading into the living room to see what Nox was doing. She carried her favorite black boots in one hand, her suitcase in the other as she walked across to where Nox was sitting at the island working on his wrist comm.

She soaked up the sight of him in his new clothes. He'd been so cute when he had come out dressed in his new clothes telling her how much better they felt. He had worried those jeans had caused serious injury to his lower body. He had wagged his eyebrows so she got his meaning.

Grinning, she sauntered over and leaned her whole body against his back as she kissed his cheek all the while her hand gently squeezed his ass as she told him, "Feels fine to me."

Jolted by her warm body pressed tightly against his, Nox's arms started to pull her in, but she danced away, telling him she was going to make him an American specialty.

Catching her, he nuzzled her neck until she shooed him out of the way, telling him, "Go back to your work. You're distracting me."

Taking stock of what she had in the refrigerator, she reminded herself to take out the trash and leave a note for her cleaning lady to take anything that looked like it was going to spoil. If there was one thing Emeline hated, it was to waste food and if she was going to be gone for a while, there was no need for anything to go to waste.

She rummaged around and found the fixings for burgers and fries. She wanted him to try an original staple of American food. It was one of her favorite things to eat— well that and pizza. *Definitely pizza!*

As the smell of onions, peppers and mushrooms filled the air, Nox moved over to the stove and leaned over her shoulder, asking, "What are you making? That smells wonderful."

With spatula in hand, she flipped a burger, telling him, "This is what we in America call a hamburger. It's something that pretty much everyone eats. In fact, if I think about it, most countries on Earth have some version of a burger. We're having beef burgers, but you can make a burger out of anything you want. My mum can make you six different chicken burgers."

Taking the fries out of the oven and placing them in a basket, Emeline lowered the heat on the fry pan. "The best thing about a burger is that you can put anything you want on it."

Piling the cooked vegetables on top of the burgers, she took them out of the pan and placed each on a bun she had piled with lettuce, tomato and ketchup.

Setting the cooked food down in front of him, she showed him how to pick it up with his hands and eat it. He gave the burger a dubious look, causing her to be a little worried he wouldn't like it. She was pleasantly surprised when a look a pure joy spread across his face at his first bite. *Okay then, he likes burgers. Good to know.*

Taking a bite, Emeline savored the juicy flavors. She always loved a good burger and this one was exceptional. Picking up a French fry, she laughed at how fast he had polished off his first one. "Good thing I made you two, huh?"

Grinning, he took a bite from his second one.

Looking him up and down, she could only wonder at the amount of food Delician males consumed.

"Tell me," she asked curiously, "what did you think of our typical American meal?"

Popping his last fry into his mouth, he wiped his hands on his napkin before reaching over and lightly caressing her hand. "It was fantastic. Thank you for preparing the food. It was delicious. We will definitely program burgers into our replicator."

She winked at him, happy that he enjoyed her cooking, telling him, "Wait until you try pasta—you will think you died and went to heaven."

Noticing the sun was starting to go down, they got

ready to head over to her lab. Finishing putting the last of the dishes in the washer, Emeline put on her boots before quickly taking out the trash and writing a quick note to her cleaning lady.

Gathering up her laptop bag and her small suitcase, she looked over at Nox as he was getting into his hoodie.

"Here, let me help you with that." This time when Emeline pulled the hood over his head, she gave in to her desire, giving him a hot searing kiss that left them both breathless. She'd been wanting to do that for the past few hours. She wasn't disappointed. He kissed her back with equal enthusiasm. *Wow! Soon I'm going to kiss more than just his lips. Em —stop it. We have a mission to get through and then decisions to make.*

Sighing to herself, she gave her loft one last long look as they headed out the door into the night.

After an uneventful walk through the streets of Boston, they were able to reach her lab without anyone noticing them. Nox told her he was going to contact Nyx and tell them they were ready for pickup.

Emeline headed into her bathroom to freshen up and do a quick check of her makeup before they left. She was nervous about going on the shuttle—more so than the fact that she was about to be introduced to a shipload of aliens. Nox had tried to reassure her that it was easy, as easy as sitting in one of her gasoline-powered vehicles. Still, her stomach wanted to revolt just thinking about it.

Finally feeling better, she opened the door to her bathroom and headed out of her office into her lab only to come to a complete standstill at the sight in front of her. Lorelei and Heather had Nox pinned up against the wall with Lorelei's knife pointed directly at Nox's private parts. The look on Nox's face showed that he didn't dare move for fear of losing his most favorite body part. If not for the look on her friends' faces, she would have laughed.

Since that was one of her favorite body parts as well,

Emeline yelled as she barreled into the room, "Heather, Lorelei, what the hell are you doing? Let him go!"

"Stand back, Em. We've got him—it—whatever the hell he is." Lorelei was showing no indication she was going to release Nox any time soon. Heather was frantically searching through drawers for something to tie him up with.

Putting herself between Nox and her friends, Emeline glared at them. "Would you put the knife down and listen to me for two seconds. He is not going to hurt anyone. He's here to help us."

Lorelei was breathing hard as she motioned for Emeline to move out of the way as she yelled at Heather. "No, get away from him, Em. Heather, you found those zip ties yet?"

"Yeah, right here. Em, get out of the way so I can tie him up." Heather tried to shove Emeline out of the way to get to Nox.

Ripping the ties out of Heather's hands, Emeline yelled at the two panicked women. "Would you two just back off and let me explain." Emeline held her hand out to her friend, pleading with her. "Lorelei put the knife down—please."

Lorelei looked from Emeline to Nox, trying to decide what to do. Pulling her knife away from Nox's crotch, Lorelei stepped back, keeping a wary eye on him. Glancing at Emeline, Lorelei was baffled at her defense of this alien. Holding up her knife, she said, "Okay, okay. But I'm keeping this ready just in case."

Emeline turned to Nox and pressed her hand to his face, asking him if he was all right.

Nodding his head that he was fine, he decided not to say anything and let Emeline do the talking. She probably didn't realize that he could have easily stopped her two friends at any time. He hadn't been in any real danger when the two women burst into the room scaring the hell out of him. When they started yelling at him, he thought it best to just go along with what they wanted until Emeline came

197

back into the room.

"What the hell are you two doing here? Why aren't you at home?" Emeline asked, frustrated that both women weren't where they were supposed to be.

Picking up her phone, Heather waved it at her saying, "*Find Friends* remember. We knew you were heading back to the lab and we wanted to know why you've been avoiding us. Guess we know now, don't we, Chica?" Heather was clearly not happy with Emeline.

"Damn that app. I'm deleting it as soon as I can," Emeline muttered to herself. She didn't need this kind of stress right before she was supposed to leave on a shuttle that was taking her to a real live alien spaceship. But, on second thought, at least she didn't have to lie to them any longer. And hey, now no one could get mad at her for keeping such a big secret. *It's not my fault that they found out on their own. This saves me from having to break my word to Liam.*

"You lied to us." Lorelei still held her knife but relaxed her stance slightly. Her expression was drawn, disappointment marring her face. It was obvious all three women were hurting right now. They had always been able to trust one another. This cut to the core.

"I know. I'm so sorry. I wanted to tell you, but I couldn't. I hated having to lie." Emeline came over and grabbed both her friends' arms, but Heather pulled away with a jerk.

"Then why did you? So what, now you can't trust us?" Heather spat out at her.

Emeline lowered her hands to her sides…taking a calming breath. She couldn't blame them, especially Heather. Trust was important to her. "It's not that I didn't want to tell you guys. I did. Ask Liam and Ami." *Oh shit!*

"LIAM AND AMI KNOW!" Lorelei bellowed as Heather just shook her head with a look that said *I knew this day would come.*

"It's not what you think." Emeline tried to talk over Lorelei's ranting.

"ENOUGH!"

Nox let out a sharp yell, silencing the three females. "I can see that some things are universal. Females—you need to listen to what Emeline is trying to tell you."

Emeline smiled at Nox as Heather and Lorelei looked at him with their mouths open for a few moments before straightening up.

When Nox had their full attention, he tried to keep his voice even, telling them, "Emeline wanted to tell you from the beginning, but she was ordered not to."

Heather stepped forward ashamed, realizing she should never have doubted her friend. Emeline would never intentionally cause her pain. She apologized for jumping to assumptions. Lorelei made the standard joke about assuming before coming over to engulf Emeline in a hug. The three of them stood arms entwined all talking at once before finally giving in to a warm quiet embrace.

Stepping back, relief coursing through her, Emeline motioned Nox to come closer. "What I have to tell you is on a need to know basis. It's a matter of national, no wait, it's a matter that affects the entire planet. This is Director Nox. He is from the planet Delicia. He and his fellow Delicians have come to save Earth from some vile aliens who want to take over our planet."

She stopped, letting her words sink in. It was almost comical to see the looks on their faces as they tried to comprehend what she'd told them.

Staring at Nox, although still not trusting him, Lorelei put the knife on the table...keeping it just within reach in case she needed it. "Okay—wait. Say that again, only slower this time. Who is here to save us from whom and why?"

Heather found a stool and slumped down quietly. Her gaze was like watching a tennis match—back and forth, back and forth between Nox and Emeline.

"I know, weird, right? You should have seen my reaction. It wasn't pretty. Unfortunately, I can't go into that right now. I know this is a lot to take in, but we haven't got much time. Nox and I are about to go up to his ship to finish working on protecting our communication satellites. Basically, in a nutshell, a group of criminal aliens are on their way to Earth. They've got a thing for our salt. And before you say anything—I know. We all said the same thing —crazy, right?"

Emeline knew she sounded insane. Hell, if she was in their shoes, she'd think she was crazy too, but she didn't have time for this right now. The shuttle would be here soon and she wanted to fill them both in before she left.

Very slowly, Lorelei mouthed, "Salt."

"Yeah, salt. Himalayan pink salt, to be exact. Evidently it has curative properties for certain species throughout the universe. A group of aliens called Hexians have been sneaking onto Earth to steal it and now they've decided to just come in and take what they want. They plan on enslaving humans to mine it for them." The note of anger in her voice at the thought of these aliens coming onto her world and taking what didn't belong to them was evident.

"So there really are aliens out there? I was right. See I told you I was right." Lorelei was babbling, which was a clear indication she was about to have a meltdown.

Heather moved over and started rubbing Lorelei's back, trying to calm her, her own breathing coming out a little hasher than normal.

"Maybe if I explained the situation to them," Nox said quietly as he moved to sit on one of the stools.

Seeing Emeline nod her head in agreement, Nox quickly explained the chain of events from start to finish, ending with emphasizing the fact that Earth's governments were adamant about keeping first contact from its citizens. When he was finished with the story, both women gawked at him, their faces frozen in shock.

While he talked, Emeline went into the kitchen to get

drinks for everyone. Lorelei and Heather definitely looked like they could use something stronger, but water would have to suffice. After passing out the drinks, Emeline took a long drink from her own bottle. The coolness of the liquid was a welcome relief on her dry throat. Her nerves were shot, convinced her blood pressure must be through the roof. *Holy shit, what was Lorelei thinking? She was thinking that there was an alien in my lab and was trying to save me. Well, it's good to know that our training has paid off. I hope Nox isn't too upset about almost becoming a eunuch. Hell, I'm probably more upset about that than he is.*

"Lorelei? Heather?" Emeline spoke quietly. The information Nox just relayed was disturbing, and knowing both women as she did, they were processing it in their own unique way. Heather was doing a calculated analysis on the situation while Lorelei, after she got over the shock that she was right about there being life out in the universe, was going to want all the information she could get her hands on. *Just wait until she gets a load of ARI. Unfortunately, that is going to have to wait. The shuttle should be here any minute.*

"Listen, I know this is a lot to take in and I promise I'm going to give you as much information as I can, but we're leaving in a few minutes."

All of a sudden, Lorelei and Heather jumped in, asking so many questions Nox and Emeline had trouble understanding them.

They were stopped midsentence when Nox's wrist comm beeped with a message from Ezio. There had been a last-minute change in pilots. He was waiting for them on the roof.

Emeline hugged both women, reminding them this was a maximum security threat. "You can't tell anyone. This stays between us. I promise to fill you in on what's been happening as soon as I can. Please, take care of the lab for me and check on my mum and Belle. I'll get in touch as soon as I can. I love you guys."

Picking up her bags, she headed over to Nox.

Opening the door, Nox took Emeline's hand in his as he exited the lab.

Turning one last time, Emeline gave both women a wide smile as she shut the door behind her. She wished she could be a fly on the wall to listen to what Heather and Lorelei had to say to each other. If she wasn't so worried about where she was headed, she might have found the situation funny.

Following Nox up the stairs to the roof, Emeline had a feeling that staying and listening to her best friends would have been easier than what she was facing.

As they reached the roof, Nox stopped and turned, looking at Emeline with a tender smile. Brushing his palm softly across her hair, he tried to reassure her that she would be perfectly fine flying in the shuttle. He would never let anything happen to her.

"Come Emeline, I will always keep you safe." He brushed his lips lightly across hers, causing her lips to tingle.

With one last look back at her lab, Emeline stepped off the roof into her future.

CHAPTER 10

Emeline glanced around suspiciously, not quite sure what she expected an alien shuttle to look like.

Noticing how steady on her feet she was, her shoulders sagged in relief. *Thank God for gravity—and no damn rockets.*

The smooth interior of the shuttle was similar to a first class cabin on an airplane only with more walking around space. *Okay, I can get used to this.*

Her broad smile had Nox smiling in relief. He motioned to the pilot who was currently staring intensely at Nox's face. Judging from his expression, soon everyone would know that Nox had found his bondmate.

Emeline chuckled to herself that people were the same everywhere. It didn't matter what planet you were from— a good piece of gossip was universal. And if the topic was as juicy as this one, well let's just say she needed to get to her brother before he heard it from some over-enthusiastic alien. She had a feeling this was something that would be talked about for generations to come.

Nox took her hand and moving forward introduced her to their pilot. "Emeline, this is Ezio. He is a member of Tarek's elite soldiers. Ezio, this is my bondmate, Emeline Cameron." The way Nox gazed at Emeline as he introduced her spoke volumes.

Ezio looked from Nox to Emeline, immediately seeing a drastic change in his friend. They hadn't known each other long, but over the course of their time together on this mission, they had formed a deep respect for one another.

Raising both eyebrows, Ezio looked Nox in the eye, his mouth turned up in surprise saying, "Bondmate."

Emeline smiled brightly at the large Delician with the cool amber eyes and short cropped hair who stood gaping at her. He was handsome even with the long scar that ran down one side of his face. He was dressed in a lightweight jumpsuit that molded to his ridiculously fit body. The utility belt he wore around his trim waist had two wicked-looking high-tech weapons attached to it.

"It's nice to meet you, Ezio." Emeline stuck her hand out in greeting, surprised at her lack of fear. It would be daunting to anyone their first time on an alien spaceship, but she only felt excitement with an overwhelming dose of curiosity.

Ezio just stared at her hand...not moving, a confused look on his face.

Nox laughed, explaining the human handshaking custom to him.

Taking his hand, Emeline gripped it firmly. She always believed in a firm handshake. There was nothing worse than when someone gave you a wimpy hand. Unfortunately, Ezio fell into that category. *Geez, fine, he gets a pass this time. Obviously, they don't shake hands.*

Looking to Nox for guidance, he filled them in on the first time Liam extended his hand to him.

After a shared laugh, Nox looked at Ezio saying, "Go ahead, Ezio. I know you have something to say."

Nox stood still as Ezio scanned his face.

"I apologize for staring. We all know how rare it is to find your bondmate, but I have never heard of bonding with another species. How—how did this happen?"

Taking Emeline's hand in his, Nox sat in the copilot's chair and pulled her down onto his lap.

She barely bothered to protest, instead opting to snuggle down into his embrace as she focused her attention on Nox's friend. Ezio was only the second alien she'd met in person and since she didn't get threatening vibes from him, she hoped that was a good sign. Especially since she was about to meet a whole lot more of them.

Nox curled his arms around his bondmate as he settled

back into his chair. Looking at his friend, he knew what an important moment this was for all Delicians. It gave people hope.

Nox smiled down into Emeline's upturned face as he told Ezio how he felt the first time he laid eyes on Emeline.

Ezio's eyes slowly followed the colors that crossed between Nox and Emeline's clasped hands. "A bondmate is something to be cherished and it will be my honor to support you in whatever way I can." Ezio nodded his head in respect.

Nox extended his arm to Ezio in the Delician greeting as he thanked him for his support, adding to please keep this information to himself until they had a chance to talk to Liam.

Ezio laughed, pointing to his face, telling him he better put his hood back on. Turning back to the console in front of him, Ezio hid a smile as he guided the shuttle into the docking bay of the *Maelstrom*.

Emeline had been glad for the diversion of Ezio's reaction to her and Nox. The ride had been a lot smoother than she had anticipated. The only time she gripped Nox's arm was when they broke through Earth's atmosphere and even that had been minor. The Delician way of travel was certainly a lot easier on the human body.

The scientist in her couldn't help but be intrigued at everything she was witnessing. She wasn't surprised that Nox and Ezio took for granted what she viewed to be almost like magic. This only drove home the point of how much she had to learn before the Hexians arrived.

She listened as Ezio filled Nox in about what had been happening on the ship since he'd been gone. Liam and Ami had been extremely busy over the last few days not only with their retrofitting assignment but also with their interactions with the Delicians. She surmised from their comments that her brother and her friend had made quite an impression on the aliens, especially with their training regimen. The opinion that humans were not advanced and therefore inferior was proving to be a false assumption on the part of the Delicians. Although, judging by the technological advances that she was witnessing even just aboard this shuttle, she knew they were indeed inferior. *How am I ever going to be of help to Nox?*

Chewing on her lip as she contemplated how she was going to fit into Nox's world, the brush of a finger across her bottom lip broke into her thoughts. Looking up into Nox's concerned face, she reached up and smoothed the wrinkle that had formed between his eyebrows. *Hmm, eyelashes and brows but no hair anyplace else. Fascinating.*

"What's troubling you?" His worried amethyst eyes searched hers.

Sighing, she leaned against him, giving in to a moment of panic. "Just about everything. This is all so new and our technology isn't even in the same category as yours. I don't see how I could possibly be of any use to you?" She had lowered her voice so Ezio couldn't hear her. She didn't want to sound whiny but this was a bit too much to take. "Why do you even need me? You certainly could have done this on your own."

"That is not entirely true. Sure, I would have eventually figured everything out in my lab with Loris, but your knowledge of how your satellites function is vital in interfacing my technology with yours. Don't underestimate your worth to this mission, Emeline. Your network array is brilliant technology." Taking his finger and placing it under her chin, he tilted her head so she could see the sincerity of his words. "We will take it one step at a time, okay?"

Nodding her head in agreement, she took a calming breath. *Okay, let's do this.* "Thank you, Nox. I appreciate you saying that. I won't let you down."

"I never had any doubt." He tried to be reassuring but he could tell she was still struggling with her own insecurities which he felt he was partially to blame for. He needed to watch what was said in the future about humans, especially now that they would be a part of his life.

Once the shuttle came to a stop, the door opened onto a whole new world for Emeline.

Ezio led them down a short ramp onto the docking bay floor.

Eyes wide like a kid on Christmas morning, Emeline didn't know where to look first. All thoughts of force fields, network arrays and being scared disappeared. Everywhere she looked there was something new and interesting that caught her attention. Her senses were on overdrive as she tried to take in everything at once.

Emeline did a quick scan of her surroundings, noting the size of the space she was in. The space was cavernous, teeming with activity. Sleek flyers in neat rows all along the floor had aliens crawling all over them. *Now I get why Liam was so excited. He must be in heaven riding around on these spaceships. Ami's probably just happy they have gravity and knowing Liam, he's been badgering Nyx to teach him how to fly. Hmmm...maybe they might want to take a trip to Delicia with me.*

She felt Nox tug on her hand, leading them towards the doors at one end of the hangar. *Something to think about.*

Smiling, she followed him out the door into the main part of the ship.

"Nox, could you slow down a bit? My legs aren't as long as yours and besides..." She looked at him a little embarrassed. "I can't see everything if you move too fast."

He stopped short, laughing. "Forgive me. I was so excited to show you my lab that I forgot your legs aren't as long as mine. Maybe I should carry you, then we could get there faster." He pretended to bend and pick her up, while she jumped back, laughing.

"No—I can walk. I just want to see everything. It's all so new."

Running her hand along the walls, she just had to know

how the light appeared to glow off the walls. *There must be some sort of sensor embedded in the material.* "How does this work that the walls glow like this? Can they change color? What is the energy source?"

She couldn't stop herself from asking and would have continued talking except for the huge alien who came up and stood behind Nox. *General Tarek.* Ezio was standing just behind him. She'd been so distracted by what was happening all around her, she had forgotten all about him.

Nox turned to greet the General. "Tarek, this is Emeline."

She wished she could have controlled her hand as it shot out to shake his, mainly out of habit. Surprised—pleasantly —when he gave her a firm but not bone-crushing or wimpy handshake in return. *I think I might like this giant of a man.* "Tarek, it's nice to meet you in person."

"You as well. How was your first shuttle ride?" Tarek asked.

"It was better than I thought it would be, especially since I didn't have to go up strapped to a rocket."

Tarek made a face at her comment, which morphed into one of horror when Nox explained how humans launched their shuttles into space. His reaction only confirmed that her fears about space travel hadn't been irrational.

"Liam and Ami—is this how they arrived at their space station?" At the nod of her head, Tarek seemed lost in thought for a moment before saying, "This explains much. Liam has been spending all of his free time down in the docking bay learning about our shuttles and star fighters."

Ezio added, "He's been particularly interested in their construction. He asks endless questions and he has shown a greater understanding than I would have thought possible for a human."

Emeline reared back, insulted.

Quickly remembering where she was, she toned down her response, still managing to get her point across.

"Gentlemen, I understand you feel that humans are not as 'advanced' as you are. I get that—however we are still intelligent beings with the ability to learn, to reason, to discover. Those are traits we all share. And remember not all discoveries are universally known, so please take that into consideration when passing judgment on first contact situations. Most people do not take kindly to being thought of as inferior."

The three Delicians had the decency to look ashamed at her words.

"Forgive me, Emeline. You are correct," Ezio said, bowing at the waist. "That was thoughtless of me."

Tarek also apologized, telling her that he had already informed the UAP that they needed to update their information on the inhabitants of Earth.

"You are forgiven, of course. We are all learning about one another and there are bound to be misunderstandings between us, but we must make sure to remember that we are all on the same side. We all want the same things. And as for Liam, he is trained as a mechanical engineer but was also a pilot in our military. Flying has been his life for as long as I can remember. I'm not the least bit surprised where he's been spending all his spare time."

Grinning at Tarek, she asked, "So has he asked to take one of your star fighters out for a test drive yet?"

"How did you know?" Tarek asked with a frown.

"I would have been disappointed if he hadn't already asked."

She laughed out loud, her hurt beginning to fade. Tolerance was going to be important for them all to remember. "You may want to think about training him because he's never going to stop bugging you until you give in."

"I will take that under advisement," he said with a wink.

Nox cupped Emeline's elbow, directing her towards the elevator at the end of the corridor. As they all stepped in, he addressed Tarek, telling him that he was taking Emeline to their quarters and then a quick visit to his lab before taking her over to medical. It was not lost on anyone when he said *their* quarters.

Tarek told them that he would see them at dinner in the officers' rec room later. They could debrief then.

Turning to Emeline, Tarek and Ezio nodded as they exited the elevator at their deck.

Nox spoke out loud, telling the elevator which deck he wanted, chuckling at the look on Emeline's face.

After what seemed like only seconds, the door opened and he ushered her down a long corridor, stopping at what looked like a door cut into the wall. Holding his hand up to a panel set into the side of the door, the door slid open onto their quarters.

The first thing to catch her eye as she walked into the large room was the long window that ran the entire length of the back wall. There was a seating area with an L shaped couch with a low coffee table that faced the windows. It was the perfect spot to sit and gaze out at the multitude of twinkling stars. A round dining table was set up just off to the left of the couch with room for four people.

An enormous bed was tucked into the corner just to the right of the door. Emeline purposely ignored that part of the room as Nox showed her the storage units for her clothes and personal items. The area to the left of the door was set up with a desk that looked unused. Not even a scrap of paper or photographs—no personal touches could be seen anywhere in the room.

The lights coming off the walls were a softer, lighter hue than the bluish gray tone from the hallways. When she asked Nox about the lighting, he told her all she had to do was ask ARI to adjust the lighting to whatever she wanted.

She couldn't resist saying out loud, "ARI, turn the lights to neon pink and increase brightness."

When the room immediately turned a bright, almost blinding pink, she yelled, "ARI, put it back to white, please."

Relieved to have the lighting back to an acceptable setting, she thought of her sister, Belle. *We could have some pretty awesome dance parties in here.*

Watching Emeline enjoy playing with the new technology, Nox mused, *wait until she sees the bathroom. I plan on getting full use out of the tub—maybe tonight after dinner.* His mind was full of all the things he wanted to do with Emeline in there.

Heading over to a door on the right, it automatically opened as he approached. Beckoning her forward, he was anxious to see her reaction as she stepped through the doorway into the bathroom.

Emeline gasped in delight. Inside was the bathroom of her dreams. Taking up one quarter of the room was a stone pool large enough for six. A large glass shower was off to the side, but she couldn't see where the water came out of.

On the other side of the room was a long vanity with a separate area partitioned off for taking care of one's personal needs—privately. Emeline was especially happy to see that. *There were just some things you liked to do alone.* But the size of the tub was the real focal point in the room. It was like her own private swimming pool where she could skinny dip—with Nox. Just thinking of Nox naked in the tub had Emeline fanning her face as her cheeks started to pinken—again.

After showing Emeline the bathroom's control panel, Nox checked his wrist comm, making sure Loris had authorized Emeline's bio signature into ARI so she would have access to authorized sections of the ship. He was anxious to see the wrist comm that he had Loris create for him. He hoped she liked it.

"Come here, I want to show you something." He walked back into the main living space to what looked to be a storage cabinet set into the wall.

Pressing the panel, a portion of the wall disappeared upward leaving an opening about the size of three foot by three-foot square box.

"This is a replicator that you can use to create whatever you need. Loris has programmed ARI with many of your human products and foods. Would you like to try it?"

He could see she was just itching to get her hands on this piece of technology.

"Are you crazy? Of course I do! Show me—please." Her excitement was contagious.

"All you have to do is tell ARI what you want and it will appear on the platform here."

"That is so cool." Her face was lit with anticipation.

Catching her excitement, Nox laughed, telling her to pace herself.

"Ha ha. You laugh, but I've got a whole list of things. What happens if I change my mind and don't want something?"

Nox told her just to place the item back in the replicator and tell ARI to recycle it. It would get broken down on the molecular level and reintegrated back into the unit.

"Amazing. How is this even possible? I mean, where do you get your energy and the materials from?"

"I was going to wait to tell you when we got to the lab, but I can give you a quick overview of how it works. It's fueled by synthetic crystals. Each crystal is created for whatever device you want to use. For example, in the case of replicators, we are able to make crystals made up of whatever elements are needed in any particular item. We can create crystals to fuel our ships and then others for use on our planet. It was an important innovative technology that our ancestors developed. I can't tell you too much about the theory behind how we make the crystals because it's a well-guarded secret. This type of technology, if placed in the wrong hands, could have massive repercussions throughout the universe."

Emeline was astounded hearing about the crystal technology and nodded in agreement, but she couldn't help but add, "Can you imagine how many lives could be changed for the better if this type of technology was available to everyone?"

"Yes, that's true, but it can also be just as harmful, especially to beings who want to exploit it. That is why the UAP makes a point to err on the side of caution. It is imperative, if at all possible, that planets be allowed to evolve naturally. I'm only telling you this because you are my bondmate. This information is not something that is common knowledge and I must ask you to keep this between us."

Emeline immediately agreed. There was so much about Nox's world that she didn't understand. As much as she wanted to run back to Earth and start making changes, Nox was right—too much advanced technology dumped on the humans could spell disaster for Earth. *Baby steps, Em, baby steps.*

Squeezing his hand in understanding, she held his gaze, telling him, "You can trust me."

Rubbing his hand up and down her arm, he grabbed her hand and kissed the back of it. "I know I can. Now go on— ask ARI to make you something."

At his words, he could almost see her mind whirling, excited with the knowledge she could create anything she wanted.

With a sly look on her face, she murmured, "Oh, I know just the thing."

Rotating her finger at him she said, "Turn around please. I have a feeling you are really going like this."

Going over to the replicator, she tapped a few commands into the control panel. To her delight within moments exactly what she wanted appeared on the platform before her.

Clapping her hands, she grabbed the items and hid them behind her back.

Turning to Nox, who was sitting on the bed with his arms crossed, Emeline smiled. As promised, his eyes were closed...waiting for her surprise.

When she told him to open his eyes, she was holding up a red thong and a matching lace bra. "Would you like me to model these for you?" Her voice took on a sultry, sexy tone as she molded the virtually transparent bra against her breasts.

Nox nearly fell off the bed. His eyes were hooded with desire for this gorgeous woman standing like a siren enticing him with her song. He growled as the sound of his comm interrupted their moment.

Asking Loris if it was important and not getting the answer he wanted to hear, Nox threw down his comm and pulled Emeline in close.

In one sweeping movement she was on her back with him pressing her down into the bed. Careful not to crush her, he touched his forehead to hers giving into a heavy sigh. "This is not what I had planned for your first few hours on board."

Picking up her thong and twirling it on his finger, he gave her a smoldering look before he took her lips in a fiery kiss. Letting her feel his desire that was hard to miss pressing against her stomach, he whispered in a harsh breath, "Unfortunately, this will have to wait until later." He was not at all happy with Loris. Thoughts of how to keep his assistant unduly busy floated through his mind.

Emeline could feel his whole body pressing her into the mattress. *God, I could wrap my arms and legs around him and stay right here forever. Screw the panties and bra and screw Loris. He and I are going to have to set some boundaries about his calling habits.*

Running her hand down the front of his pants, she could feel how much he wanted her. And judging from the hardness of her nipples that were poking him in the chest, he knew she was just as affected as he was. "I was hoping for a good ravishing before we got started in the lab, but I can see that that's going to have to wait." She pressed her hips to his, her body taking on a life of its own.

Breathing in her arousal, his body refusing to let her go —instead he gave in to his desire...for just a little while. That is, until his comm beeped again. Loris.

Looking down into Emeline's flushed face, disappointment crossed between them as they both realized the mission came first.

"Loris!" Nox's voice was rough with frustration and impatience.

Looking into her bright blue eyes, he told her fixedly, "We will finish this ravishing later, I promise."

His hand skimmed down along her curves; the softness of her skin reminded him of the petals of a Morning Zingla. A delicate pink flower found in the mountains near his grandfather's home. It grew deep in the woods in the shadow of a mighty Forlig tree. Brushing his lips across hers, he whispered, "Later."

Standing up, he pulled Emeline to her feet and after a quick once-over making sure that their clothing was presentable, he opened the door as they headed to his lab. All the while thinking he and Loris were due for a major discussion now that he had Emeline in his life.

When Emeline walked into Nox's lab, her first impression was how clean and uncluttered it was, unusually so from any lab she had ever worked in. Her lab looked practically archaic compared to his, which was hard for her to comprehend since her lab was equipped with the world's latest and greatest technology available.

Looking around, she noticed where her lab had workstations divided into wet and dry chemistry and areas for storage of the materials and the chemicals she used, Nox's lab was stark in comparison. It was clean and white and weirdly sterile.

In the center of the room was a round platform surrounded by transparent screens. A tall Delician male working on equations appeared to be talking to himself. He looked up sharply as they walked into the room. *Loris!* Emeline assumed he must be working with ARI on something.

A look of relief showed on his face at the sight of his friend. Coming toward them with his arm reaching out to give Nox the Delician greeting, he came to an abrupt halt when he saw the colors moving across Nox's face. His own face showed confusion and then shock as he processed the meaning of what he saw.

"Bondmate?"

Meeting Loris's look of uncertainty with a silly grin, Nox brought Emeline forward to meet his friend. "Loris, this is Emeline, my bondmate."

Turning to Emeline, he introduced his friend. "This is Loris, my assistant and also one of my dearest friends." Giving Emeline a knowing look, he glared good-naturedly, saying, "He's also about to be my sparring partner in the training room. Perhaps that will teach him not to interrupt us when we're in our quarters." Nox snickered, slapping Loris's back at his obvious discomfort as Emeline looked on, her cheeks splotched a bright red.

"Hi. It's nice to meet you." She put her arm out to give him the Delician greeting.

Nox smiled at her attempt to conform to his culture as he watched Loris hesitate, checking to see if Nox would want him touching his bondmate. Giving him a subtle nod, Loris's hand completely engulfed her arm, being careful to be gentle as they completed their greeting.

Emeline was pleased with herself that she remembered not to shake Loris's hand. She desperately wanted to make a good impression even though she needn't have worried when she saw Loris's silly grin matched Nox's. He was genuinely happy for his friend. They had a comfortable camaraderie between them that had developed over years of working together. Nox had told her that Loris had been one of his only friends he'd had over the years and he attributed that friendship to helping him get through the dark times after his mother's death. She had caught a glimpse of Nox's obvious loneliness, making her feel sad. *Well, he's not alone anymore.*

That thought made her smile as she took in Loris's appearance. Nox wasn't kidding when he said he was smaller than most Delician males. Whereas General Tarek towered over almost anyone, Loris was only a few inches taller than Nox, only stockier with thicker legs and definitely much thicker around the middle. What surprised her was his hair. It was dark with the telltale purple streaks but much longer—pulled up into a man bun. So far most of the Delician males she had seen, other than Nox, had sported military-style haircuts. Seeing Loris reminded her of someone who was from her parents' generation. All he needed was a tie-dyed T-shirt and some Grateful Dead playing in the background and he would've fit right in with her dad.

"It is nice to meet you, Emeline." Looking at Nox, Loris used his finger to make a circular motion around his face, indicating that he was aware how the bondmating was affecting his skin. "Looks like you're been busy, my friend."

"Yes, it was an unexpected development, but I must tell you, Loris, it has made me happier than I ever thought possible." Nox gently pulled Emeline to his side and gazed lovingly into her face. "I am a lucky male to have found a bondmate as wonderful as Emeline. She is everything I could have hoped for. The fates have been kind to me." He leaned in and gave Emeline a quick kiss on lips that smiled back at him.

"If anyone deserves to find their bondmate, it's you, Nox. Although have you considered what you're going to say to Sandovar the next time he contacts you? That's why I was calling you—sorry about the interruption. Bad timing, I guess?" Loris's cheeks glowed slightly at the thought of what they were doing when he called. "Your father's been trying to reach you for the past two days. I've been able to put him off, but he's getting pretty persistent. I think he wants you to agree to his plan for you to marry Senator Ventano's daughter."

Annoyed at his father's continued interference in his life, Nox growled, "I'll call him later. I have nothing to say to him. You'd think having your only child find their bondmate would be cause for him to rejoice. Instead, he's going to be extremely angry that I thwarted his plans. But knowing Sandovar, he'll find some way to use this as a means for furthering his own gain."

"I concur. I think you're safe for a few days. I told him you were with Tarek. That shut him up rather quickly, but you better be working on what you want to say to him—preferably before someone else tells him." If Loris had his way, he would have ARI automatically delete any communications coming in from Nox's father. Loris did not like Sandovar, especially knowing how manipulative he could be.

A feeling of dread began to grow in the pit of Emeline's stomach. Nox's father wasn't the only person who might have a problem with her mating with Nox. Liam's stern, unhappy face popped into her mind, causing her to involuntarily shiver. *Yeah, I wonder if Liam is going to go all Hank on me. Well—too bad. It's my life.*

Nox's voice interrupted her thoughts, grinding out, "Sandovar might be my father, but he has no control over me or my life."

"That might be true, Nox, but your father does have a lot of influence and he can make getting funding for our projects a lot harder to get," Loris reminded him.

"True, but after we complete this mission for the UAP, not even Sandovar will be able to have much say in my life. I have a bondmate now. That takes precedence over everything else. Besides, if he gives me too much trouble, we'll just move to another planet where he has no influence at all." Nox had already decided...if he had to, he would move to Earth and live in Emeline's loft. "Emeline is mine, Loris, and I'm not giving her up. Now enough about Sandovar. Were you able to complete my request?" Nox was excited. He wished he could give Emeline her present in private, but that wouldn't be fair to Loris, especially since he had completed it for him. He wanted Emeline to be happy working in here with both him and Loris.

Opening a drawer at a workstation in the corner of the room, Loris handed Nox a small box, a sly grin graced his face. "Here it is." Loris was eager to see Emeline's reaction to the gift that Nox had designed for her.

"Nox? Loris? Is that what I think it is?" Emeline couldn't contain herself and a small squeal escaped her mouth before she could stop it with her hand.

Laughing, Nox led her over to the platform, a knowing smile spread over his face as he handed Emeline the pretty blue box. Her reaction to his gift was immediate with her exclamation of joy as she opened the box.

Inside on a pillow made of a shiny silver material, such that she had never seen before, lay an exquisite wrist comm designed specifically for her. It was made from a material that looked similar to silver but she knew it wasn't. It was about three quarters of an inch at its widest part but tapered down around leaving a half-inch wide opening for her to fit her wrist through. It had two lines of small multi-colored gemstones that lined either side of the band, leaving the center space open with a small square for ARI's use. It was stunning and so thoughtful.

She hugged Nox and then hugged Loris, before hugging Nox again all the while thanking them both profusely on how much she loved their gift. "Here, help me put it on," she told Nox as she handed him the comm, sticking her arm out at him to place it on.

Nox held the comm in his hand for a second, inspecting the piece to make sure it was exactly as he had designed, which of course it was. Nodding his head in thanks to Loris, he turned to Emeline who was standing there still holding her wrist up to him, waiting impatiently for him to put it on her. "I am so glad you like it, my beautiful girl."

Loris's head jerked up at the endearment he heard Nox call Emeline and smiled at his friend. He had never heard Nox speak that way to anyone before. It warmed his heart that he was able to be a part, even in a small way, of helping Nox with his surprise.

Admiring her present, Emeline gushed happily, "Oh Nox, I more than love it, thank you so much. It's beautiful. Does it work like yours? Can I try it out?" She knew she sounded like a little kid at Christmas, but it wasn't every day you got a present like this one. Her friends were going to be so jealous that she had a portable ARI at her fingertips.

He chuckled at her exuberance. "Yes, it works like mine and of course you can try it out, but first we need to do the retina scan before you can get started."

Nox took the wrist comm and pressed on the small square, saying aloud, "ARI, start retina scan to initiate wrist comm for Emeline Cameron."

Holding it up to Emeline's eye, a beam appeared, completing the process in a matter of seconds.

Taking her wrist gently in his hand, he slipped the comm into place, teasing her, "Now be gentle with ARI. Try not to overdo it in the first ten minutes."

Emeline laughed up at him and threw her arms around his neck, pulling him down for a very thankful, very appreciative kiss that had Loris retreating to his corner of the room, wishing for his own bondmate. He hoped that the two of them would keep that part of their relationship contained to their room, but he had a feeling, judging by the way they couldn't seem to keep their hands off each other, that he better get used to it. Smiling to himself, he thought,

Well, at least my friend is happy. If anyone deserves it, he does.

After a few more minutes of making sure that Nox knew just how thankful she was for his thoughtful gift, Emeline was ready to start exploring Nox's lab and trying to define where she fit in to all of this. She had so many questions but still in the back of her mind didn't know how she would be able to help him with her lack of knowledge of such advanced technology. Remembering what she'd said to Tarek in the corridor about how humans had the ability to learn, she decided to cut herself some slack. She would start like she always did when she had a problem—assess, define, learn. Assess the situation, define the problem, learn what you needed to do in order to complete the task.

Nox started with an overview of the lab, how to access the consoles and then brought her over to the replicator, explaining that it was the same concept as what she'd seen in their room. He explained they still did experiments, but they were mostly done through simulations with ARI. Working on a battle cruiser was different than being in his lab on Delicia. Here you were limited in the ways in which you did experiments. You were, after all, still on a spaceship and you had to be careful that you didn't do any lasting damage that could affect the integrity of the ship and its crew.

Emeline completely understood what he was saying and kind of liked the idea of having ARI run simulations first. This gave her the freedom to have ARI do simulations of all kinds of ideas that she had running through her brain. Secretly, what she really wanted was to learn more about this synthetic crystal that Nox said they used for their fuel. That was the most fascinating thing she had ever heard of. *Imagine synthesizing a crystal that could solve all your fuel, energy, food problems. That sounded more science fiction than reality.* Laughing to herself at that thought, she shook her head. *Well, you are hanging out with a bunch of aliens. Anything is possible.*

Nox showed her his office and where the bathroom was and then set her up at one of the workstations near Loris, telling her to ask either him or Loris if she had any questions. He left her happily instructing ARI to give her a rundown on Liam and Ami's progress with the satellites.

Checking the time, he saw how late it was getting. He had wanted to make a quick stop in medical to introduce Emeline to Dr. Datrem before dinner. *I'll just comm him and tell him we'll be by in the morning.*

To say Nox was nervous about their upcoming dinner was an understatement. It wasn't the reaction of his team that worried him. They would be thrilled for him. It was Liam's and Ami's reaction to their bondmating. Liam was not going to be happy about his little sister becoming a bondmate to an alien. As the paternal figure in Emeline's life, he wondered just how much of an influence Liam would have on Emeline's decision to complete their bondmating.

Perhaps I better do some research into human mating customs. Knowledge might be the answer to understanding what I'm facing at dinner tonight.

"ARI, bring up all the information you have on human dating rituals."

Emeline arched an eyebrow at Nox with a questioning look when she heard what he asked ARI.

Shrugging his shoulders, he told her, "I thought I should prepare for our dinner with Liam. I'm not sure what his reaction is going to be when we tell him about us."

As the data started scrolling on his screen, Nox was fascinated at what he read. "Did you know that in some human cultures, a woman's family has to make a payment to a man in order for him to agree to marry her? Now, that's just wrong. He should be happy he's getting a life partner...not expect to get compensated for it." Nox's face took on a disgusted look as he continued to read through the data. "And did you know that a woman has to do everything a man says or he can beat her into submission. That's unacceptable. What kind of a world do you come from?" He was appalled.

Emeline gave him a confused look until she looked at what he was reading.

Giggling, she called out, "ARI, display human mating rituals starting in the year 2019."

A whole new set of data started scrolling onto Nox's monitor.

Trying hard not to laugh at him because she thought it was so cute that he was taking the time to research her culture, she quietly told him, "You were reading materials from the 1600s. That was a really long time ago and yes, you are right, back then being a woman was not much fun. You were at the mercy of your father and then your husband. It was all about money and power. Rarely did a woman marry for love.

"It's different in my generation. Couples nowadays marry for love, but even with that few couples remain together. The rate of divorce has been so high recently that a lot of couples are opting to just live together, avoiding marriage altogether. It makes breaking up easier if it's not legal."

Emeline's laissez-faire attitude shocked Nox. Did she feel that way about them, he thought—that their bondmating was only temporary and that when she got tired of him, she would just walk away and leave him? *No. She is a part of my soul. I could not survive without her. She must understand that once the bond is completed, she is mine forever.*

From the look on Nox's face, Emeline realized that she had obviously upset him with her careless comments. Running her hand along his face, she made him move his chair so she could sit on his lap. Putting her arms around his shoulders, she caressed his face...making him meet her eyes—her voice soft as she told him that this was not the case with them.

Looking over at Loris, who was pretending not to listen, she thought that they should be having this discussion in private. However, this was important.

"Nox, listen to me. These are just words that you are reading. Words that don't have anything to do with how you and I feel about each other. Now maybe it's the bond talking but I don't think so. The past few days with you have been the best of my life, so believe me, I will not let anyone take this, whatever it is, away from us. You and I are in this together. I feel you inside my heart, my soul and nothing or no one will ever change that. You have to trust me that there is nothing Liam and Ami can say to make me feel otherwise. Besides my parents were married for over 40 years and were still madly in love when my dad died."

Emeline's words calmed his racing heart. Her words eased any doubts that had been trying to overtake his mind. "Thank you, my beautiful girl. You make me so happy and you're right...together we can face anything." He leaned in, kissing her lips...adding a balm to his battered heart. "But I was thinking we might want to try some of these dating rituals I was just reading about. How do you feel about bowling?"

Emeline giggled again, pushing off his lap, telling him *it's a date*—then went on to explain that she had been bowling with her family since she was young.

Nox told her he was looking forward to their date and then reminded himself to learn more about bowling.

Glancing over at Loris, Nox saw him trying to concentrate on what he was working on, noting the amused look on his face.

Checking the time again, he saw that they needed to leave shortly. "Emeline, would you like to replicate an outfit to wear to dinner tonight?"

"YES!" Itching to try something new, she decided maybe tonight's dinner she should stick with her normal style. Choosing black leggings with a long blue sweater dress and black heeled boots, she headed into the bathroom to change. *I can wear heels until my feet fall off and I'll still be considered short. Gotta love this.*

Coming out of his office wearing black pants paired with a fitted long-sleeved purple shirt, Nox was glad to be back in his own clothes. He felt infinitely more comfortable than he had in those *jeans* he wore on Earth. Touching the hem of his shirt, he compared this fabric to the human clothing he had worn on Earth. Earth's fabric was grown in the ground, "cotton" Emeline had called it. Examining his sleeve, he noticed that the Delician fabric was a combination of materials that were created in the replicator. The feel was similar, but as he sniffed his sleeve, it didn't have that vanilla smell that he was becoming so fond of.

Glancing up, he saw Emeline standing outside the bathroom door, a confused look on her face.

She couldn't help asking, "Are you sniffing your shirt?"

Smiling, his eyes lit up when he took in this beautiful woman standing before him. "I was just thinking that my own clothes don't have that wonderful scent as yours did." He came over pulling her close, nudging her hair away from her neck as he took a deep breath. "Ah, yes there it is. Do we really have to go? You look so beautiful; I wouldn't mind keeping you all to myself." His tongue snaked out for a quick taste, causing Emeline to shiver.

Pulling away, she smiled up at him, "Thank you—but we're going. We need to get this over with so we can concentrate on kicking some Hexian butt." Taking his hand in hers, they headed out the door.

Stopping abruptly, Emeline peered intently into his eyes. "Nox, I want us to start our lives together. I know my brother. He loves me and only wants what's best for me. What's the worst he can do? Ground me? Not going to happen. Come on, I'll protect you." Emeline knew Liam would be upset, but eventually he'd come around to her way of thinking.

Leaning down, kissing the tip of her nose, he whispered in her ear, "I think I like it when you take charge. Let's go, my beautiful girl."

CHAPTER 11

Tarquin's office aboard
Battle Cruiser Invidia
A week out from entering Earth's
Solar system

"You wanted to talk to me." Hagen didn't bother to announce himself as he sauntered into Tarquin's office and sat heavily in a chair that had seen better days. Leaning back, he slammed his weather-beaten boots onto the desk, the sound of them hitting the scratched metal desk echoed around the room as he crossed his ankles. He dismissed the look of disdain his boss gave him—frankly because he didn't give a shit what his boss thought.

As far as Hagen was concerned, Tarquin was a means to an end—an end that led to money and power. Power being the ultimate result for Hagen above all else. He learned a long time ago that you only had yourself to rely on. A lesson he learned as an eight-year-old boy who watched his young strung-out mother die on a dirty bathroom floor in the dump his father called an "exotic" dance club. *Ha, dance club—more like sex club.* A club that was nothing more than a place for people to come in to feed their need for the ultimate high, either from drugs, sex, booze or in most cases violence. The only thing exotic about that club had died on the floor of her bathroom with a double dose of the newest and latest drug coursing through her veins. Her death had not been an easy one, vomit and snot running down her sweat-stained naked body. It was a sight Hagen never got out of his head.

Tarquin glared at his second in command, wondering again why he had hired Hagen in the first place. Sure, he was good at getting the desired results, but he wondered sometimes if it was worth the cost. Half the time, his clients complained that the cost of doing business with him was too high. Too many times the result ended in the deaths of anyone who got in Hagen's way. Collateral damage, he would say to Tarquin when he would return from a job with only a portion of his crew still intact and who knows how many bystanders were killed along the way. "Finesse" and "Hagen" were two words you didn't generally use in the same sentence.

Well, he is good in a fight as long as he's fighting on your side. Tarquin remembered the night he'd met Hagen. He didn't normally go into that part of the city by himself, but he had been hearing some rumblings about a shipment of Delician crystals that were about to be brought onto Hexia. If it was true, then he needed to find out before anyone else got their hands on them. Regrettably for Tarquin, he found out the hard way the rumors were false. Instead, he found himself in a position that proved deadly. It turned out to be a trap set up by members of General Tarek's elite soldiers. He should have trusted his gut. He had a contact within the executive committee of the Delician government that would have warned him if a shipment had gone missing. Those crystals were manufactured and secured in a facility that was nearly impossible to penetrate, and if anyone could have gained access to them, his contact would have already done it.

Tarquin would have lost his life that night if not for Hagen jumping in and saving his sorry ass. *I suppose I owe him for that, but Hagen is not the type to want to sit around and talk about feelings. Neither am I, for that matter—that's why we generally get along so well.* Unfortunately for one of Tarek's soldiers, *what was his name again? Oh yeah Ezio...*his face didn't leave as pretty as he came in. Hagen left a nice reminder of just what a prick he could be. Tarquin was sure Ezio would be looking for a way to return the favor if he ever got the chance.

Getting up and coming around his desk, Tarquin shoved Hagen's feet off his desk. The sound of them hitting the floor was like the sound of what Hagen's fist sounded like when it was hitting an unsuspecting miscreant who had gotten in his way. "What have I told you about putting your dirty boots on my desk?" Breathing deep, he could smell the sweat and dirt and whatever else clung to Hagen's filthy clothes wafting up from around his body. "Damn, man—you reek. I'm guessing it's about time for your monthly bath."

Hagen gave him a smile that Tarquin could have done without—his nasty yellow teeth looked as though they had never been cleaned. Hagen replaced his boots back on the desk all the while giving Tarquin a look as if to say, *go ahead, do it again.* "What do you want, boss man? I'm busy training the new recruits."

"Well, if you hadn't gotten the last set killed on that mission to Calor Prime, then you wouldn't have to constantly be training new ones." Tarquin was pissed that Hagen seemed to go through crewmembers faster than he could replace them. It was starting to get old since the recruits they were getting were less and less reliable.

Hagen had a sneer to his tone as he glared at Tarquin. "And maybe I wouldn't have had to go to that cesspit of a planet to get fuel if you had just used your contact to get us some Delician crystals. But that's right, you only do his bidding and you don't get much in return, do you?"

"Are you forgetting the cloaking device we got from my contact, or has the booze you got from Calor Prime clouded your mind?" Tarquin was sick of Hagen constantly rubbing his nose in the fact that other than the cloaking device, the relationship with his contact had been one-sided. Tarquin was well aware of this fact, but his contact was not someone you wanted to cross—plus the fact that his relationship with his contact was a well-guarded secret.

Hagen jumped to his feet and in one swift moment had Tarquin's back up against the wall with his meaty hand closing tightly around his throat.

Sneering into his face, he was barely even breathing hard from the effort. "You've lost your touch lately, *boss*," he said with a twisted smile. His tone showed the lack of respect he had for his boss, and the fact that Tarquin didn't make any attempt to push him away only fueled his contempt further.

Leaning in, spittle forming around his mouth, his fingers slowly tightening, "That booze is the only good thing on that planet—well, besides their females. And you know how much I love hot, dirty, sweaty females."

Not noticing Tarquin's hand move until it was too late, Hagen felt a small tube pressing into the side of his neck as a very quiet, very deadly voice said in a hushed tone, "Go ahead, move just one muscle and a toxin so powerful will hit your bloodstream so fast, you'll be dead before you hit the ground."

No one breathed for what seemed like an eternity as two dark, deadly eyes looked back at Hagen…their intent showing in their depths…just willing Hagen to move…ever so slightly.

Backing away with the slow deliberation of a man who wasn't quite sure how he managed to live past the last minute, Hagen held his palms up to the man who he thought couldn't have surprised him anymore. "Well—it's nice to see you still have some backbone in you. Although, I'm not surprised you'd stoop to using poison instead of fighting like a good Hexian male, but then again, you've gotten soft in your old age. Maybe it's time for a new leader for Hexia—to bring us back to the original purpose of this planet instead of taking us into this new direction of peace and well-being." A look of disgust crossed his face as he added, "I mean, you wouldn't want to bruise your tender hands fighting a real man."

Tarquin was on Hagen before he even finished spewing his hateful words. With one punch to Hagen's filthy mouth and another quick powerful jab to his nose, while his knee came in contact with his groin, Tarquin had Hagen on the ground with one hand clutching his nose, the other clutching his balls, crying out as pain coursed through his body.

"You think you can run this planet better than me? You think you can hold back the lawlessness, the corruption, the masses who only want one thing—to survive on this hellhole of a planet? Ha—better males than you have tried to take me on and yet I'm still here…still dealing with sorry excuses of assholes who think they're a better fit for this job than I am."

Tarquin rubbed his hand as he looked down at his second in command lying in a heap on the floor. Blood ran from his nose down to his mouth, his teeth stained red from where Tarquin's fist had landed. His blood, mixed in with all the filth on his body, gave off a sickening smell that he knew for sure would never come out of his well-worn carpet.

"Get up before you bleed all over my office. It's bad enough I have to smell your stench, now I've got to look at your blood all over my floor." Tarquin couldn't help looking at his second in command with loathing. Hagen wasn't the first one to try and kill him and Tarquin knew he wouldn't be the last. He knew one of these days his luck was going to run out. *Maybe I need a new line of work. If only my "contact" would come through with just one shipment of crystals. Yeah sure, he's been promising me that for way too long. Always some excuse as to why he couldn't get them.* "Now get up and sit down. We have a problem and I haven't got time for your bullshit."

Tarquin went over and poured himself a glass of his favorite Delician wine. *The one good thing of having a contact in the Delician government—their excellent wine.*

Picking his huge body up off the floor, Hagen stood,

wincing slightly. His hand delicately probed his groin as he smirked at Tarquin. "I guess I was wrong. You do still have a small measure of cunning in you." Hagen gave him a look of renewed respect as he righted his chair and sat down, very gingerly as to not crush his swollen balls. Swiping his arm across his face, a long streak of blood mixed in with the layers of dirt smeared across the sleeve of his shabby jacket. His Delician skin should have shown white and shiny with the telltale opalescent flecks lying just under the surface, but the years spent on Hexia had weathered his skin. Instead, it looked dirty—yellowed like his teeth.

Rubbing his hand across his bald head, he was glad he'd spent the money to have his hair lasered off. He didn't need hair with purple highlights taking away from the well-earned badass persona he had cultivated over the years.

His father would have been proud, although "proud" probably wasn't the right word... *Expected* would have been a better word for his reputation as a tough, take-no-prisoners mercenary. If things had been different, he would have been running his father's club right now. Unfortunately, his cocksure father had been careless...stepping out of his office without his guards. That one moment of weakness proved to be his last. His father had ended up like his mother, dead on the floor with only Hagen around to care. Well, those Hexians had lived to regret the day they walked into his father's club.

Snapping his fingers at Hagen, Tarquin rolled his eyes. "I haven't got time for any more of your crap. We've got more pressing matters to handle." Tarquin was so over Hagen, wishing he could just boot his ass off his ship, but he needed him. Someone had to lead his crew and right now, Hagen was all he had.

Hagen looked up sharply, his interest piqued. "What kind of problem? We're almost to Earth. It won't be long before we have control over their salt mines. Then we'll have more money than we'll know what to do with. Maybe even fix up this rust bucket."

As if the ship heard him, the lights flickered. He felt as well as heard a groan coming from deep within the bowels of the ship. The Invidia had definitely seen better days, and if they didn't do something soon, they might just end up stuck on this primitive planet called Earth.

"These beings are so backwards they don't even know how to defend themselves against our superior weapons. This is going to be the easiest mission we've ever been on. Once we get the first shipment of salt to our buyers, we can buy ten new battle cruisers and use this one for target practice."

"Well, it might not be as easy as you think. My contact on Delicia just informed me that that skizoid General Tarek somehow found out about our trip. He and his crew are on their way to Earth right now to investigate. From what I hear, they have the UAP's Director Nox onboard the *Maelstrom*. They're planning on using his force field technology to try and stop us. I heard they're even working with a human female."

"A human female? No way. They must be desperate. Why don't we use your cloaked ship? We'll sneak in and take what we want." Hagen figured it would be easy to just sneak past Tarek and his crew. "They have no idea that we even have this tech, so I don't see what the problem is."

"The problem is that they know we've been coming to Earth. If they get those force fields up and running, we won't be able to sneak past them. Their sensors will pick up our engine signatures, and if I know Tarek and his buddy Jagger, they'll have their own cloaked ships waiting for us. We need at least one of those salt shipments. That would set us up for a while anyway. We need a way to stop them or at least slow them down." Tarquin scratched his head through the cap he always wore. No one ever saw him without it. If they did, his secret would be out. *Damn, I hate this hat. It makes my head itch.*

Tarquin began pacing around his office, trying to come up with a plan to thwart Tarek. They had been constant adversaries for years, but lately Tarek and his team had been getting the upper hand. Even just one shipment of salt would change all that. He could leave Hexia and his "benefactor" behind and start a new life, far away in a place that wasn't so hellishly hot and dusty. A place where he could breathe clean air, feel free and not have to wear this disguise all the time. He could finally be himself without someone or something always pulling at him to do their bidding. He was sick of it and just wanted some peace.

"I might have a way." Hagen had been quietly thinking while Tarquin paced around. Hagen knew that Tarquin wasn't one to talk about himself. Tarquin's grandfather had been the former leader of Hexia. He had been the contributing factor in creating this current version of Hexia—a place that was a haven for anyone needing to disappear. No one knew who Tarquin's father was. It was a topic no one dared speak out loud. Tarquin had a reputation for being vicious with anyone stupid enough to try to dig into his past. Hagen knew though, but he kept that piece of information to himself...for now.

"Okay tell me." Tarquin sat down heavily in his chair—waiting.

"My cousin is a medic on Tarek's ship. I can contact her and get some information from her."

"What makes you think she'll do anything for you?" Tarquin asked him.

"Trust me—she will. I may not live on Delicia anymore, but I still have plenty of contacts through my father. She'll do what I tell her, if she knows what's good for her." Hagen's voice became deadly as he thought about what he could do to Violia if she refused him. She was nothing but a weak little bleeding heart who would do what he said or she would regret it. "You leave her to me."

"Fine, just keep me informed. Now get out of my office

and get cleaned up. Your stench is going to kill the rest of the new recruits and then you'll be fighting Tarek alone." Tarquin pointed towards the door, indicating he was done and for Hagen to leave.

"Yeah—like that's going to happen." He shot him a rude sign and stalked the door. He had a little cousin to intimidate.

◆ ◆ ◆

Violia was enjoying a few moments of peace before their lives got crazy. The medical bay on the *Maelstrom* was unusually quiet tonight, especially considering how busy everyone was preparing for the upcoming battle with the Hexians. Back on duty after Dr. Datrem had given her, Senta and Tulio, her fellow coworkers, a few days off to rest up, she was eager to get back to work. No one knew what was happening, only that the General and Captain Jagger had stressed to them that they needed the medical bay ready for whatever wounded they might have once the battle began.

Checking to make sure the crystals in the regen units were at maximum capacity, she thought about the humans that had been on the ship for the last few days. Having never seen humans before, she had only gotten a glimpse of them in the corridor. Their skin tone was different from hers and she was more than curious about their physiology. She was anxious to read the report ARI was currently compiling regarding the humans.

But what she really wanted was to have one of them come into the med bay for a personal examination, and that was about to happen tomorrow because something very exciting had occurred. One of their own, Director Nox, had found his bondmate among the humans. The Director had informed the doctor that they would be coming in to have some tests run, so the doctor wanted them to be pre-

235

pared. Interspecies bondmating was unheard of and they were all eager about the prospect of being able to examine a species that was on the Prohibited Planets list. Dr. Datrem had assigned each of them a specific body function to research and they were going to meet in the morning to discuss their findings.

Violia was excited that her task had been to discover all she could about the female human reproductive system. Getting comfortable in the medics' office, she started scrolling through the data that ARI had downloaded for her. *Umm, human women can produce an egg for fertilization once a month! And—they can have multiple births.* That was astonishing to her. Delician women only ovulated twice in their entire lives. *They can have multiple births at once.* There had never been a case of multiple births on Delicia. *Humans are a fascinating species. I hope I get to do the examination for Director Nox's bondmate.*

As she continued reading, she wondered about the changes to the human female's body that would take place. She had never met anyone who had a bondmate before, so they would all be learning together.

A particular passage caught her eye as she read out loud to herself, "Gestation for human pregnancies is nine months." *Interesting. Delician females carry for only five months. That must be hard on the human body to carry for such a long time.*

She continued reading the information that ARI had downloaded and was so engrossed in the information she didn't notice that Dr. Datrem had come into the room. Looking up and seeing the amused look on his face, she smiled at him. He was such a kind male. She had learned so much from him in just the short time she had been on the ship. Her grandmother Etha had wanted her to stay on Delicia and work at one of the local medical offices, but she had such a strong desire to go off into space.

Violia needed a change and getting the chance to serve

aboard the *Maelstrom* with Dr. Datrem wasn't something she was going to pass up. It was the only time in her life that Violia had pushed for something just for herself. Besides, the experience she got working with the doctor would go a long way towards advancing her career. She hoped that with this experience she would be able to apply to the university to complete her real goal...to become a doctor.

She had put her life on hold to take care of her grandmother. There had been no other options—not that she minded...Etha was everything to her. Ever since her cousin Hagen had disappeared, leaving her alone to care for their elderly grandmother, it had been her responsibility to provide all the support for the two of them. The only reason she was even able to go on this assignment was because Dr. Datrem had arranged for one of his granddaughters to come and stay with Etha so she wouldn't be alone. She appreciated the effort he had made for her and she wanted to do her best for him.

"Hello, Dr. Datrem."

"Hello, Violia. What has you so engrossed that you didn't even notice I was here? I've been watching you for the past ten minutes."

"Humans are an amazing species. Did you know that they can get pregnant once a month from the time they menstruate until the time they reach menopause?" Amazed, she had a hard time comprehending that fact.

"Yes. I was just reading that. I'm looking forward to when Director Nox's bondmate becomes pregnant. We will have to monitor her very closely." The doctor seemed just as fascinated as she was.

"I'll be curious as to what kind of changes the human's body will undergo once they complete the bond. I understand they haven't completed it yet because of the Hexians. They're waiting until the threat is over," Violia said to the doctor as he came and sat down next to her on the couch.

"Yes, that is true," he replied. Violia tried to stifle a yawn before the doctor could catch her, but at his expression saw she had been caught.

Concerned, Dr. Datrem inquired, "Have you not been sleeping well?" He knew that leaving her grandmother had put a lot of pressure on her. He had been happy to help Violia with this chance to serve aboard the *Maelstrom*. Her life had been put on hold for too many years and it was time for that to change.

"Yes—well, maybe I'm having a little trouble. I hated leaving Grandmother, but I needed to go. I can't thank you enough for all your help in arranging this assignment for me."

"Violia, I have known your family for many years. I know better than most how much you have sacrificed for your grandmother. It was a lot for you to take on when your cousin Hagen left the way he did and with the death of his father, it really took a toll on both of you. I was more than happy to help." And he was. He had watched her grandmother deteriorate over the years, first with the death of her husband and daughter in an accident and then the murder of her son, leaving her to raise the children that were left. It was a huge disappointment to her when Hagen turned out to be just like his parents. When he left with not so much as a good-bye, Etha took it hard. It was important for Violia to get this opportunity to further her career as a medic. He planned on helping even further when they returned from this mission. She didn't know it yet but he had already made arrangements for her to continue her studies at the university to become a doctor. It was his way of helping someone who deserved it.

"Dr. Datrem, I can never repay you for all that you've done for my family. I'm—"—yawn—"so grateful"—yawn. "Oh, my goodness. Sorry about that. I guess I am tired." She covered her mouth to hide another one that tried so slip out as she looked at him sheepishly.

"Go on, get some rest."

"I can't yet. I still have two hours before my shift is over," she protested to him.

"Go. I will be here if anything comes up. Things should be quiet tonight anyway, so get some rest while you can. I don't want to see you back here until tomorrow morning at the earliest." He took the tablet out of her hand as he shooed her out the door.

Thanking the doctor once again, she headed to her room. *A nap is just what I need. Although maybe I should comm Grandmother first.* As she walked, she thought about what Dr. Datrem had said to her. He was right about Hagen. She was glad when he left and didn't care where he was as long as he stayed there. There had been talk he had gone to Hexia. She shivered at that thought as she walked—Hexia was a bad place.

Hagen was mean, nasty and wasn't above using his considerable size against her just because he could. But she had learned though. She might be small but she was fit and had learned a few tricks of her own. You had to when you had a cousin like him. He wasn't above doing dirty tricks, especially if it was to get his own way.

She remembered one time he had stolen some money from their grandmother and lied to get out of it. Violia knew he had done it and if he thought he was fooling anyone, he was vastly mistaken. He caught her one night in the garden when she was walking home from the clinic. Stepping out from behind a tree, he grabbed her by the hair... pulling it almost out of her head...shaking her down to her bones. She actually thought that he had snapped her neck having grabbed her so hard. His threats still rang in her ears and she knew he would follow through if she didn't do what he said. He left shortly after that. She hadn't seen him in years. *If I never see him again it will be too soon.*

Stepping into her room, she looked around at the quarters she'd been assigned. It was nicer than she would have thought with a big bed, storage and her own private bath. She didn't care if she had to sleep on a cot in a corner of the med bay as long as she got to come on this mission.

Pulling off her uniform, she grabbed a night dress out of the storage unit and slipped it on. *I'll comm Grandmother in the morning before work.* Her bed looked too inviting and comfortable.

Climbing in, it didn't take long for her to drift off to sleep.

What is that beeping? Can't you see I'm sleeping?

She was deep in a sweet dream. She was at the university lab—she had been accepted into the physician's program. It was a fascinating demonstration on the use of the latest improvements to the regen device.

Seriously what is that beeping noise?

The constant noise finally brought her awake.

The room was dark except for the tiny glow of light emanating from her comm unit. Grabbing the unit, she tried to focus her eyes on the small screen. The call was incoming on a secure line.

What?

Pressing her thumb into the middle of her comm bracelet, the face that stared, no, glared back at her was her worst nightmare come to life—Hagen!

Jumping out of bed, she called for the lights to come up.

Grabbing a blanket, she wrapped it around herself, attempting to cover her body,

"What the hell do you want, Hagen?" she demanded.

Dragging his eyes up and down her body, his leer made her skin crawl. "Well, well, well, little cousin, I see you've grown a backbone since I've been gone. Or is it just that you're only brave because we're not in the same room?"

"What do you want, Hagen?" she asked again, glaring at him because he was right—it was easier to be brave when he wasn't standing over her. If she ever got in the same room as him, she was probably as good as dead. *What does he want?*

"I see you got yourself a nice little position on the *Maelstrom*. Good. I need some information and you're going to give it to me." He gave her a look indicating he wouldn't take no for an answer.

"I'm not going to give you anything. You don't own me and I don't have to do anything you say." The conviction in her voice was clear and she meant everything she said. She would not betray the General and especially not Dr. Datrem after all he had done for her.

He seemed to grow right out of the comm unit as he hissed at her, "Listen to me, you little twat. You will give me whatever I want, when I want—you hear me."

Trying not to be intimidated, she held her ground until he did the one thing that he knew would make her cave. He threatened their grandmother. He told her in great detail what he would do to their sweet, fragile grandmother, the one person in her life that he knew she would do anything for. Once he finished spewing his venom about Etha, he started on her...all the horrible vile things he would love to do to her.

Her face flushed with disgust as she ground out, "What do you want to know?"

"Now there's the smart little female I knew you could be. Tell me about the humans—have they made contact yet?"

Trying to figure out how to give him only vague information, she nodded her head.

"And?"

"And what? I'm a medic. I work in the medical bay. It's not like they're reading me in on what their plans are," she retorted back to him. Pulling her blanket up to her chin, she watched Hagen through half-lidded eyes.

With a sly smile, Hagen was well aware she knew more than what she was saying. "Ah, but you know something, don't you? I can tell. You never could lie. Your face always shows when you are lying. Spit it out or I make one call and you know what will happen."

"You are such a skizoid, Hagen. I hate you so much. You won't get away with this." She knew that she would have to give him something. *Please forgive me, Dr. Datrem.*

"Oh, I'm so much worse than that, little cousin. Now tell me what you know." He stood back with his arms crossed, waiting for her to speak.

She stood there, chewing on her bottom lip, worrying it until she could feel it start to tear slightly. Making her decision, she spoke quickly, "Fine. There are three humans on board the ship right now."

"What are they doing there?" he asked, getting impatient.

"There are two females and one male. I don't know what they're doing but I do know that one of them is the bondmate to Director Nox." She finished up in a hurry, hoping this would satisfy him.

Hagen stared at her, surprise covering his face. Without warning, he slapped his thigh, howling with laughter. "Oh, this is rich—a lowly human mating with the son of a high-ranking senator." *Oh, this is going to send his father into a rage. Now to see how to use this to my advantage.*

After a few moments where Violia just sat there glaring at him like he was a lunatic, Hagen started thinking out loud. "What's her name?"

Violia bit her lip again—the sting from the cut causing her to wince. She hesitated before finally saying, "Emeline Cameron."

"Do you have access to her?" Hagen demanded.

"She-she's coming into the medical bay tomorrow. They're not sure how the human body will handle being the bondmate to a Delician. They want to run some tests on her." She wanted to cry as she told him the information he wanted. Violia couldn't get over how life was just so unfair sometimes.

"Is she the one working with Director Nox?"

Violia threw her hands in the air, yelling at him, "How am I supposed to know that? I just told you—I'm a medic. They don't tell me anything."

"Don't take that tone with me. You're smart. I'm sure you hear things. You know a lot more than you're telling me. No matter. It's got to be her." Ignoring Violia's protests, Hagen mulled over what he should do. Tarquin didn't have the balls to take charge like he would. Deciding on a plan, he told his cousin to sit tight. He would be in touch in a few days when they got closer to their location.

Violia was horrified with Hagen's plan. He made it sound so easy, but then again it was easy...for him. She was the one who had to take all the risk while he sat back on his ass. And she told him just that. "I won't do it."

"Oh, but you will, little cousin. Unless you want our grandmother to be joining her dead family sooner than you'd like."

"You're vile, Hagen. Why are you doing this? What do you hope to gain?"

"That's none of your concern. You will do what you're told. I'm done talking."

The comm went dead in her hand...all her hopes and dreams fading into the darkness.

CHAPTER 12

Emeline's palms were clammy as her anxiety level rose —sweat formed under her clothing, adding to her discomfort. The thought of seeing Liam and Ami was enough to send her scurrying back to their room, thinking that maybe trying out the replicator would be a better idea. *This is stupid. It's my brother and my best friend. Why should I be nervous about seeing them? Okay, maybe the fact that I'm the bondmate to an alien and my skin now has colorful dots running up and down it. No problem. They'll be so happy—NOT!*

Taking her hand, Nox kissed her fingertips, trying to reassure her even though he wasn't sure himself how this evening was going to go. "It's going to be okay. If you want, I can talk to Liam and Ami—explain to them about the bondmating. How rare it is. I'm sure they'll be happy for us."

He hated seeing her so upset, especially when she looked so beautiful in the new outfit she had created. She had been so proud dancing out of the bathroom showing off her new skill at using the replicator. Her long blond hair swayed back and forth...the way it framed her lovely face made him want to find a dark corner and run his fingers through it—maybe take a little taste of her sweet lips.

"I'm not so sure about that." Giving him a hesitant smile, she pulled her hand from his. There was also the fact that she was about to meet the crew of the *Maelstrom*. Walking in draped all over Nox was not the first impression she was going for—particularly not before she got a chance to eat dinner. She might have been nervous about having to explain things to Liam and Ami, but it was Captain Jagger's meal she was really looking forward do.

She was excited when Nox told her Jagger was cooking

244

one of his special fish dishes in their honor, curious about how he was going to prepare his dish. It had been thrilling to learn that cooking was such an integral part of Delician culture. Just another item on her checklist of things their two cultures had in common. Food was a central part of human families and social get-togethers. Her own family could put together a delicious feast faster than you could say *we're coming over!* She loved that the art of cooking was a universal concept.

The corridor in front of them ended at a closed door. Nox waved his hand over the panel beside the door and it immediately opened revealing a scene right out a sci-fi movie.

Emeline's eyes swept the room, unease racing through her as she took in the scene—a room full of aliens who had all stopped midsentence to stare at the couple in the door-way.

Turning into Nox, she stopped him with her eyes telling him, *I don't know if I can do this.* She could feel multiple eyes fixated on them.

Wrapping his arm around her waist, Nox drew her forward until she rested against his chest, attempting to give her some modicum of comfort and reassurance. "It's okay," he whispered gently in her ear. "No one is going to hurt you."

"I know that." She leaned back, lightly swatting his chest, hoping he couldn't feel her racing heart. "I'm just a little nervous. For me, this—this isn't something you do every day—you know, having dinner with aliens on their spaceship." Emeline felt her cheeks redden, knowing she was babbling as she talked out of the side of her mouth hoping no one could hear her.

Remembering her mum's mantra, *Okay, Em—Breathe, Center, Focus.* Emeline could feel herself beginning to relax. Nox's hand rubbed along her spine, his gentle touch calming her nerves. "I got this." Turning around, she gave a tentative smile to the group of aliens watching her and Nox with rapt interest. "Hi everyone."

The Delicians in the room couldn't help but notice her nervousness. Ezio was the first to come forward to greet her. His hands hung loosely at his side; his sleeveless tunic allowed the iridescent coloring on his arms to shimmer softly in the light. He was slow in his approach...keeping his pace calm and easy. Stopping a few feet from her, he offered her his arm in greeting.

Stepping forward, Emeline took Ezio's arm, giving him a grateful smile as she returned the greeting. Maybe it was the fact that she had already met Ezio or maybe it was the feeling of the warm male against her back, but her nerves began to settle.

"I'm sorry. I don't know what's come over me." She looked up at Ezio, mouthing *"Thank you."*

Giving her a knowing smile, he released her arm, telling the rest of the room to back off and give her some space. They could meet her one at a time.

Nox guided her gently into the middle of the room, allowing her to get a better view of her surroundings. The room was unlike anything she had ever seen before, but seriously, what did she expect to find on an alien spaceship? It was warm and inviting—the smell of the food cooking was tantalizing.

Emeline's eyes widened as a small Delician woman came forward, a glass of clear liquid in her hand.

With a shy smile on her delicate face, she held out the glass to Emeline. "Hello. It's nice to finally meet you, Emeline. My name is Marsel. I'm the science officer here on the *Maelstrom*."

"H-hi." Emeline took the glass, looking at it carefully as she took a sip. *Water, huh. What did you think it was going to be, you idiot? Get a hold of yourself. Do you want them to think you're unstable?*

Drinking deeply, she could feel the coolness of the liquid

slide down her throat, calming her insides. "Tha-thank you. That's so much better."

Looking around the room, noticing everyone was trying their best not to stare, Emeline chuckled at their failed attempt. She couldn't blame them really. Especially considering she nearly fainted at the door. It had been a long few days for her and each day seemed to add another level of fantasy to her world. "I'm sorry. Please believe me—I'm normally not this crazed." She gave her a shy smile, hoping they would forgive her reaction to them.

Marsel reached down and squeezed her hand gently. "It's okay. Really. You've had a lot to take in recently. It's to be expected. Trust me when I tell you being around these big brutes as long as I have, it's enough to send anyone running from the room."

"Hey, who you calling brutes?" Ezio came over, gently rubbing the top of her head. The look of affection that passed between them overshadowed the obvious difference in their sizes. Clearly everyone had known each other for a long time.

Tarek came forward, his broad smile changing his normally stern-looking face into one of relaxed welcome. This was clearly a place where he could come and be himself. "Emeline, it's good to see you. I'm glad Nox brought you down to have dinner with us."

Emeline smiled back, glad to see another familiar face in a room full of new ones. It suddenly occurred to her that when she bonded with Nox, these people would become her people too. Looking around at each new face, she smiled, trying to commit each one to memory. Over the next few weeks, these were the people she was going to have to rely on if they were going to defeat the Hexians.

"Thank you, Tarek. Again, sorry for my reaction. I'm generally not this emotional, but as you can imagine, the last few days have been pretty surreal. Please forgive me."

"There is nothing to forgive, and I agree with you—finding out you're not alone in the universe would be a shock to anyone." Tarek knew she was overwhelmed, but even he could understand that without warning, her life had gone in a direction that no one could have foreseen.

"Well at least I didn't run screaming from the room, so that's a big plus." She squeezed Nox's hand that was still wrapped around her waist, giving him a grateful smile.

Looking around, she was blown away at what she saw, telling him, "Can I just say—this room is not at all what I had expected." Her cheeks reddening, she stumbled on, "In my wildest imagination, I would have never expected this on a military spaceship. It's wonderful in here."

Tarek tried not to beam, but he was pleased at her reaction. "Thank you, Emeline. And you're right, it is unusual. Most military ships in our fleet have a similar version but on a much smaller scale. There are times we carry members of our senatorial council and it's important that we have a space for socialization." Leaning in, he lowered his voice, adding, "Plus, this is my personal ship and I like to be comfortable—and I like to eat."

Emeline giggled at his words as she gave his body a quick once-over. Not an ounce of fat could be found anywhere—actually on any of the Delicians' bodies, and that included the females.

"You're in luck tonight. Jagger is making one of his famous dishes." Tarek looked over at the big Delician who was sharpening a large knife over what looked like some sort of exotic-looking fish. It was wide and at least three feet long with wet bluish green skin. Big enough to feed this hungry crew. It looked like a fish from Earth—if you overlooked the four eyes.

Jagger looked up from his task, giving her a quick smile. "Welcome, Emeline. It's nice to finally meet you. Liam and Ami have been talking about you constantly. I hope you're hungry." He winked at her as he lifted his arm and then lowered it swiftly—cleanly chopping the head off the fish.

She laughed, surprising him when she said, "Oh what, you thought I might faint. Sorry. My dad used to fish. I've gutted more fish than I can count." Her stomach chose that precise moment to make its presence known to everyone in the room. Holding her hand to her stomach, she knew they'd all heard it when everyone burst out laughing—the remaining tension that had been lingering in the air gone.

Emeline laughed with the rest of them, trying to remember the last time she'd eaten. *Oh yeah, when I made burgers for Nox and I. When was that?* It seemed like a lifetime ago but it was only this afternoon. "I'm starving." She gave Jagger a warm smile, adding, "It smells amazing in here. I still can't get over this kitchen setup."

The room itself was large, but when you considered the size of the Delician males, it wasn't surprising. The kitchen area was to the left of the door with an island large enough to seat eight people comfortably. It separated the cooking area from the rest of the room. Directly in front of her was a huge window that spanned the entire wall. A massively long table that sat at least 20 people was situated in front of it. To the right of the table tucked into a corner was a small intimate dining space for four. To the right of the door was a large seating area for lounging. This was a room that gave off a feeling of camaraderie and comfort. A room where you could sit down, put your feet up and enjoy spending time getting to know everyone. Emeline liked this room immensely and could see herself spending a great deal of time in here.

Nox gently guided her over to the island and started introducing her. Captain Jagger, who now that his fish was filleted, was crumbling some type of herb onto it. He had two helpers, one male and one female on either side of him chopping what she thought were fruits and vegetables whose shapes and colors were ones she had never seen before. The cook in her wanted to jump into the fray and get her hands dirty. The smell coming from the kitchen was so enticing, her mouth watered.

"This is Nicon, Jagger's first officer, and this is Zyanya, one of the intelligence officers on board."

"It's nice to meet you both." She smiled at them as they greeted her warmly.

Nox next introduced her to an older Delician male who was sipping from a glass filled with something similar to beer. "Dr. Datrem, this is my bondmate, Emeline."

"Hello, Emeline. I've been looking forward to meeting you." The doctor took her hand in his large wide palm. It was warm and strangely comforting as he gave her a gentle squeeze. He was slightly taller than Nox, with a leaner build, and the purple streaks in his hair were darker than anyone else's in the room. She reminded herself to ask Nox about that later on when they were alone.

"It's nice to meet you too, Doctor." Emeline's smile was coming easier now that she was feeling more at ease. "Nox told me that we would be coming in to see you in the morning to talk about our bondmating. I have to warn you, I know nothing about any of this. I'm going to be asking lots of questions." She grinned from Nox to the doctor.

Chuckling warmly, he countered, "I bet you do. I'll confess—I have quite a few myself. It's been a long time since I've met anyone who has found their bondmate and I've never heard of a bondmating amongst another species." Patting her hand reassuringly, he added, "I'm sure we will find the answers you are looking for. It is my honor to be able to work with you and Nox." Looking at Nox, he squeezed his shoulder, "Congratulations, Nox. I'm thrilled for you. Your mother would have been pleased."

Nox's family had known Dr. Datrem for years. His mother, Elara, had been very fond of the doctor. She had told Nox how sad it was that the doctor's wife had died giving birth to their second child. The child, a boy, had lived but ironically his own wife had died in childbirth, leaving him with two children to raise on his own as his father had.

"Have you told your father your good news?" Datrem asked Nox, a look of concern shadowing his face because he knew Nox's father. Everyone on Delicia knew that Sandovar had plans for his son's future and this development wasn't going to go over well with certain people in the Delician government, especially his father.

"Not yet. We haven't told many people, including Emeline's brother and her friend. I would"—he looked down at his beautiful bondmate— "we would appreciate it if you wouldn't mention it to them when they come in until we have a chance to tell them ourselves." Nox looked around the room at each face, pleased when everyone nodded in agreement.

"Thank you so much," Emeline added. "I would like to tell my brother on my—" She was interrupted as the door opened and Liam and Ami came bursting into the room, followed by a massive Delician dressed in a military uniform.

"Emeline!" They both came running over and all three tried to squeeze the life out of each other, which must have looked quite comical to the Delicians in the room.

Liam was the first to ask, "How are you?" Not giving her a chance to speak, he continued on, "How did you like that shuttle ride? Wasn't it awesome?" Excitement was clearly plastered all over his face. He looked to be having the time of his life.

Before she could even answer, Ami had her pulled into a bear hug, showing her how much she had missed her. "So how did you like the ride up from Earth? A lot easier than being strapped to a fiery rocket, isn't it?" Seeing Emeline cringe, she nudged her teasingly, "Oh that's right, you never had to do it that way, did you? You big wussy girl. You let me be the one to risk getting their ass blown out of the sky." She was kidding of course. She loved to watch Emeline's face go from red to white to red again every time she kidded her about her fear of Earth's current space travel methods.

Behind them, Nyx pushed through to where Nox was watching the humans. He slapped him on the back, crying out boisterously, "Congratulations, Nox. I see you've found your bondmate. You are one lucky male. She's beautiful." He turned to Emeline and nodded his head in respect as he introduced himself. He went on to tell her how happy he was for them that they had found each other. He continued on, telling her that he had been piloting Liam and Ami in the shuttle as they retrofitted the satellites...all the while totally unaware of the silence that had descended upon the room.

The Delicians stood rooted where they were—waiting for what seemed like an eternity for the explosion that was about to happen. Emeline watched Nyx's mouth moving but she didn't hear any of his words. She was too intent on watching Liam and Ami trying to comprehend what Nyx was saying. The expressions on their faces turned from happy to see her to one of confusion and then outrage. It was hard to say who spoke first or maybe it was all three at once. Emeline trying to explain, while Liam and Ami wanted to know what the hell was going on. Nox had at this point pushed Emeline behind him, acting as a barrier between the three humans.

It was Tarek's voice that silenced the three of them as he stepped over, his hand gesturing to the seating area. "Why don't we sit down and have a drink while Jagger finishes preparing dinner." Having spent years defusing worse situations, he said sternly, "I think we have a lot to talk about and yelling at each other will prove futile.

Giving Nyx a hard stare, he told him, "Why don't you go and see if you can help Jagger." It was hard to blame Nyx for his reaction to the situation. Everyone was excited about one of their own finding a bondmate. It was obvious Nyx was thrilled for them and didn't stop to think about his actions.

Nyx nodded apologetically to the General. Turning back

to Nox and Emeline and then to Liam and Ami, he said, "Please forgive me. I didn't mean to overstep. I was just so happy for you." Turning, he headed over to the kitchen… along the way getting nudged by his crewmembers, all of them feeling the same way he did. A bondmate was to be celebrated and they hoped that the humans would come to embrace this unique situation.

Nox took ahold of Emeline's arm just as Liam tried to pull his sister away from Nox…his face flushed with fury. "Get your hands off my sister." His voice rose as he tried to pull Emeline towards him.

Emeline planted her feet and pulled her arm away from her brother. His face showed confusion and then hurt that she didn't automatically side with him. "Wait, Liam. We can explain." Her voice took on an edge of pleading but still remained firm. She was aware this whole *bondmating* was going to be hard for them to understand. *Hell, it's hard for me sometimes and I'm the one living it!* "Can we please sit down and talk? I promise we'll explain the whole situation to you if you'll just give us a chance." She looked from Liam to Ami, hoping they would trust her.

Throwing his hands up in the air, Liam growled out, "Fine, I'll listen, but I'm not happy about this, Emeline." Emeline gulped at his dad voice.

Ami, in the meantime, stood apart, studying her friend. Finally letting out the breath she had been holding, she sat down in one of the chairs. The look on her face as she stared from Nox to Emeline belied the anger that was simmering just below the surface. Sitting back with arms crossed, she gave Emeline a pointed look saying, "This better be good, girlfriend."

Taking Nox's hand, she led him to the corner of the couch. Sitting down, she leaned her back against his front…soaking in his warmth and support. She understood their feelings—the whole situation was surreal. She only hoped she could get them to understand what was happening between her and Nox—that Nox was her future.

Looking over, Emeline watched Ami's eyes widen as she stared intently at her face. *The colors! Crap, I forgot. Oh great, now Liam's noticed.*

"What the fuck is happening to your face, Em?" He couldn't seem to move his eyes away, following the colors as they slowly rippled just under her skin.

Touching her face, trying to get it to stop, knowing full well that wasn't happening anytime soon. And even then, who knew what the colors would do afterwards. Hopefully, they would get some answers when they saw the doctor tomorrow, who by the way was watching their exchange intently, as were all the Delicians.

"Nox and I are bondmates." Holding up her hand to stop their questions, she said, "Please, let me explain what happened."

Nox interrupted her at this point and asked if he could tell them from his perspective first. When she nodded in agreement, he began by explaining about Delician bondmates and what a rare and wondrous blessing it was. He explained how he felt the first time he saw Emeline, shocked that he had found his bondmate on Earth. He concluded his story by telling them that Emeline wanted to wait until the threat to Earth was over before completing the bond.

The whole time he was talking, Emeline was watching his face. The joy and love she had for him sparkled in her eyes—a fact that wasn't lost on Liam and Ami.

Liam was the first to find his voice after listening to Nox. Clearing his throat, he said, "Em, how do you feel about all of this?"

"I'm not going to lie, at first I didn't know what was happening to me. I thought I was losing it, but once we talked about it and the more time I've spent with Nox, the more these feelings seemed to take on a life of their own."

Ami jumped up and pointed her finger at Nox, giving

him an accusing look. "Did you do something to her?" Then to Emeline, "Did he drug you?" Glaring accusingly at Nox, she looked intently at her friend, "Has he hurt you?"

"No!" That was yelled not only by Emeline and Nox but also came from multiple voices throughout the room, causing Ami to stop midsentence.

Pulling Ami down onto the couch beside him, forcing her to focus on him, Liam shushed her, saying, "Nox would never hurt Emeline."

Ami gave Nox a dubious look—her two fingers pointing from her eyes back to his. "I'm watching you."

Emeline had lost patience at this point, growling to the both of them, "That's enough. Cut it out, Ami. No one drugged anyone. What's the matter with you?"

Ami at least had the decency to look ashamed, muttering *"sorry"* while Liam sat stone-faced, not knowing how to feel.

"Dinner is ready." Jagger's call to dinner came none too soon.

Taking Liam and Ami both by the arms, Emeline led them to the table, telling them, "Jagger has made a special dinner tonight."

Stopping just shy of the table, she told them softly that everyone had worked hard preparing this dinner and she was looking forward to her first taste of Delician food. She promised they would finish their discussion afterwards— in private.

Ami nodded, sliding into a chair next to Nyx. They nudged each other, trading a few snide jokes, lightening the mood of the room. It was obvious a camaraderie had developed between the humans and aliens.

The enormous table gave everyone a panoramic view of the stars in their solar system. It was breathtaking, but so were the large platters heaped with food that were being carried over and placed on the table. The smell from the different dishes permeated the air with mouth-watering aromas. Delicians did love to eat, and since they were big, it took a sizable amount of food to satisfy their enormous appetites. It also took a lot of training to keep their bodies fit and strong and fueling their bodies with proper nutrition was a major priority to them.

Emeline slid into the chair that Nox had pulled out for her. She noted the look that Liam gave them both as Nox took the one next to hers.

Liam took the chair on her other side, still studying Nox. Turning to Emeline, he saw the look of uncertainty in her eyes...a look he knew he had put there. He gently rubbed his knuckle softly down his sister's cheek—a habit he started the first time he laid eyes on her as a baby.

Emeline knew Liam wanted to say something, but she shook her head at him, mouthing "*later.*"

Nodding, Liam placed his napkin in his lap as he continued watching the two of them out of the corner of his eye. He felt Marsel nudge his hand, motioning to the platter of food she held out to him, a look of sympathy on her face. Smiling down, he thanked her and put some of the food on his plate before passing it to Emeline.

Emeline was trying to reassure Nox that she was fine, although she knew he didn't believe her, especially when he whispered softly so that only she could hear, "I know what you're feeling, remember."

Rubbing his thigh lightly, she smiled up at him as he placed his hand over hers, giving it a gentle squeeze. She whispered back, "I'm fine—really. Let's just eat dinner and then we'll go somewhere and talk."

Both of them were totally unaware that all eyes were fixated on them, fascinated at seeing newly found bondmates interact.

It was Jagger's question that had Emeline looking away from Nox, embarrassed when she asked him to repeat it.

"I asked how you liked the fish," he asked again, laughing slightly at how flushed her face became.

Taking her first bite, her face transformed as the delicate flavors melted on her tongue. The combination of the herbs with the creamy texture of the fish sent her taste buds into overdrive as the exotic flavors flooded her mouth. "Wow! This is delicious. I mean the combination of flavors is so unique. You have to teach me this dish." Emeline loved good food and Jagger's fish was right up there with one of the best things she'd ever tasted.

"I don't know," he said, rubbing his chin as he thought for a moment. "I'll make a deal with you."

Looking at him warily, Emeline nodded for him to continue, only too glad the topic wasn't about her and Nox.

"I'll teach you this dish if you teach me how to make your chili. Ami said you make the best chili she's ever tasted. That's something I'd like to learn how to make."

Laughing, Emeline agreed, saying, "It's a deal. I love sharing and learning new recipes. One night I'll make you one of my favorite fish dishes. It's from England—fish and chips—delicious!"

"Tomorrow night then—we make some chili," Jagger told her as all his fellow crewmembers enthusiastically agreed.

The rest of the dinner continued with the humans enjoying all the different dishes. It was Tarek who suggested they end the night early so that Emeline could talk to Liam and Ami. It had been a long day for everyone and they still had a lot to do in preparation for the Hexians.

Thanking everyone for a wonderful meal and promising to meet tomorrow for a cooking lesson, Emeline followed Nox as he led them up to the observation lounge so that they could have a private discussion.

As she walked through the ship, Emeline mulled over what she wanted to say to her brother and Ami. They already knew the basics. What they wanted to know were the details and that would be tougher to put into words. She knew they were bewildered as to how she could be attracted to a tall, iridescent alien she'd only known for a few days. *Valid point.* She'd asked that same question in the beginning, but the more time she'd spent with Nox, the stronger their bond became. She was confident she could trust him with her heart. Now all she had to do was convince Liam and Ami that her feelings were true. *And I'm not suffering the effects from reading too many of Lorelei's books. Although come on—so far, all the Delicians I've met are exceptional to look at.*

Rolling her eyes, scolding herself to focus, she mentally ran through the list of pros and cons Liam would give her as to why she shouldn't just finish the mission and head home to Boston, picking up her life where she had left off. That was no longer an option for her.

Ami, on the other hand, was harder to read. She had gotten unusually upset at the thought of Emeline getting hurt. Glancing at Ami who walked in front of her, Emeline noticed she appeared reticent—thoughtful even... watching and observing. *I really shouldn't be surprised. Ami is processing this situation the way any scientist worth her salt would [laugh]—nice pun. Be serious, Em. If you want to move forward with Nox, you need Liam and Ami on your side.*

Then again, considering what Liam had been doing the last few days and the look on his face when he came in right before Nyx shot his mouth off, maybe he wouldn't be so opposed to taking a trip to Delicia. She'd never seen Liam that excited—well, okay, maybe the first time he flew an F-16 fighter jet. She swore he had grinned for a month straight. Would they understand the feelings she had inside of her? Did she even understand? Walking beside Nox, so deep in thought, she didn't notice they had reached their destination until Nox stopped and waved his hand over a panel in the side of the wall. A door opened into a room that took her breath away.

When Nox had said "observation lounge," he wasn't kidding. They were drawn, mesmerized, to the floor-to-ceiling windows that surrounded the room with its glass ceiling giving them a 360-degree view of space. They gazed out at the Milky Way in all its glory spread out before them. The humans couldn't help but to slowly turn, taking in the incredible view of swirling cosmic clouds interspersed with brightly colored lights that winked hello to them. The profoundness of this moment caused each of them to re-evaluate their thoughts and feelings.

Liam was the first to break the silence as he stood spellbound at a view that should have been impossible for anyone from Earth to see. "I would have preferred having this discussion in private, but it looks like—" He motioned towards Nox. "...isn't inclined to let that happen. Am I right, Director Nox?" Liam's tight voice might have come out quiet and steady, but inside he was a muddled mess.

How did this happen? I'm the big brother. It's my responsibility to keep her safe and instead I left her in the hands of an alien. I put her in this situation and now I don't know if I'll be able to save her or, more importantly, if she even wants to be saved. Judging by the way she's looking at him, holding his hand, caressing his face, that would be a solid no. Should I be an asshole and insist she walk away, or am I a selfish bastard because a part of me wants to spend more time with the Delicians? Mum and Belle are going to kill me.

Emeline leaned up and kissed Nox lightly on his lips, the taste of wine and sweetness giving her some courage as she walked over, her hands clasped together in front of her as she stood next to Liam. Standing side by side, the magnificence of her surroundings called to her soul. Reaching over, she hooked his pinky finger in hers, pulling slightly, just letting him know she was there.

That one little gesture reminded Liam she was still his little sister. "I'm sorry I yelled," Liam told her quietly, still not able to move his eyes away from a sight he knew he would never get tired of looking at.

"I'm sorry I didn't call you right away and tell you what was happening," she replied, giving him her best apology look.

With a sigh, Liam turned, his eyes roaming up and down her body. He was always a sucker for his baby sister, but she wasn't a baby anymore. What he saw now gave him pause —she was different. Yes, the roving dots took a little getting used to, but it wasn't only that. It was the way she held herself. Her demeanor was calmer, more assured. Granted, she was agitated because he and Ami were upset, but that was on the surface. Underneath he saw she was settled... dare he say content. His little sister was usually anything but content. She was always searching for her place in life, first as the youngest child with two older, overbearing siblings, and then in her career where she had to fight for every opportunity. Even when she started her company, she still had to prove to the science world that her theories were sound—but she'd done it. Although, if he was honest with himself, even through all her success, she was never satisfied in her personal life.

Now when he looked at her, that restlessness was gone. Begrudgingly, Liam conceded that if Nox could do that for her, then he couldn't be all bad. Granted, he thought a little too gleefully, he was looking forward to getting Nox in the training room. Not to inflict injury, mind you, although a little bloodletting would go a long way to making him feel better. Maybe just enough to get his point across that if Emeline got hurt in any way, he would be showing Nox just how a big brother took care of anyone who hurt his family.

"What are you looking at?" Emeline was looking at him with confusion in her eyes.

"You."

"I know, I know. The colors, right?" They both watched a series of dots slide fluidly across the top of her hand.

"It's more than that." He ran his fingers through his hair. "Can we sit down and talk? Honestly, I'm exhausted."

Agreeing, she grabbed his hand, pulling them both over to sit on the long couch where Ami and Nox were sitting on opposite ends from each other. Looking over at Nox, she gave him a slight smile, letting him know she was fine. She kept forgetting he could sense how she was feeling as he returned her look with a knowing smile.

Sitting down, they faced each other. Liam couldn't take his eyes away from following one particular color as it slowly snaked its way across Emeline's face...disappearing beneath her hairline. Cupping her cheek, worried, he asked, "Does it hurt?"

"What hurt?"

Hesitantly, he touched her hand.

"No, not at all," she said, shaking her head softly.

Cradling her palm in his, it was impossible to miss the color contrast between their hands. His deep tan contrasted sharply against her paleness.

"Man, Em—you got yourself in a mess this time, didn't you? I don't even know what to say about all this."

Emeline pulled her hand away and stood up facing her brother. Liam knew that look—his little sister was about to lose her shit at him. That usually led to an overly heated discussion that would get them nowhere.

Putting his hands up, he gave her a crooked smile, immediately defusing her anger. "Okay, okay. Come on, sit down. I heard Nox's side of things. Now I want to hear your side. I promise I'll listen to anything you want to tell me. You know I love you, baby sister."

"I love you too, big bro." She did, unconditionally, but on this, she wasn't budging. She needed him to really listen to what she had to say.

Emeline locked eyes momentarily with Nox. He could see she was relieved that they were finally ready to listen. Turning back to Liam and Ami, Emeline stood tall, a confident smile plastered over her shaking nerves. Clearing her throat lightly, she started, "Thank you—both of you. Okay, so to start, you were there when we first met. You got to witness my shabby performance as an enlightened scientist first hand. Yeah, I know I was a wreck." Emeline was floundering. *Ugh! Why is this so hard?* Looking at Nox helplessly, he gave her an encouraging smile just like Hank used to give Fiona when she needed encouragement.

That smile—that's it. All at once, it came to her just how to explain her feelings about Nox to them.

Determination showing on her face, Emeline leaned in, asking them both, "Do you remember how Mum and Dad would always tell us that when they met, they just knew they were meant to be together? That there was never any question, no doubts. They knew from the first moment their eyes locked, this was the person they were meant to spend their life with."

When she saw Ami and Liam nod their heads in agreement, she knew she had them. "I felt that with Nox." Glancing lovingly at Nox, the words flowed like a long-winding stream from her soul. "I know what you're going to say and it's nothing I haven't already thought about myself at least a thousand times. Trust me—I've analyzed this to death. But I kept coming up with the same conclusion. He makes me feel complete...that I've found what I didn't even know I was searching for. Do you remember Mum telling us you never knew when the love of your life would come charging in changing your life forever? She said finding dad was the best thing that had ever happened to her. That's how I feel."

She flopped down between them on the couch, her head leaning back as her eyes focused on the majestic view above her. Pressing her lips together for a moment, she spoke not only to them but to herself, "I don't know what's going to happen next. Hell, I don't know what's going to happen tomorrow. I can't make any big decisions until we save Earth. God"—she laughed— "sound melodramatic much."

They laughed knowingly but let her finish. "One thing you've got to understand, I can't, no, I won't ever leave him. Just the thought of not having Nox in my life makes me physically sick."

At that statement, Ami found her voice, "Are you sure he didn't drug you or do some kind of alien mojo on you?" She was giving Nox a death glare as she spoke.

Emeline lightly slapped Ami's arm, scoffing at her overly concerned friend. "Cut it out. Geez, Ames. Let it go, will yah? Honestly, I'm not sure why the fates would choose me for his bondmate. I mean, think about it, if the Hexians hadn't been trying to come to Earth to steal our salt, then we never would have met. He never would have found his bondmate." Looking at Nox, her eyes filled, her voice came out with a slight hitch to it, "That's too sad for me to even think about."

Nox jerked forward, but she gave him a silent hand motion asking him to wait. She knew he wanted to comfort her, but she needed to do this. Needed to make them understand what was happening to them was a good thing. Even though Emeline knew that Nox was her bondmate, Liam and Ami were her family and regardless of what happened in the future, her family would always be a part of her life and Nox knew this.

Liam leaned over and pulled her into his arms, hugging her tightly...years of memories running through his mind. *Emeline, our sweet beautiful baby girl.* She was shy and quiet...kind and one of the most empathetic people he'd ever met. She was beautiful inside and out but totally unaware of her own beauty. He often wondered what she saw when she looked in the mirror. Did she see the way her eyes sparkled when she talked about their dad? Did she see the look of genuine interest on her face when she was talking to fledgling scientists or reading stories to her younger cousins?

Looking deep into her eyes, he saw the depth of her feelings for Nox. She was happy. For the first time since their dad had died, that shadow that had been hiding just behind her eyes was gone...replaced with that spark that had been missing. "Oh, Em, I love you so much. If this is what truly makes you happy, whatever you need, I'm there for you." Liam meant every word he said. He would do whatever was necessary to ensure that look always stayed on her face. "I'll even come with you to talk to Mum and Belle."

Tears welled in Emeline's eyes. She had been trying to hold them back, but it meant the world to her having Liam's support. Laughingly wiping her eyes, she hugged him back, kissing both his cheeks.

Blinking back his emotions, Liam smiled, telling her he would always be on her side. He wished them both happiness but gave Nox the big brother look...that one that said, *mess with my sister and you mess with me.*

Nox got the message, delivering one of his own—*she's mine.*

"So, what happens now? Have you made any plans for the future?" Liam asked.

Emeline got up to go sit with Nox. She snuggled back into his embrace, her body finally relaxing. All the tension of the last few hours thankfully faded away, replaced by feelings of comfort but also ones of want...need. His hot body sent shivers of desire through her.

Tamping down her feelings, she told them, "Once we complete the bond, we're not sure what will happen. We're meeting with Dr. Datrem tomorrow to run some tests. Did you know there have never been interspecies bondmates outside of the Delician culture before? I guess we'll be learning together."

Nox finally spoke, saying, "As I told you, finding your bondmate has been rare over the last many decades." A look of happiness spread across his face as he ran his hand down Emeline's arm. "This is new territory for all of us. Delicians had all but given up on finding their bondmates. That's why it's become common to enter into arranged marriages."

When a look of horror appeared on Liam's and Ami's faces, he explained how over the years it had become normal, especially with their population dipping to such low levels. When Ami asked Nox about his own feelings on this type of arrangement, Nox related his own parents' story to them. He ended his sad tale by telling them about his father's marriage demand for him. Nox was adamant he would never agree to an arranged marriage. He had been determined to find his bondmate, and finding Emeline was a dream come true for him.

"And what is your father going to say about your bond with my sister?" Liam asked him, a seed of doubt about the whole bondmate concept crossing his mind. "If the concept of finding a bondmate with another species is so new, how do you think your people will react to yours and Emeline's bond?"

"Those are valid questions, Liam, but the bond cannot be denied. I'm not sure what they'll say. Honestly, I don't really care."

"Of course, being the bondmate of a lowly human wouldn't be acceptable, is that what you're saying?" Ami's lingering hurt over being thought of as inferior was evident.

Sighing, Nox gave Ami a sympathetic look as he rubbed his hands up and down Emeline's arms. He knew she was still feeling the sting of the initial opinion of humans. "I'm sorry, Ami. I know this has been hard on all of you and unfortunately, it's going to take a while for opinions to change. Having said that, most Delicians will be happy that I've found my bondmate. It will be celebrated and blessed, but more importantly it will bring hope to my people.

As far as how the humans will be received throughout the universe—only time will tell. Remember, most of the universe has never even heard of Earth. A lot will depend on how first contact is handled between your governments and the UAP. Once the threat from Hexia is over, some hard decisions will have to be made. On how I feel personally —" He looked down at Emeline, his eyes shining with love and admiration. "Even in the short time I've spent working with Emeline, humans are my new favorite species. And judging from the reports I've been hearing from Nyx, humans are not to be underestimated."

Ami and Liam looked at it each other, somewhat mollified at Nox's words.

"As to your question about my father, he will have no choice but to abandon his plans. Emeline is my bondmate, my life. If we are not accepted on Delicia, we will find a way to be together on Earth."

"You mean you'd give up your life on Delicia, all your technology and even your own father in order to be with Emeline?" Ami asked, a note of disbelief in her voice.

"No question. She is the other half of me...of course I would give up everything to be with her."

Holding up his hand to stop Ami's question, Nox spoke softly but with conviction, "It's not a question of denying or accepting a bondmate. The question is why would you want to? To give up being connected to the one person who will love you and support you no matter what, I know of no one who would do that. Nothing destroys the bond—ever. My mother was a firm believer in it and I wanted to honor her memory by waiting until I'd found mine and somehow, I've been blessed with Emeline." He nuzzled Emeline's neck. His body was on fire as the bond seemed to vibrate between them. It was nearly impossible to explain these feelings of wholeness to someone who had never experienced it before.

Fatigue was beginning to show on Emeline's face. It seemed like a lifetime ago that she had woken up on the couch in her loft. Yawning, she asked if they could finish their discussion tomorrow. "We've had a full day and I know you and Ami must be as tired as I am."

Liam agreed as he stood up, engulfing her in a hug and kissed her cheek. "Ami and I still have to finish retrofitting the rest of the satellites. How is the interface coming along?"

"We have a basic understanding of the concept now, so the implementation shouldn't take that long." Holding up her wrist, Emeline showed them her new wrist comm. "Now that I have ARI at my fingertips, it should be smooth sailing."

After some oohing and ahhing, they decided to meet up the next day in the training room before dinner.

Entering their room, Emeline was happy this day was finally over. Exhausted, she barely remembered getting into her nightgown. Before she knew it, she was nestled back against a very hot alien body. Her last thought before sleep overtook her was what a waste of time sleep was.

CHAPTER 13

Was it possible to be warm and hot at the same time, Emeline mused as a strong hand massaged her foot? Electric shocks vibrated up her leg, causing her core muscles to clench in a vain attempt to soothe the ache that brought her out of the sweet dream she was having. You know that ache, the one that sends you reaching for relief—relief that only a hot sexy man, or in her case, an alien, could satisfy. She felt his fingers continue their journey, leaving a path of need in their wake...only to be stopped by the beeping of his wrist comm informing them Dr. Datrem was expecting them in medical.

As he attempted to move his hand, a firm grip held him in place as Emeline gave him a look indicating that he would lose said hand if he didn't finish what he had started. Not wanting to upset his beautiful bondmate, he complied with her silent request. Dr. Datrem and his tests could wait a little while longer.

Walking into medical, Emeline's cheeks were still flushed from Nox's little wakeup call this morning. Dressed in her usual work outfit of jeans, T-shirt and a jacket, Emeline had been looking forward to visiting the medical bay in hopes of getting information on the bonding process.

Turning when he saw them walk in, Dr. Datrem came over, extending his arm in greeting. "Emeline, Nox, it's good to see you this morning."

"Good morning, Doctor Datrem." Emeline was hoping that her cheeks were starting to return to their normal color. *Who am I kidding? Ever since I've been around Nox, my face has been permanently red.*

"Come in. Let me introduce you to my team. This is Dr. Senta." He pointed to an older female. Her brown hair streaked with dark purple highlights was pulled back into a tight knot at the nape of her neck.

"It's nice to meet you, Dr. Senta," Emeline said, giving her a bright smile.

"And these are our medics, Violia and Tulio," Dr. Datrem introduced the two remaining Delicians in the room, one male and one female. The male, Tulio, was young, with lilac-colored highlights in his short-cropped hair. Serious forest green eyes with hints of amber looked at her with interest. He came forward to greet her.

The female medic, Violia, appeared to hold herself back. Her long brown hair had slightly darker lavender highlights and was pulled back into a ponytail. Her dark green eyes were hooded as she murmured her greetings to both Nox and Emeline...not offering her arm.

Dr. Datrem gave her a strange look as if wondering why she wasn't being friendlier to Nox and his bondmate.

Emeline gave them both a wide smile, although she was a little taken aback at the female medic's reaction to her. She couldn't help but wonder if it was because she was a human. Shrugging her shoulders, she dismissed her reaction as she turned to check out the medical facilities. As a scientist, the type of technology she had been introduced to since meeting the Delicians was beyond belief. She was especially interested in the regen units she'd heard so much about.

Giving them a tour of the lab, Dr. Datrem showed Emeline the regen beds, explaining how they used synthetic crystals that the Delicians had developed. The crystals fueled the nanites that healed most diseases and wounds on the cellular level, all but eliminating the need for surgery and most drug therapies.

Amazed, Emeline moved from one piece of equipment to another as Dr. Datrem continued demonstrating their uses.

Taking her over to one of the three medical beds in the

room, the doctor asked if she was ready for her examination.

"Sure." Emeline knew she probably should have been nervous about being scanned by alien technology, but her inner geekiness was coming through right now.

Asking her to lie back and relax, Dr. Datrem instructed Violia to start the scanning process. He smiled at Nox indulgently as he told him he needed to let go of his bondmate's hand so they could start the scan.

Reluctantly, Nox released her hand and then, stepping back, gave Emeline a reassuring look.

As she lay on the bed, Emeline figured the surface would be cold and hard—it wasn't. The table melded around her, infusing warmth into her body. Looking up at the doctor, her expression made him laugh as she relaxed onto the table, calming her mind as a beam of light appeared from a round box that was attached to the ceiling. It started at her head, scanning downward as a projection of her body appeared to hover in the center of the room. Her breath caught in her throat as she watched her heart pump blood through the veins of her body. The hologram unit in her lab was primitive compared to what she was looking at here. The quality and detail far surpassed anything she had ever seen before. *I am definitely going to be using this in my work!*

The details of her brain were especially interesting. She wanted to see a comparison between the human and Delician brain scans, curious at their differences especially considering she and Nox might have children one day.

Since she was the first human female to be scanned, everyone in the room was focused on the three-dimensional depiction of her body. Drs. Datrem and Senta moved in a circular path around the scan as they studied Emeline's body, pointing out what Emeline thought were the differences and similarities between the Delicians and humans.

Dr. Senta asked ARI to expand the detail on the reproductive area...the hologram highlighting and expanding the lower region of her body.

Emeline wasn't sure if she liked everyone examining that part of her body in such minute detail but as a scientist, she could understand why they would be so curious. She was equally as curious.

Dr. Senta moved slowly around the hologram, evaluating, measuring—murmuring "just fascinating" more than once. Pointing to Emeline's reproductive organs, she was surprised that humans had two ovaries whereas Delician females only had one. Dr. Senta continued her examination, speaking aloud so everyone could hear. "This must be why humans can have multiple births. Notice here"— she pointed to the pelvic area of the hologram—"the difference in the bone density especially around the pelvis. I wonder if that contributes to the fact that humans can carry multiple children at once."

Dr. Senta continued talking to Violia and Tulio as Dr. Datrem told Emeline she could sit up as he picked up an instrument that looked similar to a penlight. It was about six inches long with three raised rings around its length. The Doctor called it a data retrieval injector. He handed it to her so she could examine it as he gave her an explanation on how it worked.

Emeline listened intently to the doctor while she examined the *injector*. It felt cool to her touch and as she looked closer, it had writing on it that she couldn't decipher.

Taking it from her hand, he told her that the top ring was for injecting, the middle ring was for taking samples of biologics and the third one was for a mobile ARI for use out in the field. Pushing upward on the bottom of the device revealed a small compartment where vials could be inserted for collection or injecting substances.

Seeing the doctor and Nox share a look, Emeline got the impression they had something to tell her. Not sure what to think she asked, "Okay what's going on?"

"Emeline, the doctor has a translator chip that can be

injected into your bloodstream that will allow you to communicate with all species in the UAP. Is this something that appeals to you?" Nox asked cautiously, not sure what her thoughts were on injecting alien technology into her body.

After taking a moment to consider his words, she grinned up at him, "You know I have some questions, right." She loved how his face softened when he looked at her.

Nox caressed her cheek, chuckling, "Of course you do. I would expect nothing less. Ask me what you want, beautiful." He couldn't help himself from touching her. He loved the fact that she was so inquisitive, always trying to look at problems from all sides.

"Okay, how does this translator work?"

"The translator chip is injected into your bloodstream. It will flow through your body and lodge into the lingual section of your brain," he told her.

"Do you have one?"

"Yes. I work for the UAP and I must interact with many different species whenever I'm at their central headquarters. And because of my father's position within the government, my mother and I were given one a long time ago."

Coming over with the injector in his hand, the doctor told her, "All Delicians are injected with one when they enter the military. Since you are the first human to receive one, we're not quite sure how this will affect you. After looking over your scans, they show that our brain functions are similar. We're not anticipating any issues. Once we inject the chip, we will watch you closely for any adverse reactions. If we see any problems beginning to arise, it can be removed immediately."

Considering her options and doing her mental checklist of pros and cons, she nodded in agreement and after removing her jacket, extended her arm. The doctor, after placing a small capsule into the chamber, placed his instrument against the inside of her arm and pressed the first ring. Emeline had expected to feel a pinch, but all she felt was the coolness of the rounded tip against her skin and then a moment of minor discomfort.

Looking from Nox to the doctor, she waited for some sign, anything that would indicate that the translator chip had inserted itself properly. She felt fine, nothing out of the ordinary until a quick sharp pain caused her to grab the back of her head as she sucked a breath. As quick as the pain came, it was gone, leaving Emeline feeling slightly woozy. "I'm just gonna to shut my eyes for a minute," she slurred before pitching forward.

Nox grabbed Emeline before she could fall off the bed and laid her gently back.

Taking his hand scanner, the doctor quickly ran it over her body. Seeing that the chip had embedded in the correct location, he determined that it was probably sensory overload from the implantation. Checking her vitals, Dr. Datrem told Nox that Emeline was in perfect health and that she also had healthy reproductive organs. Telling Nox he'd like to run some more tests on her, but from what he was seeing so far, he didn't foresee any problems with them having multiple births.

At that, Nox asked Dr. Datrem to wait for any further analysis on Emeline until she woke up. He would not allow anything to be done to her unless she was fully informed and even then, the final decision was hers to make. He knew Emeline enough to know that unless it was an emergency, she would want to make her own choices when it came to her body. He felt the same way.

Emeline laid there, her eyes shut, by all appearances she looked asleep, but she wasn't—she was listening. Listening to the doctor tell Nox she was fertile. *Great. Thank you very much. So what, now I'm a broodmare?* But when she heard Nox tell the doctor to stop and wait for Emeline to awaken before he said anymore, her heart melted. If she hadn't already been falling in love with this big handsome iridescent alien, well that pushed her right over the edge. Here was this alien, so different from her, Emeline thought, and yet he understood her, not just on the surface, but what was most important to her deep down...her core values that made her who she was.

Through her barely raised lashes she watched Nox and the doctor talking to one side while on the other side the two medics and Dr. Senta were still studying her holographic projection. Watching the female medic, Violia, who kept stealing glances at her, Emeline saw a look of worry wrinkling the otherwise flawless skin between her eyes. She was a beautiful woman, Emeline thought to herself, but she acted standoffish towards her—almost as if she was distressed about being in her presence. *I wonder if she is upset about me being Nox's bondmate.*

Nox had stopped talking to the doctor and came to sit on the side of her bed. Taking her hand in his hand, he gently called her name while he stroked the side of her face lightly with his other hand.

Opening her eyes, she saw relief spread across his worried face. *God, how did I get so lucky?* Giving him a radiant smile, she pulled him down for a kiss, not caring who was there. He was hers and she didn't care who knew.

"Thank you," she whispered to him as she gently caressed his lips with hers.

"For what?" he whispered back, enjoying the attention of her sweet mouth.

"For sticking up for me with Dr. Datrem," she said, nuzzling his cheek with her nose.

He kissed her cheek and pulled her up against him. "You heard that, huh. I will always *stick up* for you." He spoke softly, gazing deeply into her eyes so she could see he was sincere.

"It's just hard for me to trust. In the past the only people I could count on were my family and my girls. This is all new to me—you know, having someone who puts me first before their own needs. Just so you know—I'm here for you too." She hugged him around the waist, her head resting on his chest...feeling his heart beating in time with her own. It had a soothing effect on her, although she wasn't feeling any ill effects from the injection. *It's weird. You'd think I'd feel different. Maybe it doesn't work on humans.*

Getting the doctor's attention, she asked him his thoughts on her supposition of the chip. He laughed, which confused her until he told her that she and Nox had been conversing in Delician since she'd awoken. Emeline looked at the doctor in surprise—she hadn't even noticed. He went on to explain that the translator chip allowed them to converse in any known language seamlessly. *That must be why I could understand what Nox and the doctor were saying about me. I think I'm going to like this!*

Impressed, she asked how it worked with the written language. Nox told her it didn't. She would have to learn to read and write in Delician if she felt the need, or she could use ARI to translate.

Eager to get to the lab and start working on their interface program, she pushed off the table, thanking the doctor for his help. She felt they had wasted enough time between dinner last night, talking things out with Liam and Ami, and then being in medical this morning.

Nox stopped her and asked where she was going.

"To the lab to get to work," she told him, tugging on his hand to move him along.

"Aren't you forgetting the whole reason we came here?" he asked her, a look of confusion his face.

"Oh shoot. Yes, I did forget. Sorry. I was just so excited to get to the lab and try out this new chip." Turning to the rest of the room, she apologized to them and asked what they needed from her.

Dr. Datrem told her they would need to take some genetic samples from both of them for analysis. They already had samples from Nox in their databases, so he asked Emeline's permission to have his medic take the samples. Emeline told him he could take whatever he needed if it would help them to figure out what was going to happen to her once they completed the bond. He asked Violia to get her kit as he pointed Emeline to sit back down onto the bed.

Sitting down and putting her arm out for Violia to take the samples, it gave Emeline a chance to study this strange Delician female. It was obvious she was nervous—her hands were shaking as she tried to turn the dial on the DRI.

Emeline gently placed her hand over Violia's and gave it a gentle squeeze. Violia looked up, startled at Emeline's touch. "You don't have to be nervous around me, Violia. I promise humans don't bite—well at least I don't anyway." She was trying to lighten the mood and put Violia at ease. Although, shouldn't she be trying to comfort me, Emeline thought.

"I- I'm sorry," Violia said. Her voice came out raspy as she stopped what she was doing. Taking a deep breath, she turned the dial to retrieve.

Emeline, wondering what was making her so nervous, finally decided to ask. "Is the fact that I'm human making you uncomfortable? I realize I'm the first human to be a bondmate to a Delician, but this information will go a long way in understanding how the human body will react to interspecies bondmating."

"Oh no, madam. That's not it. I'm happy for the Director that he found his bondmate," she assured Emeline, adding quickly, "And for you as well."

"Please call me Emeline."

Violia was taken aback for a moment before smiling —her first genuine one since Emeline had walked into the room. "Thank you, Emeline." Taking a deep breath, she took the DRI and, placing the tip against Emeline's arm, pressed the second ring, taking the samples that she needed.

"Now that wasn't so bad, was it?" Emeline looked down

at her arm and didn't even see a red mark. "It didn't hurt a bit."

Laughing, Violia replied, "I thought it was my job to reassure you instead of the other way around."

Smiling back, Emeline thought for a moment and then asked Violia if she could ask her a few questions, telling her that she had only interacted with one Delician female, Marsel, and that was only briefly at dinner. She was hoping that if she could get Violia to talk to her, she could find out more about Delicia from the female perspective.

When Violia nodded her head slowly, Emeline began by asking her why she became a medic. At first, Violia was hesitant but soon she relaxed and began telling Emeline about her lifelong desire to help the sick and elderly, explaining that when her assignment was finished, she was going to apply to the university to become a physician. Emeline asked what the requirements were to get into medical school and Violia told her anyone applying had to take a series of tests. After that you went before a review board before a final decision was made.

As Emeline listened to Violia, she got the impression that humans and Delicians weren't that different when it came to pursuing their hopes and dreams. When Violia said there were no costs associated with going to school, she was impressed. All they had to do was commit to donating some of their free time for a certain number of years to the local hospitals and all of their schooling was paid for by the government. She explained that for Delicians, giving back to the less fortunate only benefited their society as a whole.

Emeline was amazed and wondered why humans couldn't do that for their students. The amount of student loan debt that a lot of new graduates carried in her country was staggering. When she told Violia how getting your education worked in her country, Violia explained that it was because of the income generated from the synthesized crystals. Delicia was considered one of the wealthiest planets in the UAP.

Emeline started to shift topics, asking about how a Delician family unit worked when Dr. Senta called for Violia to bring her the samples, putting an end to their discussion.

As Violia turned away, Emeline asked if maybe she would like to get a drink sometime to finish their discussion.

Giving Emeline a strange look, she nodded her head, telling her she'd like that.

"Great. Let me know when you're free and we can meet up." Grabbing her hand, Emeline added, "Thank you, Violia. You have been helpful to me and very informative as well." Holding up her new wrist comm, she told Violia to call her anytime.

"Emeline." Nox motioned her over to the center of the room where her hologram was still being displayed. "Dr. Datrem was just going over some of his findings. Come and take a look."

Walking over to where everyone was standing, Emeline saw Violia inputting her biological samples into a slot in one of the machines that was located just to the right of the door. In what felt like no time at all, data began to appear alongside the hologram of her body. Drs. Datrem and Senta peered intently at the information, talking quietly to each other as Nox and Emeline stood waiting, trying to be patient but anxious to hear their findings.

After a few minutes, Dr. Datrem turned with a frown on his face. "The samples will still need some time to process, but from what we have been able to determine so far, until the bond is completed, we won't fully know what will happen to either of you."

Sighing, Nox took Emeline's hand in his, kissing her fingertips. He was disappointed, not only for himself but for her. He didn't care what happened to him, so long as they were together. It was Emeline he was worried about.

She knew nothing about bondmating other than what he had told her, which obviously wasn't much.

Sensing his anxiety, Emeline tried to reassure him, saying that it didn't matter to her what happened. As soon as the threat to the humans was over, she would be completing their bond. Although she cringed inward at the discussion they were having. She'd just met these people and having them discuss her sex life made her uncomfortable. Until she knew these people better, she would keep some things to herself. Most humans were discreet when it came to their sexual habits. It wasn't something you usually discussed with strangers. Her father would have had a meltdown hearing this conversation.

Seeing their discomfort, Dr. Datrem pointed at the hologram of Emeline that was still floating in the middle of the room. "Maybe I can shed some light on a few things that might help alleviate some of your anxiety." Turning to his assistant, he said, "Tulio, put up the hologram of Director Nox's body so we can look at them side by side."

Immediately an image of Nox's body materialized next to Emeline's. At first glance you would have thought you were looking at the inside of a human male body, but on closer inspection subtle differences became apparent.

Looking at his heart, Emeline noticed that it was larger, which made sense considering the size of a Delician male. In fact, most of his organs were larger and his bone density was considerably higher than human males, but that would be expected as well. As far as Emeline could tell there were no major differences internally other than their size.

On the outside, however, there was the iridescent skin and of course the purple highlights in their hair.

"Okay, I have just got to ask about the purple streaks in the hair. I mean, humans are always dying their hair crazy colors, but I've only seen different shades of purple on the Delicians. I'm sorry if you think I'm rude, but I've been dying to ask about this." Emeline looked around the room, hoping she didn't offend anyone.

Nox laughed, unconsciously running his fingers through his hair at Emeline's question. He had never given much thought to the color of his hair. Preferring to keep his hair on the longer side, he generally pulled it back when he was working or swimming. Pulling on the ends, he realized it was longer than he usually kept it.

Dr. Datrem ran his palm down his own hair, smiling at her. "Your question is perfectly acceptable. The separate color is an indicator of age. When a Delician is born, the color is a light purple or what you would consider lavender. As you age, the color deepens until eventually at the end of your life, the color is a very dark shade of purple. If you look at my hair, I'm older than anyone here and you can see that the color of my hair is a medium shade of purple. I am not quite so old as my colleagues would have me be," he said with a wink.

"Violia, what color is your grandmother's hair?" Dr. Datrem asked her. "She is quite elderly."

"Etha? It's a deep dark purple now. Unfortunately, she is starting to become frail," Violia answered him shyly.

"Are you close to your grandmother?" Emeline asked her curiously. She was interested in learning as much as she could about the dynamic of Delician families.

"Yes, we are very close. Actually, this is the first time I've been away from her. It's because of Dr. Datrem I've been given this chance to serve on the *Maelstrom*."

Dr. Datrem explained to Emeline and Nox, with Violia's permission, of course, how he had arranged with his grand-daughter to stay with Etha so Violia could have this opportunity. He told them he had known Etha and her husband for many years and that the only family Etha had left was Violia and her cousin Hagen.

When Hagen's name was mentioned, Violia visibly stiffened—her face turning even paler. Dr. Datrem noticed the change in Violia body language and frowned. When Nox asked where Hagen was, Dr. Datrem told them Hagen was a huge disappointment to his grandmother and that they hadn't seen him for a number of years. It had been Violia who was the sole caregiver to their grandmother since Etha's children were all gone. That's why he was glad he could do this for Violia.

The conversation turned back to the two holograms that were floating together. The brightness of the holograms gave them a star-like quality, which Emeline found apropos considering they were on a spaceship hovering somewhere in Earth's solar system.

After conferring with his team, Dr. Datrem told the couple that as far as they could tell, once the bond was completed the colors would become stationary under their skin. It was then that he dropped the ultimate bombshell on them—the simulation of their DNA showed a 98% probability that Emeline's life cycle could extend to match that of Nox.

This new information took Emeline by surprise. She didn't know what to think.

For Nox, it was more than he could have ever hoped for. He turned to Emeline, wanting to see her reaction to what the doctor had just told them.

She blinked at him as her mind whirled, trying to process the doctor's words. This was beyond comprehension for a human whose life cycle was roughly 90 years. To find out your life would be extended by hundreds of years was astounding.

Nox took both of her hands in his, feeling how cold they were, as if all her blood had frozen in place.

"Emeline, do you know what this could mean for us?" His hands pushed back her hair, searching her eyes, hoping, no, praying that she felt as he did.

Emeline shook her head, thinking that maybe she hadn't heard the doctor correctly. Whispering to him, "Did he say it might be possible I could live as long as you? Did he really just say that?"

"Yes. Are you not happy about this?" Nox asked her, his hopes for them beginning to diminish, thinking maybe Emeline didn't want this kind of life. Maybe the bondmating with a human was not as strong as it would be with a Delician. *No*, thought Nox. He knew deep down that his bond with Emeline was growing stronger every day.

Emeline looked at Nox and saw the stress forming on his face. "No, I mean—I mean I think I am." Looking around at the medical personnel in the room watching their reaction to the doctor's words, Emeline thought maybe this particular discussion should be held in private. "Do you think we could go somewhere to talk?"

Dr. Datrem stepped forward, squeezing Nox's shoulder as he looked down at Emeline. "I'm sorry if I've upset you, Emeline. Frankly, we're still not sure what the effects are going to be until you complete the bond."

"No, no—it's fine, Dr. Datrem. It's just a lot to take in." Her smile wavered slightly as she looked from Nox to the doctor.

Picking up on his bondmate's distress, Nox told the doctor, "I think we've done enough tests for today. I'm going to take Emeline back to my lab. Call me if you get any new information from ARI."

Turning to Emeline, he asked her softly, "Would you like to go lie down in our room or would you rather go to the lab? Your choice."

"The lab. I need to do some thinking and I always feel better when I'm in my lab." Turning to the doctors and medics in the room, Emeline thanked them, saying, "You've certainly given me a lot to consider."

"Any time, Emeline. It was a pleasure meeting you. Come by tomorrow and we'll have the regen device correct your vision. It should only take a few moments."

"I will. Thanks, Dr. Datrem."

Saying goodbye, Emeline and Nox left the medical bay, each of them lost in their own thoughts. Since the medical bay was only a few doors down from Nox's lab, it took only a few moments to get there. Loris was seated at one of the consoles along the far wall working on their interface program. He looked up as they walked in with a questioning look on his face.

Nox waved his hand away and ushered her into his office. "Come, let's go into my office. We can talk in there."

Entering his office, it was obvious to her that this was merely a temporary space for him. It was way too clean. She couldn't wait to see his lab on Delicia—then maybe she would see the real Nox at work. His desk was facing her on an outer wall, leaving enough room for him to be able to turn his chair and look out the window. There were two windows on either side of his desk that gave a magnificent view of a black backdrop of space. Emeline thought she would have a hard time getting any work done if she spent too much time in here.

There was a couch, a chair and a few tables around the room, but the most amazing thing was when he shut the door, the transparent glass separating them from Loris, frosted over—sealing them off from the rest of the world.

Oooh—handy. Emeline couldn't decide if she wanted to sit down or pace as she tried to digest everything. Imagine, she thought, being given the gift of a long life. It was the one thing that always bothered her—how short life could be. Thinking of her dad, she knew he would have loved this.

Stopping abruptly, she thought of her mother. What would Fiona say about all this? Knowing her mum, Fiona would think it was the coolest thing ever. The woman saw every sci-fi movie out there, and the number of alien lust novels she read—well, even Fiona had been shocked when she saw the number of books in her online library.

Her family, Emeline thought, this would mean that she

would outlive her entire family if she went through with the bond with Nox. She wouldn't age for hundreds of years and by then all her friends and family would be long gone, leaving her alone. Well, not really alone—she would have Nox and their own children. And she would be there for Liam and Belle's children and their children and so on. She laughed out loud, startling Nox out of his own thoughts. The whole concept of living for, what, another 570 years was pretty hard to accept. Could she, though?

Seeing Nox standing there studying her face, trying to get a glimpse into what she was thinking, she smiled at him. All at once, it occurred to her that with her longer life cycle, she could continue her work. With the Delicians' advanced technology there was no telling how much good she could do for humanity. Maybe living longer wouldn't be such a bad thing.

As she raked her gaze up and down Nox's body, a seductive smile formed on her face. He really was spectacular to look at. Honestly, the thought of that beautiful body —sexy, fit, strong and all hers for hundreds of years—seriously, what was the downside to that? Remembering how he made her feel every time he touched her, especially this morning, waking up to his soft caresses against her skin. *And now I'm seeing the upside to this.*

Seeing the smile bloom on her face, Nox couldn't resist pulling her in for a kiss. His lips were urgent, needing to feel hers against his. His fingers threaded through her hair, gripping the back of her head. The kiss deepened. He worried he was too rough until he felt Emeline's long slender fingers tug on his hair. Her leg snaked around his, hooking between his thighs as her hips molded to his. New emotions mixed with their combined passion drawing them closer—the spark of their bond intensifying along with their desire.

Needing skin-to-skin contact, Emeline pulled at his shirt, desperate for a way to remove it—her hands roamed his body looking for any fasteners. Alternating between pulling on his clothes and getting distracted by the curve of his muscles under her fingertips, she felt him quiver at her touch.

Emeline groaned out loud, "Please, Nox, a little help here. I want to feel you." Yearning flashed in her eyes. She wasn't above pleading to get what she wanted—a naked alien in her arms.

He stepped back and pulled at the top of his shirt. The material fell to the floor, leaving all that magnificence a feast for Emeline's eyes.

Running her hands up his smooth chest, she could feel his heart under her fingers. Her body reacted, pounding in unison with every beat. Leaning forward, replacing her fingers with her lips...caressing his heart, her tongue slipping out to taste his skin. She could feel his desire through their bond—it matched her own.

Her tongue trailed across the wide expanse of his chest, stopping here and there to nibble and taste as she criss-crossed her way down his magnificent body. The lower she went, the more his fingers clutched at her arms as he gently tried to pull her up to him. Emeline had other ideas.

"What are you doing, beautiful?" Shortening his favorite name for her—his brain was having trouble focusing.

"I'm going to taste you." Her words came out soft, sensual, with a hint of a smile as she slowly knelt before him, her fingers pulling his pants along with her.

"What! No, you can't do that." His voice sounded shocked—astonished at her words.

With the smile of a sly cat, she caught his amethyst eyes in her sultry gaze. As her fingers caressed the prize she had been seeking, she blew him a kiss. Running her hands lightly up and down his length, she asked him curiously, "Have you never had anyone taste you here?" His penis had sprung out from his pants long and hard, ready for her touch. She nuzzled her nose along his length, savoring his unique scent. *Hmmm, male with a hint of vanilla.* Smiling to herself, she moved her tongue up along his length, savoring his taste until she reached the very tip.

Nox shook his head as a long, low moan escaped his dry mouth. He swore his heart skipped a beat when he felt her hot tongue slowly lick the drop of his essence that threatened to escape. His fingers threaded into her hair as he gave in to what this scintillating female was doing to him. She wasn't deterred—teasing and taunting as she gave him the most pleasurable experience of his life. When her warm, wet mouth engulfed the head of his penis...taking him in deeply, he trembled, his legs struggling to stay upright.

Emeline delighted that she was the one to introduce Nox to this new experience. It only added to their shared intimacy. Surprised at herself—this wasn't something that she generally was into, but it felt different with Nox. Maybe it was the bond, maybe it was Nox, but touching him, tasting him—to her it was just another way that she could give herself to him. Maybe she wasn't ready to fully commit, but being here with him helped her to feed the fire that was burning slowly through her resistance, burning into her very soul.

Smiling naughtily, an ice-cream cone popped into her mind. *Hmmm, my favorite.* She devoured him as she would her favorite treat that was melting on a hot summer's day... his moans only fed her desire for him. His fingers stroking her hair as she enveloped him in her love. She felt her own desire peak at the same time a release so powerful burned through him—adding another link to the chain that bound them together.

Emeline giggled happily as she rubbed her face against his abs, his colorful dots moving quicker under her nose. She loved touching him.

Sighing against his skin, she turned her head, giving him a look of total adoration.

Nox was surprised he was still standing. Never in his

life had he felt such a physical sensation. His palm lovingly caressed the side of her face, tracing the line between her ear and chin. Hooking a stray piece of hair behind her ear, smiling as she shivered as he lightly grazed her neck. His nose flared—he could smell her sweet desire...he wasn't the only one affected.

Leaning down, he pulled her up in one motion and had her on her back on his couch as she squeaked out her surprise. She was even more surprised at the speed at which he had her pants and thong removed. In one motion, they were flung towards the door while he worked her shirt up over her head, leaving her lying open in front of him in only her bra, her lucky red bra.

"Take it off," he commanded—his desire to taste her as she had him was all-consuming. Watching her hungrily as her hands slowly undid the clasp that was nestled between her creamy breasts, Nox exhaled as she slowly peeled the cups back, exposing her loveliness to him.

Dropping her bra onto the floor, she lay back against the cushions. Her eyes were soft, expectant, waiting for what she knew was going to be a moment so intense she wondered if she would burst into flames.

"Beautiful girl—yes, that is a perfect name for you. Your body is exquisite. I will never get enough of you." Kneeling between her supple legs, he leaned over and kissed her sensual lips. She tasted of love and need...him. Nibbling slowly, her skin became hotter as his teeth scraped lightly against her neck causing her body to quiver. As he moved down to that perfect spot between her breasts, his tongue tasting her skin, loving how smooth and soft she was. Taking one hand, he toyed with one breast, while his tongue flicked the other. She squirmed under him, her back arching, trying to get closer to him. The more he feasted and rolled her nipples, the harder she prayed to her god.

His free hand roamed down, caressing her legs, her hips, around to her bottom, following all the contours of her body until he landed on her secret spot right at the juncture of her thighs. His eyes strayed to the small rectangle of light curls he had felt the first time he touched her. He ran his fingers through its softness.

"I love that you have hair here," he said with wonder, his voice bringing her back into herself, his fingers stroking her, playing with her curls.

"Yes. You only have hair on your head." She was surprised she could form words with what his fingers were doing to her.

"Touch me," she pleaded. *Am I begging? Yup!*

He continued to torture her as he told her that Delician women didn't have hair covering their *vaginas,* so this was something unique to him. He loved how her body responded to his touch. He especially loved how her soft covering held onto her scent—filling his mind with all the things he wanted to do to her. He had never been with a female in this way before. The fact that she was his bond-mate, his Emeline, made this experience all the more special. He wanted to take his time, to savor the gift she was giving him.

"That's it beautiful, show me how much you want me." His mouth kissed and nipped all the way down her body... stopping here and there to explore, to discover all the hidden sweet spots that caused her legs to tremble—her lips to sigh. His tongue swirled across her soft skin, causing her to call out even more prayers to her god until he finally reached that one spot that had her digging her fingernails into his scalp.

"Oh god, Nox." For the first time ever, Emeline wasn't thinking. She was only feeling—feeling the fire spreading up through her body, feeling Nox's hands, his tongue doing things that sent her places she'd only read about. She felt him nibbling along her hipbones, his tongue playing with that pesky mole she had never liked, wondering why it had bothered her so much as a spark of pleasure shot to her core. She felt wet and hot…wanting him to hurry to that place that was at the center of all her need.

Leaning in, the scent of her desire driving him to want more, he took his first taste of his beautiful bondmate. She tasted like the finest wine made on his beloved Delicia. Beloved. That was the perfect word for this beautiful female as she gave herself to him. His own desires flared to life again with just one taste of her, but he pushed those thoughts aside. This was for her pleasure and he was determined that when he was through, she would know just how much he loved her.

He could feel her body tense, her back arching the more he coaxed her higher. Moving his fingers inside her, first slowly and then quickly, he felt her teetering on the precipice of her orgasm. When he curled his two fingers deep inside her, nudging her passion higher, she screamed to her god as he felt her release.

Emeline wondered if she had been struck by lightning as her orgasm sent shockwaves of ecstasy rocketing through her. *I wonder—can you die from pleasure overload?*

Her eyes closed, her breathing slowly returning to normal as she lay there feeling Nox's head lying gently between her hip bones. The smile on her face was soft as her fingers played with his hair, rejoicing in the blissful feelings that radiated through both of them. The worries of the world were pushed to the side as they reveled in the love that was blossoming between them.

Looking up, Nox's face beamed with joy as he wondered again how blessed he was to find such a wonderful female to spend his life with. And now with the news from Dr. Datrem, it would be a long and happy life. He watched the blissful look on her face, loving that he'd been the one to put it there. Kissing her thigh, he saw her eyes open, giving him a look so tender he would treasure it for the rest of his days. It was a look that said *I am yours.*

"Hi there, beautiful," he said as he softly kissed her bent

knee.

"Hi yourself." Her voice was quiet as her hand stroked the side of his face.

"I guess I did okay for my first time?" he asked her with a teasing sound to his voice.

Surprised, her eyes widened. "That was your first time? How did you get so talented?" She laughed softly as she continued to stroke his face.

"It was you. I just followed where you led me."

Sighing happily, Emeline glanced at wrist comm, checking the time. "Well, I suppose we should get up and maybe get working on our program." She gave him a little nudge so she could sit up. Looking around for her clothes, she took another long look at Nox, drinking in the sight of his beautiful naked body as he stood up and reached out his hand to her. Taking his hand, Emeline's body flushed when she remembered what they had just been doing as he pulled her to her feet.

"If we don't get dressed and get to work, the Hexians are going to be on our doorstep before you know it. The last thing we need is Tarek stomping in here catching us like this," she said as she began putting her clothes back on. "And as much as I'd like to spend the rest of the day in here, I don't think Loris is going to appreciate doing all the work. Oh shit—Loris." She covered her mouth as she swore.

Whispering, she said, "Do you think he heard us?"

Putting on his shirt, he gave her a silly grin, "Beautiful, I think the whole ship heard you praying to your god."

Slapping him on his arm, mortified at the thought of everyone knowing what they had been doing, she groaned.

Giving her one last hug before he opened the door, he kissed the top of her head, saying, "Don't worry about what others think, if anything they'll just think you're very religious."

CHAPTER 14

Four days later
Director Nox's lab
Aboard the Maelstrom

Walking around the hologram platform as an image of a satellite spun slowly in its orbit around Earth, Emeline was thrilled that their interface program was working. Checking her comm, she saw that Liam and Ami had sent new data from the satellites they were retrofitting. After much trial and error, she had just this morning finished inputting her final piece to the integration program. It was hard to refrain from doing a happy dance that it was working. Currently, a simulation of the force field that surrounded the satellite was running and so far, all her calculations appeared to be correct. Nox and Loris had been impressed at how quickly she had adapted to using the Delician technology.

Emeline kept to herself what she really thought about using their technology—it was pretty straightforward. Maybe she hadn't learned all the science behind the new "toys," but she was a quick study. Having the use of a verbal command system that allowed for almost instantaneous response time certainly made learning a lot easier.

Smiling, Nox rubbed her back, asking her, "What has you so amused, beautiful?"

She grinned at him as she moved from one computer screen to another. "I was just thinking how much I love ARI."

Nox raised his eyebrows while Loris snickered, asking Nox, "She does know ARI is not sentient, right?"

Playfully slapping Loris's arm, she scoffed at him, "Not

that kind of love, you goof. I was thinking about how easy ARI has made my work. We've accomplished more in the last week than I have in the last six months. It's been awesome, but sometimes I feel like my head is going to explode."

Seeing worry cross their faces, she snapped her fingers at them, saying, "Joking here. But seriously, using such an advanced system as ARI has been enlightening. I am totally grateful for this opportunity."

Nox kissed her cheek while Loris grinned as they both returned to their work. With time running short before the Hexians were to arrive, they had been spending most of their time in the lab. It was the small snatches of free time that had Emeline's body shuddering in delight. She and Nox had been exploring their bond through talk and touch. Nox was certainly a fast learner—deciding to make it his personal mission to learn all he could about his newly discovered *talent.* Blushing at this thought, Emeline certainly had no complaints.

Loris and Nox were watching her simulation, admiration showing on Nox's face. Standing a little taller, Emeline was proud of her team—and herself.

Looking at her wrist comm, she had an incoming message from Liam. "Nox, Liam said they've finished retrofitting the last satellite and are heading back to the ship. Tomorrow they'll install the last piece of equipment on the Space Station. Then we should be able to initiate the interface program." Her face beamed with pride.

Nox came around the platform, putting his arms around her, drawing her in close. Catching her gaze in his, he put his finger under her chin, gently tipping her head back. He told her how proud he was to be her partner. "Emeline, working with you over these last few days, I see how dedicated you are. You're constantly striving to learn. You don't hesitate to ask questions for more clarification. You are tenacious when you are searching for a solution and you have never once let any of this new technology deter you. Both Loris and I have been impressed at how quickly you have adapted to our technology. In fact, I wouldn't be at all surprised if you knew more about my own process than I do before the week is out." He smiled down at her before glancing over at Loris for his support.

Embarrassed, Emeline's face turned a pretty shade of pink, his words a soothing balm to her soul. Not having to justify her work, especially from someone with as much experience as Nox, had been so refreshing. "Thank you." She beamed at him.

Glancing over at Loris, she added, "And you too, Loris. You guys have no idea how hard it's been constantly having your work second-guessed. I've spent years being judged by my appearance instead of by the contributions I've made to the scientific community. It wasn't until I started my own company that I've had even a modicum of acceptance from my peers."

Loris raised his eyebrows in surprise, asking, "Females are not accepted in all fields of study on Earth?"

Considering her words carefully, Emeline tried to rein in her passion about women's rights on Earth. "That's a tough question to answer. Women have not had an easy time finding their way in our society. Women were always pigeonholed into certain categories that were decided upon by men. It has taken many generations for women to break free of this type of stereotyping. It's only been 100 years since women have even had the right to vote in my country. Women have always had to struggle to get ahead in their careers." Giving him a wry smile, she added, "There are some males in our society that make the mistake of underestimating us—although most are coming to see that working together only benefits all of us. It's slow going but forever moving forward."

Loris looked confused. "Why has it been so difficult for you?"

Nox had at this point released her and was watching the expressions on her face. He saw that telltale rise of color start at her chest and move its way up into her cheeks. He could see her mind working as she tried to find a way to explain to Loris how appearances played such a major role in human society. Emeline had told him about her experiences with some of her teachers at school. It was hard not to judge their society as a whole, especially when he looked at this beautiful talented woman.

"Because, Loris, a lot of times you are judged on your outward appearance."

Seeing that Loris still didn't understand, she tried a different approach. "Loris, when you look at a Delician female's physical appearance, what do you see?"

Considering her question, Loris said thoughtfully, "On the outside they are small in stature and compared to Delician males, quite fragile looking, but I can tell you that looks can be deceiving."

Smiling at his description, Emeline then asked him, "Would you deny a female a position because of her appearance?"

"Of course." Seeing the disgusted look on her face, he rushed to continue. "But only if it was a position that was physically impossible for them to do."

"Would you ever think that a female was not qualified for a job because she was pretty?" she asked, curious to hear his answer.

Surprised, Loris shook his head. "No. What has that got to do with whether she can do the job?"

Emeline could have hugged him for the genuine sincerity of his question. This was definitely going in the differences column in her notes she was keeping. If only humans were as enlightened as the Delicians seemed to be.

"Loris, that is a question that human women have been asking for generations. Don't get me wrong, there have been many positive changes and the world is slowly changing its opinions of women's roles on our planet. Unfortunately, there are still instances where it's as if time has moved in slow motion."

"If you don't mind my asking, what happened to you?" Loris asked.

Hesitating for an instant, Emeline thought about the best way to illustrate her experience, finally asking him, "Loris, do you see the color of my hair?"

"Yes."

"This color hair is called blond and unfortunately if you are attractive and a blonde—well, then you are oftentimes considered lacking in intelligence." Seeing his confusion, she stated simply, "Because I'm pretty and blond, there are some people who think I am not smart enough to be in the science field."

Loris burst out laughing when he heard this. "I'm sorry to laugh, Emeline, but I find that the most ridiculous thing I've ever heard. I've worked with you for the past four days and I have found you incredibly intelligent.

Leaning up, Emeline kissed Loris on the cheek. A look of surprise appeared on his face as he looked at Nox to see his reaction to Emeline kissing him.

Nox, who had been listening intently to their conversation, chimed in, "Emeline, even though there is equality amongst Delicians, we are still very protective over our females. That doesn't mean that we find them inferior. On the contrary, our females are highly regarded. It's just a fact that there are physical differences between us. We will not hesitate to take action if we feel that any of our females are in danger. In our society is it our duty to protect our females and children."

Nodding, Emeline could appreciate what Nox was saying, and even though they could debate this topic all day, they did have a planet to save. Solving all the world's problems would have to wait for another day. "Thank you, Loris. I think you and I are going to have many interesting conversations over the next few years."

Turning to Nox, she wagged her finger at him. "I know you're only looking out for me, but you know I can take care of myself? You've seen me in the training room."

Nox leaned down and gave her a quick kiss, whispering in her ear, "Oh, I've seen you in the training room in your tight body suit." Her skintight suit showed every curve as she moved through her workout. Liam had face-planted him into the exercise mat more than once-catching him off guard watching Emeline go through her routine with Ami.

Nox was having a difficult time trying to keep his feelings contained. Between holding back his desire to drag Emeline into his office to give them both some relief or not wanting to let them get out of bed in the morning, Nox couldn't wait to get this whole mission over with. And judging by the success of the simulation he was looking at, at least their part of the mission was almost completed. Next it would be up to the General and his crew to take care of the Hexians before they even got to Earth.

Speaking of the General, Nox needed to update him on their progress. After telling Emeline and Loris he'd be in his office while they each continued with their assigned tasks, Nox grabbed a cup of his new favorite coffee drink, vanilla latte with a double shot, before heading in to make his call.

Sitting at his desk, Nox pressed his desktop comm unit requesting ARI to connect him to the General.

After a short time, Tarek's steeling gaze appeared before him. "Nox, do you have an update for me? How are the satellite retrofits coming along?"

"Yes, I do have an update." Nox went on to brief Tarek of their progress, ending that they would be ready to initiate their program tomorrow afternoon.

Pleased to hear about their progress, Tarek sat back contemplating Nox. "Tell me your assessment on working with the humans."

Nox was only mildly surprised at Tarek's interest in the

humans. These past few weeks spent in Tarek's company had Nox reevaluating his original opinion of the General. Oh, he could still be a hard ass, no doubt, but he also had a side that few people got to see. Nox was thrilled and humbled to be included in Tarek's inner circle.

Leaning back in his chair, Nox told Tarek, "Honestly, they have been a constant surprise. Their work ethic is similar to ours and they have been quick in adapting to their new surroundings. I have a feeling it's going to be hard for them to go back to their lives on Earth when this mission is over."

Tarek rubbed his chin, considering Nox's words. "I am in full agreement with you—at least with these three humans. I'm not so sure about the rest of Earth's population. Humans may appear similar in body physiology, but they are as diverse in culture as any other species we've encountered." Taking a moment to study Nox's face, Tarek asked how he was getting along with his bondmate's brother. "It has not escaped my notice that you two always end up as sparring partners."

Nox's hand unconsciously rubbed at a particularly sore muscle in his lower back. "You saw that, huh? He's just trying to make a point." Giving in to a slight groan, Nox smirked at the General, adding, "I think it's time for me to make a few of my own."

Tarek leaned back and barked out a laugh, saying, "I can't wait to watch."

Changing the subject, Nox asked Tarek if there was any updated information on the Hexians.

"Nothing as of yet," Tarek told him. "I'll make sure Jagger contacts you if anything changes."

"Thanks. Do we have any idea how many ships they have?" Nox asked.

"We have a general idea, but currently I'm keeping our mission plans on a need-to-know basis. I'm positive Tarquin is aware of our presence. I have my suspicions that he has a contact on Delicia who's been feeding him information. I'll be updating everyone at dinner tonight. I heard Ami and Emeline are cooking something called Korean beef barbecue." Tarek loved trying new foods, and ever since the humans had arrived onboard, they had been eating some unique and delicious flavors.

"Tarek, you will love it. It's the first dish Emeline made for me. Delicious." Nox could almost feel his mouth watering.

As he ended his call, Nox looked up smiling as Emeline came into his office. Closing the door with a wave of her hand, she watched as the glass frosted over, giving them some much needed privacy.

"What did Tarek have to say?" Emeline sauntered over and slid onto his lap; her hands caressed the back of his neck as she settled her body against his. Almost immediately Nox's desire pressed against her backside, prompting her to wiggle against him. She knew the effect she had on him. It was the same one he had on her.

"How can I talk about battle plans when all I want to do is strip you naked and taste you again?" He gave her a smoldering look as he moved his hand up under her T-shirt and bra while his other one moved around to massage and squeeze the side of her hip. Her breast filled his hand, soft and warm as his thumb slowly toyed with her nipple, causing a moan to escape from Emeline's lips.

"If you keep that up, I'm going to forget why I came in here." Her breathing came out haltingly the more his fingers danced across her breast. "Oh, yeah"—gasp— "I came to tell you that Liam just landed in the shuttle bay—ooohhh god—and should be here in about fifteen minutes." Trying to focus was getting more difficult by the minute and judging from the look of concentration on Nox's face, he wasn't going to finish anytime soon.

Moving his hand down along her body, Emeline's legs opened for him. He pressed hard against the seam of her pants that ran between her thighs. He could feel how hot she was even through her clothing. He loved seeing her face as he played with her body. She was so responsive to him. Neither one of them seemed to be able to get enough of each other. The more he pressed on her secret spot, the louder she prayed. It was a beautiful sound, and when he felt her body shudder with release, sighing into his neck, he sighed with her...their bond cloaking them like a warm blanket.

"Beautiful girl, I love how you feel in my arms."

Kissing his neck, she inhaled deeply, loving how their two scents mingled together, their bond creating a scent unique only to them. Her lips moving of their own accord nibbled on his earlobe as she felt him shift under her. Smiling, she continued to use her lips, showing him through her touch just how much he affected her, and considering how hard his erection was, she knew he felt the same. Moving her hips gently from side to side, she applied just the right amount of pressure, causing his own hips to move in concert with hers. The chair they were sitting in rocked and twisted with each movement. She felt his pectoral muscles tighten as they tried to take in more air, his body chasing her movements as he began to pray to his own god. The more she moved her hips, the more the chair swayed, mimicking their movements until finally stopping abruptly as she brought him to that peak that he had just brought her.

Nox laughed into Emeline's neck, happy that he had a replicator in his office considering the state of his pants.

Hearing Liam's voice coming through the door caused the two of them to giggle like a pair of teenagers who had just been caught doing exactly what they had been doing.

"Come on, Em. Open up," Liam yelled through the closed door.

"Give me a minute," she yelled back.

Nox stood up, holding Emeline as she straightened her

clothes…her back to his front so Liam wouldn't see his rumpled clothing. Nox opened the door, allowing Liam to come strolling through the door.

"Seriously? It's almost dinner time and you two are acting like—well I can't go there." Liam's face was starting to turn red as he glared at his sister and her alien bondmate.

Giving in to the slight giggle, Emeline shushed him. She was not discussing her sex life with her brother. *Not happening.* "Where's Ami?" she asked, looking towards the door for her friend.

"She's gone to take a shower before you guys make dinner." Liam came in and sat in one of the chairs.

"Shoot, I should go do the same. I'm going to head back to our room and change. I want to call Mum and check in with Lorelei anyway. You know she's worried about me—all of us actually," she said pointing to Liam, "so I have to keep her in the loop. Besides, if I don't give Mum a call, she is going to start worrying and none of us want that." She gave Liam a knowing look. He knew what a worry-wort their mother could be.

She could have talked to Fiona and Lorelei here, but she wanted to give Nox some time alone with Liam. If they were going to become a family, then those two needed to spend some time together outside of the training area. There was less blood that way.

Reaching up to drop a kiss onto Nox's lips, she turned to her brother and gave him a hug before she headed out the door.

"Be careful. Maybe you should wait for me to take you. I don't think it's a good idea for you to be walking alone. This is a very large ship." Nox started to follow her out of the door only to be stopped by Emeline's outstretched arm.

"Nox, I've got this," she told him as she held up her wrist comm. Speaking out loud, she said, "ARI will take me where I want to go and I can be in constant contact with you all the way to our room." Giving him a reassuring hug, she walked out the door saying good-bye to Loris on her way out of the lab.

"Don't bother." Nox was stopped in his tracks at Liam's words. Moving over to the couch, Liam plopped down, putting his feet up, closing his tired eyes. "Trust me, if Em felt in any danger, she would have waited. She'll be fine."

"I'm walking down the hallway." Emeline's voice came out of Nox's comm.

Both men laughed, which lightened the mood. Nox respected Liam. Considered him likeable. *He's also a worthy sparring partner as well.* Which had prompted both of them to visit medical after every training session to heal more than a few bruises they'd inflicted on each other.

"Emeline is very close to her family." Nox's statement indicated to Liam that he understood the nature of their family.

"Yes, family is everything." Eyes burning slightly, Liam got up from his spot on the couch and went to the replicator and ordered up two beers. Handing one to Nox, he clinked bottles. "Cheers." Taking a long drink from his beer, Liam resumed his spot on the couch as he studied Nox, taking in this big male with the iridescent skin. "Mum and Dad got married young and I came along pretty much right away. Mum was still in school and Dad was working and not making much money, so I went to school with my Mum for four years. Learning was something that was important to our family. Isabelle and Emeline came along one right after the other when I was about nine. By then, I was older and going off to school. They were just my sweet little sisters." Liam stopped to take another long drink from his beer.

Nox took a taste from the bottle Liam had handed him. It was delicious. He usually drank Delician wine, but this was different. It was bubbly in his mouth, similar to a drink he had at the UAP headquarters when he was younger. Listening to Liam talk, Nox gained a little insight into Liam's role within Emeline's world. Liam was their protector—even more so since their father had died. However, Nox did notice that their women lived their lives without males and did so quite proficiently. *Emeline is a gifted and talented scientist.* Nox was proud of Emeline and told Liam about how impressed he was with Emeline and her company.

"I'm in the room." Emeline's voice wafted up from Nox's wrist, eliciting another laugh from the two males.

"Nox, I want you to know I see how Em is with you and I can tell you feel the same way."

"Liam—"

"No, please let me have my say." Liam wanted to say this before they all went to dinner. He had been a little aggressive with Nox in the training room and it was time to let Emeline know that he accepted her choice. "I'm the big brother and now I'm the head male of our family. Whether Emeline likes it or not, I'm always going to look out for her. You've met her friends, so you know how protective we all are of her."

Nox wanted to say something, but he let Liam finish. He was well aware of how many people cared about his Emeline, but they had to understand he also cared. The feelings between them were genuine.

"And you know if anything ever happens to Emeline, I can hold my own against you." Liam rubbed his ribs just thinking of his training sessions with Nox. Not to mention all the other Delicians that wanted to *spar* with the human. Their healing technology had gotten a lot of use the last few days.

"Liam, you know I would lay down my life for her. She is my very existence. You have my word; I will always honor and protect your sister." The sincerity in his voice confirmed to Liam that Emeline was in good hands.

"I know you will, Nox." Locking eyes, so Nox would understand his meaning, Liam was passionate when he spoke about his feelings for his family, "I'm trusting you with my sister. I don't understand this bond you two have...maybe someday I will. I know my parents found it and they lived an extraordinarily happy life. But remember one thing, you're still going to have to get the approval of my mother and my sister." At Nox's look of apprehension, Liam reassured him, "Just keep my sister as happy as she's been these last weeks and you'll be a part of the family in no time."

"I am looking forward to meeting your mother and other sister. Just know this, you can trust me, Liam. I give you my word, Emeline will always come first in my life." Nox was equally as passionate when it came to his feelings for his bondmate.

"All right then. I'm going to go and get changed for dinner. Ami and I can fill you both in on the last of the satellites tonight." Rubbing his belly on his way out the door, he said, "I'm starved and they're making one of my favorite meals."

"I'll walk out with you." Nox headed into the lab, with Liam noticing that Loris had already gone off to meet Marsel for dinner. They had become friends and were swapping stories about their many adventures. Everyone was a bit on edge waiting for the Hexians. It's not that they didn't know what to expect. The Hexians were gnats that you kept swatting but you could never seem to get them all.

"Try to make it on time tonight. Emeline is supposed to be helping Ami cook and I don't want to hear about why you two are late. I mean, come on, man, it's my sister." Liam groaned, rolling his eyes while Nox laughed at his discomfort. He had good reason to laugh. He was the one who had the smart, beautiful female waiting for him. *Yes, Life is good.*

She knew the minute she stepped into the officers' rec

room that she was in for an earful. "I know. I know. I'm late. Don't get your panties in a twist." Emeline was yelling at Ami as she came running through the door with Nox following closely behind her. Seeing his face told everyone why they were late, which just added to Ami's annoyance.

"I don't want to hear about it and my panties are just fine, thank you very much. Not that anyone has been looking at my panties lately," Ami mumbled to herself. Although considering some of the looks she had been getting from some of Tarek's crew, maybe she could have gotten some action if not for the fact that they were trying to save Earth.

Emeline came around the corner of the island into the cooking area of the room. Grabbing an apron to cover the new outfit she had just replicated, she looked over at Ami, seeing the worried frown on her face. They had been on the ship together for the past four days and she'd tried to spend as much time with her as she could. Judging by the deep frown on her bestie's face, it apparently wasn't enough. It had been hard being pulled in all directions, trying to keep everyone happy and failing miserably at it.

Standing behind her friend, her arms snaked around Ami, giving her a squeeze, trying not to get in the way as Ami cut up pieces of steak for her Korean beef barbecue. Emeline whispered in her ear, "All right—spill your guts. What's going on? Why the long face?"

Sighing, Ami turned and gave her friend a sideways look as she put her knife down on the countertop. She had never seen Emeline look so settled, so content as she was when she was around Nox. The last few years had been ones of turmoil in all of their lives, especially since Hank had died. Combining that with trying to get their network array funded and then approved and then finally after what felt like forever, installed. It had been a hectic time but they had always been able to count on each other. Now Emeline was pulling away, not because she didn't want to be a part of their family, but because of Nox and their bond. *Where does that leave all of us?* Ami wondered.

Looking out at the people in the room, Ami should have been full of her normal quips and jokes, especially when what she saw looked like a scene out of a Hollywood movie. Liam, standing drinking a beer and laughing with five alien males that towered over him, acting like it was the most natural thing in the world. "Em, tell me what you see when you look over there?"

Following Ami's gaze, it didn't take a rocket scientist to know what she was talking about. "I see my brother and my alien bondmate laughing and drinking with his alien friends." Giving Ami a sunny smile because she knew it would irritate her friend, she added, "Why, what do you see?"

"Very funny, girlfriend. You know what I mean."

"I know. I'm only playing with you." Giving her a gentle nudge, she picked up a pan, asking, "Do you want me to start the rice pilaf?" After getting a nod from Ami, she grabbed some carrots and red peppers and started cleaning them. "Talk to me, Ames. What's going on in that head of yours?"

Blowing out a breath that she hoped would get her bangs out of her face, Ami gave her a very long, very heavy sigh. "Too much is changing too fast and I can't do anything about it. You and Nox, the Delicians, bad aliens coming to attack us—I mean, how did everything get so out of control?"

Putting down the vegetable peeler, Emeline pulled her friend in for a hug, knowing that Ami was doing her best to cope in this unbelievable situation they had all been thrown into. You could always count on Ami to lighten the atmosphere with her unique take on any given situation. It was her way of coping. But seeing her friend like this had Emeline more than a little concerned.

Not wanting to make a scene, Ami turned back to her

cooking. She had some overly hungry males who liked to eat—a lot. Finishing up the beef and pouring the marinade over it, she moved on to making the slaw she would use in her rollups. Cooking always helped her focus, and cooking with her friend, well, she wondered how long before that changed. "So, when this is all over, I suppose you'll be going to Delicia with Nox?" Ami asked, almost afraid of Emeline's answer.

"Honestly, I don't know what's going to happen. We haven't made any decisions yet—other than that we want to stay together." Emeline was nervous watching Ami's face. How did she expect her friend and even her family to understand these feelings that she was only just coming to terms with herself?

"Do you love him?"

"Yes."

"Just like that—no doubts?

"None."

The surprised look on Ami's face had Emeline laughing out loud, breaking the tension that had been building between the two women. The sound was loud enough that it silenced the jovial conversations that were taking place across the room. All eyes turned to see what was so funny.

"Anything you want to share, Em?" Liam cocked his eyebrow at the two women. He had been watching them both out of the corner of his eye. He could tell they were having a serious discussion judging by the tense body language they were giving off.

"All good," Emeline called to them. She saw that Nox was staring at her, giving her a slight smile because he could tell she was upset. This was a talk that was long overdue between her and Ami.

Noticing the looks that flowed between her friend and her alien bondmate, Ami relaxed a bit. Somehow this was different from all the other relationships that she had witnessed Emeline have. "Tell me about the bond. Does it hurt?"

Noticing the change of attitude in her friend, Emeline smiled as she went back to chopping the veggies in front of her. "The bond?"

Ami nodded her head.

"No, it doesn't hurt. It feels—how do I describe it? It's like nothing I've ever felt before. You know how whenever I would date a guy, I would always start building my wall?"

Ami nodded again, watching her friend's face, waiting because Ami knew the drill. It always started out so great with so much promise although Emeline would begin building the foundation of her wall. Then slowly as the telltale signs would pop up and little by little, the wall would start to take shape. As the time between texts would lengthen, the excuses, the broken dates, the angst that would always come every time she'd looked at her phone —each disappointment adding another brick. Until finally when all contact was ended, the wall would be finished... blocking out the pain that Emeline tried so hard not to feel. In the aftermath, lots of alcohol and chocolate would be consumed as all four girls would rehash the reasons why things didn't work out—again.

"Not even a pebble," Emeline said in a quiet voice. Ami's eyes widened at her meaning. "It's like for the first time in my life, I'm home." Holding up her hand, carrot peelings sticking to the peeler as she waved it at her friend, she scoffed at the look of disbelief on Ami's face. "Oh, I know what you're thinking and yes, I have a home with my family and with you guys, but this is different. This is a home that Nox and I are building together—a place where we'll raise our children, a place where we'll grow old together."

Looking over at Nox, Emeline's eyes fill with tears, happy tears. She watched him talking and laughing with her brother and his friends. His facial expression relaxed as he listened to Nyx tell him how Liam had been badgering him to take him flying in one of their star fighters.

Glancing down at the pot where she was just finishing up cooking the vegetables, she added the rice, wine, herbs and broth. After giving it a quick stir, she placed the cover on the pan and turned down the heat to allow the pilaf to simmer.

Watching her friend's face, Ami huffed out her exasperation. "See, this is what I'm trying to understand. Don't get me wrong, I am happy for you. It's just I don't get it. If you feel so strongly, why haven't you completed the bond? I mean, if you know he's 'THE ONE,' what are you waiting for?" Ami turned back to mixing the dressing into her slaw as she waited for the excuse she knew was coming.

Emeline stood lost in thought contemplating Ami's words as she over stirred the rice, which caused Ami to clear her throat and nudge her out of the way.

"You're going to kill that rice and then we're going to have some unhappy, very hungry aliens on our hands."

Looking up at Ami, her eyes snapping back into focus, she looked down at the pan. Saving the rice just in time, she was glad they wouldn't have to use the replicator to complete their dinner. That would defeat the purpose of actually cooking their meal.

"You know what? You're right. What are we waiting for? I was the one who wanted to wait until the Hexians were defeated. I thought it would be a distraction, but now that the program is finished and ready to be implemented, why should we wait? I mean, it's going to happen anyway and if God forbid something were to go wrong, at least Nox and I would have had some time together as bondmates." She looked over at Nox, noticing not for the first time just how well he filled out his clothing. "I mean, seriously, just look at him. What have I been thinking?"

"Honestly, Em, I'm surprised it's taken you this long." The knot in Ami's chest had started to loosen the more she listened to her friend talk about Nox.

"Well, I wouldn't say we've waited." Emeline's face was

changing color again and it wasn't from the heat of the stove.

"Oh really? Okay, now spill your guts." Ami laughed at her friend because she knew that Emeline wasn't really one to kiss and tell, but every now and then you got a few juicy tidbits out of her. "Are you going to tell me about alien dick, or is it two dicks?"

Now Emeline's face was really red as she gasped out, "All I'll say is that Lorelei's books weren't wrong."

With eyebrows raised, Ami's curiosity was piqued. "Should I be making us her new favorite drink then?" Remembering Lorelei's new creation of a Fuzzy Alien Dick—they had all decided that it was one of her more tastier drink creations.

"No," Emeline said, slapping her on the arm and looking up to see Nox coming in their direction. The smells that permeated the room were so delicious that they could hear the grumbles of hungry stomachs coming from across the room.

Nox came around the island, snaking his arms around Emeline as she stood at the stove checking out her rice. Leaning over to steal a piece of beef from the pile that Ami had been cooking, he pulled back, surprised when Ami reached over, lightly swatting his hand away.

"No tasting until it's finished." They both looked at each other—this was the first time Ami's tone was teasing. The usual note of tension she had whenever he was around was gone.

Nuzzling Emeline's neck, Nox growled good naturedly as Ami tried to shoo him out of the kitchen area telling him to go set the table. Dinner would be ready in ten minutes.

Giving Emeline a light peck on the cheek, he quietly asked her if things between her and Ami were good.

Winking at him, Emeline whispered, "Everything is fine, but I need to talk to you later." Her intense blue eyes swept him from head to toe.

Intrigued, he lightly swatted her behind as he grabbed the plates, yelling to Jagger and the rest of the males that dinner was almost ready and they needed to get the table set.

The conversation during dinner ranged from how fabulous the meal was, to which the Delicians wanted to make sure the women had put their recipes into ARI, to the Hexians and when they would make an appearance. Even though their meal was thoroughly enjoyed by all, there was the underlying tension that couldn't be denied.

Tarek informed them that he was having a strategy meeting tomorrow after Nyx and Liam finished with the last of the retrofitting. Telling Liam and Ami to join them, Tarek looked at Nox saying he was to be there as well. "I know you will be initiating the interface program tomorrow, but I would like you to be at the meeting. We could use your technical expertise in the preparation of our plan."

Looking to Emeline, Nox asked her, "Do you mind finishing up with Loris?"

Wiping her mouth on her napkin, Emeline smiled, saying, "Sure, no worries. Loris and I can manage."

"Thank you." Normally Nox wouldn't have hesitated answering Tarek, but now he had a partner not only in his life but also in his work. Emeline would always come first.

Tarek scanned the table, looking into the faces of the few people he could trust right now. They were all aware of how wrong things could go over the next few days. There was a lot at stake.

Tarek nodded to Jagger, who cleared his throat, getting everyone's attention, saying, "I have news on the Hexians." Everyone stopped mid bite to stare at Jagger. Pointing to the holographic image of Earth's solar system that appeared in the center of the table, he said, "Long-range sensors indicated they are about two days out, which is why we need to finalize our plans."

Jagger considered the hologram, wondering out loud at

Tarquin's motives. "ARI, show the position of the Invidia." A lone battle cruiser was seen heading in the direction of Earth. Jagger pointed to Tarquin's ship, adding, "I don't trust him."

"I agree." Ramola dropped his fork and had his finger pointing at the hologram.

Tarek took a swallow of his Delician ale, silently agreeing with his team. Setting down his glass, he pointed to the map in front of them. "I have a portion of our fleet holding at their current location just outside of Earth's solar system. I don't doubt that Tarquin has more ships hovering somewhere just outside of our sensor range. Confrontation is coming and we need to be prepared and I want the fleet to be accessible when needed. Liam, have you updated Earth's leaders?"

"I have." Liam told them he had talked to Leslie and that she told him the President and the UN Council were pleased that the satellites would be protected and to let her know when things began to escalate.

Tarek nodded in agreement as he took another helping of rice pilaf. "Ami, this is superb. We have a similar dish to this on Delicia called Oirza. I have very much enjoyed your cooking."

Ami giggled, thanking him with a sappy grin.

As the rest of the Korean beef was polished off, Tarek, Jagger and Nyx told the humans their own personal stories of their interactions with Hexians. Ezio pointed to the scar on the side of his face, telling them that it was a reminder to himself of just how deadly the Hexians could be.

Ami's eyes followed his finger as he traced down the length of long thin white line that ran from his right eyebrow down around the side of his chin.

Shuddering, Ami blurted out, "Who wants dessert?"

Silence was then met with a resounding "yes," while Emeline leaned over and asked, "You made dessert? What did you make?"

"I made my favorite…apple crisp with vanilla ice cream, or I should say I made the apple crisp and the replicator made the ice cream. It came out pretty good actually." Ami hadn't been sure about replicating ice cream, but apple crisp just wasn't the same without it.

"When did you have time?" Emeline loved Ami's apple crisp. She had a secret ingredient that always set hers apart from others' recipes. Who would have thought to put vanilla in with the cinnamon?

Emeline followed Ami over to the kitchen and helped her get dessert while the guys cleaned off the table. The replicator system had a recycling program, so cleaning up the table was a snap. Ami opened the oven and pulled out two pans of warm apple crisp, while Emeline grabbed two containers of ice cream out of their freezer unit.

"I had extra time on my hands while I waited for my friend to come cook with me." Ami wagged her eyebrows at Emeline as she watched her friend look away with a guilty face. Laughing at her, Ami nudged her arm. "Stop feeling guilty, Em. You know if I had a hot alien warming my bed, I would have left you cooking by yourself. Come on, let's get this served before that ice cream melts."

"You suck, you know that, right?" Emeline retorted.

"Yes, I do, and I've never had any complaints either," Ami countered.

"Do I have to separate you two?" Liam called over to them.

Laughing at her brother, Emeline and Ami both yelled, "No, Dad." It was their stock answer whenever Liam would stick his nose into their good-natured sniping at each other.

As Ami put the apple crisp on the table, the smell of baked apples and cinnamon had the Delicians eager to try this delicious-looking human dish. Nox was the first one to be handed a dishful of this apple goodness with vanilla ice cream melting like snow on a mountain. Taking the dish from Emeline, he took a deep breath of the creamy dessert, his eyes lit up when he detected a scent he knew. "*Vanilla,*" he mouthed to her, a smile forming on his face as she nodded her head.

As each Delician received their dish, the sound in the room changed from one of talking to one of lips smacking and moans of delight and sighs of satisfaction. The women were pleased that they could share one of their favorite meals with their new friends. Even when things were at their bleakest, sometimes something as simple as a shared meal could bring the most unlikely of people, or in this case beings, together, even if just for a few moments of respite.

Nox leaned in close to whisper softly in Emeline's ear, "Are you finished?"

Thinking he was being quiet, Nox was surprised when Nyx answered for her, grinning at him saying, "Yes, I am. Why, do you want to go do some training to work off some of this delicious dinner?"

Nox gave him a look as if to say *never going to happen* before Liam chimed in, rubbing his full stomach, "I could do with a little exercise. How about we go a few rounds before bed, Nox?"

Grabbing Emeline by the hand and pulling her up, he headed out the door, stopping only to address his friends, "Sorry, gentlemen, you'll have to train without me tonight. Emeline and I have some *talking* to do." He winked at them as the door closed behind him. The sound of groaning could be heard as he and Emeline laughed all the way back to their room.

CHAPTER 15

Emeline giggled, imagining the look on Liam's face at Nox's parting words, but she really did want to talk to Nox. Ami's words had been forefront in her mind all throughout dinner. *She did have a point. What are we waiting for?*

Straightening her shoulders, Emeline decided she was done waiting. Tonight, they would complete their bond. She huffed out a nervous breath, hoping Nox agreed with her.

Feeling a little nervous, she wondered what Nox was going to say about her change in attitude. Grinning slyly to herself, Emeline thought, maybe he needed a little incentive.

Going over to the replicator, she programmed in a special outfit that might just do the trick. Once it was completed, she went into the bathroom, and after taking a quick shower, she came out just as Nox was putting on his sleeping pants.

When he caught sight of her coming through the bathroom door, he lost his footing and nearly toppled over onto the bed. His heart nearly stopped as his eyes devoured her.

She stopped in front of him, a shy look on her face, her hands clasped lightly in front of her as she stood before him...her body barely covered in a red sheer nightgown with a matching lace thong.

Rather quickly, his pants felt tight as his erection pushed against his waistband in an attempt to reach his bondmate.

"Emeline?" His voice was barely audible as his eyes feasted on this beautiful creature standing before him.

"Nox," she started softly, "I want you. I don't want to wait any longer."

"Oh...beautiful girl...you're killing me here." He groaned as she came forward, her arms going around his waist, as she pressed herself against him.

"I mean it, Nox. I want to complete the bond, now... tonight." Her mouth started to explore along his chest, his muscles moving against her lips causing her core to twitch. He tasted so good. Her tongue, finding his nipples, teased and nipped at each one. She could feel him pressing against her, her feelings of uncertainty gone, replaced by their mutual desire for one another.

His grip tightened on her arms, but instead of pulling her closer, he took a step back. A look of confusion and then hurt crossed her face. "Emeline, please, give me a moment here."

She pulled away and walked over to the window, staring out at the stars, embarrassed. "I'm sorry. I thought you wanted this as much as I did."

He let her go, confused for a moment as to what prompted this change of heart. He gazed at her standing by the window. The backdrop of the stars didn't compare to her loveliness. He was lost for a moment as he gazed at her long shapely legs. They were bare except for where the top of her sheer nightgown barely touched the bottom of her perfectly shaped buttock.

Coming up behind her, he pulled her back against him. She stiffened at his touch...her hurt feelings evident as he rubbed his hands up and down her arms.

"Emeline, you know I want you. You can feel it in here." Placing his hand under her breast, he could feel her heart beating beneath his fingers. It took all his strength to keep his hands from cupping her high, firm breasts, her nipples hard, begging for his touch. "What brought this on?"

Sighing, she turned in his arms, her front pressed against his as she looked up into his eyes. "I was talking to Ami." Nox made a face, causing Emeline to cup his face, telling him, "No really, she actually made sense. She made me realize that there really is no reason to wait. I mean, I'm not going to change my mind. And I know you aren't going to change yours. What does it matter what happens with the Hexians? I will always be your bondmate." Placing light kisses along his pectorals, she spoke against his skin, "I don't want to wait any longer. I need you."

Taking her hand and leading her over to the bed, Nox sat down, pulling her to stand between his legs. What he was about to say to her was going to kill him, but this was too big a decision to rush into. Wrapping his arms around her waist, he pulled her close. He could tell that she had showered, the scent of vanilla making what he had to say all the more difficult. "Your scent drives me wild. Beautiful girl, you know what I feel for you." Rubbing his nose across her tight stomach, the softness of the material pushed his desire for her higher. His tongue snuck out to take a small taste as he felt her giggling at his touch.

Standing up quickly, he sat her on the bed while he paced in front of her. He tried to calm himself. If he didn't stop touching her, he would change his mind and give her exactly what she wanted, but this was too important. He needed to be clear in his feelings so she wouldn't misunderstand what he was trying to say.

Stopping in front of her, he took a deep breath, "Emeline, I need to talk to you and you're...umm, you're making it very hard for me to concentrate." He was trying to calm this unbelievable urge to throw her back on the bed and never let her up. By the time she could get up, there would be no doubt how much she was cherished.

Lightly swatting his erection that was waving hello in her face, she gave him a crooked smile, saying, "I can tell. Is that a problem for you?"

"Yes, no—I mean—" Nox sat down beside her, taking her hands in his.

She tightened her fingers around his, hanging on, almost afraid of what Nox was going to say to her. Didn't he understand how much she loved him, needed him.

Giving her a serious look, he told her, "I love you. I do. I want nothing more than to complete our bond, but I want you to do it for the right reason."

"I know what I want." She was worried that he was changing his mind. Her heart fell to her stomach, tears formed at the corners of her eyes. *Doesn't he believe me?*

As if he could read her mind, he pulled her tight against him, letting her feel his desire, his need for her. "I'm just asking you to take a step back for a moment and see things from my point of view. These feelings between us are like an inferno. When I see you dressed like this, all I want is to throw you on the bed and ravish you until you can't think straight."

She could feel his erection pressing between them. Slowly she rubbed her body gently back and forth against him, the motions making him even harder—as if that was even possible. "I want that too," she whispered against his chest. His muscles tightened every time her lips touched him.

"Emeline, all I'm asking is that we don't rush into this decision on emotions alone. At least take tomorrow to really analyze and run through all your probabilities."

Emeline laughed into his shoulder. Her arms came up, wrapping tightly around his neck. "Are you seriously asking me to run a scientific analysis on whether or not I want to become your bondmate?" She thought he was kidding until she looked up into his face and she saw that he was dead serious. "You do! Why?"

"Well, because when we bond, it will be forever. There is no divorce, no separations, no changing your mind. We will be together as one for a very long time. Remember how long Delicians live. You heard what Dr. Datrem said. It's entirely possible you and I will be together for more than five of your natural life spans. You must be absolutely sure of your decision."

He watched her face as she began to understand the magnitude of the step they were contemplating. "Emeline, I've watched how you work. You have an analytical mind. All I'm saying is that aside from our obvious physical attraction, we need to make sure we fit together in all aspects of our lives." He kissed the top of her head before he leaned back to look at her.

Emeline wanted to laugh and cry all at the same time. He was so darn sweet. And if she was being at all truthful with herself, maybe she was being led around by her body's need for him. Not that she was complaining. He had an amazing body and he let her do anything she wanted to him—well, except for that one last thing and it didn't look like she was getting that tonight. Well, if she did what he wanted her to do, then maybe tomorrow night. *Hmm. I have just the thing to wear.*

"You know, when you say things like this, it's just another reason why I love you so much. But you're right about one thing—500 years is a long time. I mean, what if we get sick of each other?" She gave him a worried look because really 500 years was a hell of a long time to be with the same person.

He gave her a hard kiss. "Whether it's one day, one year or one thousand years, I will always want to be with you. I just want you to be sure." Touching his finger to the end of her nose, he said playfully, "I'll make you a deal."

She pulled away and stood apart from him, her arms crossed at her chest. "All right then—give me your best offer."

Damn, she is gorgeous. Nox was having a hard time concentrating on getting his words out with her standing there...head held high in a sheer red nothing with all her glorious attributes staring at him. Didn't she know he would give her anything—everything he could just to be a part of her life?

"Okay. Here's my deal. You take tomorrow—do your

scientific analysis on the ramifications of our bondmating. Then tomorrow night after dinner, if you still feel the same way you do now, we'll complete our bond." Giving her an emphatic stare, he reiterated, "We will be one forever. No going back."

Her heart wanted to burst out of her chest. She would do what he asked, but the answer would remain the same— she wanted to be with him.

Coming to stand between his legs, she liked that she could look him right in the eye when she stood this way. *Hmm, I'm going to have to remember this when I have a point to make.* She leaned in and gently kissed his lips, her hands cupping his face. "I accept your deal. But Nox, know this... tomorrow night we will be completing our bond."

She covered his face with butterfly kisses as she ran her fingers through his hair. She loved fanning it out, watching the purple highlights dance against his shiny skin. "I love you and I want you, but I will respect your wishes. Now if we can't complete the bond tonight, can we at least enjoy each other?" She didn't want to whine but she had an ache burning through her that needed soothing...immediately.

In one move, he had her splayed out under him on the bed, their bodies straining with their need for each other. Nox grinned hungrily down at his beautiful girl thinking he would provide her with more than enough data for her analysis. *Like Mother always said, the more data you have, the better the result.* By morning, Emeline had been given more than enough quality data.

It was the end of a long and frustrating day for Violia. The biologics she had taken from the human female, Emeline, still weren't giving them any pertinent data. Her eyes burned from the long hours she'd put in reading over all the reports in the Medical Bay. Dr. Datrem had them run and rerun the tests, but the findings were all the same…nothing out of the ordinary.

Sighing, Violia sat on her bed, rubbing her tired face lightly with her hand. Wanting nothing more than to change into her nightdress and fall into bed, she didn't dare. What if Hagen called her? Who was she kidding? Of course, he was going to call. Maybe not tonight, but eventually her worst nightmare would come true. There was no way she'd be undressed when that disgusting pervert called. He'd made her skin crawl the way he looked at her when he had barged into her life wanting, no, demanding she to do his bidding. It still blew her mind what he wanted her to do. Was he insane? Well, of course he was. What kind of person uses other people's vulnerabilities to further their own gain? Someone who had no heart or soul.

Her stomach grumbled, a reminder it had been a long time since she had eaten.

Programming some fruit and sweet rolls into the replicator, she sat at her little table peeling the pink aurant. It was a deliciously sweet fruit native to Delicia—a cross between an orange and a strawberry. As each section came off in her fingers, the smell should have enticed her to put one in her mouth, but lately everything she ate came right back up. *Damn you, Hagen!*

Her coworkers were beginning to notice her appearance. Dr. Datrem had even gone so far as to call her into his office today asking if she was ill. She nearly confessed to him about Hagen. Nearly—that was until she thought of her grandmother and what Hagen promised to do to her. Instead, she had lied. Women's issues, she'd said. He offered to give her an exam, but she fluffed him off telling him she would take something later. She couldn't risk anything happening to Etha, her sweet fragile grandmother whose only dream was to raise her family in peace. Instead, what did she get…a drug-dealing son who dumped his deviant psychopathic son on her before he got himself killed in a sex club—a club that he owned, no less.

Her poor grandmother—this was going to destroy her when she found out what Violia did because she knew that there was no coming back from this. What Hagen wanted was literally a death sentence for her. Even if by some luck she did end up getting out of this alive, she'd be spending the rest of her life on a desolate prison planet. There was no way the Delicians would be that forgiving. It didn't matter that Hagen threatened to kill his own grandmother if she didn't do what he said. No one was coming out of this unscathed, she thought bitterly.

Lost in silent misery, she hadn't noticed the mangled piece of fruit in her hand until the juice running down her fingers dripped onto her plate. Her life was spinning out of control. If only there was some way she could stop Hagen before she had to comply with his plan. She'd spent the last four days wracking her brain for some kind of solution but so far, she hadn't been able to come up with any way out of this horrible situation.

Looking down at her stained fingers, she angrily dropped the battered fruit back on her plate. *Stop kidding yourself. You have no choice but to do whatever Hagen wants.*

Frustrated, she shoved another piece of fruit into her mouth, the sweetness filled her senses as she considered going to Dr. Datrem for help. Swallowing the fruit, she shook her head—no, she couldn't involve him in this. He'd already given her this chance to come on the *Maelstrom*. As it was, this was going to kill him when he found out what she had done. Hopefully he would forgive her when he learned the circumstances of her actions, but by then it would be too late.

The fruit wasn't going to stay down. Running to the bathroom, she barely made it to the toilet before it came back up. If this kept up, she would end up in medical as a patient.

Leaning back against the wall, she finally gave in to her

anguish. Sliding down the wall to sit on the floor, Violia rested her head on her knees sobbing in despair as her world fell apart. She grieved for herself, for her grandmother and even for the humans. Everyone's lives were about to be changed forever because she had no choice but to follow Hagen's instructions. If she refused him, he would kill their grandmother. He was that cruel and she would never be able to live with herself if she was the cause of Etha's death.

What was even worse was thinking about what would happen to the humans. Hagen had no idea how many lives he was destroying nor did he care. She was just a pawn in his game.

Dragging herself up off the bathroom floor, she looked in the mirror. The dark circles under her eyes showed prominently against her dull white skin—skin that was usually shiny and bright. Her hair hung limp and unwashed—her lack of personal care visible for anyone to see. The stress of the last few days was taking its toll on her. She should have been rejoicing that her dream of becoming a doctor was coming true. Instead, all she saw was her life spiraling out of control with no hope for redemption.

What is wrong with you? Are you going to let Hagen take everything you've worked so hard for and not even try to fight back? Who are you, Violia? This is not the person Etha raised you to be.

Violia remembered the lessons her grandmother had instilled in her. *What did she used to say when things were at their worst?* Violia thought back to the day her parents had died in a transport accident. It had been a horrendous day —one that seemed to never end. When she'd finally gone to bed, Etha had come in and sat beside her, stroking her hair as she cried herself to sleep. Right before she had drifted off, she heard her grandmother say that although her parents were gone, they still lived inside of her, in her heart. Violia must always remember that when things seemed at their darkest, they would be the light that would help guide her through. Why had she forgotten that? Why? Because sometimes life and responsibilities made you forget the important things that really meant the most to you.

Turning on the shower, Violia decided she needed to find that inner strength again. She knew she would have to do what Hagen demanded, but that didn't mean that she was helpless.

The hot water coming from overhead washed away some of the dread she had been carrying around inside her. A plan started formulating in her mind as she scrubbed three days' worth of dirt and worries from her hair. Steam and heat floated up all around the shower as her self-pity evaporated into the air. She felt a lightness come over her as a tiny glow began to brighten inside her.

Feeling better after getting clean, Violia finally felt hungry. Dressed in a thick robe, she sat down and started to take a bite of aurant when her wrist comm beeped. She held in her breath before slowly exhaling. She knew who it was without having to look...the inevitable was finally calling.

Staring at her comm unit on the table, she let it ring for what seemed like an eternity.

Checking her robe to make sure she was covered, she straightened her shoulders and, putting on a blank face, Violia answered the call.

Immediately Hagen's angry face appeared in front of her. His piercing eyes glared at her as if trying to burn her with his displeasure, while his mouth was pulled down into the permanent frown he always wore. He demanded to know why it took her so long to answer his call. "I have better things to do with my time than wait around for a puny weakling like you, little cousin."

Keeping her emotions in check, she blandly asked, "What do you want, Hagen? I'm tired and I want to go to bed."

Surprised at her dismissive tone, his eyes roamed over

her body, taking in her robe cinched tightly at her slim waist. They lingered on her breasts as Violia fought the urge to cross her arms over her chest, blocking his view. "Feeling brave, little one?" His tongue swept lazily across his dry cracked lips as he leered at her. "Why don't you open your robe and show me your tits?"

Revolted, her hands gave into the urge to pull the edges of her robe tighter together. Crossing her arms against her chest, her nose wrinkled up, her eyes filling with disgust. "You pathetic pig. What, you can't get any of your Hexian whores to put out for you, so you have to talk like that to your own cousin? You're sick, you know that, Hagen?" She held his gaze, not backing down. He sickened her.

It surprised her when Hagen merely laughed in her face. "Well played, little cousin. I wondered if there was any spunk in that tight little body of yours. Or whether Etha had turned you into the wilted little flower she's become."

"She's old, Hagen. Leave her alone. Let her live the rest of her life in peace." Violia would have begged if she thought for one moment Hagen would change his mind.

"Yeah, so what—she may be old, but she does have her uses." He gave her a sly smile. "And if you want her to continue breathing, then you'll do exactly what I tell you to do."

Cocking her head and tapping her finger against her cheek, she found her inner strength, telling him, "No, I don't think I will. In fact, I'm going to go to General Tarek right now and tell him what you want me to do. He'll protect Etha. He'll make sure you never get your filthy hands on her."

Surprised by her tone, Hagen gave her a smug look. "No —I don't think you will. Do you want to know why?"

She knew by his tone it was going to be bad. Sure enough, her stomach sank when he held up a holo photo of their grandmother. She was held in a tight grip up against a nasty-looking Hexian...his weapon pressed hard against her temple. A trickle of blood ran down the side of her freshly bruised face.

He snickered at her look of horror. "All I have to do is make one call and he'll pull the trigger."

"Hagen," she implored him. "Why are you doing this to your own grandmother?"

"Why? Because if this is what it takes to get you to do what I say, then so be it. Besides, what did she ever do for me? Nothing, but harp about what a disappointment my father was and how I was just like him."

"You are just like him!" she yelled back. "She did everything for you. Etha tried to give you a good life but it was never enough for you. You would rather spend all your time down at that...that disgusting club. How could you do this to the one person who loved you?"

He laughed, the bitterness oozing out of him, "Loved me? No one loved me. At best, she tolerated me and when my father died, did she care?" He jeered at her, "No she didn't. That disgusting club as you call it—that at least gave me funds to live the life I wanted."

"She tried to love you, but you were just like your mother, always wanting something for nothing," she shot back at him.

At the mention of his mother, his face turned nearly purple with fury. She knew if they were in the same room, he would have backhanded her and with his size, she would have ended up in medical or worse—dead. He gave her a cold lifeless look that scared her more than she had ever been in her life.

In a voice devoid of feeling, he said, "Don't ever talk about my mother."

Violia knew she had crossed the line at the mentioned his mother. Hagen hated it if anyone said anything about her. It was the one thing that would send him into a boiling rage. The only time Etha had made a comment about his mother had been the day Hagen's father died. Hagen had flown into such a rage, he slapped Etha, nearly breaking her jaw with the blow. That was the last time they had seen him until he had called her four days ago. Lucky for Etha, Dr. Datrem had come right away and was able to repair the damage to her face, but it didn't repair the damage to her heart. Etha had tried to love Hagen, but he didn't make it easy. It was more she felt sorry for him because of the type of parents he'd had and the environment he had been forced to grow up in. She'd tried being a good grandmother to him, but he was too damaged. Now seeing him, Violia knew that he was beyond help.

"Fine, whatever." She put her hands up but still held her ground.

Still holding up the photo of Etha, Hagen's eyes narrowed on Violia. "Enough talking." His voice was hard as he filled her in on what she was to do, threatening her if she even considered defying him. "You better not tell anyone, and that includes your mentor Dr. Datrem."

She glared back at him, ready to argue, but Hagen just stood there with his arms crossed, the muscles in his thick barrel chest pulling against his filthy shirt. He was wearing the same dirty clothes he had on the last time he'd called. Violia wasn't surprised…Hagen never was very fond of soap or water. It was the smile on his face that had her worried. It was unnatural, and that only meant one thing —Hagen never left anything to chance.

"Do you realize the position you are putting me in if I do this for you? I finally have a chance to become a doctor and do some real good. Can't you understand why I can't do this? Let Grandmother go and find another way to get what you want." Violia tried again to get him to stop this craziness. "No one is going to win."

"Now that's where you're wrong. I will win. Hexia will win. And as for you, I don't really care what happens to you."

"No, I won't do it. Forget it. I'm hanging up. Go away, Hagen. I'm going to tell the General right now. Etha would not want me doing this." Violia had had enough of Hagen.

Not backing down, she continued, her voice growing stronger, almost to a yell, saying, "Good-bye, Hagen." She reached to shut off the wrist comm, but he stopped her.

"Fine." Giving her a heavy sigh, before his eyes turned deadly, saying, "Then I guess you won't have any problem living the rest of your life with her death on your conscience."

He held up a holo video for Violia to see. It was of a young girl being held by a large angry Hexian whose filthy hand was covering her mouth. Violia's heart shattered at the sight of her terror-stricken face that was stained with tears as she fought frantically against her attacker.

Lilith, Dr. Datrem's granddaughter!

Violia had forgotten that Dr. Datrem had arranged for her to stay with Etha while they were away on this mission. Terror formed on Violia's face as she watched another Hexian male come into the picture, his dirty fingers caressing the young girl's face. The girl twisted and squirmed, screaming through the fingers covering her mouth, trying to get away. The second male stood at her side, stroking her head before running his fingers through her long ponytail. The more his fingers played with her hair, the harder the girl struggled to get away until finally he backhanded her across the face. Her head snapped back before she slumped, unconscious, in her captor's arms. The second male pulled a large knife out of the sheath that was strapped to his leg.

Violia gasped as she started for the hologram yelling "*NO,*" thinking he was going to cut her throat but instead he grabbed her head and in one swipe of his knife, he cut off her ponytail. Holding it up, he rubbed it against his face, his sadistic laugh echoing through the holo vid as he displayed his prize for her to see. Tucking the hair into his belt, he bowed to the screen before grabbing the young girl, throwing her slender body over his shoulder as he sauntered out of the picture.

"You are pure evil."

Smiling his acknowledgement of her words, Hagen crossed his arms and gave Violia a knowing look. Yes, she would do everything he said without question. "You finally understand. Good. Now you will do what I've instructed or you will be responsible for two deaths."

The screen disappeared...leaving Violia alone, staring hopelessly at the mangled piece of fruit.

Closing her eyes for a moment in a vain attempt to block out the last fifteen minutes, her mind kept replaying the interaction with Hagen. *I have never known anyone so evil. Okay, Violia, you can't let Lilith and Etha die, although knowing Hagen, he would probably kill them anyway.* That thought brought Violia to her knees. The thought of that sweet girl in the hands of those disgusting men—who knows what they were doing to her. *She must be so scared.*

Violia covered her eyes with her hands, trying to block out the images she had just witnessed. She gave herself exactly one minute to fall apart before she sat up, shaking her hair back from her face, swiping the tears from her eyes. *Crying is not going to save them. You need to think of a plan. There must be some way I can alert the General of Hagen's plan without getting Etha and Lilith killed.*

Moving around the room, picking up her hairbrush and then putting it back down, she started thinking. As she paced, touching and straightening the mementos she had brought from home, reflecting on all the sacrifices her grandmother had made to give her a good life, an idea began to form in her mind.

Going to her computer tablet, she opened a file and started dictating the events of Hagen's two conversations, detailing everything he wanted her to do. When she got to the part about Lilith, she paused, still remembering the look of terror on her young face. Violia knew that feeling. She had lived with it daily when Hagen was living with Etha. He took every opportunity he could to inflict his sadistic sense of humor on her and her grandmother. Now he had crossed the line. She would do everything she could to stop him.

When she had finished with her file, she ended it with a note addressed to General Tarek outlining her plan, imploring him to send help to Etha and Lilith on Delicia. She apologized to him for her part in Hagen's despicable plan, begging him to please make sure her grandmother was safe. Violia knew she wasn't going to make it back alive. It would be up to the General to save Etha and Lilith. She then instructed ARI to deliver this file to General Tarek at 4:30 tomorrow afternoon. It was the least she could do.

Looking at the time, she saw it was late. If she hurried, she would have enough time to set her plan in motion.

Changing back into her uniform, she put her wrist comm on and headed out the door. If her plan worked, although if she was being honest with herself, the probabilities were pretty low, she could at least give herself a fighting chance of staying alive until help came. She might be small and delicate looking, but that didn't mean she couldn't be as cunning as her cousin. If she was going down, she was taking Hagen down with her.

CHAPTER 16

Nox's gaze never left Emeline as he stepped quietly onto the hologram platform. She was dressed in her typical lab clothes—jeans and a T-shirt, but had replaced her jacket with her simple white lab coat. He never got tired of watching her. Whether it was the look on her face as she lay in his arms or when she was whipping up one of her special creations in the kitchen, each time he learned something new about her.

Like at this moment—she was so absorbed in what she was doing that he had to call her name several times to get her attention. In between waiting for her simulation to finish, she was working on the analysis he had asked her to do last night. He knew she was only doing this to placate him, but he wanted her to be absolutely sure of her decision.

Watching her upload the last bit of data into ARI, Nox couldn't contain his happiness as he looked at his gorgeous bondmate.

Emeline grinned over at him as she instructed ARI to formulate a hypothesis using the updated information. "Okay, let's see what your alien AI has to say about our bondmating."

She stood back, watching the three screens in front of her. She had thought her lab was state of the art—it wasn't even close. Transparent screens and primitive holograms aside, Nox's computer system far surpassed anything they had on Earth. The Delicians used a maxi core unit where hers was only a multi core. *Maxi core—the brain of the ship.* Nox had explained how the maxi core controlled the entire ship. It could create a core on demand when needed and shut off those that weren't in use, thus controlling the amount of energy that was used.

Emeline took a moment to allow her imagination to flow with the endless possibilities open to them. The thought of her and Nox brainstorming together was definitely appealing to her.

Chuckling to herself, she looked up when Nox asked her what was so funny. "I was just doing some comparisons of our computer systems."

"Interesting, and what did you discover?" Nox asked, giving in to the temptation to twine his fingers through the thick strands of her ponytail.

"Well, aside from the maxi core unit, which, by the way I am totally jealous of, I still end up impatiently waiting for results. Come on, ARI, let's get a move on."

Nox had to admit even he was a little nervous. There was still a small part of him that worried something would go wrong between them. Although after last night, it was a very small part...she had not been shy in showing him that this was what she wanted.

Not wanting to get into another discussion about the UAP's misconceptions of humans, pulling lightly on her hair, causing her head to bend back, he kissed her nose lightly saying, "I suppose I'll find you in my lab on Delicia when you should be in my bed, beautiful girl?"

"Probably." Laughing, she ran her finger down his chest. "Maybe we should put a bed in the lab?" She wagged her eyebrows at him, knowing he would get her meaning.

Pulling her close, Nox nuzzled his nose into her hair, inhaling the enticing scent of vanilla that sent shivers through his body. He murmured that there was already one in there and then proceeded to whisper all his secret *experiments* he wanted to try with her.

Blushing, Emeline looked up at Nox, a silly grin plastered on her face. A grin he had put there this morning before work and that didn't appear to be going away anytime soon. Nudging him in the side, she joked to him, "So what happens when ARI rejects us?"

Shaking his head sadly, he lamented, "The crew will be very upset when ARI meets a terrible end."

Leaning into him, she giggled. Emeline knew they would be completing the bond tonight. Yes, as scientists they would examine the results and assess the outcome that ARI would give them. *But we will still be making the final decision—not some artificial intelligence. Geez, like I'd let some AI make a life-changing decision for me.* It wasn't like they weren't prepared for what the future held for them. They had already witnessed some physical changes...their skin spoke for itself. All they knew was that they were in this together.

"And I was becoming so fond of ARI. He—she...what do you call ARI anyway, male or female?"

Emeline didn't give him time to answer because at that moment ARI signaled that the analysis was complete, "Whatever—*he* just posted the results. Oh look. See, I was right. ARI agrees with me that our bond is— 'The Correct Solution.'" Excited, Emeline's smile radiated her happiness. She jumped up and gave him a quick kiss and a hug then broke into her happy dance.

Nox watched her gyrate her hips, her hands moved gracefully above her head before she extended her leg, toes pointed as she performed a perfect pirouette, finishing up into a low bow. Looking up at him, her face glowed with happiness before she jumped into his arms, covering his face with kisses. He held her tightly, her body melding to his. He could feel the love she had for him through their bond, so it was a good thing Loris chose that moment to walk through the door. Otherwise, they'd be completing their bond on his office floor and that was definitely not how he wanted their first time to be.

"I take it you got good news." Loris chuckled as he looked at the two of them. Anyone could see that they were celebrating something, although those two never seemed to stop touching each other.

Emeline watched Nox, who was sending the data from ARI to his personal comm. Smiling to herself, she thought how alike they were. She was just going to do the same thing—no one needed to see their personal information. Just because they were the first interspecies bondmates didn't mean their lives were open for everyone to examine.

"Yes, ARI gets to live another day." Emeline shot back at him as she straightened her hair.

"I'm sure ARI thanks you." Loris grinned at her as he moved past her to get to his workstation.

She sniffed the air as he passed. With her hand on her hip, she glared at him accusingly. "Is that beef I smell? Was someone cooking and didn't tell us? I'm starving, you know."

Loris put his head down in an attempt to hide his face as he answered her. "Ezio was trying out a new dish he wanted to make for everyone tonight and I was his tester." Looking up at her, he continued, "It's similar to the beef you have on Earth. I think you call it a cow. What Ezio was cooking is called a Bubuli. It roams the forests of our mountain region. It's delicious when cooked with a sauce, and Ezio's is outstanding."

"I wonder if it's similar to a deer on Earth."

"I'm not sure," Loris replied.

"I know—ARI, do a comparison of a Delician Bubuli and Earth's deer and display the results on screen 2. This is just like Google."

Loris and Nox looked at each other curiously.

"What is a Google?" Nox asked.

"That is what we call a search engine on our internet. Remember how I told you that we have the world wide web that holds our data on servers we call the cloud?" The two males nodded their heads. "Well, Google is one of the search engines we use to access the data. Only ARI is so much better. I would spend hours doing searches on the internet, but now all I have to do is tell ARI what I want and he does the searches in a fraction of the time. Not to mention the display is incredible."

The images of the two animals appeared on the screen in front of them. Both animals were similar in appearance except one had six legs and was twice the size. It had the same rack of antlers and the same soulful eyes when it looked at you as a stag would on Earth. Loris told her that the six legs allowed it to move at incredibly fast speeds through the forests. It was hunted for pleasure on Delicia.

"It's the same on Earth. My mother has deer wandering through her backyard all the time," Emeline told them.

"And does she kill them for food herself?" Loris asked.

"Oh god, no. My mother would rather eat a salad than kill an animal. Although she thought about it last summer when one ate all her lettuce that she had carefully nurtured from seed. I have never seen her so mad." Emeline was wistful at the memory of her mum. She missed her terribly.

Nox was thinking about food too but remembered he did have a meeting to go to and then afterwards he and Emeline had plans. "Loris, will you tell Ezio to save us some food? We won't be able to make it to the rec room for dinner." Giving Emeline a wink, he added cryptically, "But we're definitely going to be hungry later."

Emeline snorted at Loris's bewildered expression as she watched him head over to his workstation, muttering that he wasn't going to even ask—he had work to finish up. Liam and Ami had just completed the last of the retrofits on the Space Station and had sent Loris the new data for him to run the last of the simulations. The duo were due back any time now to attend Tarek's strategy meeting with Nox.

Emeline turned back to the computer console and started to read through Liam's notes. Glad that the retrofits were finished, now all they had to do was initiate the program and the communications network for Earth would be protected. She was so absorbed in what she was reading she hadn't noticed Nox until she felt his hands on her shoulders.

"I have to go meet with Tarek and the team. Are you going to be okay?" Nox had reached down and taken her hand in his before pulling her into his office. The table in the corner was laden with small dishes of exotic-looking foods.

"What's all this?" She grinned at him then laughed as her stomach growled at the different smells coming from the foods.

"You said you were starving, so I made you some food."

Kissing him on the cheek, she went over to check out what he had prepared for her. "This is so nice of you. It looks amazing."

"Well, as your bondmate, it is my pleasure to see to your needs." He walked over and started pointing out the different foods. "This is similar to the sushi you were telling me about, only I used some Delician seafood for you to try. I hope you like it." The look of delight on her face as he put the first piece in her mouth was priceless.

"Wow, that is fantastic. What kind of fish is that? It has such a buttery taste to it." Her smile at his thoughtfulness lit up the room. "Aren't you going to eat?" she asked, her words muffled with food.

He walked over to the replicator, giving her a silly grin as he brought over a cheeseburger, fries and a vanilla shake and set it on the table. "I think I've found my new favorite Earth food."

Laughing, she dug into her own meal, marveling at the different flavors and textures. When she was finished, she sat back patting her stomach. "I am so full. That was delicious—I'm going to have to find time to get to the training room today."

Finishing the last of his shake, he cocked his eyebrow at her, giving her a hungry grin. "There's no need for that. In fact, I think you should get some rest. You're going to have a very busy night."

Emeline's cheeks felt hot when she thought about her and Nox completing their bond tonight.

Sauntering over and pulling him to his feet, she wrapped her arms around his waist as she nestled her head against his shoulder. She loved the feel of his hard body against hers, and the smell of vanilla from his shake made her relax into him.

Holding her close, Nox drank in her warm body heat like a thirsty male. Kissing the top of her head, he asked her, "Will you be staying here in the lab with Loris?"

"No. I'm going to go take a bubble bath. I've been wanting to soak in that tub ever since I first saw it." She hugged him close, inhaling his very air…sighing with happiness.

Nuzzling her neck, he couldn't stop himself from finding her lush lips. They were warm and inviting as he pressed his gently to hers. They were a perfect fit. Kissing was his new favorite thing—well, one of his new favorite things. Everything about Emeline was his favorite. As he started to deepen the kiss, his wrist comm began to beep. *The meeting!*

"I wish I could be in the bath with you. I could massage your sore muscles, but it looks like I'm going to be late to Tarek's meeting. I'm not making a good impression with my colleagues," Kissing her forehead, he headed towards the door. "They'll just have to understand. Shall I meet you in our room after the meeting?"

"Yes. I think I might take a nap before my bath." She yawned at him.

Coming back in and kissing her lightly, he whispered in her ear, "Why don't you wait on that bath and I'll join you after my meeting?" He kissed her nose before gazing into her deep blue eyes as he waited for her answer.

Emeline's eyes glistened with love. *A bath with this beautiful alien male who could melt my insides when he looks at me with that smoldering look—HELL YES!* "I like how you think. I'll rest up while you go and make a plan to save the world."

She caressed his lips, murmuring, "I'll be waiting for you."

Stealing one last kiss, Nox groaned. This meeting was going to be torture for him. Grabbing her hand, he kissed each finger—tonight would be amazing. Yeah, he was going to be late to the meeting. With one last look, he walked through the lab, asking Loris to send the latest simulation results on the data to his comm unit before the lab door closed behind him.

Judging by the silly grin that seemed permanently affixed to his face, Nox was going to have a hard time concentrating. Not to mention the ribbing he was going to get from his colleagues when all he could think about was his beautiful girl and their plans for tonight.

Leaning against the door jamb of Nox's office, Emeline laughed watching her bondmate grin from ear to ear as he ran out the door.

Standing up, she had her own things to do. First up, the nightgown design she had in mind for tonight needed to get entered into the replicator.

Loris gave her a distracted smile and waved his hand at her when she told him she was going back to her quarters. If he needed anything from her, feel free to call, but she was going to take a nap.

Walking along the corridor, Emeline marveled at the design of the ship. The *Maelstrom* was massive, with lots of corridors and different decks. The ship wasn't exactly what she had thought it would be. The places she'd been so far —the interiors seemed more attuned to a cruise ship than a battle cruiser. Having spent most of her time working in Nox's lab, she couldn't wait for when she and Nox had some free time to do some exploring. She was eager to get a look at the engine room and see how they used the Delician crystals as their energy source.

Since the distance from the lab to their room wasn't far, in no time at all she was in her room. Looking around the stark space, she decided it was time to put some human touches to the place.

Pressing her wrist comm, she brought up her file with the list of items she wanted replicated. Champagne was at the top of the list along with roses, lots of roses, and strawberries with chocolate fondue. She was looking forward to introducing Nox to a unique way of tasting chocolate.

Smiling to herself, she looked over at their bed and decided a little housekeeping was in order. She loved how easy having a replicator made her life, especially when it came to laundry.

Once her chores were done, she settled herself on the couch under her favorite blanket ready to take a nap while she waited for Nox to return. She wanted to be rested for tonight, and considering he had kept her up most of last night— *[Yawning] I could use a couple hours of sleep before he gets here. I'll just shut my eyes for a few minutes.* Her eyes drifted shut, her mind thinking about Nox—tonight was going to be so special.

Beep beep

Groaning, Emeline opened her eyes to see who was calling. *Violia? Huh. I wonder what she wants. Maybe she has an update on my test results.*

Pressing receive, Emeline smiled as she remembered Nox giving her this unique and functional gift as Violia's image appeared before her. "Hi, Violia. How are you?"

"Hello, Emeline. I hope I'm not disturbing you."

She had on a friendly smile and Emeline thought she looked better than she had since the last time she'd seen her. "No, I was just taking some time to myself while Nox is at a meeting." She didn't want to make Violia feel bad if she knew she was about to take a nap.

"I was wondering if you would like to take a tour of the ship with me. I know you said that you'd wanted to see more of it and I thought we could continue our discussion on Delician families. I'm free for the next few hours if you have time."

Emeline looked into Violia's dark green eyes and saw that they were clear. The dark smudges that had been under them lately were not as pronounced.

Checking the time, there was plenty of time for a tour and she could still get back well before Nox got here. Besides, she couldn't resist a tour of the ship. After all, she would be living on it for a while and it would be good for her to learn her way around.

Violia didn't wait for her to answer, saying, "I have a special place on the ship I'd like to show you. I just know you are going to love it."

"That sounds great. Where do you want me to meet you?"

"I'll come to you. It will be easier and it's closer to where we're going."

Ending their call, Emeline took the time to freshen up before Violia arrived. She was looking forward to getting to know her better. She remembered how standoffish Violia was when they first met, but their friendship had started to show improvement with each time Emeline had gone to medical. *I really want to ask Violia about life on Delicia. I need to learn as much as I can before we get there. I'm going to have to meet Nox's father eventually and I want to make a good impression. I'm going to need as much info as I can about my new life.* Nox had been telling her about life on Delicia, but she wanted to learn more about their dynamic from a woman's point of view. Learning about Delician male interactions had been eye opening. She laughed to herself, thinking about their training sessions and then cooking and eating each night with the Delician males. *Man, can they eat!*

Emeline checked herself out in the mirror. She loved how she was looking lately...those training sessions were really paying off. *That and all the "exercise" I've been getting with Nox.* It was more than that though. She was happy.

Smiling, she turned at the sound of her door beeping.

Violia, right on time.

Opening the door to Violia, she invited her in. "I just needed to grab my purse." She considered leaving a note for Nox, but knew she would be back well before him, so she didn't bother.

Turning to Violia, she motioned towards the door, saying, "Are you ready to go?"

"Yes, follow me." Violia walked out the door, heading off in a direction Emeline had never been before.

Catching up to walk beside Violia, Emeline told her, "I'm so glad you called. I've been wanting to see more of the ship, but there just hasn't been much free time. I'll be glad when this threat is over and we can start living our lives."

Violia nodded in agreement.

Looking around, Emeline was disappointed all they seemed to be doing was walking down one corridor after another with nothing interesting to see except the strange writing over the doors. *I think I need to start learning to read and write Delician. It doesn't look that difficult.*

As they walked, they passed multiple crewmembers, all of whom turned to stare at Emeline, some never having seen a human before. She couldn't blame them really. She was definitely looking back, but so far all she had seen was muscle-bound males with gorgeous faces. She wondered about what the males were like back on Delicia.

"Violia, are all Delician males this jacked and good-looking or is it just General Tarek's training methods?"

Stepping into a small alcove off the hallway, Violia turned and shook her head as she chuckled at her. "No, that's all General Tarek's doing. Delician males are mostly as tall as the soldiers here, but they are definitely not as *jacked.*" An image of Hagen came to mind—definitely not good-looking.

Understanding her meaning, Emeline told her, "It's the same on Earth. Humans are all sizes, shapes and colors. But I think it's more than just physical characteristics that determine what a person looks like. Temperament, economics, climate—they're just a few of the factors that can shape a person physically."

"That's true on Delicia as well."

"Can I ask you about Delician families?"

"Of course. What would you like to know?"

"Everything." Emeline laughed broadly. "I'm going to be living on Delicia with Nox, and I have no idea what it's like there. I only know how life is on Earth. I mean, to me the idea of family should be universal, but as a scientist I need more data in order to complete my findings. Where I'm from in the United States, family and work—a sense of accomplishment—those are what's important. Of course, you will always have those people who go against the norm."

"It's the same on my planet. Most want to have families and fulfillment in careers, and of course finding your bondmate is the ultimate goal, but as you are well aware—that is rare." Violia saw the color start to rise on Emeline's cheeks.

"Do families live in separate houses once they marry, or do they all live as a unit?"

"That depends on what the family wants, I suppose. I can tell you that for me and my parents, we had our own house. My mother was a medic and my father was a biology teacher at my school. As an only child I was spoiled—of course." Violia always had bittersweet feelings when she thought of her parents. She considered her words thoughtfully before she spoke again, "If I could tell you one thing about Delicians, it would be that because we have no poverty on our planet, we are free to pursue whatever career paths we choose. Most Delicians are quite satisfied with their careers. The Delician crystals have afforded us the opportunity to provide for every citizen."

She stopped, giving Emeline a sorrowful look, telling her, "I don't want to give you an unrealistic view of my planet though. Most planets have an unsavory aspect to them, wouldn't you agree?"

Emeline nodded her head. She had lived in the city for a long time and had to agree with Violia.

"Delicia is no different."

Violia continued her story. "My parents were always going off on excursions to find new plants. Every room in our house was filled with different scents from all the pots of fresh herbs crowding every spare surface. They even had a drying room off the kitchen for making medicines and teas for natural healing."

"It sounds like you had a wonderful life," Emeline told her.

Shrugging her shoulders, Violia answered sadly, "It was for as long as it lasted—they were killed in a shuttle accident when I was 12. I had been away at camp with my friends when it happened. After that I went to live at my grandmother's."

Emeline put her arm around her shoulder, giving her a small hug. She was all too familiar with what Violia was feeling. "I'm sorry for your loss."

Violia gave her a pained smile. Losing her parents had created a hole in her soul. No matter how hard she tried, the hole never filled in.

"How was it living with your grandmother?" Emeline asked softly. She wanted to know more about Violia's life but didn't want to appear too pushy.

"It was okay at first. My grandmother is a sweet caring person and tried her best to be both father and mother to me. That changed whenever my uncle would show up. He was nothing but trouble. He was, as I said before, from the unsavory aspect of our planet. He had a son, Hagen, who is a little older than I am. He is not a nice person. After his mother died of a drug overdose, he came to live with us for a while."

"That must have been terrible for him to lose his mother that way. Were you close?" Emeline asked.

"Close?" Violia let out a sharp laugh. "Scared to death is more like it. He was a bully. I was never so happy as the day he moved back to live at his father's 'exotic dance club,' but he would still show up on a whim just to terrorize me and my grandmother."

"What happened to him?"

"He worked for his father until my uncle got himself killed—in his own club, no less. After that he disappeared." Not wanting to say anymore, Violia didn't volunteer any more information.

"Wow—that is so sad."

Having stuck to most of the facts about her life, Violia squeezed Emeline's hand, telling her, "Yes, it was awful for a while but look how good my life has turned out. I have a career I love and now I have a new friend."

Touched, Emeline squeezed back. "Yes, you do. And who knows, maybe Hagen found what he was looking for and turned his life around."

"And sometimes people are just plain evil." Violia sighed before she tugged on Emeline's hand and continued on to the next opening. Turning right, she pointed to the door at the end of a small corridor.

Violia grinned at her as she pulled Emeline forward. "You are going to love this. I was shown this place when I first came on board and now, I come here all the time. You're going to be so surprised."

Emeline followed her, but had to wonder about her comment about her cousin. It was an unusual response, one that Emeline had never heard before. Her cousin Hagen sounded like someone she definitely never wanted to meet.

The melancholy look on Violia's face was replaced with one of delight as she pointed toward the door in front of them. Emeline was curious as to what she was so excited about—that was until the door opened in front of her...the sight was magical to behold.

A botany lab but not just any lab, oh no. This lab was

filled with all sorts of colors—deep greens, various shades of browns, reds and oranges and yes, even some blues and purples. There were trees filled with different kinds of fruits and nuts.

Looking closely, Emeline recognized a few of the fruits the Delicians had been using in their dinners. "This place is fantastic. Now I know where Jagger and Tarek have been getting their produce. I thought they were using the replicator."

Emeline was looking around trying to decide where to go first. There was too much going on—every square inch of the room was used for some specific function. Long raised beds held a variety of vegetables in different stages of growth. Several workstations were positioned around the room for the ease in caring for the plants. Long tubes ran across the ceiling that had tiny hoses dropping down for watering. It had a similar feel to some of the botany labs on Earth that Emeline had been in except that this one was on a SPACESHIP! Floating out in Earth's outer solar system.

Emeline laughed with joy. Who would have thought to find a botany lab like this on a battle cruiser? This was definitely going on her pros list, Emeline thought to herself. She could see herself spending a lot of time in here. *Mum is going to love this. I hope I can talk her into coming to Delicia with me!*

"Dr. Senta showed this room to me when I first arrived. She wanted to make me dinner and needed some ingredients." Looking around, Violia gently guided Emeline into the center of the room. "Come over here and look at this— these are the climate-controlled rooms."

Along the far-left wall were four glass-partitioned rooms that were used to grow plants and trees that require different types of climate. Walking into one of the rooms, Emeline saw that it was dedicated to crops grown in the coastal areas of Delicia. Plants loaded with fruit hung down from hooks—the different scents mingled together, making Emeline's mouth water.

"Can I take a taste?" Emeline reached up, palming a round fruit similar to an orange.

"Certainly. Eat whatever you want. Of course, you will have to spend an hour of your time in here helping out in order to eat anything," Violia told her.

"Is that all? Sign me up. I love growing my own vegetables and herbs. I wonder if they'd let me bring in a few plants from Earth?" Emeline was hopeful. That would be fantastic to be able to eat fresh foods from home.

"I'm sure General Tarek wouldn't mind. You'll have to ask him." Noticing Emeline's questioning look, she added, "He runs this lab."

"You're kidding? These are the General's gardens?"

Laughing, Violia said, "I know it's hard to believe. He can be so intimidating. You'd think he would spend all his time working out or commanding everyone, but he loves to work in here creating plants and foods. He will probably be very amenable to growing some vegetables and fruits from Earth. I heard he was interested in something called an apple."

Hearing that made Emeline feel pretty proud of the apple crisp Ami had made for Tarek. She told Violia about the recipe for apple crisp and promised to make some for her soon.

They wandered around, stopping in each of the rooms, sampling the different fruits, nuts and vegetables. Some tasted familiar to what she had eaten on Earth, including the ones she didn't like—peas and beets. One tree in particular grew something that looked like a grapefruit, only the color was teal. Thinking it would be sour and tart like a grapefruit, Emeline was shocked when it tasted sweet like a plum. It was called a *prunova*.

"I'm going to have to talk to Tarek. I can make jams to spread on bread out of these fruits." Picking one up, she put it in her purse. "I could spend hours in here working. I'll save this for later."

"Take as much as you like. I can tell you'll be spending a lot of time in here." Violia had picked a vegetable that was similar to a carrot and was washing it off in the sink. "There is a schedule on the computer console in the office, but it's usually pretty casual. Just sign up when you want but you can come in anytime. Come, I'll show you the office." She broke off a piece of the vegetable and handed it to Emeline before taking a bite of the crunchy vegetable.

They passed a large storage area along the back wall before coming to the office. Violia showed Emeline how to access ARI through the botany lab's console. They signed her up for the hour after lunch for the next few days. Emeline figured she could schedule more time once she began living on board.

Violia asked Emeline if she would like to continue the tour.

"Sure."

The next section of the room was different from the rest of the room. It was more like a large section of metal with a large door cut into it. A console panel was inserted into the wall to the right of the door.

"Want to see what an escape pod looks like?" Violia went to the panel and punched in a series of commands, causing the door to open.

Standing in the doorway, Emeline paused for a moment. For some unknown reason her inner voice screamed caution, however, checking out alien technology was enough to tune it out.

Walking inside, she realized it was a small space, maybe only big enough for four Delician males or eight females. It had seats that could be pulled down along the sides with a small cockpit area in the front. "This is cool. I just hope we never have to use one of these. Have you ever had to use one before?"

Her words had just passed her lips when Emeline felt

346

something cold press against the side of her neck.

"What the hell!"

Holding Violia's gaze, Emeline could feel the drugs begin to course through her body.

"Why" was all she could get out before she slowly slid to the floor...unconscious.

Swallowing hard, Violia hit the button to close the door. She couldn't risk anyone finding them before they made their escape.

After making sure Emeline was comfortable, she took a seat in the cockpit. Leaning her head back, she took a moment to calm herself. Beads of sweat formed across her forehead. Swiping her arm to clear the moisture, Violia prayed she was doing the right thing. *Please somebody help me out here.* Praying wasn't something she generally did. With the way her life had been lately, no one had been listening to her anyway.

Glancing at Emeline lying on her side on the floor, her peaceful face made Violia feel shame. Shaking it off, she tried to assuage herself that there were two lives at stake.

Disabling the sensors with the codes she had been given, she input the coordinates that Hagen had sent to her this morning. With any luck, it wouldn't take too long for General Tarek to rescue them. If not, then she had a few surprises planned for Hagen. Determined, she swore to herself to keep both her and Emeline safe from Hagen's evil plans.

Giving Emeline one last look and mouthing a silent "*sorry*," she pushed the eject button before moving to sit next to Emeline on the floor. She could hear the clamps of the pod release and then a feeling of falling made her clutch her stomach until the gravity sensors came online, causing the escape pod to stabilize. She only wished her stomach would follow suit.

Picking up Emeline's wrist to check her pulse, Violia noticed a bracelet slide down her arm. It was beautiful. No way was she going to let Hagen take this from Emeline.

Slipping it off Emeline's arm, she put it in one of the hidden pockets she programmed into her uniform. The nanite technology they used in making clothing was useful for creating this new and improved uniform. She had used the replicator in the medical bay that allowed her to use advanced materials for a more upgraded version but still looked like a standard medic's uniform.

Checking her for any more jewelry, Violia removed a ring from one of her fingers and a necklace and placed them in her pocket with the bracelet. Folding her hands across her chest, Violia leaned back against the wall to wait for Hagen. She didn't know how long she would have to wait —only hoping she would stay under the *Maelstrom's* radar and didn't end up getting blown up in the process.

Emeline hadn't moved since Violia had used a DRI to inject her with enough of a sedative to keep her out for at least three to four hours. *It will be better this way for both of us.* Hagen was cruel and it was better if Emeline stayed unconscious for as long as possible.

The pod jerked unexpectedly, causing Violia's head to bang sharply against the wall, the impact nearly causing her to black out. Emeline's body slammed hard against the wall, causing Violia to cringe...thankful she was unconscious. That had to have hurt, she thought. Hopefully she didn't break any ribs. *Damn you, Hagen. You did that on purpose.*

Violia staggered to her feet, her head spinning as she struggled to stand up straight. The movement of the pod indicated they were being pulled forward, but when Violia looked outside she didn't see any ships. The only thing visible was the twinkling of stars staring back at her. *That's odd.*

Tucking her hair up into a bun at the base of her neck, she straightened her uniform, rechecking to make sure her pockets were concealed as she waited for the pod to stop moving.

Checking the window again, this time she saw that they were in the cargo bay of a small shuttle. Violia wondered why she hadn't seen Hagen's ship when she had first looked out the window.

They were moving again, so she stood there, waiting, her stomach doing flip-flops from too much adrenaline.

After what felt like an eternity, the shuttle slowed before setting down, the vibrations from the engines that had been a constant hum dissipated. She knew it would only be a matter of minutes before she had to confront Hagen. The fruits and vegetables that she had eaten earlier were burning a hole in her stomach.

Looking at Emeline lying on the floor, totally unaware of the terrible danger she had put her in, Violia knew she needed to be strong for both their sakes.

Squaring her shoulders, Violia swallowed her nerves, ready for whatever Hagen meant to do to her and Emeline.

When the door abruptly opened, Violia's breath froze in her throat at her first look at Hagen in many years. What she saw was right out of one of her father's scary stories he would tell her on their family camping trips. The ones that had her begging to sleep in their bed.

Hagen looked nothing like he did when they were children. He was bald, for one thing. Growing up, his brown hair had hung long...limp and stringy around his broad oval face—always looking like it needed a good washing. Observing him closely, it was his skin that had changed the most—it was no longer the shiny white iridescent skin of the average Delician. His skin was yellowed, aged, like he had spent too much time in a hot dry climate, which meant only one thing—he'd been on Hexia all this time. Violia wasn't at all surprised that's where he had ended up. It was natural he would migrate towards the kind of element he was used to.

It was his eyes that scared her the most. They were still the same dark green mixed with amber that gave them a muddied look. Worst of all, they still had the same cruel glint to them. Violia swallowed hard, knowing in her soul that Hagen had only grown meaner over the years.

His lewd grin was sickening, making her feel unclean. "Little cousin, you've filled out nicely, I see. Come and give your old cousin a hug." He came at her with outstretched arms, expecting her to comply.

She took a step backwards, dodging just out of his reach. "Are you serious? I'm not here for a family reunion. I came because you threatened to kill our grandmother, so now I'm here. Let Etha and Lilith go." She stood with her hands on her hips, Emeline's prone body lying silently at her feet.

Looking down at the human, Hagen ignored Violia's request, focusing his attention on Emeline.

Violia didn't like the way he was looking at Emeline, so she stepped in front of her body, blocking Hagen's view, a move that caused him to growl.

Pushing her out of the way, he reached down and grabbed Emeline, flinging her over his shoulder. Her head slapped against his back as her ponytail swung back and forth. He rubbed his hand slowly over her bottom, which infuriated Violia. He had no right to lay his hands on her, but at this point she couldn't challenge him. She had to bide her time until help arrived.

Turning to follow Hagen, she suddenly found herself seized around the waist by a dirty muscular arm. He held her tight against his body as he turned and strode out the door of the pod carrying both women. She squirmed, kicking her feet as she yelled at him to let her down. He squeezed her tight against his side, telling her to cut it out before he dropped her on her head. She stilled, her body going limp as he carried both women through the ship. With each step, Violia could tell that she would be one massive bruise by tomorrow. Glancing over, she cringed at the thought of how much pain Emeline was going to be in when she woke up.

He didn't speak to her as he stalked down one corridor after another. It was obvious the ship was in desperate need of attention. It was nothing like the *Maelstrom,* whose meticulous care was evident throughout the entire ship. This ship reflected the same type of care Hagen took in his bathing habits—none. The smell emanating from his unwashed body made her gag.

Stopping in front of a door that had rust encased along the edges, he pushed a button and the door opened inward, revealing a small room with two cots against one wall. Violia could tell by the musty smell that it wasn't a room that was used very often. At least it had a small washroom off in one corner. Hopefully Hagen wouldn't use restraints on them. His enormous ego was such that he probably didn't consider they would dare to resist him.

Hagen threw Emeline's unconscious body onto one of the cots, not caring how rough he was being; her body bouncing several times on the rickety cot. Landing on her stomach, Emeline's head was turned so that only the side of her face was visible. Hagen ran his filth-encrusted fingernail down her serene face, almost mesmerized at the swirl of colors moving along her cheek. "A human bondmate." He snorted, his lips forming a sneer, "And from a backwards planet like Earth. I love it. This is really going to piss off the purists on Delicia." Running his hand down along Emeline's body, he stopped at her breast, squeezing it hard before he ran his hand down her long legs.

Seeing Hagen violating an unconscious Emeline was too much for Violia. She might have to follow his orders, but this—this was not going to happen. Having no regard for her own safety, she pulled at Hagen's arm, yelling, "Leave her alone, you disgusting pig." She wasn't at all surprised when he backhanded her across the face. The force was so hard she flew backwards, landing hard on her butt, a trail of blood running down her chin. Fury shone in her eyes as her hand swiped across her mouth, causing a smear to form on her cheek. She could feel her lip was split in two places from his blow.

"You don't get to tell me what to do. Remember your place, Violia, or maybe I'll just give you to some of my crew to play with." Leering at her, he gloated, "Believe me, you won't be the one having fun. It's been a long time for some of them—it wouldn't matter to them that you're a puny little thing. They'll fuck anything." He rubbed the hand he hit her with against his dirty pants before grabbing his crotch, laughing at the look of revulsion on her face.

At least he'd stopped touching Emeline. So what if she had a few cuts and bruises, Violia thought. "You would do that to your own cousin. Nice to see some things don't change. You're still the heartless bastard you always were."

Grabbing her up by the front of her uniform, he barked into her face, "That's right, so don't forget who holds your future in his hands." He threw her onto the other cot, not caring where she landed. "You will do what I say, when I say it and I don't want to hear any more out of your mouth."

The cot nearly collapsed with the force with which she landed on it. With the way he was throwing her around, Violia knew she needed to take a different approach with him, otherwise her body wouldn't be able to take much more of his brutal treatment. Once he left them alone, she could use the handheld regen device she had hidden to heal the bruises. Her split lip and facial bruises would just have to heal on their own for a while.

"Fine, fine." She held up her hands in surrender, but they both knew she didn't mean it.

He stood with his arms crossed as he studied her, his eyes taking in the typical Delician woman—small and meek, needy, so damn needy. He hadn't met one Delician woman he could respect, well other than maybe his cousin, he supposed. She always stood up to him. They both knew he could overpower her physically—that was a given. He could snap her neck in a heartbeat, but he wouldn't—not yet anyway. He hadn't seen her in years. She was beautiful, he'd give her that, but there was something else about her. She was never one to back down until he physically threatened her and even then, she would concede but never quit.

It was unfortunate she allowed her life to be ruled by emotions. Hagen lived by one simple rule—you could only rely on yourself. Emotions like love weren't something he believed in. His father had always told his mother how much he loved her. If he did, it was a twisted kind of love, one that only fueled her misery. When his mother was high on drugs or booze, she would tell Hagen she loved him, but that didn't stop her from leaving him with strangers who would use him in ways that no loving mother should have allowed. Not one person in his family had cared enough to find out what was happening to such a young child living in those horrid conditions. It wasn't until after his mother had died when he moved in with his grandmother that the abuse stopped. But by then it was too late.

Seeming to make a decision, he told her, "You do look different. What have you been doing with your life other than being a medic?"

"I'm going to school when I get home to be a physician."

"Yeah, always the ambitious one, weren't you?" He snickered.

Sitting up, she sighed—calm always worked best with Hagen. Pulling herself up against the wall, Violia pulled her knees into her chest. Resting one arm on her knee, she casually examined her split lip with her finger.

Looking Hagen directly in the eye, she simply asked, "What would you rather I do? Become a mercenary like you? No, never mind. You know what? Did you ever stop to think that maybe I liked what I was doing? I happen to be very good at it. I understand it and I like helping people. Why is that so wrong?"

"What's wrong is that you're helping the wrong people.

You could come and work for me on Hexia. No one would touch you if you were under my protection."

Keeping her face bland, she told him that she'd give it some thought. Glancing over at Emeline, she saw she was starting to wake up. Violia needed to get him out of here.

Standing up and walking over to check out the washroom, she wet a towel and began wiping the blood off her face. She asked cautiously, "So what happens next?"

She tried to hide her surprise when he answered, "My captain will be in to see you. It will be up to him to decide what happens to the human. Probably ransom her."

"Hagen, can I ask you a question?

His nod turned into a glare when she asked why the Hexians had come to Earth. "That's none of your business." He growled, turning towards the door, "I'll be back later." Looking over at Emeline's still form, he licked his lips, clearly salivating as he murmured, "I'm looking forward to interrogating the human."

Violia's body tensed, visibly shuddering at the thought of where Hagen's mind was going. No way would she allow that to happen to either of them, but she had to be careful. Hagen was shrewd. He hadn't lived this long with his type of lifestyle without being extremely careful. *I'll just have to be equally as careful.*

CHAPTER 17

Maelstrom's conference room

"Nox—are you with us? I get you have plans tonight with your bondmate, but this briefing is important." Tarek was trying to be understanding, but it was proving difficult. This meeting was vital to their plan to protect Earth. He needed his entire crew at their best and having his top scientist on this mission looking like he'd rather be somewhere else was not what he needed right now.

"Sorry." Nox's face flushed from being caught daydreaming. Tarek was right—he was distracted. Nox reminded himself that the quicker this meeting was over, the quicker he could get back to Emeline.

Leaning forward in his chair, he pushed the image of Emeline's luscious body lounging in the bath to the back of his mind. The rosy color that was usually present on her cheeks wasn't just limited to her face. He shook his head, forcing his attention back to what Tarek was saying.

Standing at the head of the table, Tarek studied his team. Aside from Nox being distracted, Liam was talking to Nyx, his hand movements indicated to Tarek that it had something to do with flying. Ami was scrolling through the console in front of her—who knows what she was looking at. Most likely it was the specs to one of their handheld blasters that had her so absorbed. Jagger had that stupid sphere in his hands again, lobbing it from one hand to the other as he appeared to be studying Ami...his face thoughtful. Tarek could understand the fascination with the human. She was the first human female he had ever seen. She impressed him. Aside from her exotic beauty, she was unique in her straightforward demeanor, her ability to adapt and her honesty. It was quite refreshing.

With his hands relaxed at his sides, his piercing green eyes caught the attention of each member of his crew... making eye contact as he scanned the table. What he needed from them was their full attention. Not only were the Hexians being a nuisance, but his instincts told him there was a mole somewhere on Delicia. It wasn't confirmed, but Tarek had his own suspicions as to who was selling out his planet. The feeling that there was much more behind this issue with the Hexians gnawed at him. He couldn't do this alone. He needed his elite team if they were going to be successful. They were the ones he could truly trust...alien and human alike. Now all he needed to do was light a fire under their asses.

Speaking with authority, his voice rang clear as his words commanded their attention, "I need everyone to focus on the here and now." That was all it took. "It's imperative that you are at your absolute best. Once this battle starts, that has to be your total focus. Liam and Ami, Delicians have experience with the Hexians. You do not. You must remember, Hexians do not have a regulated military like we do on Delicia. Most of their soldiers are hired mercenaries who have no code of honor. It's about money and killing. You will have to put your emotions aside and remember you are part of a team. Working together is vital if we are to be successful. Every detail will be planned out and followed accordingly. Does anyone have any questions or comments?"

Tarek encouraged feedback, no matter how small. You never knew what piece of information would be pivotal to a mission. But in the end, he was the one who had the final say.

Ami was the first to raise her hand.

"Yes, Ami." Tarek knew what she was going to say but he let her say it anyway.

"I would like to request that I be allowed to accompany Liam and Nyx on their star fighter during the battle. I could be on weapons." She paused, her eyes flashing as she geared up to state her case. "I've been doing the simulations and I've passed them all—first time. Okay maybe a couple of them it took me twice, but in all fairness, it was my first time using alien weapons." Learning alien weaponry had ignited a passion in her. Her desire to be a part of this mission had consumed her. She had spent every spare moment in the simulator sharpening her skills. She stopped just short of telling the General it was her video game prowess that had been really helpful in how proficient she had become. It wasn't the impression she was going for.

Liam jumped to her defense, telling Tarek that she actually had a great eye. He told him that Ami would have passed her marksmanship badge in the military with high marks. If he was honest with himself though, he didn't want her to go on this mission with them. The situation was going to be too dangerous, and besides, he needed her on the ship monitoring the network array for them.

"Anyone else have anything to say?" Tarek asked.

Nyx raised his hand. "I have also witnessed Ami's weapons skills. They are impressive."

Ezio added his two cents as well. "I too have watched

Ami in the simulator. She has a very keen eye when it comes to shooting." He smiled at Ami, who was sitting in her chair, grinning from ear to ear.

Tarek could see how much this meant to her. In any other circumstance, he would have acquiesced to her request, but he needed her skills here, on the *Maelstrom.* "I'm sorry, Ami, but the mission must come first. I need you here more than I need you in a star fighter." Seeing the defeated look flash briefly across her face, Tarek knew she was disappointed. "You have impressed me with your initiative and I value you on my team. However, for this mission I need you to work with Loris feeding information to Liam and Nyx. It's vital that they be kept informed. They are the last line of defense before the Hexians get to Earth."

Ami couldn't decide whether she felt happy or sad at Tarek's words, but at least she got to do something important. "Of course. I will do my part, and thank you for making me part of the team. I promise to do my best. You can count on me, sir."

"I know I can, Ami," Tarek said with a satisfied smile. Turning to Liam and Nyx, he told them, "Liam, I want you to keep working in the simulator. Nyx, make sure all the star fighters are ready to go at a moment's notice." Both males nodded in agreement.

"Nox, how long will it take to bring all the satellites online?" Tarek asked.

"It should only take about two hours. I have the latest simulation results from Loris. ARI, display Loris's last entry."

Everyone watched as the enhanced network array formed a force field around the Space Station.

"Good work, all of you. Jagger?" Tarek looked over at his friend, who was using the hologram to display his battle plan, his annoying sphere finally put away. Tarek watched the interaction among his team as they listened to Jagger outline every member's assignment. Liam and Nyx would be with two other fighters while the rest of the ships would form a perimeter around the *Maelstrom*. Ami and Loris would work from the bridge to stay in contact with Liam and Nyx. Tarek could see the friendships that had already formed between all of them. He encouraged this amongst the members of his team that were closest to him. He needed to be able to rely on them for their honestly and more importantly their courage and trust, especially with what was coming. Finding out the identity of the mole was going to be their top priority once they dispatched the Hexians. Hopefully their mere presence would deter Tarquin, but from past experience, Tarek doubted it.

A notification on his personal comm unit interrupted Tarek's contemplation. It was marked urgent—sent from the medic assigned to work with Dr. Datrem. He wondered why she would be contacting him, questioning how she was able to get access to his personal comm unit. *This can't be good,* Tarek thought to himself. There wasn't much that rattled Tarek, however as he stared at the accept button, he hesitated. His instincts never failed him and right now they were on high alert. With great trepidation his finger pressed accept, first making sure the audio was set for his ears only.

The image of a highly agitated Delician female appeared on his screen. Tarek could see that she was trying hard to be precise as she detailed the circumstances of her message.

Her face was drawn, showing the torment that she had been under. It was obvious she hadn't had much sleep by the dark circles under her eyes—the furrow between them was too deep for someone so young, indicating she was under a tremendous amount of stress.

As he listened to her story, Tarek's whole body pulsed with the anger. Anger at her for not coming to him first but also for the position her cousin had put her in. If she had only trusted him, but as he listened to her impassioned plea for help, the feeling that she had no choice but to follow her cousin's demands was evident. She ended with an apology and a prayer that he would find a way to rescue everyone.

Tarek pinched the bridge of his nose as he absorbed what he had just seen. He knew who was responsible for this—Tarquin. It only reiterated his feeling that there was a mole somewhere in their midst. With his long years of military service, it had ceased to surprise him the depths that people would stoop to for personal gain. A few individuals came to mind, but that would have to wait. Right now, they had a rescue mission to plan. But first he had to tell Nox and Liam. After their initial reaction, they would want to immediately rush to launch a rescue. That wasn't his style, preferring instead to take the time to run through multiple scenarios first.

It was Jagger's voice calling his name that brought Tarek's focus back to the room. Steeling himself for the explosive reactions he was about to get, Tarek got to his feet. All eyes turned to stare at him, noting the grim expression on his face. "We have a situation."

Holding up his hand as everyone started talking at once, his expression silenced them. He pushed the play button, knowing that once they saw this video, everyone would go ballistic.

"*General Tarek, my name is Violia. I'm a medic onboard your ship. I need your help. By the time you get this file I will have kidnapped the human, Emeline Cameron. Please believe me when I tell you I didn't want to. My cousin, Hagen—he's working for the Hexians. He contacted me last week and told me I was to kidnap the human. I told him no of course, but then he did a despicable thing—he threatened our grandmother. He's a bastard and I told him so, but he told me I would have to do what he said or he would kill her. I don't know why he wants Emeline but I told him I wouldn't do it.*

"*He called again last night and this time he had two men at my grandmother's house. They had a knife to her throat. I told Hagen again I wouldn't do it. I honestly didn't think he would hurt her. I was right, he didn't, but one of his men had Lilith. She's Dr. Datrem's granddaughter. The man was cruel... he...cut her hair off. If I didn't do what Hagen said they were going to hurt them. Please, you have to help them. Lilith is very young—she must be so scared.*

"*Hagen told me I was to drug Emeline and put her in an escape pod. I used the one attached to the botany lab. He told me to disable the sensors and then input coordinates he gave me. That's all I can tell you right now. I promise I will do my best to keep Emeline safe. I've programmed some hidden pockets into my uniform and filled them with some tools that should help keep us safe until you can find us.*

"*I'm sorry, truly I am, but what choice did I have? Hagen is evil. I hadn't seen him in years. I don't know much about what he has been doing all these years, but if I had to guess, I'd say he was a mercenary. I promise to do my best to protect Emeline.*

Please save my grandmother and Lilith. I pray that you will get to us in time."

The momentary silence from the shocking news was short lived as the room exploded into activity. Nox had been trying to get Emeline on his wrist comm ever since the words "kidnap" and "Emeline" were said. His bond immediately reached out—searching for its mate.

Stunned, Liam gazed at the hologram, his mind racing frantically. How could this have happened? Em—his baby sister—kidnapped by aliens. *She must be so scared!* They needed to find her and fast.

Seeing motion in front of him, his reflexes worked automatically as he caught Ami before she fell out of her chair, her eyes fluttering closed as she cried out Emeline's name, her fear echoing around the room.

The Delicians sprang into action. Jagger, Nyx, Ramola and Ezio jumped up and started yelling orders at each other.

A loud whistle silenced them. Tarek gave them a steely look. "Everyone, sit down." He looked down at his console and began inputting commands. He didn't need to see them sit back down and give him their full attention. He had earned their respect, but more importantly they knew when things looked impossible, Tarek was the one who usually had a solution. Even Ami had managed to pull herself together and pay attention to the General. If anyone could find Emeline, it would be him.

"First thing—Nox, any luck reaching Emeline?"

Closing his eyes, Nox tried not to give in to the terror in his heart. She was there along the edges—just out of reach. He was afraid for her, but knew she was smart—maybe too smart sometimes. He prayed she would be savvy enough to stay alive until they could get to her.

Shaking his head, he locked eyes with Tarek, the devastation reflected back told Tarek all he needed to know.

"Can you track her movement up until the escape pod ejected?" Keeping Nox busy was imperative at this moment.

"I'll have Loris track her wrist comm." Nox got up and moved over to the corner of the room as he contacted Loris.

"Jagger." Tarek addressed his captain.

"Sir."

"Can you explain to me how a medic was able to disable sensors and launch an escape pod on my ship and not one alarm was sounded?" Tarek was furious that his own personal ship's security protocols had been circumvented. "I've already checked—one of the escape pods is missing. I'd also like to know how she was able to get access to my personal comm."

"I'm on it." Jagger was incensed that not one person on his ship had been alerted when the escape pod had deployed. This was a serious security breach.

Inputting a few commands into the console in front of him, Jagger sat back and waited. It wasn't long before Yilmaz, his security officer, came rushing into the room, weapon drawn, his facial expression showing that he was on high alert as he surveyed the room. A room where all of its inhabitants, all except one that is, stood frozen, staring at the massively muscular male with startling bright amethyst eyes holding a pulsar rifle pointed at them.

Jagger jumped to his feet before anyone could react, yelling, "Put that rifle down, you fool, before someone gets hurt."

Lowering the rifle, Yilmaz shot back, "Well what did you expect when you send me a high security alert? You know how I'm going to react." His adrenaline had spiked when he first got the alert from Jagger and continued skyrocketing as he stood pointing a rifle at General Tarek, who stared back at him, his eyebrow cocked. He knew he would be spending lots of time in the training room. "Sir, is everything all right?" Yilmaz's eyes moved from Jagger's to Tarek's, the tension in the room could be felt the moment he'd walked through the door.

Yilmaz had been a trusted member of Jagger's crew for years and his chief security officer aboard the *Maelstrom* for the last several missions. Although not a member of Tarek's elite crew, he had been offered the opportunity but had chosen to serve with Jagger. They had a bond that had formed years ago when they were fighting the Hexians as young recruits. Serving on the same ship, they had watched their sister ship be destroyed by a ship commanded by the then leader of Hexia, Tarquin's grandfather. It was safe to say that there was no love lost between them and Tarquin. Especially since it was Tarek who had retaliated by destroying the Hexian ship, killing Tarquin's grandfather and all on board. It had been that event that had allowed Tarquin to assume leadership of Hexia. Yilmaz still felt the loss of his friends who had perished that fateful day.

Jagger began filling him in on what had happened with the kidnapping of Emeline. He already knew the Hexians were after the special pink salt on Earth, now they were resorting to kidnapping humans right off their ship. Yilmaz's jaw was visibly clenching by the time Jagger had finished talking. He was a tall, well-built, middle-aged male whose deeply lined face reflected the many campaigns he had participated in with the Delician military. He stood at attention, his rifle hanging down his side while his sharp mind was already prioritizing who would provide him the necessary information that his superiors requested. He was also interested in finding out who within his ship had been helping the Hexians. When he found that person, they would regret ever having stepped on board the *Maelstrom*.

Tarek took over, asking him questions and giving orders all at the same time. He demanded to know how this could have happened. Tarek was adamant when he told Yilmaz, "I want whoever did this found. I know someone had to have helped Violia. I want that pod found and I want to know where the Hexians are. Yilmaz, I want you to be in charge of the investigation here on the ship. You will report directly to me or Jagger. I need information and answers. You should have just received the access codes to all the files pertaining to this situation. Review them and give me your assessment as to how these events were allowed to happen on board my ship."

"Yes, sir." Yilmaz moved to sit in one of the empty chairs and began scrolling through the information the General had given him.

A rescue plan was beginning to form in Tarek's mind as he watched Liam and Ami discussing Emeline and what she must be going through. Nox, his head reclined back against his chair, had his eyes closed as he tried over and over to feel the bond between him and Emeline. "Nox, I need you to hear this."

Nox sat up abruptly, his eyes going immediately to Tarek. An empty feeling sat heavy in his gut, but the look in Tarek's eyes told him he would definitely want to hear what he had to say.

"I've got an idea that I think might work, but we need more information." Looking from Nox to Liam to Ami, trying to convey to them that he understood their anger and frustration at Tarquin and the Hexians. "We will get them back, but we're going to need everyone's help to do it."

Nodding to Tarek, Nyx spoke up as he uploaded the information he had been gathering to the center table screen, "I've already started gathering information on Hagen, cousin to Violia, grandson to Etha. Parents—both deceased. Father was the owner in a sleazy dance club but ran protection scams all throughout his small region of the city. Mother was a dancer who died of an overdose at the club. Hagen was eight and at the scene at the time of her death." He went on to list Hagen's activities in the following years, being stopped not even halfway through by Tarek who told him they got the picture and to get to how he came to work for Tarquin.

"After Tarquin's grandfather was killed, Tarquin was made leader of Hexia. Apparently, he's close to his mother and grandmother and it was their counsel that encouraged him to become the leader. He didn't want the job and even though he was close to his grandfather, they didn't always see eye to eye. After the grandfather's death, Tarquin decided there was a better way to make money. He had been trying to get his grandfather to change the way he did business. My sources say he had been considering it before he was killed. However, there were some of the more prominent crime families that wanted to keep the status quo. Tarquin needed Hagen's reputation as someone you didn't want to cross to keep those organizations in line. Tarquin hired Hagen soon after he became leader, but it says here that things have begun to sour between the two males lately. Apparently, Tarquin was using money to build communities for the families that reside on Hexia. Over the years, the number of children, females and elderly have multiplied and Hexia is now faced with a population of people native to the planet. Tarquin has appointed himself their protector."

Tarek and Jagger looked at Nyx as if he had lost his mind. Tarek didn't think he could trust this information. Tarquin was, after all, a Hexian. All Hexians were evil and vile and only wanted one thing. A thought occurred to Tarek, Hexia may have at one time been uninhabited, but that obviously had changed. It would seem that over the many generations of Hexia, children were born, people grew old and families were created. Tarquin could genuinely care for his fellow Hexians, but that didn't excuse his methods of providing for them.

Tarek shook his head saying, "It could very well be that Tarquin could be helping his people, however kidnapping and stealing—black marketing, that's still illegal even if it is for the right reasons.

"But at least we know he won't hurt Emeline. If he's as they say he is, she should be safe as long as he keeps Hagen away from her." Nox clung to any thread of hope he could hold onto.

"Do you think he'll keep her safe?" Liam's spirits rose

slightly with a glimmer of hope. Ami squeezed his hand , giving him a hopeful smile.

Tarek wasn't sure what to say to them. "I don't know." Turning to Jagger, he asked, "Did you know this about Tarquin?"

Jagger couldn't have been more shocked at this information. "No, I didn't. I knew more about his less than legal activities. He has always been one step ahead of the law. It's got to be his advisors—they must be influencing him. I have heard some grumblings that there's been some unrest and infighting amongst the organizations on Hexia. Although honestly, I've never equated Hexia and family."

Tarek felt the same way. "It gives us hope that the females will be treated well." He focused his gaze on Yilmaz, who had been working furiously sending commands through his wrist comm.

Yilmaz stood, getting the General's attention, "Sir, I need to go to my office."

"Do what you need to do, but I want an update within the hour."

"Yes, sir." He nodded his head and turned towards the door.

"And Yilmaz"

Turning back to face him, "Yes, General."

"This will never happen again. Am I clear?"

"Yes, sir." He turned to walk away before stopping to look the General in the eye asking, "What time should I meet you in the training room, sir?"

"I'll let you know. Right now, we have Nox's bondmate to save, but when that's over we'll have the entire journey back to Delicia to discuss how this was allowed to happen."

Groaning, Yilmaz turned to take his leave, his face flushed as he barked orders into his wrist comm, hurrying away before the General could inflict any more pain on him. He, however, was about to inflict his own brand of pain on his security team. This was unacceptable and he would get to the bottom of who was responsible.

Nox's wrist comm signaled he had an incoming message. "I have the route that Emeline took before she was taken off the ship." His voice was laced with worry for his bondmate. His fingers flew over the console, inputting commands as the highlighted route of Emeline's steps appeared on the screen. She appeared to meander through the ship, ending up in the botany lab. They could see her path as she walked through the lab, spending a few moments here and there at the different stations as she made her way around the room before suddenly disappearing... completely.

Trying desperately to hold it together, Ami reached over and squeezed Liam's hand as she looked at Tarek, quietly asking, "Isn't Violia the medic who was working with Emeline on her medical tests?"

"Yes, she is," Nox answered for Tarek.

Ami recalled Emeline talking about the medic she had met when she was having her tests taken. "Em said that she had been kind of bitchy to her at first—well she didn't say bitchy, but you know what I mean. It bothered her—a lot, but I guess lately Violia has been nicer. If her cousin has been threatening her for over a week, I suppose her attitude towards Em makes sense." Turning to Liam, she reminded him how compassionate his sister was. "You know Em. She is always trying to solve everyone's problems. If she thought Violia needed help, she would do whatever she could to help her."

Nox looked at Ami thoughtfully. He knew Emeline was sweet and caring, but this was a different side of her. "Has Emeline always been like this?"

Not meaning to sound snarky, but come on, thought Ami, you've only known her for, what, a week and she had no problem telling him that. "You've only scratched the surface with our Em, right, Liam?"

Liam, who had been trying hold back his fear and anger, ground out, "Yes." His voice was curt as he glared at Nox.

Tarek saw the signs of tension building between the two males closest to Emeline. He was glad when he saw that Marsel and Paulo, the chief engineer, at the door requesting entry. "Enter."

Hurrying into the room, they stood before Jagger and told them they had some information on the escape pod. Directing them to the console along the side wall, it wasn't long before a simulation replaced the map Nox had displayed on the center table screen.

Marsel's voice was all business, any antics she and Jagger were used to were replaced with the seriousness of their current situation. "The pod was ejected here, in the botany lab at precisely 3:02. We were able to track the exhaust particles from the pod along this route." All eyes followed the movement through the solar system. "This is the intercept point here. It's at this location we lose all contact with the pod. No exhaust particles from any type of vessel. It's like they simply vanished."

"What do you mean they just vanished?" Ami asked warily.

Tarek's hand silenced the room. Staring at the intercept

point, he carefully thought out his next question. "Marsel, if you were to add in the variable that they were picked up by a cloaked ship, would that make any difference in your search?"

Looking at Liam, Ami mouthed to him, *"A cloaked ship? What the hell?"*

Liam wasn't at all surprised since Nox had brought up the possibility in their first meeting. Shrugging his shoulders at Ami, he waited to hear what Marsel had to say.

For a slight Delician woman, she carried herself tall with the responsibilities she had on board this ship. As the science officer, it was her job to solve mysteries using whatever means necessary. Her eyes were solely focused on the screen in front of her as she gave ARI command after command.

Paulo was talking softly into her ear as her fingers moved over the console. She was nodding her head as he continued talking until finally, she stopped for a second, staring into his eyes, unsure of what he was saying. He nodded at her and she gave one last command to ARI. Smiling slightly at the results, she cried softly before nudging Paulo in the stomach, "Gotcha!"

The center table screen began to show them the path that Hagen's ship had taken. It seemed their cloaking device lacked all the new upgrades that the *Maelstrom* ships had. There had been a slight bug in the code that allowed for certain particles to be emitted through the device. That particular nasty error had recently been corrected, but evidently whoever had given Tarquin the cloaking devices hadn't been in the loop for the new upgrades.

"We were able to trace Hagen's ship from this intercept

point to the Invidia, which sits right now behind this planet here. It's called Uranus." Paulo stood, waiting for more orders from his captain.

"Uranus?" Ami said, frowning slightly at Liam. Even she was too upset to come up with a joke to that although to herself she wasn't surprised "asshole" was included in this whole situation.

"How many vessels do they have with them?" Tarek asked.

"There is only the one." Marsel was searching her data for any other vessels that might be in the area. "Since cloaking technology is still limited to the size of the vessel, the Invidia is too large to be cloaked. I'm not picking up any other particles in the area, General."

"So, from this we can assume Emeline and Violia are on board the Invidia." Tarek asked.

"Yes, sir."

Nox had been listening intently to Marsel, and once he knew where Emeline was, he demanded to know when they would be leaving to rescue her. Liam and Ami both stood with him waiting anxiously for the General's answer.

Ignoring Nox, Tarek spoke to his officers, "Thank you, Marsel, Paulo. That will be all." Tarek waited until they left the room before speaking sharply. "I know you are impatient, but if we go in there unprepared, we could cause harm to Emeline, and I know you don't want that. You need to get your emotions in check and think this through methodically."

Nox struggled to contain his anger. He needed to be strong for Emeline and this wasn't what any of them wanted to hear. Emotions were stretched thin.

Liam and Ami knew they were in uncharted territory here. They had no choice but to trust Tarek's judgment. Emeline's safety was their first priority. They nodded their heads to Tarek and waited for him to continue.

Tarek studied the Invidia as it sat hidden behind the planet the humans called Uranus. It wasn't the largest planet in their solar system, but according to the information that Marsel had given him, it certainly was the coldest. Its size was equal to 15 Earths and had 27 moons, which certainly gave Tarquin plenty of places to hide.

Tarek asked out loud, not to anyone in particular, "What I don't understand is why Tarquin only has one ship with him and it's not even one of his newer ships. Nyx, I need you to start gathering as much information as you can on the specs of the Invidia and the type and number of star fighters it's carrying. Liam, Nyx will show you how to help him access the data, although I'm sure you're already familiar with it."

The tips of Liam's ears reddened at Tarek calling him out on his unauthorized access to Delician military data files. The fact that he wasn't in the brig indicated to him that Tarek approved of his tenacity at wanting to learn everything he could about all things Delician. "Yes, sir. I will do anything and everything it takes to rescue my sister."

Tarek turned his attention to Ami. "Ami, I want you to work with Nox researching Hagen and Tarquin. Learn all you can—how they fight, what their favorite weapon is, if they have any flaws—anything you can learn that might help give you an edge when you encounter them." Tarek knew that Ami would keep Nox focused for the moment.

Ami's deep brown eyes burned hot with anger as she

told Tarek, "Anything you need for me to do, I'll do it." She would do whatever necessary to rescue her *bestie*. Violia, on the other hand, Ami huffed to herself, *She and I are going to have a long talk about asking for help before kidnapping defenseless women and giving them to aliens.*

Nyx and Liam sat huddled together at one end of the table, each with their tablets open to blueprints and specs of the Invidia.

Moving over along the wall to a separate console, Nox began commanding ARI to put together profiles on Tarquin and Hagen. "Ami, have ARI create profiles on any known associates of those two—*[grrr]* assholes."

Ami snorted at his curse. "I feel the same way." She gave his arm a quick squeeze before turning back to her tablet.

Nox swallowed the bile that was lying in the back of his throat. He needed to be ready when they left to rescue Emeline. Tarek hadn't specifically said he was going, but one way or another Nox would be on that team. He would not fail Emeline again. Information began filling his screens. Soon he was absorbed in learning anything he could that would help save his bondmate.

Tarek scanned the room as everyone concentrated on their part of the mission planning. Ezio and Ramola were deep in discussion on the type of firepower they would need for this rescue mission. Jagger, who was squeezing the life out of his sphere with one hand, was scrolling through multiple screens, making notes on assembling a team.

It gave him a moment to reflect on the events of the last hour. There were still so many unanswered questions before he could finalize his plans. One thing he definitely had to do was inform Dr. Datrem about his granddaughter. Tarek sighed, knowing that was going to be a hard conversation, but they would do everything they could to save everyone.

His eyes felt gritty, wishing for a brief moment he was lying in the surf on his favorite stretch of beach on Delicia, longing for the warmth of the sun on his skin...a few moments of solitude. Instead he sat pondering his theory on who the mole was on Delicia. Considering all that had happened lately, he knew in his gut someone on his ship was working with the mole and he was determined to find out who it was. The thought of someone on his crew working against the UAP and Delicia infuriated him. Even though he had shared his theory with Jagger, Tarek felt he needed to keep his suspicions quiet, especially since it was possibly coming from the highest level in the Delician government. If true, the scandal would rock Delicia and the UAP to its core.

The sound of the door opening broke Tarek out of his rumination as Yilmaz came hurrying in. Looking up, Tarek saw uncertainty on his face. The other members of the team, seeing Yilmaz come in, came over and stood by the table, eager to hear what he had to say. Nodding his head to Yilmaz, Tarek indicated he should begin.

"Sir, I've found out whose codes were used to help the medic circumvent the access codes." Yilmaz's fingers were twitching, a clear indication he was nervous. Beads of sweat formed on his brow even though the room was slightly on the colder side.

"Out with it, Yilmaz. Who's getting skinned alive today?" Tarek's voice was hard, indicating he would show no quarter to whoever it was.

Squeezing his eyes shut for a moment, he spoke directly to the General. "The codes were yours, sir."

Audible gasps reverberated around the room as all eyes were focused on Tarek...waiting for his reaction.

The deadly stare Tarek gave Yilmaz would have rattled a lesser male, but Yilmaz had known Tarek for a long time. He continued on, saying, "I've traced the authorization inputs to the docking bay, so whoever stole your codes was smart enough to know that that was one of the few blind spots on this ship."

Tarek smiled knowingly. Of course, turn the focus on him. When he finally caught whoever was behind this, it was going to be a pleasure to take them apart piece by piece. And he would catch them—after he recovered the human and made sure Tarquin and Hagen spent a very long time on the coldest prison planet he could find.

Tarek's reaction startled the group, all of whom had expected fireworks. Not understanding what was happening, Ami asked Tarek to explain what Yilmaz was talking about.

"Ami, whoever is working against us on my ship was smart. By focusing the blame on me and by doing it in one of the busiest places on this ship, they made it virtually impossible to pinpoint exactly who was responsible."

Ami's face fell at Tarek's words. "There is no way of finding out who helped Violia kidnap Emeline."

"I didn't say that." Turning to Yilmaz, he asked him if he had anything else to report.

"Yes, sir. I was able to find the exact console that was used, and even though we don't know who was using the console at the time, I do have a list of crewmembers who were in the docking bay at that time. Unfortunately, the list shows over 87 crewmembers."

"Send the list to my console. Assign someone from your team to begin quietly investigating each person on this list. I don't care who they are and what rank they have. Everyone is to be considered a suspect. Am I clear?"

"Yes, sir." Yilmaz nodded and left the room, wiping his sleeve across his brow. He was just thankful he still had his head as he rushed out to complete the General's orders.

With the door shutting behind Yilmaz, Tarek motioned with his hand for his team to get back to their assignments. Gazing out the panoramic view screen at the millions of tiny lights, Tarek considered the information that Yilmaz had just given him. Running his fingers through his short hair, he could feel the beginnings of a headache forming behind his eyes. The addition of a second mole stuck in his throat. Why had they targeted his ship was a question he kept asking himself. Whoever this person was, there had to be a connection to the Hexians, but it begged the question again for why Tarquin would only bring the Invidia. Tarquin obviously knew that the Delician military would try to stop him. What was he up to? That was the question that Tarek played over and over again in his mind.

Nox sat back in his chair, his mind losing focus on what he was supposed to be doing. The more time that passed that Emeline wasn't by his side, the more his body felt the effects of her absence. He was irritated with everyone, nearly biting Ami's head off when she asked him a simple question. He needed to hold it together, but all he could think about was Emeline and how scared she must be. If anyone touched his bondmate, he knew he would rip them to shreds.

Nox could see Liam was having similar feelings. He didn't fault Liam for feeling this way. Emeline was his responsibility to protect and he'd done a piss poor job at it. *If only I had insisted she stay in the lab with Loris.*

"What are you looking at?" Liam had seen Nox studying him.

"It's nothing. I was just thinking." Nox stood and walked over to where Liam had been working with Nyx.

"Thinking about how you allowed my sister to be kidnapped?" Liam retorted angrily. Deep red was beginning to rise slowly up his neck, staining his cheeks, his anger level increasing. "I told you if anything happened to her, I would hold you responsible." Liam was standing face to face with Nox, his hands clenched, trying desperately to keep his anger under control.

"I know. It is all my fault," Nox yelled, his frustration bubbling over the edge as his voice rose with every sentence. "If only I had made her stay in the lab with Loris, she would still be on this ship."

"You should have. I trusted you to keep her safe and where is she? On an alien spaceship with a bunch of ruthless mercenaries. You were supposed to protect her." Even though Liam was shorter than Nox by a good six inches, he managed to get within an inch of his face.

Nox stood his ground, knowing every word Liam spoke was the truth. "You think I don't know that? It's making me sick just thinking about some sick bastard putting his hands on her."

The two males glared into each other's eyes, their bodies rigid, ready to tear each other apart at the slightest cue.

Liam's voice was low, almost deadly. "I never should have trusted you." His fist came out of nowhere, catching Nox in the stomach.

Nox doubled over—the sound of air rushed out of his mouth as pain radiated outward from where Liam's fist had caught him unaware. It would have been worse if not for the strength of his ab muscles from the years of swimming, but he never expected Liam to actually strike him.

Ami rushed over, pushing Liam out of the way as she put her arm around Nox's back, helping him straighten up. Her eyes were bright with anger as she berated the two of them, calling them a bunch of idiotic men who thought fighting amongst themselves would help save Emeline. "Liam, what the hell is wrong with you? You think Em would be happy to see you two fighting? This is so not helping. I get that you're upset, we're all upset, but you two punching the shit out of each other is not going to bring her back any faster." Ami's face was flushed with anger, her nerves strung tight.

Shaking her finger at the two males, Ami called them out on their behavior, "Evidently, an overabundance of male testosterone is a universal thing. Stupid jerks." Ami's voice showed her disgust. "Let me tell you, if anything happens to Em because you two can't keep it together, well I'm not going to be the one who tells Fiona what happened to her baby girl. That's on you two." She turned away, disappointed with them both.

Hanging his head in shame, Liam stepped back and looked around at all the faces watching this scene with keen interest. Shit, he thought. Being viewed as a hothead was not the impression he wanted to give to the Delicians, especially the General. "Sorry." He spoke out loud to everyone. Shooting a glance to Ami, he spoke softer, "I'm sorry, Ami." To Nox, he shook his head and then offered Nox his arm, Delician style.

Nox took it, saying, "I don't blame you." He desperately wanted to punch something too, only he was thinking maybe a punching bag, not an actual person.

"Sorry, man," Liam said to Nox before he moved over to grab Ami's hand in his, pulling her into an embrace. Within the Cameron family, affection was a part of everyday life. It took a lot to be welcomed into the family, but once you were, the hugs never stopped. Rubbing her back, Liam whispered how right she was...Emeline would not be happy with him for losing his cool. She was counting on him to work with Nox and everyone to rescue her.

Glancing over her shoulder at Tarek, he apologized to him, adding that they could count on him for this mission. It was a momentary lapse but he was more than ready to be part of this mission.

Tarek nodded his head at Liam, silently accepting his apology. However, to Ami he smiled, congratulating her on defusing a potentially volatile situation. "I'm impressed, Ami. You handled that exactly the way I would have." Giving her a wink, he added, "Although I probably would have been a little more forceful."

Thrilled at the General's words, Ami straightened her shoulders as she went back and took her seat, ready to complete her assignment.

Settling into the seat next to Ami, Nox brought up the data on Tarquin's family when his wrist comm beeped again. Assuming it was Loris with more data, he hit receive as he continued to peruse the information in front of him.

They needed as much data on Hagen and Tarquin as they could get before they left to rescue his beautiful bondmate.

CHAPTER 18

Storage Room
Aboard the Invidia

Violia slid down the door to the washroom—the urge to tremble was hard to ignore. Putting her head on her knees, she began to take measured breaths. *In, out, in, out.* Movement from the cot caused Violia to jerk her head up—Emeline was finally waking up from the sedative. It was time to face the human's wrath, but it wasn't anything she didn't deserve.

Emeline's hand moved up across her forehead. Her eyes first blinking then squinting as she tried to focus on her surroundings. Wondering why she was looking at a metal ceiling, she shook her head in an attempt to clear her fuzzy mind. Hearing a noise beside her, she looked over and saw Violia sitting on the floor.

Sitting up quickly, she groaned in pain, almost losing her breath as she pressed a hand to her aching ribs. *What the hell?*

"Violia, what's going on? Where are we? And why do I feel like I've been run over by a car?"

Violia gave Emeline a long look before saying, "I don't know what a car is."

Emeline huffed out a breath, muttering, "Never mind."

An expression of regret crossed Violia's face. She was ashamed for hurting this human female who had only shown her kindness. "Emeline—please, I'm so sorry for what I have done to you, but I honestly had no choice."

"What exactly have you done to me?" Emeline's breath was coming out in shallow pants, each one as excruciatingly painful as the next. "My body feels like it's on fire."

Rising slowly to her feet, Violia came over to Emeline, pulling a handheld regen device out of her pocket. "Please lie back and let me heal you before any more damage is done."

Pulling away, Emeline glared at her, "Why should I trust you? I can see by our surroundings that we're not on the *Maelstrom* anymore, correct?"

"That is correct. I will explain everything to you, but first let me fix your injuries." Kneeling on the floor beside Emeline's cot, Violia gently pushed her backwards and began to run the device over her ribs. Thankfully the data showed they were only cracked. As she held the device steady so it could complete the repairs, Violia filled Emeline in on the entire story. She deserved the whole truth, and that's exactly what Violia gave her.

As the pain in Emeline's body began to lessen, she slowly inhaled and exhaled, marveling as each breath became easier. *Amazing!* Now that the pain was gone, her mind was able to focus on Violia's words. *Kidnapped?* She wasn't sure how to feel. *Kidnapped by aliens, I mean, seriously, I have become a cliché.* Only this was real—not a novel you could read ahead to find out what happened next.

Violia shut off the regen device, saying, "You should be fine now. I know you're strong and train often, but you need to keep that to yourself. You may need to use that to your advantage. Hagen is very cunning. Do not trust him."

"Yeah, I don't see that happening." Emeline was still trying to wrap her head around everything that Violia had told her.

"And please, I beg you, try not to piss him off because I can guarantee you, he will hurt you. Stay on your guard."

"Not a problem. Did he say anything else—like how long we have to stay in here?"

Violia lay down on her cot and started to run the device over her body. "He said that his captain would be coming in to see us soon."

Emeline got up and held her hand out, saying, "Here, let me help you."

Giving Emeline a grateful look, she put the device in her outstretched hand. "Just don't touch my face with it." She winced as her lips pulled on the cuts, feeling them start to bleed again. "I need Hagen to think he's hurt me badly. As I said, he's ruthless, but I spent my childhood growing up watching him. If we want to get out of this alive, we have to be just as ruthless." Her body was beginning to relax as the pain began to dissipate.

Handing her back the device, Emeline was surprised when the device appeared to meld into Violia's uniform. "What else have you got in there?" She pointed to Violia's pocket.

"Just a few surprises." Violia patted a few spots on her chest. "It's nanite technology that uses some new materials that are just being developed on my planet."

"We've been using nanites in our textiles on Earth as well." Touching Violia's sleeve, the feel was surprisingly soft.

"As I'm sure you are aware, Director Nox has been working on trying to enhance our armor with his force field technology, although I don't think he's had much time to work on it lately."

Emeline dropped her hand, her eyes widening—*Nox! He is going to be so upset. The bond!*

Closing her eyes, she concentrated on Nox and their bond. *Please, please, please, Nox—come on babe—where are you?* "Dammit!" Sitting on the cot, she finally gave in and hung her head in her hands, whispering to him, "Nox, where are you?" *Okay, Fiona, I need you here. Breathe, Center, Focus.* Breathing deeply, she visualized Nox's face. The way his lips curved up in a sexy smile when they were lying together talking about nothing and everything. He was there and he was worried. It was faint—just out of reach. "It must be because we haven't completed the bond yet." She muttered to herself.

"What did you say?" Violia asked.

"Nox—I can just barely feel him but I can tell he's worried. He's probably searching everywhere looking for me." Emeline got up and started trying to pace, but the tightness of the room limited her strides. Frustrated, she gave up and sat down across from Violia. "Look, I get why you did what you did, but why didn't you tell someone?"

"I did."

Emeline's eyebrows shot up in surprise. "You did? Who?"

Violia sat up and took Emeline's hand in hers, patting it gently, saying, "I sent a video file to General Tarek last night after Hagen called me. I set it to be delivered at 4:30 today. I don't know what time it is now, but I'm assuming he has gotten it and that's why Nox is worried."

"What did you tell him?"

Violia held her chin high. She knew that the General would come for them, but he needed all the facts. "Everything."

Surprised, Emeline considered Violia. She wanted to throttle her for kidnapping her in the first place, however if she was in Violia's place, she might have done the same thing. Still, she had put them in terrible danger, and if they weren't careful, they could get hurt or worse. With that in mind, Emeline knew they needed to proceed with caution but also be prepared for anything.

Remembering Liam and his training, Emeline steeled her inner core and started to think logically. "Okay, so what's our plan? Do we know who is behind this kidnapping and what they want from me? Did your cousin say anything about what he planned to do with us?" Emeline was starting to use her skills as an analyzer to assess their best strategy.

Dumbfounded that Emeline could be so calm, Violia asked, "So, you're not upset with me for having to follow

Hagen's orders?"

"Oh, I'm definitely mad at you, but we'll deal with that *after* we get rescued. Until then, it's just you and me, so what's our plan going to be?" Emeline leaned back against the wall, resting her head. She wished for an ibuprofen for her pounding headache.

Violia reached into a pocket and pulled out one of the DRI injectors and waved it at Emeline. "I can give you something for your headache if you want."

Giving her a suspicious look, Emeline replied dryly, "Like you gave me something to knock me out—umm, no thank you."

Violia couldn't hide her look of shame. "I know—I can't apologize enough. I promise this will only take away your aches and pains. I have a feeling we're going to need all our strength the next time Hagen comes in." Violia took the DRI and injected herself before she handed it to Emeline, saying, "Just push the top button. It's only a mild painkiller."

"Fine, but know this, if I end up knocked out again, I will kick your ass when I wake up—if I wake up." Taking the injector, she pressed it against her forearm and pushed the top button. Immediately the pressure behind her eyes started to abate as well as the pain in the back of her head, her mind swiftly beginning to clear.

When Emeline handed the DRI back to Violia, something Violia had said earlier clicked into her mind. "What did you mean when you said we were going to need all our strength when your cousin came back?"

It was Violia's turn to pace. Did she tell Emeline what Hagen wanted to do to her or not? Violia felt that lying to Emeline would only cause more friction between them. They needed to trust each other and work as a team.

Stopping in front of Emeline, she hunched down, looking her directly in the eyes, "This is not going to be easy to hear, Emeline, but I'm not going lie to you. When I told you Hagen was evil, I meant it." Taking a deep breath, Violia forced Hagen's horrible words out through pursed lips, "He wants to use you as his sex slave."

"WHAT!" Pure panic raced through Emeline before morphing into anger. *That is so not happening. I'll die fighting before I allow that to happen.*

"What else?" She needed to hear all of it.

"Um…he took liberties with your body."

Emeline felt her skin begin to crawl. "What kind of liberties?" Doing an internal check of her body, she was relieved to know that his *liberties* didn't involve rape. Not yet anyway.

"He…he rubbed your bottom and squeezed your breast. I tried to stop him." Her finger gently touched the cut on her lip. "It worked, but I don't know what's going to happen the next time he comes in. Trust me, he is mean and thinks that all females are only good for one thing—fucking. Sorry to be vulgar but Hagen is that and so much more. You need to be prepared for when he comes in because he's going to do everything he can to make you fear him. It's how his father taught him and Hagen was really good at it. I've found the best way to handle him is to remain calm but stand your ground. Well, that is until he tries to physically hurt you." Violia's Delician skin, already ethereal looking in the dim, dirty light, dropped another shade lighter. Swallowing hard, she said softly, "Then you have no choice but to give in."

Squeezing her hand, Emeline thanked her for stopping Hagen from going further. She pushed down the need to bathe in disinfectant—she would definitely be taking a hazmat shower when this was all over. *Note to self—guys can be scum all over the universe.*

"All right, so we've established that Hagen is a pig and evil. What else did he say?"

"He threatened to hand me over to his crew to use as their new sex toy."

Emeline's eyes got huge at the level of depravity this guy would stoop to as Violia continued, "But he got weird all of a sudden and then offered me a job working for him. He said they always needed healers and I would be under his protection."

"And what did you say to that?" Emeline asked her, still not fully trusting her. Violia's answer would be insightful.

"I told him I'd think about it."

Snorting, Emeline looked at her in disgust. "I'll just bet you did."

"No wait—of course I'm not going to go work for him. I love my life on Delicia. I would never give that up to go live on Hexia with a bunch of mercenaries and especially not Hagen. Believe me, I want as far away from him as I can get." Sitting down heavily on the cot, Violia sighed in resignation. "I know if we make it back to Delicia, I'll be spending the rest of my life in prison. I'll serve my punishment gladly as long as everyone is safe." Slamming her fist on her knee, she told Emeline, "I'd much rather spend the rest of my life in prison than working on Hexia for Hagen."

Emeline wasn't sure why she believed her, but she did. "Okay so what—we just wait for him to come back? Do we try to escape?"

"No, I don't think we should try to escape just yet. Let's rest up and see how the next few hours play out. I'm not familiar with this ship. At least we're safe here for now. Who knows what would happen if we got caught by some of Hagen's crew?" She shuddered just thinking about it.

Emeline agreed, leaning back against the cot. Looking down at where she had been lying, she sat up and leaned against the wall. The filth from the mattress flaked off in spots, falling silently to the floor. *Gross.*

Rubbing her arm, she felt for her wrist comm. Gone. Looking around, thinking maybe she dropped it, Emeline's spirits sank even lower when she came up empty handed.

"What are you looking for?"

"My wrist comm is missing. Did you see it?" Emeline was looking through her pockets.

"Is this what you are looking for?" She held up the brace-let she had taken off Emeline's arm.

Gasping in delight, Emeline grabbed it from Violia's hand and held it to her chest. "Yes—thank you. Phew, I thought I'd lost it. Nox gave it to me."

"You can't keep it on you. If Hagen sees it, he'll take it, and besides, we might be able to use it. Mine was the first thing Hagen took from me when we got here." Pointing to Emeline's bracelet, she said, "I didn't realize that was a wrist comm. I've never seen one like that before."

"Nox had it designed for me."

Happy that she had a connection to Nox, Emeline rubbed the engraving, his words giving her a glimmer of hope. *To the beautiful girl who holds my heart.* She hoped that they would be able to get through to the *Maelstrom*. It would all depend on whether or not the Hexians could disrupt the signal. She was tempted to call Nox right now, but she may only get one chance, so she needed to wait for just the right time. Kissing the words one last time, she handed it back to Violia to put it away.

Violia had just sealed her pocket when the door slammed open.

Hagen stood in the doorway, his amber eyes squinting at Violia as she sat on the cot. She immediately jumped to her feet as he moved into the room, kicking the door shut. His eyes moved to Emeline, a nasty glint in them as they roamed her body before settling on her breasts.

Pulling her jacket closed, Emeline sat up straight on the bed. Keeping her distance from the gigantic troll who was leering at her was uppermost in her mind. When Violia had described her cousin, she was right on the money. This guy reminded her of the villain with the chainsaw in the horror movies that she never wanted to go to but Heather always talked her into. Emeline stared back at Hagen, trying not to show her fear, although she was sure he could hear her heart pounding in her chest.

Laughing out loud, Hagen slapped his leg, a layer of dirt wafted off his pants as the smell of grime and filth permeated the already stale dry air.

Unconsciously, a brief look of disgust showed on Emeline's face, causing him to abruptly stop laughing. His anger could be seen rising as his skin began to flush.

"Oh, excuse me if my appearance isn't pleasing enough for you, human." Sarcasm dripped from his mouth.

Emeline's adrenaline started to rise as she tried to soften her features. She was doing her best not piss him off like Violia said, but it was hard. This guy was just a plain asshole as far as Emeline could see. Swallowing hard, she shook her head at him.

Looking at Violia, he asked, "Does the human have a translator chip?"

Answering for her, Emeline spoke, her voice coming out surprisingly steady, considering the terror that raced through her. "The human has a name. It's Emeline Cameron and yes, I can understand every word you say."

"Good. Then let me be clear, human, I'm in charge. You will do what I say, when I say it."

"And if I don't?" Emeline said, unsure why she was pushing her luck. Violia's eyes widened at her in fear, silently telling her to shut up.

Hagen leaned his huge body down close to hers. She could feel his hot nasty breath on her face as he whispered, "Go ahead, defy me." He stood up straight, the glare on his face daring them to question him. Violia's face remained passive as she tried to keep as calm as possible, while Emeline fought to keep the revulsion off her face as she took small breaths to clear his stench from her nostrils.

"Fine, you're the boss. Now can you please tell us why we're here and when we can go home?" Emeline decided on a different approach.

"Good. It looks like you are smarter than I would have expected for a human. Keep it up and you might just make it out of here alive. As for why you're here, I'll let my captain explain that to you. When you're leaving—well, that depends on how much your bondmate wants you back. I guess we'll just have to see. Of course, I can't guarantee what condition you'll be in when and if he does get you back. He might not want you once I get finished with you."

"What's that supposed to mean?" Emeline shifted her body farther away from him, but he moved closer to her, his big body trying to trap her as she moved to avoid him.

"Leave her alone, Hagen. There is no need to scare her. You know she hasn't been around other species before." Violia was trying to defuse a situation that was threatening to get out of hand.

"Shut up, Violia. No one asked you for your comments."

"No, Hagen, I won't. I've got my own questions. Look, I already know if I get out of this, I'll be spending the rest of my life in prison. You've successfully blown up my life. Hope you're happy." She threw her hands up at him.

"I told you to come work for me. Think about it, Violia. You would have so much money. You could live like a queen." He waved his hand at her. "And you wouldn't have to deal with all those sick people." The disdain in his voice was apparent—as if he was doing her a favor.

Desperate to keep him talking, she said, "I'm still thinking about it. I mean, aren't you worried about the UAP? They will never let you get away with kidnapping a human."

Wiping his hand across his mouth, he spat out, "You think I care what the UAP says? They mean nothing to me." He turned, his gaze landing on Emeline who was quietly watching their interaction. His hand twitched at his side. He had never seen a human female before and she was intriguing.

Violia, seeing Hagen's attention focused on Emeline,

called his name. "Hagen."

He turned, glaring at her.

With her hands on her hips, frustrated, Violia yelled at him, "You're Delician. Why would you go live on Hexia?" Not that she really cared. As far as she was concerned, he could stay on Hexia or any other place as long as it was far enough away from her.

Outraged, he took a step towards Violia, "Why? Why do you think? Wealth...power. Did you know that I'm second in command of an entire planet?" His chest literally puffed out as he smugly dropped that bombshell on her.

Stunned, Violia stared at him in disbelief. "You mean that you're second in command to Tarquin, the leader of Hexia?"

"Yup. And you, little cousin, always thought I'd end up like my father, but you were wrong." Coming over, he grabbed Violia's chin a little too firmly between his two fingers. "You could be the healer to the leader of Hexia." This was Hagen's habit—always applying just the right amount of pressure to make it hurt, but not enough to show an injury. It was his way of proving his power over her.

Bright forest green eyes squinted her defiance of him. Leaning in, Hagen laughed in her face, saying, "You never back down. I always liked that about you."

Trying to stay calm, Violia asked how he came to be on Hexia. Hagen was proud of himself. He had no problem bragging to her how he came to be Tarquin's second in command. It involved a lot of killing, stealing and betrayal. None of which surprised Violia—it was all he knew.

Noticing his gaze straying to Emeline, Violia tried again to keep him talking. "Hagen, what do you want with Earth and the humans?" Adding quickly when she saw his expression harden with her question, "I'm just curious as to why you would want to be bothered with them. I mean, they are kind of primitive, don't you think?" She glanced over at Emeline, giving her a slight smile, immediately acknowledging her error.

Hagen turned and began to study the human female. "You're right, they are primitive, but this one here—she's interesting to look at. She certainly is strong looking." He was starting to get excited the more he looked at Emeline, causing her to push farther to the end of the cot. "She has big tits—I like that and her legs...I could wrap them around me as I pounded into her. Probably get more than one fuck out of this one." He licked his lips, his hand unconsciously rubbing the bulge in his pants that had grown considerably larger the more his face became twisted with lust as he considered all the ways he could use Emeline's body.

Violia stepped in front of Hagen, blocking his view of Emeline, asking him again what was so fascinating about Earth.

This gave Emeline the opportunity to at least attempt to mask her look of revulsion at the thought of Hagen putting his slimy hands on her. A thin sheen of sweat covered most of her body, causing her clothing to stick to her. Emeline knew from her training with Liam that she had to stay alert. He warned many times there was a difference between training and facing real danger. *This is beyond anything I could have ever experienced. We're going to need a miracle here.*

The air around Emeline was beginning to swirl. The stress of the last 24 hours was beginning to take its toll. She tried pinching different areas of her body—anything to thwart the rising hysteria she was trying desperately to curtail. Narrowing her eyes at Hagen, Emeline was thankful that Liam had drilled these calming techniques into her brain. He had been relentless, nearly fanatical at times when it came to training Emeline and her friends. Almost like he knew that one day it would save their lives. *Well, it looks like today is my day.*

Hagen became caught up in the moment as he told Violia how Tarquin had been able to obtain a small sample of the Himalayan salt. That even though most of it had been used up in their analysis, the results had been staggering. He boasted that by selling the salt on the black market it would give them wealth beyond belief.

Rubbing his hands together, Hagen was nearly salivating as he boasted about what life would be like once he controlled all of the salt mines. That was why they couldn't allow Earth's satellites to go online with Nox's force field. They planned on destroying the satellites, which would disable Earth's global communications networks. In essence, bringing Earth to its knees.

"If it hadn't been for the UAP finding out about us going to Earth, this wouldn't be happening." Turning to Emeline, he said accusingly, "You can blame your bondmate and Tarek for this. If they had just left us alone, we would have been gone already." One side of his mouth pulled down into a sneer as his eyes narrowed at Emeline. "If it wasn't for them, my plan would have already been set in motion." He complained like a petulant child when he told them Tarquin didn't want to dominate Earth, only wanted a few shipments. "He's gotten soft over the years thinking that he could use the money from the salt to make Hexia into a more productive place to live." The sarcasm just oozed out of him as he continued maligning his boss.

As if Tarquin could hear his second in command, Hagen's comm signaled an order for him to report to his office. Violia was thankful that they would soon be rid of him, although Hagen just snorted his displeasure as he disregarded the message. He wasn't in any hurry to comply with Tarquin's summons. In fact, he was more interested in continuing his tirade on how ineffectual a leader Tarquin was.

As if he didn't care who heard him, Hagen went on to tell them about his plan to take out Tarquin. Violia always knew that Hagen teetered on the edge of reality at times. How could he help it considering his gene pool, but this was beyond even that. This was flat out insanity.

Hoping to get Hagen to leave, Violia motioned to his wrist comm, asking, "Don't you need to go see your captain?"

Hagen barked out a laugh at her question, his spit flying out in all directions. "It won't be long before he'll be obeying my summons, or on second thought, maybe I'll just shoot him out the closest airlock."

Locking eyes with Emeline, Hagen ground out, "Your lover may have slowed me down a bit, but in the end, I'll get what I want. I know you have the knowledge on how to build force fields. Tarquin may think he's going to ransom you back, but that's not going to happen. You'll be working for me from now on. Once I have control over the salt mines, I'll have more than enough money to control this entire sector. My new base will be on Earth and the humans will have no choice but to accept me as their new leader."

Emeline jumped to her feet; her face flushed with anger.

Violia shot her a pleading look, but her rage was too great when she thought about what Hagen meant to do to her planet. She would do everything in her power to stop him. He was not going to use her to help enslave mankind. He was well on the way to considering himself a demigod and she wanted no part of it.

However, Violia was right about one thing, no need pushing this moron's buttons.

Taking in deep breaths, she tried to calm down. *Stupid, stupid, stupid Em. So much for Liam's training. Crap, he's watching me, waiting to see what I'll say or do. Is he baiting me to get a reaction, or does he really think his plan has merit?*

She had every intention of keeping her mouth shut, but when the fate of humanity rested on your shoulders—yeah, well, that wasn't going to happen.

Unable to stop herself and knowing her sarcasm was probably wasted on him, she ground out, "You don't honestly think that Earth is just going to lay down its weapons, saying, 'Sure Hagen, do whatever you want to us,' do you?"

Moving to stand in front of her, he tipped her chin upwards so she had no choice but to look into his eyes—hard eyes that drove home the point that he was dead serious in his plans. "The money I'll get from just one shipment will be more than enough to pay for an army of mercenaries that will have your planet on its knees in one day. So, you have a choice to make, human, and you better choose carefully."

His eyes bored into hers. He didn't seem at all interested in her answer because in his mind, he knew she would do what he said. Females were easy to control—that was one of the lessons he'd learned from his father. A good slap or a pinch in a soft spot generally had any female he wanted bending to his whims.

Emeline's deep blue eyes burned with fury, causing him to flash, just for a second, a rare smile. He couldn't seem to look away—as if she was the most fascinating creature he had ever seen.

Moving closer, he reached up, stroking her hair. Pulling her ponytail through his fingers, he spoke almost reverently. "I've never seen hair this color before. What do you call it?" He twirled the strands around his finger as he pulled her head not so gently towards him.

Trying to pull away, she ignored him, until he pulled harder, making her huff out, "Blond."

He leaned in and sniffed her hair. Emeline was trying to pull away, but he held on tight, causing her roots to scream in agony. "Nice. And blue eyes—that's something I've never seen before. Yes, human, I think I will be keeping you."

Terror unlike anything she had ever experienced began to fill her body. The urge to flee took over as she screamed in his face, "No—never. I will never help you destroy Earth. I will never help you ever hurt the human race. And I will never let you touch me." Her hands balled into fists as she readied herself for his attack.

She didn't have long to wait, although she should have listened more carefully to Violia's warning. His brute strength was unlike anything she had encountered before. He simply grabbed Emeline up under the arm—she squirmed and twisted but he held her fast like she weighed no more than a feather. His hand moved so fast that she couldn't stop him before he ripped her shirt down the front, leaving her breasts exposed in only her lucky red bra —lucky in the fact that it was constructed of sturdy wire, causing it to remain intact. His hand reached out, grabbing one of her breasts—twisting her nipple through her lace bra.

Furious, Emeline kicked at him...her free arm swinging, trying to hit anywhere on his body—anything to stop this evil man from molesting her.

"Yes, that's it. Show me how mad you are." Hagen was trying to get her bra off by pulling and tugging on the middle. The hooks dug grooves into Emeline's back the more he pulled. He finally got fed up and began to pull her bra down, her breasts beginning to pop out the top. Hagen's tongue moved slowly across his lips in anticipation of seeing her naked flesh.

Violia chose the perfect moment to spring into action. Jumping on Hagen's back, she dug her nails into his neck.

As Hagen turned to get Violia off his back, his grip loosened on Emeline.

Liam's teaching came to mind. *Go for the weak spots— eyes, ears, balls.*

Not having an opening, she opted instead to kick him as hard as she could behind his knee, causing him to lose his balance. He fell...hard, landing on top of Violia, whose head made a terrible sound as it smacked against the floor. By the angle of her head, Emeline prayed that she hadn't broken her neck.

Jumping up, Hagen backhanded Emeline across the face, causing her to fall back across the bed.

Scrambling up away from him, her face burned where he had struck her. Blood trickled down her cheek that she swore was broken or at the very least cracked. But Emeline knew she had more to worry about than damage to her face —Violia might be dead and she was inches away from getting raped.

A moan escaped from Violia, giving Emeline a moment of relief before she found a meaty hand tightening around her throat as she was lifted off the bed...her back slammed against the wall. Pain radiated from her skull down her back as metal rivets dug into her spine. Her hands pulled at his, nails digging into his skin, trying desperately to loosen his hold...gasping for air.

The horrid smell of Hagen's hot breath filled her nose, as she tried in vain to escape him. He leaned his enormous body into hers, grinding his erection against her stomach. Hot tears formed at the corner of her eyes as she tried to contain her panic.

As one tear escaped...slowly making its way down her cheek, she felt his wet tongue lick it off her face. She gagged. Bile made its way up into her throat, and if he hadn't had such a tight grip on her throat she would have vomited in his face.

"Ah little human—that's it...fight me. I like feisty females. You are going to be lots of fun to play with." Nuzzling her face, he licked more tears as they fell from her eyes. He laughed at her look of disgust as his other hand moved around her body, pinching, squeezing, pulling—not caring that he caused her pain. Hagen didn't know the meaning of the word "gentle."

Closing her eyes, she knew she had to do something to stop him. Spying the washroom, she figured it might be her only chance to get away from him.

Remembering what Violia had said about staying calm, she pulled her head back to look into his bloodshot eyes... bright with lust as he ground his rock-hard erection into her.

Swallowing her revulsion, she purred at him, "So, you want to play? I'm surprised that you would waste your time on a lowly human. I thought we weren't good enough for you." Her voice came out raspy, so he loosened his hold slightly at her words.

"Oh human, I am going to have so much fun fucking you." When he saw her recoil, he laughed and bit her earlobe. "Go ahead, fight me. I like a female with spirit. You might just like it and decide to stay here." He continued his biting kisses up along the side of her face and neck.

The sting of each bite was just the motivation she needed to put her plan into motion.

With Liam's voice guiding her through the motions, relaxing her body, she slowly moved her arms up around his shoulders and pressed herself to him. Liam's words echoed in her mind, *"Do whatever it takes to stay alive."*

Feeling her submission, Hagen arrogantly assumed he had won. "That's it, human." He removed his hand from her neck as he set her on her feet. His voice was muffled as he continued peppering bites along her neck and ears as he moved towards her breasts.

Praying to god, gods, anyone who would listen, Emeline did the one thing Liam said never failed—she slammed her knee as hard as she could up into his balls as she pushed him backwards. He fell to the floor, his hands holding his crotch...an ungodly roar of pain ricocheting off the walls.

Thinking he would be down for a few minutes, she scrambled up past him, trying to get to the washroom. The door was right there. Her fingers grazed the handle just before her foot was jerked backwards by a rough hand.

He dragged her across the floor towards him, her heels digging into the floor as she frantically reached for anything to grab onto.

Straddling her legs, he pulled her hands up, capturing them in one of his huge paws. Laughing down at her,

Hagen's finger reached out to stroke her face as he taunted her, "So you like it rough. Good, I do too."

Releasing one of her hands, he pressed it against his injured groin. "I know my cousin is the healer, but since you inflicted the injury, you can make me feel better." He then went on to tell her all the things he had planned for her. Taking special care to elaborate on the things he would do while she was tied to his bed. The whole time he talked, his hand moved her unwilling fingers over the ever-hardening bulge in his pants.

She stared at him through half-masted eyes, no longer hearing his words. He was going rape her. *What would Liam do? I mean it's obvious he's got balls of steel, so that didn't work.*

Deciding on her only option, Emeline spit in Hagen's face. Screaming obscenities at him, she squeezed his crotch with her free hand, digging her nails in as hard as she could...her adrenaline giving her strength she didn't know she had in her.

The look of lust on his face gave way to rage as he dragged her hand away with such force, she felt her wrist snap.

Immense pain shot up her arm causing her fingers to release her solid hold on him.

Seeing his fingers move in and out of a fist, she knew she wouldn't survive the powerful strike she knew was coming.

As his arm came up, Emeline sucked in a ragged breath, readying herself for the pain that was to come.

Closing her eyes so she wouldn't see his fist coming, she was shocked when without warning his weight was suddenly lifted off of her.

Quickly opening her eyes, she tried to comprehend what was happening. She didn't know who this new guy was nor did she care. At this moment, she was just grateful that someone had come to save her. Her only thought was that

Hagen was lying flat on his back with a very large boot pushing down on his chest.

Trying to control her rapid breathing while struggling to get to her feet, she looked down at Hagen, who was shooting daggers at the large male, whom she assumed must be Tarquin. It wasn't his clothing that gave her that impression—it was more the aura that surrounded him. She was just thankful he had shown up when he did.

Tarquin turned his gaze from Hagen to Emeline. "Forgive me and my idiotic second in command." Glaring at Hagen, he said dryly, "I figured you were up to no good when you disregarded my order." Seeing Emeline holding her wrist and the condition of her clothes, he cursed out loud. "When I said that I needed a way to stop Tarek, I guess you didn't understand that didn't include assaulting defenseless females."

With a disgusted look at Hagen, Tarquin spoke directly to Emeline. "Abusing females is not tolerated on my ship and he knows that. You must be Emeline Cameron. My name is Tarquin, leader of Hexia."

Wiping the blood off her face with the back of her uninjured hand, Emeline huffed out, "Well, I'd say it was nice to meet you, but considering the circumstances, I'm not."

Cocking his head at her, Tarquin replied, "Can't say that I blame you." Pointing to her injuries, he asked, "Are you badly injured?"

Shaking her head, Emeline bent over her knees, taking in deep calming breathes. Her body was bruised and shaken. Her wrist was broken, but looking over at Violia, the fact that she was still unconscious worried her. "I'll heal but I'm not so sure about Violia."

Feeling a little braver now that Tarquin was here, with her wrist held tight against her chest, she moved past Hagen to where Violia lay in a bloody heap on the floor. Checking her pulse, Emeline felt a steady beat, relieved that she was still alive.

Glaring down at Hagen, Emeline couldn't help herself. "No thanks to you, you disgusting pig, your cousin is still alive."

Not that he cared. He lay there under Tarquin's foot watching her, his eyes burning with the retribution that was to come. This was not over between them—they both knew it.

Tarquin shot Hagen a nasty look before telling Emeline, "I will send a regen device to heal her and your wounds. Hagen will no longer be looking after you. Once I've sent my message to Tarek, I will be back to escort you to my office. If all goes as planned, you should be back with your bondmate sooner than you think."

Removing his foot from Hagen's chest, he reached down and grabbed him by the arm. Hauling him to his feet, Tarquin's hand was clenched tightly around Hagen's arm as he pulled him towards the open door. Hagen jerked his arm out of Tarquin's grasp and stormed through the opening, but not before giving Emeline a silent warning.

Tarquin scowled at Hagen's retreating back. "Again, I apologize for—" He nodded his head towards her and Violia, indicating their injuries. "I should have known Hagen would abuse his power." Sighing to himself, Tarquin knew his problem with Hagen needed to be dealt with, and soon. "I will send some food and drink along with the medical supplies. If you need anything else, please let me know."

"What I need is to go home. When can that be arranged?" Emeline demanded.

Tarquin smiled at her. "I like you."

"Yeah? Well just don't tell me you like feisty females. I might have to show you the move I used on Hagen." Emeline wiped the beads of sweat forming on her forehead. She really needed to sit down for a second.

Shaking his head at her, Tarquin laughed, "I've been observing humans for a while now and I have to say your species is fascinating. I've never seen a female take down

Hagen in quite that way. As you can probably tell, he did not take kindly to that. I will do my best to keep him away from you, but I can't guarantee anything when it comes to him." Going to the door, Tarquin shot a perturbed look at them before shutting it hard behind him.

Holding her wrist in her other hand, Emeline shoved one of the cots in front of the door. Trying to control her shaky legs, she looked over, noticing Violia's eyelashes were beginning to flutter. Dropping to her knees in front of her, she pushed the hair from Violia's face and softly called her name. "Violia."

Giving Violia a few moments to come back to reality, Emeline finally asked, "How are you feeling? Is anything broken?"

With Emeline's limited help, Violia sat up and leaned against the wall, careful not to hit her head. Running a mental check of her body, she was grateful there didn't appear to be any internal damage. Reaching into her pocket, she handed the regen device to Emeline. "Here. Do your wrist first. I'm not sure if anything is broken, but there might be a few cracks here and there." Her fingers carefully examined the large bump that was forming on the back of her head.

Emeline was having a hard time trying to keep her hands from shaking as she ran the scanner over her wrist. Once finished, she turned to Violia, joking that she must have a hard head to have survived Hagen landing on her.

When Violia's wounds where healed, Emeline had Violia run the device over her neck and cheek. Hagen's finger marks had created deep bruises along her neck. Emeline noticed that Violia didn't say a word as she healed the bite marks along the side of her face, but her lips were pulled into a tight grimace. Emeline was surprised Hagen hadn't snapped her neck.

Glancing down she tried to pull her shirt closed but it was beyond repair, opting instead to button up her jacket in an attempt to cover herself. Satisfied her breasts were at least covered, she slid down next to Violia and rested her head against the wall.

"What happened after I got knocked out?" Violia wasn't sure she wanted to know.

Emeline exhaled, telling her sharply, "I don't want to talk about that right now."

"Ok." Violia didn't push her. It made her sick to see the damage her cousin had done to this human female who had done nothing to deserve this kind of treatment.

Emeline knew Violia was only trying to be kind and she felt bad hurting her feelings. However, now was not the time to fall apart—she had to be on guard. "What I will tell you is that Tarquin came in and—" Her voice dropped almost to a whisper. "He...he saved me."

"Tarquin—as in leader of Hexia? He's here on this ship?"

"Yeah, I was shocked too. He was totally different from Hagen. He said he would be bringing us to his office and Hagen won't be allowed near us."

Violia laughed in disbelief, "Yeah, well I don't believe that for one second."

"Neither do I. You should have seen his face when Tarquin dragged him out of here. He was furious. I guarantee he'll be coming back for us." Emeline clasped her hands together to keep from wringing them. "Tarquin said he was going to send a message to Tarek and then he would be sending a regen device with some food and drinks."

"We won't need his regen device, but we do need food and water," Violia said. She then asked Emeline if she thought they could trust Tarquin.

Emeline shook her head no.

Hearing a knock at the door, Emeline got up and approached it cautiously. "Hello?"

A deep voice could be heard telling them there was food and medical supplies on the floor outside the door. Waiting until she heard his footsteps moving away, she moved the cot away from the door before slowly opening it. A tray loaded with food, drink, and a regen device just like the one Violia had sat in front of the door. Pulling the tray in, she quickly closed the door, pushing the cot back into place, motioning to Violia to come and sit with her on the cot.

Sitting down gingerly, her body still aching from the beating it took, Violia picked up a piece of fruit that looked similar to a banana and began to peel it open. "I know I need to eat but I'm not that hungry. Ever since Hagen contacted me after all these years, I haven't been able to eat much except some fruit here and there."

Emeline was surprised to see that the inside was purple. "What is that called?" she asked, reaching out to take the piece offered to her by Violia. It was soft and tasted starchy like a banana.

"This is an arieri. It grows in the southern coastal regions on Delicia. They can be kind of bland, but they're soft and easy on the stomach." She offered Emeline another piece, but she declined.

"We need to try to call Nox. We have to get out of here before Hagen comes back. He has a score to settle." Emeline rubbed her arms nervously. She was trying to keep down the small piece of the arieri that Violia had given her. It sat precariously in her stomach just like her tenuous grasp on her courage. Her mind was trying to forget the feel of Hagen's breath on her skin or the way he had rubbed himself against her. Running to the washroom, Emeline just made the toilet before everything came up. The stress finally taking its toll on her, Emeline gave in to her tears.

A soft hand brushed her hair away from her face, while the other one held a towel to wipe her face off. "Emeline— did he—did Hagen hurt you? I know you don't want to talk about it, but I don't know if I can live with myself if he did."

Wiping her eyes, she blew her nose into the towel, not caring how disgusting she sounded. "I'm okay. Tarquin stopped him before he could do too much damage." Laughing harshly and with more than a little satisfaction, she added, "Although I'm surprised that he could walk after the damage I inflicted on his balls."

Violia's eyes widened at that. "I wish I could have seen that." Offering her arm to Emeline, they went back in and sat down on the cot. Handing her a cup of water, Violia took Emeline's wrist comm out of her pocket and held it out to her.

"We need to talk to General Tarek and Director Nox."

Emeline agreed until she looked down at her filthy clothes. "Wait, I can't let Nox see me like this. He can't know what happened—not yet. I'll tell him...I'll tell him when we're safe."

Putting her hair up into a fresh ponytail, Emeline thought at least her hair looked better, but unfortunately, her clothes were ruined. She knew what Nox would think when he saw the state of her clothing. She couldn't worry about that now. She only prayed that somehow her comm device would work.

Holding up her wrist comm, Emeline asked Violia how to contact Nox.

"Just open up your comm and ask ARI to connect you to him. If nothing is blocking the signal, it should work."

"That's all? Too easy." Taking a deep breath, adding, "Fingers crossed," she asked ARI to connect her to Nox.

Emeline didn't know who was more shocked, Nox when he saw her face, or her and Violia that it had actually worked. Both bondmates started talking at once until General Tarek interrupted them, telling them they might not have much time.

"Emeline, Violia, are you both all right?" The General was all business. They didn't know how long the signal would hold. So far, they were lucky—their signal hadn't been detected.

Tarek told them that they were working on a plan and to be ready at a moment's notice. When both women replied in the affirmative, he continued asking them to describe in as much detail as they could about their surroundings.

Keeping her voice low, Violia told Tarek about releasing the escape pod and how Hagen picked them up in his shuttle. "It was odd though when he put a tractor beam on us, because when I looked out the window, I didn't see his ship. It was very strange."

Glancing back behind him, Tarek nodded his head. "That proves my theory." Not elaborating any further, Tarek took in their appearance. At first glance both females had no wounds, but when he took a closer look, he could see they had been traumatized. Stepping out of the screen, Tarek whispered something to Nox before Nox spoke to Emeline.

"Beautiful girl, are you well?" His eyes were clouded with worry.

Emeline's mouth tightened as she tried not to cry at his endearment. Her eyes closed briefly as she willed herself to hold it together. Opening her eyes, she told him, "I'm better now that I can see you." Trying to decide what to tell him, she knew that they had to know about Tarquin. Later on, when she was back in Nox's arms, then she could fall apart and tell him about Hagen. Now was not the time. "Nox, I will tell you everything when I see you, but right now, I have more important information.

"Tell me."

"This is Tarquin's ship," Emeline exclaimed.

Tarek came into view saying, "I knew he was behind this." He wasn't at all surprised this was Tarquin's doing.

"Hagen told us Tarquin just wanted a shipment of Himalayan salt and then he would release us. Only, Tarek, Hagen has this crazy plan to get rid of Tarquin and take over Earth. He's dangerous and right now he's not happy with me." Looking at Nox, she knew what she said next was going to really upset him. "Tarquin saved us—me and Violia."

"WHAT?!"

Tarek's voice cut through Nox's yell, "What do you mean he saved you?"

"Hagen decided to knock us around, but Tarquin came in and stopped him. He said that abusing females was not allowed. Only I don't think Hagen got the memo." She shrugged her shoulders, not wanting them to read too much into it, but she should have known that was a pipe dream.

"Emeline, what did he do to you?" Nox was frantic, his eyes wide with concern... his mind running through scenario after scenario, none of them good.

Trying to reassure him, she said, "Babe, I'm okay. Tarquin stopped him before he could do too much damage." Making her voice sound lighter, she gave a little laugh as she said, "Trust me, he didn't walk away unscathed."

Liam pushed Nox out of the way, his eyes searching out his sister. Giving her the once-over, he saw her clothes were in tatters, but otherwise there were no visible cuts or bruises. "I hope he's not walking upright."

Winking at him, Emeline said, "Let's just say he went down hard." None of them needed to know how fast he got back up. She was trying hard to forget that fact.

Tarek interrupted them, saying that they shouldn't stay on too long. He ordered them to get as much rest as they could and be ready.

Nodding in agreement, Emeline held up her finger, saying, "Nox, wait. Have you initiated the interface program yet?"

"Not yet. We were just talking about using your retina scan to initiate it. Liam has your authorization. Do you give your consent to initiate the program?"

"Yes of course. I totally agree. Liam, you have my permission to access my file."

Motioning for Nox to pick up the wrist comm and move away from the group in the room, she whispered, "Babe, are you okay? I've been so worried about you."

Shaking his head as he gave her a sad smile, saying, "Here you are the one that's been kidnapped and you're worrying for me. It's you I fear for. Do you have any weapons?"

"I don't know. I can't find my purse. I had the knife that Liam gave me for my birthday, but I don't know where it is. It might still be in the botany lab."

"What were you doing in there? I thought you were going to take a nap and wait for me," he grumbled.

"I was—only Violia called and asked if I wanted a tour of the ship. You know me, I couldn't pass that up. I guess I got the more extended tour." She was trying to keep it light, but she knew they had to hang up before they got caught. She didn't want to think about what Hagen would do if he found her wrist comm. "Nox, I have to go."

"I know—please stay safe, know we are coming for you. Do whatever you have to do to stay alive." Holding his palm up to the screen, he whispered, "I love you, Emeline. No matter what—I always will."

Reaching her hand up to his, she answered, "I love you too. Don't take too long." Kissing her fingers, she waved them at Nox.

"Stay strong, my beautiful girl." Those were Nox's last words before Emeline ended the call.

Turning her attention to Violia, Emeline saw that she was eating some of the fruit, trying not to listen in on her conversation with Nox.

Handing her back the wrist comm for her to put away, she asked, "Violia, what else have you got in those pockets that we can use as weapons? We're going to need something if we're going to have any chance against Hagen."

Standing up in front of her, Violia opened up one pocket after another, showing Emeline her surprises. Handing Emeline a DRI, Violia told her it was loaded with a high dose of sedative that would knock out anyone in a matter of seconds. You just have to get close enough to inject it." Handing her a long thin sliver tool, Violia said, "This is a laser scalpel."

Turning it on, a thin laser beam shot out one end, Violia demonstrated how it worked.

Handing it to Emeline, she told her, "I think this would be your best weapon. If necessary, you could distract him with this, while I inject him with the sedative. I only hope we get rescued before we have to use any of this stuff. I really only see two outcomes here...either he gets knocked out or he doesn't, in which case we're dead. "

Dread rolled off of Emeline as she murmured, "You got that right."

Lying down on one of the cots, Emeline suggested they both try to get some sleep. They would need to be rested when Nox and Tarek got there. Taking her mind to her happy place so her body could rest, Emeline managed to shut out the echoes of pain and humiliation that she felt from Hagen's brutal assault. Those could wait for now.

CHAPTER 19

Nox's body shook with relief—*she's alive!* Leaning back, his hand covering his eyes, he fought back the emotions of seeing his beautiful girl. He tried not to read too deeply into what lay behind that hard look in her eyes. Something bad had happened…it was there in her face if you knew where to look, which he did. Ami may think that time mattered in how well he knew Emeline, but she was looking at their relationship from a different viewpoint. Not until she experienced her own bondmate would she truly understand the immediate connection that happens.

His bond had reached out, catching a glimmer of a thread. He felt her love but also her fear. She was trying to be brave, but she needed him. They had to act soon. Every minute they waited, she was in more and more danger.

He felt a hand squeeze his shoulder.

"Nox! Hey, man, she's alive!"

Nox quickly lowered his hand, giving Liam a relieved look. "Thank the stars."

Looking around, he saw Tarek talking to Jagger. They were having ARI run a simulation incorporating the data that Emeline and Violia had given them. A diagram of the Invidia showing where the two females were being kept instantly appeared.

Nox didn't want to interrupt him, but he was anxious to get to Emeline. "Tarek, when do we leave?"

Tarek paused then pointed at the holographic image of the Invidia. "When the time is right. Now that we've spoken to the females, they have given us valuable data that will help in the finalization of the plan."

Looking at Liam, he continued, "Your sister is remarkable. Most females would not have survived as well as she has. I've watched you training with her. I like your methods."

A look of pride flushed across Liam's face. "Thank you, General. I run a training class for both males and females back on Earth. Em and her friends are my star pupils." He gave Ami a wink, the pride he felt for his *girls* showed.

Tarek directed their attention back to the hologram, saying, "With this information, Jagger and I have been weighing our options."

Nox leaned in, his skin color beginning to return to normal. Ever since the kidnapping, his skin had turned paler than normal, giving him an almost ghostly appearance. Feeling a hint of cautious optimism, he was eager to get this rescue mission started.

As Tarek began his explanation, Farzie, the communications officer, interrupted him on his console. "Sir, incoming transmission from the Invidia asking to talk to you. Should I connect?" She waited silently for the General's orders.

Everyone looked at each other, waiting. No one was surprised since Violia had mentioned Tarquin was going to call.

Addressing the room, Tarek said, "I need everyone to remain calm. We cannot let Tarquin know that we have spoken to the females. That would only put them in more danger." Hitting a button on his console he told Farzie, "Send it to the center table console."

Tarquin was at his desk, leaning back in his chair as if he didn't have a care in the world. His cap was pulled down almost to his eyebrows, leaving only his dark eyes staring out. His right hand was playing with a knife—Emeline's knife. He knew Tarek could see it; his expression smug as he saw Tarek's eyes glance from the knife to the red leather purse that was lying there out of place on an otherwise stark metal desk.

Tarquin's lips curved into a slight smile as Tarek's jaw

tightened, watching as he ran his two fingers down the blade from the tip to the hilt. "General, what a strange place for us to meet."

"Tarquin." Tarek's voice came out hard as he stood in front of the hologram. Arms crossed over his wide chest; years of experience had taught Tarek how to keep his anger in check. "Let's not waste time. I can see you have the human scientist. What do you want?"

Before he could answer, Nox jumped out of his chair, his hands clenched as he stared into the eyes of the male who had ordered the kidnapping of his bondmate. Aware of Tarek's warning, he couldn't stop himself. He had to see for himself the infamous Tarquin. Ready to speak his mind, he was stopped by the look of surprise on Tarquin's face.

"Director Nox, it's a pleasure. I was just talking to your female. She is very beautiful." With a look of mocked innocence, Tarquin asked him, "Tell me, Director, are you sure she's your bondmate? I mean, I wouldn't mind keeping her. Human females are amazingly resilient. It was fascinating watching her attempt to take down my first officer." He knew his words only enflamed Nox.

"What have you done to her?" Nox shouted at him.

Rushing over, Liam shoved Nox out of the way as he spoke to the hologram, his voice low and deadly. "If anything happens to my sister, I will personally take you apart limb by limb as slowly and as painfully as I can."

Taken aback by the venom oozing out of Liam's voice, Tarquin cocked an eyebrow at Tarek. "A human male. Interesting. Tell me, General, have you decided that Earth should be brought into your precious UAP?"

Looking Liam up and down, he addressed his next remarks to him. " Human, I give you credit for being brave, but you do not want to engage a Hexian. The outcome would not be in your favor."

"Once you return my sister, I look forward to giving it my best shot." Liam gave Tarquin an equally smug look.

Tarquin might think he knew about humans, but he was like all the aliens he'd met so far, always underestimating them. *I'll just have to use that to my advantage.*

"Enough." General Tarek took control over the room. If there was a way that they could negotiate the release of the females, Tarek might consider it. This was not the time to be ruled by emotions. "Tarquin, name your demands."

Snorting, Tarquin shook his head at Tarek. "Always to the point. You never change, do you?" Not waiting for him to answer, Tarquin's face hardened, "If you had just minded your own business and left us alone, this wouldn't be happening."

Tarek smirked back, "As usual you put the blame on everyone except yourself. What did you think was going to happen? The UAP would never have allowed you to attack Earth and steal from them."

"Who said anything about attacking Earth? You really need to check where you get your information, General. It might be time to do a little in-house investigating." Tarquin knew he was getting under Tarek's skin. He knew who the mole was but wasn't inclined to share that information.

A frown crossed over Tarek's face. "Regardless, Earth is still on the prohibited list, so it's off limits to you. Return the two females and go back to Hexia."

Ignoring Tarek's demands, Tarquin countered, "Since Hexia isn't a member of the UAP, we don't have to follow their edicts. Just because you follow them like a loyal lapdog doesn't mean that I do."

A stifled laugh came from the other side of the table, followed by Jagger murmuring loudly, "Follow, my ass." Everyone knew that Tarek made his own decisions, especially if it involved endangering any member of his crew needlessly. The glare that Tarek shot in Jagger's direction quieted the room.

"This is tiring, what do you want?"

"I want two shipments of Earth's pink salt. I'll release

the human once I've received the shipments and cleared the solar system. The female will be placed back in your escape pod. You'll get the coordinates as to where to pick her up once I leave this system."

"And how do I know you'll release her unharmed?" Tarek said warily.

Tarquin pretended to be offended, saying, "You question my word?"

Tarek almost laughed, but his face remained expressionless, replying, "History is an amazing thing, wouldn't you agree? So again, what guarantee do I have that you will keep your word?"

"You don't. You'll just have to trust me." His words hung in the air because there wasn't anyone in the room that did and Tarquin knew it.

Appearing to think about Tarquin's demand, Tarek looked over at Jagger, who was just out of the sightline of the hologram. A silent communication passed between the two friends, leading Tarek to tell Tarquin that fine, he would accept his demand only with a few changes. "We will be the one to get the salt shipments from Earth, and then we will make the exchange for both females."

Frowning, Tarquin didn't appear to be at all happy about this change in his plans, but he knew he needed that salt. It was the only way he could get the funds for the Hexian families. He needed that money and quickly. Looking at Tarek, he told him he would agree to his changes with one exception—Violia stayed with him. "I need her skills. She comes with us. That is nonnegotiable." Medics were in short supply for his people.

Ami, who had been sitting quietly listening to this whole exchange, surged to her feet at his words. She knew that Tarek was going to have her head for interrupting, but she had heard enough.

Coming into view of the screen, she got her first glimpse of the leader of Hexia. She took in his rugged appearance that told her he spent a great deal of time out of doors. Locking eyes with the man who held her best friend hostage, she was mad enough to rip his head off, but something held her back. She didn't know if it was the widening of his eyes as he took in her appearance or the slight softening of his face when he scanned her body, taking in every detail, but she stood there drinking him in—transfixed.

Seeing the interaction between Ami and Tarquin, Tarek took control. "Ami."

His voice broke through her haze, her skin reddening as she realized she had been standing there *checking out* the enemy. Mouthing *"sorry"* to Tarek, she sat down next to Liam, her eyes still glued to the hologram.

"Tarquin," Tarek barked out, mindful of Tarquin's eyes flickering back and forth between him and the back of Ami as she moved out of sight. "Violia is a member of my crew, so she will be returned along with the human female. I don't care why you need her. Unless she is willing to stay, she will be coming back to the *Maelstrom*." Tarek was not willing to negotiate when it came to any member of his crew. He added, making his point clear, "Of course, if you want me to involve my entire fleet that could certainly be arranged."

Anger flashed in Tarquin's eyes, there would be no negotiating with Tarek, he thought to himself. He would get the salt himself. "We're done here. Call me if you change your mind." Tarquin's image disappeared into the table.

Silence settled around the room, everyone lost in thought as to what had just taken place.

Nox was the first to speak, his mind made up...he was ready to take action. They needed to act soon before Tarquin took off to Hexia, taking Emeline with him. "We have to do something. If Tarquin had even an inkling of how valuable Emeline was to him, he'd never let her go. Tell me you have a plan," he implored Tarek.

Smiling sympathetically at Nox, Tarek nodded his head.

"We will not be negotiating with anyone. Keeping one of my crewmembers is not an option. I'm not saying that what Violia did was right, but it's apparent she's a victim in this as well. We will proceed as planned…only the timetable has been moved up." Looking over at Jagger, he asked, "When can your team will be ready for deployment?"

Rechecking the console in front of him, Jagger, replied, "Minimum three hours."

Turning to Nox, Tarek asked, "Nox, I need you to get your interface program initiated immediately."

"On it."

Asking Liam to give him the authorization codes from Emeline, Nox moved over to the side console to contact Loris. It was time to see if all of their hard work paid off.

The mood in the room hummed with excitement. Finally, they were going to engage the Hexians and rescue Emeline and Violia.

Tarek told Jagger to contact Dr. Datrem and fill him in on what was happening. Then, turning to Liam and Nyx, he began reviewing his plan for them. They were going to lead a team of three star fighters towards Earth acting as the final barrier from the Hexians. Nyx would be piloting, with Liam on weapons. They were to use any means necessary to keep the Hexians away from Earth. "Nyx, I want you to set up a perimeter away from Earth's orbit. It is imperative that Earth's inhabitants remain unaware of the danger they could be facing. As far as their leaders are concerned, we have taken care of any problems."

Liam raised his hand, "General, shouldn't we inform my superiors on Earth?" He hadn't gotten in touch with Leslie Merriman since the kidnapping. He didn't want to cause needless concern until he had more information, but now that they were moving forward with a plan, he wondered about the General's thoughts.

Tarek took a moment to consider his options before replying. "I was going to say no, that we should wait until this is over, but now I think you should contact your superior. If we are to proceed in good faith, they should be informed in case something unexpected was to happen."

Making eye contact with Nyx, Tarek told him, "I'm counting on you as mission leader to make sure that nothing does." At Nyx's nod, Tarek turned back to Liam, "Inform Ms. Merriman of the facts and relay our plan. We'll let her know the outcome once the mission is over."

Nodding his head in understanding, Liam moved over to the corner of the room to call Leslie. He could only imagine what she was going to say when he informed her that a major battle was about to take place in the skies above Earth. This was uncharted territory for Earth and he was unsure how much he should tell her. Asking ARI to connect him to NASA headquarters, it wasn't long before Leslie's face appeared before him. She started to ask why he was calling, but stopped short as she took in his appearance.

"Liam, what's happened?" Leslie's voice was sharp, concern showing on her face.

"We have a situation."

"Go on."

Lowering his voice, Liam began to explain what was happening. "The Hexians kidnapped Emeline. They want two shipments of Himalayan salt in exchange for her release."

Leslie's deep brown eyes widened the more Liam went on to explain the entire chain of events. "Liam, I need to inform the President about this latest incident, but I'm positive he'll want you to do whatever it takes to keep this battle away from Earth. He and the UN council members are already concerned, and this will not bode well for any alliances that might come out of this first contact."

"I agree with you, but in all honesty, Leslie, I think we've gone well beyond ignoring that we're not alone in the universe. Change is coming and Earth is going to have be prepared—maybe not now but sometime in the very near future. Why don't we table this discussion for later, after we get my sister back? Getting her out of the hands of the Hexians is my first priority."

Glancing over, Nox gave him a thumbs up, indicating that the interface program has been initiated. "Leslie, I just received notification that the force field technology that Nox and Emeline developed has been initiated. Within the next two hours, all Earth's major communication satellites will be protected from being destroyed in the event that we are unable to stop the Hexians."

Leslie smiled, glad for some positive news. "Well done. That will go a long way towards reassuring the President and the council members. I'm going to call the President right now. If there are any changes, I'll call you back. Otherwise call me when you have completed your mission."

"Yes, ma'am."

Leslie's dark eyes softened as she paused for a moment before saying, "Liam, I'm sorry to hear about Emeline. I know I told you to keep this on a need-to-know basis, but have you told your mother and sister about any of this?"

"No, I haven't called Mum yet. There is no point in making her crazy with worry when there isn't anything she could do. You know Fiona, she'd be on your doorstep asking for a ride up to the Space Station if she even suspected one of her kids was in trouble. When this is all over, I'll have a long talk with her."

Seeing Nox out of the corner of his eyes, he gave a short laugh, "Once she hears about her kids meeting aliens—well let's just say that's going to be a lively conversation."

Leslie's eyes crinkled at the corners in laughter. "To be a fly on the wall when that happens, but in all seriousness, Liam, please be careful. I wish you success in your mission. Take care of yourself."

"I will. I'll get in touch with you when it's over, but frankly, Leslie, I'm worried about Em. If they figure out the kind of knowledge she possesses—man, I can't even think about that right now."

Gazing at her, his bloodshot eyes laced with worry, Liam inhaled sharply. Breathing out softly, he asked, "Before you go, do you still have the letter to my family in my file?" Liam didn't want to think about the letter all military members who left on a hazardous assignment had to write in the event that the unthinkable happened. He had every intention of surviving this mission, but he knew better than most...sometimes unforeseen circumstances happened.

"Of course." A frown crossed her face as she considered Liam's question. "Liam, I don't plan on having to send that letter, so you better keep your ass safe. Do I make myself clear?"

Sighing, Liam answered in the affirmative.

"Now go kick some alien butt and then I want to see you back on Earth as soon as possible. Are you hearing me, Lt. Commander?" Her tone was hard because any other option was not acceptable.

Grinning at her, he saluted her, saying, "Ma'am, yes ma'am." Adding, "Thank you, Leslie. I'll be in touch. Cameron out."

Liam ended the link to Earth and leaned his head against the wall for a moment, thoughts of his mother and sisters ran through his mind. He didn't dare let his mind think of how his mother would feel if something happened to him and Emeline. She would be destroyed.

A firm hand landed on his shoulder.

Tarek had been watching Liam's interchange with Leslie Merriman. "Is there a problem?"

Liam was surprised at the concern in Tarek's voice. Turning around, he shook his head, not only to answer him but to clear his mind. "No. She's going to inform the President and the council members. We were just talking about my mother. Leslie was wondering if I had called her about Emeline. I told her that calling Mum and telling her that her youngest daughter was kidnapped by aliens was not an option."

"I understand. That would be hard for any mother to accept." Tarek said, frowning.

"Ever since my dad died, my Mum has been a little on the overprotective side." Sighing, Liam remembered his parents fondly. "They were together for almost forty years— I know she misses him." Seeing a confused look on Tarek's face, Liam asked him what he was thinking.

"It's difficult to understand because our life cycles are so different. We live for close to 600 of your Earth years, so forty is not that long on my planet. Humans are a relatively young species, whereas Delicians have been around for many millennia. My parents have been together for over 350 years."

Liam's eyebrows rose up in surprise. "Wow that's— that's incredible. How did they meet?"

Tarek told Liam they met through mutual friends. Even though they weren't bondmates, they were deeply committed to each other.

Liam told Tarek how his parents had met. It was in computer class, second year of college. Hank came in late to class on the first day of the term and fell into the seat next to Fiona's. From that moment on, they were inseparable and within two years had married and had Liam. "I spent most of my childhood going to classes with my mum. Her idea of a playgroup was study groups with her computer nerd friends."

"Your mother is also a scientist?" Tarek was curious about the woman who had raised these two interesting humans.

"Yes." Seeing Nyx at the table going over their part of the plan, Liam excused himself to join him.

Ami and Nox were studying the diagram of the Invidia, discussing their role in Tarek's plan. They would be going with Tarek and his team to the Invidia. Their mission would be to rescue Emeline and Violia while Tarek and his team took over the ship. Jagger's star fighters would create a diversion, distracting Tarquin and the Invidia. Once the Hexians opened their docking bay doors to deploy their fighters, Ezio would slip a cloaked shuttle carrying a contingent of Tarek's elite soldiers right in under their noses.

"Ami." Jagger called her over. "I need you to go with Ramola. He will assist you with your battle armor."

Ami stopped mid step, her excitement rising, "I get my own armor? Just like Liam and Nyx have?"

Jagger rolled his eyes, chuckling at the delight on her face. "Yup. Only this armor has a few more modifications. In fact, Liam?" Jagger called him over. "I need you to go with her to get yours upgraded as well."

"Yes, sir." Liam was focused on the mission and anxious to get moving. "I'm ready to go." He headed towards the door, not waiting to see if Ami followed.

"Wait up, Liam." Ami turned, running after Liam, with Ramola following behind grumbling at the overexuberant humans. "Ramola, what kind of cool stuff does the armor do?" You could hear her ask another question as the door closed behind them.

Jagger and Tarek turned to look at each other, amusement on their faces. "Ami certainly does love using our gear. I think she's going to have a hard time going back to Earth and giving up our technology," Jagger murmured to Tarek. "In fact, I think it's going to be hard for all three of them."

Hearing Jagger's comments, Nox looked up. Pointing to the hologram of Earth's satellite retrofits that were suspended in the middle of the table, he said, "You're right about that. Emeline has said many times she couldn't imagine giving up our *cool stuff*. If it were up to her, there would already be regen units in all their medical facilities." His face took on a lost look as he watched one satellite after another be encased in a protective force field. *She would have loved seeing our program working.*

Jagger rubbed his chin thoughtfully as he watched the product of the first human and Delician collaboration come to life in front of him. "We were totally wrong about the humans, at least these three anyway. If the rest of the humans are like them, we have been doing a disservice to the human race."

Nyx looked up from where he was checking the readiness of his star fighters, chiming in, "Liam and Ami are constantly asking how things work. Every time I go looking for Ami, she's in the simulator shooting everything she can. If I didn't hate the Hexians so much, I'd almost pity them when they come up against her."

Tarek had been listening to his crew discuss the humans. "Nox, can I speak to you alone for a moment?"

Nox looked up, surprised, as Ezio, Nyx and Jagger moved down to the other end of the room giving them some privacy.

Standing in front of Tarek made Nox anxious. His biggest fear was that Tarek would make him stay behind on the rescue mission. He couldn't let that happen. Squaring his shoulders, Nox focused his gaze on Tarek.

"Nox, I'm sending you and Ami to get Emeline and Violia and bring them back to the shuttle. I know how badly you want to go on this mission, but I have to ask—are you up for this?"

Flashing amethyst eyes told Tarek of course he could count on him. The plan was burned into his memory. Rescuing Emeline was the only thing he was thinking of. Nothing was going to stop him from rescuing his bondmate. "Yes." Planning this rescue was the only thing keeping him from stealing a shuttle and going after her himself.

"Are you prepared to follow your team?" Tarek had been noticing Nox's body language. Tarek didn't get where he was by not being able to read people. Even though Nox was a civilian, when he was on his ship, Nox was his responsibility...along with every other member of his crew. He knew Nox was capable. Nox just needed to realize it.

"Yes."

"Good. We leave in eight hours."

"WHAT?" Nox's voice roared out at them. He couldn't believe they were going to make his bondmate wait that long before they got to them. "Why aren't we leaving now?" Turning to Jagger, he demanded, "I thought you said you could be ready in three hours?"

Jagger raised an eyebrow at Nox, telling him, "Calm down. We can't go off unprepared. We need time to coordinate all the pieces. I'm confident we have at least that long before Tarquin can leave the solar system. Besides, I need time to get my star fighters and crewmembers read in on the mission."

"But you don't know what they might be doing to her," Nox blurted out. Hearing his own words out loud caused him to stop, realizing that his control was slipping and that would not help Emeline.

Running his fingers through his hair, Nox blew out his frustration muttering, "Sorry. I'm trying to keep everything contained inside, but sometimes it's hard. You're right. We're a team. I know that and I really appreciate you allowing me to go on this mission. I realize everyone has to be prepared. It's just frustrating feeling like this—knowing that she's in danger and there's nothing I can do to help her."

Tarek spoke quietly to Nox. "Have some faith in your bondmate. She has already proven she can take care of herself. She's a fighter."

Nox looked up, surprised at Tarek's insight into his bondmate. "Yes, and that's what worries me." The worry for Emeline was eating at him. Under normal circumstances, he considered himself to be cool-headed when faced with adversity, but knowing what Emeline was facing tore at his soul. Tarek was right—she was strong. It was the waiting and worrying that was torturous.

Taking a different tactic, Tarek asked Nox, "Haven't you noticed in training how Liam is constantly making corrections and pushing them, making them think? Her brother has prepared her well."

"He has."

"I have enjoyed watching these females spar. I do understand now why they wear pads. I haven't seen them draw blood, but they certainly don't hold back either." Tarek rubbed his hand across his massive chest, each pectoral muscle was clearly outlined through his tight uniform as he mulled over an idea. "I'm considering implementing new training methods for our females."

Jagger grinned, liking where Tarek was going with this. "I like it. I know Marsel is always bugging me to train with her. I've been too afraid I'd hurt her, but after watching Liam with the human females, I think you're right. The way he taught them to use their weaknesses to their advantage was brilliant. I think Marsel will be the first one to sign up, especially if she gets to see Ami take Ezio down as fast as she did." Laughing at Ezio, whose expression had turned sour, Jagger knew he had hit a sore spot.

"She caught me unaware, that's all." Ezio's hand unconsciously rubbed his groin. It still hurt where her knee had clipped him. She said she had misjudged her aim because of his height, but the smug look on her face every time she saw him made him think otherwise. He wouldn't make that mistake twice.

Tarek laughed along with the rest of them. His team needed to blow off a little steam before they embarked on this mission. He knew he was in desperate need to hit something or someone.

Turning his attention to Nox, who was lost in thought, he clapped him on the back, saying, "I know exactly what you need—what we all could use before the mission."

As Tarek stalked towards the door, he called over his shoulder, "Call Liam and Ami. Tell them to meet us in the training room when they're finished with Ramola. A good workout will help take the edge off."

He chuckled going through the door at the collective groan coming from behind him.

◆ ◆ ◆

Two hours later

Nox dragged his exhausted and bruised body down the corridor towards his room. It was the one place he'd been avoiding. It felt like years since he had been back there. Had it only been this morning that Emeline had been laughing about staying under the covers and spending the whole day in bed? He should have listened to her. Maybe if he had, she would be with him now, completing their bond...instead of fighting to stay alive on a ship full of mercenaries.

Standing in front of the door, he leaned his head down... the coolness of the surface didn't calm the rage that burned inside him. He knew he needed rest. Tarek and Emeline were counting on him.

Tarek questioning his competence had been insulting. Snorting to himself, Nox shook his head in disbelief. Did Tarek seriously think they would be going on this mission without him? He knew Nox better than that. Granted they weren't exactly friends before this mission, although they had known each other for years. Tarek had been instrumental in getting Nox to use his ship for the first installation of his force field technology. Tarek was well aware of how determined Nox could be when he wanted something.

Steeling himself against the onslaught of emotions that were about to assail him, Nox waved his hand at the panel. As the door opened, he walked hesitantly into the room. The door closed silently behind him, leaving him alone...in the dark—even the window had been darkened.

Disoriented for a brief moment, he remembered Emeline had said she was going to take a nap while she waited for him. If only she had told Violia no. *Stop it!* He couldn't think like that. Violia had been desperate enough to find a way to get Emeline to do what she wanted, and desperate people had a tendency to do rash things.

The cold feel of the room fueled Nox's discomfort at being there without Emeline's warming presence. Unable to see anything in the darkened room, Nox's nose twitched as he tried to identify some of the scents that surrounded him. It really was true when you lose one sense, the others become more enhanced. There was a heady perfumed smell that stood out the strongest—a rose.

Smiling to himself, a memory of Emeline holding up a red rose formed in Nox's mind. He remembered how lovely she had looked leaning over the large planter of her favorite flower she had growing on her patio. The sun had shone down golden on her hair, a wisp of a smile on her lips as she inhaled deeply from the fragrant flower. She was so beautiful standing there. A hot August breeze blew off the water, causing her light dress to blow up, revealing her long shapely legs. Emeline had been totally unaware of the effect she had on him.

Taking another breath, the smell of strawberries and something else—*oh yeah, chocolate. I like chocolate.* The thought of reliving Emeline's introduction to chocolate should have been a memory that he took out and savored, only not this time.

Needing the distraction, Nox called out wearily into the room, "ARI, bring lights up twenty-five percent."

The light was still low enough that his eyes were able to quickly adjust. Glancing at the bed, he saw rose petals formed into the shape of a heart. He laughed bitterly at her joke to him. They had talked about how he made her feel —what was the word, oh yeah, corny. Over the past week they'd lived in such a small space, they were able to get to know some of each other's habits and quirks. He found out that she loved silly romantic gestures and it didn't matter whether she gave them or got them. He'd spent more time thinking up ways to surprise her when he should have been focusing on his work. He had even asked Ami to help him with a design from Emeline's favorite lingerie store that he was going to surprise her with tonight. He never got the chance to replicate it. Maybe he should do it now, so it was ready when he brought her home.

Looking down at his uniform, the state of which showed the extent of his long day, a shower was probably a good idea.

Using his finger, he ran his nail down the front of his shirt, causing the nanites to create an opening, leaving Nox's sweaty chest exposed as his shirt fell to the floor. His pants followed as he stepped into the bathroom.

Looking back at his clothes lying on the floor, he stopped and turned around to pick them up. A bad habit Emeline had said to him about dropping his clothes on the floor. He usually picked them up, eventually, but it was one of Emeline's pet peeves as she would call it. He was getting better at it. His mother had always been after him to take care of his clothes.

He stopped and looked at his reflection in the mirror. His mother's eyes stared back at him as he thought about how much she would have liked Emeline.

Setting the shower on hot and hard, he let the water pound against his skin. It felt like a futile attempt to remove some of the sorrow and fear that he felt at this moment. A large purplish bruise could be seen darkening just along his left shoulder—a slow reaction to one of Liam's flips. Not a move Nox was likely to forget again. He'd have to run a portable regen device over it after his shower. On second thought, he figured he might as well run it over his entire body. Sparring with Tarek's elite soldiers on a good day was difficult. Considering how high everyone's emotions were at this moment, this particular sparring session was brutal. There wasn't one person who didn't feel some kind of responsibility for Emeline's kidnapping. The fact that she was stolen right under their noses—that didn't sit well with any of them.

Reaching for the shampoo, the scent of vanilla wafting softly through the steam, Nox poured some into his hand and began rubbing it over his entire body. It sank into his pores as Emeline had seeped into his very soul. As he massaged his hair, the foam slid down his long body, his thoughts on the woman who had burst into his life, changing it forever. Having her scent surround him gave him comfort, allowing him to feel closer to her.

She would want him to keep Ami safe during the rescue. He didn't agree with Tarek sending Ami with him, but there would be no stopping her. He couldn't blame her. She was just as invested in saving Emeline as he was. Normally, Delician females would remain out of combat, but human females were different, especially Ami and Emeline. At least Ami would be outfitted with Delician armor, unlike Emeline who was unprotected.

Rinsing off, Nox stepped out in front of the dryer that removed all the water from his skin. Grabbing the portable regen device, he ran it over his shoulder, waiting patiently as the bruise slowly faded away, leaving his pearly white skin shining in the soft light. Pastel-colored dots could be seen moving across his healed skin.

Slipping into a pair of sleeping pants, he moved into the main room, noticing for the first time the framed picture on the table.

Picking it up, his insides clenched as he gazed at the picture of Emeline and himself. A selfie, she'd called it. Their heads touching, the laughter shining on her face as she had tried several times to get him to look at the right spot as she snapped picture after picture with her cell phone.

Surveying the room, he found her subtle touches everywhere. There was a picture of her family on the shelf beside the couch and another one of just him, sitting in his office, giving her what she said was his *sexy alien* smile. If she only knew it was really his *I want to rip your clothes off and have my way with you* smile.

Remembering he wanted to replicate a surprise he had been working on for Emeline, Nox saw that there was something already in the replicator. It appeared that he and Emeline had been of a similar mindset.

Gently taking the delicate nightgown out of the replicator, it felt as if the rock that had been holding back the dam of his emotions finally broke free. He rubbed the soft material against his face. The scent, unique to Emeline, filled his very being. A lone tear dropped from his eye onto the silky fabric, marring the beautiful design.

Pulling it away from his face, he carefully laid the nightgown on the bed. Running his hands over it, he smoothed out all the wrinkles as best he could. It would be there waiting for when he brought Emeline home.

It wasn't right that she was gone. Emeline was an innocent human who up until a few weeks ago was only interested in eliminating Earth's solar flare problem. Instead, she was fighting for her life—counting on him to rescue her. Hagen was a dead man as far as Nox was concerned.

Just the thought of that worthless scum touching his beautiful girl—Nox couldn't keep his anger contained. His fist slammed into the wall, the impact taking his breath away as pain shot up his arm. Probably not the brightest move on his part, Nox thought, trying to shake the pain out of his hand. It did little to defuse the rage that had been building since he saw Violia's message. He wondered what Emeline would say when she saw the fist-size hole in the wall when she returned. Knowing her, she would be more concerned about his bruised hand than a hole in the wall.

Lying down on the couch, after using the regen device

yet again, he tried to convince his body to rest. Unfortunately, his mind had other ideas. Tarek's words about the mission ran through his mind. Was he right in thinking *I'm too emotional to be of any good to the team and to Emeline? No. I have to do this. I will save her*

Focusing, he mentally ran through the sequences of the mission, determined to be prepared.

Finally, his body gave in to exhaustion. Unfortunately, he quickly sank into a nightmare that had him chasing demons. It looked as if Nox would be running on pure adrenaline for this mission. Rest would have to wait until he saved his love.

CHAPTER 20

Docking Bay
Battle Cruiser Maelstrom

Liam hurried across the docking bay floor as he saw Ami waiting for him in front of the star fighter he and Nyx would be flying on their mission. Her helmet was on with the visor pulled down over her eyes. He could see she was reading the outputs from the internal computer that was designed into the suit. All of Tarek's soldiers wore similar suits, linking them together. The suit itself fit snugly over her curvy figure—a fact noticed by all the Delician males around her. She wasn't totally unaware of the effect she had on these aliens—both male and females alike. Aside from being the only human female in the room, she stood out not only because of how vastly different she was from Delician females, but also because of her exotic beauty. Ami had groused to him on numerous occasions how uncomfortable she was with all the staring. Liam reminded her that it was because she was different—heck, they were all different. It was going to take time for them to get used to seeing such a dynamic and hot-looking female. Rubbing his shoulder, he remembered how she had scoffed at him before punching him.

Ami waved excitedly at him as she waxed on about how amazing it was that she could see the readout of her biological signs displayed on the screen in front of her.

"Watch this."

She did a few jumping jacks, watching her heart rate steadily increase the more she did. Stopping to take a breather, she saw her heart rate slowly start to decrease, although with them about to leave to rescue Emeline, her heart rate was higher than normal. "Isn't this the coolest thing ever? Do you think they'd let us take one of these home with us?"

Giving her a thoughtful look, Liam said cryptically, "Maybe—who knows? They are definitely cool."

"You got that right," she grinned happily. "Watch how easily I can move." Moving through a series of stretches, she marveled to Liam just how deceiving the suit was. "I really thought it was going to be stiff and hard to move in, you know, similar to our space suits, but this material is amazing. When Ramola told us how flexible the suit was, I didn't believe him, but he was right."

Laughing at her acting like a little kid showing off, he was happy for the distraction. He was uncharacteristically nervous, which bothered him. "You know, Ames, early in my military career when I was in Afghanistan, I had to do some scary stuff. I can't go into the details—you know why —but I can tell you that I've had my share of close calls from enemy fire."

Ami stopped playing with her suit at Liam's words. Walking over, she leaned into him, trying to give him some much-needed comfort, whispering, "We were so scared for you every time you went over there. I can't tell you the number of times we sat up doing all-nighters when we thought you might call."

Liam made small circles with his hand on Ami's back. "So many nights I tried to call, but those were dangerous times. I was young and thought I could save the world." Snorting, he shook his head, saying, "Man, did I have a lot to learn, and hopefully, what I learned then will help me with my mission today."

Ami squeezed him tight. She had no idea what they would be facing—only that they would both need to be strong. "You're going to do great. Just like I'm going to go over there, rescue Em and hope I don't get my ass shot off in the process."

A nervous giggle escaped as she leaned away from his shoulder...staring directly into his eyes. "Liam, listen to me. We are the only humans involved in this whole mess. It's up to us. Whatever it takes. Nothing matters until we rescue Em. So that means we go out there and show those alien assholes exactly what it's like to tangle with us lowly humans."

Shouldering her new blaster rifle that was fast becoming a close friend, she turned away. Looking back, she called out to him, "Come on, let's go show them just what happens when they give us shiny new toys to play with, shall we?" She grinned at him through her helmet visor.

Grabbing her arm, he gave her a lopsided smile, agreeing completely with Ami's analogy of the alien weaponry.

Getting serious, Liam reminded her of their training and reiterated some of the rules of engagement with her.

She listened carefully to his words and when he had finished, gave him an indulgent smile. "Yes, Dad. Come on, I've done my homework. Don't worry...you've taught us well."

Seeing the regret in his eyes, knowing it was about Emeline, she squeezed his arms, saying softly, "Liam, she'll be fine. Em's been training with you a long time." Trying to lighten his mood, she quipped, "Knowing her, she's probably already brought a few of those dirt bags to their knees."

"I know, you're right. It's just that look in her eyes when we saw her." A look that spoke volumes to him.

Shaking off unwanted negative thoughts, Liam changed the subject. "When you both get back, I'll cook you anything you want for dinner."

Grinning from ear to ear, she told him that she wanted Fiona's lasagna, the one with all the meat and mozzarella and yummy sauce—and garlic bread. "And you better make a double batch."

"Planning on being that hungry, are you?"

"Not me." She giggled at him, pointing to General Tarek,

who was striding through the door heading towards his shuttle. "You've seen him eat. In fact, you better triple it." It still amazed her at the amount of food these huge alien males put away.

"Once this mission is over, I'll gladly cook for the entire crew."

Looking around the cavernous room, Liam normally saw Delicians diligently going about their assigned jobs keeping the large contingent of spaceships always at the ready. Not today. Tarek's shuttle was front and center on the shuttle platform, opposite to the docking bay doors. Today there were only a few of Tarek's elite soldiers preparing it for launch. Tarek ran a well-organized and efficient ship, and judging by the interactions with his crewmembers, he was well respected. But there was someone who was working for the Hexians on this ship. Liam knew that Tarek was being extra cautious in limiting who knew about the entirety of their mission. He had come to know Tarek fairly well over the last couple of weeks and had tremendous admiration and respect for him. He would do whatever it took to succeed at the mission Tarek was sending him on.

How hard could it be, Liam thought, as he gazed up in wonder at the object that held his affection right now—a Delician star fighter!

Releasing Ami, Liam put his hand on the nose of the ship, giving it a gentle pat. Grinning from ear to ear, his bright green eyes alive with the excitement of a teenage boy getting his first car, Liam spoke almost reverently, "I can't wait to fly one of these babies. You know that Nyx has been holding off letting me take the controls."

"Only because he knows that if anything happened to it, Tarek would have his balls." Ami watched as Tarek gave orders to his crewmembers. "That's not someone I want to get on the bad side of."

Nodding his head, Liam moved all the muscles of his

body, noting some of the sore spots he could still feel from their last *training* session. "You got that right, but a guy can dream," he said with a sigh.

"Sure you can, but I'm thinking we've moved way past dreaming—heading straight into nightmare mode. I mean, come on, seriously, we're in space about to go on a mission with aliens who have kidnapped our girl. How much more nightmarish can we get?" Ami gave him a meaningful look just as she heard Tarek call her name. "Coming, sir," she called back.

Turning to Liam, she gave him one last hug. "I'll bring her back, I promise."

Liam squeezed her hard, not wanting to think this might be the last time they saw each other. Swallowing his emotions, he said, "I know you will." The confidence in his voice belied the feeling of uneasiness he felt inside. "Just make sure you come back in one piece. I am not going to be the one having to call home saying how I lost you to a bunch of alien mercenaries. One person in my life who wants to torture me in the training room is enough."

Laughing out loud at his comment, Ami saw that the Delicians were staring at them—again. "Oh, come on, my dad's not that bad."

"I was talking about your mother. My head would not survive her hitting me with her favorite frying pan if anything happened to her baby." Liam recalled how Ami's mother might be little, but when she got mad, she didn't hesitate to pick up anything within her reach and throw it at you.

"Yeah, my mom can be quite feisty for such a little lady." Chuckling, Ami gave Liam one last hug. "I could say the same for you. I am not calling Fiona, so make sure you bring that fine-looking ass back here in one piece." Slapping said ass, she gave him one last smile before heading over to where the rest of her team was assembled in front of Tarek.

Watching Ami walk away was hard, but all he could do

was pray that the mission would go smoothly. At least Ami was in good hands with Tarek and his team.

Looking up at the star fighter again, it boosted Liam's confidence in the success of the mission knowing Nox's enhanced force field technology had been installed on all of the Delician star fighters. From the last briefing Liam had sat through, the Hexians had acquired an earlier version of shield technology, meaning their ships weren't as up to date as the *Maelstrom*. Maybe that would work in their favor.

"Liam," Tarek called over as he walked toward him, Nyx and Nox on either side of him. "I'd like a word before you leave."

"Yes, sir."

Tarek pulled Liam aside so he could speak to him in private. In a low voice, Tarek told Liam he had the utmost confidence in his abilities. Humans had shown to be extremely resourceful. He was counting on Liam to use whatever means necessary to stop the Hexians, short of destroying Earth or killing themselves.

Liam listened intently to the General's words. "I'll do whatever it takes, sir," he promised the General.

Tarek turned to Nox, saying, "I'll meet you onboard the shuttle." Nox nodded his head as Tarek walked away, only to stop and call over his shoulder, "Oh, and Liam, you better quadruple the amount of lasagna you're making. I'm going to be famished when I return with the two females." He gave Liam a half-grin as he sauntered away towards his ship.

Shocked, Liam looked from Nox and Nyx. "Geez, what kind of hearing do you guys have?"

Nox and Nyx burst out laughing, telling Liam that he had no idea just how sensitive their ears were.

Not wanting to think about how much of his and Ami's conversation Tarek had overhead, Liam spoke quietly to Nox. "I know I've been angry and I took a lot of it out on you

—I'm sorry for that. I just feel so guilty for not protecting her."

Nox's face relaxed at Liam's words. "Thank you for saying that." Rubbing his hand, he gave Liam a rueful smile, saying, "You're not alone in your guilt. I too have failed her. It is a mistake I will not make again." Even though the regen device had healed his hand, he still recalled the pain from hitting the wall. "Good luck in your mission, Liam. I will not come back without her—I promise you that. She is my life."

"Thanks, Nox. And Nox—tell Em that I love her."

Nodding his head, Nox turned and jogged over to where Ami and Tarek were getting ready to board their shuttle.

"You ready?" Nyx had been watching Liam's interaction with Nox, glad that the tension between the two males was finally resolved. It was time to focus on their part of the mission.

"Let's do this." Liam put on his helmet and climbed aboard the star fighter. Taking the seat to the right of Nyx, he situated himself at his workstation. He would be on weapons and navigation as well as anything else that might be needed. Glad that he'd been working closely with Nyx, plus all the hours he had spent in the simulator, Liam was confident in his abilities.

Already familiar with the weapons controls, Liam made sure to double-check their weapons inventory. They had an assortment of plasma torpedoes, particle cannons as well as striation plasma guns. Upon command, ARI could automatically set the target locking mechanisms and fire the particle cannons and torpedoes, although on some of the weapons Liam preferred to shoot the old-fashioned way.

Jagger commed in asking if they were finished with their preflight. Their mission was to head towards Earth flanked by two star fighters. If any Hexians star fighters came towards Earth, they were to stop them by whatever means necessary. He reminded them to keep the General's main directive in mind—safeguard Earth while keeping the human population unaware of the Hexian threat.

As Nyx was powering up the fighter, Jagger's exasperated voice interrupted them with an urgent message. "Change of plan. A Hexian freighter has been spotted heading towards Earth accompanied by two Hexian star fighters. You are to head out immediately to intercept them before they get to Earth's moon."

"Fuck!" Liam exclaimed not so softly.

"Fuck is right," Jagger answered back. "Nyx, do whatever you have to do to stop those assholes. But remember, do not let them get close to Earth."

"Affirmative," Nyx replied to Jagger.

Changing comm signals, he addressed his star fighters. "Fighter 2 and fighter 3, are you ready to launch?" After hearing an affirmative reply, Nyx led the way while Liam continued the navigation check as they discussed a new plan.

Clearing the docking bay doors, Liam shook his head at the gall of the Hexians. "Nyx, what do you think Tarquin's plan is here?"

Nyx's voice came through Liam's helmet, saying, "Tarquin seems determined to get that salt. It must be worth quite a bit to risk pissing off the UAP like he is. I don't know what he's thinking, especially now that the Delicians have made contact with Earth. If he thinks Earth is fair game, he's in for a world of hurt. We will never let that happen."

Nyx engaged the fighter at top speed in order to intercept the Hexians' freighter.

Liam could feel that familiar rush of adrenaline surge through him as his military training kicked in. Instructing ARI to bring up the coordinates of the freighter on the screen in front of him, the data indicated they would reach the intercept point in approximately seven minutes. The spatial map on his screen displayed all the moving objects in their area based on sensor input, one of which matched the last known speed of the freighter. This allowed Liam to also track the movements of the two support Hexian fighters that were shadowing on either side of the freighter.

Nyx ordered his two support fighters to stay in formation as he stopped just within contact range of the freighter. He sent out a prepared message informing them that they represented the United Alliance of Planets. That they were in direct violation of the UAP for contacting a planet on the Prohibited Planets list. They were to immediately stop, turn around and leave Earth's solar system.

Nothing. The Hexians were ignoring all communications.

Nyx, shook his head in disbelief and promptly replayed the message. Again, all they heard was silence. However, the two Hexian support fighters moved off away from the freighter towards the Delicians' star fighters, firing on them as they flew past. Luckily, they had Nox's advanced shielding so there was no damage to any of their ships.

Watching the two Hexian fighters disappear around the back of the freighter, Nyx barked out commands to his own team. "Fighters 2 and 3, pursue and engage. Make sure you keep them away from Earth."

"Affirmative, Commander."

Nyx gave Liam an aggravated look...it was obvious the captain of the freighter was not going to comply to his commands.

Pressing the comm button, Nyx sent out a different warning, "Stand down or we will fire."

When again he got no response, Nyx winked at Liam, saying he had another way to get their attention.

Following Nyx's orders, Liam had ARI lock onto Nyx's targeting coordinates and fired on his command. They watched the shot streak across the dark sky, crossing just in front of the freighter.

Nothing.

The freighter never deviated from its course...Earth.

Liam was dumbfounded that the freighter didn't even react to narrowly escaping the beam of a particle cannon. "What the heck? What do we do now?"

Spying a Hexian star fighter slip around the far side of the freighter, Nyx checked their force fields to make sure they were still at maximum. "Judging by what's coming at us now, it looks like we'll be busy for the next few minutes."

The Hexian fighter fired a series of volleys straight at them as it flew by.

Calling out to Liam, "Inform the Captain of our situation and then get ready to return fire," Nyx grabbed the helm, yelling at Liam to hang on as he spun their ship around, giving chase.

Immediately following Nyx's orders, Liam turned his attention back to the Hexian star fighter. It had swung around to the left and was making a direct pass at them —their particle cannons firing barrage after barrage. Years of experience had Nyx banking a hard left, the shots barely missing their right wing.

"Where the hell did they get particle cannons?" Nyx grumbled loudly. He didn't have time to be shocked as the Hexian came around to make another run at them. "I shouldn't be surprised," Nyx muttered to himself. "Liam get ready—they're heading back towards us."

"On it."

Nyx could feel that he was pushing his ship's engines hard, but this was his ship. He knew its capabilities. The Hexians' shields had limited capacity, unlike Nox's newly upgraded ones. "It shouldn't take too many hits to bring down their shields," Nyx told Liam.

"Okay. How do we do that?" Liam grimaced, seeing that this time the Hexian fighter was heading straight for them. Their particle cannons were trying to make contact, but Nyx weaved and rolled the ship, trying to avoid as many of the hits as he could. Unfortunately, the Hexians were able to get a few shots past, but their shields were holding steady at 88%.

Liam was using a particle cannon as well and was able to hit his mark every time, but the Hexians' shields still held.

Looping back around, Nyx tried to come up behind the Hexian star fighter, but the Hexian pilot anticipated his move. Doing something totally unexpected, he dropped down just as Nyx flew by, leaving themselves exposed, allowing the Hexian ship to come up behind them.

Switching to rear cannons, Liam aimed for the cockpit of the Hexian flyer, but again it felt like the Hexian pilot was reading their minds. He dipped down sharply, causing Liam's shot to go high as they came up underneath Liam and Nyx, making a direct hit to their shield core. Their star fighter shuddered as their shields fought to deflect the Hexian weapon's energy away from them. Liam's head slammed against the side wall as their ship was batted about.

Holding the helm steady, Nyx yelled out to ARI, "Reroute all auxiliary power to the shields."

Finally, after what seemed like an eternity, the ship stabilized and held steady.

"Shit. How the hell are they doing that?" The frustration was evident in Liam's voice as he pounded his fist on the console. He didn't notice the blood running down his cheek from the cut over his eye. Thankfully his helmet had taken the brunt of the hit.

Checking the shields, Liam noticed that their levels were at 45%.

Nyx was quiet as he watched the Hexian fighter turn and hover just out of weapons range. He knew they were assessing their damage as well.

"Our shields are at 45% and our weapons power is down to 63%. How is it that this guy is all over our ass?" Liam was pissed. He'd flown a few combat missions in his time but never anything like this.

Nyx finally broke his silence, his voice sounding deadly, "I can almost guarantee you that whoever is piloting that ship trained in the Delician military." His face was filled with disgust at the thought of one of their own, or worse, someone that Nyx himself had trained, was working for the Hexians. Where was the honor, the duty, the loyalty that you would sell out your own planet, and for what? Greed—plain and simple.

Liam winced internally...betrayed by one of your own, that was harsh. "So, this guy knows all your tricks?"

Nyx grinned sadistically at Liam, saying, "I wouldn't say all my tricks. I think I might have held one or two things back—you know, just for myself."

Liam's fist punched the air as he cried out, "All right then. Let's go show this asshole what he missed in class."

Nyx was lost momentarily, gazing out at the Hexian fighter. He swore the pilot was taunting him.

Turning to Liam, he outlined his plan. "Okay, here's what we're going to do. I'm going to fly straight at them."

Liam's mouth fell open. "And see who blinks first? Seriously? You mean, you're going to play chicken with them?" Shaking his head, he muttered out loud, "I hope that's not your whole plan."

"Play chicken? I don't understand what you mean?"

Exasperated Liam said, "It's an Earth term meaning that you drive straight at someone and see who blinks first." Liam was really hoping that wasn't the plan.

"Blink as in who moves out of the way first?" Nyx asked.
"Yes."

"Then yes—we are playing chicken, only we will be the first ones to blink," Nyx said in all seriousness. "Once we get close enough, I'm going to bank a hard right. I want you to bombard their shields as hard as you can. Find their weak spot and aim for that. Give it as much as you can."

"You got it." Liam's fingers sped over the weapons controls, using the information from ARI on the specs of the

Hexian ship to pinpoint the weakest point in their shields.

With their weapons armed and ready, Liam looked up and inhaled sharply as he watched the Hexian ship moving closer and closer. He didn't have time to think about how crazy this was...being in a space battle with a bunch of aliens as he fought for his life and the survival of humanity. Glancing over at Nyx, Liam could have sworn he saw Nyx grinning from ear to ear, causing Liam to think Nyx might be just a little bit insane with this plan of his.

When they moved into weapons range, moisture formed on Liam's brow as he fired volley after volley at the oncoming ship. Nyx was maneuvering their ship, trying to avoid as many hits as possible as the two ships hurtled towards one another. For the moment their shields were holding, but who knew for how long.

Time moved in slow motion for Liam as he watched the Hexian star fighter move so close he was able to make out the serial number written above the cockpit window. If Nyx didn't turn soon, both ships would be making a fiery blast in the dark sky.

"On my mark," Nyx called out to Liam, who was relieved to finally hear Nyx's command.

Liam steadied his hand on the controls.

"Three, two, one—FIRE," Nyx yelled as Liam fired his weapons with great aplomb.

Nyx rolled their battered star fighter a hard 180 degrees...just missing hitting them head on as five particle bursts hit the direct center section of the Hexians' fighter, every shot hitting their mark, causing the Hexian shields to immediately collapse.

"Hooyah!!" Liam yelled, jumping up and down.

Turning in his seat, he laughed when he saw Nyx put his hand up to high five him. "That was awesome!" Liam slapped Nyx on the back. "Scared the crap out of me, but totally awesome. You know you're nuts, right?"

Laughing at the human's reaction to his flying, Nyx

cocked an eyebrow in agreement. "Probably. Nice shooting by the way."

"Thanks." Liam's face reddened slightly with pride as he appreciated the praise that Nyx gave him. Liam was loving alien technology. Life was going to be boring when he went back to Earth, Liam thought. If he went back, that is.

Checking on the Hexians, Liam watched as they turned tail and limped back to the freighter. "Shouldn't we go after them?" Liam asked Nyx.

"No. They were just a distraction. Look where the freighter is. They're almost to Earth's moon." Nyx was tapping his fingers on the console as he considered the situation. "We don't have enough firepower to knock out a ship that size without help."

Bringing up the specs of the freighter, Liam asked ARI to calculate the amount of fire power it would take to stop them before they made it through to Earth. Seeing the answer, Liam shook his head at Nyx. "Not happening. We need to call for reinforcements. Where are star fighters 2 and 3? Are they close enough that they could get here in time? If we could combine our weapons."

"No, they're not." Nyx saw that they had dispatched the two Hexian fighters but would never make it to them in time. "We have about 15 minutes to stop that freighter and it will take at least double that for them to get here."

Taking his helmet off, Liam finally felt the sting coming from his eye. His hand swiped across his cheek, leaving a trail of red across it.

Getting up to grab a portable regen device to stop the bleeding, he noticed the last of Emeline's network arrays tucked back beside the airlock.

Thinking for a second, he yelled over his shoulder, "Hey, Nyx, I have an idea."

"What?" Nyx asked him, a look of surprise was on his face.

"How many Delician crystals do you have on board?"

"Five—two for fuel, two for the shields and one for the replicator. Why? What are you thinking?"

Liam came back, pulling the network array behind him. It was the last one that had been fitted with Nox's force field technology. "I know we need one crystal for our shields —that's important. But the other four crystals, I'm thinking we put them into this array and drop it in front of the freighter."

"I see where you're going, but you'd have to hit it right on the mark for it to have any effect. Are you up for that?" Nyx pointed to Liam's eye.

Liam shrugged, not seeing any other alternatives. Short of ramming his star fighter into the side of the freighter— something he definitely was not up for—they were running out of options.

"I'm willing to give it my best shot." Liam gave Nyx a sly grin. "I always was good at thinking on the fly." Seeing the confused look on Nyx's face, Liam explained, "Thinking on the fly is when you're out of options and you need to come up with a new plan fast or you die trying. I'm sure you've done it tons of times." Liam knew that Nyx had spent the majority of his adult life in the military so he was familiar with having to improvise in life-threatening situations.

"Ah, I get it. Thinking on the fly, I like it. The human language can be quite colorful at times."

"Yeah, especially if you're having a conversation with Ami. She loves using colorful language." Liam was quick to laugh, but at the thought of Ami and where she was right now, his mood quickly turned darker. He couldn't worry about her now. He had an alien freighter to stop.

After laying out the network array, he looked around for the crystals. "Where are the spare crystals?"

"Give me a moment and I'll get them for you. They're locked up and need my bio print to open the compartment."

Having ARI hold their position, Nyx moved over to a concealed compartment and opened a small door, revealing a green oval light. Removing one of his gloves, Nyx pressed his thumb over the light. Once his print was accepted, a panel slid open showing a larger container with five glowing crystals in it. Two were quite large, each about the size of a soccer ball and they were red, while one was slightly smaller and glowed blue. The last two for the force fields were green, about the size of a tennis ball.

Nyx explained that the red ones were used for fueling the ship and the blue one was for the replicator. "The red ones will cause the biggest explosion since they have all the essential elements to run this ship. If your theory works, the chain reaction created should cause the freighter to lose forward propulsion."

Handing Liam the crystals, Nyx took a green crystal and stared at it thoughtfully. "It might be a good idea to install a new crystal to our force fields since our shields have dropped to 36%.

Nodding his head in agreement, Liam took a well-used red tool out of his pocket. Using his thumb, he pulled a metal piece out of the side and started to open the front of the array doors.

Curious, Nyx asked him what he had in his hand.

"Oh this? My dad gave me this when I was a kid. It's a Swiss Army knife. I carry it with me all the time. It has all kinds of tools you can use for just about anything."

Liam's eyes glazed over for a quick second as he thought about his dad. He remembered the day Hank had given it to him. It was the summer he turned 14 and they were camping up at Dolly Copp in the White Mountains. Every summer the family would pack up for five days and go off the grid. It was Dad's way of recharging and getting in tune with nature. Mum said it was his way to get the kids out of the house and off their electronics.

This particular summer, they had been setting up the camp site when Liam asked to use Hank's knife to cut some rope. Reaching into his pocket, Hank pulled out a shiny red knife and handed it to Liam. It was newer than the old worn used one that Hank always carried with him, and Liam remembered looking at it with awe. *Now that you're almost a man, I got you one of your own.* Liam swore he grew two inches when his father called him a man—well, almost, but close enough. What stuck with him the most were the words of caution his father had given him. *A knife was still a weapon and it was to be taken care of and used cautiously.* It was to remain at home when he was in school or out with his friends until he was older. He had listened to every word his dad had said that day because he didn't want to lose his new cherished possession. Now that he was older, he rarely went anywhere without it. Although using the knife in space to stop an alien freighter probably wasn't something Hank would have ever considered Liam using it for, but Dad would have been proud as hell, Liam thought to himself.

He removed the door off the front of the array and nestled the crystals against the cache of Lazonium that was used to deflect the solar flares. Liam theorized that shooting a particle cannon at this precise point just as the freighter was within range should cause enough of an explosion to stop the freighter. That's what he was hoping for anyway.

Closing the compartment door, Liam sat back on his heels and surveyed his handiwork. "Fingers crossed."

"Another Earth saying?" Nyx asked, a hint of humor in his voice as he looked over Liam's work.

Chuckling, Liam nodded. "Humans are full of them, but in this case, I might just rub a rabbit's foot if I had one." Seeing the baffled look in Nyx's eyes, Liam just clapped him on the shoulder, saying, "There are some people on my planet that can be superstitious. They say things like that to give themselves luck. I'm sure Delicians have sayings that mean the same things."

Getting his meaning, Nyx thought for a moment. "Yes

—you are right. We also have sayings like that, although I do not rely on them. I rely on my training and my instinct. General Tarek has instilled that in all of his soldiers."

Liam stood up as he slipped his knife into the pocket of his armor. He could see the seriousness embedded on Nyx's face. "How long have you been in the military?" Liam asked.

Nyx knew the one major difference between them was their different life spans and was hesitant to tell Liam exactly how long he had known Tarek.

Grabbing the other end of the array, he nodded to Liam to start moving it towards the airlock. "When this is over, we'll sit and have one of your human beers. I'll tell you the story about how I met the General. All I'll tell you now is I've known Tarek longer than you've been alive."

Liam's mouth formed an "O" as he pushed the panel to open the inner airlock door. He couldn't imagine what it must be like to live for such a long time. A thought came to him about his sister. What would Nox do when Emeline grew old and died long before he would be considered elderly? He couldn't imagine what it would be like watching the person you love grow old right before your eyes. He needed to ask Emeline some important questions before she completed the bond with Nox. First though, they had to rescue her. Well no, first they had to stop this damn alien freighter.

The array was arranged in such a way that when Nyx opened the outer airlock doors, it would float out through the doors into space.

Jagger's voice came over the comm, interrupting their discussion. "Nyx, what's happening out there?"

Nyx filled him in on what had happened and what their plan was to stop the freighter.

"Do whatever you think will work. We can't allow them to get past Earth's satellite network. We're a little busy right now helping out Tarek. Keep me informed." Jagger's voice was tense, as if things weren't going well on his end.

Concerned, Liam asked Jagger, "Have they located my sister?"

"Not yet. Listen, I need to keep this channel clear. Get back to me when your mission is complete. Jagger out."

Liam felt sick in the pit of his stomach thinking about his sister, but he had other worries right now. He had to trust that Nox and Tarek would take care of her and Ami. He had a freighter to stop.

Taking his seat, he nodded to Nyx to set a course to intercept the freighter. They had to move fast. They were running out of time and they weren't sure if there were any more Hexian star fighters onboard the freighter.

Nyx maneuvered their ship in front of the freighter just far enough away that they could stop and open the airlock, allowing the network array to slip silently out into position. Not wanting to wait around giving the Hexians a chance to challenge them, once the array was clear of the ship, Nyx brought their ship a safe distance away from the freighter but close enough to be in weapons range.

Adjusting his helmet, Liam exhaled slowly, silently centering himself before focusing on the firing coordinates ARI had set in place. They appeared before him on the screen as Nyx checked the time, giving him a quiet countdown. The room was still, the only sound was Liam's breathing as he steadied himself to take the shot. The red light indicating the freighter on his screen flashed faster and faster as it approached the seemingly innocuous array. When the red light suddenly stopped, Liam exhaled slowly, and with the mindset that he was about to save mankind, boldly squeezed the trigger.

With heart-stopping anticipation, Liam and Nyx watched as the particle cannon's beam shot out from their ship. It streaked across time and space like a lightning bolt thrown from Zeus's mighty hand.

KABOOM!!

Direct hit!

The array lit up like a mega celebration on the fourth of July. Only one problem, the freighter didn't stop dead in the water like they thought. Instead, it created a cascading effect that blew the freighter into millions of tiny pieces.

The debris from the blown freighter was hurtling everywhere, including towards their small ship. With their shields at 100% now, in theory they should be able to withstand the energy given off from the blast. They weren't about to wait around to find out. Nyx pushed their engines full throttle away from the blast. Judging from the size of the explosion, it appeared as if the freighter was carrying more than a few weapons on board. That didn't bode well for Earth since they had limited capabilities against the Hexians.

"Go, go, go," Liam yelled as he scanned the screen in front of him. ARI had all the available power sources uploaded for his review. At the press of his finger, he was able to transfer power to their rear shields and so far, it was holding. At least the ship was still in one piece, but the ride was rough and jarring. The farther away they got from the blast, the constant push from behind began to lessen, allowing Liam to return power levels to normal. The ship would need a major overhaul, but they were alive and relatively unscathed.

Removing his helmet, Liam leaned back in his chair, his face ashen. Turning towards Nyx, making sure he wasn't injured, Liam put his head between his legs, trying to stop himself from hyperventilating. *Thank God we didn't die.*

Not sure whether he had said that out loud, Liam was surprised when Nyx abruptly put the ship on autopilot. He was even more surprised when Nyx leaned over and put his head in his hands, taking in deep, even breaths. Liam watched, mesmerized, as Nyx's body began to relax, quickly calming itself. *I need to learn how to do that. I'm totally freaking out here.* He was having a hard time taking in the impact of what had just happened.

Staring intently at Nyx, Liam expelled all of his anxiety in one large burst. "What the hell kind of weapons were they carrying? That was one big-ass explosion! I mean, hell —I didn't expect the whole thing to blow up. I was just trying to make it stop. Those must be some crazy-powerful crystals you Delicians make."

Standing up to stretch out his sore body, Nyx didn't hesitate in telling him, "There is no way those crystals would have caused that much damage." He grabbed a water bottle and handed it to Liam. "Here, drink this."

Liam gave him a knowing look. Blowing up an entire freighter—well, this was a first for Liam, apparently one of many firsts for him. It certainly was an eye-opener at the amount of firepower these aliens had. This was an important fact for him to tell Leslie. She needed to let the President know just what they were up against.

After taking a long swallow from the tepid liquid, bile still burned in the back of Liam's throat. He couldn't help but contemplate his recent actions. "How many people do you think were on that freighter?" He knew the question was rhetorical. This was war after all—instigated by the Hexians. Was it supposed to matter, he wondered? Was he supposed to care?

Seeing how shaken Liam was, Nyx knew he needed to stop Liam's descent into self-recrimination.

Speaking harshly, he let loose a few of his own demons regarding the Hexians. "Save your pity. Do you think they would've had any for your planet and your people? Not a chance. You saw the size of that explosion. They had enough firepower to cause some serious damage to your world. Think about that before you beat yourself up over a bunch of mercenaries who wouldn't think twice about slitting your throat if it meant more in their pockets."

Pulling his braid through his fingers, Nyx muttered to himself, "Humans—so emotional." Arching his eyebrow,

Nyx gave Liam a deliberate look. With contempt lacing his voice, he reminded Liam about the pilot of the star fighter they fought against. "It's hard for me to feel remorse for anyone who would betray Delicia by selling our military secrets to the Hexians. They got what they deserved."

Unsurprised at Nyx's attitude, he'd had more than one discussion with Nyx on how despicable the Hexians were, Liam huffed out, "I know, I know. You're right. It was just so unexpected, that's all. I never expected that whole freakin' ship to blow up. Do you think they could see that from Earth? Crap. I hope not."

He had ARI bring up the debris field from the destroyed freighter to see how close to Earth they'd been when it exploded. Studying the field, he was relieved to see that most of the pieces were small enough that they would burn up in the Earth's atmosphere.

Liam took another sip of water—this time it soothed away some of his inner turmoil. He felt better knowing Earth was safe—for the moment at least. His tight muscles began to unclench as he considered Nyx's words. Nyx was right in that the Hexians would've had no qualms about hurting his people.

"Thanks, Nyx. You're a good friend. Honestly, just the thought of anyone going after my mother or my sister Isabelle—," Liam banged his fist on the console, "I won't let those bastards near my planet."

Nyx grinned back at Liam, knowing exactly how he felt. Saving people who were being taken advantage of by others had been a lifelong passion of his. That's why he joined the military in the first place. "It feels good to be able to protect others from low-life scum like the Hexians. Hold on to that feeling the next time you get the urge to feel any empathy towards the Hexians. Trust me when I say they're not worth it."

"Now all I have to do is figure out what to tell Leslie when she wants to know what that big explosion was in the sky." Liam wasn't looking forward to that video call.

Slapping Liam on the arm, Nyx turned back to his console, saying, "Just tell her you saved her from becoming an alien love slave. That should give her something to chew on for a while." Both males laughed at the thought of seeing the look on Leslie's face.

As they headed back to the *Maelstrom,* the activity coming from the comm told them that Jagger was busy creating a diversion for Tarek. The two star fighters that had been accompanying Nyx and Liam had already radioed ahead that they were back onboard the *Maelstrom.* They'd taken some heavy damage but were mostly intact, unlike the two Hexian ships that were left floating out in space, their ships damaged beyond repair. They still had life support, so once this was over, Nyx told Liam, they'd send a team over to retrieve their sorry asses. "Not that I wouldn't mind just leaving them there," Nyx said under his breath.

"Nyx, Liam, what the hell was that?" Jagger's voice came over the comm. He did not sound happy.

"Sorry, Captain. I guess Liam didn't know his own strength out there." Sensing things were not going well, a worried Nyx tried to lighten the mood.

"Not funny," Jagger barked at them. "Get your asses back here right now. Any injuries?"

"No, sir," Liam said. The cut over his eye had healed quickly once he'd used a regen device on it. The rest of his aches and pains would have to wait for a while.

"All good here, Captain." Nyx replied.

"Good. Do you think you could go help out Tarek?" Jagger asked. Liam and Nyx both agreed immediately. "Great. I'm waiting to hear from him. They've landed on the Invidia and have commenced with the extraction. I'll meet you in the docking bay as soon as you land and bring you up to date on what's happening."

"Yes, sir," both males replied together.

"And Liam."

"Yes, sir." Liam gulped at Jagger's tone.

"I'll want a full explanation on how a human who just learned about alien weapons could bring down an entire freighter with one shot." There was a slight note of awe in Jagger's voice. "And I know the General is going to want a full report. Jagger out."

Liam leaned back hard in his chair, mumbling about getting his ass whooped in the training room again.

Nyx stood beside his chair watching Liam mutter to himself. Even with Nyx's seven-foot frame, there was still about a foot clearance between him and the ceiling. With his helmet off, his thick dark braid dropped down to lie just in the middle of his back. The contrast of his dark brown hair with his highlights looked as though his braid was laced with light purple threads.

Leaning down, his large hand slapped Liam on the arm, shooing him out of his chair. "Go on. Take the controls. You earned it."

"Really?" A note of disbelief sounded in his voice. Not waiting for an answer, Liam jumped over into the other seat. "Awesome." *Okay, calm down, Liam. You've got this.*

"If you can blow up a freighter, I think you've got this." Nyx leaned back in the chair; his long legs stretched out in front as he closed his eyes. "Oh, one more thing though, don't hit anything when you land in the docking bay. I'd hate to have to explain that one to the General." A twisted grin formed on Nyx's lips as he heard Liam swallow hard.

No way was Liam having that conversation with General Tarek. He'd land this baby on a dime if he had to and damn well enjoy doing it too.

The wide smile on his face as he landed their battered and bruised star fighter safely in its assigned spot could be seen by everyone.

Seeing that Tarek's shuttle wasn't back yet, Liam was anxious to get an update from Jagger about Emeline. As the door opened, Liam made his way down the ramp, heading over to Jagger who was by the main interior door of the docking bay talking to Wayra, the *Maelstrom's* navigator.

Without warning, a thunderous noise sounded in his ears. Looking around...awestruck—the entire crew of the docking bay was clapping and cheering for him.

Coming up behind him, Nyx grabbed him by the neck, shaking him roughly, grinning with pride. "That's for you. They heard what you did."

Letting go of his neck, Nyx extended his arm and grasped Liam's forearm, speaking loud enough for all to hear, "Liam Cameron, it has been an honor to serve with you. You have more than earned your place on our team."

Squeezing Nyx's arm, Liam beamed. "Thank you, Nyx. I could never have done any of that without you." Looking around, Liam said aloud to them, "Seriously, I mean that was freaking awesome!"

Jagger's sharp voice cut through the laughter. "All right everyone. We still have a mission to finish. Liam, Nyx— over here. After I'm done talking with Wayra, I'll fill you in on what's happening." He pointed to the navigator who stood out only because his small stature was so dramatically in contrast to other Delician males. It didn't seem to bother him as he stood talking comfortably to Jagger. It was Jagger who was clearly in an agitated mood. He was demanding to know how a Delician freighter could just suddenly appear out of nowhere heading to Earth.

Liam watched the exchange between them with interest. In most of the Delicians he had observed, they were always respectful and clearly knew about proper military procedures. This Delician appeared more laidback, almost bohemian in his style with his shaggy hair that came down to his shoulders and his loose-fitting clothing. It was a stark contradiction from the normal tight-fitting uniform usually worn by his peers. Liam remembered being introduced to him when he first came on board, but hadn't had any real contact with him. Wayra had never been to any of the nightly dinners in the officers' rec room and was not a member of Tarek's elite circle.

Listening to Jagger's terse, almost interrogation-like attitude towards Wayra, Liam was eager to hear his answer, but it appeared Wayra didn't have any answers as to why the freighter was able to get past all their advanced technology. *Maybe things could have ended differently if they had been better informed.*

Clearly displeased, Jagger sent the navigator to go get him some answers, yelling that he wanted them ASAP. Turning to Liam and Nyx, he led the way back to his conference room.

Telling ARI to seal the door, Jagger held up his hand. "As you know, we have limited the number of people who know the full extent of the mission. I am waiting for a report from Tarek. Nyx, I know you're tired, but can you to take a shuttle over and report to Tarek?" Nyx nodded in agreement. "Liam, do you feel up to going with him?"

"Yes, sir." Liam would have stood and saluted but he was saving his energy. He watched Jagger go to the replicator and order two vitamin protein shakes. Handing one to each of them, Jagger told them to drink up—it would give them a much-needed boost.

Taking the dubious-looking thick, chalky drink and placing it to his lips, Liam was pleasantly surprised at the delicious cool taste that soothed his dry throat. It had a similar taste to strawberries and pineapple and he could smell a hint of nuts in the background. Settling back in his chair, Liam could feel his body start to rejuvenate the more he drank. He had taken a beating from the aftermath of the explosion and this was making him feel renewed.

Jagger's comm lit up. It was Tarek checking in. Liam and Nyx immediately sat up in their chairs, anxious to hear every word.

"Ja—can—hear?" There was so much static that it was almost impossible to hear what Tarek was saying.

"Hold on a second, Tarek." Jagger's fingers moved across his console as he shouted. "ARI, enhance the signal from this comm."

"...hear me?"

"We're trying to clear up the signal." Jagger prayed Tarek could understand him.

"Jagger, you there?" The signal had finally cleared enough for them to hear each other.

"Tarek, what's going on?"

"They knew we were coming. We've taken some heavy fire, but we've been able to push them back."

Jagger pounded his fist in fury. "They knew you were coming? That bastard. How many casualties?" They all held their breaths, dreading his answer. That was the worst part of war...lost crewmembers.

"None, but I've got three with injuries. It's nothing we can't handle."

An audible sigh was heard in the room. Liam couldn't stop himself from asking about Emeline. Tarek told them that Nox and Ami were able to make it into the main part of the ship with Ezio and Ramola. He hadn't heard anything as of yet.

"Jagger, have Nyx and Liam take the last cloaked shuttle and start over here towards the Invidia. Bring Dr. Datrem and Tulio with you. I'm going to need medics before this is finished. I'll signal you when it's clear for you to land." Rifle fire sounded in the background. Tarek could be heard giving orders as he fired his gun, shots going off in rapid succession.

Coming back on quickly, Tarek yelled into the comm, "Sorry about that. As you can tell it's a little hectic here. Wait for my signal. Tarek out."

All three males looked at each other, each thinking the same thing. Someone on this ship had sold out their fellow crewmembers. That was unforgivable.

Liam was the first to speak. "Once this bastard is caught,

I want first crack at him." Cracking his knuckles, the drink having done its job, Liam felt more than ready to go kick some more Hexian ass.

"Only if there is anything left after the General gets through with him." Jagger gave a hollow laugh as they headed through the door back down to the docking bay. *Or after I'm through with him*, Jagger thought to himself as the door closed silently behind him.

CHAPTER 21

The Invidia Battle Cruiser

Jolting upright, Emeline's head swung around confused at her surroundings as her mind fought through the haze of sleep. Grim reality set in rather quickly, bringing her to full awareness of her dire situation. She hadn't meant to sleep, but apparently her body disagreed with her...the events of the last 24 hours having finally taken their toll.

Doing a quick body scan, mainly for her own piece of mind that nothing bad had happened during her unexpected nap, Emeline then stretched her arms over her head. The fatigue she had felt before her unplanned nap had lessened somewhat, but she was bone weary, her muscles sore and achy. How long did I sleep? Emeline wondered.

Seeing Violia asleep on the other cot, Emeline patted her inside jacket pocket, reassuring herself that her wrist comm was still where she had hidden it. She had retrieved it from Violia right before they had fallen asleep last night. She debated trying to contact Nox, even for a brief second, but didn't dare. *He may be on his way. I have to be careful. I don't want to screw anything up. But how will I know if I don't turn it on?* She could only hope it would be obvious when the opportunity presented itself.

While she waited for Violia to wake up, Emeline decided keeping her body ready and her mind sharp had to be her top priority. With Liam's words rolling around in the back of her head on how physical activity was the best cure for relieving stress, she slowly began her morning warm-up. At first her stiff muscles rebelled, but after working slowly through her routine, her muscles began to loosen up…moving fluidly from one stretch into another as some of her more stubborn kinks began to release. Wishing her mind responded the way her muscles did, Emeline tried unsuccessfully to push Hagen's attack from her thoughts. *Just be glad you're still alive and in one piece. Nox will be here soon. Just hold on. You can do this, Em.*

When she had finished, Emeline reached for one of the water containers, greedily draining the whole thing. The thought of eating turned her stomach, but eating and staying hydrated were key to her survival. Also, it helped knowing she wasn't totally defenseless as she patted the laser scalpel she had hidden in another pocket. She would have preferred one of the guns she had seen Ami using—sleek units that molded securely to your hand. They were powerful weapons that could either stun the recipient or, if set on high, maim and even kill.

Moving into the center of the room, she looked down at the floor, figuring what's a little more dirt to her already filthy clothes. Crossing her legs as she sank slowly to the floor, Emeline began her meditation in the hopes of quieting her mind. *Breathe, Center, Focus.* She slowly recited her mantra over and over, trying to get her mind to settle as she willed herself to relax and focus on her happy place. Not so easily done when every breath she took smelled like stale, moldy air—not to mention the stench that was left over from Hagen.

Feeling she was being watched, Emeline turned her head to see curious dark green eyes staring at her intently.

"What are you doing?" Violia had awoken to see Emeline sitting quietly in the center of the room, legs crossed, back straight, hands lying lightly upturned on her knees—eyes closed, totally still.

Turning back to her position even knowing this was a pointless exercise, Emeline sighed, saying, "I was meditating. It's supposed to help clear my mind and center myself." Opening her eyes, she looked over at Violia who had moved to sit on the edge of the cot, running her fingers through her tangled and knotted long dark hair.

"Did it help?" she asked, giving up and opting to braid her hair to get it out of her face. Rolling her neck and shoulders, Violia could feel the pain in her muscles radiating throughout her body. As a medic she knew a regen device could only do so much. What she needed most was rest and hydration for her body to heal properly, but given their current situation, that wasn't an option. Staying alive was. Etha and Lilith needed her.

"Somewhat." Getting to her feet, Emeline stood over Violia and brushed her hand away from her hair. "Here, let me help you. Turn around."

Giving Emeline a guarded look, Violia turned and presented her back to Emeline, asking, "Why are you being nice to me? I don't deserve it."

Shrugging her shoulders, Emeline gathered up Violia's hair, wondering how to answer such a loaded question. As her fingers began sectioning the hair at the top of her head, forming the beginnings of a French braid, a skill she had acquired from years of dance recitals, she mulled over her question. "Look, Violia, I get why you did it. I mean, I probably would have done the same thing if it was my family— I don't know. Do I wish you had picked another option before kidnapping me? Hell yes."

"Yikes." Violia's winced as Emeline pulled a little too hard on one particular section of hair.

Seeing Violia's face contort in pain, Emeline murmured "sorry" as she loosened the section a bit before continuing. "We will table that discussion until we get out of here." Turning Violia's head so she could look directly into her eyes, she added empathically, "But trust me—you and I will be having a long conversation about this once we get out of this mess. Right now though, we need to be ready for anything, and I don't know if that's possible."

"What do you mean?" Violia's eyes were beginning to

water—thankful that Emeline was almost finished with her hair.

Tucking the end of the braid neatly up under her hair, Emeline started her own braid. *Don't give them anything they can grab onto.* Liam had drilled that into her head enough times. "The thing is, Violia, if we're going to get through this, we're going to have to trust each other and honestly, I don't trust you." She held up her hand at Violia's protest. They didn't have time for excuses. Emeline's brow creased as she fought to control her frustration at their situation. "Yes, I know you're sorry, but being sorry isn't going to help when Hagen comes for us." Just the thought of that vile piece of crap terrified Emeline. She knew he was looking for revenge, and one way or another, she had to be ready to defend herself. "We need to be prepared. Am I going to be able to count on you or are you going to take Hagen up on his offer?"

Violia jumped to her feet, her hands clenched at her side while her insides burned with misplaced indignation. "No. I am not. I already told you I would never work for the Hexians." Her body shuddered involuntarily just at the thought of breathing the same air as Hagen.

"Sshh." Emeline put her hand out to signal Violia to keep her voice down. They could hear heavy footsteps stop just outside their door. They froze when they heard a sharp knock.

"Can I come in?" Tarquin's low voice came muffled through the door. Pushing on the door and not getting it to open, he asked again if he could come in.

"Should we open the door?" Violia asked in a hushed voice. "Maybe we can just hide in here for a while."

Getting exasperated with the whole situation, Emeline moved Violia out of the way and pushed the cots away from the door, calling out "You can open the door now." Turning to Violia, Emeline shook her head, saying, "What's the point? At least he saved us from Hagen. I'm sticking with him for now."

Tarquin, having slid quietly into the room, watched the interchange between the two females. He'd seen Delician females many times, but human females were a novelty. He found them intriguing. His mind went immediately to the beautiful human female he had seen in Tarek's office. She was unlike any female he had ever seen before.

Noticing the two females staring at him, he cleared his throat, telling them he was moving them to his office. It appeared Hagen was making noises that he was planning on having some fun with the human female and that Tarquin would never allow. Emeline was too valuable to the Hexians. Hagen was just too shortsighted to see that. The Delicians, especially Nox, would stop at nothing to get their revenge if she was hurt in any way. He had too many people counting on him to allow Hagen to ruin everything just because some female got the better of him. Smiling to himself, he thought it was fitting that Hagen got his balls handed to him, literally, by a female—a human female no less.

Motioning them through the door, he hustled them quickly down the corridor into a waiting elevator. Tarquin had made sure his crew was otherwise engaged before he moved the females. If he moved quickly and quietly, his hope was to have everyone thinking the females were still in the storage room. He wanted to laugh at the irony of his situation. Hagen's obsession for this human bordered on manic, which only added to his problems. Now Tarquin was forced to figure out a way out of this mess, preferably with a shipment of salt and without hurting the human. One thing he knew for certain as he ushered both females into his office—Tarek was not going to cooperate.

As Emeline walked into Tarquin's office, she couldn't help but compare his office to Jagger's on the *Maelstrom*. From what she had observed while being rushed into his office, this entire ship was in need of a serious overhaul.

Not that it mattered to her. She'd be happy if she never saw another Hexian again in her life. Why they had kidnapped her in the first place had been nagging at her. "Tarquin, can I ask you a question?"

He was seated at his desk, checking what looked like data on an older version of a console similar to the one that Emeline had used in Nox's lab. He looked up at her expectantly. "Go ahead."

Staring into dark eyes, she asked innocently, "Why did you kidnap me? What did you hope to accomplish? I mean, I'm a lowly human. What gain could I possibly bring to you?"

Tarquin gave her a wide smile. "Don't sell yourself short, human. You are of great value to me." Seeing Emeline's eyes widen in fear, Tarquin quickly added, "Not in the way you think." Knowing she was thinking about the treatment she had endured so far, he again apologized for Hagen. "Again, I'm sorry for the way Hagen treated you. I should have known he would take things to the extreme. He always uses his fists before engaging his mind. When he said he had a plan, I should have demanded more details."

Appearing lost in thought, Tarquin stared at her with a gleam in his eye before murmuring out loud, "Hmm, maybe there is a way we can both get what we want."

"So, what do you want?" Emeline asked, sitting back in her chair, her curiosity getting the better of her.

Deciding to humor her, Tarquin told her, "I wanted to stop you from getting your force fields online. At least Hagen was able to accomplish that. Now my plans can proceed without being hampered by the humans and the UAP." Tarquin paused to look down at his console for a moment.

"Yes, our pink salt. I heard that it was valuable to aliens." Emeline couldn't keep the disdain from her voice.

At her tone, Tarquin looked up, frowning. He appeared distracted, as if he hadn't heard her speak. Whatever news he had just received didn't make him at all happy.

"Is something wrong?" she asked with quiet apprehension.

"Well, it would seem that kidnapping you was a waste of time. When did you get the force fields online?" Tarquin's mouth was pulled into a flat line.

Secretly thrilled that their interface had worked, it really wasn't that difficult for her to look surprised at Tarquin. "It is? It worked? Sweet."

A slight glimmer of an idea was beginning to formulate in her mind. She knew that when Tarek and Nox came for them, she wanted to help in any way she could.

Thinking if she kept Tarquin talking, maybe he would slip up and reveal anything that might be useful for her to use against him, she feigned surprise saying, "Oh, you didn't think that it was my doing, did you? All I did was give them the housing for their equipment. The whole force field thing—that was all Nox's doing. I'd never even seen computers like what you have before. I mean, most humans still have to manually input their commands and it takes hours to get results. I can't tell you how amazing it's been watching Nox verbally command their computer."

Not looking at her, Tarquin scrolled through his tablet, going from one screen to another as he shook his head...his frustration growing. Almost to himself he muttered, "Director Nox—I should have known." Evidently his contact in the Delician government didn't know everything, Tarquin mused to himself. "It seems the Director has been having a lot of success lately—first his force field tech and now with you—his bondmate. From what I hear, not all Delicians have been so lucky over the past generations."

Forgetting about his computer for a moment, Tarquin sat back, taking in the alluring features of this human. "Bondmated to a human—that is going to cause quite an uproar on Delicia, especially when they get a look at you."

"How do you mean?" Emeline asked, not sure she really wanted to hear what he had to say.

Snorting, Tarquin gave her a look as if to say *seriously.* "Aside from the obvious." His eyes scanned her body. "One of Delicia's leading scientists, son of a senator, has a bondmate from the Prohibited Planets list. I hope you are ready for the implications that presents."

Glaring at him, Emeline surprised herself by giving him an honest answer. "No, I'm not ready for any of it. Actually, I'm already sick of hearing about it. It's all anyone can talk about. How unbelievable it is to have found a bondmate with a human. Humans are so…so archaic, too underdeveloped. How about how unbelievable it is to be bondmated to an alien? No one ever stops to ask me how I feel. I'm the one expected to give up my home, my family, my career and go off to be the dutiful little wife all because of some invisible bond. What am I supposed to do all day? Oh, that's right —I'm to acclimate to my husband's culture and be a good wife and mother. What if I don't want to do all those things right now? What about my work?" Emeline's voice was rising, her face flushed, not meaning to vocalize the very same questions that had been running around in her own head before she had been kidnapped.

Seeing the amused look on Tarquin's face, Emeline winced as she got up and began to pace around the room, trying but failing to calm her emotions. She couldn't blame Tarquin for being curious, especially since interspecies bondmating was unheard of. She reminded herself that these were questions for Nox, not her kidnapper, although for some reason she found it easy to talk to Tarquin. Unlike Hagen, Tarquin showed genuine interest in what she had to say.

Stopping mid-step, she turned to look at him, her cheeks flushed with embarrassment, muttering softly, "Sorry for my outburst. You kind of touched on a nerve. It's been an interesting couple of weeks."

"And getting kidnapped by aliens wasn't on your list of priorities?" Tarquin asked with a bite of sarcasm.

Emeline laughed at his attempt at a joke. "No, it wasn't. Didn't even make the top ten. All I can say is aliens have got a lot to learn about humans."

Wanting to change the topic of conversation, Emeline wandered around the room, ending up next to Tarquin.

Sniffing lightly, she was surprised at the light scent of cinnamon. Tarquin and Hagen smelled nothing alike and that wasn't the only difference she was discovering.

Pointing down at his computer console, she commented on how amazing their technology was. She lied that Nox hadn't allowed her to use any of the equipment in his lab. Telling him she was only given access to a tablet they had set up for her to use. She innocently asked when a series of commands popped up onto the screen what they all meant. Half expecting him to push her hand away telling her to go sit down, he surprised her by walking her through some basic functions. Emeline theorized it was probably morally wrong to deceive Tarquin, but he had allowed Hagen to kidnap her. *Hey, work with what you've got.*

Tarquin's lesson was cut short when an alarm suddenly sounded throughout the ship. Pressing the comm button on his console, Tarquin demanded to know what was going on.

"Captain, you are needed on the bridge. The *Maelstrom* has come into range. They've launched a squadron of star fighters headed in our direction. We're awaiting your orders, sir."

Swearing to himself, Tarquin shot back, "Who's in charge on the bridge? Where's Hagen?"

It was a moment before the voice came over the comm saying, "Sorry, sir, we don't know what to do. Hagen hasn't arrived for his shift. We don't know where he is. We also have an update on the freighter."

"Idiots—they're all idiots. Fine, I'll be right there. Find Hagen. Tell him to report to the bridge immediately. And make sure our shields are stable. I want all star fighters ready to launch on my command. And shut off that damn alarm! Tarquin out."

Tarquin stood with his hand on his hip, his steady gaze landing on the two females, his voice loud and rough against the sudden quiet as he told them, "I see Tarek didn't waste any time." To himself he thought it was a good thing that his contact onboard the *Maelstrom* had alerted him that the Delicians were planning a rescue. At least his crew was prepared and ready for whatever the Delicians had planned, and knowing Tarek like he did, it would be something unpredictable.

Emeline and Violia were startled at hearing Tarek's name. Emeline spoke first. "Tarek? What do you mean?" Emeline knew this was the signal she was waiting for. Maybe they would get a chance to help out with their rescue after all.

Turning off his console, Tarquin headed toward the door. Facing the females, Tarquin's eyes grew darker with an inner rage—the planes of his face hard and unmoving as he told them, "I contacted Tarek with my ransom demands."

Emeline interrupted him. "What did he say?"

He didn't hesitate in telling them, "He refused to negotiate."

Both women gasped. "Did he give a reason?" Emeline countered, not for a minute believing Tarek wouldn't come for them.

Laughing sharply, Tarquin replied, "Tarek isn't the negotiating type." Lost in thought for a moment, Tarquin's fingers tapped rhythmically on the door, talking more to himself then to either of them. "I should never have listened to Hagen. Kidnapping the bondmate of a prominent Delician was suicide. Now I have to go clean up his mess."

Feeling the ship lurch hard to the left broke Tarquin out of his thoughts. *Damn you, Tarek.*

Looking up, he focused on the two females who were

holding on to the desk trying to steady themselves from his shuddering ship. "I have to go. Stay here. It's for your own safety. The last thing I need is for Hagen to come in here."

Emeline gave him a worried look. She didn't want Hagen coming in here either. "What will happen to us?"

Tarquin stood in the open doorway, his fingers inputting a code that would open the door only on his command. "No need to worry…I'll be back for you. If necessary, I'll put you back in the escape pod." On that note, the door closed, leaving the two females alone again.

After first making sure the door was secure, mainly for her own peace of mind, Emeline hurried over to Tarquin's computer console. Seeing that it was protected, she swore under her breath. *Why can't things be simple for once in my life?*

Violia came over, pushing Emeline's hand away, checking to see what kind of security protocol was needed to access the console. "It requires an index fingerprint to activate. Crap—we'll never get in." Violia's face fell. She had hoped to be of some assistance to Emeline, proving to her that she could be trusted.

Smiling to herself, Emeline shook her head, thinking maybe things could be that simple. Taking her wrist comm out of her pocket, she turned it on and asked the portable ARI to scan the desk for fingerprints. Next, she had ARI eliminate hers and Violia's prints. This left only Tarquin's prints, and after instructing ARI to show only his index fingers, Emeline had ARI flash the print from his right finger onto the console.

Violia breathed a sigh of relief when Tarquin's console activated. "That was brilliant. Where did you learn how to do that?" Her delight in Emeline's ingenuity brightened her face.

"TV." Seeing the confused look on Violia's face, Emeline laughed. "It's an Earth thing. I'll tell you later."

Instructing ARI to translate the Hexian text for her,

470

she scrolled through the Invidia's directories trying to find something that could help with their rescue. Muttering out loud, she wondered, "What would help take out the shields but not make it seem that it was too deliberate?"

"Here let me." Violia nudged Emeline out of the way, taking command of the console. Glancing back, Violia felt even tinier with Emeline leaning over her shoulder trying to follow what she was doing. "Their system isn't that hard to understand. I should be able to locate their shield generators."

"Can you show me the Delician star fighters? I wonder if my brother is on one of them" The thought of Liam being on one of those fighters was enough to make Emeline's insides clench with fear. She knew him and if it meant rescuing her, she'd bet her last box of chocolates that he'd be on one of those fighters.

"I could try, but I don't want to stay in here too long. Okay, I've located engineering but I'm not sure how to disable the shields. Give me a minute to think. I'm a medic not an engineer."

"Let me have a go at it. I might not be an engineer, but I've worked with enough of them that I should be able to come up with something."

Emeline began scrolling through the shield information when she remembered something that Nox had shown her about shield generation. "If I remember correctly, if I overload this particle stream at this junction here, it should cause their shields to buckle. Tarquin would have to physically send someone down to replace the particle pack in order for the shields to come back online. Hopefully this will give Tarek the opening he needs."

After a few tense moments, Emeline exhaled slowly as she initiated the overload process. "That should do it. I'm estimating that in about ten minutes it's going to get really crazy around here." Closing out from Tarquin's console, Emeline allowed herself a moment of satisfaction that she had contributed in some small way to their rescue.

"Now what do we do?" Violia looked at Emeline with uncertainty in her eyes.

Plopping down in one of Tarquin's office chairs, Emeline took out her wrist comm. Checking it over carefully, she took a deep breath and turned it on to receive transmissions before slipping it onto her wrist. Placing her hand into her pocket, she fingered the laser scalpel. "Now we wait."

Nox shifted impatiently from side to side. *What was taking so long?* He understood that Jagger's timing for the diversion had to be precise in order for Ezio to slip the cloaked shuttle unnoticed into the Hexian docking bay. It was Emeline that had him on edge. The silent anguish on her pale face fueled his determination to hurry this mission along.

Once they made it on board, the plan was for Tarek and his soldiers to neutralize Tarquin's crew without causing too much damage to the ship. They were all aware this would not be an easy in and out. The Hexians were fierce fighters, and since their training was predicated on fear and reprisal for poor performance, they fought hard and dirty.

Through Loris's research, it was disclosed that Hagen was in charge of training and acquiring new mercenaries for the Hexian "military." Because Hagen was known for his use of brute force, fear and harsh methods of punishment, the majority of his crew were criminals and outcasts grasping at the promise of wealth and a place to belong. Mixed in amongst them were those unfortunate miscreants who were taken in raids from other worlds. For them, their choice was taken from them. For them, it was a kill or be killed life.

Nox glanced around at Tarek's soldiers. You couldn't

miss how well prepared they were—not just physically but mentally. Tarek spent a great deal of time on the overall conditioning of his men. Honor and duty were instilled in each member of his team. That's why it was so hard to imagine any one of them being a traitor.

Standing beside Tarek, Nox could feel his bond with Emeline getting stronger the closer he got to the Hexian ship. He would stop at nothing to save the love of his life. Since she'd been gone, his heart had recognized how much he loved and needed her. She gave so much of herself to him.

Guilt rippled through him. It was his fault she was taken. He should have been more vigilant.

His eyes closed for a moment, silently promising he would stop at nothing to protect her for the rest of their lives. The first step in that promise was about to happen and he was more than ready.

Nox's hand gently hovered over the blaster that hung from his utility belt. This was the first time he would be going on a mission where there was the real possibility for him get injured or worse—killed. *Saving Emeline is the only thing that matters.*

Ezio's tense voice talking to Jagger on the comm broke through Nox's thoughts. Tarek was staring out the window, his visor was up so only hard green eyes could be seen clearly as he listened to his pilot.

At a break in the conversation, Nox asked Tarek, "What's happening? Shouldn't we be trying to board?"

Keeping his voice low, Tarek spoke quickly, "There's a problem. They knew we were coming." Tarek's rigid posture displayed how furious he was about the traitor in their midst. "I will catch whoever it is, you can be certain of that, but right now we need a new way in."

"Why don't we just shoot our way in?" Nox was frustrated and so close to taking the controls and landing the ship himself, except he didn't know how.

Frowning, Tarek shook his head. "Not unless you want us to get our asses blown off and take your bondmate with us. We need to minimize the damage to the battle cruiser, at least until we get Emeline and Violia out of there."

Putting his hand to his head, Nox realized how irrational he sounded. "Sorry. It's just so hard to be this close and not be able to get to her."

"Look out there and tell me what you see." Tarek pointed to the front viewscreen of the shuttle.

Scanning the area before him, Nox was dismayed to see the Hexian battle cruiser with their shields up with no movement coming from their docking bay. It appeared that Tarquin had already launched most of his star fighters because they had formed a ring of defense around his ship. "Okay—since we're cloaked, shouldn't we be able to slip right by them?"

"We could, except for the fact that they've got the docking bay doors blocked." Tarek said, scrolling through the data results of the simulations ARI had run on the possible courses of action. "Ezio—suggestions," Tarek queried his pilot. If anyone could get them on board that ship, Ezio could.

Ezio was scanning the Hexian vessel looking for a way to sneak past into the docking bay. There didn't seem to be any way to get through their force field unless he shot his way in. Not a viable option.

As he quickly ran through a number of scenarios, without warning, some of the Invidia's star fighters began to move off in the direction of the *Maelstrom*. Jagger's ships had finally arrived and were engaging the Hexian star fighters. This left plenty of room for Ezio to maneuver the shuttle, but the shields were still up.

Staring down at his console, Ezio's head snapped up, giving the battle cruiser a quick scan. His amber eyes widened in shock as he turned to Tarek, saying, "It appears that someone on board the Invidia is helping us." Seeing the confused look from his teammates, he replied, "Their shields just dropped. I should be able to maneuver us right into their docking bay without them seeing us. Hang on."

Smiling, Ami cheered to herself, knowing deep down this had Emeline's hand all over it. "That's my girl."

Tarek couldn't believe it. Winking at Ami, he told his crew to never underestimate a human. Smiling broadly at Nox, he said, "Let's go get your bondmate back."

Addressing his team, Tarek's voice was hard and deliberate, demanding their full attention before they went into battle. As with any mission, injuries and even deaths were always a possibility. It was for that reason alone he was so hard on his men. The occasional injury he could deal with, but death—that was unacceptable. All of his soldiers were important—a fact many of his counterparts seemed to forget. "All right everyone, listen up, slight change in plans. Nox, you and Ami will go get the females. Ezio and Ramola will be with you. Ezio, you're in charge. The rest of you, you're with me. You know the drill—once we secure the docking bay, I want a deck by deck search done. The goal is to take control of the ship and capture Tarquin and Hagen."

Giving Nox a subtle nod before telling his team, if at all possible, he wanted them taken alive. "I have plans for them. The rest of the Hexians can be put in the detention cells."

Tarek had Yilmaz divide the team in pairs and had them check and recheck their weapons. Each pair would work together as a unit when engaging the enemy. Tarek always said it was the most effective way of engagement that he had found, although he knew there were times that you had to improvise in order to stay alive.

With the Invidia's shields down, Ezio maneuvered the cloaked shuttle towards the docking bay doors.

Using manual controls, he slid silently past two Hexian star fighters poised on either side of the opening.

The docking bay was as large as the *Maelstrom's,* and

since most of the Hexian ships were out engaging the Delicians, the docking bay was empty except for a pair of shuttles. Heading to the far side of the bay, Ezio hovered the shuttle a few feet off the floor. To anyone looking, the space would appear empty.

The air inside a cloaked shuttle packed with soldiers in full battle gear was stifling, no matter the state-of-the-art circulation system. Ami stood wedged in between Ramola and Nanga, another huge Delician soldier she knew from the training room. For the first time in her life, she felt tiny, which was an altogether new feeling for her. At 5'10" she was normally the Amazon in the room. Instead, her body was being pressed on all sides by hot muscular males whose adrenaline simmered just under the surface as they prepared to go kick some Hexian ass. Eager faces stared back at her—most she recognized, a few she didn't. Those were the faces that peered at her strangely, probably wondering why she was even on this mission. She had been thrilled when Tarek had placed her on the team. She wasn't about to let him down and she certainly would be showing these Delician males that she could hold her own. Her plasma rifle was lined up in the weapons rack just like everyone else's, but she had two small hand blasters attached to her belt as well as her knife hidden in one of her pockets. No one on Earth would ever believe where she was —well, maybe her father would.

Her upbringing was unique compared to most kids. Her dad had started training her in self-defense as soon as she could walk. Being the daughter of a petite Korean woman and a tough as nails African American Navy Seal had a tendency to cause issues with other kids at the different military bases where they had been stationed. Her dad had been pleased when Liam stepped in to continue her training regimen. A picture of her dad's smiling face flashed into her mind. *He is going to be so mad he missed all the fun.*

Rubbing her gloved fingers together, she knew he'd have

been so jealous of her new armor, something she was grateful for. It wouldn't make her invincible—after all, nothing was foolproof—but it sure felt like it. She'd still have to be careful if she wanted to get out of this in one piece. Rescuing Emeline was her main priority. Maybe she'd even catch a glimpse of Tarquin, she thought wistfully, then quickly chastised herself for thinking of the enemy in such a way. *What is wrong with you, girl? He's the bad guy, remember. There is no lusting after the bad guy, no matter how much he makes your girly parts tingle. Stop thinking about how manly and rugged he looked, especially with that smile of his—whew! Enough. Focus.*

Tarek's quiet, commanding voice interrupted her musings. Glad that no one could see through her visor, Ami gave Tarek her full attention. She was to wait until Tarek and his team had created a diversion, then she would go rescue her bestie. A thought occurred to her about Emeline's wrist comm, so she pressed a button on the side of her helmet. "General," she said, trying to keep her voice low.

"You have a question, Ami?"

"Has anyone tried to contact Em through her wrist comm? I mean, if she was able to lower the shields, she must have been moved to a different location that has computer access."

Tarek looked over at Nox, relaying Ami's question. Nox immediately went to his comm and tried to contact Emeline. At first the hologram was wavy. All he could hear was her sweet voice coming through sporadically.

"Nox—Nox, is that you?"

"Yes, yes, Emeline—it's me. Are you all right?" He was overjoyed at the sound of her voice. Adjusting the frequency, the figures of two females came into view.

"Yes. We're all right. I'm here with Violia." Emeline's voice was hushed—an indication she was afraid she might be overheard. "Where are you? Are you all right? I tried to lower the shields for you, but I'm not sure if it worked yet."

Speaking equally as soft so as not to be overheard, Nox drank in her appearance like a flower soaking up a summer rain storm. Other than her clothes needing to be burned, she looked slightly better than the last time he'd seen her. "We're on the shuttle in the Invidia's docking bay." With a big smile, he told her, "I knew that was you. Dropping the shields was brilliant, Emeline, but we don't have much time. You can tell us later how you did it. Right now, we're coming for you and Violia. Where are you? You've changed locations."

"We're in Tarquin's office." Emeline bent down lower, whispering, "He said that Hagen was looking for me." Her body visibly shuddered at the mention of his name. "We're locked in here alone. When Jagger's guys started shooting at them, Tarquin went to the bridge. He said he would come back for us, but we haven't seen him in a while."

Relieved that she was safe, Nox told her to leave her comm on but shut off the hologram. They would be there as soon as they could. "Ami is here. She's coming with me to get you."

"Ami," she squeaked out. "Are you sure it's safe?"

Glancing back quickly at Ami, Nox replied with a chuckle, "Like she would let us go without her? Not likely. It was easier to bring her with us than to find her sneaking onto the shuttle anyway."

Emeline laughed at the thought of her beautiful friend giving the Delician males a hard time. "I would have liked to have witnessed that conversation." Getting quiet, Emeline's anguish showed on her face. "I miss you so much."

"I miss you too. I'll be there soon."

"Nox, I love you. Never forget that."

"I love you too and I'll tell you in person very soon." Seeing that Tarek was ready to disembark, Nox told Emeline to hang on, they'd be there soon. He was glad she hadn't asked about Liam. The last thing he knew, Liam and Nyx were chasing down a Hexian freighter. He hadn't heard from either of them in a while.

Tarek spoke to the team. "As soon as we set down, the Hexians in the docking bay are going to know we're here—so be ready to move on my mark." Tarek saw Yilmaz handing out the plasma rifles to everyone while Ezio kept the shuttle hovering quietly. "Ezio—life signs?"

"Eighty-three Hexians on the ground here—another 263 throughout the ship." Ezio had ARI continuously send updated information on their surroundings to each team member. "Firepower is similar to ours. ARI is detecting particle cannons, so be on guard."

"Hell, are they insane?" Nox couldn't believe how stupid people could be. "Are they trying to blow up the entire ship?"

"We need to take them out. Ezio, how many particle cannons do they have?" Even Tarek was surprised at the Hexians' advanced weapons. Those weren't cheap. No wonder they wanted Earth's resources.

Ezio held up two fingers. "Two, sir. They've got one on each side of the docking bay doors."

"When we get back, our top priority will be finding out how Tarquin is getting his hands on UAP technology." Tamping down his anger, Tarek leaned his huge frame over Ezio as he studied an updated diagram of the Invidia. It was displayed on a screen projected out of the console in front of Ezio. Small white heat signatures were moving throughout the ship. The weapons that ARI could detect were in red. Some weapons, such as particle cannons, gave off measurable neutrino residue that ARI was able to detect.

Tarek knew they needed to act immediately. "Yilmaz, as soon as we set down, you and Owin take out the particle cannons. After that, the rest of you pair up and spread out." Each soldier nodded in the affirmative to Tarek, their weapons at the ready, mind focused.

Ami and Nox were moved toward the back of the shuttle where they would wait until given the go signal.

Just as Tarek was ready to give the command, Jagger's voice came over the comm.

"Tarek, what's your status?" His voice sounded strange, agitated.

"Perfect timing, you got any star fighters near the docking bay?"

"I do. Need a diversion?"

"Yes. Have them fire a series of blasts at the doors. Not too much, just enough to get their attention." Tarek was watching the Hexians, and so far, they were unaware of their presence. A few Hexian mercenaries were patrolling the outer area of the room, but none had ventured over to their side of the docking bay. Taking note of Jagger's tone, Tarek asked, "Jagger, is there something I need to know? Have you heard from Nyx?"

Jagger spoke hastily, "They're on their way back now. The freighter was destroyed. I'll know more when I see them. Your diversion should be happening just about now. I have to go. I'll check back in a few minutes. Be careful."

The comm was silent for only a few seconds before weapons fire could be heard firing at the docking bay doors, causing the Hexians inside to panic. Seizing the opportunity, Ezio set the shuttle down as smoothly as possible. The shuttle door opened immediately on the far side, allowing Yilmaz and Owin to take their positions. On Tarek's mark, their shots simultaneously took out the Hexian mercenaries holding the particle cannons. It was at that moment all hell broke loose. Not being able to see through the cloaked ship, no one knew where the shots came from. Hexians were running around in chaos, yelling and pointing towards the docking bay doors.

Using the cloaked shuttle as cover, the remaining members of Tarek's team moved into position. Being as outnumbered as they were, Tarek was using stunners that were small enough to be thrown into a crowd. One stunner might only take out one or two Hexians for a few hours, but multiple stunners should incapacitate enough to make it a fair fight.

Holding up his hand, Tarek waited patiently. The Hexians had finally quieted and were grouped together trying to figure out where the shots had come from. Dropping his hand, 12 stunners were lobbed towards the majority of the Hexian mercenaries, exploding on contact causing the desired effect. Not waiting, Tarek's team began firing at the remaining Hexians still standing.

Confused and disoriented, the Hexians tried to return fire, but Yilmaz and his team were too much for them and it wasn't long before the remaining Hexians were overpowered.

Hearing the discharging of weapons, Nox and Ami stood together, plasma rifles primed and ready, anxiously waiting for the signal for them to move out.

Tarek appeared at the door, his hand moving in rapid motion for them to leave, stopping Ezio as he passed through the door saying, "Report in every five minutes. As soon as we've secured this area, we'll be right behind you."

"Yes, sir." Ezio nodded to the general and then disappeared around the side of the shuttle, followed by Nox and Ami, with Ramola bringing up the rear.

Since Emeline and Violia were being held on deck two and the docking bay was on deck six, they had to get up four decks from their current location without being seen. The route they were to take had been mapped out before they left, but unfortunately, there were 20 Hexian mercenaries headed in their direction. Not wanting to engage that many with just the four of them, Ezio reported to Tarek what was headed their way as he pulled them into an empty storage room. The door closed shut just as the first Hexian came around the corner. It was a tight fit, but it wasn't long before they were able to leave the room and continue on their way. Not wanting to draw attention to themselves, Ezio found a maintenance shaft that would keep them off the main corridors. It would take a little bit longer, but hopefully it would allow them to move through the ship undetected.

Opening a door on their left, Ezio led them into a tunnel that was surprising wide with a round opening at the end. It opened onto a shaft that ran the length of the ship and measured at least ten stories high and approximately six feet across. Each deck had tunnels and ladders on either side, allowing crewmembers easy access between decks. After making sure the shaft was empty, Ezio had Ramola go first.

Ramola swung his huge body out onto the ladder, his hand reaching down to grasp Ami's. Shouldering her rifle, Ami grabbed his hand and stepped out behind him, a small gasp escaping her lips as she looked down, "You have got to be kidding me."

Gripping the sides of the ladder with both hands, she muttered under her breath as she willed herself not to look down, "The things I do for my friends. Aliens, bonding, mercenaries—then getting yourself kidnapped by evil dudes. I can tell you one thing for sure, Emeline Cameron, you and I are going to have some serious girl talk when this is all over."

"Did you say something?" Nox asked. He had climbed out right behind her, crowding her on the ladder.

"Nope, nope. Everything's just fine. Fine, yup—fine, fine, fine." Letting out a calming breath, Ami concentrated on putting one foot securely on each rung as they all climbed upwards in unison. With Nox practically up her butt, Ami had a crazy thought that if she fell, at least she had a couple of large Delician males to land on. That is if she didn't get killed in the process. Staring straight ahead, she was thankful they only had to go up four stories—no problem, piece of cake!

With those thoughts ringing in her head, she moved cautiously up the ladder, trying to avoid getting kicked by

Ramola. Hearing loud footsteps coming up from below, she felt Nox lean his large body against hers as he pushed her head against the ladder. Plasma rifle fire shots careened past Ami's head, making her glad Nox was at her back. Looking up, she saw Ramola lean down past her, taking aim at a Hexian who was firing from a tunnel two floors down and across from them. The Hexian jumped back into the tunnel, causing Ramola's shots to just miss him.

Two more Hexians were charging up from several floors below, firing handheld blasters at them. Ezio was the last on the ladder, leaving him the most exposed. Yelling "go, go, go" to Ramola, Ezio took aim and was able to take out the Hexian closest to him, although he took two direct shots in the process. Luckily his armor absorbed most of the damage. Seeing two Hexians getting closer, Ezio moved up the ladder and ducked into a tunnel they were passing. Motioning for Nox to continue on, Ezio told him he'd cover them. Plasma bursts shot out of his rifle at the two males on the ladder, hitting the closest one, causing him to fall off down the shaft. The second male jumped off into a side tunnel, Ezio's shot easily missing him. Ezio continued to fire his rifle, giving the rest of his team a chance to get up the ladder to deck two.

Speaking through his helmet, Ezio told them, "Nox, you and Ami go get Emeline. Ramola and I will finish up here and then come find you. Stay in Tarquin's office until I get there."

Nodding his head at Ezio, Nox saw Ramola reach down from the tunnel at deck two and pulled Ami up beside him. Nox stepped into the tunnel just as a rifle shot slammed into the wall just above his head. Grabbing Ami's shoulder, he pushed her farther back into the tunnel, trying to shield her from the weapons fire. Shoving his rifle at her, he grabbed a blaster off his belt and started firing at the Hexians who were in one of the tunnels above them. Skill or luck seemed to be on their side, because he got one in the arm and the other one—a direct hit causing him to fall from above.

The sound of his screaming as he fell like a rock down a well would be something Ami would never forget. Feeling Nox grab her arm, she grunted as she felt a sting on the back of her upper thigh. A Hexian was firing at them from the tunnel across from them. As Nox was reaching for Ami, she acted instinctively, firing the rifle in her hands killing the Hexian without any thought.

Ramola, who had been trying to cover Nox, paused in surprise as he watched the Hexian across from him fall into the shaft. Thinking it was Nox who had fired, his face broke out into a huge grin when he saw Ami lowering her rifle. "Nice shooting."

"Thanks." Ami gave him a hollow smile. To Nox, she whispered, "Am I supposed to be happy that I just killed someone?" Ami was hanging on to his arm, standing on one foot as she tested how much weight she could put on her wounded leg...surprised when she felt no pain.

"Happy, no, but since he shot you first, now you're even." Nox was watching Ramola as he moved carefully back to the end of the tunnel, watching for enemy fire. Confident that Ezio and Ramola could handle things here, he was anxious to get to Emeline.

Ami gave him a half-smile then pointed towards the door. "Come on, let's go get our girl."

Nodding at her, Nox lowered the handle on the door and slowly opened it—just barely enough for him to check if it was safe. The tunnel door was at the junction of two corridors. One short one in front of them and another longer one to the left. Seeing nothing to the left, Nox heard muffled noises coming from one of the rooms. He knew one of those voices.

Yanking open the door, Nox lunged forward only to be pulled back by Ami. It took all she had to hold him back from barging into a situation without thinking. "Stop. Nox

—you have to stop. Think about what you're doing."

"I must—get to her." He was trying to get away from Ami without hurting her, but if she didn't let him go, he would drag her with him.

"I know you do, but you might get her killed if you go barging in without knowing what's going on." Ami was pulling on his arm, trying to get him to think before he acted. "You could get us all killed. Let's check it out first."

At the thought of hurting his bondmate, Nox stopped short at Ami's words. Keeping his voice low, he relented, "You're right. We need to find out what's happening first. Come on, stay behind me."

Ami shouldered her rifle and pulled one of the blasters off her belt. She marveled at how perfectly it fit into the palm of her hand. Brushing past Nox she whispered, "Nope, I've got this," as she slowly crept towards the door.

CHAPTER 22

Tarquin's office

Emeline's body hummed with excitement—anticipation rolled through her. *He was here, just a few decks away.* It was only a matter of time before they were together again and she could get off this horrid ship. Her eyes filled with tears as she focused inward to that place where their bond lived. Ever since they'd been apart, a thin barrier had formed, closing off their bond, separating them. Now that barrier was weakening. *It must be because he is so close.* She could feel his love reaching for her. That familiar warmth —that comfort that only he could make her feel was slipping through the barrier like holes through a watering can spout. Nox had told her that once they completed the bond, they would always feel connected no matter where they were. Emeline longed for that, unhappy with herself for not completing the bond when they had the chance. She would be rectifying that mistake as soon as they got back to their room on the *Maelstrom*.

"Crap—Nox." Emeline frowned, thinking of all the surprises she had placed around their room. Had it really only been a few days—it felt like a lifetime. *He must have been so devastated.*

The entire ship vibrated again, causing both females to jump. The sounds of chaos echoing throughout the ship heightened her anxiety for Nox and Ami. Being stuck in here waiting while everyone was out there fighting was driving her crazy.

Still seated in Tarquin's chair, Emeline needed something to keep her thoughts occupied, so she began snooping through Tarquin's computer. Using her wrist comm, she began downloading as many files of Tarquin's as she could. ARI would translate them for her when they got back to Nox's lab. She was looking for anything that might help the humans keep the Hexians away from Earth. She didn't feel the least bit guilty for snooping, especially with everything she'd been through over the last few days. The few files she'd stolen weren't even a down payment for what Tarquin had put her and her planet through. *All this bullshit for pink salt. BUT if what they say is true—that it's a curative substance for species throughout the UAP—then holy crap. This changes everything. We need to think about this very carefully before the powers that be inform the rest of Earth. This has disaster written all over it.*

"Why the serious face? Director Nox should be here soon and then we'll be rescued." Violia stood for a second, one eyebrow cocked before shaking her head and turning back to her task. She had been rummaging through all the cabinets and closets looking for anything that they could use as a weapon. So far, she hadn't found anything of much use to them—just a couple of bottles of some nasty-smelling stuff that she found undrinkable. No wonder Hexians were so foul if that's what they drank.

"I'm just worried, that's all. You've seen the Hexians. What do you think—they're just going to throw down their weapons and say 'oh no, the big bad Delicians are here'?" The sarcasm coming from her mouth surprised even herself, especially when she saw the look of dismay written all over Violia's face. "I'm sorry. I'm not usually this cranky. You have as much to worry about as I do. I really am sorry about your grandmother and Dr. Datrem's granddaughter." A genuine look of sympathy softened Emeline's face.

"I need to find out what's happening. Do you think Tarek's soldiers have rescued them yet?"

Emeline shrugged her shoulders, compassion etched on her face as she thought about Etha and Lilith and what they'd had to endure. "I'm not sure, but knowing Tarek, he'll make sure they're safe."

Violia nodded her head in agreement. "I can't help worrying about them."

Pushing her chair back, Emeline walked over, engulfing Violia's shaking body in her warm embrace. Feeling such a tiny delicate body felt strange to Emeline because Violia always appeared so much taller...stronger. Maybe it was because of the heavy burdens she had been carrying, she'd had to be strong in order to survive. But at this moment, with the thoughts of Hagen's mercenaries doing unspeakable things to her grandmother and a young girl, Emeline could feel her struggle. "Trust Tarek. He won't let you down." Rubbing her arm gently, trying to give Violia even a modicum of comfort, Emeline quietly told her that everything was going to be okay. They had renewed hope now that the General and his team were on board the Invidia. He would rescue them and keep them safe from Hagen and the rest of the Hexians.

Emeline wasn't sure who she was trying to convince, herself or Violia.

Giving Violia's arm a light squeeze, she stood up, tucking the remnants of her shirt into her jeans. She would have taken it off after Hagen ripped it down the front, but it gave her comfort having even a small barrier across her back. With her jacket buttoned all the way, she cringed thinking what Nox and Tarek must have thought when they had seen the state of her clothing.

Looking down at Violia, Emeline fingered her torn shirt, saying with disdain, "First thing I'm going to do is burn these clothes." Then her voice softened. "Then I'm going to take a long hot shower followed by a long soak in a tub filled with lots of bubbles." Blushing slightly, she added with a soft laugh, "And a hot sexy naked Delician."

"That sounds wonderful." Violia's small hand vainly tried to brush some of the dirt and stains from her own uniform, her tone not as wistful as Emeline's. There would be no hot bath for her. She'd be lucky if she got a cold shower before they put her in a detention cell, which is where she belonged, Violia thought bitterly. It would be worth it as long as Etha and Lilith were safe.

Picking up on Violia's feelings, Emeline could feel her own heart beginning to soften towards this sad woman standing in front of her. It would take a while to work through some of her lingering anger, but having your family in danger made people do crazy things. She considered for a moment what she would do for Liam or Belle—not to mention Nox and her mother. Yeah, Emeline thought, I can understand why she did what she did. *I guess I can forgive her, but I can still be mad about this whole thing.*

For some reason, Emeline felt compelled to tell Violia her thoughts. "Violia, I wanted to tell you, I..." The door opened unexpectedly, interrupting her midsentence. *Shit, shit, shit—Hagen*

His huge body filled the doorway, a blaster gun in his hand, his eyes glaring at them while waves of anger rolled off of him. His face was hard, lips pulled tight into a sneer as if he could smell their fear.

"Hagen, what are you doing in here?" Emeline stood back from Tarquin's chair, her finger covertly pressing the off button on the console she had been using. Putting on a mask of bravery, she spoke loudly, hoping to cover her pounding heart. "Tarquin said he was the only one who could open that door." She could feel the terror radiating off of Violia, who had moved to stand beside her in an attempt to keep a united front.

Hagen ignored Emeline, his focus on someone else. He moved into the room bringing with him a feeling of foreboding as the door closed swiftly behind him. With his blaster pointed directly at Violia's heart, Hagen was agitated, verging on panicked. "You didn't keep your word, little cousin." Spittle formed at the corner of his mouth as he spoke, making him appear almost rabid...definitely dangerous.

Trying to hide the fear on her face, Violia's words slid out cautiously. "What do you mean?" A slight sheen of sweat began to form across her brow.

He reached out, trying to grab her hair, only to get more furious when his hand came up empty. When Emeline tried to slap his hand away, he jabbed her in the shoulder with his blaster, roaring at her. His other hand came out lightning fast, slapping her hard across the face before pushing her away from him, "Get back. NOW."

Emeline stumbled backwards, just managing to remain on her feet. The pain in her shoulder wasn't nearly as intense as the pain on the side of her face. That nearly took her breath away, but Emeline was done being abused by this asshole. She could see that he was barely holding it together, reminding her of a cornered animal. She'd have to tread carefully, but she was through being intimidated any longer. Emeline was sure part of the reason for her small boost of courage was knowing Nox was nearby.

Standing up as straight as she could, she moved slowly over towards Violia, who had fallen to her knees. In her calmest voice, she said, "Hagen, please—be careful with her. She's still recovering from the last beating you gave her."

Finding a gun pointed at her head, Emeline stopped and put her hands out. "Okay, okay. Just please don't hurt her anymore," she implored him.

"Shut up, bitch."

Grabbing Violia roughly by the arm, Hagen pulled her tiny body up an inch from his face, screaming the whole time that she was like all females—liars. She hung there like a trapped mouse caught in the jaws of an enraged rattlesnake as he spewed his caustic venom at her. He paused for a second, growling in her face while he shook her several more times before flinging her to the floor. Her body bounced twice before she landed face down on the hard surface. She lay there panting, each breath more painful than the next while Hagen ranted on and on how it was her fault for what was going to happen next.

Violia's head snapped around to glare at him. She groaned as the muscles in her upper body rebelled at her movements. Deep in her heart, she knew what he was going to say. Anger filled her battered body. He was going to hurt their grandmother. "What are you going to do, Hagen?" Her voice was raspy as she tried to drag oxygen in her lungs.

"Don't move. Stay right where you are." Hagen's words were directed at Emeline, who had started to move towards Violia.

Emeline froze at Hagen's glare. Holding up her hands, showing him that she was complying with his orders, her eyes flicked quickly towards Violia. She had to be hurting with the force at which Hagen had thrown her. She heard Violia demanding Hagen tell her what he had done to their grandmother and Lilith. This was not going to be good.

Emeline steeled herself when she saw Hagen had turned...his gun trained on her. Waving it around all over her body as if he couldn't decide where to shoot first, his voice oozed with contempt. "Because of you, human, there are Delicians all over my ship." Hagen jabbed his gun in her direction as he made each point. "Because of you, human, I lost a freighter going to Earth. Blown up by a lone Delician fighter." *[Jab]* "And because of you, human, I won't be getting a shipment of Earth's pink salt, which means you have cost me way more than you are worth. It's time I get some payback." *[Jab]*

Almost as if he was trying to rein in his rising anger, he paused for a moment, breathing deeply before giving her a sick smile. His voice almost purring, his eyes darkening as they raked over her body. "I've had enough of you, human, and once I've finished with my cousin here, I'm going to show you what I do to females who fuck with me." Sneer-

491

ing, he began to list a few of the ways he planned on punishing her for fighting him, just like he had a punishment in store for Violia for defying him.

Ignoring his vile words, Emeline only heard "freighter" and "blown up." *Wow, one of their freighters got destroyed.* Secretly pleased that they had stopped the Hexians from getting to Earth, Emeline pretended to listen to Hagen's delusional rant, her face bland, emotionless. His words would have sickened her if she didn't know that Nox was coming. All she had to do was stall Hagen long enough until Nox and his team got here.

With his blaster still pointed at her, Hagen motioned her over to Violia, telling them both to sit in the chairs in front of the desk.

"Little cousin." Hagen's mouth twisted into a sick grin as he pulled out a comm unit. Barking in a command, a holo vid appeared, showing the same two nasty Hexians who were holding Etha and Lilith hostage.

Violia felt hot tears fill her eyes as she watched the two huge Hexians drag a struggling Lilith and Etha into the view of the screen. Both Hexians towered over the two small females whose clothing was ripped and filthy. Violia's heart broke as she looked at their faces which were covered in bruises and smears of blood and tears from the abuse they had received. The stub of Lilith's hair stood crooked like a broken tree after a storm - the light purple highlights dulled from days' worth of dirt and grime.

Violia's body began to tremble, terror unlike anything she had felt before raced through her body. "Hagen," she implored. "Please don't hurt them. I'm begging you. Please —"

Etha looked worn, tired. The wrinkles in her face were deeper than the last time Violia had seen her, but that fire still sparked in her eyes as she looked directly at her grandson. "Hagen, what do you hope to gain by hurting your family?" Shaking her head at him, she sighed, telling him

492

sadly, "I tried my best to raise you right and give you a decent home and this is how you treat me. I always knew you would be just like your father. You'll probably end up just like your mother, too." Sorrow filled her face, showing the disappointment she felt. She had done all she could for him. "At some point, you must take responsibility for your own actions."

It was that last part that seemed to push Hagen over the top. "Shut up, old woman. Don't—don't talk about my mother. My father, hah—he was small time compared to me. Soon you'll all be wishing you chose to stick with me." Looking at his cousin, she looked small huddled in her chair...her eyes never wavering from the image of Etha. Fear, fury, compassion—those were just some of the emotions Hagen could sense from her. She always had a soft heart—that's what made her so easy to control.

However, right now, everything was closing in on Hagen. He had moved beyond the rational...about to lose everything he had been working for. His only hope was to escape with the human and his cousin in Tarquin's cloaked shuttle. He would take them to Earth and retrieve a shipment of the pink salt himself. He'd use the human as leverage if necessary. Not to mention, she owed him. His balls still hurt from where she'd kicked him. He was so going to enjoy punishing her.

Relishing his cousin's distraught face, his yellowed teeth formed an evil smile before he turned back to his grandmother, saying menacingly, "Violia didn't follow my commands. I gave her every opportunity to come and join me, but she refused. Hexia isn't good enough for her. One day soon she'll be sorry for that. Right now though, she defied me and for that she has to be punished. Unfortunately for you, Grandmother, the best way to punish her is to punish you." He nodded his head at the screen.

Violia jumped up, her small hands clinging to Hagen's arm as she yelled, "No. Please. Don't touch them." She turned and looked at her grandmother as the Hexian holding her began to lift his arm to deliver a blow across her face. "Please, please Hagen—don't let them hurt her. I'll do anything you want. I promise. I won't defy you again. Please, please, I'm begging you, please don't hurt her." Frantic, her face covered in tears, she pleaded with her cousin not to hurt their grandmother.

Watching the holo vid, Violia's face froze in horror. The silence in the room shattered by that horrible sound— the sound of bone snapping...her beloved grandmother lay motionless in the arms of her killer.

Violia turned to her cousin, disbelief on her face, her mouth opening and closing, trying desperately to comprehend what she had just witnessed. No one moved— stunned at what had just happened.

"You killed her." Violia's broken voice came out so softly Hagen had to strain to hear her words.

"I didn't." Glaring at the Hexian holding his dead grandmother, Hagen bellowed at him, "What's wrong with you? I told you not to kill her."

Shrugging his shoulders, he said, "Sorry, boss. I mean, I didn't hit her *that* hard. Besides, she was old." Walking over, he callously dumped Etha's body onto a nearby couch, causing Violia to hiss at him. Looking into the holo vid at the fury on Hagen's face, he grabbed a blanket and threw it over Etha's body before moving quickly out of the room.

Violia's mind clouded with grief and outrage at the actions of her grandmother's murderer. She blindly reached out for her grandmother only to fall forward onto the floor. Her arms saved her battered face from taking yet another beating, but the force of the fall knocked the breath out of her, leaving her sprawled on the hard unforgiving floor. Her mind embracing the dark abyss...even for just a little while.

Emeline had tried to catch Violia, but Hagen moved between them, blocking her path. "Leave her," he barked as he turned to the video and began giving orders to the Hexian who had killed his grandmother. That one brief moment following the death of his grandmother when a glimmer of remorse had appeared on his face was now replaced with one of renewed vengeance. Maybe in that one moment he had felt sorrow, but it was fleeting at best. Anger and hate were the normal constants in Hagen's life and now he had even more reason to hate. He hated the Delicians. He hated Tarquin and he especially hated her.

Emeline could feel her insides churning. Bile formed in the back of her throat when Hagen told them to leave Etha's house and take Lilith with them, giving them permission to use her as they pleased.

She wanted to hurt him—wanted him to feel real pain. Never in her life had she felt this much hate, but now she knew that feeling intimately...thanks to Hagen.

Emeline became puzzled as she watched Hagen's angry expression turn to confusion as the holo vid tipped and appeared to drop to the floor, as if a struggle was happening.

Finally, Tarek's soldiers had arrived, albeit too late to save Etha.

Hagen's eyes squinted, trying to make out what was happening on Delicia. One of Tarek's soldiers grabbed the comm unit and turned it, showing both Hexians lying dead on the floor. Lilith was safe—her sobs could be heard as she buried her head in the chest of a Delician soldier. Turning the comm to show his face, the Delician growled into the unit, "You're next, Hexian." The holo vid disappeared, leaving just the three of them in the room.

If Emeline had thought she had seen rage before, she was sadly mistaken. It's said that everyone had their breaking point—well she was about to see Hagen's. She was looking at a desperate alien whose world was spinning out of control. The sounds of a battle could be heard through the door, which only fueled his fury.

Feeling her laser scalpel through the pocket of her

jacket, she slowly reached in until she felt the cool smoothness of her only weapon against her fingers. Deciding to leave it where it was, waiting for just the right moment, Violia still had two injectors loaded with enough sedative to take down two Hexians. They had talked earlier, agreeing that if they got the chance to use them, they wanted it to work fast. Looking at Violia still unconscious on the floor, Emeline wished she could do something to wake her. Two against one would be helpful right about now.

Hagen let out a roar as he turned towards his cousin as she lay in a heap on the floor...his blaster pointed at her head. He paused for a split second before his massive foot pulled back, kicking her in the stomach—her slight body jolted upwards from the blow. A small cry escaped Violia's mouth as the pain brought her back to reality. Her arms moved up, trying to protect her middle while Hagen continued to scream obscenities at her.

When Emeline saw his foot pull back for yet another kick, she knew she'd seen enough of Hagen's brutality. She had to do something before he killed Violia. Moving quickly in front of him, she slapped him as hard as she could across the face. She knew she was provoking an enraged grizzly bear, but if she didn't, Violia would be dead. No way would she survive another one of Hagen's savage kicks.

Hagen's head snapped back from the unexpected blow. His eyes burned with rage as he swung his arm out, trying to swat Emeline away, infuriating him even more when she danced out of his way. He came at her, his hand reaching for her throat.

She knew she was dead if he touched her, so with Liam's words ringing in her ears, she readied her stance. Raising her right forearm, blocking his oncoming hand before it could reach her throat, her left fist connected with his eye, pushing him backwards as her knee connected with his unprotected groin.

Not anticipating her attack, Hagen fell backwards, his finger instinctively squeezing the trigger of his blaster, the shot catching Emeline in the right shoulder. The force of his shot flung her body backwards, causing her to hit the edge of the desk before she slid across the hard surface. Her left hand clamped onto the end of the desk, stopping her momentum…saving her from further damage.

Hagen cried out in agony, his hand clutching his throbbing balls. He was out for blood—hers.

Her hand automatically went to where he had shot her. Her fingers came back red from the blood that seeped out of the black hole the blaster had made through her jacket. Emeline didn't have the luxury to tend to her wound, especially when she saw Hagen stumble to his feet, his blaster pointed at her head.

"Don't move." His voice was deadly.

As her breath caught in her throat, her eyes never wavered from the weapon in his hand. The pain in her shoulder was intense—a sharp reminder that maybe she should rethink her situation. *Where the hell is Nox?*

Blood dripped down Hagen's face as he glared at her. His hand let go of his groin long enough to swipe at the blood, creating a red smear across his face, only adding to his fearsome appearance. His blaster was still trained on the middle of her forehead, but at least his breathing had slowed, his control quickly returning.

Looking down at his cousin, he saw her watching him, her eyes clouded with pain and grief. She tried to sit up, but ended up hunched over clutching her ribs.

Looking up at him from the floor, Violia spit her words out at him. "Haven't you caused enough pain for one day? First you kill our grandmother and now this." Glancing over at Emeline, Violia saw her checking the damage to her bleeding shoulder. Grunting as she struggled to get to her feet, Violia managed to pull herself upright, using the desk for support.

"Sit down," he commanded. Moving his gun away from Emeline, he began waving it at Violia.

"No."

Hagen's eyebrows knit together at her defiance. She ignored his words—mocking him as she taunted, "What are you going do, kill me too?"

Hagen growled at her, "Now is not the time to grow a backbone, little cousin." Interrupted by his comm, he glanced down, obviously unhappy at what he saw.

Glad for the momentary reprieve, along with hoping he didn't shoot her in the back, Violia leaned over to Emeline, quietly asking, "How bad is it?"

"Bad enough but I'll live." Her shoulder burned like a smoldering coal from a campfire. "Nothing a regen device wouldn't take care of."

Violia gave her a small smile as she glanced back at her cousin, who was still reading his comm device. He was getting more agitated by the minute. "We don't have much time," she whispered. "We need to do this now. Are you up for it with your shoulder?"

Nodding her head, Emeline stole a quick glance at Hagen, shocked at the look of pure hatred staring back at her. "Just give me a nod," she whispered back as Hagen stormed over and pulled his cousin to his side.

"Come here. We need to leave and we're taking the human with us." He pushed her into one of the chairs near Tarquin's desk, not caring that he was causing her further pain.

Emeline sat up on the desk, her left hand pressed tightly to her wound, trying to stop the bleeding. The pain was beginning to dull as adrenaline began to pump through her as she watched for Violia's signal.

"Where are we going?" Violia was trying quietly to reach into her pockets for the injectors without him noticing. Her body froze as Hagen stopped in front of her. He brought his head down, looking deep into her eyes. Crap—

she wasn't ready yet.

"We are going to Earth to get a shipment of their pink salt."

A sharp laugh erupted from Emeline's mouth before she could stop it. At both their startled looks, Emeline shook her head at them. "All this because of salt." Sliding her legs off the desk, swaying slightly, she managed to stand up straight. In an attempt to get Hagen to move away from Violia, Emeline inched her way towards the door, hoping to distract him. "You know what we do with that salt? We cook with it. It means nothing to us—just something to season our food with."

Hagen swung his blaster around as his big body blocked Emeline's path. Violia seized the opportunity to inject Hagen while Emeline pressed the button of the laser scalpel in her hand. *Go for the soft spots.* Okay, face it is.

Unfortunately, Violia never even got near him with the injectors. He had caught her movement, shoving her harshly to the floor.

Hagen's unexpected turn caused Emeline's hand to miss her intended target...his eyes. Instead, the laser beam skimmed the side of his bald head.

Crying out like a wounded animal, Hagen grabbed her wrist, crushing her bones in his steely fist, before flinging her backwards where she landed hard on the floor.

He stood over her, his massive chest heaving...his furious eyes skimming her body as she lay splayed out in front of him. With one hand on his bloody ear, the other on his blaster, it took only a split second for his mind to decide... he pressed the trigger, shooting her in the upper thigh.

Blood was everywhere. Emeline's screams turned to groans as pain wracked her entire body. She knew she was in serious trouble. She cried out to Violia, "Help me. I think he hit an artery. Violia, please help me."

"No!" Hagen yelled to Violia as she started in Emeline's direction. Blood dripped down the side of his head, soaking into his shirt. The laser scalpel had burned into the side of his head, slicing off the upper half of his ear. In a hate-filled voice, he growled, "I want you to suffer. You deserve to die, human."

Not surprised at Hagen's attitude, Emeline knew she was losing blood fast and needed to act. Quickly considering her options, Emeline removed her jacket, which wasn't easy one handed but she managed to get it off. Pulling off the rest of her ripped shirt...her creamy white breasts were a sharp contrast to the blood that still dripped from her shoulder wound. Struggling while she tried to ignore the searing pain, she managed to get her shirt under her leg. Twisting it tightly, she tried to stem the flow of blood that seeped slowly out of the gaping hole in her thigh. By the time she was finished, she was wrung out, barely able to hold herself up, but at least she had somewhat slowed the blood loss...for now anyway.

Even lying in a pool of her own blood, Hagen leered at her...his tongue moving slowly back and forth across his dry, dirty lips. *This guy is a piece of work.*

Emeline recoiled in disgust. *Where the hell are you, Nox?*

The ship shuddered violently—the lights flickered... growing dim as disruptions were happening throughout the ship, shaking Hagen out of his lurid thoughts. Reaching out a hand to Violia, he said roughly, "Time to go, little cousin."

Ignoring him, Violia took a quick assessment of Emeline's condition. If Emeline didn't get treatment soon, she would die. Struggling slowly to her feet, her back to Emeline, Violia tried to play to Hagen's practical side. "Let's just leave the human here. She's not in any condition to go with us. She'll probably bleed out before we get to your ship anyway. We're better off leaving her here for the Delicians and getting the salt ourselves."

Hagen paused, giving Violia a suspicious look. "Why the change of heart? I thought you couldn't stand to be around

Hexians."

"Easy. Now that Etha is gone, I have nothing left. At least with you I won't be spending the rest of my life in a prison cell."

Watching her face for signs of deception, he conceded. "Fine, whatever. Let's get moving." As he moved towards the door, Hagen stopped to consider Emeline. "You're right —we don't need this human anymore." Pointing his blaster at Emeline's head, he pulled the trigger.

Emeline knew Hagen was going to kill her even before he pulled the trigger. His cold cruel eyes had clearly telegraphed his intension. Her body would not survive the next blast. In these last moments before death, a collage of images flooded her mind. Everyone she loved smiled at her, with Nox's big sexy grin front and center. She was happy her last thoughts were of all the people that she loved. When he pulled the trigger, a sudden movement caught her eye.

Violia moved instinctively, her only thought was saving Emeline. Stepping in front of her, taking the total impact of Hagen's blaster discharge, she noticed several things. First was the door abruptly opening and two figures standing in the doorway. The second was the flash of a weapon hitting Hagen directly in the heart and thirdly, the immense pain that flooded her body. Good, she thought as darkness overtook her, at least we're both dead.

Nox and Ami crept quietly down the corridor, their weapons at the ready. They had to be cautious. One false move could mean injury or death, not only for themselves but also for Emeline and Violia.

Listening at the door, they could hear angry voices but couldn't make out what was being said. With their fingers on their weapon triggers, Ami held up three fingers, indicating to Nox to open the door on her signal. When the door finally opened, the scene being played out before them happened so fast, Nox hadn't even realized Ami had fired her weapon until he saw the look of surprise on Hagen's face before he slumped to the floor...dead.

Pushing past Ami, Nox's only thought was getting to Emeline. He rushed over to where she was lying on the floor —the red stain under her legs was growing larger by the second. Violia's prone body was lying face down across the lower half of Emeline's body.

Shoving Violia's body off to one side, he stifled a sob as his eyes skimmed down the battered body of his bondmate. "Oh, my beautiful Emeline." With red-rimmed eyes, he took in her torn shirt tied around her leg as a makeshift tourniquet. At least there was a reason she was dressed in just a bra and jeans. He had to admire her fast thinking. It's probably what saved her life, but it would only work for so long. She needed a regen device and a transfusion fast.

"No—x? You ca—me." Her voice was thin...reedy, her body shaking from both pain and the cold from losing too much blood. With her last bit of strength, she gave him a weak smile. *I knew he would come.*

His voice broke, "Of course, I came for you, my beauty. I will always come for you. Em—I need you to hang on. I'm going to try to stop the bleeding." With shaking hands, he worked frantically, trying to get the regen device out of his belt, the feeling she was slipping away motivating him to move quickly.

Finally getting the device working, he held back the burned edges of her jeans as he concentrated the device over the hole in her thigh. From the amount of blood he was seeing, it was obvious a major artery had been nicked. At least the pool of blood that had formed under her injured leg hadn't gotten any larger, the tourniquet having done its job, but she was going into shock. Glancing down into her agony-riddled face, her eyes were closed, her lips tinged with blue as she struggled for each breath.

Opening a pocket in his uniform with his fingernail, Nox withdrew a DRI injector and pressed it against Emeline's arm. The pain meds went to work immediately, the pinched look of pain softening as the medication began to work its way through her body.

Nox's shoulders eased slightly when the device indicated that the damaged artery had been sealed...stopping the bleeding. Next, he moved on to healing the surrounding tissue and muscles that were burned black and raw down to the bone, which thankfully was not broken. Nox sent a silent blessing to the universe but knew her situation was still tenuous.

Leaning in carefully, his hand barely skimming the side of her face, Nox took in her overall appearance. Her color was almost as translucent as his—not a good sign. When he saw his colors slide across her hand, his heart sighed a little. It gave him a glimmer of hope.

Very gently he pressed his head to hers, reaching out slowly through their bond. "Please, my beautiful girl—I need you to stay with me. Come on, Em—stay with me."

She whimpered at the sound of his voice.

Breathing deeply, he ignored the other scents around him—death, burnt flesh—blood. Instead, he found what he was looking for—his Emeline. That faint scent of vanilla was still there. Homing in on it, he closed his eyes for the first time in days...allowed himself a brief moment to be surrounded by all that was Emeline.

Pulling his head back, he inspected her face. What he saw infuriated him—cuts and scrapes littered her skin, a deep purple bruise bloomed on her upper cheek. The imprint of a large hand circling her neck caused Nox's face to harden. His fists clenched as he fought to hold on to his growing rage. The regen device would heal the bruises on the outside, but it was the damage on the inside that worried him the most.

Not wanting to move her, he looked around for something to support her head. Her burned and bloodstained jacket lay discarded on the floor, causing Nox to growl in Hagen's direction. Swallowing his anger, he grabbed her jacket and after a quick fold, gently placed it under her head...desperate to give her even the smallest amount of comfort. Gently, his lips barely touching her, he softly blew feather-like kisses across her brow.

Her eyes fluttered open at his caress. Nox could feel her anguish as her tear-filled eyes clouded with sadness and sorrow. As her tears spilled down, disappearing into her hair, he spoke softly, telling her how proud he was of her. "Your strength and will to live is amazing. I know you're tired, sweetheart, but I need you to keep fighting. Liam will be here soon." Her eyes brightened at the mention of her brother's name.

Brushing a stray strand of hair from her cheek, he murmured over and over how sorry he was that he hadn't been there to protect her. She had been through hell and back. He would have to be careful with her, handle her gently, but his Emeline was strong. They would get through this, together. It would take time, but he vowed to do whatever was necessary, whatever she needed to become whole again. One thing he was certain of—he wasn't letting her out of his sight ever again. She would have to get used to having him around all the time. He was practically growling at the thought of anyone taking his bondmate from him again. "I love you so much," he whispered to her.

Emeline tried to smile at Nox's words, but she could feel herself fading in and out. It was hard to say which part of her body hurt the worst—she felt like she was the cream in whipped cream—beat to hell. She was just thankful the pain meds were working. *Thank god for alien technology.*

Nox's heartfelt words meant everything to her. He was right about one thing—she was alive. A sudden thought came to her. "Viol—a?" *Oh no. She stepped in front of me.*

Why?? Why did she take the shot that was meant for me? Whether it was the medicine or the shock of what Violia had done, Emeline had had enough and finally surrendered to the numbness.

Nox tried to stem his rising panic when he saw Emeline lapse into unconsciousness. This was not a good sign. Her skin felt pasty—cold. He pulled her jacket out from under her head and draped it carefully over her chest, giving her some much needed warmth. It would also cover her breasts, leaving her less exposed, but it also covered the deep purple handprints that marred both her arms. Just the thought of Hagen touching his bondmate sent Nox reeling. *A quick death had been too good for Hagen. A simple procedure of a destabilization of his body's molecules would have been better served. Watching yourself being taken apart molecule by molecule would have been a fitting ending to someone who never valued life.*

Emeline's raspy breathing had Nox muttering to himself, "Where the hell is Liam and the doctor?" Yelling harshly over his shoulder to Ami, he asked, "Where is Ezio? She needs a transfusion immediately."

Not getting any response, he put in a call to Tarek, giving him a quick rundown on what had happened and that they needed Liam right away. Since Ami's and Emeline's blood weren't compatible, Liam was their only option and he was still 10 minutes away. Before he signed off, Tarek told him that Ezio and Ramola would be there momentarily.

Hearing a beep, Nox saw that the regen device had completed repairs on Emeline's leg. Her skin was still an angry red, but once they got her back to the ship and into a full-body regen unit, her skin would return to its normal smoothness.

Trying to decide which injury to do next, he held the device over the wound at her shoulder. The damage to her wrist was too severe for a portable regen device. It would require extensive time in the regen bed to regenerate her crushed bones. Maybe it was a good thing, he thought, that she was unconscious. At least this way she didn't feel any pain.

Now all they needed was Liam. *Where the hell is he?* Looking towards the door, his eyes narrowed at Ami. She was leaning against the frame, a dazed look on her face. He followed her eyes to where Hagen lay dead on the floor, his face forever frozen in a look of disbelief. Nox was glad he was dead. He was only sorry he wasn't the one to do it.

When the door had opened, all Ami's eyes could see was the larger than...well, she wasn't exactly sure what, but this guy was massive and mean looking. He had an alien blaster in his hand, having just shot at the Delician medic who had stepped in front of Emeline, saving her. *What the hell is going on?*

Instinctively, Ami fired her own sleek alien weapon, aiming right for the bastard's heart. Her shot stopped that evil asshole right in his tracks. The best part of the whole thing was the look of disbelief on his face as he looked up and saw where the shot had come from. Just before death took him, his eyes widened...a human and a female to boot had taken down the mighty Hagen with only one shot. Going wherever he was going in the afterlife, at least he had that to think on for all eternity.

Thinking on eternity, Ami was shaken at the thought that in the span of ten minutes she had killed two people. She looked down at the gun in her hand—it had looked so shiny only this morning. Now it had lost its sheen. It hadn't taken long for its true colors to come out. It was a lethal killing device, not a new shiny alien toy.

Lost in her thoughts, it wasn't until Ami felt a hard body pulling her into the corridor that she became aware of the Hexian who had been haunting her thoughts day and night. "Tarquin." The word came out in a small gasp, her eyes pulled into his dark gaze. Eyes that looked back at her in wonder, lust even, but something else—was that longing?

He reached up and removed her helmet, tossing it onto the floor. "Call me Quin." His words were a mere whisper as he leaned down, touching his nose to just underneath her ear. His chest pulled in as he breathed deeply, almost as if he were savoring his favorite dish.

"But—" Ami could feel his breath tickling her skin. He smelled like a man should, with heat and sweat and that something else—cinnamon, yeah that's what it was. It clung to his clothes and that silly hat he wore. The hat looked way too big for him and she wondered what he was hiding under there.

Quin pulled his head away; his rough fingers ran down the side of her cheek contrasting against the softness of her face. Taking a light hold of her chin, he leaned his mouth close, his breath mixing with hers insisting, "Tell me your name."

"Ami" flew out before she could stop herself.

"Ami."

She shivered as he said her name back to her, loving how exotic he made it sound. Gazing into his eyes, she realized they weren't totally black as she'd first thought. Up close there were flecks of amber, amethyst, even a little green interspersed throughout the darkness. Ami couldn't help herself. She was lost when she looked at him. Reaching her hand up, her fingertips traced his eyebrows. With a light graze, her fingers moved slowly down along his cheek. His skin felt weathered but strangely soft. She didn't understand what it was about this alien that fascinated her so much. He was a bad person. Everyone said so. But if that was the case, then why couldn't she stop this feeling of wanting to find the nearest closet to explore his alien assets?

"You are amazing, human female. So fierce, so beautiful." His words sounded almost reverent as his eyes roamed her lovely face as if committing it to memory.

The very tip of her pink tongue snuck out quickly—flicking back and forth, moistening her ruby lips before quietly slipping back in.

Quin watched it with longing, dying to taste her. Not one to hold back, he leaned in and took his first taste of this beautiful female. She had a unique flavor, bold, spicy—with a little bit of floral mixed in. He pulled back slightly, watching closely for her reaction. When he didn't get the slap he'd expected, he pressed his lips to hers again, only this time her tongue came out to meet his. Quin didn't know where these feelings were coming from, but from the look on her face, he saw that she was feeling the same thing he was.

There wasn't time for a long exploration. Their kiss deepened quickly—each taking what the other gave and then giving everything in return. Maybe it was knowing that this was their only chance to have this moment and neither of them wanted to miss it.

It felt like a lifetime when in reality it was only a matter of seconds. Trailing kisses down the side of her face, he felt her trembling in his arms. Giving her one of his wide smiles, he shook his head lightly before confessing to her, "Ah, lovely Ami. You tempt me badly. If only we had more time." Looking over his shoulder, Quin heard the hatch door beginning to open. Lightly dragging his knuckle over her swollen lower lip, he leaned in for one more taste before darting down the corridor, disappearing into a side door.

Watching his back disappear, Ami leaned heavily against the side of the doorframe. If anyone were to ask her what had just happened, she'd finally have a reason to use the word "thunderstruck" because that about covered it. Except for the fact that she could still taste him on her tongue, she would have thought she'd hallucinated the last

508

two minutes. Quin—*holy moly can he kiss!*

Seeing Ezio and Ramola coming out from the hatch snapped Ami out of her dream world. Waving at them, she leaned against the doorframe as she surveyed the room. Hagen was dead on the floor while the little medic was lying on her side like a discarded doll, too broken to play with. She knew Nox had headed straight for Emeline, but as she looked at her dearest friend lying in a pool of blood, Ami was afraid the worst had happened.

Feeling Nox's eyes on her as she walked over to where he knelt by Emeline's side, Ami's focus was totally on her friend...thoughts of Quin pushed into the background. "How bad is it?" she asked, squatting down beside him, her eyes taking in Emeline's still face.

Leaning back on his knees, Nox turned to her. Worry lines etched in his normally smooth face. "I don't know. I was able to stop the bleeding, but—" He looked at her bleakly. "She needs Liam here to give her a transfusion. I hope he gets here soon. She's lost a lot of blood."

"And we're not the same blood type, so I'd be more likely to kill her than help her." Ami felt helpless at this moment. "What can I do?"

"Nothing right now." Looking over, he saw the bodies of the two cousins lying in a heap on the floor. "Nice shooting, by the way."

"Thanks—I think. Honestly, Nox, I didn't even realize I had fired until I saw him collapse on the ground."

"Well, if you hadn't, I would have, but I don't think I would have killed him in one shot." Hatred burned in his eyes as he looked at the Hexian who had caused his love so much pain. Moving his gaze to Violia, his hatred dissolved into pity. "I can't believe she took the blast meant for Emeline." He shook his head in disbelief. "First she kidnaps her and then she sacrifices her life for her. Unbelievable."

Ami was sorry that Violia had died, although if she was being honest, she felt that Violia bore some responsibility for this mess. Regardless, she was very brave saving Emeline like she did. Standing up, Ami's long legs stepped over Hagen's prone body, his open eyes unnerving her as he stared unseeing at the floor. Reaching down to straighten out Violia's body, she made a startling discovery. "Hey, she's not dead! Nox, she's still alive. Help me! What do I do?" Rolling her over, Ami's fingers searched for a pulse. It was hard to find, but after a moment, Ami felt a faint throb.

Ezio hurried into the room at Ami's pronouncement, heading quickly over to where she was leaning over Violia checking her wounds. "I have a regen device. Let me do a diagnostic on her." He was all business as he set his pack down and started pulling out the items he would need.

While Ezio and Nox were busy taking care of the wounded females, Ami and Ramola turned their attention to Hagen. Ramola kept looking from Hagen to Ami, finally shaking his head in wonder. "Humans—you certainly are an interesting species." He gave Ami a wide grin as he leaned down and hefted Hagen over his shoulder.

"Where are you going with him?" Ami asked, following him, her curiosity getting the better of her.

"I'm taking out the trash," he grunted as he walked through the open door, dumping Hagen's body onto the floor.

Looking down at the face of the alien she had killed without even a thought, she shuddered, remorse flickering through her. *You wouldn't be human if you didn't feel something.* Ami slapped her hand over her mouth, trying to stop the nervous laugh that threatened to escape. Alien, humans, death, greed—the events of the last few weeks were enough to send her into years of therapy, or more likely a stay in a home for the delusional.

Not wanting to linger in the corridor for very long, Ami headed back into the office. The room smelled like the warzone it was. The scent given off by the blaster guns gave the room a burnt electrical smell. Between that and the smell of blood and burned flesh, Ami covered her nose with her hand as she fought off her rising nausea. Finding a chair to sit in, she slumped over, putting her head between her knees, trying to contain the urge to throw up.

Ramola moved over to her, placing a canteen in her hand. "Here, drink this. It will help settle your stomach."

Giving him a grateful grimace, Ami put the container to her lips, allowing the cool liquid to slip down her dry throat. It took a few seconds to hit her system, but to her amazement, rather quickly the clammy nauseous feeling began to fade. Wiping her hand over her mouth, she handed the canteen back to Ramola.

"Keep it. It's a vitamin drink. It will help restore you."

Taking another sip, she leaned back in her chair. "Thanks. This stuff is great. I don't know what's in it, and right now I don't really care. All I know is I feel better already."

Ramola was hovering beside her, giving her a slightly uncomfortable feeling—especially the way he was grinning at her. *Please don't tell me he's going to hit on me. That it's some kind of weird alien ritual that you get the girl who kills the most aliens.* "Um, Ramola, are you all right?" She spoke with a certain amount of hesitancy in her voice.

"I am well."

"Then why are you looking at me like that?" Ami wasn't sure she wanted to know.

Squatting down in front of her, Ramola's expression turned serious. "Taking a life is not something to take lightly. It will live inside you hidden in the shadows." When he saw Ami's eyes start to fill, her body trembling slightly, he took her free hand in his and squeezed lightly. "Ami, listen to me. I am in awe of you. Never in all my life have I seen a female as brave and fearless as you are. What you did today was necessary. You saved your friend and you fought well with your team. Remember that when your mind wants to take you to that dark place."

His words made all the difference. He was right. She had done what she was supposed to do. "Thanks, Ramola. I appreciate you saying that. You're right—I did do good. I guess all that practice really paid off." Then she added shyly, "I thought maybe you were hitting on me."

Letting out a huge laugh, Ramola patted her knee. "As tempting as you are, I have other plans." Looking at Nox hovering over his bondmate, he said with a note of wistfulness in his voice, "I want that." Standing to his full height, he became all business as he told her, "Now I need to find out where Tarek and the rest of our team are. Sit and take a rest. Liam should be here very soon."

Taking his advice, Ami leaned back and took another sip from the canteen. Closing her eyes, she sent up a silent prayer, "Please hurry, Liam."

CHAPTER 23

"Where the hell is Liam?" It wasn't the first time Nox had growled out his frustration...Emeline needed him badly.

Hovering at her side, his large hand held her nearly colorless one lightly in his. He gently rubbed her fingers, trying to infuse some of his warmth into her.

Ezio, glancing over quickly—his focus had been on trying to save Violia—called towards the door. "Ramola, what is Liam's location?" Ezio held a regen unit steady as it worked to repair Violia's immediate life-threatening injuries. Being so close to the blast, her wound was the size of a tennis ball that had hit just below her midsection. Once the bleeding was contained, it would then concentrate on repairing the surrounding damage. Considering how much of a beating her small body had taken, it was a miracle she still lived.

Ramola, who had been watching the corridor from the doorway, turned, telling everyone, "Tarek just called. Liam and Dr. Datrem should be here any second now. He also said the bridge is secure."

The mood in the room immediately turned to one of relief—the Delicians had won.

Nox asked about Tarquin. Ramola relayed that Tarek had teams searching the ship, but so far, he seemed to have vanished.

At the sound of Tarquin's name, Ami couldn't refrain from gently biting her lower lip. It didn't take much for her to remember the feeling of his firm lips on hers. The urgency...the need that had swept through both of them. She could feel her face heat, glad that everyone was too preoccupied to notice. She allowed herself a second to wonder where he was...hoping he was safe, before she scolded herself to remember he was a bad alien who had kidnapped her friend. *What kind of person are you, Ami?*

Ramola interrupted her self-deprecation with the news that Liam was here with the doctor and his medic, Tulio.

Liam burst through the door only to stop short at the sight of his baby sister lying bloody and broken on the floor looking like the loser in a street fight. Sinking to his knees, a quiet sob escaped his lips as he took in the horrific scene. "Oh, Em." The nearly black bruises on her face, neck and arms brought tears to his eyes. *How did I allow this to happen?*

Without warning, Emeline began gasping for air. Her mouth opening and closing, straining as her lungs searched desperately for oxygen.

Fear gripped Liam as he looked across to Nox, who was kneeling on her other side, wild panic in his eyes as they both screamed for the doctor. "Help her, help her."

Liam's voice broke as he pleaded with his sister. "Em, please don't die."

Dr. Datrem shooed both males out of the way as he began calling out orders. "Tulio, inject her with the respiration meds. That should calm her lungs. Ramola, get the portable stretcher out of my bag so we can get her off the floor."

The sound of her heart racing could be heard through the device they had placed on her forehead that allowed the doctor to monitor her vital signs.

All of a sudden, the room felt very small as they all stood there—Nox, Liam and Ami—helpless as they watched the medical team work on Emeline.

Ramola pulled a large square out of one of the bags. Placing it down beside Emeline on the floor, he pushed a small indentation on the top. The square started growing lengthwise, stopping at around six feet. With Dr. Datrem at her head and Tulio at her feet, Ramola leaned over as they gently slid Emeline onto the stretcher.

Placing his palm under the stretcher, Datrem slowly lifted upwards, stopping at waist level. With the stretcher hovering in a stationary position, it allowed easy access for him to begin treating Emeline.

Seeing the looks on the three solemn faces, the doctor smiled encouragingly as he ran his diagnostic scanner over Emeline's body. "I forget that you humans don't have this type of technology yet."

No one responded to him—their focus solely on Emeline. Whatever they had given her appeared to be working. Her breathing evened out, allowing her body to relax. Her heartbeat slowed, the sound becoming more rhythmic.

"What the hell happened to her?" Liam ground out. "How did she get shot?" Liam knew he sounded demanding, but hell, this was his little sister lying half naked with two blaster shots and multiple contusions to her body.

It was Nox who was standing beside him that told him what they had witnessed when they opened the door. He couldn't tell him how Emeline got her other injuries, saying they'd have to wait for her to wake up before they got the full story.

Liam glanced at Violia, whom Ezio had placed on another of the portable stretchers. Looking like she had taken quite a beating, she had a medical monitor on her forehead as well. He would be forever grateful to her for saving his sister.

Now that Emeline had been stabilized, Tulio moved over to help Violia. He installed a line into one of Violia's veins to start a transfusion of Delician blood he had in his supplies.

Dr. Datrem interrupted Liam, telling him that he would have to get his answers later. Right now, he needed him to roll up his sleeve so they could start the transfusion.

"Sure thing, Doc. Anything you need." Liam plopped down in a chair and began pulling off his armor. "Take as much as you need," he told Datrem.

Amused at the shortening of his title, Dr. Datrem prepared Liam's arm for the transfusion. "That's very admirable of you, but after what you've experienced today, if we had another alternative, the last thing I'd be doing is taking your blood."

Wincing at the needle, Liam watched his blood start to flow into his sister. Acknowledging Datrem's words, he agreed. "It's been a tough day for all of us." Leaning back, his body relaxing for the first time in days, he asked the doctor, "Have you heard from your family? How is your granddaughter doing?"

"Yes. My son sent word that she was safe and at home." His lips were pressed into a thin line. "As you can imagine, she is extremely traumatized. She refused to go to the hospital, but they were able to give her something to help her sleep. My son said that Etha had shielded her from most of the abuse and for that I will be eternally grateful."

He paused, thinking of his old friend, adding sadly, "Etha didn't deserve to die like that. This is going to be a long journey of healing for Violia and Lilith—and Emeline as well. Once we return to Delicia, I'll be taking a leave of absence to spend some time with her." Looking over at Tulio monitoring Violia, Datrem sighed. "If only she had confided in me or someone, things might have ended differently."

Nox was winding a strand of Emeline's hair around his finger, watching Liam's blood flowing in her body...saving her life. He considered Datrem's words, arriving at a similar conclusion. "As mad as I am at her, it's easy to say in hindsight what anyone of us would have done in the situation she was placed in. The fact that she tried to save Emeline shows that her intentions were noble, however misguided her actions were."

"I'm surprised you can be so forgiving?" Liam countered.

"Probably because I watched her take the blaster shot meant to kill Emeline." Nox's eyes were glued to Emeline's face, watching for any signs of consciousness. Leaning down, he whispered encouraging words to her, telling her that Liam and Ami were here waiting for her to wake up.

Overcome with emotion, he turned his head away, murmuring sadly, "I don't know what I would do if I had lost her."

Liam couldn't tell if Nox was talking to himself or to him, but he could see the extent of Nox's feelings for his sister. Liam was glad that Emeline had found love, even if it had come from such an unlikely source—an alien from a planet millions of light years away from Earth. Man, was their mother going to have a lot to say about this when they finally got around to telling her.

Hearing a commotion out in the corridor, Tarek appeared at the entrance to the room. His commanding presence filled the doorway as he surveyed the scene. His armor had a few visible dings in various places, but on the whole, he looked unscathed from the battle. Calling over to the doctor, he asked, "How are the females?"

Datrem looked up from where he was using the regen device on Emeline's shoulder. The blast area—the size of a golf ball—had turned from black to a dark pink, indicating that it was healing nicely. She should have no visible scars once the healing process was completed. "Emeline was lucky Nox and Ami arrived when they did, but she probably saved her own life with her quick actions." He nodded his head towards Emeline's bloody, torn shirt that had been removed once the nick in her artery had been sealed. Glancing over to Violia, he shook his head. "Unfortunately for Violia, we're still not sure. We've stopped the bleeding, but she's lost a lot of blood. We'll just have to wait and see. Aside from the damage to her abdomen, she has a concussion, several broken ribs and multiple contusions."

Ami jumped into the conversation, her voice strained as

she looked down at Violia, "This is all my fault. I should have checked on her sooner. I honestly thought she was dead from that blast she took from Hagen." The feeling of guilt was added to the heaviness on her already battered soul.

Tarek clasped Ami on the shoulder, giving her a long, serious look. When he had her full attention, he reinforced Ramola's words, adding his own, "You are wrong, Ami. From what I hear, you acted instinctively—taking out Hagen to save Emeline. Impressive." Looking down at Violia, he added, "She's lucky to be alive, both of them are, and that's thanks to you."

Ami gave him a slight smile. She appreciated Tarek's praise, and if the circumstances were different, she'd be doing her happy dance. Ami didn't feel like dancing.

Tarek gave her shoulder another comforting squeeze before moving towards the door. Seeing Ezio hovering over Violia's body, Tarek frowned. This was odd behavior for his friend to be so concerned over the injured medic. Normally he would have been asking about his team or out leading the search for more Hexians. "Ezio, can I see you out in the corridor?"

After a reluctant pause, Ezio followed Tarek out of the room. Tarek, taking in the bewildered look on Ezio's face, asked curiously, "Are you all right?"

Ezio scrubbed his hands over his face as he looked down at Hagen's body. His finger traced down the old scar, remembering how he had gotten it. "I'm not sure. I mean, I'm glad the bastard is dead. I only wish I had been the one to end him." Studying Hagen's bloodied face and sheared off ear, Ezio smirked, "At least someone got in a few good shots."

"True, but that's not what I meant. Why are you hovering over the medic?" Studying his friend's face, he noticed a slight movement just under the skin. His eyes widened as he recognized the implication of what he was witnessing.

Ezio threw his hands up in the air, grinding out, "I can't explain it. For some reason, I have this overwhelming need to protect her."

Tarek pointed down at Ezio's hand just as a wave of colors swirled slowly across the top. They both stared at it as the full impact of the meaning left a heavy silence between the two males. Raising an eyebrow, Tarek again pointed to Ezio's hand, telling him quietly, "We'll speak about this later. For now, when Datrem gives the all clear, I want you to escort the two females to the medical bay on the *Maelstrom*. I don't trust the med bay here. Ramola will stay here with me until we have all the Hexians secured. After that, I will return to the *Maelstrom*. Nicon will take control of the Invidia until we head back to Delicia. Check with him and Yilmaz on how many soldiers they'll need to send over."

"Yes, sir."

"And Ezio—congratulations."

"Thank you, sir—I think." Ezio nodded his head at the General before returning to Violia's side.

"Nox?" Tarek knew that Nox was reluctant to leave Emeline, but Tarek wanted to speak to him.

"Yes, Tarek?" Stepping out into the corridor, he saw Tarek looking at Hagen's corpse.

Crouching down, Tarek took an inventory of the wounds on Hagen's body. There was the obvious blaster wound that was Ami's kill shot. A black hole could be seen through his dirty shirt, blood congealed around the edges of the wound. The long burn mark on the side of his face and the cut over his eye intrigued Tarek.

Standing up as Nox came over, Tarek pointed to the battered remains of the male who had caused so much pain. "Looks like your female left a few marks of her own on him. You should be proud of her. You know, for a planet that we thought was so primitive and backwards, they certainly showed us we were wrong."

This was the first time Nox had been able to get a hard look at the perverted deviant who had hurt his bondmate. He wished he could have been the one to fire the killing shot. The longer he stared at this monster, the harder it became to hold back his rage. "She should never have been put in this position. I should have protected her better," he spat out.

Nox's eyes closed—his hands tightened into fists as he fought and failed to keep his emotions contained. Looking down at the person who hurt his Emeline, he snapped. His fury let loose on Hagen—kicking him multiple times about the groin and body. By the time he was finished, he was breathing hard, a light sheen glistened across his forehead.

Tarek stood there, watching, a nonchalant look on his face. When he saw Nox stop and lean his head against the wall, he quietly asked, "Feel better?"

Looking down at the dead male at their feet, Nox huffed out a short laugh, telling him, "Maybe, not really, okay maybe that did feel good. I just wish he was alive as I was doing it."

Looking over, Nox saw Liam leaning against the doorframe, watching him with a look of grim satisfaction.

Pointing to the wounds on Hagen's head, Liam asked, "Em do that?"

"I believe so," Tarek answered with a look of pride on his face.

"Good."

"There is no way Violia is strong enough, and I know she's not large enough to have caused that much damage to his ear." Tarek came over and placed a hand on Liam's shoulder. "Liam, you trained her well. She might not have been able to take him out completely, but at least she's alive. How is she doing?"

"Stable—for now. Once we get her back to the *Maelstrom*, the doc says he may need to give her another transfusion." Liam leaned his head back against the wall, grabbing a moment's respite from an extremely exhausting day. His face was drawn, deep worry lines wrinkling his forehead. "All I can say is thank God for your medical equipment, otherwise she'd be dead." Liam shuddered at the thought.

Nox moved to stand in the doorway, his watchful eyes on Emeline waiting for any sign that she had regained consciousness. He glanced at Liam, saying, "I'm just grateful this is over and we have her back. You better believe I'm not letting her out of my sight ever again." Staring intently into first Liam's eyes and then into Tarek's, he said quite emphatically, "I can't risk losing her again. I won't survive without her."

Liam straightened at his words, saying, "I'm glad to hear you say that. I'm holding you to it." Looking at Tarek, who was getting information from his team through his helmet, Liam waited until Tarek was finished before asking, "What's going on with the Hexians? Has Tarquin been located yet?"

"Nicon just confirmed that all the Hexians on board have been contained but there is still no sign of Tarquin."

"Damn it. We need to catch that bastard. He's got a lot to answer for. Regardless of how he helped my sister and Violia, I blame him for this." Liam's face turned slightly red as he slapped the wall at the thought of Tarquin getting away. Liam wanted him to pay for all the pain he had caused.

Dr. Datrem called out, telling Nox and Liam that Emeline was starting to come around.

As Nox rushed into the room, Tarek grabbed Liam's arm, holding him back from following Nox, "Hold on a second, Liam."

"Sir."

"I have to go sort things on the bridge, but I'll be heading back to the *Maelstrom* shortly. I've already given orders to Ezio about transporting all of you back to the ship once Violia and Emeline are stabilized. Once Emeline is cleared from medical, I want my senior staff to meet in the officers' rec room for a debrief. That includes you and Ami as well."

A look of surprise appeared on Liam's face. "Really?"

Tarek let out a small chuckle at Liam's expression. "Yes, Liam. You have more than proven yourself to me and my team. Not everyone can say they singlehandedly blew up a Hexian freighter."

Even the tips of Liam's ears pinkened from the unexpectedly high praise from one of the fiercest generals in the universe.

"Besides, didn't I hear something about you making a dish called 'lasagna'? From what I understand it is something special and I am very much looking forward to tasting it." Tarek rubbed his stomach in anticipation. He loved trying new foods and so far, the food the humans had prepared for him and his crew had been delicious.

Liam grinned back at him. "Looks like I'll be spending some time in the kitchen when we get back."

Hearing Tarek being called through his comm, Liam nodded as Tarek turned and headed towards the bridge.

Ami poked her head out the door, calling Liam's name—Emeline wanted to see him.

Liam came hurrying into the room...the people around her stretcher parted so that he could see for himself that his sister was indeed improving. She lifted one hand to him, her other one was completely encased in what looked like clear bubble wrap. Only this stuff was flashing thin blue electric shocks all around her hand and wrist similar to the plasma globe his friend had in college. Careful not to jolt her, Liam couldn't stop his eyes from overflowing, his emotions laid bare for her to see. "Hey sweet girl, how you doing?" His voice came out choked as a tear worked its way down his cheek.

Emeline's thumb gently brushed away the wetness on his face. Her own tired eyes took in his disheveled appearance. He looked thinner than the last time she'd seen him, not to mention the exhaustion plastered all over his face.

"Hey big brother." Her voice shook with emotion as tears ran down on either side of her head. "I remembered what you told me."

Brushing back the thin wisps of hair from her forehead, his smile wavered between pride and sorrow. "I saw. You did good. I think you might be ready to move up to the next level." Tamping down his desperate need to sob, knowing it was not really a manly thing to do, Liam looked away for a moment trying to collect his thoughts.

Once he managed to gain some control of his emotions, he caught her gaze in his saying, "I am so damn proud of you. You got your shots in, but what was the main thing I always stressed?"

"Do whatever to stay alive. And I did, Liam. I did." Her face pulled down into a frown as she remembered having to pretend to give in to Hagen's advances. Her body visibly shuddered at the thought. "I didn't want to—I didn't, but I got him, Liam. I got him right where you said." She gave a watery hiccupped laugh, saying, "I think I sent his balls up into his throat."

"I bet he didn't like that."

The image of Hagen's fury as he came after her flashed into her mind. She had to keep reminding herself that Hagen was dead. "He was pretty pissed." The words barely a whisper on her tongue.

"Em, look at me." Liam's voice urged her to focus on him. He saw the fear lingering in her eyes. "Listen to me. He can't hurt you anymore. He's dead. Ami took care of that." Seeing the relief spread across her pale face, Liam gave a quick smile to Ami who was standing beside Nox at the foot of the stretcher watching the exchange between the two siblings. "Ami has become quite the shot. I hear she took out a Hexian who was about to shoot your bondmate."

Emeline's eyes flew to Nox at Liam's words. "You were shot?"

Nox glared at Liam before stroking her head reassuringly. "Almost. I was saving that tiny tidbit for later and I figured Ami would be filling you in on all her exploits during girl time." He knew that Emeline and Ami required a certain amount of girl time whenever possible.

"You got that right." Ami winked at Emeline. "There might be hope for him yet." Ami gave Emeline a meaningful look. "Seriously, girlfriend, I'm glad you're all right. Had me worried there for a while."

"You and me both, but you left me no choice. I had to have something exciting to bring back home to tell Heather and Lorelei. I couldn't let you have all the fun." Emeline's attempt at a joke showed she was gaining some of her strength back. The blood transfusion, along with the infusion of nutrients that Datrem had given her, had helped accelerate the healing process.

Emeline's eyes drifted over to Violia wondering aloud how she was doing.

Overhearing Emeline's comment, Datrem came to her side, telling them Violia was stable at the moment, so they could leave any time. Both injured females needed to be placed in the regen beds on the *Maelstrom* as soon as possible.

Ramola contacted Tarek, telling him they were heading to the docking bay. Ami and Liam turned and followed behind him as he took the lead. Tulio and Ezio took a hold of Violia's stretcher while Nox and Dr. Datrem took Emeline's. Nyx, who had come to check on everyone, took up the rear.

Leaning down, Nox brushed a soft kiss across Emeline's forehead, whispering, "You ready to get off this rust bucket and go home?"

Squeezing his hand with her good one, Emeline blew out of sigh of relief. "Home—I like the sound of that."

Nox frowned at her words. "Home as in your apartment on Earth?" He held his breath, waiting for her answer. Considering what she had just endured, he wouldn't blame her for wanting to go back to Earth.

Giving him a shy smile, her eyes alight with love, she told him, "No silly. Home is wherever you are."

Nox let out a sigh, the horrors of the last few days fading momentarily into the background. Giving her a huge grin, he grabbed the side of the stretcher, saying, "All right then, home it is."

◆ ◆ ◆

Tarquin was livid. Not only had he lost a ship and its entire crew, but because of Hagen's stupidity, he still didn't have the shipment of Earth's pink salt that his people so desperately needed. How the hell had his life spun so much out of control?

Peering carefully out the door of his sleeping quarters, his body was tense as he listened for any sounds. Hearing movement, he managed to close the door just in time before being caught. Barely breathing, Tarquin froze until the movement passed by.

Cracking the door slightly, he saw a group of Delicians and humans moving quickly down the corridor carrying stretchers with the injured females. His eyes landed briefly on the backside of the tall dark-skinned human female. *Ami! What is it about you? Why are you always in my thoughts?*

He didn't have time for distractions. People were counting on him and right now he was failing everyone. It was time to get off this ship and figure out what his next move was. Good thing he'd had the foresight to have his cloaked ship ready for just such a circumstance as this. *Trust your instincts, mother always said.*

Thoughts of his mother were always followed by memories of his grandfather. Growing up, they had been close, spending all their time together. That all changed when his grandfather started antagonizing members of the UAP. That decision caused more devastation than anyone could have realized. His grandfather hadn't wanted to deal with the ever-growing population of women, children and elderly that were starving and needed housing and medicine. He left that distasteful task to his wife and daughter. He was still stuck in the old ways of Hexia, and nothing Tarquin or anyone could say would change his mind. But the old male was dead, killed the way he lived his life.

Now Tarquin was the leader of Hexia and he was determined to make sure the new *native* Hexians were taken care of. He had a plan, but he needed a bargaining piece in order to get them what they needed. Earth's salt would be the perfect thing to use—the only problem was how to get it.

Tarquin mulled over some of his options as he made his way through the hidden panel set into the back of his closet. He had installed a short tunnel that led directly to an airlock where his personal shuttle was currently docked.

Crawling on his hands and knees, he quickly reached the airlock. Inputting his personal code, the door slid open and he made his way into the cockpit. He wasn't concerned about the Delicians finding him. The only other person who knew about his contingency plan had gotten himself killed.

Hagen—what the hell was he thinking? All he had to do was keep the females locked in a storage room. Give them food and water. Follow orders and leave them alone. We could have ransomed them, gotten a salt shipment and been on our way. Not hard. Well, the moron got what he deserved.

All these thoughts swarmed around in Tarquin's head as he eased his ship away from the Invidia. Aside from all the other crap he had to deal with, the question was, did he go for the salt and hope that the humans wouldn't detect him? Or did he head back to Hexia to face the wrath of some of the more influential crime families as well as his mother and grandmother? Well, the first thing he needed to do was get as far away from the Delicians as he could, then he would decide.

Looking down at his instrument panel, Tarquin switched over to manual as he maneuvered his ship he had affectionately nicknamed *Cosmos* away from the battle cruiser. The name he picked didn't mean what you would expect. It was actually the name of one of the few flowers that grew natively on Hexia. They were hard to find because the burnt orange flowers tended to blend in with the reddish soil. His grandmother and mother used to take him out searching for the flowers when he was a boy. They were some of his happiest memories before duty and responsibility took over his life. Right now, however, he felt like his life was spinning out of control trying to keep both sides satisfied. It was all going to blow up in his face. It was inevitable.

With thrusters at minimal, Tarquin held his breath as he skimmed just underneath the belly of a Delician star fighter. He had spent a lot of time and money making sure *Cosmos* was top of the line. The final piece was the newly upgraded cloaking device his Delician benefactor had finally given him. A benefactor who until recently had maintained a distance from Tarquin—interacting mainly with his mother and grandparents. However, as of late, the Delician had been getting creative in his methods of trying to gain some influence over Tarquin—the cloaking device being the main one. Tarquin had to admit it gave him the freedom he desperately needed to complete supply drops for his people, but at what cost? The Delician wanted a share of the salt shipment and was going to be displeased with this latest turn of events. Well, he could stand in line with everyone else, he mused unhappily to himself.

With the Delician star fighters taking up positions all around the Invidia, Tarquin saw an opening in one of the lines. *Looks like Jagger is letting his recruits get soft.* Tarquin glanced over, spotting the *Maelstrom* just off to the starboard side, which meant that Tarquin would be heading in the opposite direction. Hiding out behind this solar system's biggest planet, Jupiter, sounded like an ideal spot to make some decisions.

Once he had a clear path away from his former ship, he increased his speed slightly, still not wanting to leave any trace of his escape. Taking one last look at the Invidia, he couldn't lie to himself—losing his ship was a huge loss, one he would have to justify to his people on Hexia. For too many years, Hexia had been ruled by whichever family could maintain control over the masses. Originally a haven for anyone who wanted to live by their own rules, Hexia quickly turned into a battleground of who could control the money and power. Tarquin's family descended from one of the original settlers coming from a small planet within the UAP and had been in power for numerous generations. When his grandfather had been killed, Tarquin had no choice but to step in. He had been groomed from a young age to take over as leader...a role he didn't want, but more importantly, a role most of the more influential crime families didn't think he could handle.

Setting a course for the far side of the planet Jupiter, Tarquin pulled off his hat and threw it against the wall. *I really hate wearing this stupid thing.* With his hat off, Tarquin ran his fingers through his hair, separating out the dark strains and massaging his scalp. A sigh of satisfied relief escaped his mouth as his scalp no longer carried the combined weight of his hair and the hat. His curly brown hair fell to just below his shoulders. Purple highlights glowed in the light, giving anyone who saw his hair the knowledge that Tarquin was half Delician. He didn't think much about his Delician side, but he didn't want anyone questioning who his father might be. As far as he was concerned, he was a native Hexian. It's where he was born—where his mother and grandparents had been born. If things went according to his plan, Hexia was about to undergo a transition that could possibly change the entire course of their planet. The ratio between the *criminal* population and the *native* inhabitants had shifted. The voices of the women and children born and raised on Hexia were growing louder and stronger for change. They were coming to a crossroads and it seemed that Tarquin had made himself their self-imposed leader, much to the chagrin of his benefactor.

Shaking off his heavy thoughts, Tarquin grabbed a bottle of liquid nutrient and settled back into his chair. Taking a long drink, the cool liquid slid down his parched throat, giving relief along the way. Staring out at the blackness, dotted only by the millions of tiny lights, Tarquin could feel the fatigue pulling at him but knew he couldn't rest until he was safely out of reach of the Delicians. At least taking it slow would allow him to save on fuel. He didn't have the luxury of having an endless supply of Delician crystals. He had only been able to obtain a small shipment before he left for Earth this time. *Come to think of it, there always seems to be delays whenever I ask for Delician crystals. But if I go for the salt, I won't need to ask. I can purchase whatever I need. Hmm, something to consider.* Normally Tarquin could get whatever he wanted on Hexia. There was always someone with a connection—well, except when it came to Delician crystals. They were elusive and costly.

As Tarquin nestled his shuttle in between two of Jupiter's 79 moons, he powered down his engines and stood, stretching his long body, allowing his tense muscles to begin to loosen. What he really needed was a nice long soak and 24 hours of uninterrupted sleep. *No, what I really need is a nice long soak with a certain exotic human beauty. Agh, stop thinking about her—Ami. Enough.*

Tarquin headed into the galley to find something to fill his empty stomach. Not sure what he would find, his wide mouth lifted in a smile at the sight of a new upgraded replicator. Hagen must have installed this.

Frowning, Tarquin wondered why Hagen would have bothered. *I wonder what else he did.* Programming the replicator for a bowl of Sulkis stew, he considered Hagen's recent demeanor. He had dropped more than a few hints that he was planning something, which Tarquin had promptly brushed off, figuring Hagen was just mouthing off as usual. Maybe there was more to it.

Seeing his food appearing, hot and smelling delicious, Tarquin's stomach grumbled as he inhaled deeply over his bowl. This was one of his favorite comfort foods his mother used to make for him using the succulent breast meat of a domesticated Sulkis. Mixed with lots of vegetables and covered in a thick brown savory sauce, his mouth watered in anticipation of his first taste. Sliding into a chair at a small table that was bolted to the floor, Tarquin ordered his onboard computer to compile an inventory of all the recent changes made to his shuttle.

He ate heartily, savoring each bite, while he read through the list wondering what the hell Hagen had been thinking and where he had gotten the funds for all this. There were upgrades on a whole litany of items from a specialized sleeping chair to the food replicator, of course, but also an increase in the weapons inventory by half.

What was Hagen up to? Tarquin replayed some of the conversations he'd had with Hagen recently. Certain comments began to make sense. It was obvious he had been too caught up in trying to appease everyone that he neglected to keep a tight rein on Hagen. That was something he sorely regretted.

Putting down his bowl, Tarquin thought back to his last confrontation with Hagen. Hagen had been furious at the human for tricking him. He swore he was going to teach her a lesson. When he was ordered to stay away from the human, he changed his rant to how this was just another example of how inept a leader Tarquin was. It had taken Tarquin's not so gentle reminder of exactly where Hagen's place was on Hexia for Hagen to even begin to calm down. But Tarquin saw how Hagen continued to obsess about the human female. You could see it in the way he spoke about her, his eyes almost maniacal in movement.

Tarquin knew Hagen would ignore his orders and go for the human. That was why when Hagen didn't show up on the bridge, Tarquin knew where he would go. Too bad he had been too late to stop Hagen—although in some ways his timing had been perfect. Hagen got exactly what he deserved, especially since it looked like he was planning to kill Tarquin and take over Hexia. He laughed out loud, loving the irony of it all—killed by a human female.

Ami! She was amazing. I hope she's okay. Fuck—where did that come from? Tarquin couldn't stop his mind from thinking about her. She was beautiful with her sweet lips...soft and tasting of passion. Sighing, Tarquin leaned forward in his chair, his bowl of food left half eaten in front of him. Picking up his spoon, his eye caught a slight movement across the top of his hand. *Huh?* Holding his breath, he waited to see if it happened again. It only took a few moments for another set of dark colors to move subtly just beneath his skin.

Tarquin did not move for a very long time. His mind was blank, his body numb.

The image that finally filled his mind was one of a certain human female, *Ami.* He was holding her in his arms having just kissed her with everything he had to give. Her face gazed up at him, her eyes glazed with heat and passion...her lush lips swollen from his kiss. The realization that came to his mind was staggering, adding another layer to his already complicated life.

He struggled trying to wrap his mind around what was happening to him. Sure, he'd been with females—who hadn't?—but it never meant anything. Come to think of it, there never were any females that had ever caught his attention for more than a few hours. But Ami—she had more than occupied his mind. She consumed him. It had been that way since the moment he'd first seen her on the *Mael-*

strom. Now it made sense as to why this human female fascinated him so much. *Ha!* She was an amazing creature—tall, curvy, with a face that constantly invaded his dreams. Brave and beautiful, she had been fearless when she had shot Hagen...not hesitating at all, didn't even flinch. He had been awestruck watching her in action.

Being the one to catch her when she had realized what she had done, well, that was something Tarquin would dream about for a very long time.

An alarm blaring broke through Tarquin's thoughts. Jagger must have sent patrols out looking for him.

Making sure his cloaking unit was working properly, Tarquin wasn't concerned about getting caught. With all the new upgrades to his shuttle, he was confident he was safe for now.

Shutting off the alarm, he decided to forgo the bedroom and instead settled into the new sleeping chair Hagen had installed. Stretching out, the chair conformed to his body, giving off a comforting warm heat allowing his stiff muscles to relax. He was dead on his feet. Any major decisions could wait until he had gotten some much needed rest. His last thought before drifting off was of the beautiful human female who had gotten under his skin in more ways than one.

CHAPTER 24

Back on board the Maelstrom

After an uneventful ride back to the *Maelstrom*, both females were whisked off to medical followed by the entire crew of the shuttle. Nox had never let go of Emeline's *good* hand the entire ride. He regaled her with a story about a time when his mother had taken him to Tyrax Prime. The sister planet to Calor Prime, Tyrax Prime was a humid planet with a wide variety of rare plant life. "Mother had been curious and suggested a small excursion. I was always eager to visit new places. However, once there I had the misfortune of getting stung by a Volucar."

Emeline raised her eyebrows, asking, "What is that? It doesn't sound very pleasant."

"It wasn't." Unconsciously rubbing his arm, Nox explained that a Volucar was a flying insect with a stinger about the size of his thumb that secreted a nasty poison. He winced remembering how he had spent four days lying in a tent covered in red welts withering with pain. The local healer had given him a nasty milky-looking tea, assuring his mother he would heal him. "Of course, I would have healed a lot quicker with a portable regen device." Nox smirked, remembering it had been his responsibility to pack the medical supplies for their trip and in his haste to get to the surface had forgotten half of their supplies. "It was a painful mistake I swore to never make again."

Emeline gave him a sympathetic smile as Nox visibly shuddered, remembering his awful experience. Her smile turned into a yawn, prompting Nox to urge her to close her eyes a while.

Now that he had her back, he wasn't leaving her—ever.

Oh, he knew she would have a whole plethora of things to say when she discovered his plan for keeping her safe. He welcomed it. As far as he was concerned, it would be music to his ears listening to her yell at him about how ridiculous he was being. *Wait until she finds out that if I can't be with her, someone else sure as hell will be.*

Skimming his tormented eyes down her broken and abused body, his mouth flattened as he watched her forehead crinkle in pain. The sudden urge to do terrible violence was a feeling Nox was becoming all too familiar with. The tightening of his stomach, the set of his posture, the vengeful voice whispering in the back of his mind—those were all indications that he was on the verge of losing control. He'd only done that twice in his life—once when his mother died and then again just yesterday.

A soft caress across his hand calmed his raging emotions. Flicking his eyes from her hand to her red-rimmed eyes, he saw her studying him intently. "Why don't you try to get some sleep?"

"I'm afraid."

He ran his hand lightly over her head, trying to reassure her. "You don't have to be afraid anymore. I promise—I'll never leave you."

Speaking low so that only he could hear, she confessed, "I won't make it if this is all a dream." Her eyes filled with tears as she tried to blink them away.

Emotion filled Nox as his eyes matched hers. "Oh, Emeline." He kissed her trembling lips, letting her feel just how real he was.

Clearing his throat, Dr. Datrem moved over to stand across from Nox. Holding up a DRI injector for Emeline to see, he told her, "I'm going to give you something to help you sleep."

Shaking her head, Emeline's vital stats spiked as she struggled to sit up. "No." Her anxious eyes shot to Nox. "No more drugs."

Leaning down close, his breath gentle on her face, Nox spoke her name over and over, trying to calm her. "Em, it's okay. It's only a mild sedative. I promise it's going to be okay. Sshh—look at me. That's it—look at me. You've been through so much and your body needs to rest. Please, let the doctor help you."

Too tired to resist, Emeline relaxed back onto the stretcher, her eyes pleading with Nox. "Stay."

Like he could ever leave her. "I promise I'll be right here. I'm not going anywhere until I take you back to our room. I swear to you, I'll be right here when you wake up." Gazing into her drooping eyes, he lightly brushed a kiss to her lips. "Rest and when you wake up, I promise to be right here beside you."

Upon arrival to the Med Bay on the *Maelstrom*, Datrem had both females placed in regen beds.

Emeline's treatment would take approximately eight hours, and if she was doing well, he would release her in the morning.

Kissing her forehead, Nox gave her hand one final squeeze before the regen bed's transparent cover descended from the ceiling, completely encasing her in the healing process.

With his chin in his hand, Nox stood, gazing thoughtfully at his bondmate. She looked infinitely better now that she was clean...her ruined clothes gone, Senta having deposited them in the recycle bin. None of them needed another reminder of the last few days.

The room itself was beginning to feel crowded as more returning soldiers came in to have various injuries healed. Ami and Liam had moved off to the side, trying to stay out to the way.

Once the medical team had Emeline situated, the two of them came over to stand on either side of Nox.

Liam looked down helplessly at his sweet baby sister lying in an alien healing device. "Will she feel any pain?" he asked, his face awash with concern.

Standing at the foot of the bed typing into a medical tablet, Datrem adjusted the beam that emanated out of a rectangular device that protruded from the ceiling. Without taking his eyes off the three of them, he explained how the process would work. "This beam will assess her injuries... sending all her data to ARI. ARI will then map out a series of healing therapies needed for Emeline to make a complete recovery. Once the diagnostics are completed, we will begin healing her injuries on the cellular level using nanotechnology. When her healing is completed, all the nanites will be extracted. As I said, it should take approximately eight hours and no, Liam, she will not feel any pain. She will sleep through the entire process."

Leaning into Liam, Ami pursed her lips, watching the beam move back and forth along her friend's body. "Doctor, how is she going to feel when...that thing finishes?"

Making a final check of the unit, Datrem turned to look at the three of them—each face as somber as the next. Giving them his typical grandfatherly smile, he tried to reassure them. "Emeline will be fine...thanks to her quick thinking. That's what really saved her life. She will feel some fatigue for a few days. Physically, she will fully recover, but I must caution you, emotionally, only she will know. Just take it easy with her. Let her set the pace. She's strong—quite remarkably really. Her survival skills are impressive."

Datrem rubbed his chin as he regarded Liam. "I've heard about your skills at training females. If you have time later, I have a proposal I'd like to run by you."

Liam pulled back, surprised, not to mention flattered. "Thanks, Doc. I'd like that. I'll contact you later." Looking at his sister, Liam was pleased that she was improving, but he had to agree with the doctor—it would take a long time before any of them recovered from this.

Not taking his eyes off his beloved, Nox wished desperately to crawl in beside Emeline and hold her tight, but he knew he had to allow the machine to do its job. He too agreed with the doctor's assessment—it would take a long time for any of them to recover from this terrible ordeal.

Sighing deeply, fatigue rolled off of Nox. Promising Datrem she would get plenty of rest, he emphasized, "Whether she wants to or not."

Giving Nox's shoulder a pat, Datrem gave him a wry smile. "I have every confidence that she will get the best care. My concerned is that she may get too much care. I would recommend that she take it easy. Try to keep things calm. No lectures." This was directed at Liam, whose face reddened.

Spearing Nox with a knowing look, Datrem continued his instructions. "Maybe let her get a full night of sleep before making any important decisions."

The embarrassed look on Nox's face matched that of Liam's. Ami, who had been listening intently, burst out laughing, causing a chain reaction from the males around her. It was a welcome sound after so much misery.

Coming into the room, Jagger was surprised to hear laughter. "I take it the news is good—Emeline is better?" He moved over to stand beside Nox.

With a weary smile, Nox extended his arm in greeting. "It's good to see you, my friend." Jagger had played a vital role in the rescue mission. His mastery at coordinating so many star fighters resulted in the disabling of all the Hexian ships. "She's better. The doctor was just telling us that eight hours in the regen bed will heal the rest of her wounds."

"That's terrific news." Turning to Liam and Ami, Jagger could see that the humans were exhausted. "Liam, Ami— it's good to see you." Looking them up and down, he inquired, "Did either of you sustain any injuries?"

Liam shook his head no.

Ami pointed to the back of her leg where her armor had

taken the hit from the Hexian mercenary she'd killed. "Just minor. The guy who did this got the worst of it."

The looks she got from the males around her were a mixture of curiosity, pride, and a healthy dose of awe. Feeling slightly uncomfortable, Ami turned to look at Emeline in the hopes of shifting the focus away from herself.

Seeing her discomfort, Nox quickly asked Jagger if he had any updates from Tarek. "Has there been any word on Tarquin?" Nox's tone was unforgiving. Tarquin would pay for what he did to Emeline and Violia. He glanced over to where Violia lay receiving treatment. He knew he had to find a way to forgive her. She'd earned it.

The entire room went silent—everyone anxious to hear the report from Tarek. "There's still no sign of Tarquin. It's like he's vanished. They're searching the ship for him, but so far nothing. He will fill us in when he gets back. He wants all elite team members to meet in the officers' rec room for dinner tomorrow night at seven sharp. I believe he said something about Liam and his mother's famous lasagna." Jagger gave Liam a piercing look as he asked hungrily, "What is lasagna?"

Ami nearly drooled on herself describing to Jagger how yummy it was with layers of pasta, different meats, two difference sauces, red and white. Add to that lots of gooey cheese. "Garlic bread—right, Liam?"

"Of course."

"And lots of it, cause I'm really hungry for some reason."

More laughing lightened the mood of the room. Jagger rubbed his abdomen, informing Liam he was looking forward to dinner. After telling them to get some rest, he left the room, followed closely by Ramola and Nyx.

Pulling a chair close to Emeline's bed, Nox sat down heavily. With his head in his hands, elbows on his knees, he closed his eyes, just for a moment.

Ami stood back with her hand on her chin, pondering Nox, his body swayed first to one side, then slowly back, wondering how long before he fell on his face. "I don't know, Liam, you think he's gonna fall over?"

Liam turned, following her eyes. Giving her a short laugh, he shook Nox's shoulder. "Hey, man. Why don't you go get some sleep? I'll stay here with her."

Nox jolted awake, his eyes slightly unfocused. "Huh. What?" Confused for a second, he focused on Emeline before looking from Ami to Liam. "No—thanks anyway. I promised her I'd be here when she woke up." Nox pushed a button on the armrest. The top of the chair elongated at the same time as a footrest appeared, turning the chair into a sleep lounger. Settling back in the chair with his arm over his head, Nox couldn't help but gaze longingly at Emeline. "I won't leave her."

"I know how you feel." Liam moved closer to his sister's bed. It felt like a miracle watching her bruises start to fade, leaving behind white unmarred skin—almost as if she had never been beaten or shot.

Ami was inspecting the beam, making a mental note to ask Loris about the properties of the device. He had a wealth of knowledge. Between him and ARI, Ami had learned so much in the last few weeks, she thought her head would explode. "You know, this stuff is so surreal. Just look at her wrist. It's almost back to normal." Lowering her voice, Ami fought back the horror at what her friend had faced, "God, that had to have hurt—I don't know if I want to know how she got that."

Liam looked over and saw that Nox had fallen asleep. One of his arms had fallen onto his lap, while the other rested atop his head. Taking Ami's hand, he pulled her out into the corridor. "Let's let them rest. There's nothing we can do right now." Grabbing her by both arms, Liam gave Ami the once-over. "How are you?" Pulling her in for a tight hug, he murmured into her ear, "I am so damn proud of you."

Squeezing her arms tight around him, Ami leaned in,

letting out a long breath. "That was some crazy shit."

"Don't I know it." A shadow crossed his face. He couldn't stop thinking of all those people on the freighter.

Noticing the curious looks they were getting, Liam knew this probably wasn't the best place for them to talk. Besides, they both looked ready to keel over. "Ami, let's talk tomorrow. We both need to clean up and grab some shut-eye. Meet me in the kitchen tomorrow at five?"

"Sure."

"Will you do the salad?"

Rolling her eyes because she knew he hated making salads—it's just easier to buy them already made was his usual answer—she agreed, but with one condition, "Only if you make chocolate gelato for dessert."

"You're on."

They both headed towards their rooms, each one worn out, but very relieved that their ordeal was finally over. Emeline was home. "Now my only problem is how many pans of lasagna to make."

Ami giggled, "Well, whatever you're thinking, better double it."

"Better meet me at four then."

Emeline woke to two things. First, the excruciating pain that had been coursing through her body was gone. Second, the sound of her alien bondmate lightly snoring in the chair by her side. Her heart did a happy dance watching his face relaxed in a long-overdue rest. He was stretched out, still dressed in his armor. There were scuffs and dings dotted in various spots all over him, causing her to resist the urge to jump out of bed to do her own inspection.

Lying back, she did a quick inventory of her injuries. Shocked at the condition of her wrist, she wiggled it back and forth and then in a circle, marveling that it looked normal. She was sure she would never have full use of it again, especially the way it had been crushed. Still, considering he shot her twice, *the asshole*, she was lucky to be alive. *Violia!* The full memory of what happened came crashing back.

Looking across the room, Emeline could just make out Violia's still form lying in a bed similar to hers. Ezio was hovering around her bed, watching her intently. His face was creased with worry, which perplexed Emeline. She didn't realize that Ezio even knew Violia. It made her wonder why one of Tarek's elite soldiers would be assigned to guard Violia, especially considering her current condition. She didn't look like she'd be up to kidnapping anyone at this moment.

"You're awake."

Emeline was startled out of her thoughts at Nox's voice. "Hey." Her dry throat had her voice coming out in barely a whisper. In one fluid motion, he was out of his chair and leaning over her, his hands poised just shy of her face, too afraid to touch her.

"How are you feeling?" His eyes searching hers for any lingering pain.

Clearing her throat, Emeline tried to answer, but her words kept getting stuck.

Seeing her discomfort Nox reached for the water container that had been placed on a table beside him. With his body half on and off the bed, he helped her into a sitting position, supporting her in the crook of his arm so she could take a drink.

She'd obviously lost weight during her ordeal—the shirt that Dr. Senta had replaced her ripped and bloodied one with hung around her shoulders.

When she'd drunk her fill, Emeline pulled the glass away and leaned in to Nox's big warm body. God, how she had missed his touch, his smell—although taking a quick sniff, she thought it was time for both of them to hit the showers.

Pulling away, she swung her legs over the side of the

bed, her hand automatically rubbing the spot where Hagen had shot her. *No pain! Not even a twinge. Amazing.*

Nox reached out, taking her hand in his, unable to stop himself from touching her, and again asked, "How are you feeling? Do you have any pain?"

Testing out her voice again, this time it came out clearer. "No pain, which is weird considering I got shot—twice." Seeing him flinch, the residual anger he felt crept dangerously close to the surface, which he instantly tried to hide from her, but she wasn't fooled.

Quickly changing the subject, Emeline told Nox she needed to see how Violia was doing. Sliding her feet towards the floor, without warning, she found herself scooped up into Nox's arms. "What are you doing? I can walk you know."

"I know, but Dr. Datrem told us that you had to take it easy." He kissed her temple as he carried her over to Violia. "Please, Em, let me do this."

"Fine," she conceded. Besides, she didn't know what she was complaining about. She was exactly where she had been wishing to be—back in Nox's strong arms.

Standing next to Ezio, Nox turned so she could look down at Violia's sleeping form. They had removed her torn and dirty clothing and placed her in an outfit similar to Emeline's.

"How is she doing?" It was hard to imagine Violia looking any smaller lying so still on the bed. The only movement was the steady rise and fall of her chest. Her hair was still in the braid that Emeline had done for her—geez was that only yesterday? Emeline felt like she had lost all sense of time lately.

Ezio shook his head, seemingly unwilling to tear his gaze away from Violia. Speaking in a hushed tone, Ezio told them Datrem felt Violia would pull through, although Hagen's shot had done some major damage to her lower abdomen. They had been able to repair most of it. "She's been placed in a medically induced coma. She suffered so much blood loss." Ezio's hand covered his face for a brief moment before looking at Emeline and Nox, saying, "There was damage to some of her reproductive organs. They're not sure if she will ever be able to have children. Her ovary took most of the impact from the shot."

Emeline felt sick. "I'm so sorry. I don't know what to say." Looking from Nox to Ezio, tears welled in her eyes. With a heavy heart and a broken voice, Emeline looked down at Violia. "This is awful. It's going to destroy her. You know, she told me it was her dream to one day have a family of her own." Tears ran down Emeline's face. "Even dead, Hagen is still destroying lives."

Nox held her close as she cried into his shoulder. "What's going to happen to her?" Nox asked Ezio.

"I'm not sure. That will be up to the General to decide. I just hope that he'll show her some mercy—take into consideration the circumstances before he passes judgment." Ezio's bloodshot amber eyes locked on Emeline's. "Will you speak on her behalf to General Tarek?"

Ezio's voice, uncharacteristically pleading for such a war-hardened soldier, had Emeline's eyes widening in surprise. Wiping away the remainder of her tears, she assured Ezio that she would be having a long conversation with Tarek about his plans for Violia. "I know she kidnapped me, but she also saved me. That has got to count for something."

Unable to stop her curiosity, Emeline just had to ask, "Ezio, I didn't realize that you and Violia were close?"

His eyes were drawn to the tiny female lying so still on the bed. Gently caressing her hand, Ezio spoke softly, "We're not. I saw her for the first time yesterday on the Invidia." Exhaling a hard breath, he turned to face them, blurting out, "She's my bondmate."

Well, that declaration was met with shocked silence. They all stared at each other open-mouthed as Ezio held up his hand to them...pastel colors swirled subtly under his skin. Emeline squealed in delight...thrilled that she wasn't alone in the whole bondmating experience.

Ezio's head jerked up at Emeline's cry of happiness just as Dr. Datrem came out of his office, interrupting the moment.

Heading in their direction when he saw them, Datrem smiled broadly, saying, "Emeline, how are you feeling?"

Emeline gave Ezio a pointed look, letting him know this conversation was far from over before taking Datrem's hand in hers. Telling the doctor how much better she felt, she added her thanks to him for all that he had done to save her.

When her gaze dropped to Violia, Emeline's voice was quiet. "Ezio was just telling us about Violia. Do you think you'll be able to help her?"

Datrem shook his head dolefully, saying, "I'm not sure yet. We'll do everything we can. We just have to wait and see how well her body reacts to the healing." Moving over to one of the med bay beds, he patted the surface, indicating that Nox should put Emeline down. "Let me examine you."

Setting Emeline down on the bed, Nox was reluctant to let her go.

Datrem pulled in a breath as he gave Nox the once-over. Nodding his head in the direction of a door, he said, "Nox, why don't you go in and get cleaned up while I examine Emeline? You'll feel better and trust me, you'll smell better too."

Nox looked at Emeline, hoping she would tell him she didn't want him to leave her. He was sadly mistaken.

Giggling, which made him smile, she agreed with the doctor...giving him a gentle nudge, telling him, "Babe, seriously, go take a shower."

He sighed, growling out fine, he'd shower, but she wasn't to go anywhere or do anything until he got back.

Winking, she countered, "I'll be right here. Save me

some hot water. I plan on showering after you."

Nox shook his head, muttering to himself about humans and didn't they know they had unlimited hot water.

Emeline chuckled after him...a blissful sigh escaped her lips watching his very fine backside walk to the bathroom. Soon, she told herself, soon she would have Nox all to herself. Hearing a throat clearing, Emeline knew her cheeks were scarlet, but she didn't care. Not turning her eyes from Nox until the door was closed, she murmured wistfully to Datrem. "I honestly thought I would never see him again."

A warm hand landed on her shoulder, interrupting her musings. Turning, she saw understanding in his deep amber eyes. "How is Lilith?"

"She is safe." Patting the table, Datrem asked her to lie down so he could examine her. "Let me see how you are healing."

As he scanned her body, Datrem explained that even though her wounds were healed, she still required lots of rest. "I want you to take it easy for the next few days. No training and no major decisions until you've gotten at least a few good nights' sleep." He raised one eyebrow at her at that last part, adding, "I know you're eager to complete your bond with Nox."

"Yes, I am."

Frowning at her tone of determination, Datrem put down his scanner and crossed his arms. Waiting until he had her full attention, he said, "All I'm asking is that you give yourself some time to recover. You've had a major trauma to not only your body but to your psyche as well. Emeline—I'm talking to you not just as your doctor but as someone who has come to care for you as a friend."

Gently holding her hand, he urged her, "Take the time you need to come to grips with what has happened to you. I've been studying Earth's medical information. I believe you could experience post-traumatic stress disorder."

"PTSD." Emeline had seen first hand how devastating

PTSD could be having been around her brother and his military friends for so many years. She listened carefully to what Datrem was telling her.

"We have something similar that I have witnessed countless times over the years. You must allow not only your body to heal but also your mind as well. You were kidnapped and treated brutally—that is a fact that must be accepted."

Emeline couldn't keep her eyes from tearing up as some of the worst of the memories swirled through her mind. "I know." It came out in a harsh whisper. "Sometimes I can't stop the memories. They come in flashes when I least expect it." Her voice dropped low, causing Dr. Datrem to have to lean closer to hear her words. "It's like I'm caught in a riptide that I can't get out of. I feel like I'm drowning."

Gently rubbing her hand, trying to comfort her, Dr. Datrem told her that it was a perfectly normal feeling. "When you are ready, let me know. I'd like you to spend some time talking with Senta. She is one of our leading experts on the subject. I think it would be beneficial for you."

When the door to the bathroom opened in what was probably the fastest shower in the history of showers, Datrem leaned in, whispering, "I think it would be beneficial for the both of you."

Nodding her head in agreement, she turned to Nox, amusement dancing on her face. "That was quick. Was the dryer not working?"

He was clean but it looked like he hadn't bothered to dry himself. His hair dripped water randomly all over his shirt, which in turn got her wet when he sat beside her, pulling her tight against him. Kissing her temple, he whispered, "I saved you lots of hot water." Looking over at Datrem, Nox was anxious about Emeline's condition. "How is she, Doctor?"

After Datrem reassured him she was fine, he turned, asking if she was ready for a shower.

"Oh yes. More than ready."

Scooping her up in his arms, smiling at the squeak she let out at his unexpected move. Nox moved towards the bathroom.

Tapping him on the shoulder, she scolded him, "Nox, I can do this." Grabbing his cheeks in her hands, she made him stop and listen to her. "I need to do this—on my own. Babe, I know you want to help me, but I've got this. If I need any help, I'll yell for you." She wiggled in his arms to get her point across.

Nox wasn't convinced, assuring her he would be standing right outside the door in case she needed him.

Emeline made her way into the bathroom, ignoring the scowls from both Nox and Datrem. Closing the door behind her, she leaned heavily against it, fighting back the onslaught of tears that threatened to escape. This was the first time she had been alone since this whole ordeal started. *Let's just get through this. Now is not the time to have a freak-out meltdown. The last thing I need is the entire medical staff barging in here.*

Squaring her shoulders, Emeline turned on the shower and removed her clothes. Looking down at her naked body, there were only faint reminders of her injuries, and Datrem had said those would fade pretty quickly. Her finger traced the spot on her leg where she had almost bled to death. Alien technology really was quite remarkable.

Reaching up, she adjusted the shower spray, loving the feel of the hot water beating down on her. Standing there feeling the pounding of the spray washing away not only the blood and grime but also taking with it some of the pain and sorrow she still carried within her, she had to agree —Datrem was right with his assessment. This was something she would carry inside forever, but she would learn to live with it. It would be hard. It would take time. *Maybe talking to Senta wouldn't be such a bad idea.*

Grabbing the shampoo, she vigorously scrubbed her

scalp, determined to remove all reminders of Hagen. She had her life back. She was alive and back with Nox and her family. She just had to keep reminding herself that she wasn't alone and Hagen was dead. Thanks to Ami, his reign of terror was over.

Hearing a gentle knock on the door, Emeline smiled to herself. *Nox.*

"Emeline, are you all right?"

"Yes." Silence. She knew he wanted to be in here helping her, but he was respecting her space. Her heart melted in her chest. Grinning, she called out, "You can come in if you want."

The door opened and closed almost immediately, Nox's large body filling the steamy room. "Can I help you with anything?"

"I'm almost done. Is there anything clean for me to put on?" Shutting off the water, Emeline stepped out and was immediately pulled into Nox's warm embrace.

Pressing her body into his, her words muffled against his shirt, "I missed you so much." Holding back a sob, she fought for control. "I knew you would come."

Pulling her up tight against him, not caring that his clothes were getting soaked, Nox took his first full breath in what felt like days. She was back where she belonged—in his arms where she would stay forever. He held onto her, tight, vowing never to let her go. "I was so afraid I wouldn't get there in time." His voice was rough as he tried to tamp down his emotions, but it was like trying to hold back a leak in a dam.

Clinging to him, she cried into his broad chest, "Oh Nox, I never had any doubt."

Her lips found his, gentle at first, but she wanted more, needed to feel alive. Pressing her lips hard to his, her tongue demanded he open for her...he did. Their kiss became frenzied, wild and untamed.

"Emeline, Nox, is everything okay?" Datrem's concerned

voice called through the closed door.

Pulling back, both of them breathless, she managed to call out, "Umm—be right out." Giving Nox a sexy smile telling him that they'd pick this up later, she tried to extricate herself from his embrace.

Grabbing the clean shirt and pants that Nox had gotten for her, she slipped into them. Giving up trying to tame her hair, she pulled it into a wet ponytail.

Leaning into Nox as he stood watching her with hooded eyes, Emeline ran her hand down his long beautiful body. Feeling his desire hard against her fingers, she winked up at him as her fingers began a naughty dance.

Swallowing hard, he put his hand over hers, gently prying her fingers away. Kissing each fingertip, his hot breath ignited her senses. His silky voice warned her she was playing with fire.

"If you keep that up, we'll never leave this bathroom." Leaning down, he growled softly into her ear, "I don't think you want all of medical to hear me making you scream my name."

Giving him a sassy look, which made Nox's heart stutter, Emeline giggled as he reached over and scooped her up. She shrieked in surprise as she hung on tightly to his neck. "We better get out of here before they send in the troops."

Nox opened the door, his arms full of his giggling bondmate. The sight of the two of them caused smiles to break out around the room.

Datrem patted the table he was standing next to, indicating where Nox should put Emeline down. "I want you to have a nutrient drink before you leave."

Motioning for Tulio to bring one over to him, Datrem turned, telling them, "This won't take long, and then I promise to release you. But only if you promise to remember what I told you—the both of you."

They both nodded, promising to consider his advice.

Datrem smiled, glad that they were taking his words

seriously. The twinkle that appeared in his eye as he watched the two of them together gave him hope for his granddaughter Lilith. If she was half as strong as this human female, with love and support, she would come through this. He'd do everything he could to help her.

After finally getting her walking papers, Emeline and Nox walked hand in hand down the corridor towards their room, eager to get their life back to normal. First up, a long hot soak in the arms of her sexy alien.

But as the door to their room opened, reality slapped her—hard—in the face. Everywhere she looked were re-minders of her interrupted plan. They were supposed to have completed their bond—become one forever. *Do I even know what I want now?*

Emeline's eyes took in the rose petal heart in the center of their bed. It made her sad to see it now. What was supposed to signify hope and love instead looked lonely and forgotten. The petals no longer supple...their bright red color dulled to a dark brownish rust, their edges curled tight. Specks of dried flowers dotted the stark white bed like the blood on her shirt that she had used as a tourniquet to save her life.

Emeline instantly flashed back to Tarquin's office. Blood —Hagen.

Inwardly shuddering, she shook off the memory, her fingers gently stroking the nightie she had created for Nox. *He must have found this in the replicator and put it on the bed. Oh Nox, what you must have felt when you came in and saw all of this.*

Looking up, she saw him standing just inside the door. Her heart ached for the unwitting pain she had caused him. Not moving, his hands clenched at his sides...watch-ing wordlessly as she wandered around the room tenderly picking up all the small touches she had created for their bonding.

Putting down the framed picture of their selfie, Emeline

rushed over to him. Slipping her fingers into his, she asked softly, "Will you hold me?" She was desperate to be surrounded by his warmth.

When he hesitated, Emeline reached up, looping her arms around his neck. Pulling his eyes down to hers, his emotions warred with his body, unsure of what to say or do...waiting to take his cues from her.

What a sweet, caring person. Never has a man loved me like he does. I want him. [laugh] I guess that would be a YES to my question.

Her feelings for Nox were akin to a glowing ball of energy that she could hold in her hands. As she moved the ball, encircling her body with it, a thin stream of golden energy particles followed, encasing her in a shiny cocoon.

Smiling at her image of how the bond would bind them together, Emeline melted into Nox's arms. "It feels so good to be back in your arms again. I've missed you so much," she said softly.

They clung to one another, basking in the simple joy of being together again.

Turning her head to the side, her eyes landed on the fist-size indentation in the wall next to the replicator. "Um, Nox?" She pulled back, gazing up at him with more than mild curiosity.

"Hmm." He was peppering her neck with kisses, sending shivers coursing all the way to her toes.

"Why is there a hole in the wall?"

She felt his body stiffen, then relax as he blew a sorry against her skin as he continued his mission to reacquaint himself with her lovely body.

"Did it help?" Her arms stretched around his body, squeezing him tight.

Pulling his head back and then resting his chin on the top of her head, he huffed out, "No."

Emeline laughed into his shirt as she explored his back with her hands, letting him feel her...letting him know that she was here with him.

Stepping back, she asked curiously, "Which one was it?" Seeing his right hand clench, she leaned down, gently kissing each knuckle. "Good thing you had a regen device, huh?"

He looked away embarrassed, murmuring, "It wasn't my finest moment."

She knew exactly what he meant, having experienced a few of those herself in the past few days. Getting herself shot—twice—was a prime example. Her finger moved unconsciously, pressing first to her shoulder before moving to her thigh. She should have died. If not for the portable regen device, she would have bled out on the floor of Tarquin's office.

"Where did you go just then?"

His question caught her by surprise. "You saw that, huh?"

Nodding, he released her when she pressed on his arms.

She moved over and stood by the window, gazing out, lost in the moment. Having been stuck in windowless rooms for the past few days, she had missed this—this familiar view of the stars. She'd gotten used to all those twinkling lights being the last thing she saw before falling asleep each night in Nox's arms. A happy sigh escaped her lips knowing this would be her view when she closed her eyes tonight.

Turning back to Nox, she headed in the direction of the bathroom, calling over her shoulder to him, "Come on. That shower in the med bay was nice, but what I could really use is a nice hot soak...with you." She grinned as Nox stalked toward her, saying her wish was his command.

Walking over to the tub, she reached for the control panel only to be stopped by Nox.

Taking her gently by the arm, he guided her over to the small fabric-covered stool that sat in front of her vanity table. "Here, why don't you sit and rest. Let me do this for you." Kissing the top of her head, he caught her eyes in his, silently imploring her to let him take care of her.

Turning back to the panel, Nox selected a few commands. Water began to flow into the tub from a wide faucet that had appeared from a hidden pocket set into the wall. Pouring their favorite vanilla-scented bath soap into the tub, the room was soon filled with the delicate fragrance he loved so much.

Murmuring a thank you, Emeline was more than ready for someone else to be in charge. After the horrors of the last few days, it was time to replace all the bad memories with new ones.

Relaxing into the chair, she could feel the tension in her body begin to loosen as steam filled the room. The faint scent of vanilla wafted up, causing her eyes to drift shut. Smiling, she allowed herself a brief moment to just breathe in that wonderful aroma that reminded her so much of Nox. With her clothes beginning to stick to her body, Emeline reached her hand up to undo her shirt.

As the tub started to fill, Nox came over and hunched down in front of her, gently brushing her hand away as he touched her shirt. Her eyes snapped open at his touch, her body jerking slightly.

Stilling his hands, he waited for her to settle. In a quiet voice, he told her, "It's okay. I've got you." Peering into her eyes, he was wary at what he would see. So many emotions whirled through the both of them, but looking into her startled blue eyes, his heart broke a little more when he saw her trying to hide her anxiety from him. He knew she didn't want to burden him with all the turmoil that rolled through her. It was so like her, but right now, it needed to be about her.

Emeline pressed her hand to his chest. "I know. I'm sorry. I guess I just—I don't know what." Swallowing hard, she stood holding onto Nox's shoulder, saying softly, "Let me do it."

Her shirt and pants hit the floor leaving her standing naked in front of him. Her body shivered, but not from the cold. She felt exposed...vulnerable.

Nox drew her into his strong arms and held her close until her body relaxed against his, his fingers stroking lightly along her side trying to reassure her. "Whenever you're ready, I will be here to listen to anything you want to tell me."

"I know you will. I just don't know what I'm feeling right now."

"I can tell."

"What do you mean?"

"Our bond—it's very strong even though we haven't fully completed it yet." Peering into her eyes, he chuckled at the suspicious look she gave him. "Since I've never had a bondmate before, this is all new to me, too. I'm not sure if it's the fact that you're human or if this is normal, but your feelings have a tendency to shout at me at times."

Emeline's mouth dropped open. *Oh god. Not all of them, I hope.*

"Yup, even those too." He watched her face flush a lovely shade of pink at some of the more indecent thoughts she'd had about him.

Mortified, she hid her face in his shoulder, her voice muffled. "I'm sorry. I'll try to rein it in some."

"Don't you dare." His hands came up around each of her biceps, pulling her back slightly. "I want all of you, good, bad, happy, sad." Staring down at her naked body flushed from the heat of the steam, Nox's voice came out husky, "Especially your thoughts of us being together. Please, don't ever try to hide your emotions from me."

Looking deep into his beautiful amethyst eyes, Emeline nodded her head, whispering, "As long as you never hide from me."

"I promise." He could feel their bond strengthening the more they were together. His hand moved to cradle her chin as his thumb moved slowly over her bottom lip. "I love you so much." Leaning in, he brushed his lips lightly against hers.

Her lips tingled at his touch...her tongue snuck out, stealing a quick taste from him. There wasn't enough time to complete their bond right now—that would come later tonight when they would have no interruptions. *Damn you and your lasagna, Liam.* Pressing herself against his hard body, Emeline pushed all thoughts out of her mind...focusing her full attention on what was right in front of her.

Deepening their kiss, she groaned into his mouth. This was what she needed, to take back her control, and being here with Nox, knowing how much he loved her, needed her—this was the first step.

Stepping back, she pulled at his shirt. "Clothes. Off. *Now.*"

His eyes never left hers as his clothes fell to the floor. In a flash, they were in each other's arms, skin on skin, their bodies trembling with need. He loved how easily she gave herself to him, trusted him.

Frowning, Nox knew deep down he didn't deserve her trust. He had failed her...failed at protecting her from the Hexians, failed at protecting her from Hagen's abuse. That was on him. Unconsciously his body tensed as he tried to silence his inner voice.

"Nox?"

Fully aware she could feel his unease, Nox silently shook his head, not ready to share his thoughts just yet.

Feeling the sudden heaviness that hung between them, Emeline cupped his face, murmuring, "I think we need to slow down for a minute."

Nodding, Nox walked over to the tub, climbing in as Emeline clung to him.

Settling back against the side, he slid them both into the soothing hot water. Sighing at the same time, they both laughed, letting their bodies adjust to not only the heat of the water but to being together again.

Nuzzling her nose into the crease of Nox's neck, she breathed in his scent...her tongue snaking out slowly, savoring his taste. *God, how I missed this.* She felt his hands holding her, letting her set the pace, although, he did have a pretty firm grip on her backside. Not that she was complaining. She loved the feel of her big sparkly alien, his muscled body hard against her softness. Snippets of hot water tried to find space between where her breasts were pressed tightly against his broad chest.

Closing her eyes, Emeline looked deep within herself at their bond and for the first time felt the tremendous fear and heavy guilt that surrounded her bondmate. A sudden realization slammed into her—it wasn't just her and Violia that has been affected by her kidnapping. Everyone around her was suffering. Hagen and the Hexians tried to ruin so many lives. Even Tarquin, regardless of how he had saved her, deserved his share of the blame. Whatever his reason for wanting Earth's salt, it wasn't worth killing for it.

As Emeline lay contemplating this new insight, she could feel Nox's body stiffen. Glancing up, she saw by his expression that he was deep in thought. She knew he dwelled in a place that only led to continued pain. It was time they opened up to one another and cleared the air between them, knowing in her heart it was the only way they could move forward. She also knew some of it was going to be hard for Nox to hear.

Like how she had allowed Hagen to touch her. In her defense, though, it was just to get close enough to cause damage. Emeline grimaced at the image of Hagen lying on the floor in the fetal position, his hand covering his groin. He hadn't stayed down though. If Tarquin hadn't come in...her body shivered as memories started playing like a scary movie. She tried to stop them, but images of the last few days began whirling through her mind. "I'd never met anyone so cruel before."

It came out in a mere whisper. If Nox hadn't exhaled sharply at her words, she might have thought he hadn't heard her. When his arms tightened around her body, she could feel him desperately trying to contain his swirling emotions. A feat easier said than done, especially knowing his feelings at the thought of another male touching her.

Gathering her courage, Emeline quietly began to speak. Maybe it was the soothing bath or maybe it was because she felt safe in his arms, who could tell, but the words began to flow. When she came to the part where Violia's grandmother died, her voice broke—tears streamed down her cheeks.

He listened, never interrupting her, even through the hard stuff. She felt him trying to shield his feelings from her, but she felt every single one of them. Some made her sad at his anger, his fear and helplessness. While others gave her strength and courage at his pride in how she had defended herself and Violia. And still interlaced throughout was an overwhelming feeling of guilt.

When she'd finished, Emeline lifted her face to his. Sitting up quickly, her fist to her mouth, she stifled a sob at the sight of the tears staining his devastated face. She flung her arms around his neck, crying out his name, only to be soothed hearing her name in return. They clung to one another, their mingled tears a balm to their battered souls.

Emeline was the first to sit up, the warm water coming up just above her breasts, hiding them from view. She needed him to understand the facts about her kidnapping. They were scientists after all—examining facts was what they did. Fact number one: Her kidnapping was not his fault. Fact number two: He couldn't put her in a bubble for the rest of her life.

With gentle fingers, she smoothed away the wetness on his cheeks, telling him, "Babe, you really don't think that my kidnapping was your fault, do you? I mean, come on, you're the one who saved me. If you hadn't come along when you did, I would be dead."

Nox turned his face into her palm, shuddering at the mere thought of losing her. "It is my fault for what happened." He sat up straighter, causing Emeline to tilt backwards, losing her balance. His arm shot out, catching her before she fell backwards, causing water to splash up into their faces. They looked at each other, water droplets hanging off their eyelashes, making it hard to see. Bursting out laughing—the happy sound echoing off the walls.

Swiping at the water on her face, Emeline leaned in, kissing the skin over his heart. "It feels so good to laugh with you again."

Running his hand down his face, Nox took several cleansing breaths. "Yes, it is." Taking a more serious tone, Nox felt he owed Emeline an apology. "Em, I'm sorry for not protecting you. It's my fault that you were left alone on the ship that day. I should have been more diligent."

"No, Nox. You know that's not true. There was nothing you could have—"

He silenced her with steely look—he needed to have his say whether she agreed with him or not. "I never should have left you alone. If I had taken more precautions then Violia never would have been able to take you. You almost died." That last word came out harsher than he'd meant.

Emeline didn't know if he would listen to reason, but she had to try. "Nox, you can't control everything. I mean, come on, what are you going to do, lock me in a room, or better yet keep me tied to your side all day?"

Not hesitating for a second, Nox yelled, "Yes—if I thought it would work, that's exactly what I'd do."

Getting her dander up, she retorted, "Well I'm a grown-ass woman. I make my own decisions."

"Not if it means I can't keep you safe," he shot back intensely, showing just how agitated he was. The laughter from a few moments ago was gone, replaced by the anger and guilt that had been festering inside him.

Normally an independent woman like Emeline would never let anyone speak to her this way, but this was Nox, her bondmate. She could see that the stress of the last few days had finally taken its toll. Deciding she needed to take a calmer approach, Emeline ran her hands up and down his arms, trying not only to soothe him but also her own nerves. "Nox," she said quietly, "I know you want to protect me. Trust me, I can feel you. I'm not the only one whose feelings get loud." She quirked her eyebrow at him. "But sometimes things happen, people happen, shit happens." She held her finger against his lips as he tried to interrupt her. "Let me finish, please."

"Fine," Nox said begrudgingly, giving in and kissing her finger.

Smiling inwards, Emeline tried to drive her point home. "Let's say you knew I was going to the botany lab with Violia that day. Say I called you and you said great, we'll meet back in our room. You know what? Violia still would have kidnapped me. There was nothing anyone of us could have done. And trust me when she gets better, she and I will be having a long discussion about some of her recent choices. But besides all that, we can't be together all the time." Taking his cheeks between her hands, her eyes beseeching him to hear her words, she said, "I love you so much and I know you love me. I know you want to protect me, but you can't be with me all the time, no matter how much I want you to."

Placing his hands on her shoulders, Nox leaned in, pressing his forehead to hers. "Oh, Em, I know I'm being irrational. I was just so scared for you. It's been eating at me —all that you've had to go through. I just want you safe and happy. When I found out that Violia had taken you, you can't imagine how helpless I felt—how afraid I was for you. Then when I saw you on the comm unit, I saw your pain. I felt it in here." He tapped his hand over his heart. "I can't help but to take some of the blame. You were new on this ship. Not only that, you had just found out that there were other species out in the universe. It was my—"

"Don't you dare say I'm your responsibility or so help me I will smack you."

"I wasn't, but it's a good word."

Emeline crossed her arms, her lips pulled down annoyed at where this was going. She was beginning to lose patience with him. There was more than enough blame to go around, and Nox wasn't even on the list. She started down the list of all the people she could blame for what happened as he lay there making harrumphing sounds at every name.

"Nox, don't you get it? You were the only thing keeping me sane. Seriously, babe." She leaned in and kissed each of her points across his smooth skin, leaving goosebumps in her wake. She knew she was getting through to him as she leaned forward, rubbing against his growing desire that was pressed hard against her belly. "There were times thoughts of you were the only thing keeping me alive. You have nothing to feel guilty about. It was knowing how much you love me—that's what helped get me through the worst of it."

Sighing reflectively, Nox knew she was only trying to make him feel better. He watched her expressive eyes... accepting that she truly meant every word. It still amazed him that this human female had somehow become the love of his life. "Thank you for saying that."

Taking her face in his hands, holding her as if she were a delicate flower, Nox caught his gaze with hers. "My Pulmina, you have been through so much in the last few weeks. You were so brave, so fierce."

"Pulmina?" She let his words flow through her, expelling some of the sorrow that had been weighing her down. "Pulmina." She tested the word on her tongue. Her translator chip didn't have a translation for it, but she liked the word. It had a sensuous feel to it, especially the way Nox let it roll off his tongue. "What does that mean?"

A soft laugh escaped his lips. Leaning down, he whispered into her ear, "It means beautiful girl."

"I've never heard that word before. How come my chip doesn't translate it?"

"It's a very old word that isn't used any longer."

Crinkling her forehead, Emeline asked, "So where did it come from?"

Brushing featherlike kisses across her nose, he said, "Delicians have been around for many millennia and so their language has evolved over time. My father's family can trace their lineage back to ancient times, and trust me when I tell you their homes are overflowing with heirlooms. One rainy day, I was rummaging through the library when I found a small book. The writing was faded but a few words were still legible. The word Pulmina stood out dark against the faded pages. It means someone having a beautiful soul."

Looking deep into her shining eyes, his lips curved into a tender smile, his voice laced with the love he felt for her. "That's what you are to me—my Pulmina...beautiful inside and out."

The soft light from the room illuminated Emeline's face...alight with her first real smile since her kidnapping. Reaching over, she drew Nox's head down to hers, her lips devouring his, loving how firm they felt against hers.

As she stretched her body out along his, her need for him grew. Her hands smoothed up along the contours of his hard body, marveling in the fact that her alien didn't have an ounce of fat on him...anywhere.

Tangling her fingers in his hair, she deepened their kiss. Her tongue danced with his...tasting, sucking, loving the flavor that was all Nox. That familiar ache that only he could elicit from her began as a slow burn...quickly building into a fiery blaze.

Sitting up, her legs straddled his hips as she rubbed

her core against his growing hardness. Her smoldering eyes letting Nox know exactly where her intensions were headed.

A small gasp escaped as Nox's fingers danced up and down her smooth back before moving up to cup her breasts. Her gasp turned into a full-out moan when he rolled her nipples between his fingers. When his tongue replaced his fingers, it created a spark so strong, it pulsed directly to that bundle of nerves, causing her body to rock back and forth searching for more. As pleasure shuddered through her body, a massive orgasm started to build.

Holding her lover's gaze as his fingers roamed down along her hip...a trail of fire followed in their wake, she became breathless in anticipation of his final destination.

Beep, beep, beep

They froze, their ardor cooling immediately at the unexpected sound. The events of the last few days were still too fresh for them not to be on high alert.

Beep, beep, beep

Reaching over and picking up his wrist comm, Nox pushed audio only when he saw it was Liam. "What?"

"Sorry. Didn't mean to interrupt but dinner is ready and everyone is waiting—and hungry, if you catch my meaning."

Emeline giggled when Nox playfully squeezed her butt.

Dropping a kiss to his nose, she sighed heavily before pushing away from him. "Looks like we'll have to pick this up again after dinner."

Climbing out of the bath, she stood before the dryer, amazed at how quickly the water evaporated off her skin. "We'll be there in ten," she yelled as she ran out of the room to get dressed.

Nox sat in the cooling bath, watching the lovely backside of his bondmate disappear into their bedroom, sarcastically telling Liam thanks for calling. Hearing a sharp laugh before the call ended, Nox slapped the water hard, willing his overstimulated body to calm. Blowing out a heavy sigh, he wasn't sure how he would get through dinner tonight. Maybe they could eat fast.

"Hey, babe, we gotta get moving."

Nox's mouth dropped open, his desire flaring back to attention at the sight of her. She wore a simple cocktail dress that fell to mid-calf. It was a blue and white floral print that matched perfectly to her eyes. Her blond hair fell softly around her shoulders as she came in to push him along. Personally, he would have been more than happy to stay right where he was, but he knew she was anxious to see Liam and Ami.

Standing up, he saw the way Emeline straightened, her gaze locked on his body as he stood there, the water cascading down his long torso. He loved the look on her face when she realized she gotten caught staring. Giving her a sly smile, he asked, "How hungry are you?"

Laughing out loud, Emeline turned to leave, calling over her shoulder, "I'm starved...and not just for food."

CHAPTER 25

Officers' rec room

Quickening her pace, Emeline knew they were in for a major ribbing for being late. "You realize that Ami and Liam are going to give us so much grief for being late for dinner—you know that right? I can already hear the wisecracks now from Jagger and Nyx." Groaning, she lightly slapped her hand to her head, telling him, "Oh god, don't even get me started on what Tarek is going to say."

Rolling his eyes, Nox knew she was right. "Yes, I'm well aware. In fact, why don't we at least make it worth the aggravation?"

Which is how Emeline found herself backed up against the wall with Nox's fingers in her hair, plundering her mouth like a thirsty man finally given a drink. Not that she was complaining, mind you. With her senses on overload, so into Nox's kiss, she didn't notice the hidden smiles of the crewmembers who had to scoot around them to get by.

General Tarek just happened to be standing by the door pouring himself a glass of Delician ale as it swooshed open. His normally serious expression was replaced by one of amusement as Emeline floated into the room. Her lips red and swollen, her hair mussed, with that unmistakable dazed giggly look on her face telling everyone, yup I just got ravaged by my sexy alien. "It's about time you two got here. If I had to stand here smelling this lasagna much longer, we'd be starting without you." His chuckle had Emeline's cheeks flaming red, especially when Jagger and Nyx along with Ramola started trying to outdo each other with their bawdy jokes.

It was Liam who came to the rescue, pushing his way

through the group who had crowded around Nox and Emeline, calling out, "All right, you clowns...that's my sister you're talking about." He ignored their laughter and joking as he reached for his sister.

Liam! She launched herself at him, knowing he would catch her because that's what big brothers did. The rest of the group stepped back, giving the siblings a moment of privacy for their family reunion. With her arms wrapped tight around Liam's neck, Emeline pressed her cheek against his, breathing in his familiar scent of home. Swallowing her urge to bawl like a baby, she whispered against his skin, "I thought I'd never see you again."

"That was never going to happen." Liam's overzealous bear hug elicited a yelp out of her, a sound that silenced the room, getting Liam a guarded frown from Nox. Ignoring Nox, Liam set Emeline down gently, kissing the top of her head. "Don't ever scare me like that again, brat."

"Hey—don't blame me," Emeline mumbled defiantly. Stepping back, she playfully swatted his arm, giving him the *I'm the little sister and you have to love me* look. "I was just minding my own business."

"Yeah right, and I just flew an alien spaceship. Oh wait, that's right—I did just fly an alien spaceship." Liam smirked at her, crooking that one eyebrow that for some reason only he and their mother could do. The one that mimicked the look Fiona gave you when she knew you were trying to put one over on her.

"What?" Covering half her mouth with her hand, she whispered, "No way! Nyx let you fly?" Giving Tarek a quick side glance, she asked covertly, "Does the General know?"

Whispering to each other like little kids telling secrets, he replied, "Yes, he knows."

"And wait until you find out what else he did." Ami came over, pulling Emeline in for a tight hug before she pushed her away, swatting her in the arm.

"Ouch. What did you do that for?" Emeline rubbed her

arm mainly just for show, knowing Ami would never deliberately hurt her—well, unless they were in the training room. Then all bets were off. Seeing Nox start in her direction, she shook her head at him, mouthing *"I'm fine."*

"That was for getting yourself kidnapped and almost killed," Ami snapped back.

"Well, it's not like I did it on purpose," Emeline returned.

Sighing like the martyr she felt like, Ami countered with, "Just be glad I am such a good shot."

Emeline's middle finger playfully started to rise, causing all three of them to burst out laughing.

The two women began chatting away in the kitchen, happy to be back together again, while Liam put the finishing touches on dinner. Ami threw a barrage of questions at Emeline from how she was really doing to what it felt like being in the regen bed to how she and Nox were doing. The whole time both women dodged the flick of Liam's fingers as they tried to steal a taste of his meat sauce. Emeline admired Ami's burgundy dress that accented the deep brown of her eyes, teasing her about playing with the replicator.

Ami and Liam filled her in on what had been happening since her kidnapping. Emeline was curious to hear all about how Ami ended up with Nox on Tarek's team. Hearing Ami describe how she had mastered the weapons simulator, Emeline congratulated her on showing the aliens just how badass human females could be.

All three humans were totally unaware just how fascinating they were to the Delicians. "Did you understand any of that?" Jagger nudged Nox who was watching the interaction between the humans, his gaze mostly focused on Emeline. Jagger leaned forward in his chair at the kitchen island, cupping a glass of Delician whiskey called Capum. It was similar in taste to an aged Scotch whisky, although the color was darker—more like a rich deep mahogany. The speed at which the humans were conversing in their native tongue confused Jagger. His translator implant was having trouble keeping up.

"Not at all. Must be a human thing." Nox shook his head in confusion, causing more laughter from the humans. "It's just refreshing to hear laughter again. If not for Ami's quick action, the outcome could have been very different." Nox quickly pushed that thought out of his mind.

Hearing Nox's compliment, Ami beamed with pride, feeling satisfaction at the praise for her recently acquired skills with their weaponry. "It's all in the practice."

Tarek shook his head in disagreement, telling everyone the humans played a vital role in defeating the Hexians.

Emeline looked at her brother, curiously asking, "What's he talking about? I know that Ami shot Hagen—what'd you do?"

"My human copilot here—well, he was just responsible for taking out a Hexian freighter that was trying to get to Earth." Nyx had come over trying to steal a piece of garlic bread that Ami had just taken out of the oven. "With one shot!" he said emphatically, popping a piece of the hot bread into his wide smiling mouth, groaning and holding his stomach as the delicious flavors melted on his tongue.

"Oh, this I've got to hear." Emeline wasn't about to let this go.

Embarrassed, Liam tried to shoo Nyx out of the kitchen area. "We can talk about that later. Right now, dinner is just about ready."

Nyx dodged Liam's swat as he went back to join the Delicians who were all trying to snag a piece of the yummy bread from Nyx's hand as he shoved the rest of it into his mouth.

"Em, can you pour the wine?" Liam asked, changing the subject, laughing at her giving him the two fingers to the eyes motioning *I'm watching you.*

After mouthing *"I'm sorry"* to Liam, Ami continued putting big hunks of buttery garlicky Italian bread into two huge baskets. The smell coming off the hot steamy bread was so mouthwatering it was a wonder she was able to even get it to the table with all the hungry males in the room.

But the real centerpiece to the entire meal were the steaming pans of Fiona Cameron's version of authentic Italian lasagna.

Taking the last pan out of the oven, Liam set it down next to the three other ones already on the counter. It was so hot, the mixture of beef, pork and veal married with seasoned tomato sauce covered in cheese that had crusted brown on the top, it bubbled up over the sides.

While Emeline had been talking with Ami and Liam, Nox had been discussing the UAP's reaction to the Hexian situation with Tarek.

Fatigue crept into Tarek's voice as he spoke. "I just finished up a long conversation with them. Needless to say, there is much concern within the Alliance." Fixing Nox with a serious stare, he asked, "Have you spoken to your father lately?"

Shrugging his shoulder, Nox told him Sandovar called a few times, but he'd been a little busy. "I will call him later—maybe tomorrow."

"See that you do. He's been stirring up controversary with the UAP about you going on this mission. Telling them that you're too valuable a scientist to be put in a combat position defending a primitive species." Tarek leaned back in his chair, running his fingers along the top of his glass of ale as he contemplated Nox's father. "This seems totally out of character for Sandovar, don't you think?"

Nox considered Tarek's question, knowing he was making a valid point. "I don't get it. I haven't heard from him in ages. Why now? And why all of a sudden does he play the concerned father?" Nox cocked his head at Tarek. "Makes me wonder what he wants."

Silence hung between them as they each contemplated Sandovar's sudden interest in his son's life.

Voicing his concerns to Nox, Tarek said, "It's his timing that makes me suspect his motives. Just something to consider before you speak to him. I haven't told anyone yet about Emeline being your bondmate. I assumed you'd want to do that yourself." Tarek's eyebrow quirked up questioningly.

With a relieved look, Nox nodded, saying, "Thank you. I will have to tell him, but I'm waiting until after we complete the bond." Giving Emeline a tender look, Nox told Tarek it was happening tonight.

"I thought Datrem said you should wait?" Nyx, who had been pouring himself another ale, reminded Nox. "I mean, she's only been back one day."

"You know young love, Nyx—or maybe you don't." Jagger winked at Nox before taking a sip of his own drink.

"It's also none of anyone's business either." Nox tried to look vexed, but the thought of finally having Emeline all to himself—well, his silly grin said it all. Tonight, he would make her his forever, a thought that caused the subtle colors to quicken along his opalescent skin.

Jagger pointed to Nox's face as a swathe of colors swirled across one cheek, disappearing into his hair. "Whoa, that's quite some color pattern you got going on there."

Batting Jagger's hand away from his face, Nox chuckled good naturedly to his friends, "Just wait until you find your own bondmates. We'll see who's laughing then."

Ignoring Jagger, Tarek returned to the topic of Sandovar. "You're going to have to talk to your father. You know this is going to anger him and why. In fact, I'm not even sure how the humans and the UAP are going to feel about this. There are going to be huge ramifications about interspecies bondmating." Tarek rubbed his hand down his tired face. "Emeline hasn't told anyone other than her brother and Ami, has she?"

"No, and I know—I know." Nox glanced over at Emeline, her lovely face relaxed as she teased Liam about whether his sauce was as good as their mother's. "I haven't had a chance to talk to her about my father yet. She has been dealing with so much. I wanted to give her at least one day without adding more drama and let's face it, Sandovar is all about drama."

"I know you want to protect her," Tarek said as he watched Emeline reading something on the side of a bottle she held in her hand. "At least consider what Datrem said about letting her set her own pace."

Standing at the sideboard, Emeline grabbed the two bottles of wine Liam had replicated and uncorked them. Picking up one of the corks, she put it to her nose, breathing in the aroma. Loving the heady bouquet, she smiled— *God how I love alien technology.* Bringing the bottles to the table, she poured a small amount into one of the glasses. Swirling the dark burgundy liquid around and around, she watched how the wine clung to the side of the glass, leaving a slight film in its wake. Putting her nose inside the glass, she closed her eyes, breathing in the smell given off by the fruitiness of the grapes mixed with oak from the barrel and possibly a touch of currants and plums.

Taking a small sip, allowing the wine to roll around on her tongue, she smiled at the hint of chocolate she tasted. The deep rich flavors showed themselves to her before she swallowed—loving that velvety feeling as it slid smoothly down her throat. A small sigh escaped her lips as she reveled in the delightful taste of the wine. Her pink tongue snuck out unconsciously, making sure to catch every drop. *It's good to be alive.* Looking up, she was surprised to have six pairs of multicolored eyes watching her...spellbound.

Flustered, Emeline's cheeks flushed, either from the wine or the unwanted attention, she wasn't sure. "What? Haven't you ever done a wine tasting before?"

"No," was the collective answer from the Delicians whose expressions ranged from thirst to curiosity, ending with lust. That last one coming from Nox, whose bright amethyst eyes stared hungrily at her mouth.

"Really? Wow. You guys don't know what you're missing." Emeline made a mental note to make sure she collected a good selection of wines to bring with her when they left for Delicia. Smiling at Nox, who was moving towards her, she was surprised to find herself bent her over his arm...her lips set ablaze in a searing kiss.

His back to the room, Nox reluctantly released her. Grinning from ear to ear at his success in stealing a kiss...a kiss that put a look of lustful wonderment on her beautiful face, Nox had never felt such happiness. Her body trembled in his arms, causing him to lean in for another taste— that was until the mood was shattered by the *woo hoos* and whistles, along with Liam yelling at Nox to stop mauling his sister.

Knowing her face was the color of Liam's sauce, Emeline rolled her eyes at them. Pushing out of Nox's arms, she picked up the wine and began pouring some into all the glasses.

Carrying a steaming pan of lasagna over to the table, Liam told everyone to grab a seat. No one had to tell these hungry Delicians twice as they all scrambled into empty chairs.

As the last pan was placed in front of Tarek, Liam asked if Ezio was coming.

Nodding his head yes, Tarek leaned down, his eyes closing as he savored the delicious smells wafting up from the pan in front of him.

"Do you think we should wait for him?"

Tarek shook his head as the door unexpectedly opened.

Ezio rushed in, his face drawn, haggard—bordering on frazzled. "I'm sorry I'm late." He had finally gotten out of his armor and cleaned up. Slipping into the empty chair next to Emeline, he slid an apologetic look to Tarek.

The table normally sat as many as 20 people, but now it was set for ten. Tonight's dinner was not open to their usual group of crewmembers. Tarek had specifically invited only a select few of his closest and most trustworthy team members to dinner. They still hadn't caught the mole, so Tarek wanted a tight rein kept on security. Tarek sat at the opposite end from Jagger, with Loris and Nyx on either side of him. Nox, Emeline and Ezio were across from Liam, Ami and Ramola.

Leaning back comfortably in his chair, Tarek toyed with his wine, studying the color as it swirled rhythmically in his glass. Following Emeline's guidance, Tarek savored the flavor of the wine. Pulling the glass from his lips, he murmured his pleasure, "This is delicious."

Emeline couldn't hide her smile as she noticed everyone following the General's lead. Picking up her own glass, she took a sip as she watched each of their faces as they inspected their wine. Loris was very analytical in his approach to the taste, making notes into his wrist comm. Emeline was sure by tomorrow he'd have a complete molecular breakdown of the wine. Nyx's approach was more of *let's just get to the drinking and save the smelling for later*. Jagger and Ramola were similar in that they mimicked Emeline's instructions exactly.

Seeing Ami watching the General's closed eyes, wide mouth pursed together savoring his wine, Emeline knew an outburst of laughter was coming. Shaking her head slightly at Ami, she saw her hesitate, instead taking a long slip of wine, smiling into her glass.

"What are you all doing?" Ezio asked, having missed Emeline's little show with the wine earlier.

Jagger pulled his nose out of his glass, telling him, "We're tasting a human drink called wine. You have to savor the smell before you can drink it." Seated next to Ezio, he pushed at the glass in front of Ezio. "Try it."

"You don't *have* to do this every time, but it is fun," Emeline teased.

"And we've been seriously lacking in fun lately." Tarek's words surprised everyone, since fun and the General wasn't any everyday occurrence. Standing up, Tarek set down his glass, looking directly at Emeline. "The UAP wanted me to extend its apologies to you. I would also like to give you my own apology as well."

"Tarek, please—you don't—" She paused when she saw the sincerity on his face.

"I do. You were on board my ship. Every person on this ship is my responsibility—no exceptions. Emeline, you are one of us now, and not because you are Nox's bondmate. It is so much more than that. You showed great courage when you were faced with extreme danger. I find you to be an amazing individual. I for one am happy that you'll be joining our little family here."

Tarek's heartfelt words only added to the love and acceptance Emeline had felt from the moment she had walked through the door. For the second time today, she realized how many people had been affected by the Hexians. Liam, Ami, Violia, Dr. Datrem—too many lives changed forever. But Tarek was right in that they were a family and she knew about families and how wonderful they were. With a bright smile, she thanked him. "That really means a lot to me."

Tarek raised his glass to his team, telling them, "I would like to propose a toast to all of you. You are why we are here tonight celebrating. It's because of your dedication and loyalty to this team—this family such that we are— that we were victorious. So, here's to many more successful missions, new and old friends"—then pointing his glass to Emeline and Nox— "and new loves. Now can we please eat that lasagna? The smell is driving me insane."

Tarek's toast had the desired effect on the people around the table. The mood was upbeat, a welcome change from the thunder clouds that had been hanging in the air over the last few days.

Emeline watched with great curiosity as Tarek picked up his fork, taking his first bite of lasagna. She hid her smile behind her own fork as he practically groaned at the delicious goodness in his mouth. The reactions were the same from everyone at the table.

Blowing on the steaming bite of pasta before sliding it slowly into her mouth, the rich flavors reminding her of home, she murmured to her brother, "Liam, this is out-standing. God, how I've missed this. Mum would be so proud."

Liam dug into his own plate, closing his eyes briefly as he tasted the results of his hard work.

At the end of the table, Jagger let out a moan as he de-voured a huge plateful of the delicious pasta. Between bites he asked about their mother, Fiona. He knew she liked to cook but wondered what she was like as they were growing up.

The two siblings jumped in wholeheartedly, regaling them with funny stories about their mother. One story in particular that had everyone laughing was Fiona's views on table manners.

Pulling up a picture of Fiona on her cell phone, Eme-line passed it around the table, telling everyone Fiona even went so far as to teach the neighborhood kids proper be-havior at the dinner table. "Liam, remember Mum telling us that just last year she ran into Tina who used to live next door? Mum had loved it when Tina confided to her that she still used her table manners and was teaching them to her own kids."

Liam and Ami were both nodding, telling them Fiona took proper manners very seriously.

"Bad manners equaled no food," Emeline giggled at her brother, remembering him missing one or two meals on occasion.

"Watch yourself, brat." Liam grinned as he stabbed his fork in her direction causing his little sister to laugh harder.

Tarek studied the woman on the device that Nox had handed him. She was standing next to Emeline, their arms around each other next to a large box filled with colorful flowers. The difference in their height was obvious as was the love glowing between them. Fiona was small—around 5'2", slightly taller than the average height of Delician females. That was the end of the similarities, he considered. She was strong, muscular—the shape of her arms and legs indicated that she was an active female. She was dressed in a black and white sundress that came to her knees. Her face was radiant with joy, her smile wide, showing her happiness at the moment. "She is lovely," Tarek murmured.

"Yes, she is," Liam answered. "She's always doing something. I think the only time she sits still is when she's reading or sleeping." He told them how Fiona's job as a programmer allowed her to work from home. "Mum liked to work, but she liked being a mother more." Liam smiled at the thought of how his mother never missed a single one of his games.

With most of the lasagna and bread gone, only a few bits of salad remained in the bowl. The Delicians had pretty much demolished all the food. Tarek was wiping his plate clean with his last piece of garlic bread, commenting on how Italian food was superb. Jagger sat back, rubbing his full stomach, letting out a satisfied sigh, while Loris and Nyx were fighting over the last piece of bread.

Ami stood up, asking who wanted dessert as she began stacking the dirty dishes to be put into the recycler. Having a replicator combined with a recycler made clean-up a snap. With a resounding *"me"* coming from the entire table, Ami chuckled at them, saying, "I don't know why I bothered asking."

"Can I help?" Emeline followed Ami into the kitchen carrying the last of the dishes.

"Sure. Can you put those Italian cookies on a couple of plates?" Ami took the two gallons of gelato that Liam had replicated out of the freezer drawer that was located in the island. One was her favorite chocolate and the other one was his favorite—mint chocolate chip.

Emeline teased Nox when she placed a bowl of the creamy cold gelato in front of him along with a plate of Italian cookies—almost as good as the ones she got in the North End of Boston she told him.

Seated beside her, Nox's fingers squeezed her thigh—just hard enough for a spike of desire to shoot right to her core. *Damn that man. Well, two can play that game.* Smiling innocently at him, she slipped her hand onto his thigh, her fingernails caressing back and forth, creating friction against the fabric of his pants. When she felt his hand grip hers firmly and place it back on her leg, she knew she'd hit a nerve. Well, that and the huge bulge in the front of his pants. Smirking to herself, she sucked the creamy chocolaty goodness into her mouth, murmuring to Nox how delicious it was.

Leaning down, Nox's lips brushed her ear, his amethyst eyes flashed hungrily at hers as he whispered, "Soon, Pulmina." Those two words elicited an involuntary quiver from his bondmate and it had nothing to do with the coldness of the gelato.

With the meal winding down, the conversation around the table eventually turned to Violia with Tarek asking how she was doing.

Putting his spoon down, Ezio told them that she was doing better. Dr. Datrem was running more tests and said they'd have to wait to see how her body responded to the treatments. His eyes creased with worry as he asked Tarek, "What's going to happen to her?"

Tarek took a bite of the cookie he held in his hand, contemplating Ezio as he chewed. The chatter around the table had quieted as everyone was anxious to hear what he had to say. "After much discussion and consideration, the UAP has left the decision up to me since she's under my command."

"Sir, have you made a decision?" Ezio asked anxiously.

Reclining back in his chair, Tarek took a sip from his wine before looking from Ezio to Emeline. "I have. It was a difficult decision because there were many mitigating factors to consider. After evaluating all the facts, I've decided she will be placed on probation. Given that she saved Emeline and lost her grandmother as a result of Hagen, I don't feel going to prison would be a just punishment. Datrem said that he was willing to have her continue working in the med bay, but only with constant supervision. The rest of the time, Ezio, you will be responsible for her."

Ezio agreed immediately...he would do anything for his bondmate.

Tarek nodded his head, informing him, "I want weekly updates on her progress. She has a long way to go to gain back my trust and the trust of the people she's hurt." That last sentence was directed to Emeline, who nodded in agreement. "I am glad for one thing though—she did point out a major flaw in our security system when she disabled the sensors on the escape pod. New procedures have already been put in place so this cannot happen again. The new codes have been given to Jagger, Yilmaz and myself. We still have a mole in our midst, and until that person is found, this information stays in this room."

"Thank you, sir." Some of the tension in Ezio's body visibly dissipated, knowing Tarek had been more than fair. "I'll tell her after dinner. She'll be relieved and thankful for what you and the doctor are doing for her. I know she carries tremendous guilt. She's expecting to spend the rest of her life in prison. I'm sure she'll be grateful for this second chance."

"Regardless, she still has a lot to atone for. Just make sure I don't regret my decision."

"You won't, I promise you that." Ezio picked up his wine glass and took a long drink, smiling for the first time since finding his bondmate.

Once the meal was over, the group moved over to the

seating area while Jagger and Ramola went to help Ami clear the rest of the table. Nyx continued as bartender, picking up a bottle of port, asking who wanted to try another human drink.

Emeline put her hand on Ezio's arm, getting his attention. "I'd like to talk to her tomorrow if she's up for it." Seeing his forehead crease with worry, Emeline smiled softly at him. "Don't worry. I just want to talk to her and see how she is doing. She did save my life, Ezio. I don't take that lightly."

Ezio put his hand over hers, squeezing lightly. "Thank you. I think she'd like that."

"Besides, I want to know how she feels about finding her bondmate." Emeline wagged her eyebrows at him, surprised at his reaction. "What? Wait. Don't tell me you haven't told her?"

He hesitated slightly, saying he hadn't had the chance yet. "She thinks I'm there to guard her. I didn't want to burden her with this news on top of everything else she is going through."

Emeline could sympathize with him. "I'm sorry. I wish I could do something to help you both." Her eyes shot to Nox, who was passing out glasses of port to everyone. "I understand better than most what you're going through."

"Can I ask you something?" Ezio asked as he slid over on the couch so Emeline could sit down. At her nod, he said, "There is something I don't understand. How is it you can be so compassionate, have so much empathy for Violia after what she did to you?"

She considered his question carefully. She didn't know about most humans but she did know her own feelings. When she finally answered him, the hardness in her voice wasn't surprising, "When someone steps in front of a blaster meant to kill you, compassion and empathy is the least that you're feeling." Her fist lightly pounded on her knee, unintentionally drawing the attention of everyone in the room.

Looking around, Emeline figured no time like the present for her turn at debriefing everyone. Glad that the bulk of her rage was gone and knowing she was among friends and family, the words flowed easier than she had expected. "Yes, Violia kidnapped me and we all know the reasons why. But what you don't know is that when she stepped in front of Hagen's kill shot, it wasn't the first time she'd tried to save me."

Nox, who had moved to sit next to Emeline, pulled her into his embrace, whispering into her hair. "You don't have to do this now. You can wait until you are ready."

Pulling back, Emeline cupped his cheek. *What a sweet man.* "No, babe, it's fine. I want to tell them."

Turning back around, Emeline started her story from where Violia had lured her into the escape pod and injected her with a sedative. Knowing how hard this was to hear, she was relieved that Nox knew most of it. When she got to the part about the first time Hagen had tried to assault her, she could feel Nox's hand clench her thigh. She didn't dare look at Liam because she would never be able to get through this if she did.

As she told them about Tarquin saving them and then giving them the regen device, the Delicians uttered their disbelief. "I understand your surprise, but he was actually kind of nice." She shrugged her shoulders at their comments of disdain for Tarquin. "Believe me, I'm just glad he showed up when he did. Violia took quite a beating trying to stop Hagen from attacking me. If she hadn't, things would have been much worse." She explained how Violia had created hidden pockets within her uniform with a regen device, a DRI injector and a laser scalpel.

Ramola muttered unhappily, "She should have taken a blaster."

It was Ami who spoke up, surprising Emeline as she came over and plopped down in a chair across from them.

"Now we all know that's not possible. Chief Koralo keeps his weapons locked up tight. No way was she getting any weapons."

"She still should have told someone," Nyx growled while Ramola nodded his head in agreement.

Jagger had the same sentiment, stating that it was her duty to tell the General or someone on their team *before* following Hagen's plan.

"I agree and I told her that several times, but regardless of what she should have done, it is what it is. We can't change any of that now. I'm just glad she had the mindset to bring a regen device."

She continued her story, telling them how Tarquin had food and water sent and that he moved them to his office where he could keep them safe, especially after hearing that Hagen was bragging to the crew about *having some fun* with the human female. That last statement was met with more than a few growls from around the room causing Emeline to move quickly onto how she had tricked Tarquin into allowing her access to his computer. They all thought she was pure genius hearing how she was able to get his fingerprint off his console. She explained that when the battle started, Tarquin had supposedly locked them in his office, which gave her the perfect opportunity take down their shields. "We thought we were safe until Hagen used some kind of override to get into the office. He went ballistic when he realized that Violia had disobeyed him. He wanted to punish her, but I honestly don't think he expected his men to kill Etha."

Turning to Tarek, Emeline's voice softened as she told them about Hagen's reaction to his grandmother's death. "After that, all he wanted to do was get off the Invidia as fast as he could. He told us he had a plan."

"And what was that?" Tarek asked. His lips had thinned into a straight line as he sat listening to Emeline's story.

"He was going to steal Tarquin's shuttle—which, by the

way, had a cloaking device—and take me and Violia with him to Earth to get a shipment of Himalayan salt. He was going to use me as a hostage to get what he wanted. But I was hurt, so Violia tried to convince him to let me go. She said she'd go with him and help him get the salt. She even told him that she'd go to Hexia with him if he would just leave me alone. He must have believed her but at the last minute decided I'd be more of a liability. Next thing I knew he's pointing his blaster at me and well—you know the rest," she trailed off.

Tarek broke the silence, knowing this was a memory that was still too fresh to dwell on right now. His expression was not that of the hardened general who had seen too much war and death. Instead, it was the face of a friend, someone you knew you could count on to help in any way he could. "Emeline, you were very brave. Again, I am sorry you had to experience such terrible things. If there is anything I can do to help you or anything you need, please just ask."

"Thank you, Tarek. Honestly, being here with all of you has been exactly what I needed. For a while there, I wasn't sure I was going to make it." Nox's body tensed against her back at her words. "But I did, thanks to all of you. You put your lives on the line for me and I'm grateful." Her words were spoken with such warmth and affection. There wasn't one person in the room who wasn't affected by her story.

Giving her brother a look of gratitude, she said, "Liam, I really have to credit you and your incessant nagging about my training for helping me through the worst of it." Her expression darkened, recalling how intimidating Hagen had been. "I just kept running through everything you drilled into our heads a million times. Especially the parts about dealing with impossible situations—that proved vital to my survival. I used every dirty trick you taught me and a few that just came to me in the heat of the moment."

Ami piped in, agreeing with her. "You got that right. If I said *Breathe, Center, Focus* one more time, I was going to hurl."

The girls giggled while Liam beamed with pride. He quickly explained to the Delicians about Fiona's mantra for handling stress. That produced a lot of laughs all around, except for Tarek. He sat pondering Fiona's words.

Emeline laughed at Ami telling her she felt the same way. "But honestly those three words helped me from hyperventilating more than a few times."

A thought came to Emeline—there was something important she needed to tell Tarek. Rubbing her forehead with her three middle fingers, trying to think, she muttered aloud, "I feel like I'm forgetting something." Looking from Nox to Tarek, Emeline burst out, "He knew—Tarquin knew about my network array. I never told him, but somehow, he knew. Violia said that Hagen mentioned it to her when he first contacted her."

When everyone started talking at once, Tarek held up his hand, quieting the room. His lips pursed tight, needing a moment to consider her words. When he finally did speak, his anger was tightly contained. "It's confirmed then. Someone on my ship is supplying information to the Hexians. Finding this person is my top priority and trust me, when I do, I will enjoy doling out his punishment—very slowly. Emeline, what else did Tarquin say?"

Hesitating slightly, Emeline shot a glance at Nox, "Just that being the bondmate to another species was going to cause lots of problems on Delicia and with the UAP."

Seeing Nox's face flush with anger, Emeline nudged him with her arm, "Hey, it's okay, but can we not go there right now? I honestly don't have the energy for it."

Nox stole a glance at Tarek, agreeing they could talk about it later.

Instead, Emeline continued on telling them how after she and Violia got into Tarquin's console and took down the force fields, she downloaded a bunch of random files from Tarquin's console. "I'm not sure what's on them. I have ARI translating them right now."

"You stole files from Tarquin? Unbelievable." Jagger looked at Emeline with a renewed sense of awe. "Forget about being a scientist, Emeline. We should use your skills as a spy."

"Um—no thanks." Emeline scoffed at Jagger. Clutching Nox's hand, she told him, "I prefer the lab with Nox and Loris, if you don't mind."

Pressing her tight against him, Nox growled at Jagger to keep his ideas to himself.

Seeing Liam agreeing with Nox, Emeline rolled her eyes at the both of them. *Men!* "Okay, Liam, it's your turn. I want to hear all about this freighter you blew up." Emeline snuggled up against Nox...engulfed in his warm safe arms, relieved it was someone else's turn to speak.

Nyx caught her attention with a wink. "Wait until you hear. This is going to blow your mind." Emeline chuckled at Nyx's use of human slang.

As Liam launched into his story, Emeline really was blown away. Between the *oh my gods* to all the *no ways*, she was riveted. Her emotions flipped from trying to keep her mouth from hanging open to being scared to death, especially at the part when the Hexian freighter exploded.

The whole time Liam was telling their tale, Nyx was giving them a running commentary from his perspective, causing lots of jokes to be thrown around—mostly at Liam's expense. It ended with Liam blurting out, exasperated at their teasing, that he seriously never expected the damn thing to blow up. "What's in those crystals anyway?"

Laughter filled the room as he continued telling them that he and Nyx were just as shocked as anyone. "It was Nyx's quick thinking that saved our asses from the shockwave."

Wiping her eyes from laughing, Emeline got up and

pulled Liam in for a hard hug. Leaning back just enough to see his eyes, she whispered, "Did you need clean underwear when you got back to the ship?"

Liam looked at his sister appalled but then sheepishly whispered "*maybe*."

Laughing, she cupped his cheek, searching his eyes. "You okay?"

"Yeah, I'm good."

"Good, because I'm telling Mum."

Ruffling her hair, Liam laughed. "Better you than me."

Liam felt Tarek's hand on his shoulder, causing him to release his hold on his sister and turning gave the General an expectant look.

"Liam, your ability to function under extreme pressure, especially the kind of pressure you'd never encountered before, was impressive. Not only was your shooting ability outstanding but your integrity and ability to adapt was top notch. I have spoken to the UAP and told them of a decision I've made." Everyone waited expectantly for him to continue. "Liam, I would like to offer you a position as a member of my elite team of soldiers."

Emeline and Ami gasped as Liam stood there astounded at the General's offer. His stunned face almost comical as he moved from one emotion to another at being offered a chance of a lifetime.

"Yes!" Liam exclaimed before he could stop himself. He tried but failed to contain his joy at getting his heart's desire. Rising to his feet, he extended his arm to Tarek. "General, I don't know what to say. Of course, I'll have to consult with Leslie about getting released from my contract with NASA, but absolutely...it would be an honor to become a member of your team."

Taking Liam's forearm, Tarek grinned, telling him, "We'll discuss the details tomorrow, but for now, welcome to the team."

Emeline studied Liam's face as she considered this new

opportunity he'd been given. Everyone at this point had crowded around her brother. There was no doubt in her mind that this offer was something that Liam only dreamed about. His blue eyes sparkled with happiness as she watched Nyx and Ramola tease him about being the new guy and how now all the crap jobs would go to him.

Extricating himself from his new teammates, Liam's mood became a little sober as he tried to judge Emeline's reaction to Tarek's offer. When she winked at him, giving him one of her bright happy smiles, he relaxed, letting the joy and anticipation of this new adventure sink in. "So, Em, what do you think?"

"What do I think? Are you kidding me? I'm thrilled for you." Although if she was being totally honest, her joy was tinged with maybe a smidge of selfishness. Now she would have Liam along on this journey with her to Delicia.

Liam's face was flushed with joy. Blowing out a breath, he tried to calm his voice, but who was he kidding. What he really wanted to do was run through the ship screaming "*Hoorah*" at the top of his lungs. Falling into a chair, he looked up at her, asking in disbelief, "Can you believe it?"

"A duh—of course I can. You're going to do so awesome." Emeline sat on the arm of his chair, ruffling his hair.

Gently rubbing the back of her hand, Liam considered his words, finally telling her, "Just so you know, I was planning on coming with you when you went to Delicia anyway."

"You were? Seriously?" With a relieved smile, she added, "I was hoping—I mean, I kind of figured if you got the chance to go to Delicia, you would jump at it."

"What made you think that?" Liam was a little surprised at his sister's attitude to Tarek's offer.

"Are you kidding me? I haven't seen you this happy since you got accepted into the astronaut program for NASA." Biting her lower lip, Emeline confessed to Liam, "Actually I was hoping you'd come to Delicia with me because I was thinking about asking Mum to come, but I wasn't sure how you'd feel about that."

"Mum?" Narrowing his eyes at her, Liam sipped his port, savoring the thick heady flavor. He took a moment to think about it. "You might be right. I think a change might do her good. I've been worried about her being alone so much since Dad died. Maybe an adventure is exactly what she needs."

Emeline's eyes lit up with excitement. "Oh Liam, I'm so happy you said that. I totally agree. She's been like a lost soul these past two years. Besides, you know how much she loves to travel." Giving him a small laugh, she squeezed his arm, mischievously adding, "I'm going to love seeing her face when we tell her just where we're taking her."

"Liam?" Tarek had come over and stood behind Emeline.

"Yes, General." Liam stood up, leaving Emeline cracking jokes with Ami about Fiona's reaction to meeting the Delicians.

"I would like to meet with you tomorrow to discuss a few other things."

"Yes, sir."

"Datrem mentioned to me that he asked to speak to you about training his granddaughter in self-defense."

"Yes, he did. I'm meeting with him in the morning," Liam said.

"Good. I want you to take that one step further and start developing a program that can be implemented for all female crewmembers. We can discuss this more after your meeting with Datrem."

Nodding his head in agreement, Liam was astounded at how much his life had changed since first receiving Nox's message on the Space Station.

When Emeline saw that Liam and Tarek had finished their conversation, she figured before she told Fiona anything, she had better clear it with the person in charge first. Giving Tarek a wary look, her fingers twisting in the hem of her dress, she asked him, "Tarek? Can I ask you something?" At his nod, she said, "I was wondering if you would be okay with us bringing our mother to Delicia when we leave?" Her lower lip caught between her teeth as she waited for his reaction.

His answer surprised her. Not only was he amenable to Fiona coming, he also invited Ami and anyone else to journey back to Delicia when they left. Sometimes it was hard to get a read on Tarek, she thought. *Now all I have to do is convince Mum and hope that Belle doesn't kill me.*

Emeline glanced over at Ami, noticing the worried frown on her face. "What's wrong?"

Swallowing hard, Ami was still unsure of her feelings about leaving Earth. "We have some decisions to make regarding EAC, especially now that you'll be going to Delicia."

Emeline smiled at her friend. Giving her a reassuring hug, she said, "I agree. How about we meet tomorrow afternoon?" Ami agreed, returning her smile.

Getting Nox's attention, Emeline pulled him into the conversation. "I want to continue my work with EAC, but I also want to continue working with you and Loris. I can't see any reason why we can't do both."

"I agree," Nox said, locking their fingers together. Brushing a kiss along her temple, he added, "Loris and I can meet with you and Ami tomorrow as well to figure things out."

Ami relaxed slightly, causing Emeline to study her friend closely. Ami's uncertain expression at Tarek's invitation had not escaped Emeline. Her brave friend had been nothing short of heroic in her eyes. It had been chilling hearing about Ami's experience fighting the Hexians. Knowing Ami's feelings on the sanctity of life, Emeline wasn't surprised at the shadows lurking behind Ami's eyes. *Looks like it's time for a girls' night.*

Emeline knew when they got back to Earth there was going to be hell to pay from Heather and Lorelei. Being left out of their adventure was hard on all of them. They were a team and now part of their team would be on the other side of the universe. Even though Ami had been keeping them apprised on what had been happening, it wasn't the same. It was clear to Emeline they had a lot to talk about before any decisions could be made.

"I would like everyone's attention." Tarek moved away from the group, his commanding voice immediately stopping all conversation. "I want to give you an update on some new developments." He waited until everyone had taken a seat before continuing. "As you know I have apprised the UAP of the results of our mission. Now that the imminent threat has been neutralized, they have authorized me to speak to the humans on their behalf."

The three humans in the room crowded around one another, knowing the seriousness of Tarek's words would change the lives of humans forever. When people said they were carrying the weight of the world, that was an understatement. If not now, then in the very near future, the people of Earth were going to have to come to terms with the fact that they were not alone in the universe.

Tarek explained that the UAP wanted him to meet with the humans and extend an offer to visit the UAP headquarters to discuss possible membership into the Alliance. "They want the humans to send a delegation, escorted by us, to their headquarters to meet with the council." Tarek turned at their collective gasp. "They feel it is necessary. Word has already begun to spread throughout our sector about the valuable resource that Earth possesses. I can think of more than a few species that will try to come to Earth."

Emeline paled at Tarek's implication, while Ami blurted out a few of her more colorful words.

Tarek held up his hand, telling them Earth had nothing to fear. "We will not be leaving you unprotected any longer. And if Earth decides to decline our offer, we will still make sure your planet is left untouched." Turning to Liam, Tarek asked if he had given his report to Leslie yet.

Liam quickly replied that he had. "I debriefed her on the mission. She was going to contact President Jenkins with her report. I'm supposed to contact her tomorrow at 0800 her time, but I can call her now if you want."

"No, the morning is fine. Ask her to set up a meeting with Earth's leaders. They can set the time and place, or if they wish, we can do it over vid comm."

Liam took notes on his wrist comm as Tarek talked. "There's no rush. We'll give the humans as much time as they need to make a decision. We're not on any timetable. Besides, we're still trying to get the Invidia sorted out." A sly smirk formed on Tarek's face. "I have decided to add Tarquin's ship to my own personal fleet." The Delicians cheered at this, with Nyx trying to high five Jagger.

"How did you manage that?" Jagger grinned at his friend, knowing exactly how he did it. The UAP rarely said no to anything Tarek wanted. "Strange the hold you have over them," he mulled to no one in particular.

A flash of fury replaced by total calm came over Tarek's face as he thought about why he always got his way. The UAP owed him. "It's because my team is so proficient at their jobs that I'm able to succeed where others have failed. The Invidia is just another tool in our arsenal." Focusing on the three humans, Tarek told them it was important they attend the meeting with Earth's leaders. "I would like the three of you to tell your stories to the human leaders. Emeline?"

"Yes."

"I will leave it for you to decide how much of your experience you wish to tell them. I don't think it's necessary to share everything." He gave her a meaningful look, adding, "However, they do need to understand that the universe is full of dangerous species." Tarek told her that it was also her decision to tell them about her and Nox, although it would be better coming from the both of them.

Emeline swallowed her discomfort, telling him that she and Nox would discuss everything and let him know before the meeting.

All three humans agreed to help in any way they could —each willing to tell their individual stories to Earth's leaders.

With Jagger still muttering about the Invidia and what Tarek had to promise the UAP in return, Tarek merely smirked as he sipped his port. Liam and Ami had drifted off, discussing what he would tell Leslie about quitting and joining Tarek's team. Loris looked to be taking notes on his wrist comm as he tasted more of the port wine, while Nyx had Ramola laughing with his story of Liam's use of a pocket knife on their mission.

Covering her mouth with her hand, Emeline tried to stifle a yawn. Embarrassed, she turned her head into Nox's shoulder.

Gently lifting her chin, he couldn't help noticing how tired she looked. Her long dark lashes were a match in color to the smudges under her eyes. "Time for bed, Pulmina" he whispered low enough for only her to hear.

Smiling with her eyes, Emeline noticed that it wasn't a question but more of a statement from him. "Yes."

Nox pulled on Emeline's hand, tugging her to her feet. "It's getting late. Emeline needs to get some rest."

Liam came over and kissed Emeline's cheek, telling her that she did look tired and she should get some sleep. He cocked his head at her, his meaning evident on his face.

Ami was next, pulling her friend in for a long hug, whispering in her ear to take her time but do what she felt was right for her. Ami gave her a final squeeze, then winked at her, knowing exactly what Emeline had planned.

Assuring Liam and Ami that she was fine, Emeline smiled dreamily at Nox, who had gone over to speak to Loris. Giving them each another hug, telling them she was perfect and would meet them sometime tomorrow. She quickly added not too early, which in turn generated groans from Liam and a gagging sound from Ami. They could be heard laughing as they headed out the door to go to bed.

Emeline, catching Nox's eye, nodded towards the door, indicating that she was ready to go.

Nox, not being a stupid male, cut Loris off midsentence, telling him their discussion could wait until tomorrow. Nox locked eyes with sparkling blue ones, drawing him to her like food to a starving man. He swiftly closed the distance between, engulfing her in his embrace, neither of them conscious of the comments thrown their way. Bending his head down, Nox took her lips in a deep kiss — one that promised more—oh so much more—to come. Walking out the door, giggles could be heard fading down the corridor as the door silently closed behind them.

CHAPTER 26

"It's too bad you don't have a transporter. We'd be there already." With Nox's arm pressing Emeline tightly against his side, they hurried along the corridor...their passion rising with each passing step. "Wait—do you?"

"Do I what?"

"Have a transporter."

Seeing the confusion in his eyes, she explained. "It's a device that changes you into a particle beam and can send you from one location to another in the blink of an eye." Snapping her fingers, she exclaimed, "You know, kind of like magic." Her excited smile faded at the look of horror on Nox's face.

"N-no. Why would anyone want to do that?"

The way Nox was shaking his head in total disbelief made Emeline feel that maybe all the science fiction she'd read or watched had gotten it all wrong. "So, I guess that's a no on the transporter. Bummer."

Stopping abruptly, Nox gave her a troubled look. "Would you really allow a device to take your body apart at the subatomic level, shoot the beam out who knows where and then trust that everything would be put back together precisely the way it should be?"

The way he said that spoke volumes. "Well, when you put it that way, I guess not," Emeline mumbled unhappily. "This is really going to bum out a lot of the real hardcore sci-fi fans—I can tell you that."

Seeing the dejected frown on Emeline's face, Nox couldn't help chuckling at this whole conversation. Humans really were fascinating.

Finally making it to their room, Nox stopped her before opening the door. Pulling their joined hands to his chest, his love for her shone brightly in his eyes. "Come, Pulmina, let's create our own magic and I promise you; life will never be the same." Kissing her lips softly, he whispered, "For either of us."

As soon as the door closed behind them, Emeline found her back pressed up against the wall, Nox's mouth devouring hers. One hand slapped against the wall beside her head, his other hand cupped her curvaceous bottom. Pulling her legs up around his waist...his hard body pinned her in place. The scent of her arousal enflamed him...setting his senses on fire.

Her dress pooled around her middle exposing her wet thong. Rocking rhythmically against the hard bulge in the front of Nox's pants, her body was awash with anticipation. His commanding kiss pushed her hunger for him beyond anything she had ever felt before.

Nox could feel her moist heat pressed against him...the potency of her desire spurred him to demand more from her. Each time his tongue caressed hers, he could feel how her body answered back to him. The tender sighs and tiny spasms had morphed into long groans and deep shudders.

With her head tilted back against the wall, Emeline's eyes fluttered like butterfly wings as Nox skimmed his teeth down her neck...sampling the tender patches of her creamy skin. In his wake, he left a trail of sparks that had Emeline groaning to her god.

Moving in harmony, his hardness stroked her clit with each roll of his hips; pleasure skyrocketed through Emeline as her climax began to peak. Nox's hand slipped down the front of her dress finding her nipples stiff and wanting— begging for his touch. His fingers rolled and pinched her hard nubs sending jolts of lightening straight to her core.

Screaming out, "Oh god, I'm coming," a wave of euphoria crashed over her leaving her clinging helplessly to Nox's biceps.

Straightened up...his arms full of this uniquely sensuous woman, Nox ignored her small cries of protest when he dropped her feet gently to the floor and slowly pulled her dress over her head. Clad only in a tiny white lace thong, Nox nearly lost it at the incredible sight before him. "You are so beautiful," he purred, his eyes darkening with naked desire at this gorgeous woman who for reasons known only to the fates, wanted him.

Swiftly removing his own clothing, the luminous glow of his skin highlighted the swirls of color that now moved along the surface of his body. His stomach muscles clenched watching Emeline lick her lips as her eyes lingered on his erection.

Still riding the high from her orgasm, Emeline's mouth curved into a playful smile as she raked her gaze up and down her hot alien lover's delicious looking body. Her body took on a life of its own when she flung herself at him, knowing he would catch her. Sealing her lips to his, she felt cherished as he gripped her backside in his strong wide hands while he matched her kiss for kiss.

Pulling back, breathless, Nox rested his forehead against hers, fighting to maintain some modicum of control, but Emeline was relentless. She ran the tips of her fingernails down his back leaving a scorching trail of fire in their wake. His body shook uncontrollably. When her hands continued downward, grasping his butt cheeks; his smooth muscles flexed unwittingly at her touch causing them both to let out a deep sound filled with need.

Staring deeply into her soulful eyes, the doctor's words floated through Nox's mind. Datrem was right. There was no need to rush things. They had plenty of time.

"My beautiful Pulmina. We need to slow down. I am trying to make this last."

Already too far down that road to stop now, Emeline panted out, "Don't want to." Lost in the moment, her core pressed snuggly against his erection...her hips moving in constant motion reaching for what...she wasn't sure. All she knew was that a continuous flow of heavenly sparks, like fireworks exploding in the night sky, sprinted straight to her aching center. She was so close.

All at once—a sharp gasp, clenched muscles, exquisite pain and then immense pleasure spread from the inside out as her body bowed into his. A feeling of pure bliss raced through her as her release sent her shooting into the stratosphere.

Nox's strong arms held her close to him, anchoring her body to his as she floated on the sweet aftereffects of another release.

Her forehead dropped to his chest, taking a moment for her breathing to steady. With a lazy smile, she brushed her lips across his smooth skin, murmuring sheepishly, "Sorry, I didn't wait for you."

"I noticed," he said with a grin, nuzzling his nose into her sweet-smelling hair. "Seems like I have a little catching up to do."

"Here, let me see what I can do to help." She reached between them circling her finger through the wetness that pebbled at the slit in his penis.

Removing her hand before things escalated past his point of no return, he had been trying to take things slow but it appeared his *little minx* had other ideas.

Nox loved how she snuggled up against him, her legs still wrapped tightly around his trim waist. Her nose was flush up against his neck; her warm breath sending goose bumps rippling across his skin.

He carried her over to their bed—the white duvet that had been covered in the rose petal design was gone. In its place was a plush new red one. Nox smiled at the thoughtfulness of Ami, wondering when she had found the time. He made a mental note to thank her for removing what would have been a painful reminder of the last few days for Emeline.

Feeling her silky tongue drawing circles against his neck

sent a tremor racing down his spine. A harsh moan erupted from down deep within his body. Her fingernails flicked his nipples causing them to stand at attention. It looked like his Pulmina was doing her best to torture him and it was working—his control was teetering on the edge, like walking a tightrope over a deep crevasse. Gritting his teeth, Nox had every intention of taking his time, savoring this life changing moment.

With a wicked glint in his eyes, Nox dropped his beautiful bondmate none too gently into the middle of their bed; his lips curved into a devilish smile at the surprised look on her face.

"Hey!" Emeline giggled up at him as she bounced a few times before settling back into the softness of the pillows. Fanning out her arms, her body arched into the bed, loving how the silkiness of the material felt cool against her overly stimulated skin.

Grabbing the sides of her thong, she slowly teased each side down, inch by inch, down her long shapely legs. With a mischievous smile, she dropped her legs open revealing her hidden treasure to him.

Nearly choking on his tongue, Nox devoured his sexy vixen as she offered herself up to him. He was humbled by her beauty. She was magnificent and somehow fate had brought her to him. Call it destiny. Call it the will of whatever gods there were, he didn't care. He gave thanks for every moment he had Emeline in his life.

Lifting her eyes to his deep amethyst ones, she was reminded of sunsets over Cape Cod. That perfect moment when the deep purple sky was awash with the last rays of the sun before nighttime took its turn. A moment of pure peace. That was how she felt being with Nox.

He was so gorgeous, she thought happily and all hers. *Every last luscious inch.*

Stretching her body into the bed, she beckoned him to her. "You are so damn sexy," she whispered sucking the end of her index finger into her mouth. Trailing her wet finger down her neck, circling one rock hard nipple and then moving on to the other, her breasts ached, desperate to feel his hot mouth on her sensitive skin. Her breathing hitched as he moved to kneel between her open thighs and began gliding his hands slowly up her legs. When he moved in to taste her, Emeline basked in the ripples of pleasure that shot straight to her core.

He took his time savoring the rich essence of his bond-mate. Each throaty sigh and soft moan drove him further, pushing Emeline to give him her all. Even after wringing yet another orgasm out of her, he didn't give her time to recover. He nibbled his way up along her long smooth body. The fine blond hairs covering her skin stood tall with each passing touch of his soft lips.

His gaze skimmed slowly across her body, following the red blush that rippled across her flawless skin. Full pale breasts with deep rose-colored tips called to him. His mouth descended upon them—insistent, unrelenting as he drove his sweet Emeline to cry out again to her god. Her cries of passion became louder as his fingers discovered the sweetness between her thighs. It wasn't long before Emeline screamed his name in pleasure as her body surrendered to his touches.

Nox's body throbbed with need. With his erection nestled between them...her arousal glistening on her thighs, it took all of his inner strength to hold himself back from ramming into her with wild abandon.

Resting his arms on either side of her head, his nose brushed at that sensitive spot behind her earlobe. Breathing deeply...her delicate scent surrounded him...taunting him to take her; to stop wasting time and complete the bond.

Pulling back, he locked eyes with her asking, "My Pulmina, are you ready to become mine forever?"

Still riding the high from multiple orgasms, her brain

was clouded with passion. *What kind of question is that?* Of course, she was ready. Her senses were so electrified, she was lucky her lungs still functioned.

Wiggling her hips, feeling his weight settled perfectly right where she needed him, she knew he could feel her wetness, smell her arousal. She was beyond ready.

Moving her hand between them, she curled her fingers around his hard length and started to guide him into her.

When he stopped her hand, her face scrunched up in surprise. *What's going on? Why did he stop?* Every nerve ending in her body was poised and ready. Couldn't he feel how much she needed him? Feel how her hips molded to his sending sparks to her core. Feel his weight pushing her into the bed—her girly parts quivering with the promise of what was to come. Feel the way their bodies touched—well, except in that one crucial way that she longed for. *What is the hold up here?!*

"Babe," she panted, "please."

Nox's shoulders shook as he tried to hold back his un-bridled desire for her. His voice sounded gruff as he confessed, "Pulmina, you have been through so much pain and suffering. I can't bear to cause you anymore."

"I trust you," she said trying to reassure him. True, he was a big man, much bigger than she was used to, but he was always gentle with her. It's one of the reasons she loved him so much. But seriously, if he held back much longer... *can you die from sexual frustration?*

Slipping her arms around his neck, she decided enough was enough. It was time to play dirty. Wiggling beneath him, tingles electrified her body, intensifying her need. With slow strokes, she brushed her breasts across his wide chest loving how his body tensed against hers.

"I'm trying to be gentle with you," he blew out.

Gazing longingly into eyes that were filled with a pent-up hunger so strong it should have scared her. It didn't. Teasing his lips with her tongue, she whispered, "Nox, I love you. Make me yours."

Her words sent all his hesitations drifting off into space. Giving her a sweet lingering kiss, he gently entered her.

Yeah, gentle was not what Emeline wanted right now. She was done being treated like she was made of glass. Knowing that from this moment forward they would be one for eternity, Emeline craved fire...passion. With a quick thrust of her hips, she took every bit of him into her, not caring how full she felt. "Nox," she growled at his look of surprise, "stop holding back. I'm not going to break."

Letting out an animalistic growl, she flipped him over and took control; riding him with an intensity that had her eyes rolling back in her head. Passion whipped through her body as she leaned forward, digging her fingertips into his pecs. Throwing her head back, she moaned over and over, *OH MY GOD, OH MY GOD* as Nox gripped her hot flesh between his fingers.

Grinding their hips together, a powerful feeling began to pulse through her. It was so strong, she had to squeeze her thighs tighter around his waist just to stay upright.

Nox was in awe of his glorious golden goddess who soared above him. Seeing how flushed her skin was; the beads of sweat dotting her forehead; her color deepening with each erratic breath was the final straw that pushed Nox to succumb to her demands.

Seeing that Emeline was close to another orgasm, Nox flipped them over in one smooth movement. She arched up into him, whimpering out a breathless sigh of desire. The rapture on her face was too much for him to resist. His lips descended on hers taking her swollen red lips with his. He tasted sweetness and sunshine...the flavor unique to his beautiful bondmate. Intoxicated by her taste, he increased his pace.

Their movements became fluid; their kisses deepening...fingers entwined; their breathing becoming ragged as their tempo built.

"Oh god, Nox. Don't stop." Her shaky voice fluctuated from high to low with each movement of their jointed bodies.

Widening her legs, Emeline nearly passed out from ecstasy when Nox twisted their bodies and began concentrating on that bundle of nerves that only she had been able to find when she used her vibrator. Black spots dotted her vision. Each thrust sent a zing through her body that had her teetering on the edge of reality.

His breathing quickening, Nox's hand skimmed across the curve of her hip cupping her butt cheek firmly as he drove them to new heights. Her skin felt dewy under his fingers as he felt his own orgasm building. Her nails scraped up his back as she cried out in ecstasy.

Nox growled out a sound that started at his toes. Feelings so intense, his legs trembled, his lower body stretched taut—sending him careening over the edge...filled with the most amazing sensations he'd ever felt. As if all the stars across the universe aligned for that one perfect moment —the impetus that completing their bond meant...sealing their fate together forever.

The ball of energy that Emeline had envisioned representing their bond became a reality. At the moment they reached the pinnacle of their climax, her ball of golden particles swirled around them, binding them together—their souls now joined side by side. Each soul still separate, but no longer alone. There would always be someone loving you, accepting you, supporting you—even crying with you when there was a need.

Emeline didn't know how much time had passed—her body still reeled with the delicious aftershocks from their lovemaking. Somehow, she'd ended up sprawled across Nox's broad chest, her head resting in the crook of his neck. Her breasts were tender along with a few other places, causing her to smile against his skin. Her finger trailed along his collarbone as she took stock of how her body was feeling. Did she feel any different? Yes—an emphatic YES. Aside from how wonderfully satisfied she felt, she didn't feel alone. For the first time ever, she could feel his emotions intertwined with hers.

Looking down at her hand, she saw that the colors under her skin were stationary. Huh. Well, she thought, Dr. Datrem had told them he wasn't sure what to expect once the bond was completed. Normally between two Delicians, the colors were bolder, not outlandish but subtle enough for anyone looking to see that the individual was part of a bonded pair. *I thought there would be more.*

Picking up on the subtle change in the body underneath her, she knew Nox was awake. Giving him a silly sated grin, she noticed his colors no longer swirled but were stationary like hers. Her eyes were drawn to the side of his face.

Pushing his hair back off his forehead, her eyes widened in surprise. The imprint of a cord ran up alongside his hairline. It was thin, maybe half a centimeter wide and twisted with three colorful lines; pink, purple and blue. *That had not been there before. I would have remembered something this beautiful.* She traced her finger along the cord where it started, at the corner of his ear. Following it up across his forehead, it ended at the same spot on the other side of his face.

Nox, shivering at her touch, gently grabbed her hand, bringing her fingertips to his mouth. He kissed each one, finally asking her what she saw.

"It's like a tattoo of a thin cord. It has three distinct colored threads...pink, purple and blue. It's beautiful." With a look of wonder, her fingers skimmed along the cord, amazed at the symmetry of his new mark.

A sudden thought occurred to her. Slipping her hand out of his, she ran her finger down the side of her face. "Do I have one," she wondered out loud.

Not waiting for his answer, she slid off his body and sat up. Pulling her hair away from her face so he could get a good look at her, she demanded, "Do you see it?" Seeing his face light up with pleasure, she jumped off the bed, hurrying into the bathroom to see for herself. Pulling up short, Emeline squeezed her eyes tight—preparing herself for whatever changes she might see.

Cautiously opening one eye, she peeked at her reflection. "Oh—my—god." Emeline could hear Nox chuckling at her exclamation.

Opening both eyes wide, she turned her face from side to side, checking out the mark that was an exact replica to Nox's. The blue was the same color as her eyes, while the purple matched Nox's sparkling amethyst ones.

A feeling of contentment washed over her like a warm spring rain. She was reminded of home—the way things were before her father had passed. Their house was always filled with unconditional love, total acceptance and friendship. That's how she felt right now deep down inside, but there was something more, another dimension, more layers to her connection with Nox. A warm flush spread through her body at the memory of how thoroughly she and Nox had loved one another.

Running quickly back into the bedroom, Emeline was oblivious to the sight she presented to her new bondmate. He had moved up and was quietly lounging against the headboard, watching as she stopped at the foot of the bed. *She is lovely.* Her skin had taken on a slight luminescent sheen that caused her naked body to glow in the low light of the room. Her hands had her hair pulled back on either side of her face so he could see their matching marks.

"Can you see it?" she asked, daring him to tell her that she was mistaken at what was on her face.

"I can." Nox held his breath, waiting, trying to get a read on what she was feeling, but her emotions were all over the place.

"It matches yours."

"It does."

Throwing her head back, a soft laugh escaped her mouth, taking Nox by surprise.

"You're happy about...about this?" His finger hovered in the air tracing her mark.

Standing facing the end of the bed, Emeline's lips were curved up into a radiant smile. "Of course. Why? Aren't you? No, wait—!"

Grinning, she closed her eyes, searching deep within their newly completed bond. There it was—Nox's love for her along with a slight worry about her reaction to the changes her body would experience.

While she was searching his feelings, Nox scooted down to sit at the end of the bed. Placing his hands on her hips, he pulled her to stand between his spread legs. His eyes roamed her body, looking for any more changes.

Leaning down slightly, Emeline captured his lips in a tender kiss. She showed him through her touch exactly what she thought about the changes they were both going through. "I love you," she whispered when she pulled back.

Taking ahold of his hand, Emeline placed it against her heart. "On Earth or at least in my country, when two people fall in love and commit themselves to each other, they get married."

Intrigued, Nox ran his hand down along her hip, smiling as she shivered at his touch. "And how do they do this?"

"Well, there are tons of ways that people can get married. It's basically a ceremony with someone officiating it. Once the ceremony is finished, there is always a party with lots of dancing and drinking and eating. Oh, and cake— always some type of cake. Anyway, the whole point is to pledge themselves to each other."

Gazing deeply into Nox's eyes, her voice clear and confident, Emeline took a deep breath before saying, "I, Emeline, take you Nox to be my husband—bondmate. I vow to love you forever. I vow to always listen to anything you want to tell me, even if I don't like it." Leaning in, she brushed her lips gently across his. "I give you my body and my soul to protect. This I pledge to you forever." Pressing her lips to his, she sealed her vows with a searing kiss that left them both gasping.

Nox was, as Emeline had put it, *"blown away"* at her declaration to him. Knowing that her parents had been married for many years, he knew it was a secret wish of hers to have a similar loving relationship as theirs. That was a feeling he could definitely understand. Finding your bondmate, as rare as it was, was incredible. Finding it across the universe, in the most unlikely of places, was unimaginable. The fates had blessed him with this gorgeous *woman*. He liked the human word for females. *Emeline is my woman.*

Pulling her delicious body tightly up against him, his arm circled around her waist, caressing her toned backside. Nuzzling his nose at that sweet spot just between her breasts, his lips pressed against her soft skin. Her heart beat wildly against his lips, sending tiny vibrations drumming through his body. Her words affected him deeply. Her love and loyalty were things he would cherish forever.

Smiling inwardly, it was his turn to express how he felt.

Wanting her full attention, Nox moved quickly, catching Emeline totally off-guard.

"Nox!"

One minute he was snuggling her breasts, the next, he had one half of his body pressing her down into the mattress.

Grinning down into her upturned face, Nox felt her hand playfully slap at his bicep.

"Hey, give a girl a little warning next time." Emeline rubbed where she had swatted him, soothing the spot as if she might have caused him pain.

His eyes turned serious as he cupped the side of her face in his large hand. The sincerity of his expression had her eyes locked to his. His voice was husky as he started and then stopped in his attempt to convey to her the feelings that filled his heart.

"Pulmina." He felt her shiver at his endearment for her. "I love you more than life itself. I know you can feel that deep within you, but I want to say the words to you. Tell you how you make me feel—only it's difficult for me."

Looking away for an instant, he felt Emeline's hand pulling gently on his cheek, bringing his eyes back to hers, an encouraging smile on her face.

"I have never loved anyone before you." His words came out in a rush.

Surprise flashed across Emeline's face. "You've never been in love?"

"No. Other than the love of my mother and her mother, I never gave it much thought. As you know, all Delicians dream of finding their bondmates, but as time went by and it never happened, I stopped thinking about it. Instead, I focused on my work, putting it out of my mind. When my mother died, I was filled with such anger and pain—finding love was the last thing I wanted."

"Wow. Aren't you like 140 years old or something?" Emeline tried to keep the touch of sadness out her voice. "That's an awfully long time to be alone," she said, caressing his cheek.

Giving her a short laugh, he murmured into her hand, "To humans that is a long time, but to Delicians I'm still considered young. To be honest, Pulmina, I didn't realize I was lonely until I found you. You, your family and friends fill up my life."

Squeezing his cheek, Emeline felt tears forming at the corner of her eyes at the depth of his emotions.

He started softly, his voice a mere whisper. "Your vows were beautiful. I will keep them here in my heart—always."

A fleeting memory crossed his mind as he thought about how marriages were celebrated on his planet. "On Delicia we have a custom similar to your wedding. I have only ever been to one, when I was very young. Father insisted Mother and I accompany him. I don't remember too much about the ceremony itself. Only that it was very lavish with many important people, so of course, my father expected a certain behavior from us. He spent most of his time with his colleagues, leaving us to fend for ourselves. Mother had felt as out of place as I did. Most of the people there were political colleagues of my father's and certainly not friendly. I remember how she had snuck a plate of food and found us a quiet spot out on one of the balconies. We sat there eating and watching the sun set over the water talking about all the things we were going to invent when I became a scientist and we could work together. She could always find ways of making fun out of my father's political commitments he insisted we attend.

I'm sorry now that I was too young to appreciate how special a moment that was. I do not remember the Delicians words, so instead I will use your human ones. I, Nox, take you Emeline to be my bondmate."

"Wife," she interrupted with a grin.

Kissing the tip of her nose, he amended his vows. "I, Nox, take you Emeline to be my wife. I vow to love you until all the stars disappear from the sky and even then, I will love you. I vow to go where you go. No matter where it is, I will always be at your side."

Pressing his body tightly up against hers, connecting them from toes to breast, his desire hard between them, he continued with a quiet intensity, "I vow to worship your body completely, thoroughly—always." Moving his hips in slow circles, he leaned down, caressing his cheek against hers. Closing his eyes, he took slow, deep breaths, filling his senses with her exotic scent. He trailed loving kisses up along her bond mark, feeling her body tighten against his, her breathing coming out in short bursts as he moved up along her face. "I vow to never leave you wanting—for anything." Sprinkling kisses across her nose, he promised, "This, I pledge to you forever."

Not giving her time to respond, Nox took her mouth in a kiss so deep, so fiery, it gave her no cause to ever doubt his commitment to her.

Emeline knew it was a cliché to say that she had never felt like this before, but it was true. She could honestly say that their bond was right out of a fairytale and she was never letting go. What she thought had been love the handful of times she had considered herself *in love* in the past was nothing but at best infatuation.

"Fiona was right again."

Distracted by her words, Nox, who had her leg pulled up over his thigh, stopped mid-squeeze of the soft flesh that filled his hand. "What was that, Pulmina?" he asked in a low voice.

Wiggling her butt against his hand for him to continue what he was doing, she huffed out and then squealed as his fingers pressed to the spot that was causing her to ache. Groaning loudly as his fingers caressed her, she panted out her words. "She—said—I'd—know. Ooh yeah, right there. YES. Oh god, don't stop."

"Know what, my beauty?" Nox could feel her passion wet against his fingers knowing she was well on her way to losing control. He smiled with satisfaction as he continued to push her higher.

She rubbed her breasts against his massive chest, her nipples creating friction, trying to assuage the need that was burning through her. It matched what Nox was doing with his magic fingers.

What was I saying? Oh yeah. 'The one.'

Yes, Nox was definitely the only one who could make her feel like a firework being shot into the sky as her body exploded into a million tiny colorful flickering lights.

They loved one another long and slow. Each demonstrating their deep love and affection through tender touches intertwined with all the emotions that could be felt coming through their bond. This time their need wasn't driven by pent-up desires or the long-awaited anticipation of when they would complete their bond. This was different—more of a discovery of their innermost wants and needs that now connected them. It culminated in a glorious sharing of not only their bodies but of all their hopes and dreams for the new, exciting future that awaited them. Their past disappointments and loneliness replaced by love, acceptance, and most importantly a deep respect for one another. Now that their bond was completed, there was nothing holding them back. The entire universe was waiting for them to explore, new discoveries to find, but also a new family to share their adventure with.

"Babe. Hey babe." Emeline had meant her words to come out soft. Unfortunately, Nox didn't hear it that way. Jolting to a sitting position, his quick movement sent her careening off towards the side of the bed.

"Huh." Nox's long arm reached out instinctively, pulling her back on top of him. With his eyebrow cocked, he grunted at her, "Wife?"

Feeling his body underneath hers...still warm from being snuggled up together under the covers, she got goose bumps at hearing what he'd called her. "I'm hungry." Her voice was slightly muffled, her smiling face pressed into his chest.

Nox laughed into the top of Emeline's head. "Well, we can't have that now, can we? We need to keep your strength up." His fingers danced up and down her spine, his body beginning to react as hers shimmered against his. "What's on the menu tonight?" Nox's own stomach could be heard rumbling, which elicited a giggle from Emeline.

"How about I make us some nachos? They're kind of messy but really good. I think you'll like them."

Pushing up out of Nox's arms, chuckling as he groaned,

not wanting to let her go even for such simple necessities as food. Bending down, picking up the clothes that were scattered across the room, she dumped them into the recycling bin before heading into the bathroom.

Calling over her shoulder, she told him, "Just give me a few minutes. I'll make frozen strawberry margaritas to go along with the nachos. Why don't we eat over at the coffee table?"

After freshening up, Emeline emerged from the bathroom dressed in a short silky robe. Her long hair combed and put up out of the way into a high ponytail, she had never felt so content.

Nox, finally out of bed, walked in her direction. Meeting halfway, he stopped to steal a quick kiss before heading into the bathroom to take care of his own needs.

Unable to resist, her hand snuck out to squeeze one of his hard butt cheeks as he passed her. Staring as he made his way across the room, a small sigh escaped her mouth. His shoulders were wide—well-developed from years of swimming in the ocean near his home. His long torso, tapered at the waist, ended in the finest ass she had ever seen. She imagined him swimming through the water, his powerful strokes propelling him gracefully through the currents.

Lost in thought as he disappeared into the bathroom, she giggled happily at his retort that he hoped she liked what she saw.

"Damn straight I did." Emeline voiced her thoughts loud enough for him to hear…glad he couldn't see how rosy her cheeks were.

Going to the replicator, she programmed in their late-night snack along with placemats, napkins and utensils. *Not gonna lie, I can so get used to this.* The fact that she didn't have to do dishes anymore, or for that matter cook if she didn't feel like it, thrilled Emeline.

While she waited for their food to be completed, she

moved over to stand by the wide windows. Her thoughts turned to her family and friends wondering what their reactions were going to be with all the new changes that were coming. Decisions were going to have to be made regarding her company. Decisions that both she and Nox were going to have to make regarding which direction both their careers were going. Did he want to continue working together or would they both branch off into their respective fields?

A delectable smell broke Emeline's train of thought. Opening the replicator, she couldn't help but be amazed that their entire meal was ready and waiting in mere minutes.

Seeing Nox come out of the bathroom clad only in a thin pair of sleeping trousers that hung low on his hips, Emeline breathed out an *"oh boy."* Too bad the growl from both their stomachs ended that thought quick enough.

"Can I help?" Nox reached up to take the hot platter from her hands.

"Sure. Just put it on the coffee table." Emeline, tucking the utensils under her arm, grabbed the drinks and headed over to place them on the low table that sat in front of the couch.

Sniffing the air, Nox's eyes glazed over with delight. "My mouth is watering from this smell. What is this?"

She pointed out the different ingredients to him. "It's tortilla chips, spicy chicken, salsa and cheese. This white stuff is sour cream and the green stuff is guacamole. I'll show you how I eat nachos."

Picking up a chip covered in chicken and cheese, she dipped first in the guacamole and then in the sour cream. Taking her first bite, her eyes closed as she groaned in pure bliss.

Following her lead, Nox scooped up one of the loaded chips and popped it in his mouth. His eyes widened in surprise at the combination of hot and cold goodness that assailed his taste buds. "This is delicious. I like these nachos."

He reached down and began piling his plate with food.

Handing him a napkin, she couldn't hide her grin as Nox began eating in earnest. "Here, use this. These can get pretty messy."

Filling her own plate, she leaned back into the corner of the couch. With her plate nestled between her legs, a margarita glass in one hand, Emeline picked up a loaded chip and examined it before placing the tasty tidbit in her mouth. "So good. Even better than I can make and so much faster."

After a few moments of silent eating, Emeline stopped long enough to take a breath before taking a long pull from the frozen concoction that cooled the spices that gave her mouth a slight burn.

"I love Mexican food." She watched him nod his head in agreement. He was obviously enjoying this new experience. "Remember how I told you that on Earth we are divided up into countries? Each country has their own governments, cultures, laws and so on. Most have their own languages, although English has come to be a standard around the world."

Picking up a chip, Emeline noticed that the cheese had formed a semi-hard coating that stuck to the chicken... exactly the way she liked it. After swallowing the delicious bite, followed by a sip of her cold drink, she continued her story. "Mexico—it's a large country located on the southern border to mine. They're just slightly north of the equator, so their weather is usually warm and sunny and they have the most amazing beaches. Maybe someday I can take you there."

Wrinkling her nose, hating that she was limited to the places she could take Nox on Earth, she added, "I guess we'll have to see what happens at the meeting." Frowning, she popped the chip in her mouth, unable to stop the sliver of unease that crept over her.

"Hopefully they won't keep us waiting too long," Nox

said in between bites.

Emeline shrugged her shoulders, changing the subject. This night was about them. The rest could wait until tomorrow.

Once the nacho platter was pretty much licked clean, their stomachs satisfied, they both leaned back, gazing out at the myriad of stars that dotted the black night. Being on a spaceship meant that it was always nighttime outside, which made it difficult to keep day and night straight. Emeline wasn't sure what time it was back on Earth. She'd had to rely on her internal clock to help her know when it was time to sleep and eat, but even that had been thrown off. Her ordeal on the Invidia had her all messed up.

Thinking about Earth, she figured it was as good a time as any to get Nox's thoughts on their future. "Nox, what happens now?" She moved closer, her fingers brushing at his hair.

"What do you mean?" He lifted up his arm so she could scoot in next to him.

Snuggling into his warmth, she asked, "What happens now that we've bonded? Do we have to tell someone, I mean, other than our families?"

"Like the UAP or the Delician government?" Nox looked down into her serious face. He had hoped to save this discussion for another time, wanting to keep tonight just for them, but he could feel her heavy thoughts. He knew as well as she did that both their worlds would have something to say about their interspecies bondmating, especially since Earth was on the Prohibited Planets list.

Nodding, Emeline tucked her head under his neck as she waited for his answer.

"I'm not really sure what to do. I mean, Tarek knows, but he's leaving it up to us to decide. I'm thinking he should be the one to tell the representatives at the UAP. I'm not sure what they're going to say. Considering everything that's happened over the last few weeks, I don't think they're going to try to separate us. If anything, the Alliance is used to dealing with different species, so at the most we'll probably have to fill out tons of forms and they'll want to check in on us every so often."

Feeling somewhat relieved, she said, "Okay. That doesn't sound so bad. Now what about Delicia? What are they going to say?"

He hesitated briefly before saying, "That might be a little different."

With a worried look, Emeline asked how so.

Looking away, he thought for a moment. Not wanting to scare her, especially since he had no idea what they were facing when they arrived on Delicia, he decided to take a more optimistic approach until proven otherwise.

Kissing the back of her hand, he watched her expression as he told her, "You know there has never been a bondmating between different species. We will be the first. Honestly, Em, I'm not sure what their reactions are going to be. I'm assuming that most will be happy and hopeful that more people will find their bondmates. I mean, look at Ezio and Violia. They're the first Delicians in more than a few generations to form a bond. This is exciting news for Delicia."

Nox reached over to run his fingers up along her bond mark. "Once they get to know you, they will love you—just like I do."

Taking his finger, he gently lifted her chin so she looked direct into his eyes. "Do you want to know how I truly feel, my Pulmina?"

At her nod, he said, "I don't care what they say. If anyone has a problem with it, we will leave and find a place where we can live without judgment."

Emeline's eyebrows turned inward, knowing that Nox was thinking about his father. "You're worried about what your dad is going to say, aren't you?"

At the mention of his father, Nox's voice became terse.

"What he thinks does not matter to me."

Lost in thought for a moment, Nox exhaled, releasing some of his frustration at his father. "I learned a long time ago not to trust my father. The fact is, he doesn't get a choice in this. Bondmates are chosen through the fates and once completed, the bond can never be undone. He will have no other option but to accept you." Running a finger down her cheek, he told her, "I don't want you to worry about him. We will rarely see him and we won't be living anywhere near him. I have not allowed my father to have any say in my life for many, many years. That is not going to change just because we are bonded."

Nox's words were unsettling to Emeline. They highlighted the differences between their families' dynamics. It was sad to her that father and son barely spoke.

"Where will we live?" Emeline's voice held a note of uncertainty, causing Nox to frown at her.

"Where would you like to live?"

"I don't know. That's what I wanted to talk to you about. I need to decide what to do with my company and the girls. I have so many unanswered questions."

Nox understood that Emeline had a lot to deal with. Not only with their new bond but also staying committed to her company and her friends, not to mention her family.

Pulling her onto his lap, he smiled as she snuggled up against him. Squeezing her hand, he knew it was time to make some plans for the future. "Tell me, Pulmina, what is it you would like to do?"

Stilling at his question, Emeline's lips curved into a smile. *This bondmating thing isn't so hard.*

The words flowed naturally as she told him what she had been thinking about. "I really want to continue working with the girls, but I also want to work with you. I know you have your own work, but I really liked working with you and Loris. What do you think? Would you be up for that?" Hopeful eyes bored into his as she barely breathed, waiting for his answer.

Smiling, Nox watched Emeline chew on her bottom lip —a sure sign she was nervous. Wanting to put her mind at ease, he told her, "I would love that and I know Loris feels the same. I wouldn't be surprised if you already had a few new projects in mind?" He quirked an eyebrow at her because he already knew her answer.

Sinking back against him, huffing out in relief, she muttered, "It's weird that you know me so well."

Taking her hand and kissing it, Nox leaned in, nudging her shoulder. "You forget, beautiful, I can feel your emotions and right now they're telling me exactly what you're feeling."

She snorted at him. "This can be both good and bad. When I'm having a grumpy day, you may wish you had a filter you could turn off and on."

"Never, my Pulmina."

"Yeah, you say that now. We'll talk when it's my time of the month."

Nox was confused. "What is your time of the month?"

Emeline's face turned bright red as she tried to figure out an easy way to tell Nox about human females and their menstruation cycle. "Um, well it's all part of the female reproductive cycle." She gave him a quick overview, ending with the one important question that had been troubling her. "I know we want to have children, but I was hoping that we could wait for a while—just until we can get settled. Are you okay with that?"

"Of course, but you do want to have children?"

Placing her hand on his face, she softly caressed his worried brow. "Yes. I want lots of children. My only worry is that Delicians live a much longer life than humans. What will happen when I age and you don't?"

"What? Did you forget what Dr. Datrem said? Now that we have completed the bond, we will age at the same time."

Confusion clouded Emeline's eyes. "Say that again."

"ARI's analysis confirmed that you will live as long as I do."

To say that Emeline was flabbergasted was an understatement. It took her a minute to absorb what Nox was saying. Sure, Datrem had mentioned it was a possibility, but she hadn't really believed him. *I mean, come on, who lives to be 600 years old? Apparently, I do. Oh, the possibilities!*

With a twinkle in her eyes, Emeline nearly shouted with joy. "You mean it's definite—I'm not going to grow old and gray while you still look like a hot babe?"

Delighted at her playful mood, Nox wagged his eyebrows asking smoothly, "You think I'm a hot babe?"

Elbowing him in the side, she couldn't help but tease him. A huge weight had been lifted from her shoulders. "You know you're gorgeous." Her lips came down hard on his, taking him in for a steamy kiss.

Pulling back, breathless, she pressed her forehead to his. "I can't believe this. That had been my greatest fear, that I would only have you for such a short time. I was worried that I wouldn't be around to see my children grow and have children of their own. This changes everything. Oh Nox, I'm so happy."

Relieved, Nox wrapped her tightly in his arm. Grinning down, he asked, "Are there any other concerns you have that I can help alleviate for you?" He nibbled on her lips, tasting the strawberries from their drink.

Turning her back to lean against his broad chest, she stared out the window at the twinkling stars, considering his question. Her eyes blinked as a shooting star shot across her line of sight. It left a trail of golden particles in its wake, which only served to add to the wonder of how much her life had changed in such a short time. Whatever decisions she made about her company needed to be discussed with Ami, Heather and Lorelei. They were as much a part of its creation as she was and deserved to be consulted in any changes that were going to be made.

Ami in particular worried her. She had filled Emeline in about the rescue mission, but something was off. She knew her friend and she was never this quiet and withdrawn. Deciding to talk to her first thing in the morning, Emeline was determined to get to the bottom of why Ami was acting so strangely lately.

Telling Nox her thoughts, Emeline reminded him that she wanted to stop in to see Violia before they met with Tarek. Even with everything that had been going on, Violia was never very far from Emeline's thoughts. She wanted to see for herself just how well she was recuperating. Acknowledging that their friendship may have started out in a precarious way, Emeline was hoping they could build a true friendship out of the hardship they had endured together. Not only that, she was curious to find out if Ezio had told Violia about their bond and what her reaction had been.

Yawning, Emeline pushed up off of Nox's lap. Picking up the remains of their meal, she dumped it in the recycle bin—dishes and all. Again, unable to hide the smile that crossed her face every time she thought of the convenience of her new life, Fiona popped into her mind. Her mother was going to love not having to do dishes anymore. Now all she had to do was talk her into coming with them.

Feeling Nox press his hot naked body against hers, she squealed when he picked her up and carried her to their bed. He loved her long into the night, stopping only when they drifted off into a blissful sleep entwined in each other's arms. With the bond completed, she wasn't just Emeline Cameron anymore. She was Emeline, bondmate to Nox, son of Sandovar and Elara, daughter of Henry and Fiona—bonded together for all eternity.

CHAPTER 27

The sound of feet pounding against hard metal echoed off the walls. She had to run faster.

Glancing over her shoulder, she didn't see anyone, but she could hear his footsteps getting closer. Hagen was gaining on her.

Her chest hurt with each ragged breath. Fear, unlike anything she had ever felt before, held her in its grip. Sweat dripped down her back, her T-shirt sticking to her body like Hagen stuck to his relentless pursuit of her. With her heart pounding loud in her ears, she sprinted through his dilapidated ship, trying desperately to control her rising panic.

Hurry, Emeline, hurry. He's coming for you.

"Human female—there is no escape." His gravelly voice caused her fear to spike as a sob escaped her mouth.

The distance between them was closing...the sound of his footsteps got increasingly louder as she took a sharp left turn, hoping to throw him off her trail. Unfortunately, the corridor she chose ended with a door that refused to open.

Shit, shit, shit.

Banging on the door, crying out for help, her panic bordered on hysteria. Drops of blood slipped quietly to the floor from the cuts and scrapes that littered her hands.

Turning around quickly, she meant to double back only to find a large unmovable alien blocking her only escape route... Hagen.

He stood there laughing, totally aware he had her cornered. The clearly maniacal sound bounced around the empty corridor as he moved toward her.

One foot at a time, Emeline moved backwards until there was nowhere else to go. Pounding her fists frantically on the metal door, hoping and praying that someone on the other side would open it. Would save her from what she knew was going to be horrific retribution from Hagen.

"Nowhere to run, human." Hagen stopped in front of her, his hands on his hips as his massive chest heaved up and down, winded from their chase. What was unnerving was that he was surprisingly calm.

Moving his hand down, he stroked his cock as his hungry eyes roamed her body. "I've waited too long for this moment. No one is going to save you this time. Finally, I will take what I am owed." He swiped his tongue across his dry lips. "You are mine to play with." His grin turned sadistic—his yellowed teeth contributing to the demented, wild look in his eyes. "I hope you like it rough."

Emeline's face was masked in horror at the bulge that tented the front of his pants. Turning back to the door, Emeline resumed her pounding, screaming at the top of her lungs for someone to help her. "Please, please, somebody...help me."

She gagged feeling his hot fetid breath on her neck.

A heavy hand landed on her shoulder, causing her self-defense instinct to kick in. Bringing her elbow up sharply, she knew she had connected with his nose when she felt his blood on her arm, at the same time she heard the crunch of bone along with a yelp of pain.

"Damn, I think you broke my nose."

Emeline jolted awake to find Nox leaning over her, his hand covering his nose, crying out in agony. Blood poured out from between his fingers down onto his chin and chest. His eyes were filled with pain and anxiety.

"Oh crap." Jumping out of bed, Emeline grabbed the closest thing she could find, Nox's discarded pants off the floor. Shoving them at him, her hands still shaking from a nightmare that had felt all too real.

"I am so sorry," she sobbed out, holding one hand over her mouth. Her other hand was pressed tight against her heaving chest, trying to dispel the terror that clung to her like wet sand. Glancing frantically around the room, a look of wild panic still lingered in her wide eyes.

Pressing his pants against his face to stop the bleeding, Nox motioned her over to him, but she shook her head, refusing his outstretched hand.

Instead, she stood with her arm clutched tight to her middle staring helplessly at him.

"Pul...ia, co...re." Nox's words were muffled as he tried to comfort her through the blood-soaked pants. "Mmffmmm...mf."

"Bhahahahahaha." Emeline couldn't stop herself. The sight of this huge shiny alien standing stark naked with his bloodied pants held tightly to his face trying to comfort her should not have been funny—only it was.

Her laughter only intensified when he dropped his pants to the floor and stood with his hands on his hips. Smears of dried blood clung to his mouth and chin, making him look like a vampire, albeit a naked vampire, who had just finished feeding.

"I'm so happy I could entertain you," he said with dry amusement. He'd take her laughter over her anguished pleas for help any day.

Dragging huge gulps of air into her lungs, trying to steady her breathing, Emeline wiped the water from her eyes. Giving him a sheepish grin, she blew out a heavy breath, saying, "Sorry. I really didn't mean to lose it like that."

Looking down at himself, Nox couldn't help but chuckle with her. "I like hearing you laugh."

Aw, what a guy. But now it was time to repair some of the damage her nightmare had caused. Pointing to his nose, she asked, "Can I take a look?"

Sitting back onto the bed, Nox reached out and pulled her to stand in between his open legs, telling her to do whatever she wanted.

Smiling at his clearly misguided trust in her, Emeline inspected the damage. "Huh."

"What?"

"I'm just surprised, that's all." Gently taking his chin in between her fingers, she moved his head slowly from side to side, inspecting his injured face. "Your blood is red."

Wincing from the movement, Nox looked at her, confused. "Were you expecting something different?"

"Actually—yeah. I figured it would be purple or pink. I never considered that we'd have the same color blood, but it does make sense." Shrugging her shoulders, she asked, "Do you want me to get a regen device?" Focusing on Nox's injury was helping to push away the last lingering remnants of her nightmare.

No longer caught up in its fierce grip, Emeline couldn't help but feel sympathy for Nox. He had only been trying to comfort her and got a bloody nose for his kindness.

"Please."

While Nox waited for her to retrieve the device, he took in her appearance. If it wasn't for the wide-eyed crazed look still lingering on her face, he might have laughed at the sight of the two of them—both naked and covered in blood.

With device in hand, Emeline held it steady to Nox's nose allowing the nanites do their thing.

Nox sat quietly as sharp tingles moved across nose. Thinking back to being woken up abruptly by Emeline's thrashing and frantic calls for help, it might have been safer to take a gentler approach to waking her up. But hearing her cries for someone—anyone—to save her nearly killed him. This episode only proved Dr. Datrem's diagnosis...Emeline suffered from PTSD.

In no time at all, the swelling was gone and Nox could breathe freely through his perfectly repaired nose. Unfortunately for him, his first smell was the faint metallic scent of blood mixed in with dried sweat and tears.

Wiping off as much of the blood from his face as he could, Nox threw his soiled pants onto the floor. Pulling his trembling mate down onto his lap, he tucked her head beneath his chin, cocooning her in his strong arms all the while murmuring that she was safe.

Peeking up at him, feeling more than mortified, she apologized again. "I didn't mean to hurt you."

"It's okay." Nox brushed off his injury but continued to send calming thoughts through their bond, anything to help soothe her troubled emotions.

Sitting up, she pulled his hair back from his face. Doing a quick scan, she considered his face thoughtfully. "You were lucky. If we were on Earth, it would take weeks, maybe months for this to heal."

Shuddering at that nasty prospect, he changed the subject. "How's your elbow?" His thumb rubbed at his blood that had dried on her skin. "Liam teach you that move?"

Nodding her head, Emeline sank back against Nox's wide chest. Her body shivered at the memory of her nightmare. Latching quickly onto the feeling of Nox's firm hands gliding gently up and down her arms...his gentle touch soothed her mind. Her anxiety levels began to recede along with the abject fear that had nearly paralyzed her. She decided that now was not the time to do an in-depth analysis of her nightmare. Her ordeal with Hagen had no place rearing its ugly head, especially when she just experienced *the* best night of her entire life. "I don't want to talk about this right now."

Knowing when to back off, Nox simply tightened his arms around her.

"I know I need to—eventually. But not right now."

Straddling his legs, she curled herself against Nox's chest, smiling as she watched his skin pebble into goose bumps at her touch.

Reaching up, her fingers caressed his cheek. She could feel the hardness of his cheekbones through the pads of her fingertips. Feeling a pang of guilt at his bloodied nose, she leaned up blowing soft featherlike kisses along the bridge of his newly repaired nose. "Babe, I'm so sorry. What can I do to make it up to you? Ask me anything—anything you want."

Pressing his face lightly into her hand, Nox turned his head and held her eyes in a hungry gaze. "Anything?" At her nod, he smiled. "I'll have to give this some thought." Closing his eyes, soaking up her touch, he told her, "You do know that the regen device healed me completely."

"Yeah, I know, but I still feel bad. Between the sound of your nose crunching and the scream that came out of your mouth, I thought I'd killed you."

"I did not scream," Nox huffed out indignantly.

Sitting up quickly with her arms crossed, a playful look of feigned shock danced across her face. "Oh, my bad. I guess I was mistaken. It must have been that other guy in the room who was screaming like a baby."

"Baby! Baby! I'll show you who's a baby." His fingers dove to that familiar ticklish spot, causing Emeline to squirm and twist in his lap, shrieking in laughter for him to stop.

Standing up quickly, his arms full of his beautiful bond-mate, Nox headed into the bathroom. A nice hot shower to wash away the remaining vestiges of her nightmare would do much to recapture their earlier bliss. His voice lowered when Nox went into in-depth detail on all the different ways in which he planned on showing her just how manly he was. He took delight in hearing Emeline giggle at each of his promises.

It was a long time before the water was finally turned off and the body dryer could be heard. Their skin had pruned from the prolonged time spent under the shower, but their souls were renewed at the reminder of the intimate bond they shared.

"I really do need to call my mum and tell her about all of this." Emeline turned her back to the dryer, cognizant of the various sore spots in certain areas, blushing slightly at just how thoroughly Nox had proved he wasn't the only screamer in the family. In fact, he'd made her scream more than a handful of times just to prove his point...he had merely grunted from the unexpected pain. That was the story he was sticking to.

Nox's mind drifted to Sandovar at her comment. His father had commed him again. *What's he up to?* This was unlike him. "I know what you mean. I have to call my father and tell him about our bonding." Grimacing at the thought of that conversation with Sandovar, Nox ground out, "I'm not looking forward to his reaction."

A worried frown creased across Emeline's forehead. "What do you think he's going to say?"

"Honestly, Pulmina, I don't care." Coming over, he gathered her in his arms, nuzzling her hair before kissing along her new bond mark. She tasted like a warm vanilla cookie. Like the one that she had made for him late one night when they were testing out the food replicator with human recipes. "You are my bondmate—mine."

"And you are mine. No one, I don't care who they are, no one will ever take you away from me again." She playfully swatted his backside as the air from the dryer swirled warm around them.

He pulled her sweet-smelling body tight up against his. His kisses became sensuous, leaving no question as to whom she belonged.

When he could speak again, Nox kissed the tip of her nose, saying, "I'm sure he will have plenty to say. I just choose not to listen." He knew Emeline had never been exposed to someone as calculating as his father before, which was why he was not in any hurry to introduce Emeline to Sandovar.

Reaching over to shut the dryer off, Emeline heard one of their comms beeping in the bedroom. "Someone is calling one of us. I better go see who it is. It might be Tarek with an update on the meeting with President Jenkins." Grabbing her robe off her vanity chair, Emeline tied a quick knot before heading out to see who was calling.

"Um, Nox."

"Yes, Pulmina?" Nox came into the room, seeing Emeline pointing to his comm link, mouthing "*Sandovar.*" Nox reached down to terminate the call, but Emeline stopped his hand.

"No, don't do that. Talk to him. He's already mad that he hasn't been able to get in touch with you. He's probably just worried." Leaning her body against his, she gently pulled his hair back from his face. "What's the worst that can happen? He yells and you get to hang up. I mean, it's not like he has any power to separate us. Besides, he may surprise you. At least give him a chance."

Rolling his eyes knowing he was acting like a petulant child, Nox sighed. "You're right. But don't say I didn't warn you." Nox knew just how unscrupulous Sandovar could be when he wanted to get his way. Emeline didn't. She was about to find out just how manipulative his father could be.

Sitting at his desk, dressed only in a pair of loose-fitting sleep trousers, Nox pressed the button and his father's face appeared before him. "Hello, Father." He kept his face neutral, devoid of all emotion. It was the same expression he had been showing to his father ever since his mother's death.

"Nox, you have been avoiding me." The face on the screen was that of an extremely attractive older male. His hair was swept back from his forehead, cut short across the nape of his neck. The color was a deep brown with even darker purple highlights threaded throughout. He was similar in size to Nox but didn't have near the muscular structure of his son. It was obvious to anyone who saw them together that they were father and son. It was also obvious from the scowl on his face that Sandovar was extremely unhappy with his son.

"I've been busy."

"I have heard. Regardless, when I call, I expect you to

answer. Did you think I wouldn't find out about your mission to Earth?" Sandovar gave him a knowing look. "Tell me everything."

Even though Sandovar's tone demanded he answer him, Nox knew him only too well. His father liked knowledge. What was that human saying? *Knowledge is power.* The humans' description described his father perfectly. Sandovar was all about power and how he could use it to benefit his ambitions. It didn't matter who got hurt. Sandovar didn't care. Nox had seen firsthand some of his father's dirty dealings...even trying to pull Nox into a few of his less than politically correct deals. Nox never allowed himself to get involved in any of his father's schemes. How he continually got away without getting caught always puzzled Nox, but his father had a knack for always finding ways of turning things in his favor or placing the blame on someone else when necessary. He was either the smartest male Nox had ever known or the luckiest. Nox was leaning towards the latter and everyone knew, eventually your luck ran out.

Until that time, he knew exactly how to piss off his father.

"No."

The groove between Sandovar's eyebrows deepened at Nox's refusal. "No? You can't say no to me. I'm your father." He pointed his finger at Nox, seriously annoyed, reminding him, "I am also a Delician Senator. I have a right to know why our top military general has disappeared along with half our fleet."

Nox knew he was irritating his father by the tightening of his jaw. Sandovar always made a point to keep his emotions in check. *Never give your adversaries any advantages over you.* There was only one person who could rattle Sandovar's carefully erected façade—Nox. He knew full well how to get under his father's skin. "Don't expect any details from me. If you want information, ask General Tarek." Nox fought to hide his smug look, knowing full well that Sandovar and Tarek did not like each other.

Sandovar tried his usual death stare on Nox, only to break into a smile as his eyes moved to look over Nox's shoulder.

Emeline stood behind him, her soft lips turned up into a gentle smile. With her hair pulled back into a ponytail, her bond mark was proudly on display.

Giving Emeline an affable smile, Sandovar turned to his son, asking him coolly, "Who is this beautiful female?"

Turning around, Nox arched an eyebrow at his bondmate. He'd had every intension of introducing them—eventually. Not surprised she was there—it was her choice of clothing that was the surprise…a traditional Delician celebration dress.

His eyes roamed her from head to toe, taking in the silky, flowing, sleeveless dress, the blue color matching her eyes as well as the blue in their bond marks. It hung gracefully from her shoulders—two thin, rectangle, sparkly, crystal pins adorned each shoulder. The V-neck front with delicate folds fit snugly, accentuating her full breasts before falling elegantly around her ankles. Even the soft sheen of the material couldn't compare to the happiness that emanated off of Emeline. When she smiled, she glowed like moonlight on a lake, serene and stunningly beautiful.

"You look amazing, Pulmina. This dress suits you."

Emeline beamed at Nox's compliment. "Thanks, babe. I'm in love with it. It reminds me of my favorite French designer Madame Alix Grès. I think it brings out my feminine side." Whispering so only he could hear, she chuckled, "Big change from my usual jeans and T-shirt, huh."

Whispering back, Nox wagged his eyebrows at her. "You look good in anything—or in nothing at all."

Clasping her hand in his, Nox tried to pull her down for a kiss, but she resisted, making *stop eyes* at him before stealing a glance at his father.

Ignoring the look of indulgence on his father's face, Nox

slid his arms around her...kissing her mark at the side of her ear, asking if she was ready for this.

Nodding, they turned together and faced the screen. Nox pulled Emeline tight up against his front, his arm snaked across her waist. "Father, this is Emeline Cameron." Kissing her temple, he faced his father, stating flatly, "My bondmate."

Nox waited for the normal disappointed rhetoric he knew was coming.

"Congratulations."

Narrowing his eyes, he glared suspiciously at his father.

Giving Nox a cursory glance, Sandovar smiled at Emeline. "It is a joy to meet you, Emeline. I'm happy for you both."

Scoffing in disbelief, Nox saw right through his father's pretense. "Now that's hard to believe." Emeline's elbow nudged his side. The thing was, Emeline didn't know Sandovar like he did—had never experienced the depth of his duplicity.

"Forgive my son, Emeline. He's obviously under the assumption that I would not be happy that he has found his bondmate. That couldn't be further from the truth." Ignoring his son's snort, Sandovar continued, his voice softening, "It is a rare thing to find your bondmate. I am very happy for the both of you."

"Thank you."

"Although, I am surprised that you are human. It was my understanding that humans are on the Prohibited Planet list. I take it you two met on this mission you can't speak about." He didn't bother to hide his displeasure at being excluded from knowing any of their mission details.

Annoyed, her smile quickly faded at Sandovar's tone at her being human. Per usual, it was assumed humans were lacking in—well pretty much everything. It was getting tiresome, Emeline thought. Biting back the urge to set Sandovar straight, he was after all her father-in-law and this was new to him, she decided to give him the benefit of the doubt and ignore his disparaging tone. Plastering a smile on her face, she replied, "Yes, we did. The only thing I can tell you is that it was a total surprise to the both of us." Tilting her head, she grinned up at Nox when he dropped a kiss onto her upturned nose. "But a happy one."

Nox wasn't fooled by Sandovar's supposed acceptance of his bond with her—the look behind his indulgent smile said it all. His father was up to something. Nox made a mental note to keep a close eye on him. "Father, I'm surprised you are so accepting, especially considering how hard you pushed for a union with Senator Ventano's daughter." Nox felt Emeline suck in a breath as he kept his steady gaze on his father.

Sandovar's eyes widened slightly at Nox's comment, admitting, "Yes, that is true. It would have been an advantageous union—for all of us. We would have had a strong alliance with Ventano's region and you would have been able to start a family."

Nox blew out a disgusted breath. The only one who would have benefitted from that doomed union was Sandovar. Nox never would have agreed to father's *request* because he knew the real reason Sandovar was pushing so hard. Senator Ventano's region was vastly populated and extremely wealthy. Whereas Sandovar's region, even though larger, was mountainous and covered in dense forests with limited financial resources.

"Enough," Nox growled out. "My bondmating with Emeline ends this discussion. We both know the real reason you were pushing so hard." Nox had learned a long time ago how to hold his ground against his father. It was ironic that it had been Sandovar himself who had taught Nox how to stand firm against an adversary. Being a quick study, he knew exactly how to annoy his father. The real reason Sandovar pushed for this *arranged* union was personal greed. One of the largest and most profitable trade ports on Delicia was located on the border adjacent to Sandovar's region—on Senator Ventano's land. Sandovar had coveted a piece of that action for longer than Nox could remember. Now it had once again slipped through Sandovar's fingers. His father was not the least bit happy with his bond with Emeline, no matter what kind of a happy guise he put on.

Sandovar gave his son a warning look.

Deciding he could only push his father just so far, Nox changed the subject. It was, after all, the first time Emeline was meeting his father. She would have a lifetime to find out exactly the kind of person Sandovar was. "Fine."

Trying to dispel some of the tension, Nox told Sandovar Emeline was a scientist on Earth. "When we return to Delicia, we'll be working together in my lab." Glancing at Emeline, he added, "Our lab now."

"You're a scientist?" Sandovar's disbelief oozed unconsciously out of his mouth, giving no thought to how Emeline might interpret his tone.

Sadly, his reaction didn't surprise her. It wasn't anything new to her. Apparently, more than a few things were universal.

Pulling her shoulders back, her gaze met Sandovar's straight on. "Yes, I am. I run my own company with a group of female friends. We are the leading company on Earth for solving global networking solutions." She smiled inwardly, knowing her new father-in-law didn't have a clue what she was talking about.

"Fascinating, and what about your family?"

Emeline hesitated, not sure what she should tell him. Her eyes darted to Nox's. At his nod, she answered, "I have a brother and sister and, of course, my mother." Nox's warning about his father resonated in her head. She trusted Nox, and if he said to be wary of his father, she would be. Of course, his annoyingly pompous attitude made that easy enough. Still, she told herself, he was Nox's father and she didn't want to cause any more friction between father and son.

"And what does your family say about your bonding with my son?"

"Liam—that's my brother—well, I'm not going lie, it came as a complete shock. It took him a while to get used to it, but he's fine now. As for my mother—her name is Fiona—I haven't had a chance to tell her and my sister, Isabelle, yet." Squeezing Nox's hand, she leaned up and kissed his cheek, "Once they get over the initial shock, I just know they're going to love him, just like I do.

"I look forward to meeting your mother and your siblings. What about your father?" Sandovar asked. "What does he do on Earth?"

Emeline bit her lip, her face paling slightly as she glanced back at Nox. "My father was an engineer who worked on scientific instruments." Attempting to hide the hitch in her voice, she added, "He died of a heart attack two years ago."

"I'm sorry to hear that." Sandovar said with compassion, "Your mother must miss him."

Emeline saw the sincerity in his eyes. "Yes. She has been lost without him."

"I can imagine. I'm sure you know we lost Nox's mother, Elara, some time ago. I still miss her every day." Sandovar's head dropped in sadness. It was Nox's cough that brought his head up with a start. He glared at his son, silently telling him not to go there.

Ignoring his father's silent directives, Nox snapped back, "Please, don't even think to tell Emeline how much you miss my mother. If you had even bothered to spend a fraction of your time with her or me, for that matter, she might still be here."

"Nox." Sandovar's tone became hard, almost menacing.

A soft hand on his arm stopped Nox from responding. Seeing her worried expression, Nox knew Emeline was right. No point in rehashing old wounds. His mother was gone. The gaping hole she left in his life was now being filled in by his beautiful bondmate. Who did Sandovar have? No one.

Catching his father watching them intently only re-affirmed what his gut was telling him...Sandovar was up to no good. Only someone who really knew his father could see there was an edginess in his demeanor. The slight tightening around his eyes, skin pulled taut across his jaw, the superficial smile on his face—Nox had seen that look many times before. Add to it his insistence on knowing Nox's location was more than enough to make Nox feel uneasy.

"Father, it was nice of you to call, but Emeline and I have a meeting with General Tarek."

"Of course. Do you know how long it will be before you to return to Delicia?" Sandovar's face appeared nonchalant as he probed for even the smallest amount of information.

Nox's nostrils flared, shaking his head at his father—some things never changed. Raising an eyebrow at his father, Sandovar knew perfectly well that type of question was classified. "Was there something you needed from me?" Nox asked.

"Actually, I did have a project I wanted to get your thoughts on, but it can wait. We can discuss it later—when you have more time." Sandovar waved his hand in an attempt to dismiss Nox's question.

Sandovar next turned his saccharine smile onto Emeline, again welcoming her to the family. Adding that he was looking forward to when they could meet in person.

She returned his sentiment as Nox ended the call.

Sighing against one another in relief that that was over, Nox sank into his chair, pulling Emeline onto his lap...each lost in their respective thoughts regarding Sandovar's call.

Emeline was the first one to break the silence, telling Nox that she thought Sandovar was nice.

Snorting out loud, Nox rolled his eyes as he started nibbling on Emeline's earlobe, telling her he didn't want to talk about his father. He'd rather pick up where he left off before his father had rudely interrupted them.

Agreeing wholeheartedly, she ran her hands up along Nox's smooth chest, encouraging him to continue—his nips were sending tingly shivers down her spine. Squirming in his lap, she could feel her senses begin to overheat from his thorough attention to detail.

Of course, Tarek had to choose that exact moment to send out an alert to all elite team members that the meeting with the humans would be in two days. He wanted everyone to report to his conference room in one hour to discuss the details.

Nox groaned into Emeline's neck. Tarek was killing him.

Murmuring into her ear, Nox scooped her up in his arms. Placing her onto the bed, Nox followed her down, whispering, "I better get busy if we only have an hour."

Ami rested her forehead against one of the panoramic windows that lined the observation lounge. The coolness of the glass did little to alleviate the turmoil that was raging through her.

The heavy sigh that started from the depths of her soul had her wondering for like the millionth time, what was it that drew her to stare longingly out into the vastness of space? Her stomach was in knots, her appetite gone, which was saying something because eating was a passion of hers. It was the main reason she constantly struggled to keep her booty in check.

So much had happened to her over the last few days. Between killing two people and then there was the whole *Quin* episode...emotions so raw filtered continuously through her mind, she felt dizzy.

Quin. What was it about him? Never had she been

so fixated on a man before. Especially one that was considered the most dangerous male in the universe. Seriously, he was the leader of a nefarious planet that wanted to conquer and enslave her own people, for heaven's sake. *What is wrong with you, Ami?*

It was that damn kiss they had shared. That had to be the reason why she was so obsessed with him.

And as far as sleeping—well, that was the worst. He invaded her dreams. And man, oh man, were they steamy. So real and vivid, she'd had to take a cold shower—twice and even that did nothing to take the edge off. Just the mere thought of him had her body humming with pent-up desire. Her mind kept replaying his sultry words over and over—*beautiful, fierce…tempting.* Remembering the feeling of his warm breath against her neck, she shivered. *Phew!*

Ami wished her besties were here. She was in desperate need of a girls' night. Yeah, that wasn't happening, not with Heather and Lorelei in Boston and Emeline being otherwise engaged for the foreseeable future, it looked like she was on her own.

For a scant moment she had considered talking to Liam, but he was such a dude. She could hear him now—*Let's just go work up a sweat. You'll feel better.* Well, she was tired of hitting things and shooting weapons—well, maybe not that last one because let's face it, shooting alien guns was *AWESOME!*

Speaking of aliens, maybe she could talk to Ramola. They had formed a sort of a bond while on the mission. He had been so understanding after she killed Hagen—coming over, lending his support. It meant a lot her that he had reached out trying to make her feel better. Guilt was a heavy burden to carry around, even though it was self-defense.

Quin had said he was impressed with my shooting. Now see…here we go again. Quin—[sigh] His name is Tarquin, no matter what he said to call him.

What is wrong with me? Why can't I stop thinking about his eyes? The way he looked at me—so intense...like a bee to a pretty flower. [Snickering] More like a grizzly bear drawn to a river full of salmon. Then he had to go and kiss me—HOLY MOLY. I mean, what a kiss.

Leaning back on her arms, Ami took stock of the situation she had gotten herself into. She had always considered herself to be pretty streetwise. After all, she was tall, strong and mouthy as well as extremely well trained in self-defense. That probably had a lot to do with her tendency to date bad boys, but come on—everyone knew bad boys were much more fun.

Well, she reminded herself, kissing Quin was over the top even for her. *Ami, you've stepped in some serious doo-doo this time.*

Standing up, she caught her reflection in the window. Startled, she barely recognized the woman staring back. Her dark hair was loose—hanging in long, leisurely curls down over her shoulders like water trickling along a quiet stream. Whatever they put in their hair products certainly agreed with her hair. It had never looked so good—all soft and shiny.

Pulling her hair back tight, Ami carefully examined her face. Where she expected to see deep lines creasing her forehead with dark bags under her eyes, instead, her skin was flawless. Her deep brown eyes sparkled, her red lips were soft and plump. *What the hell is happening to me?*

She couldn't help wondering if anyone else had noticed the changes in her or if she was just being paranoid. One thing she did know for certain, if Tarek and Jagger found out about her encounter with Quin, they would be furious. They might even send her back to Earth.

No!

She couldn't—wouldn't let that happen, not when she had come this far. In a lot less time than she had imagined, Ami had confirmed her decision—she was going with Emeline and Liam. They could run the office remotely, even from millions of light years away. It had been impressive how seamless it had been keeping in touch with Heather and Lorelei using the Delician technology.

Grinning at herself in the window, it would appear a meeting of the board of directors for EAC was in their future with some interesting changes about to happen. Not exactly sure what her role would be in the upcoming mission to introduce the human delegation to the UAP, one thing was certain—she would not be left behind.

Shivering, Ami's arms crossed tightly across her middle as she moved to stretch out on the long sofa. Closing her eyes, she really needed to talk to someone about these crazy feelings that held her in such a tight grip. Maybe she could steal Emeline away from her new bondmate for a quick girl talk. *She did say that Quin had saved her—maybe she would be more understanding. I need to talk to someone about this.*

Rolling over, with her head nestled into the crook of her arm, her mind drifted to Quin, wondering where he was. Was he thinking about her the way she couldn't seem to erase him from her thoughts?

This is silly, Ami laughed, painfully. More than likely he was halfway to Hexia, probably curled up with some sexy alien temptress—maybe even two of them. She was confused at why the thought of him kissing someone made her want to puke. It didn't make any sense.

Swallowing her unease, she realized that nothing made sense anymore.

Her eyes drifted shut. *There it is.*

Soon after Quin had kissed her, whenever she shut her eyes, a spark of gold flickered at her. Staring into the bright flame was mesmerizing, like staring into a campfire.

It was in those moments that she found an inner peace —a sense of comfort. She held on to those feelings knowing she would need them in the future. An uncertain future as they waited for word from Earth's leaders. It was mind-boggling to realize that she was no longer just Ami Jefferson from the United States of America. Now, she was Ami Jefferson, human from the planet Earth...one of the many planets under the jurisdiction of the United Alliance of Planets.

Stretching out her arm in front of her, the soft glow from the stars gave her mocha skin a satiny sheen to it. Curiously, she noticed a strange shadow moving just under her skin, trailing down along her arm, disappearing around her hand. Turning her hand over, she was surprised to see a quick swirl of color melt into her palm. *That's weird. I didn't think Dr. Datrem used nanites when he was healing my leg. I'll have to ask him about that tomorrow. I'm not crazy about having rogue nanites roaming around my body.*

Her wrist comm broke into her thoughts, signaling an incoming message from General Tarek. It seemed her people were ready to talk.

Jumping up and hurrying from the room, Ami pushed all her jumbled thoughts into the background of her mind. Her future was calling and she needed to be ready. One way or another, she was going on this mission and nothing and no one was going to stop her. *You're just hoping Quin will find you. Shut up, Ami!*

CHAPTER 28

Settling back against her seat on the shuttle, Emeline marveled at how perfectly it molded to her body. She sat in quiet wonderment, watching Earth's continents taking shape right before her very eyes. This view from space really drove home the point that their lives had been forever altered.

Nyx was piloting the shuttle to the coordinates Leslie Merriman had sent to Tarek—coordinates to a place that would ensure the privacy they needed. Leslie had quietly let Liam know that the leaders were nervous and skittish, especially since the destruction of the Hexian freighter. While they were appreciative of the Delicians' help in stopping the Hexians, they were still apprehensive about the motives of the Delicians and UAP and what it meant for Earth's future.

Emeline was still processing everything they'd discussed in the meeting with the team. Tarek had explained that he'd been through numerous first contacts and was aware there were risks, but he wasn't anticipating anything unusual happening. She smiled inwardly, remembering the look she and Ami had shared at Tarek's seemingly innocuous statement. Tarek should know better than to think that humans were like all other species he'd encountered before, especially after spending so much time with the three of them. The next few hours would prove interesting, Emeline mused as she stole a glance at Nox.

He was seated across from her, talking to Tarek about his call with Sandovar. Catching her eye, he reached over and squeezed her hand reassuringly.

Smiling into his sparkling eyes, Emeline thought they looked a deeper purple than usual. Maybe the effect came from the sharp contrast between his luminescent skin against the dark blue color of his knee-length tunic. All Emeline knew was that he took her breath away.

Nox's role at the UAP required him to dress according to diplomatic standards. Although, he would have preferred wearing a military uniform like the rest of the Delicians. He did, however, opt to wear a set of light armor underneath his clothing.

Nox had stressed to Emeline that you could never be too cautious as he had urged her to wear a set as well. Considering what she had just been through with Violia and the Hexians, it had surprised him when she told him no—it was fine. She didn't foresee any physical altercations happening at this meeting. Instead, she had worn black slacks paired with a matching jacket and overcoat. Her only pop of color was the red blouse she always wore to important meetings.

Reaching over, she couldn't resist rubbing a section of Nox's hair between her finger and her thumb. He had decided to leave it down for the meeting. Normally when he was working, it was pulled back into a short ponytail. Emeline loved it like this…his purple highlights shimmered in the light whenever he moved his head.

Breathing deeply, she caught a hint of vanilla. Nox had insisted on using her shampoo, which for some reason made her feel all goofy inside. His reasoning was simple… the scent always kept her close to him. *God, is he just the best thing ever! Look at him, all concerned. He's worried that I'm going to pass out from being on the shuttle.* She winked at him, giving him a bright smile, wondering when it had happened…not panicking at just the mere thought of riding in a space shuttle. More likely it was because this was much more pleasant than being strapped to a fiery rocket.

A lot had happened over the past month. The quiet scientist, who had struggled to conquer the scientific world at the same time building her company, had been transformed. The transformation had not been an easy one for Emeline. It had required her to dig deep within herself to find that inner strength to survive not only first contact with aliens, but also the horrors Hagen and the Hexians had put her through. She had learned a lot about herself, but the most important thing she learned was that she wasn't alone anymore. Not only did she have the love and support of her family and friends, now she had Nox. From the moment she had laid eyes on him, he had consumed her life. And he hadn't been sneaky about it either. Oh no, that wasn't his style. He was definitely a straight-to-the-point kind of male. *You're mine.* She shivered every time he said that to her.

Putting her hands up, her cheeks felt hot just thinking about how he had spent a monumental amount of time showing her just how well they fit together. Giving him a heated smile as his eyes moved lovingly along where her bond mark was hidden by her hair she thought, *no matter what happens tonight at this meeting, nothing will separate us.*

And now that her initial meeting with Sandovar was over, she'd thought it had gone fairly well. Nox had been right when he said his father took some getting used to. Never had she met a more condescending person in her entire life and she'd met more than a few over the course of her career. But he was Nox's father and therefore would be in their lives, albeit not very often, she hoped.

Glancing over, she saw Ami talking to Liam. They were deep in discussion about what they were going to tell the President and the UN Council. She already knew what she would say, but didn't want to think on it too much. Instead, she took these few moments of quiet to digest some of the things that Ami had told her, some of which were pretty shocking.

Ami!

In that moment, Ami just happened to look up, and catching Emeline's eye, stuck her finger in her mouth, pretending to barf. Laughing good-naturedly when Emeline stuck her tongue out at her, Ami turned back to Liam.

The two women had finally been able to have some girl time after Tarek had adjourned the meeting. The males had gone off to let off a little steam in the training room, while the girls had opted for some time alone in the kitchen. They were making hoagies for the guys to eat when they got through beating the crap out of each other. Ami had wanted to know, in great detail, how the *bonding* had gone.

When she tried giving Ami the PG version of her bonding experience, Ami had teased her endlessly, demanding juicier details. Of course, the mention of extra appendages had managed to work its way into the conversation causing Emeline to quickly change the subject, ignoring Ami's pout. Instead, she shifted the focus off of Nox's private parts to the physical changes she was experiencing from the bond. Ami had been awed by her new bond mark and had traced it with her finger.

As happy as Ami was for her and Nox, Emeline sensed that something was bothering her. So, being the good friend that she was, she had endlessly nagged Ami until she had finally spilled her secret. And, boy oh boy, was it a doozy. Tarquin had kissed her—and she'd kissed him back! Now she was having all kinds of mixed feelings and didn't understand what was happening to her.

Intrigued, Emeline had asked her to describe her feelings. When Ami told her how restless she was, she couldn't eat or sleep, how *Quin* was constantly in her thoughts, Emeline hid her alarm. If what she suspected was true, then all hell was about to break loose. *How was it even possible?* She had thought bondmates were a Delician thing. Emeline made a mental note to do some research on the origins of bondmating. She would need to keep a close eye on her friend.

Ami had pleaded with her not to tell Nox. That was a

hard request for Emeline to agree to. Even though Ami was like a sister to her, she would not lie to Nox. She did, however, agree to keep Ami's secret for now, but if Nox asked, she would tell the truth. It was hard enough keeping secrets from him anyway. One thing she did wholeheartedly agree on was to keep this from Tarek and Jagger, at least for now. Neither male would be happy about her interactions with *Quin*, especially considering their long history together.

The one thing Emeline did stress to Ami was that if there ever came a time when she felt Ami was in danger, she would tell everyone—in a heartbeat. No way would she let anything bad happen to Ami if she could help it. She didn't think Tarquin would intentionally hurt Ami, but he was someone to be wary of. Charming one minute, ruthless the next—anything to get what he wanted. *I need to get ARI to translate those files for me once things settle down. I think it's time to do a little research on "Quin."* She had made Ami promise to be careful and let her know if anything else happened, which made Emeline feel somewhat better.

When she said she would be coming with her and Liam when they left Earth, Emeline smiled, remembering how they had nearly choked the life out of each other. Squealing like teenagers as they talked about all the things they were going to do on their new adventure. Ami was determined to learn more about alien weaponry. Plus, if and when they were allowed, she wanted to have a hand in adapting Earth's weapons with alien technology. Emeline was more interested in advancing Earth's medical equipment.

Studying Ami, who sat lost in thought, Emeline couldn't help but wonder if maybe there wasn't another reason why Ami was so eager to come along to Delicia. It would be interesting to see what Heather and Lorelei had to say about Ami's decision. Which begged the question right now, where the hell were Heather and Lorelei and why were their phones turned off? Even *Find Friends* had been disabled, which was deeply concerning.

She had even resorted to calling Fiona, who hadn't heard from them in a few days, which was highly unusual. They always made a point of texting her at least once a day. Not wanting to worry her, Emeline said they were probably busy in the lab. When Fiona asked when she was coming home, she was missing her baby girl, Emeline had swallowed a pang of guilt, telling her soon...she would be home soon.

Concerned as to where her friends were, Emeline put that thought on hold the closer they got to Earth. She could see Nyx at the controls, Liam of course hovering right beside him.

Looking out through the view screen, Earth with its billions of inhabitants stared back at her. People were going about their lives totally unaware that within the next few hours, decisions regarding their very lives would be made —without their knowledge. Decisions made by people who had the souls of an entire planet to consider. A chill ran through her. She couldn't shake the feeling that over the next few hours her future was going to be decided and the outcome might be different than what she wanted.

Straightening her spine, Emeline reminded herself to be alert and prepared for any situation. She reached down to her boot, realizing at the last second her knife was gone. *Damn you, Hagen.*

Pushing that thought away, Emeline saw that it was Liam who was actually piloting their shuttle. She couldn't contain her grin. Lately, it was like he had a whole new aura about him. Gone was the restlessness, the always looking for the next assignment, the next thrill. Now when she looked at him, a calmness emanated from him. He was self-confident, grounded. Being asked to join Tarek's elite team was a perfect fit for him...like a key that unlocked the door to infinite possibilities.

Looking him over, she wasn't surprised to see him wearing his dress blues or that his jacket was slung over the back of his chair. He even had on a layer of light armor under his uniform like Nox. Knowing his plans to leave Earth with her, Emeline wondered how long before he swapped out his Navy uniform for a Delician one.

Which brought up that all-important question on everyone's mind—what were the President and the council members going to say to the aliens? With the first face-to-face meeting between the humans and the Delicians about to happen, this was a historic moment and somehow, she had ended up right smack in the middle of it all.

Liam turned to look at Emeline. A silly grin lit up his face as he told them all to get ready—they were about to land.

Grinning back, she waved her hand at him, "Hey, eyes on the road, dude. What do you think you're driving—a spaceship?"

Nyx picked up on Emeline's joke, taking it one step further, teasing Liam about his driving, asking if he needed to shoot anything out of the way before he could land.

Flipping Nyx the bird before turning back to the controls, Liam scoffed at him, telling him to just wait until he took him for a ride in his Mustang. Ami and Emeline both groaned out loud.

"I'll pray for you." Ami bowed her head with her hands pressed together.

"What's that supposed to mean?" Nyx looked around at the humans, confused. "And what's a Mustang? Isn't that some kind of animal?" He wasn't the least bit happy when all he got for an answer was laughter.

Feeling the vibration of the thrusters, their joking quickly ended. Emeline felt the shuttle slow, hovering a few feet off the ground. With barely a whisper of noise, Liam expertly set the cloaked shuttle down. Shooting him a thumbs up, smiling proudly at him, she had never seen her brother look so happy.

The shuttle landed on the grounds of an isolated chateau in northern France. Tarek had agreed to meet at a location chosen by the human leaders. He understood their need for bilateral cooperation. It would be essential in promoting trust in their new relationship.

Knowing that their location had been completely vetted before they had left the *Maelstrom*, Emeline felt safe. It also helped knowing Tarek was in charge. Having watched him in action over the last few weeks, especially in dealing with the Hexians, her money was on him keeping most of the impending chaos in check.

Tarek had chosen Ezio, Ramola and Yilmaz to provide security, along with Nyx and Liam. Jagger remained on board the *Maelstrom*, keeping an eye out for any stray Hexians. There was still no sign of Tarquin, which really pissed off the Delicians, especially Tarek. He had been hoping that Tarquin was halfway to Hexia along with the rest of his fleet. Emeline wasn't so convinced that was the case. He had talked about needing a shipment of salt too badly to give up so easily. She just couldn't shake the feeling that *Quin—God, would she ever get used to that?—*still lurked in the area.

Pulling her coat tighter around her, Emeline stood to take Nox's arm as they exited the shuttle. Shivering, she looked up at the dark sky. She could just make out small glimpses of stars as they peeked out through the fast-moving clouds. Shadows from the many trees that lined three sides of the large field where they had landed took on the shape of giant wooden warriors standing guard against the oncoming upheaval that Earth was facing.

A lone figure stood at the edge of the field closest to the main house waiting for them to disembark. Leslie Merriman. She was taking the lead in the negotiations between the humans and the Delicians.

Dressed in a sleek black suit, Leslie watched as both humans and aliens made their way across the small expanse of grass from where they had parked the shuttle. Holding a small LED light in her hand, the soft glow highlighted the worry lines on her light brown face. At her first live look at aliens, Leslie's emotions ran across her face so fast, it was almost comical to watch. Having five gigantic, well-built alien soldiers look her up and down was beyond intimidating.

Ami grabbed Leslie's arm securely in hers when she noticed Leslie start to sway slightly. Laughing to lighten the tense moment, Ami joked about their size, "Vid comms don't do them justice, do they?" Wagging her eyebrows, giving Leslie a sly smile which in turn elicited a sharp laugh followed by a quick bobbing of her head.

The color was starting to return to Leslie's face as she saw Emeline give her a small wave. Waving back, she frowned, watching Nox hovering directly behind Emeline.

The windy weather caused a puff of air to swirl around Emeline. The hairstyle that she had spent way too much time and effort on was ruined as her hair danced in the wind. She couldn't help but giggle as Nox's big hand managed to catch almost every strand. Giving him a quick thank you, she unconsciously turned and gave him a lingering kiss on his cheek.

Taking a hair band off her wrist, Emeline twisted her hair into a loose bun at the back of her neck. Pulling the front of her hair forward, Emeline reluctantly covered her mark. She was not happy having to hide her relationship with Nox, but knew it was better to keep it to themselves for right now. If and when the time came, she would stand against anyone who tried to separate them.

Straightening her shoulders, Emeline walked over to Leslie, extending her hand in greeting. "Hi Leslie. How have you been?"

Having witnessed the exchange between Nox and Emeline, Leslie's eyes strayed to Emeline's forehead. "Not as good as you, I see," she quipped softly.

Emeline felt her cheeks heat up. Glancing at Nox, she

replied with a smile, "Long story."

"I look forward to hearing all about it," Leslie said eagerly, her gaze drifting over Emeline's shoulder. Her eyes grew round, her pupils dark and large as she stared at the Delicians.

Emeline turned to see Tarek striding towards them. Squeezing Leslie's hand, she confided in a low tone, "He's actually really nice, once you get to know him. Well, unless you piss him off." Whispering out of the side of her mouth, she added, "Seriously, you don't want to piss him off." Raising her eyebrows, she gave Leslie a meaningful smile as she turned to speak to Tarek. "General." Purposely addressing him using his formal title, she said, "You remember Leslie Merriman."

"Yes, I do." Tarek took Leslie's small hand in his and gently shook it in the style of the humans, telling her that it was a pleasure to finally meet her in person.

Liam took over the introductions, setting a name to the faces she had met over vid comm. Each one in turn shook her hand, imitating Tarek.

Emeline couldn't help nudging Ami as they watched the look of surprise on each Delician's face as Leslie squeezed their hands harder than they had expected. They kept forgetting human females were different than Delician females. Leslie might be a small compact woman, but she had a reputation as being a tough, no-nonsense director of NASA, who was very committed to her job and country.

Tarek motioned Emeline over to him before they entered the chateau. He had worn his formal uniform, looking imposing as befitted his position, but he too had his armor on underneath. He was another one who was rarely without it, especially on first contact missions. Experience had taught him many things over his long life, he had once told Emeline. It had only taken a few times in a regen bed to remind him to listen to his instincts. He would approach the humans as he normally would any other newly introduced world, with one exception. He admired the humans he had worked beside, so he would be more open-minded when he met with their leaders.

"Emeline, I would like you to stay close to Nox."

Looking at him curiously, she normally wouldn't question Tarek, but she wondered if he knew something she didn't. "Okay. Can I ask why?"

Tarek leaned in, keeping his voice low. "I just want to make sure that you're not made to do anything or go anywhere unless it's of your own choice. Just keeping our options open in case things take an unexpected turn."

Emeline's brows creased at Tarek's warning. He was wise as well as canny—she would be a fool not to follow his advice. Nodding to the general, she looked back at Nox. He had moved over to stand behind her, making a conscious effort not to touch her until they were assured of the reception they were going to receive from Earth's leaders.

Her brother, taking up the position in front of her, gave her hand a reassuring squeeze before following Leslie into the mansion.

On any other occasion, Emeline would have loved to have explored the two-hundred-year-old smaller version of a French castle, but not tonight. Tonight, she followed closely behind Leslie as she led them through the extensive gardens into the main house. Their interesting group made their way down the main hallway into a large opulent room that had been transformed into a conference room.

Looking around at the beautiful room that would provide the setting for this historic occasion, Emeline's love for all things French had her sighing with delight.

It was an overly large room with high white ceilings —typical of a French chateau built in the late eighteenth century. Darkened with age, intricate wooden beams were laid out in a symmetrical pattern across the entire length of the room's ceiling. The marble floor had the same rich dark tones as the beams, while the walls contrasted in an antique white finish. The inlaid moldings trimmed in gold were reminiscent of the period of the chateau.

What ruined the look were the tall windows along one wall that were sealed tight with heavy metal brown shutters giving the room a gloomy feel. Even the six large Venetian chandeliers that hung throughout the room didn't do much to lighten the room. It was obvious great effort had been taken to keep this meeting private at all costs.

Two Italian marble fireplaces were on opposite sides of the room from each other, neither one of them lit. Emeline would have liked to have seen at least one of them burning. A chill ran up her spine at the cold and slightly unwelcoming feeling in the room. She was careful not to read too much into that particular notion.

Two balconies ran the width of the room opposite each other, giving the humans a strategic advantage from above. Emeline purposely refrained from glancing in the direction where she knew there were security agents hidden... watching their every move. The humans obviously hadn't considered that the Delicians were continuously scanning the building and surrounding area. They knew exactly how many life forms were on the premises and their location.

Leslie slowed her pace as she approached a group of six people who were crowded around one corner of a large horseshoe-shaped table. The expressions on their faces didn't disappoint Emeline as she hid her smile at two of the council members who staggered into each other. She supposed she should cut them some slack, totally agreeing that the Delicians standing in front of them were massively impressive, if not a bit terrifying to look at. In fairness she had had some time to get to know Tarek and his crew and considered them close friends and definitely her saviors.

This was the moment she had been excited about and dreading all at the same time. These next few minutes of this first contact meeting would set the tone for Earth's new relationship with the Delicians. All she could do was hope that the outcome would be positive for everyone. Now if only she could shake off this feeling of impending doom. *Stop being so melodramatic—geez.*

Stopping just far enough away that the humans and Delicians were able to get a good look at one another, Leslie stepped forward. Her hand extended to a large physically fit middle-aged gentleman with gray hair. Emeline knew from seeing him on television that this was the United States President, Gregory Jenkins. She had never met him in person but from all accounts he was a fair man who stood firm for American values. Known for being a shrewd businessman before venturing into politics, he was currently three months into his second term and the country was experiencing a rare moment of peace and prosperity. It was a much needed break from the last several years of economic turmoil and worldwide dissension. Emeline hoped that President Jenkins was up to the enormous task of guiding Earth into a new phase in human evolution.

"President Jenkins, may I introduce you to General Tarek, head of the Delician military and liaison for the United Alliance of Planets." Leslie turned to General Tarek, saying, "General, this is Gregory Jenkins, President of the United States of America."

General Tarek stepped forward and extended his hand to the President, who didn't hesitate to clasp the General's large, calloused shiny white hand in his. They greeted each other eye to eye. Both of them commanders who were used to having their every order obeyed.

President Jenkins spoke first. "Welcome to Earth, General Tarek."

"Thank you. It's an honor to meet you. I would like to extend a welcome from the members of the United Alliance of Planets." Tarek spoke the UAP's standard first contact greeting in perfect English.

Having all of Earth's languages downloaded into ARI's

database, eliminated the Delicians from having to inject translators into the human delegation. Emeline had really tried to drive home to them that humans would not appreciate being injected with alien technology so soon in the meeting process.

Tarek had made a rare joke about how the three humans he knew hadn't seemed to mind.

Emeline had laughed, reminding him that at the time she had willingly left Earth in a spaceship with an alien she had just met, so her judgment was questionable at best.

President Jenkins turned to the five individuals who were hovering in the background. Motioning them forward, he introduced Ming Zhu from China, Margaret Mower from the United Kingdom, Claude Lanoue from France, Ivan Orlov from Russia and Neha Dewan from Pakistan. None of the five moved forward to take Tarek's hand, which he didn't seem offended by.

Tarek introduced his elite team before introducing Liam, Emeline and Ami as the newest members of his team who had been vital in stopping the Hexians in their recent attack.

After acknowledging them, President Jenkins turned toward a doorway and nodded to an unseen person. The three humans gasped as they saw two women being brought in by a burly Secret Service Agent.

"Lorelei, Heather? What are you doing here?" Emeline and Ami rushed over to hug their friends. "We've been calling and calling. We've been so worried about you."

Heather let off a string of what sounded like a lot of nasty Spanish words at the agent, who didn't seem fazed in the least. He was too busy shooting glaring looks at the Delicians.

Lorelei tugged Emeline into a hard hug, whispering fiercely into her ear, "Em, we need to talk. These guys just showed up at my apartment without warning. Told us we had to go with them or they'd put us so far into a hole, no one would ever find us. Scared the crap out of us."

Hurrying over, Liam put his arms around Heather's and Lorelei's shoulders, pulling them close. Trying to keep his anger in check, he asked the President, "Sir, with all due respect, was this type of treatment really necessary?"

"Not to that extreme, no." The President gave his agent a reproachful look before turning back to the four women and Liam. "That was never my intention. I felt it was in everyone's best interest to have all the players in one room for this meeting."

Ami couldn't stop her mouth, grounding out hotly, "You had no right to take them against their will. What kind of a person does that?"

Leslie gave Ami a warning look as President Jenkins explained that he and the other members of the council had to think of what was best for the planet and not just a few individuals. "Although, I do apologize for the anxiety you experienced. Again, that was never our intension. I can assure you this matter will be investigated."

The agent, paling at the President's words, moved back to take up a position against the far wall.

Ami shook her head, not at all appeased by President Jenkins's assurances. She quickly reminded them that it was her, Emeline and Liam that had put their asses on the line to save this planet. Heather and Lorelei were an integral part of their team. They should have been treated with more respect. "Just saying."

Ami knew Leslie was giving her the death glare, but Ami couldn't seem to keep her emotions in check. *Ever since that damn kiss, I've been a mess.*

A solid but gentle hand squeezed her shoulder, offering support, allowing her emotions to settle...Tarek. *For a huge scary war-torn General, he's such a softie for human females.*

"Miss Jefferson, why don't we take our seats? We would all very much like to hear about your experiences." President Jenkins pointed to the table, motioning for everyone to take a seat.

Yilmaz and Ramola took up positions near the door, their eyes constantly scanning the room. The portable ARI wired into their helmets linked them to the *Maelstrom*, who was giving them details on all the heat signatures in the room. Ezio stood behind Tarek, who was flanked on either side by Emeline and Liam. Nox stood behind Emeline, not wanting to be too far from her side.

Once everyone was settled, President Jenkins stood at the podium addressing the room. "On behalf of my fellow humans, we would like to welcome you to Earth and thank you for all that you did in stopping the alien invasion. I have been elected by the other council members as the spokesperson for this first contact meeting. I know we have a lot to discuss and we especially want to hear Miss Jefferson's, Lt. Commander Cameron's and Miss Cameron's stories.

"Before we do that however, I'd like to inform you that while you were dealing with the Hexians, we came to a preliminary decision regarding the worldwide notification of first contact." President Jenkins paused for a moment to look around the room.

Emeline swore he did it only for dramatic effect. All that was missing was the music. But in fairness this was a decision that affected billions of lives—not a decision she wanted to be in charge of. *Okay, maybe he's allowed a little drama.*

"We have decided to wait—at least until we have more information before we inform the public." When no one objected to his statement, he continued. "We feel that when the time does come, the more information we can give them might help to contain the chaos that is unquestionably going to happen. Giving them only half a picture will only feed into people's fears and insecurities.

To that end, we have formed a fact-gathering committee called First Contact Exploration Council. Our first order of business is to understand the threat that just occurred."

Looking at Liam, President Jenkins asked if he would give them his report.

"Yes, sir." Liam had been in the military long enough, having given too many of these briefings, to be nervous. However, looking out seeing such serious faces, maybe he should be. This had been no ordinary mission. Regardless of the intent of the Hexians, he had been responsible for the deaths of countless individuals. All of which still weighted heavy on his shoulders.

He started at the beginning when he and Ami had first encountered Nox's holographic message. The council listened intently as he moved through the chain of events. He'd kept his comments strictly on the professional aspects of his experiences, purposely avoiding all the personal relationships he had cultivated with the Delicians. Unfortunately, the council members were like a dog with a bone when it came to the details of the destruction of the freighter.

After what felt like a lifetime of being peppered with questions, Liam was finally dismissed by President Jenkins and thanked for his dedication to service.

Taking a seat next to his sister, the coolness of her hand on his, the familiarity of her fresh scent as she leaned in giving him a reassuring smile, pushed the shadows from his haunted eyes. He replayed Nyx's words about the Hexians' plans for Earth over and over in his mind, reminding himself that he had saved his people.

His body relaxed as he felt Ami squeeze his shoulder, adding her support along with Emeline's.

With an expectant look from President Jenkins, Ami tried to center herself as she made her way to the podium. Never one to miss out on making a quip or a joke whenever she felt the need, public speaking on the other hand, was not something Ami looked forward to. She was a woman of action, not words.

Her stomach tightened as she silently berated herself. *Just pretend they're naked.*

Looking directly into President Jenkins's eyes she thought *Oh god no—anything but that. Come on, Breathe, Center, Focus.*

Griping the podium tightly, the wood dug into her fingers. She had gone over her speech so often it was stuck in a loop running over and over in her mind.

Gazing out at her audience, her mind suddenly went blank. As she opened her mouth to speak, nothing came out. Her tongue felt like it did after she'd eaten an entire bag of beef jerky...thick and dry.

"Ami"

Her head snapped up—her eyes focused on Tarek.

"Ami." Tarek paused. When he had her full attention, he asked, "Do you remember what you said the first time we met?"

Her dark brows shot upwards, surprised at his question. An unexpected laugh escaped her lips. "Yes—I said I win. You weren't little green men." Snickers erupted from different sections of the room.

"Yes, that's right. So, tell me, now that you've spent time with us, what would you say is the most important thing you've learned?" Tarek watched Ami's face—her dark almond-shaped eyes creased at the corners as she considered his question.

"There are so many things—it's hard to choose just one. I guess if I had to pick one, it would be the way you guys are so dedicated to helping—anyone. I mean, if one of your team members needs you—boom, you're there. Earth being attacked by aliens—there again. You even took in a few stray humans and treated us like one of your own. I learned that I could trust you with my life. And even you have to admit I was pretty good at adapting to a lot of your alien tech." Ami's mouth crooked up into a grin at Tarek.

He went on to prod her into telling her entire experience

to him. The council members were particularly interested in her time on the Hexian vessel and gasped when they heard that she had been the one to kill Hagen. Tarek didn't press her about her knowledge of alien weaponry. That was her decision when and if she ever decided to tell them.

Ami appeared to settle, answering as best she could. When she had finished with the council, she returned to sit with her friends, visibly relieved her part was over, whispering as she sat down to please leave her in the lab where she belonged.

Nox smirked, watching President Jenkins murmur "nicely done" to Tarek on his handling of Ami. Tarek merely nodded at the compliment. He had a knack for reading people.

It was a skill that Nox also excelled at. One of the many talents he'd picked up from his father. Like right now, for instance, Nox was keeping his eye on the agent who had brought Heather and Lorelei into the room. His demeanor was concerning—his attention never wavering from the Delicians. He appeared particularly interested in him and Emeline...intensity burned in his eyes as he watched their every move.

Nox had to fight back the impulse to pull Emeline closer to him when he saw the agent's hand wasn't exactly on his weapon, but it was clearly visible on his belt allowing for easy access.

Shooting a look over to the door, trying to catch Ramola's or Yilmaz's attention, he saw it unnecessary. They had also picked up on the agent's *unfriendly* attitude towards them.

Turning back, his eyes strayed again to the agent before looking at Emeline. She had reached back discreetly, squeezing his pinkie on her way over to the podium. Her fingers were cold. He knew she was anxious, wanting this over as quickly as possible. He recalled her telling him, "Honestly, babe." He loved when she called him that. She'd told him it was her special name only for him. "How long am I going to have—15 minutes, maybe 20 to tell them everything that happened in three weeks?"

Taking Emeline's chair, Nox rested his arms on the sides. Curling his hands around the sculpted ends, he admired the workmanship of the humans. All the chairs were exactly the same, made of a material that ARI told him was called wood that was grown in a forest. The back of the chair was tall and was crowned with an ornamental scrolled cap. The burgundy leather cushion was soft yet firm against his back as he leaned back, keeping a vigilant eye on Emeline.

Emeline knew that Nox was not happy, his tension radiated through their bond. Standing at the podium with her tablet open, she shot him a quick smile before launching into the list of talking points she had created to keep herself on task.

After explaining their work on the satellites, she quickly moved through her kidnapping since everyone already knew about it and her subsequent injuries. There were a few of the council members, however, who were persistent in their questions.

"What was it like being on an alien spaceship? Did you see lots of aliens? What did they look like?" The UK's member Margaret Mower was sitting on the edge of her chair, hanging onto Emeline's every word.

"I only saw a little bit of the ship. I was unconscious when I was brought on board. The only two Hexians I saw were Hagen and their leader Tarquin." She was trying to be vague, but the questions kept coming.

Council member Lanoue wanted details of what Tarquin was like, finally asking the question that was on all their minds, "During your time with the Hexians, did they touch you inappropriately?"

Murmurs swept around the table. Liam voiced his displeasure, telling Lanoue he should be ashamed for asking such a personal question. Margaret Mower nudged Lanoue in the ribs, telling him it was none of his business.

Lanoue responded that it was a perfectly reasonable question. It would give them insight into the character of the Hexians.

Tarek conceded that it was a fair question, but told him it was Emeline's choice if she wanted to answer him.

Watching Emeline's face, Nox wondered if she realized how often she had glanced in his direction. She was furious. The main telltale sign, other than her flashing eyes, flushed cheeks, and pursed lips was her outrage that blasted through him like a foghorn on a murky morning... loud and long.

Her face softened when she looked at Tarek, telling him thank you...she would be more than happy to answer Mr. Lanoue's question.

Uh oh. Nox held his breath—someone was about to get their ass handed to them.

Narrowing her eyes at the human leaders, Emeline's voice was clear, her sarcasm unmistakable as she slowly repeated Mr. Lanoue's question out loud. "Did they touch me inappropriately? Well, Mr. Lanoue, I guess in order to answer that you will have to define for me what you mean by inappropriately. Was it inappropriate when I was drugged...beaten...shot?" She raised an eyebrow at him, waiting for his answer.

"Yes." Mr. Lanoue's voice was a mere whisper.

"How about when I had to watch Hagen's goons kill an innocent grandmother and then terrorize a young girl? Would you consider that inappropriate as well? Or how about when I had to watch Hagen beat and threaten to molest his own cousin for no reason other than because he could? If your answer is yes, then I guess my answer would also have to be yes—yes, he did touch me inappropriately."

Council member Lanoue evidently was smart enough to take that for an answer, opting instead to sit back and close his mouth. Apparently, the warning look Tarek gave him was working, Nox thought as he gave Tarek a grateful look.

Scanning the human leaders, Emeline's voice dropped low. In a chilling tone she told them, "Let me put this into perspective for you. You all know what organized crime is." All of their heads nodded. "Most major countries around the world have one or more in some shape or form. Now consider for a moment an entire planet run solely by multiple crime families." The room got quiet as more than a few faces paled at the truth Emeline outlined for them. "That is what the planet Hexia is—only infinitely worse. They have weapons you've only seen in movies. But this is not *Star Wars*. This is real, and trust me, they will stop at nothing to get what they want. And right now, we have something they want."

Emeline shot a quick glance at Ami as she told the council more about Hexia. "Their leader, Tarquin, was unlike Hagen in that he never hurt us. Instead, he offered us his protection from his crew. Made sure we had food and use of a regen device. He tried to keep Hagen away, but Hagen wouldn't listen. He had his own agenda." Looking directly at Ami, Emeline said, "As accommodating as Tarquin was, I have no doubt he can be just as ruthless."

The human agent had slowly moved along the wall, inching ever closer to Emeline. Feeling uncomfortable, she glanced repeatedly over her shoulder at him.

Noticing her faltering, Nox asked if she needed a drink of water. Leslie pointed to a pitcher that sat on a silver tray surrounded by tall clear glasses. Pouring her some water, he carried the glass around the table to her at the podium.

The agent shifted on his feet. His body tensed like a panther stalking his prey as he zeroed in on Nox's attention to Emeline. His face contorted in anger, clearly appalled at the tender smile Emeline gave Nox as she thanked him for the water. The agent's hand clenched into a fist when he saw their hands touch briefly as she took the glass from Nox.

President Jenkins asked Emeline if she could expand on

the reasons why the Hexians wanted the Himalayan salt. More than a few heads went up as she explained about the money that could be made on the black market. The numbers were staggering.

To say the human leaders were angry was an understatement, demanding to know how Hexia had learned about Earth and its resources.

Emeline turned to Nox and Tarek for their input. Nox stood, saying that he could shed some light on that. He and Loris had just finished their preliminary findings.

Emeline returned to her seat as Nox replaced her at the podium. He looked at her sheepishly, knowing his bondmate was going to be shocked at what he and Loris had recently discovered. Evidently, shortly before Nox's mother, Elara, was killed, she had been sent to Earth on a secret assignment for the UAP. She was to evaluate Earth's natural resources and assess how humans were caring for their planet. Elara was the one who brought the initial samples of the salt back to Delicia for testing. When she discovered its potential for creating vaccines, she had immediately informed her superiors of her findings. For some reason, nothing was ever done and after her death, her samples had mysteriously disappeared along with all of her notes. "We have theorized that someone must have read the report and told the Hexians—someone who had access to my mother's work."

Emeline gave Nox a pointed look at just hearing this new information for the first time.

When the question was posed as to why Earth had not been informed until now, Nox explained to them about the Prohibited Planets list—or at least he tried to. The more he talked, the more incensed the human leaders became. Even President Jenkins was taken aback at the criteria for being on the list. Nox tried to assure them that a full report had been sent to the UAP updating the evolution of Earth's inhabitants. It wasn't surprising it did nothing to mollify any of them.

Ami couldn't help herself from smirking at Nox's unease as he brushed by her to take his seat. He shook his head, giving her a chuckle in return. "Never going to let this go, are you?"

"Nope." Ami grinned back at him, most of her lingering hurt had faded the more she gotten to know the Delicians.

Nox had come to really care for Ami. Not only was she a loyal friend to his love, she was honest and forthcoming —maybe sometimes a little too much. In truth, he appreciated her honesty. It was a welcome change from some of the sycophants his father had fawning around him. He laughed again at her until he felt eyes that burned with hatred focused directly on him. The Secret Service agent had moved back along the wall when Tarek moved over to stand at the podium. It seemed not even he wanted to mess with a massively built alien General who could vaporize you with one look.

Nox settled back into his chair as Emeline leaned over, her elbow digging into his chest, making sure she had his full attention. The news about his mother was troubling. The questions in her eyes told Nox that he would be getting an earful when they got back to their room. Covering his mouth with his hand, he murmured that he and Loris had only found out right before they left. "I promise to fill you in later."

Emeline sat back, her hands clasped together in her lap as she nodded, mouthing *"You've got that right."*

Tarek began speaking, which meant everyone's attention was focused on him. He began by giving the human leaders a brief overview of the UAP. He attempted to defuse the misconception regarding the Prohibited Planets list by explaining some of the theories the UAP had relating to planetary interference. They were committed to allowing planets to evolve at a natural progression. He assured them that his report indicated that the list needed to be reevaluated. "That being said, I feel that Earth is still a few decades away from becoming a full member."

Surprised, President Jenkins looked at Tarek, asking, "Can you elaborate, General?"

"Certainly. Although you have global space flight, you are still many years away from interstellar travel. Up until our arrival, your knowledge of life outside your solar system was nonexistent. This whole situation is unfortunate, which is why going forward, we will proceed cautiously. There is no telling the amount of damage that could ensue if humans are exposed too quickly to the universe and all its inhabitants."

The President nodded in agreement, murmuring, "That's fair."

"I understand your hesitation to inform your people. You have every reason to be worried. I've been involved in many first contact situations. It can be challenging, which is why the UAP is mindful in its decisions regarding new planet membership. They have authorized me to offer you a few choices that they are willing to allow." Tarek took a tablet and instructed ARI to display the UAP's contract for Earth.

Gasps could be heard from the human leaders as individual holographic displays appeared in front of each council member. A list of the options the UAP was offering to Earth were written in their native languages for easy interpretation for each member. Ami showed them how to maneuver through the screen as they read through the material.

President Jenkins frowned as he read through the list. "Tell me if I'm reading this right, General Tarek." At the General's nod, President Jenkins enlarged the font as he read out loud. "Option 1—The Delicians will leave our solar system and Earth's inhabitants will continue on as if nothing has happened. However, the UAP will periodically check in on Earth's progress and will keep all recordings of this interaction on file.

"Option 2—A delegation from Earth will be sent to the UAP headquarters for an exploratory meeting to determine the possibility of a limited introduction into the Alliance. Earth's population will be kept unaware of first contact for the foreseeable future.

"Option 3—Earth's population will be informed that first contact has been made. In which case, the UAP will send in troops to help with the chaos that will unquestionably occur. You don't mince words, do you, General?"

Tarek shrugged back, telling him, "You need information—the UAP is willing to give it to you."

"But why?" The Chinese council member Zhu was looking at Tarek with distrust. "Why does this UAP even care about a lowly planet like Earth?"

Emeline nudged Nox's arm, whispering how amazingly authoritative she thought Tarek was. *"He's got them eating out his hand."* With her hand covering her mouth, she continued her running commentary. *"Notice how Tarek raises his voice just slightly reiterating what he already told him. Not too loud but just loud enough to keep their attention. Watch Councilman Zhu's face. He can't take his eyes off Tarek. Can you see how scared he is—and well he should be. Good, Tarek is reminding them they don't know who else will try to come to Earth. Yeah, I don't think Zhu liked that. Heck, I don't like that. Oh, phew, he's got ships patrolling our solar system —excellent. See—everyone is happy. Oops, wait, now he is reminding them about the salt and how lots of people are going to want it. Yes, that's true, there is no going back. Oh, good, the UAP is investigating the breach. Yeah, well—I can't wait to hear what you and Loris found out. Looks like he gave them lots to think about, don't yah think?"*

Trying not to laugh at Emeline's critique of Tarek's presentation, Nox was more than happy when President Jenkins asked for a short recess to confer with the other members. He couldn't wait for this meeting to be over. He had plans with his lovely bondmate. There had been a promise of a new outfit she had created for him...something to do with cowboy boots and a hat. Nox couldn't hide his smile, intrigued about something called chaps.

The council members moved over to a seating area that was set into a small nook off to the side of the room, arguing the entire way. President Jenkins was doing his best to encourage them to speak one at a time when voicing their concerns, but it didn't look like anyone was listening to him.

Turning his back on the human leaders, Nox had more interesting things to look at. Emeline and her girls were finally together. After lots of hugging and a few tears, everyone laughed as they all tried to out talk each other. It was fascinating to watch Emeline interacting with her friends. She was relaxed, happy—the wide smile on her beautiful face coming easily. He smiled at the sound of her laughter. He also knew the exact moment they started talking about him...four pairs of eyes focused their gaze in his direction.

With a lopsided smile, Emeline made her way over to him with her girls following close behind, silly grins plastered all over their faces. They were thrilled to see Emeline so happy, but that didn't stop them from teasing Nox, unmercifully, about taking care of their girl.

"Nox, you remember Heather and Lore—," Emeline's words turned into a shrieked when a beefy arm snaked around her middle, dragging her back away from Nox.

The enraged agent yelled for everyone to get back—his gun pointed directly at Nox's chest.

"What are you doing?" Emeline cried digging her fingernails into the agent's arm as she twisted her body trying desperately to get away from him. "Let go of me," she screamed, her cries drawing the attention of everyone in the room.

Nox's only thought was keeping Emeline safe. Feeling

confident that his armor would protect him, he pushed the agent out of the way and grabbed Emeline by the arm, pulling her behind him.

The agent, heedless of the alien weapons that were pointed at him, demanded Nox release Emeline. "Leave her alone, you filthy alien. I'm not letting you take our women."

Emeline cried out to the agent to lower his weapon so they could talk about this, but he ignored her pleas.

Nox, aware of the agent's rising panic, yelled for her to stay behind him. It was clear to him that things were escalating out of control.

"No! Don't listen to him," the agent bellowed. "Come to me. You need to stay with your own kind." The agent was motioning to her with his free hand, all the while waving his gun at Nox.

Emeline didn't know what to say to get through to this guy. Huddled behind Nox, begging the agent not to shoot, she could see he was too far gone to listen to reason.

CRACK

Hearing the sound of a weapon discharging, Nox was just thanking his lucky stars that he had worn his light armor when pain exploded across his chest. A pain so intense it was reminiscent of a similar pain he'd gotten years ago. He had been stabbed in the chest by, of all things, a plant. His mother had warned him to be careful, but as usual, he knew better. What was it called again? Oh yeah —Calano Hastom. Deceptively beautiful with large graceful pure white petals lined with red. Its unique smell called to you...until you touched it. Then the lovely petals dropped away, leaving a foot-and-a-half-long reed with a wickedly sharp end that it shot at unsuspecting prey. *Strange what runs through your mind when you're dying.*

An invisible force tugged at his body, dragging him backwards as he reached for Emeline. Her horrified expression worried him as she frantically called his name—

her hands reaching for him, but he couldn't seem to move his arms. A sharp pain radiated through his head as he watched her lovely face fade away right before his eyes. His last thought before the darkness overtook him was that, at least this time, he had protected her.

Tarek tamped down his fury as he took control of the situation. He should have seen this coming. His team had been watching this particular agent.

President Jenkins was also trying on his end to defuse the situation by demanding the agent stand down. The crazed agent roared back that it was his duty to save her from the aliens.

Seeing the agent about to fire another round into Nox, Yilmaz stunned the agent with his blaster. He collapsed in a heap on the floor, his gun skidding across the polished marble stopping just shy of Ramola's foot. He bent down, scooping the gun up just as agents came out from their hidden locations with weapons drawn, pointed at the Delicians.

In unison, Nyx took out the agent that appeared on the right balcony, while Liam got the one on the left. Ezio stunned the one that stepped out from behind a wall panel, while Ami neutralized the agent that came out from a hidden door that was set into the wall.

Smiling sheepishly at Tarek before grinning at Leslie and Liam, Ami smoothly slid her blaster back inside her pants pocket. Her smile quickly faded when she saw Emeline kneeling beside Nox, who was lying in a pool of blood. She rushed over asking what she could do to help.

Tarek shook his head as he looked around the room at the five human agents lying unconscious on the floor. He motioned for his team to stand down as Yilmaz and Ramola went around collecting all the weapons from the fallen agents...Liam showing them how to unload the weapons. Tarek ordered all weapons sent to the *Maelstrom* for analysis. Catching President Jenkins's eye, he let him know that having one of his own shot was unacceptable.

President Jenkins ran his hand through his hair as he tried to apologize to Tarek, however his council members were shouting at him to do something. When he uncharacteristically yelled at them to shut up, not surprisingly, they did. He pressed them to stop and think. Didn't they realize what had just happened? One of their own agents had shot one of the aliens. "You better pray Director Nox doesn't die."

CHAPTER 29

Peering around Nox's shoulder, Emeline felt like a by-stander as her life slowly unraveled right before her eyes. Terror swept through her as she watched the agent's finger squeeze the trigger on his gun. Her eyes were drawn to the flash of light as the bullet left the chamber. Later, she would swear she had actually watched as the bullet slowly spun towards Nox's body.

"NOX!" Her hearing sounded muffled in her head as she screamed at Nox to move out of the way.

He twisted his body to the left, but not fast enough. The bullet hit just off the center of his chest, piercing his alien armor.

She watched, horrified, as Nox's body jerked sideways from the impact of the shot. What surprised her more was that he still managed to push her to safety before hitting the marble floor...headfirst. The sharp crack of bone hitting stone echoed throughout the cavernous room.

Frantically grabbing for him, her hands caught nothing but air. With his last bit of strength, he had protected her. She would never forget the look of determination in his eyes before they snapped shut when his head hit the floor.

Blood began to pool immediately from Nox's head and chest wounds. His breathing was raspy and shallow as his lungs fought for air.

"NO-NO-NO! NOX!" Emeline screamed as she reached for Nox's head, only to stop herself when she saw all the blood. *Breathe, Center, Focus. You got this.* Taking a deep breath, Emeline knew if she wanted to help Nox, she had to act fast and keep it together.

Taking in the scene around her, it was apparent her friends and family had jumped in to eliminate the remaining threat as the seriousness of Nox's injuries became apparent.

Snapping out orders, there was no way she was letting the love of her life die. At this moment, she'd kill anyone who came near him. "Ezio, get me a regen device stat."

Ezio stepped up, a regen device in each hand.

Ignoring the sights and sounds around her, Emeline pushed at the top of her wrist comm and a holographic screen appeared in front of her, a portable ARI ready for her commands. Not hesitating, Emeline instructed ARI to begin scanning Nox to determine the extent of his injuries and initiate a treatment protocol.

A beam of light immediately projected out from her unit and began scanning Nox starting at the top of his head. The pool of blood under him was growing larger by the minute. She didn't like how his skin had grown even paler than normal as she waited for ARI to finish with the scans. Patience was never one of Emeline's strong suits, but Nox needed her not to fall apart. She would do that after they saved him.

"Liam, give me your knife."

Liam, who didn't hesitate, slipped his knife out of his boot, placing it in her upturned hand. She quickly began cutting away Nox's tunic, revealing his light armor with a circular hole in it. Blood still seeped out from around the edges of the wound.

Muttering out loud, she wondered why the hell his alien armor hadn't stopped the bullet.

Leaning in helping to remove Nox's damaged armored shirt, Nyx told her it should have stopped any projectile from the human weapons.

"Yeah, well it didn't." Emeline snapped.

Gently patting her shoulder, the remorseful expression on his face thankfully pulled Emeline back from the angry tirade she felt coming.

Sighing, she apologized to Nyx. It wasn't fair of her to

take her rage out on him. "I'm sorry, Nyx. It's not your fault." Glancing over to the President and the council members, she redirected most of her anger at them. "It's theirs."

Agreeing that they should have vetted their security personnel better, Nyx picked up the remains of Nox's shirt. Looking closely at the entry point, he scowled at it. "It doesn't make any sense. We researched human weaponry and this armor should have been sufficient."

Stroking his chest thoughtfully, Tarek considered Nyx's words. "Yilmaz. Talk to Koralo. Find out what happened. I want to know why Nox's armor didn't stop the human weapon. Make this a top priority. I want every piece of armor inspected."

Yilmaz reached over and took Nox's shirt from Nyx. "Yes, sir," he said, putting it into a small pouch that was attached to his utility belt.

Confused, Liam looked down at his own armor. "You mean this isn't bulletproof?"

Tarek shook his head grimly. "Evidently not, and I'd like to know why. Is your human military using experimental weapons?"

"I wouldn't know, but if I had to guess, I'd say yes." A worried frown crossed his brow as he looked up, saying, "I think we need to talk to President Jenkins."

Glancing over to where President Jenkins was talking to his members, Tarek ground out, "Oh, I intend to."

Tuning out the noise of the room, Emeline needed to examine Nox's wounds. "Ami, get me that pitcher of water off the table. Oh, and grab a bunch of those napkins."

Blood trickled down along Nox's long torso like rivulets that meandered down a mountainside in the summertime. The deep red color so prominent against his pale skin. His normal shine had dulled, turning more ghostly by the minute.

Her future lay motionless in front of her...slipping away every second as she waited for ARI to finish its scan.

"Nox, stay with me, babe. Come on, you're not going to let a little thing like a small human bullet or a bump on the head keep you down."

Wiping at the blood on his chest, Emeline reminded him what a good nurse she was. After all, when she broke his nose, she was able to fix him right up. "No need to worry, babe. I've got this."

She continued talking to him, wishing he would smile back at her. The way one side of his lips curled up just a tiny bit higher than the other. No one would notice it, unless you were looking for it and had kissed it a thousand times.

"Just so you know, Nox, I'm not letting you go. You promised to show me the universe and I'm holding you to it." A lone sob escaped her trembling lips. "I need more time."

At Ari's alert, Ezio handed her one device while he used a second one on the hole in Nox's chest. His breathing was becoming labored and he was still losing blood.

The damage to his chest was extensive. He had a collapsed lung along with major tissue damage, but miraculously the bullet hadn't broken any bones. By him twisting out of the way, the bullet managed to pass through only muscle and tissue, exiting out through the side of his back. Yilmaz had found the bullet lodged in one of decorated wall panels. He secured the bullet to analyze later back on the ship.

Liam gently lifted Nox's head, holding him steady while Emeline held the unit to the wound on the back of his head. Watching the beam penetrate Nox's skull certainly was a sight to behold. The naked eye couldn't detect the multitude of nanites that were repairing the damage to Nox's body. It truly was a miracle to anyone witnessing it for the first time.

After roughly fifteen minutes of holding the device, Emeline's arms were shaking badly, but she refused to let anyone else tend to Nox. Ami had tried to relieve her, but she refused.

It wasn't until Nox's eyelids started to flutter that she finally allowed herself to exhale the breath she hadn't realized she had been holding.

Glancing up, she saw the faces of the President and the UN council members as they all leaned in to get a closer look, transfixed on the scene before them. To say they were stunned was an understatement as they watched Nox appear to heal right before their eyes. Yilmaz had to repeatedly ask the council members to step back to allow his team space to work on healing Director Nox.

It took no longer than thirty minutes for Nox to be remarkably recovered for someone who had been knocking on death's door. Of course, he would need to be checked out by Dr. Datrem and spend some time in the regen bed once he returned to the *Maelstrom*. And he would definitely need a pint or two of blood to replenish the amount that currently stained the antique floor, but by tomorrow, Nox's body would be as if he'd never been injured.

As Nox opened his eyes and tried to sit up, Emeline felt tears silently flow down her cheeks. Pressing gently on his shoulder to keep him in place, she urged him to stay down. "Don't move," she insisted.

Of course, he resisted, instead curling his body into hers, his arms going tight around her waist.

Placing her arm around his shoulder, she pulled him tenderly against her. The cadence of his beating heart was slowly replacing the fear that had taken up root in every cell of her body.

"Give yourself a minute to get your bearings." Feeling his head nod, she whispered, "I was so scared I was going to lose you." At her words, their arms instinctively tightened around each other as love and strength flooded their bond.

Pushing back, she brushed at the tears escaping her eyes before reaching up taking a stray lock and tucking it securely behind his ear. Locking eyes with him, she spoke quietly. "You saved me. If you hadn't pushed me out of the way, that bullet would have gone right into me."

As the full impact of what could have happened rocked through her, her words came out in broken spurts. "Thank you, thank you, thank you," she panted into his neck.

Holding her close, Nox gently rubbed her back, reminding her that he was here and they were alive. Her breath tickled his ear, sending shivers throughout his body, eternally thankful he'd been able to save her. "Always, my Pulmina, always."

He couldn't wait to get her away from these humans and back on board the *Maelstrom*. Although, he sadly reminded himself, he hadn't been able to keep her safe there either.

Giving her a tender smile, he brushed a lone tear that still trailed down her cheek. "I should be thanking you. You healed me—again. I hope this isn't going to become a habit." He tried to make a joke, but Emeline only harrumphed at him. Laughing wasn't high on her list of feelings right now.

Nyx brought a chair over and with Liam's help managed to get Nox up off the floor.

Sitting down heavily, Emeline handed him a glass of water, which he downed in two gulps. Picking up the pitcher she asked him if he wanted any more.

Shaking his head, he pulled Emeline down onto his lap, hugging her to him. He was done caring what others thought. They were lucky that neither of them had been killed by that crazed zealot. Their lives together were just starting...the adventures they'd planned so close to being over before it even began.

Tarek cleared his throat, breaking into their quiet moment.

Jumping off Nox's lap, Emeline's eyes narrowed on President Jenkins and his council members, who were making their way over towards them. Their eyes were trained on her and Nox...watching their every move.

Grabbing Nox's hand, Emeline didn't bother trying to rein in her anger and she was certainly done playing nice. Turning toward the human delegation, she let loose a tirade so strong, it was a wonder they all didn't get whiplash as she lambasted them for their carelessness. "What is wrong with you people? You could have killed us. If we hadn't had the use of the Delician technology, Nox would be dead. And if he hadn't pushed me out of the way, I'd be dead too. Did you even bother vetting your agents?"

President Jenkins held up his hand, silencing the council members who had all started shouting at once. "Quiet."

He addressed the Delician delegation, ignoring the mumblings from behind him. "Please, General Tarek, Miss Cameron, forgive my security team."

Turning to Nox, the sincerity in his voice matched his eyes, "Director Nox, I cannot express how sorry I am about what happened. My agents were under strict orders not to fire their weapons."

Looking around at his fallen agents, he ran his hand down his troubled face as the full impact of what had happened sank in. "Our weapons may be inferior to yours, but they're still lethal. However, from what we just witnessed, your technology healed wounds that should have killed you. I am at a loss for words. Humans would benefit greatly from that device."

Emeline jerked out of Nox's arms, appalled that her president would use him getting shot as a way to create a gain for Earth. "Seriously? That's how you want to play this? You don't honestly think that the UAP would grant you use of their technology when this is how you treat them—at the first meeting no less? It's this type of behavior that only reiterates that humans still belong on that list." Emeline stood with her arms crossed, glaring at the President. His council hung back at least having the decency to look somewhat contrite.

Leslie stepped up beside Emeline, interrupting her before she could continue. "It might be wise to take a break right now. I think everyone could use a little breather."

Nodding his head in agreement, Present Jenkins and his council moved over to a corner of the room where a table of refreshments had been set up.

Emeline snorted as she saw them talking animatedly until the president silenced them. With his back turned to the room, Emeline could see that the rest of council was hanging on his every word. *Good. Maybe he can talk some sense into them.*

Practically falling into a chair, her head cradled in her hands, Emeline's breathing finally returning to normal as she felt Nox through their bond. He was healing, slowly, but he would be fine, thanks to the Delicians' technology. It was his head wound that had worried her the most. Except for the dried blood caked in his hair, you'd never know he had been injured. *Amazing.*

Coming over to stand by his chair, Tarek leaned in, catching Nox's eye. "I had a feeling something like this might happen. I'm sorry you got caught up in the crossfire. This is partly my fault. I gave the humans more leeway than I normally do. I should have had their weapons removed the moment we got here. Most species that I've encountered invariably have individuals or groups who do not approve of interspecies interactions. Unfortunately, even on Delicia you will find a few with a similar sentiment."

It was Lorelei who spoke up, surprising the group. "We humans understand discrimination, as we like to call it, better than you'd think. I find it interesting that now that we've made first contact with *aliens* from outer space, we designate ourselves as humans."

Turning to General Tarek, Lorelei pointed to herself. "You see, humans have been discriminating against each other since—well, since forever."

Seeing his frown, Lorelei asked him, "General, when you look at Emeline and myself, do you notice how different we look?"

Tarek and their group looked closely from Emeline to Lorelei. After taking a moment to consider Lorelei's question, he replied, "I see some physical differences, but those are inconsequential. What stands out to me are your human female characteristics." The Delicians who were standing around all nodded in agreement.

Lorelei smiled at Tarek. "Well said, General. It's too bad humans don't always think the way you do. They put a great deal of importance on appearance, status, wealth. Wars have been fought, families torn apart, misery and sadness all in the name of what was considered right at the time." She told them some of the history of her people, which caused the Delicians to gasp in horror.

Tarek's forehead creased as he listened to her story. "Lorelei, I wish I could tell you that this type of atrocious behavior is limited to Earth. Unfortunately, I can't."

Lorelei gave him the smile her wise grandmother used to give her when she was teaching her the stories of their ancestors. "That's why it's important for me to show the world that I am important. I can make a difference."

Smiling over at Ami, Emeline and Heather, Lorelei told him. "And that's why meeting these three women changed my life. The four of us have made a difference by accepting who we are as individuals and building and learning from each others' strengths and weaknesses."

Ami came over and pulled Lorelei into a hug, whispering, "God, have I missed you."

The four women embraced as one, together for the first time in what felt like a lifetime.

Emeline had missed her friends and never wanted to lose this closeness, even if it had to survive over thousands of light years. Lucky for her, her bondmate had good communication technology, so she would always be able to stay in contact with her best friends.

Turning to Tarek, Emeline couldn't let the actions of

a few scared fools ruin what could be beneficial to their planet. She had to convince Tarek to give the humans a chance to prove they were worthy of being in the UAP. "Tarek, I don't know what decision they're going to come to." Nodding over to where Earth's leaders appeared to be arguing about something, she continued in earnest to plead her case. "All I know is before you make any decisions regarding Earth, please hear me out."

At his nod, she let out the breath she was holding. "Okay great – thank you. I know that what happened was awful – sickening actually. All I'm asking is to not let a few phobia-crazed individuals ruin what could be an important alliance. Deep down, humans are inherently good, decent, hardworking people who value family and loyalty. If given the chance, we humans might surprise you."

Nodding, Tarek told her he would consider her words. Winking at her, he added that he was well aware of just how surprising humans could be.

Looking over Tarek's shoulder, Emeline saw President Jenkins heading in their direction, his eyes landing briefly on her and Nox. *I know that look. [sigh]*

Looking around at the mixed group of aliens and humans, Jenkins's gaze stopped briefly on Leslie before turning to speak directly to Tarek. "My colleagues and I have come to a consensus. If the offer still stands, we would like to send a diplomatic delegation to your headquarters for an exploratory meeting."

Emeline looked up suspiciously, her eyes narrowing as she wondered what he was up to. She didn't trust him, not after what had just happened. Waiting to see what Tarek would say, Emeline wondered if maybe he shouldn't retract the whole deal and go home. Humans obviously had a bit more growing and evolving to do.

Tarek studied the man, who from all appearances was trying to do what was best for his world while trying to please everyone. "What assurances can you give me that a similar incident won't happen with the members of your diplomatic team?"

Frowning, the President took a moment to consider before responding cautiously, "There is no way I can guarantee that a human won't act irrationally at times. It's part of our human nature."

Tarek's response surprised everyone when he chuckled loudly, saying, "I have to agree with you there and I appreciate your honesty."

Giving Ami a knowing look, her face reddening, he smiled at her, saying, "I have witnessed your human nature."

Mumbling under her breath, Ami huffed out, "Is it my fault that sometimes my mouth engages before my brain?"

"However," Tarek said, shooting Ami a sly smile, "I have decided that in light of what happened with Director Nox, I will be making a change to the UAP's offer."

The room appeared to hold its collective breath, waiting either to be given its heart's desire or told to go home, no one wanted to play with you.

"I will accept Earth's delegation, but I will be limiting the number of security agents you send and my team will vet them before they will be accepted on this mission." Tarek's commanding gaze scanned the human leaders to see if any of them had any disagreement with his decision.

The Russian and Chinese council members looked as if they wanted to challenge Tarek, but one look from President Jenkins quieted their rumblings.

Clearly relieved at Tarek's decision, President Jenkins agreed to his terms, adding that he would like Liam to be the head of Earth's security team.

Liam's head popped up sharply, surprised at the President's request. After getting a nod from Tarek, Liam responded to the President, his voice tight, "Respectfully, sir, I'm afraid I'm going to have to decline. I am resigning my commission effective immediately."

At the stunned look on the human leaders' faces, Liam hardened his features. There was no way he was letting anything get in the way of this opportunity to join Tarek's team. "I have been asked by General Tarek to join his elite team and I have accepted. I have already informed Leslie and submitted my letter of resignation to her."

President Jenkins was visibly upset at this turn of events. "I'm disappointed, Lt. Commander. I was counting on you being there for Leslie and the delegation. You know that I could deny your request—but I won't. All I ask is that you fulfill one last assignment for your country, or should I say planet."

"And what would that be?" Liam asked, knowing full well what he wanted.

Glancing from Tarek to Leslie and then back to Liam, President Jenkins responded with a slight sigh, knowing that he was losing a valuable asset. "Since you have made it clear you are no longer interested in being in our military, would you consider acting as military liaison between the delegation team and the UAP? At least until the conclusion of the exploratory meeting. After that, I will formally release you from your duties."

Getting a quick approval nod from Tarek, Liam agreed to the President's proposal, adding, "Just so you are aware though, I will not be returning to Earth unless directed by my new commander."

Unhappy with Liam's decision, but given his military record, the President had no choice but to agree to his terms. Turning to Tarek, he sighed unhappily. "I'm sorry to be losing such a valuable member of our military. Congratulations, General. You are getting a highly skilled man."

Tarek knew what it was like to lose a valued member of your team, telling the President, "I'm well aware. He has been an asset to my team."

Red began to creep up Liam's neck, embarrassed at all

the praise. He only hoped he could live up to it.

The President then asked Tarek, "When do you plan to return to the UAP?"

General Tarek looked at his team before answering. "I'd like to depart in two of Earth's weeks. Can you have your team ready by then?"

Seeing Leslie nod her head, President Jenkins replied, "That should be sufficient." Turning his attention to Emeline and Nox, his eyes landed briefly on their clasped hands. "Miss Cameron."

"Mr. Jenkins." Everyone in the room could tell by her tone that she was still upset about what had happened to Nox. *Here it comes.*

"We would like to thank you for all that you and your company have done for Earth. Without your Deflector Network Array in conjunction with the Delicians' technology, our communication network could have been compromised or even worse, destroyed, and for that you have our sincerest thanks."

"You're welcome, and although your thanks is appreciated, it's totally unnecessary," she replied through pursed lips. "EAC Global Networking Solutions is committed to doing whatever we can for the betterment of our planet, especially now that Earth will be moving forward in a new level of evolution."

"Yes, about that." Clearing his throat, President Jenkins leveled his gaze at her. "As much as we appreciate all that you have done for Earth, in light of all that has happened to you with your kidnapping and the severe wounds that you received, we will no longer be requiring your services. I have asked Leslie to terminate your company's contract with NASA and authorized her to pay your company a generous bonus. It is the least we can do for all that you have given to Earth."

The only thing holding Emeline back from laughing in his face was the sharp intake of breath from her friends and family. It was obvious his reasoning.

Crossing her arms, Emeline looked down at her fingernails before looking up, mildly asking President Jenkins, "So, what you're telling me is that after all that my company and all of us"—pointing to her team— "have done for Earth, we're expected to what, just go home and forget this all happened?"

President Jenkins appeared genuinely surprised that Emeline wasn't going away like a good little girl. "Well yes. As I said, your services are no longer needed. You four women are cleared to return to your normal daily lives. All we ask is that you not discuss any of the events that have occurred until such time as we determine the public should be made aware that first contact has been made. We also require that you cut all contact with the Delicians and the UAP. We will, of course, have you sign a non-disclosure agreement agreeing to this."

Dropping her hands to her sides, Emeline's face flushed with anger. She could feel Nox's hand trying to pull her back down onto the chair beside him. Shaking his hand away, her eyes looked at Ami, who was being shushed by Liam.

Stealing a quick glance at the Delicians, they were just as confused as she was. Nyx was quietly asking why, especially after all they had done to help save their planet.

Taking a deep cleansing breath, Emeline tried to keep her voice from sounding shrill. Screaming at the President of the United States was not going to help anyone. "Would you care to explain to all of us why we are being *dismissed*?" Her hand motioned to the Delicians and her friends, who were still trying to make sense of the President's decision.

President Jenkins looked around at the angry faces, both alien and human, baffled at the tension in the room. He wasn't used to his orders being questioned. Smiling indulgently at both women, he softened his tone saying, "I— we"—pointing to the council members— "feel that it is not in the best interest of Earth and yourself that you continue having any contact with the Delicians. We feel that considering the traumatic experience that both you and Miss Jefferson had to endure during your time with the aliens that you be allowed to rest and recover here on Earth. Again, your country—the world—thanks you for your service."

It did not go unnoticed to Emeline that President Jenkins specifically didn't mention Nox by name.

Trying to curtail her rising resentment and after a quick check with Tarek, who gave her a slight nod, Emeline knew the time had come for the world to learn about Delician bondmates.

Gracing the human leaders with a bright smile, they all smiled back at her, happy that she appeared to accept how they had dictated her future for her without giving any thought to her feelings.

Sitting down in the chair next to Nox, she leaned over, catching his lips in a steamy kiss. She kissed him long and hard. Long enough that it had Liam clearing his throat and Ami laughing out loud. Long enough that it had the council members gasping at them with a mixture of fascination and revulsion.

Nox's eyes drifted shut as he savored her kiss before he lazily opened them, giving the human leaders a very satisfied smile. If his Emeline wanted to make a statement, he was more than happy to oblige her.

With a wicked smile on her lips, Emeline leaned back and crossed her arms, addressing the stunned group. "Is the reason you don't want me involved with the Delicians is because you think I'm *hooking* up with one of them?" Their faces said it all. "You judge without knowing the facts," she told them. "And furthermore, even if we were, it would be none of your business."

"Miss Cameron, it is for this exact reason—" President Jenkins was using his fatherly voice on Emeline.

Emeline held up her hand silencing the president. His condescending tone had her blurting out hotly, "Let me just stop you right there, Mr. President—although I am beginning to regret voting for you."

"Miss Cameron." The warning tone in the President's voice showed he was losing his patience.

"No. It's my turn to talk. You all have had your little confab and evidently, I was one of your main topics of discussion—without my knowledge or you even knowing the full facts. Let me ask you, Mr. Jenkins, is America still a free country?"

The President raised his eyebrow, nodding his head warily.

"And am I still an American citizen?"

Again, he nodded his head.

"Then as a free citizen, isn't it my right to be able to make my own decisions on where my future lies?" Emeline kept her eyes trained on the President.

Frowning, he thought for a moment before reminding her, "Yes, however, when it could affect the entire planet, then it becomes my responsibility. I'm sorry, Miss Cameron, but I cannot allow you any more interaction with the Delicians, especially Director Nox. And especially not after that display you've just shown us."

Pointing to Nox, Jenkins ground out, "I cannot allow the fate of all humanity to be undermined by this infatuation you have with someone who saved your life. I have an entire planet to think of, not just one human woman who thinks she is in love with an alien." Those last words were tinged with more than a little anger.

Emeline was furious. *Who does he think he is? So what, now I'm suffering from Stockholm Syndrome! Standing here insulting each other is getting us nowhere. Maybe if I explain about bondmating they might just get it. Otherwise, I'm leaving Earth and never coming back.* This bothered Emeline deeply. She wasn't ready to give up her planet just because some misguided dignitaries didn't have all the facts.

Nox's hand grazed her lower back. Looking into his eyes, she drew strength from him. It also helped having the Delicians, including Tarek, move to stand behind them lending their support. When Liam and the girls stood intermingled with the Delicians, showing where their loyalty lay, Emeline knew whatever happened next, she had plenty of people in her corner.

This left Leslie stuck between the two irate groups. She looked helplessly at Emeline, silently imploring her not to allow their negotiations with the aliens to end before it even got started.

Nodding her understanding to Leslie, Emeline felt Nox's arm snake warm and heavy across her chest as he pulled her hard against him.

Taking a deep breath, she ignored the metallic smell of Nox's blood, instead focusing on the small hint of vanilla that came from his hair that lay against her shoulder. Leveling her tone, she addressed the human leaders, "With all due respect, why don't we all sit down so that I can explain to you the relationship that Director Nox and I have? Once you hear what we have to say, it will give you a better understanding of our connection to one another."

Seeing their hesitation, Tarek took command, ordering everyone to take their seats at the table, much to the chagrin of the human leaders.

Nox and Emeline sat together at the head of the table beside Tarek. The human leaders chose to sit bunched together on one side, showing a clearly divided room.

Ivan Orlov, the Russian council member, was visibly agitated; his bald head was shiny with moisture, while his breathing was erratic. His color had turned pasty gray as he rubbed his chest, obviously in pain.

Emeline looked up as Tarek leaned over discreetly, telling her that Orlov appeared to be in medical distress. Her eyes shot to the Russian as he slumped over onto the table.

Jumping up, she grabbed one of the regen devices and hurried over to where the French council member Claude Lanoue and President Jenkins were placing him on the floor. He was barely conscious, clearly suffering from a heart attack.

Stopping just shy of his body, Councilman Orlov's shaky hand came up in a feeble attempt to stop Emeline from coming any closer. His fear was palpable as he eyed the device in her hand.

Allowing her compassion to overrun her anger, she watched him trying to make sense of everything that was happening to him. It wasn't hard to feel empathy for him, especially considering that up until a few hours ago, he had only seen an alien on a holographic image. To actually see one up close took some getting used to. *I suppose to them Nox and I make this whole thing all too real.* She couldn't help but feel she was living inside a comic book come to life.

Smiling gently down at him, she held the regen device up as she softly began explaining how the device worked. "I'm just going to place this over your heart. It won't hurt you. You will feel some tingling, but I promise—this will fix you. I know you're feeling pretty sick right now but please let me save you." Seeing him hesitate, she leaned in and whispered, "Besides, you don't want to go down in history as being *that* guy who died at first contact, do you?" She grinned at him as she turned on the device and slowly moved it over his heart.

"How come you didn't scan me?" He held still, his eyes never leaving the regen device.

"It wasn't necessary. We know it's your heart. Have you been having issues lately?"

Nodding, he looked up at her.

In no time at all, the Councilman's chest relaxed, his breathing beginning to level out. His face gave her a look of amazement as he exhaled with ease. "This is a miracle device, yes?"

"Yes, it is." Emeline continued to hold the device at his chest, only this time the Russian seemed to be studying her. A look of curiosity crossed his face, prompting Emeline to tell him, "Go ahead. Ask your question?" She figured he would go right for the heart of her relationship with Nox—sex with an alien. He surprised her, causing her to look at him with raised eyebrows.

"Will you sell me one of these devices?"

Emeline's mouth quirked up at the corner—capitalism at its finest. "I'm sorry, Ivan—can I call you Ivan since I'm saving your life and all?" Not waiting for an answer, she instead continued talking softly to him, allowing the device to repair his damaged heart. "This device will never be for sale. If and when the UAP and Earth decide how alien technology can be integrated into our world, it will be free for everyone to use. Now Ivan, don't you agree that something this life saving should be shared with everyone?"

Having the decency to look abashed, Ivan replied, "Forgive me, please. I was only thinking of my people and how many lives this could save."

She smiled, understanding his thinking. "There is nothing to forgive. I had the same reaction the first time I saw one in use. All I could think of was how many lives could be saved. You know, Ivan, this whole experience has been so surreal, not just for me but for all of us. The technology that I have seen in my time with the Delicians would honestly blow your mind."

Pointing to the regen device, the excitement in her voice captured everyone's attention. "If you think this is great you should see their medical bay. It has three of these devices, only the size of beds that you lie down in. And don't even get me started on the replicator. You can have a complete meal or an entire outfit within minutes. Plus, you don't have to do the dishes or the laundry. All you have to do is put everything back in the recycling container and everything gets broken down and used again and again.

Totally amazing."

The room was quiet. The only sound was Emeline's voice, the cadence rising and falling as she described some of what her life was like living on the *Maelstrom* over the last few weeks. They had already heard about her kidnapping, so she focused on her daily life—her work with Nox and Loris and their evenings with everyone taking turns cooking meals.

As she spoke, Ivan relaxed and she could see that his color was improving. Instead of a pasty gray, his skin had moved onto pale white. Giving him a glass of water, she changed the topic to her and Nox.

"I know that you don't understand my relationship with Director Nox." She looked up to find the council listening intently. "You see there is a certain aspect to the Delician culture that none of you have been made aware of."

A murmur ran through human leaders as Ivan encouraged her to continue, "What do you mean?"

As she saw that her audience was riveted to her story, Emeline knew that this was her one chance to fight for her and Nox and there was no way she was going to blow it. Feeling Nox's love and support through their bond, she took a moment to consider how best to make them understand her feelings for Nox. *Hell, it's been hard enough for me to understand them, let alone telling someone else how it feels to find that one person who just gets you.*

An idea began to form in Emeline's mind that might just do the trick. Leaning back on her heels, she asked Ivan, "Can I ask—are you married?"

Raising his eyebrows, Ivan replied with a wary tone, "Yes."

Emeline smiled at him. "Awesome. Can you tell me how you met your wife?"

Ivan smiled, nodding his head, telling her that he and his wife had grown up in the same apartment complex in Moscow. They had known each other from when they were babies, even going to school together.

"Have you always known that she was the one for you?" Emeline asked him.

Ivan didn't hesitate, "Oh yes. I always knew that my Anka and I would be together."

"Would you say that she is your soul mate?" Emeline asked, holding her breath.

Again, he didn't hesitate, "Oh yes. Anka is my life."

Thrilled at his answer, she smiled softly, saying, "The Delicians have something similar to soul mates. They're called bondmates."

Seeing the interest on Ivan's face, Emeline pushed on. "The difference is that once the bond is completed, their bodies go through a physical change."

"What kind of change?" President Jenkins, who had been kneeling on the other side of Emeline, asked.

Emeline had forgotten he was there, her focus solely on helping the council member. She gave him a cursory look before turning her attention back to Ivan. "Bondmates are connected through an internal force from the moment they meet that can never be broken. Just like your Anka is to you, Nox is to me. Our bond is eternal, marked by fate."

"How so?" Ivan was curious as to what she meant.

With a smile as bright as a summer's day, Emeline turned to her bondmate asking, "Nox, could you come over here for a second?"

Nox moved slowly towards her, bending down so his large body didn't appear so threatening to the injured man.

Asking Nox to lean down, Emeline asked Ivan to look closely at Nox's chest. "Can you see the colors there?" Since Nox's tunic had been removed, his bare chest was exposed, showing the deep colors of their bond.

"Sure. I can see deep purples, pinks and blues and lots of shimmery white." Ivan's eyes were transfixed on Nox's perfectly smooth chest—no hint of the bullet wound could be detected.

"Good. Now look over at General Tarek. Do you see the difference in the colors between them?"

Everyone's head turned from one to the other, checking out the difference in the colors.

Margaret Mower pointed with a shaky finger from Nox to Tarek, blurting out, "His colors are darker, more pronounced than his."

"Ah" Everyone was nodding in agreement.

Satisfied that she was leading them down the right path, Emeline continued. "That's right. The difference in colors means that Nox has found his bondmate and the General has not."

Again, there was a collective "ah" from the human leaders.

Nox reached over—the back of his hand gently caressed her blushing cheek before locking eyes with her. The smoldering look she gave him conveyed the intensity of her love for him. Giving him a quick wink, Emeline turned back to the human leaders.

President Jenkins was staring at Emeline intently, finally asking her, "Since you are Director Nox's bondmate, what would happen if you two were separated?"

A brief kaleidoscope of memories from her time apart from Nox filled her mind. Shuddering, she replied confidently, "That's never going to happen unless it's of our own choosing. We will not allow anyone to separate us again. Nox, do you mind showing them your bond mark?"

With his eyes never leaving hers, he lifted his thick dark hair just as she pulled back hers, displaying their matching bond marks for all to see.

Only council member Zhu appeared appalled at their marks. The other members, President Jenkins included, were totally intrigued. They all began throwing questions at them, bombarding them with wanting to know was it a tattoo, did it hurt, will it wash off, to being utterly fascinated that it had just appeared.

Emeline did her best to try to answer all their questions, finally saying it might be a good idea for everyone to sit down. "I don't think I'm the best one to tell you about Delicians and their bondmates. Nox can do a much better job at it than I can."

Shutting off the regen device, she turned to Ivan, asking, "How are you feeling?"

Ivan inhaled deeply, showing no sign of impairment. When he exhaled, a faint scent of tobacco permeated the air. Rubbing his chest, amazed, exclaiming loudly to everyone, "I have no pain." Pulling in a few more deep breathes, he smiled at his colleagues. "It's a miracle."

Emeline and Nox each hooked an arm under Ivan's armpits and lifted him to his feet. It took a moment for Ivan's legs to steady themselves, giving him an opportunity to get a closer look at their bond marks. "They are exactly the same," he murmured, totally amazed. "So, you just woke up with them? Did you have to do something to make it happen?"

Thinking back to her conversation with Nox, they had both agreed there was only so much they were willing to share. "Umm." Emeline's face was blushing a pretty shade of pink as Nox gently patted her hand.

"Of course, they did, you fool. They had to make mad passionate love to one another. Isn't that true, mon ami?" Claude Lanoue stood wagging his eyebrows at them.

Margaret Mower again tried to quiet the Frenchman, but he waved her off. "Do not shush me. I am from the country of amour. It is in our blood."

The Delicians laughed at Nox's embarrassment as Emeline pulled her hair down, covering her mark.

After passing Ivan over to Council members, Lanoue and Zhu, Zhu not in the least bit happy, Emeline and Nox took their seats.

Taking Nox's hand in hers, the contrast may have been apparent to others, but it had ceased to exist to Emeline.

Everyone took their seats, including Ivan who was frowning into his glass. He could be heard grumbling that he hadn't asked for water.

Emeline shot Ivan a *don't you dare* look, telling him, "Ivan, you've been given a second chance on life. Please try to make better choices—think of your Anka."

He waved his hand at her, hiding a smile when she gave him the two fingers to the eyes.

Nox sat in his chair as he addressed the group. There was still a divide in the room, but now the human leaders had moved closer, eager to listen to what the Delicians had to say.

Emeline mused that apparently watching how alien devices can heal could quickly make the aliens a lot more tolerable. She tried to look at things from the human side as she watched Nox give a brief description about bondmates and its connection to Delicia. He described how arranged marriages had become common into helping rebuild the Delician population since bondmating had become so rare. The Pakistani council member Dewan inserted how it was a common practice in her country. Nox ended by telling them that he and Emeline were the first interspecies bondmating that he knew of.

The members peppered him with questions—all except the Chinese council member, Ming Zhu. With a snort of disbelief at Emeline, his tone dripped with condescension. "Do you take us for fools, Miss Cameron? We have eyes. We can see the real reason you have aligned yourself with these aliens."

Scoffing at Council member Zhu as the Delicians growled their displeasure at his question, Emeline knew this guy considered her just another crazy overindulged American. "You think I'm just infatuated with the Delicians like those crazy fan girls who dress up like Wonder Woman and hang out at Comic Con. Well let me tell you something —you know nothing about me. You know only what you've read in my dossier and that's not even a fraction of who I am."

Considering the looks the Delicians were giving to Council Member Zhu, it was no wonder Zhu shrunk lower into his chair. The nasty looks he was getting weren't only from the aliens.

Pinching the bridge of her nose, Emeline had had enough. She was tired and wanted to go home. With a determined look in her eye, Emeline announced in a loud voice to the group, "I'm going with Nox to Delicia."

Ami jumped in, announcing, "I'm going with them as well."

Not to be outdone, Lorelei blurted out she was going too, which garnered her the stink eye from her three friends.

Hearing the three women's statements caused President Jenkins' eyebrows to rise almost up into his hairline. "Before you all make any decisions, could I speak to you in private for a moment, Miss Cameron?"

Wrinkling her forehead, Emeline hesitated for a moment before nodding. Since Nox refused to let her go alone, they walked side by side as they followed the President over to stand in front of one of the antique fireplaces. Smiling, remembering her mother's no touching priceless artifacts rule, Emeline stopped her hand just shy of touching such an extraordinary beautiful piece of history. *Where's a set of gloves when you need them?*

Facing each other, Emeline and President Jenkins paused for a long moment studying one another, wondering if it was possible for them to develop some form of trust.

Emeline already knew her answer—he would have to prove himself to her and so far, he was severely lacking in the acceptance and protection part of being a leader.

Exhaling softly, the President knew he owed this woman a huge apology. Feeling more than a little ashamed for his treatment of her—he wasn't known for being narrowminded. Although, all things considered, his life had never been this out of control before. "Ms. Cameron, I'm sorry for—"

"Being an ass." The words blurted out.

He laughed, surprising them both. "I guess I deserve that."

Getting serious, he apologized again, telling her that he really wasn't a bad guy. "I guess the events of the last few weeks have affected all of us. When I first became president, I was given all the details of encounters with aliens. With all the other duties as president, I really didn't give it much thought. We knew someone was out there but we'd never had anyone try to make contact with us—that is until now. When Leslie contacted my office and gave the code word, I was—"

They could see him searching for just the right word that described his feelings, but there wasn't just one. "Scared, excited, fascinated, worried, terrified, curious—I could go on. However, I kept coming back to one word, uncertain. There is too much that we don't know and that is what really concerns me."

Nodding her head in agreement, Emeline added her own thoughts. "I understand better than you think. Over the last few weeks, my very life hinged on uncertainty. But when you think about it, it's that uncertainty that drives us to try new things, take risks, learn, even survive. We have been given an opportunity to bring our people into a whole new era. Will there be uncertainty? Of course. I don't envy you the decisions you'll be facing. I just want to help in any way I can. I want to be a part of this."

Contemplating her words, President Jenkins agreed but asked if she was truly prepared for the new life she was embarking on.

Emeline looked back over her shoulder at Nox, replying that she'd never been more *certain* in her life.

He laughed at her choice of words, accepting her decision. He then went on to discuss some of the medical devices that she thought could be slowly integrated into Earth.

Nox interrupted, reminding him that the UAP must first approve any alien technology beforehand. He did, however, tell the President that he and Emeline would make it a priority as soon as they got the approval from the UAP.

Stealing a glance at Tarek, who was flanked by Yilmaz and Nyx, Emeline saw that he was listening to the Russian, Pakistani and French council members. They were discussing the salt and the impact it would have with Pakistan and the rest of the world. They were wondering if perhaps the aliens had technology that could be used to harvest the salt without doing any damage to the environment. She smiled at Tarek, telling them he was impressed that they were willing to work together, but reminded them that the UAP would initially only allow limited access to any advanced technology. When the council members protested, he held up his hand, defending the UAP and its policies regarding membership into the Alliance, reiterating that they always erred on the side of caution.

Catching her eye, Tarek made a motion that he was ready to leave. More than ready, Emeline excused herself and Nox before moving over to stand beside Tarek along with Liam and Ami.

As Tarek shook hands with the President, telling him that he would contact him with the details of their departure, the President again apologized for his security team and Nox's *unfortunate injury.*

Seeing that Heather and Lorelei were determined to leave with their friends, Tarek offered to drop the two women on the roof of their lab in Boston.

Lorelei was bubbling over with excitement at the thought of riding in an alien shuttle, chattering to Heather that, "See, I was right all along. There really are aliens and not just in my books."

Heather hung on tight to Lorelei's arm, the words *charla loca* audible under her breath.

Leslie walked them out to the shuttle, still trying to absorb the fact that she would be leading a diplomatic team to another universe. "I'll call you tomorrow, Liam, to talk about logistics." Stepping back, she watched awestruck as their alien spacecraft disappeared into the night sky.

After dropping off Lorelei and Heather and promising that soon she would give them a tour of the *Maelstrom*, Emeline asked Tarek if it would be all right to visit her mother. "It's time I told her about Nox." She also needed time to meet with the girls to make some decisions before they left for UAP headquarters. Lorelei was making arrangements for everyone to meet at Fiona's house since her property was secluded.

Tarek took a few moments to consider her request before finally giving his consent, adding, "Nyx, make sure you do a complete scan of the area before you leave."

As Nyx maneuvered the shuttle back on board the *Maelstrom*, everyone looked as if they could use a drink.

Jagger met them in the docking bay, announcing that he had made Emeline's favorite dish of poached fish in wine sauce—just the way she liked it. Hearing her stomach growl as he described how he had made the dish caused much laughter, considerably lightening everyone's mood.

Emeline looked over at Nox before shaking her head sorrowfully at the captain. "I'm sorry, Jagger, you'll have to save dinner for us." The crushed look on Jagger's face pushed Emeline to rush out her words. "Nox was shot by a human gun and I think he should to go to medical first."

Nox's stomach protested loud enough, stopping Emeline's words as he pulled her into his arms telling her, "Pulmina, I'm fine. What I really could use is something to eat. Besides, you don't want to hurt Jagger's feelings, do you?"

They all laughed as Jagger tried but failed to hold a pouty face, telling her that he'd been slaving over a hot stove all day. "I even made ice cream."

Oh, now he hit her sweet spot. Grinning at him, she asked hopefully, "With chocolate sauce?"

"Of course." Jagger knew he had her at the word "chocolate."

It was easy for Emeline to give in, especially when she looked up at the faces of the people who had come to mean so much to her over the last few weeks. "Okay then, let's eat. Just promise me, afterwards you'll go straight to the med bay."

Pulling her close, Nox bent down to kiss her forehead, agreeing to her demands, adding a few of his own before he released her, "Promise me as soon as Dr. Datrem is done examining me, you will attend me with one of your long hot bubble baths."

Squeezing his waist, loving how his hard muscles twitched under her fingers, Emeline couldn't help giving him a sultry look. Her cheeks flushed red at the thought of ending this long grueling day in the arms of her sexy bondmate. "Let's eat fast."

More laughter and more than a few bawdy remarks could be heard as they hurried towards the officers' rec room. Emeline didn't care. She was happy and looking forward to her future with Nox—well, that and a hot steamy bubble bath. *Ah life was good.*

CHAPTER 30

Cameron family home
New Hampshire

It was the kind of night Emeline always hated going out in—inky black and definitely spooky. Driving home from class on nights like this was generally a sweaty palm experience for her. You couldn't see five feet in front of you and on top of that, the roads were slick from the wet leaves that littered the ground.

Lucky for her, they were flying and not driving, but it was still hard to see. It wouldn't have mattered if the moon was full—nothing was getting through the massive black clouds that swirled past her family's home. You could almost see the moisture hanging heavy in the air.

Bad weather—God, I hope it's not an omen. Emeline was praying that this first meeting between her mother and Nox went well. She really wanted Fiona to like Nox. *What am I saying—of course she's going to love him. I mean, who wouldn't? He's awesome. She just has to get past the whole alien from another planet thing – and she will [sigh] eventually.*

Glancing over, Emeline watched Nox talking to Loris on his wrist comm. They were discussing a possible upgrade to his force fields to include armor. She smiled inwardly, loving that she and Nox were so alike—always into one project or several. Neither one of them could sit idle for very long. Life was moving in fast forward especially now that the human delegation was getting ready to head to the UAP headquarters with them. She was excited at the prospect of going on this new adventure with Nox and the rest of the crew.

Thinking back to earlier in the day, she had loved showing Nox and Nyx one of her favorite places on Earth. With Liam piloting the cloaked shuttle over the upper part of New Hampshire where the colors were at their brightest, it was hard to believe it was already October. That meant the leaves were going through their seasonal transformation —their deep greens magically morphing into the myriad of rich fall colors before falling haphazardly wherever the wind took them.

Her face had lit up at the spectacular view as she told them, "This is my favorite time of year. Every year we would make our annual fall trip to the apple orchard. They fry apple cider donuts right in front of you—and then dip them in cinnamon sugar. So amazing!" All the humans groaned, remembering the pleasure of the hot donuts. Nyx made Emeline promise to get him some.

Nox and Nyx had been thoroughly impressed at the layout of the land beneath them, with Nox telling her, "I can see why you love this area. We have similar seasonal changes on Delicia. The mountain region where my father is from has the most breathtaking color changes. I can't wait show you."

From their vantage point, Emeline had mused out loud that it looked as if all the different shades of reds, oranges and yellows had exploded into colorful patterns spreading out over the landscape. "This reminds me of the patchwork quilt Dad's Memé made as a wedding present for them. It's put away now, but I think I might bring it with me when we go to Delicia. It's something I can pass down to our children."

The subject of moving to Delicia weighed heavily on her mind. She knew it was asking a lot of her mother to accept her decision to become Nox's bondmate. *Hey, Mum, I want you to meet Nox, my alien husband. Oh, by the way, if you're not doing anything for a year or so, want to fly off to an alien planet with me? Yeah, I can already see how this is going to go.* Emeline smiled inwardly—if she could convince the President of the United States and his council members, how hard could it be convincing one overprotective mother? *Yeah, how hard indeed!*

They had told Fiona they would be arriving sometime after dark. She was used to her kids and their friends coming and going at all hours of the day and night. You just had to make sure you called first to let her know. They had learned the hard way what could happen when you showed up without calling. Emeline cringed as she thought of how many times they had interrupted Hank and Fiona during *sexy* time. Yeah, calling first was always wise, especially once she and her siblings had moved out.

That thought was interrupted as Nox came up behind her, his hands gently massaging some of the tenseness out of her shoulders and neck. He spoke into her hair, his breath causing spikes of pleasure to ripple through her. "Don't be nervous, Pulmina. Everything will work out. You'll see."

His voice calmed her as she relaxed her neck, dropping her head to her chest, enjoying the soothing sensations his fingers were sending up and down her spine.

Nox's lips brushed warm against the sensitive skin of her neck, murmuring softly into her ear, "Beautiful—you and your world."

Her body temperature rose as she leaned in to his touch. "Thanks, babe. Having your support means everything to me, but you gotta stop touching me like this. You're making it very difficult for me not to want to jump you right here. Mum will take one look at me and just know." Lust was a hard emotion to tamp down, and Nox wasn't making it easy.

Straightening her up and turning her around, he nestled her against his body. "You are too tempting as well." He pulled her in tighter, letting her feel for herself her effect on him.

Her smile was tight as her hand came up to caress his

chest where his wound had been. Now that he had been cleared by Dr. Datrem from that fiasco in France, she was slowly beginning to let go of her anger. Insisting they stop in medical after they had finished Jagger's delicious dinner, the doctor had said it was fortunate that Delician males had such unusually strong bone density. Otherwise Nox's head wound could have been infinitely more serious. Datrem explained that because of Nox's size, the actual blood loss was minimal and he wouldn't require a blood transfusion.

Nox had insisted he was fine. In fact, he had *insisted* on showing her just how fine he was...several times during the night. She giggled, remembering Nox's reaction when she accused him of showing off. The wicked smile he'd given her had pretty much melted her into a puddle and she'd loved every blessed minute of it.

Nox's fingers gently resumed their search for any hidden knots along Emeline's back, stopping whenever he'd hit a spot that brought out a yelp. "I know you're worried about her reaction. I can feel how tense you are." His strong fingers continued their dance up and down her spine as her body shivered at his touch.

Dropping her head lower, she tried to keep her moans of satisfaction quiet as she rotated her neck while he worked on a particularly tenacious knot. "Oh man, keep doing that. As for Mum, I'm not sure what she is going to do. Make sure you have a regen device nearby just in case she faints. She's not a young woman anymore. The last thing we need is for her to have a stroke or a heart attack."

Last night at dinner Emeline and Liam had asked for suggestions for the best way to tell Fiona about Nox and the Delicians. Everyone had given their input, but it was Nyx's suggestion that they send Tarek in first that got the most reaction. Ami had laughed so hard, wine came out her nose, which caused even more laughter from around the table. It was finally decided that Nox would wait on the deck while Nyx hung out in the shuttle until given the word that it was okay to come in.

Lifting her head, Emeline saw Heather and Lorelei were peppering Nyx with questions about the shuttle. They had eagerly accepted to ride with them rather than make the hour-and-a-half drive out to New Hampshire. When Nyx had ARI bring up the shuttle's navigation system, Heather hung on his every word, determined to learn as much as she could about the Delicians and their computer systems.

Lorelei nearly wept with happiness when ARI displayed a star map of Earth's solar system. She was able to identify objects that she'd only been able to guess at in her research before. Nyx became her new best friend when he offered to download a copy to her computer.

Straightening up, Emeline reached up, kissing Nox on the nose, telling him, "Thanks for distracting me during the ride down."

"Always, Pulmina." Nox lightly kissed the top of her head as a large clearing surrounded by woods came into view through the screen in front of them.

Home!

Emeline let out a contented sigh as Liam expertly set the shuttle down close to the edge of the trees that lined their property. The Cameron's two-story L-shaped colonial house was situated in the middle of a large forest. Their closest neighbor was about a mile away on either side.

Thinking back to the day her parents had found the land, Hank had barely given Fiona a chance to get out of the car before he was calling the realtor to put in an offer. He loved his little piece of heaven, as he had called it. They had spent many happy years here. Sadly, it just hadn't felt the same since her dad had died. Fiona had been holed up here alone for the last two years. It was time for her mother to move forward with her life. *Hopefully this will be just the thing for her.*

Bursting through the French doors off the deck, Fiona's

face lit with joy as Emeline headed straight at her mother. Leaning down, nearly crushing the life out of the little woman for her much needed *Mumma hug*, her whole body visibly relaxed as her mother didn't disappoint by squeezing back just as hard.

How long had it been since she had seen her mother? It'd been hard on Emeline—keeping her out of the loop. Fiona had a close bond with all of her children and surprisingly there was no jealously between the three siblings. Emeline loved that Fiona always knew when you needed a hug, to *vent* or just to talk things out. She also had a way of knowing when to leave you alone, but this wasn't one of those times.

Emeline trembled in her mother's arms.

Tightening her arms around her mother's tiny body, she couldn't help noticing that she was definitely a lot thinner than the last time she'd seen her. Fiona had never been skinny—saying she loved to eat too much. Well, it was apparent that Fiona hadn't been eating lately.

Pressing her face into her mother's neck, soaking up her soothing words, Emeline was happy to be home.

Fiona pulled at her daughter's hands, trying to loosen the death grip Emeline had on her, but Emeline was hanging on for dear life. Patting her back, Fiona strangled out, "Okay, Em, need some air here."

Loosening her arms slightly, Emeline laughed into Fiona's neck, eliciting a giggle before letting go of her mother. "I just missed my mummy so much." She rubbed her nose against Fiona's skin, soaking up her familiar scent.

"I missed you too, baby girl." This time when Fiona pulled away, she used more force, causing Emeline to pull back, giving Fiona a good look at her daughter's face.

"What's going on, Em? Did something happen?"

Brushing the hair off Emeline's face, her hand stilled as her eyes landed on the colorful mark that ran up along her daughter's hairline. "What's this? Did you get a tattoo?"

The tinge of disapproval was evident in Fiona's voice. Everyone knew Fiona's feelings on her daughters inking their bodies. It wasn't that she didn't like tattoos. It was more of a hating needles thing. "Heather? Lorelei? Ami? You couldn't stop her from doing this? I expected better out of you three. And you Liam—seriously? On her face?"

Her anger rising, Fiona looked around at each of the familiar faces that were watching her intently. "Nothing to say for yourselves."

"Mum, it's not a tattoo," Emeline insisted, her eyes practically crossing watching her mother trace her finger slowly from one end of her bondmark to the other.

Fiona's face flushed red, not even bothering to hide her disappointment in Emeline. "If that's not a tattoo, then what is it?"

Emeline fidgeted with her fingers as she stepped back out of Fiona's reach. "Mum, please—let me explain."

The atmosphere in the room grew even quieter, prompting Fiona to burst out, "You're creeping me out here. What the heck is going on? Liam, you're the oldest. Spill your guts," knowing full well her kids hated when she said that. That last part came out more as a nervous laugh, knowing that something was seriously wrong. Her kids never acted this way.

Liam came over and took his mother's hand in his. Guiding her gently towards the couch, he smiled down at his frowning mother saying, "Why don't we sit down?"

Pulling away, Fiona stood...hands on hips, exasperation sparking in her bright blue eyes. "Stop scaring me and just spit it out. What's going on? Nobody's dying, are they?"

Rolling her eyes at her mother, Emeline let out a long sigh. *Geez, I always knew Belle got her feel for the dramatic from Mum.* "Mum, stop. No one is dying."

Sagging into a chair, Fiona breathed out a sigh of relief. "All right then, if nobody's dying then what's the big secret?" Pointing to Emeline's head, she huffed out, "And it better explain that mark on your face, young lady."

"Geez, Mum—chill, will ya. Okay fine. Stay here. I'll be right back." Emeline raised her two hands, indicating they should wait while she ran out the deck door. Her mother's voice drifted from behind her asking where the heck was she going.

"Nox?" Emeline called out softly.

"I'm here," he said pulling his hoodie down revealing his face to her, his luminescent skin lighting up the dark gloomy night.

Cupping his cheek, she peered up into his worried eyes asking, "Are you ready?"

"I am. Are you?" he wondered placing his hand over hers?

"No. She saw my bond mark. She thinks it's a tattoo. I told you how she feels about them. Needless to say, my mother is not happy. We better get in there."

Taking his hand in hers, she headed towards the door, stopping just shy of the entrance, whispering softly, "Remember whatever happens—I love you. I'm going to be with you forever." Giving him a quick kiss, she turned to open the door, saying, "Let's do this."

Walking in, Emeline heard Ami telling Fiona about her family. She had maneuvered Fiona so that her back was to the door as she explained how her mother had been driving her father crazy now that he was retired. She hadn't seen much of them but was planning on taking a trip home soon to spend a few days. The whole time she was talking, Ami kept one eye on the door.

The door banged shut behind Nox, causing him to flinch as the loud sound stopped all conversation.

At the sound of the door, Fiona turned around, asking Emeline, "Where did you—?" Her eyes narrowed, then she shook her head as if she was trying to refocus on what she was looking at. She stared wide-eyed at the tall, massively fit, shiny colorful man who was standing in her kitchen grasping her daughter's hand as if his life depended on it.

"Mum? Mum—you all right?" Emeline took a step towards her mother only to be pulled up short by Nox's immoveable body.

"Yes, Emeline Agnes Cameron, I'm fine."

Ami covered her mouth quietly scoffing, "Uh oh, Agnes —you're in trouble."

Nox's brow creased at Ami's words. Leaned down, he whispered to Emeline, "Why are you in trouble? Is it because of me?"

Squeezing his hand, she whispered, "No, babe. It's not you—well okay, maybe it is you. Mum just says that when she wants your attention." She'd explain later how being called by your full name usually meant you were in trouble.

"Ah, I understand." Nox smiled at his bondmate's mother. He recognized her from the photographs Emeline had in their quarters on the *Maelstrom*.

"Mum—this—is Nox." Emeline was watching Fiona's reaction with trepidation, "Nox is from the planet Delicia." Holding up her hands, she yelled softly, "Surprise! You were right. There is life out there just like you always said."

Speaking in perfect English, Nox smiled down at Fiona, saying, "It's a pleasure to meet you, Fiona. I have heard so much about you." Knowing he was a large man, he moved toward Fiona slowly, trying to be as nonthreatening as possible as he extended his two hands towards the tiny woman.

Fiona's mouth opened and closed, mimicking a feeding fish before a hysterical laugh bubbled up out of her mouth, her eyes round and wide as she watched her small hand disappear within Nox's two enormous ones.

Nox looked down into astonished blue eyes that were a shade darker than his Emeline's. They were looking up at him with curiosity mixed with more than a hint of apprehension.

Coming up behind Fiona, Liam placed his hands on her

shoulders. Squeezing them lightly, he explained that Nox was part of an alien force that came to protect Earth from some bad aliens who wanted to steal Earth's resources.

Pulling her hand out of Nox's, Fiona spun around to face Liam in disbelief.

Finding her voice, she shrieked out, "You mean to tell me there are more than one."

Clueless as to what to say, Liam mouthed to his sister, *"What do I say?"* Shrugging her shoulder, she mouthed in return, *"How should I know?"*

"God, this is better than TV. We should've made popcorn," Ami observed loudly from the couch, where she was nestled into the corner with Heather and Lorelei watching with rapt fascination. "It's like being part of a reality TV show."

Snapping her fingers, she cried out, "Oh—oh, I've got the perfect name for it—*Meet My Alien Boyfriend*, or how about *Ma, I Married an Alien.*"

Heather giggled, hitting Ami's arm, chiming in, "No, no wait—I've got one. How about *The Alien Who Came to Dinner*?"

Ami held her sides as if pained from all the laughing as Lorelei, not to be outdone, added her own title to the mix with *My Baby Daddy is an Alien.*

The girls hooted even louder when they saw the nasty looks coming from the two Cameron siblings. Emeline growled at her friends, "Not helping."

Nox's expression showed that he was totally baffled as to what the three females were laughing about.

Ignoring them, Emeline focused on her mother, telling her that it was a long story and why didn't they sit down so they could talk.

Fiona's head bobbed up and down like her husband's prized bobble-headed figure of his favorite Red Sox player, David Ortiz. Shaking off Liam's hand that was wrapped tightly around her arm, she finally found her voice. "Liam,

I'm fine—really. Why don't you get me a drink?" Pausing for a second, she added, "Bring the good stuff." Her eyes drifted over to Nox, who was towering over her daughter, never more than an arm's length from her. "Better make it a double—ah fuck it—bring the whole damn bottle."

"MUM! You kiss your mother with that mouth?" Emeline scolded her mother, chuckling to herself at their role reversal.

Fiona merely smirked back as she stood near the fireplace, her gaze constantly going back to Nox.

When Liam handed Fiona a Jameson's and diet ginger ale made just the way she liked it, his hand shot out to snatch it back when she grabbed the drink, draining it in one gulp. Handing the empty glass back to him, she squeaked out, "Thanks. I'll have another." She smiled sheepishly up at him as she took a chair at the large dining table that overlooked the deck.

Taking a seat across from her mother, Emeline grasped Nox's hand under the table as she took in her mother's demeanor. To say she was rattled was a given, but Fiona was surprisingly calm—well, considering what she'd just downed was probably a contributing factor. If anything, her mum was leaning forward in her chair, her hand wrapped tightly around her glass...observing her and Nox.

Emeline kept her voice gentle, watching her mother's face for any adverse reactions as she started talking. "Mum, I know this is weird. I'm sorry to spring this on you this way. We were trying to be as gentle as possible."

"Just pull the Band-Aid," Fiona murmured as her eyes kept straying to the elephant in the room.

With a startled laugh, Emeline agreed. "Yup, just pull it fast and hope for the best. Okay, here goes. Honestly, I can't even begin to tell you how crazy our lives have been. Never in my wildest dreams would I think I'd meet an alien—well, a lot of aliens actually." Emeline leaned across the table, taking Fiona's hands in hers.

Squeezing back gently, her daughter's bright shining eyes told Fiona all she needed to know about Emeline's feelings for Nox.

"Mum, we had the craziest adventure. Seriously, you can't imagine all the fantastic things we saw and did. We flew on an alien battle cruiser—IN SPACE. If I hadn't experienced it myself, I wouldn't have believed it."

She knew she was babbling, but it was because her mother was freaking her out. Fiona was never one to hold back on her opinions, and right now, she was way too quiet.

Looking them all in the eyes, Fiona leaned back in her chair. When her eyes homed in on Nox, Emeline had to give him credit, he sat there not moving, allowing her mother to look her fill.

Without warning, *BAM!* Fiona's hand slammed on the table, causing them all to jump as she blurted out, "Aliens! Ha. I knew I was right! Man, do I wish your father was here. He would have loved this."

Piercing them with a steady gaze, Fiona leaned forward, her glass nestled in her hands, watching as the rest of the room scrambled to take seats at the table. Taking a sip from the icy cold glass, she waited until the burn from the whiskey had settled into her stomach before using her mom voice. "Now why don't you all just start at the beginning? I'm sure I'm going to love this story." She would have no idea the wild ride she was about to go on.

They sat for over an hour as each one took turns telling their stories. Fiona sat slowly sipping her drink as she took in the fascinating tale her children and their friends spun for her. She didn't interrupt—just let them talk—that is until they got to the part where Emeline was kidnapped and Liam had to blow up the freighter. Tears gathered in her eyes at the thought of the terrible danger her children had experienced.

Liam covered her hand with his, catching her frightened blue eyes with his, gently telling her, "Mum, that's why we almost didn't tell you."

Pulling back, Fiona lightly slapped his hand, retorting, "Yeah, cause that's worked so well for you in the past. You know I would have found out anyway—then I would have just been mad." They all knew eventually someone would slip up and the whole story would come out. "It's better this way."

Leaning in, Liam kissed his mother's cheek, saying, "You're probably right."

"Of course, I am. I'm the mother. I'm always right."

The girls had put out the snacks that Fiona had made earlier as they'd been talking. Nox seemed partial to the bruschetta and Mexican dip with tortilla chips, quietly asking Emeline if this would go well with her Margaritas.

By the time they were finished with their story, Emeline was happy that her mother appeared to accept Nox. She no longer worried that Fiona was going to faint dead away just looking at him. The one omission Emeline had purposely left out was her bonding with Nox. This was one discussion she wanted to have in private with her mother.

Getting up from the table, Emeline stretched her back, asking Fiona if she could speak to her upstairs.

Squeezing Nox's shoulder, she turned and followed her mum up to her old room.

As soon as the door was shut, mother and daughter reached for one another. Caught up in a tight embrace—the fear and terror of all that they had experienced with the Hexians really hitting home.

Fiona was the first to pull away, wiping her eyes before reaching up to brush the tears from Emeline's face. "Oh Em, what you went through. You must have been so scared. Feel my heart. It's pounding just thinking about it. You were so brave. I am so proud of you."

"Oh, Mum. It was awful, but I'm working through it. If Liam hadn't been such a nag about training, I honestly don't think I would have made it without him or Nox. He's been so awesome."

Crossing her arms, Fiona took in the blush that started to creep up Emeline's neck. "Nox, huh. So, tell me about him. It's obvious something happened." Gently brushing the hair from Emeline's forehead, exposing the bond mark, she crooked an eyebrow at her lovely daughter. "I would assume it has something to do with this?"

Emeline's cheeks turned from pink to a deep shade of candy apple red.

"Hmm, okay, this I gotta hear. Out with it. Obviously, you're in love with him and I would definitely say he's in love with you."

"Oh, Mum, I love him so much. He is the most amazing person. But Mum, before we talk about Nox—where is Belle? She was supposed to meet me here. I've wanted to tell you both so bad, but they said we couldn't. It killed me not having you to talk to when all this was happening—especially with Nox."

Fiona cupped her daughter's face, understanding her feelings. "Stop feeling guilty. You did what you had to do. As for your sister, she was supposed to be here but she got a call from LA this morning asking her to be in a movie. She had to fly out tonight in order to start shooting in two days.
"

"What? She got a movie? When did this happen?" Emeline was nearly bursting with happiness for her sister. Belle's dream was coming true and this was the first she was hearing about it. "Why didn't she tell me—oh wait, because I wasn't here," she lamented sadly answering her own question.

Sitting on the bed, Fiona patted the spot next to her. "Oh baby, she didn't even know. Remember that casting director she took a class from in college?"

"Yeah."

"Well one of the directors of a short film she did called asking her to be in a movie she was filming. I guess the woman's done pretty well out in California. Said she was going through some old films she had done and remembered your sister. She had a part that she thought she'd be perfect for. "

"That is so awesome. When is she leaving?"

Looking at her smart watch for the time, Fiona replied, "She's at the airport now. FaceTime her."

After a few dropped connections, making Emeline wish she could use her alien vid comm, they were finally able to connect to her sister.

"Hey Em—sorry I missed you. Can you believe it—I'm going to be in a movie. They're even flying me out there on a private jet!"

Emeline was thrilled for her sister. This was such an amazing opportunity. Belle was a successful writer of historical fiction, however, performing was her first love. "I'm so excited for you. I'm dying to hear all about it. When are you coming back?"

"They said maybe a week, possibly two. Why? You going somewhere—again?"

Fiona spoke softly into the phone, saying, "Your sister met a guy and is getting married."

"WHAT?" That was yelled by both girls as they looked at their mother as if she was insane.

"Of course, you're getting married. I saw the way that—" Fiona searched for words while Emeline held her breath. "... guy looks at you."

"Well, we're kind of already married." Emeline covered her mouth, knowing *oh shit I just stepped into it.* Just then the flight attendant told Belle it was time to board the plane.

Hurt, Belle gave her sister a look of disbelief, whispering hotly, "And I'm just now hearing about this—why? Look, I gotta go, but you've got a lot of explaining to do, little sister. We can FaceTime when I get in the air. Give me about an hour or so to get situated."

"Belle, wait. It's not what you think." Emeline knew that face. They hadn't lived in the same house for 18 years for nothing. *I'll be getting some major shit next time we're alone.* "Go. I'll explain it all to you when you call back. Belle—I love you."

Letting out a harried sigh, Belle gave her sister a half-smile, saying, "I love you too."

"Good luck. I'm so proud of you. Break a leg!" Emeline yelled before the call was disconnected.

"Mum, why did you say that?" Emeline gave her mother an exasperated look.

Shrugging her shoulders calmly, Fiona countered, "Why did you say you were already married?"

"Well, the thing is, Nox and I are bondmates."

Fiona gave her daughter a bewildered look. "Bond-mates? What the hell does that even mean? Is that an alien thing?"

"Yes. Come here."

Lying across her old bed, she launched into Delician bondmates and all that she had experienced with it. If there was one person in the entire world, other than Nox that Emeline felt comfortable telling her most private thoughts to, it was her mother. They giggled like teenagers discussing Emeline's first reactions to Nox, which led to Fiona making no apologies in asking about alien genitalia.

Shaking her head, Emeline tried delicately to deflect her mother's questions, knowing full well Fiona would not give up until she got the answer she was looking for.

Fiona couldn't help but be fascinated at the entire concept of being able to feel your partner's thoughts. "Does it ever get weird, like when you don't want him to know what you're thinking? I mean, what if you want to just rant for a while—he'll always know, right?"

Laughing out of the side of her mouth, Emeline murmured, "You have no idea."

Sitting up, she was glad to finally be able to talk about

some of the crazy things that had been happening. "It's like I can never just be in a bad mood because he can feel what I'm feeling. Of course, then he tries to cheer me up...well, I guess there are some benefits to it." Blushing profusely at how he tried to cheer her up just this morning in the shower, it was hard to be in a bad mood after getting all that attention to one's lady parts.

"Anyway," she said, clearing her throat, "it's still new. I haven't tried to block him because—well, because I haven't wanted to. When we were separated it nearly killed me not knowing if I was ever going to see him again."

Seeing the look of understanding on her mother's face, Emeline reached out to her, "Oh Mum—I'm so sorry. I know you feel that way about losing Daddy."

"It's okay, baby girl. You know at first it was—well, you know my world collapsed. But I have to tell you, it's been getting easier as time goes on. I've decided not to sell the house. I don't want you kids to lose your home base. I have been thinking that I might go spend some time with my sister out in California. Just to get out of here for a while. It's time for a change."

Picking some imaginary lint off the bedspread, Fiona looked up, warily telling Emeline, "I finally went through all of your dad's stuff. I put a box away for you in the basement. There's one for each of you kids."

Rolling over, Emeline wrapped her arms around her mother, pulling her in for a tight hug. Fiona fit perfectly under Emeline's chin. Resting her chin on her mother's head, the fragrant scent of lavender filled her nose. She knew that Fiona always put lavender oil in her shampoo. Said it was good for your scalp, plus the added bonus of having nice-smelling hair.

"You know, Mum, I'm glad you're feeling better. I just wish you had waited for us to help you."

Snuggling closer, her mum whispered sadly, "No. It was something I had to do on my own. It made it real for me.

I'll always love your dad. He was my life, but now he's gone and I'm still here. I still have a lot of living to do." Her voice became husky, saying, "I just miss him so much."

"I know, Mum. But you know he would be the first one to tell you it was time to move forward."

Pushing away and coming to her feet, Fiona laughed at her daughter. "Who you kidding? He wanted me to grieve him until the day I died. I told him it wasn't going to happen so he better take care of himself." Sighing, Fiona said, "He wouldn't listen. Anyway, it is what it is. I have to get out of New Hampshire for a while. I need a change."

"Well actually, Mum, Liam and I wanted to talk to you about that."

"What? Is Liam okay? He's been through so much. I can tell the incident with the freighter still bothers him. There's something else though, isn't there? He's different somehow. It's like there's an air of excitement about him that I haven't seen in a long time. Something is up with him."

"He's fine—great, actually. But yes, the whole freighter thing aside—that he'll probably carry with him forever, but he is excited about the future. Why don't we go downstairs so we can talk to him?"

Emeline turned to open the door when she felt herself hugged from behind.

Pulling her mother's hands tight around her middle, Emeline felt lighter for the first time in a long while—that knot in her stomach finally loosening. "I was so afraid to tell you about Nox," she whispered softly to the door.

"Why?"

Fighting back tears, Emeline replied, "I don't know. I thought you would be mad that it happened so quickly. I wanted to talk to you about it so many times. It really bothered me—not being able to tell you the truth or even ask for advice. Trust me, there were times I could have used a Mumma hug."

Fiona turned Emeline and pulled her into her arms, her hands gliding soothingly along her daughter's back. "Oh baby, you did just fine. Although I have to say—an alien. Really?" They both laughed as she continued, "If I'm being totally honest, I find your relationship with Nox intriguing. It sounds like the force created between the bondmates is physical as well as spiritual. I've been watching you two. It's as if your souls have somehow aligned themselves to each other."

Emeline sniffled into her mother's neck, feeling her worries dissipate the more her mother spoke her heartfelt words.

"Even in the short time I've been around both you and Nox, I see the love you share. If you feel for him what I felt for your daddy, then that's all I could ask for. Come on now. Let's not keep your bondmate waiting."

Leading their way back downstairs, Emeline smiled at Nox, who was waiting at the bottom, concern showing on his face.

Coughing into her hand, Fiona muttered, "Yep, no hiding anything from this one."

A surprised laugh burst from Emeline as she turned to Nox, telling her mother to behave. Fiona of course pretended she didn't know what her daughter was talking about as she headed in Liam's direction.

After reassuring Nox that everything was fine, she stood on the stairs quietly observing the room. Ami was sitting at the island talking to Heather as Lorelei was rummaging through the fridge. It looked like she was starting to make a salad as she chatted with the girls. Nyx must have gotten tired of waiting alone in the shuttle, since he and Liam had turned from their conversation to greet Fiona who was shyly making her way over to them.

"Liam, who's your friend?" Fiona's face was priceless. Her eyebrows were almost buried into her wispy bangs, while her eyes were wide and round, looking a deeper blue in contrast to the paleness of her skin.

Liam stopped midsentence to look at his mother. Hastening over, he put his arm around her shoulders...their size difference evident as he tucked her up underneath his armpit. "Mum, you feeling okay? Maybe you should sit down for a while."

Patting his chest, Fiona soothed his worried expression, saying, "I'm fine. Introduce me to your friend." Her body bent backwards as she looked up at the massive alien with the long dark braid who was stalking towards her, an eager smile on his face. He had similar characteristics such as skin and hair color as Nox, but that's where the similarities ended. Where Nox was built more like an Olympic swimmer, this guy was huge all over and carried an air of authority about him. He definitely had military training.

Looking down at her, Liam smiled saying, "Mum, this is Nyx. He's the one I was telling you about."

Looking Nyx up and down, Fiona laughed, asking Liam, "Are they all this big?"

"Yup. Some are even bigger."

Fiona swallowed hard at her son's comment as Nyx reached out, taking her hand gently in both of his, squeezing it with a sense of familiarity that surprised Fiona.

That was until he said, "Fiona—it is so nice to finally meet you. I have heard so much about you. Liam and Emeline talk about you all the time. Everyone on board the *Maelstrom* just loves hearing them tell Fiona stories."

With a gasp of alarm, Fiona looked up into the most unusual eyes she had ever seen. They were a combination of amber, amethyst and forest green and filled with humor and genuine affection. Groaning, she cried out, "Great. Just what I need—an intergalactic reputation."

Spearing her two children with a stinging glare, Fiona turned back, smiling up at Nyx. "I can only imagine what they've told you. In my defense, I had to be strict with the three of them. It was the only way to survive, especially since their father could drive me just as crazy."

Emeline and Liam both protested loudly—each one blaming the ones that weren't there to defend themselves.

Ignoring her children, Fiona pulled her hand from Nyx's, saying, "It's nice to meet you as well, Nyx." She surprised him by stepping in and hugging him tight around the waist. Tilting her head way back so she could look into his eyes, she whispered sincerely, "Thank you for saving my son."

Bending down close to her ear, Nyx murmured, "You're very welcome. Your son is an exceptional male. I am proud to call him my friend."

"Thank you, Nyx. I can tell he feels the same way about you." Fiona liked this alien.

Stepping back from him, Fiona asked if anyone was hungry as she headed into the kitchen.

When everyone hollered back yes, it was Emeline who stepped up to stop her saying, "Mum, Liam and I have something to ask you first. Could you come over and sit with us for a second?"

"Sure, honey. What's up?"

Taking a deep breath, Emeline and Liam laid out their plan, emphasizing that they wanted her to come with them when they left for the UAP.

"Really? You want me to go to another planet with you? Seriously? You're not just teasing me, right?" Fiona stood with her hands on her hips, glaring at everyone.

Jumping up, Emeline hugged her mother reassuringly. "Of course, we want you to come. We wanted Belle to come too, but there is no way she'll leave right now."

"Go all the way to—what was it, Delicia?" This was a lot for Fiona to take in.

"Mum, think of it as an adventure and we know how much you love adventures. Besides, you said yourself that you wanted to get away."

Rolling her eyes at having her words thrown back at

her, Fiona said, "Yeah, well, I'd say going to another planet is definitely getting away." Laughing as Emeline's mouth turned down slightly, batting her eyelashes with that pleading look she would give when she wanted something really badly. "Liam, she's doing it again." Looking at her son, his face a perfect match to his sister's, she finally conceded. "Now you're just ganging up on me. Fine. You win—I'll go."

"Yah!"

Fiona jumped at the surprised sound coming from everyone in the room.

Emeline and Liam sandwiched their mother between them, both talking at once as they told her how much fun they would have. Liam teased her about going easy on her when he flew her in the shuttle up to an honest-to-god spaceship.

Laughing back at them, she pleaded, "Please, just be gentle with your old mum."

Giving her mum a quick hug, Emeline teased her. "Oh, so now you're old? Don't try and fool us. You know you're all about traveling and adventure. Who do you think we got it from?" She motioned her hand between her and Liam, who was nodding in agreement. "It wasn't Dad. He liked to stay home too much. Trust me, Mum, you are going to be so amazed."

Fiona, like everyone else, was caught up in the lighthearted atmosphere of the room. Her dark blue eyes shined bright with hope for the future. "You're right. Why not? Let's go do something fun and daring. I guess going into space is more on the daring side than I'm used to, but what the hell—I'm in!"

Emeline squeezed Nox's hand, grinning at him from ear to ear. Turning back to Fiona, she joked, "Mum. It's going to be great. Nox has the coolest job. He's been to all kinds of different planets. He's like an alien Indiana Jones. Well, if Indiana Jones was a brilliant scientist and a whole lot sexier."

She giggled as a quick burst of shine from Nox's face nearly blinded her. He was obviously embarrassed at her comments. Leaning in, caressing his cheek, she cooed softly, "Oh babe, I'm sorry. I didn't mean to embarrass you. I did warn you how open our family is about certain things." Lowering her voice, she exclaimed, "Your face—is that what happens when you blush? I've never seen you do that before."

Cocking his eyebrow, giving her the *cut it out* look, Nox leaned in, brushing a quick kiss across her upturned lips. "Yes," he replied, only mildly annoyed as he straightened up, looking directly into Fiona's laughing eyes.

Fiona wagged her eyebrows at Nox, throwing her head back laughing at his discomfort. Patting his arm, she headed into the kitchen to start dinner, giggling out loud that Nox looked nothing like Harrison Ford—well, except for the sexy part.

She could be heard laughing even louder when Nox demanded to know who Indiana Jones was. Ami laughed so hard, she had to cross her legs, yelling to stop before she peed herself. Heather and Lorelei hung onto each other, tears of laughter running down their faces.

Nyx looked just as confused as Nox, looking to Liam who just shook his head at the crazy women.

Emeline explained as best she could in between fits of laughter, finally promising to have an Indiana Jones movie marathon on the trip back to Delicia.

Nyx found his way into the kitchen, getting in Fiona's way while she bustled about getting dinner ready. Drilling her for details on what ingredients she used in the dish she was putting into the oven; she must have decided she liked him when she pulled out her secret spice she used in her seafood casserole.

As their dinner cooked, the house became filled with the delicious smells of fresh seafood and, of course, lots of garlic bread.

"Liam, look at Mum and Nyx. I think they're bonding." Emeline winked at her brother as she watched their mother standing at the counter explaining how to make her seafood casserole to the huge alien elite soldier. "Do you think we're doing the right thing? I mean she does look happy."

"She's always happy when she's talking about cooking. But to your question, yeah, I think this will be good for her. You do realize that Belle is not going to be happy about this." Liam frowned at what his sister was going to say when they told her.

"I know. I feel bad. I haven't told her any of this yet. I was going to tell her tonight, but I totally understand why she had to leave. She's supposed to be calling us soon." Emeline glanced at her wrist comm for the time. "We better eat. Mum, is dinner almost ready?"

Fiona looked up from her conversation with Nyx, telling them yes as she watched Nyx carefully take the large casserole dish out of the oven and set it on the counter.

He leaned in, savoring the smells of butter and lemon that permeated the air from the steam rising from the golden brown dish.

Emeline and Liam both growled watching their mother holding up a fork with a steaming scallop to Nyx's mouth, giving him the taste she had denied her own children.

Dinner was lively with Nyx and Liam trying to outdo each other in regaling Fiona and the girls with stories about some of the meals they had made on the ship. Fiona was fascinated to learn that they had a fully stocked kitchen on a battle cruiser. Nyx explained that on long missions it was important for them as a team to share common activities.

Nox told them that even though most homes had food replicators, cooking was a vital part of their Delician culture. "Liam and Emeline have told us that humans have similar traditions about food and family."

Taking a sip of her crisp glass of Riesling, Fiona was happy to hear even across the universe some traditions still held. "I'm so glad to hear that. Cooking has always been a way of life for us as well. There are recipes that I still make that have been passed down from my great-great grand-mother."

"Grammy's Mac and Cheese." Emeline slapped Liam's arm as they both blurted out at the same time.

With the watchful eyes of a parent, Fiona sat back in her chair, her fingers gently swirling her wine glass as it rested on the table in front of her. Her gaze shifted around the table as she listened to Liam giving Nyx the rundown on how to make one of his favorite dishes. Emeline giggled at her brother's attempt, interrupting him with her own ver-sion of past recipe disasters.

Picking up her glass, Fiona cleared her throat, getting their attention. "I'd like to propose a toast."

Everyone picked up their glasses as Fiona smiled at each one individually. "Nox and Nyx, I'd like to welcome you to our home. I have to admit, this was not how I saw my day playing out. Definitely didn't see the whole alien coming to dinner scenario, but then I guess who would?" Shrug-ging her shoulders, she shook her head in disbelief, saying, "It really is mind boggling that first contact with aliens happened all because of pink salt. Just freakin' amazing. Anyway, here's to friends, old ones and new. Here's to Eme-line and Nox. May your future be as bright as the smiles I've seen you give each other. To creating new traditions and bonding over simple things such as great food and de-licious wine. Here's to many more dinners in our future. Cheers!"

"Cheers!"

Nyx leaned his glass towards Fiona's, clinking them to-gether, saying, "Thank you, Fiona, for a lovely meal. I look forward to cooking for you when we are on board our ship. I have several dishes I think you will enjoy." The two of them were soon lost into another conversation when he began asking her how to bake a chocolate cake.

The meal ended quicker than anyone would have liked, especially the guys. Emeline had suggested a sleepover—ladies only—and Nox was not at all happy he would be sleeping alone tonight, but he understood Emeline needed this time with her mother and her girls.

After several rounds of goodbye hugs, they were finally able to get Nox to agree to return to the ship with the promise they would come back for breakfast. Nyx had even gotten Fiona to promise to show him how to make blueberry waffles with real maple syrup.

When Nyx went out to get the shuttle ready with Liam, Emeline tried to reach Belle, but the call wouldn't connect. It looked like she'd have to wait until after her sister returned from LA. No point in screwing with her mind right now, especially when she really needed to focus on her work.

After one last goodbye kiss that had all the girls whistling at them to save some for tomorrow, Emeline shut and locked the door behind Nox.

Flipping through the apps on her phone, she found her playlist. When the opening to "Uptown Funk" blasted out of the wireless speakers, Emeline danced her way into the kitchen, shouting over the music, "Lorelei, make me a drink!"

CHAPTER 31

While Emeline and the girls danced around the room, Lorelei rubbed her hands together as she headed over to the liquor cabinet. "You know, guys, strangely enough, I've been doing a lot of thinking about aliens lately—Delicians, in particular." Bending down, she opened the cabinet door, perusing Fiona's liquor selection. Sorting through all the different-shaped bottles, she grabbed three of her favorites —Baileys, vodka and Frangelico. Taking a cocktail shaker filled with ice, Lorelei smirked as she picked up one of Fiona and Hank's shot glasses from their travel collection. Holding up one from Devil's Tower, she giggled thinking, *how apropos.* The girls all laughed as they took seats at the kitchen island.

"What are you calling this one?" Ami licked her lips as Lorelei began lacing the inside of a martini glass with chocolate that hardened on contact.

"That's my surprise." Shaking the container vigorously, she poured the contents into the glass. The frothy concoction looked delicious, however Lorelei wasn't finished yet. Searching through Fiona's baking cabinet, she squealed in delight at finding exactly what she needed. Flipping the top on a jar of sprinkles, she dusted the top of her drink, adding just the right amount of color.

Placing the drink down in front of Emeline, she proudly presented her creation. "Voilà! I call this the Dirty Delician." The pastel sprinkles immediately started melting into the cold drink, creating swirls of color throughout.

They all giggled as Emeline took a small sip from the glass, her eyes watching the pastel-colored sprinkles melt into her delicious drink. Laughing out loud, she exclaimed, "You are so funny. Lorelei, you're really good at this."

"Thank you, thank you. I couldn't help it—it just came to me. Remember the first time I saw a Delician—when Heather and I had Nox pinned in the lab. We didn't know what we were looking at. Here was this huge... I didn't know what, with really pretty glowy skin. I was convinced he was an alien. Although, I really thought I was hallucinating. If you hadn't come along when you did, it was going to get ugly. Now—I suppose you all want one?" Lorelei laughed as the rest of the girls yelled "yes."

Lorelei made the drinks as she and Heather told Fiona and Ami the story of when they first met Nox. Ami had known they knew about Nox, but she had never heard the entire story with all of them together before. Emeline laughed along with them, filling in Nox's side of the story.

"He was just as shocked as you were. We didn't expect anyone to be in the lab. But man—you guys were intense. It was truly awesome to see. Liam would've been so proud of you both. Nox on the other hand—he didn't want to hurt you because he knew who you were, but he wasn't about to let you take him down. Ami will tell you—these guys love to train. Worse than Liam."

Jumping up from her seat, Ami flexed her body into a body builder pose for the girls, bragging to them, "Just look at this body. Have you ever seen me look this good? Okay, well, except for my butt. But hey, I'll always have a nice booty." She twerked her tushy at them as they all laughed hysterically. Sitting back down, wiping her eyes, she told them, "Seriously though—these guys are so much like Liam. I can totally see why they all get along so well. They all have that whole learning through training mentality."

Lorelei groaned as Fiona sat back, relieved that she was too old for that kind of activity. "Sounds like I'll be excused cause you know I have a bum knee and a bad back. I think I'll stick to my current exercise plan."

"Sure, Mum. Whatever works for you." Fiona didn't know that as soon as she was aboard the *Maelstrom*, Dr.

724

Datrem would be giving her a complete physical. Emeline had already filled him in on a few of her mother's medical issues. He had assured her it would be his honor to look after her mother. Besides, he was thrilled to have more humans to study. Being a scientist, she could totally understand that point of view—she just wasn't sure how Fiona was going to feel about being poked by an alien.

Once they all had their drinks, Ami held up her hand to get their attention. "Ladies, ladies, now that one of us has decided to get down and *dirty* with an alien." That brought out the giggles while Emeline's face scorched red especially with her own mother wagging her eyebrows at her. "I wonder who will be the next one to fall victim to one of those big hunky Delicians. Maybe it will be Fiona and Nyx? What do you think, Fi? How'd you like to take old Nyx for a ride?"

"Ami!" Fiona was protesting, but the color on her face told a different story. "I'm old enough to be his mother. Heck, I could probably be his grandmother."

"Actually, Mum, that's not quite true." Emeline tried but failed to keep a straight face as she licked the rim of her glass.

"What do you mean?" Lorelei, who had just finished cleaning up the drink mess, came around to sit at the table with her drink in hand.

"Delicians have a long lifespan."

Fiona cocked her head at Emeline, asking curiously, "What do you mean? How long is long?"

Taking a sip from her drink, Emeline looked over the rim of her glass at them casually, saying, "600 years—give or take."

Their faces were priceless. Setting down her glass, Emeline went on to tell them that on Delicia they'd be considered adolescents.

"So how old is Nox?" Ami inquired as she licked at a drop of creamy goodness that slid down the outside of her glass, her eyes boring into Emeline's.

"One hundred and forty-seven."

The room got silent for a second before Ami jumped up, yelling, "Are you freakin' kidding me? Geez, Em, I never knew you had a thing for older guys." She moved over to sit next to Lorelei who was snorting into her drink.

"Damn, Em—sugar daddies? I guess you can never truly know a person," Lorelei snickered as she clinked her glass with Ami's. "If that's what 147 looks like, sign me up. I can't wait to get me some of that old alien booty."

"Lorelei!" Fiona tried halfheartedly to look shocked at Lorelei's comments, but even she was having trouble comprehending the whole age thing.

"What? I mean, come on, Fi—you can't tell me that having Nyx fawn all over you didn't get your motor running even just a little bit. We saw you checking out his fine backside." Lorelei winked at Emeline, who was protesting that she didn't need to hear this about her mother. "Oh, come on, Em—this from the girl who is getting it on with her own *Dirty Delician.* You don't have to be greedy. It looks like there are plenty of delicious males to go around. And who knows what we'll find when we get to the UAP Headquarters. You're talking a whole new set of species to check out. The possibilities are endless." Lorelei sighed as she sank back into her chair, a look of pure bliss crossing her face.

"Save me, please." Ami slapped the side of her head at Lorelei's comments.

Glancing up, Lorelei glared at her saying, "What? You've been awful quiet on this subject. You see any action on your little adventure?"

After a moment's hesitation in which Emeline and Ami shared a brief glance, Ami scoffed at her. "I was too busy learning how to shoot alien guns and saving Emeline's ass."

"You mean to tell me that you didn't even get a taste of all that hotness?" Lorelei looked at her friend in disbelief.

"It's not that I couldn't have if I'd wanted to. Trust me, I had more than a few requests to *train with me,* if you know what I mean. However, we were a little busy—you know, trying to save the world from being overrun by aliens." Seeing Emeline squirming in her seat, Ami couldn't resist adding to her friend's discomfort, adding slyly, "Not all of us were lucky enough to get a little action on the side."

This prompted Lorelei to innocently ask Emeline, "So are they even close?" The twinkle in Lorelei's eye should have been Emeline's first clue as to where this conversation was going.

"Is what close?" Emeline frowned at her friend.

"You know, the books. Any ridges, knobs, spurs, swirls—you know does he have one or two?" Lorelei side eyed Fiona and Heather, who were giggling behind their hands. She tried desperately to keep a straight face...totally failing as she asked, "Anything vibrate?"

Emeline's face burned, watching her mother and her friends kill themselves laughing at her expense. Boy, did she love them, but sometimes...she'd known it was only a matter of time before the subject came up. She had even created a whole scenario in her head as to what she would say when the questions started coming...knowing full well they wouldn't stop until she gave them something to assuage their curiosity.

"Don't believe everything you read—well, wait. I take that back—there might be one or two things that were spot on. Hey, Mum, let's make cookies." Emeline jumped up from her chair and headed around the island and began gathering ingredients, enjoying the brief moment of silence. Sure enough, it didn't take long for the comments to start flying around the kitchen.

Studying her friends as they debated the meaning of her words, Emeline brought out the mixer and started creaming butter for oatmeal chocolate chip cookies. It gave her a moment to reflect on the past few months. Even after everything she'd been through, these women were still here supporting her, loving her, teasing the crap out of her, and she loved every minute of it.

Letting Lorelei finish her theory on the benefits of having two penises, in which even Fiona's face turned a pretty shade of red, Emeline took pity on them. Scraping the bowl of dough, realizing she'd added way too many chocolate chips, she raised her head, catching her mother's eye. Giving her a quick wink, Emeline cleared her throat, which got its desired effect—everyone's complete attention. "Okay, okay. I get it. You're curious. Have to admit, I would be too, but I'm not going to give you any details about Nox." Her pointed finger was met with groans when she told them emphatically, "So don't even ask. But...I'll give you some general hints. The other stuff"—she wagged her eyebrows mischievously, a happy sparkle in her eye saying,— "that, I'll let you find out for yourselves."

After a few groans and a couple of "never going to happen" thrown her way, Emeline took pity on them. "Okay first up—Ami. To your question about size and stamina." Arching an eyebrow, she reminded her curious friend, "You know how fit the Delicians are. Do I need to say more?" Putting a pan of cookies in the oven, Emeline winked at her friend. "Just saying."

Turning to Fiona, she cringed outwardly. "Mum, as to your way-too-blunt question—seriously. You ask your own daughter that?"

Sticking her tongue out, Fiona held her ground. "Not in the least bit sorry. Nope. I mean come on, even you know it's a valid question. Besides, I'm your mother. It's not like you don't know me. We're talking *ALIENS* here—of course I'm going to ask." Giving her daughter a look of disbelief, Fiona stopped when Emeline held up her hand, grumbling, "Fine, don't tell me."

Laughing, Emeline grabbed her mother's hand across the island, giving her a quick squeeze. "You're right. Okay, sorry to disappoint all of you, nothing abnormal."

A collective groan had them all bursting out laughing at

the crushed look on Fiona's face.

Fiona sighed unhappily, muttering, "Oh man, I was really hoping they had that forked tongue thing going on. It sounded so amazing."

"Mum, have you been borrowing books from Lorelei again?" Emeline wondered why she even bothered asking when she already knew the answer, especially when Fiona gave a quick glance in Lorelei's direction.

Moving on to Heather's question next, Emeline took a long look at her. No amount of makeup could cover the dark smudges under her eyes. She looked so thin, almost as if a brisk wind could just pick her up and whisk her away. Heather, on a good day, could be broody, but this went beyond that. Something was going on and she was determined to find out. Pushing the guilty feeling down that she'd obviously been a neglectful friend, Emeline steadied her voice, stating in a matter-of-fact tone, "Bondmates don't cheat. It's just not possible. The bond makes it so neither one has any desire to be with anyone else.

"But what happens if you're already married and you find your bondmate?" Lorelei asked.

"It's an automatic divorce."

This news stopped them all cold.

A look of surprise showed on Heather's face, prompting her to ask. "But what happens to the other person? Do they just, what, go away? Just say, 'sorry, found my bondmate. See yah!' What if they have kids?"

Emeline's brows wrinkled as she thought about Heather's questions. "Honestly, I don't know how the whole thing works. I don't even know if the Delicians really know because finding bondmates has become such a rarity that people just started getting together and having children. What I can tell you is that children are a vital part of Delician society. Since Nox isn't married, it wasn't an issue. That's all I really know about it. Why don't we ask ARI?"

"What's ARI?" Fiona asked.

Pulling out her wrist comm, Emeline showed her mum how it worked. Of course, they all fell in love with it, making Emeline promise to replicate one for each of them once they got back on board the *Maelstrom*. She had ARI bring up a hologram of Delicia, along with a description of Delician marriage laws. Sure enough, the law was exactly as Emeline had stated.

"That doesn't sound fair." With a heavy sigh, Heather's mouth dropped slightly. "This is not very encouraging. I guess it sucks on all planets."

Fiona reached over, squeezing Heather's hand, softly asking, "What does, honey?"

"That someone gets left hanging." Sitting back in her chair, Heather was lost in thought, only to be brought back into the present when Ami lightly kicked the leg of her chair, calling her name. Her eyes snapped to Ami as she barked out, "What?"

Emeline interrupted their staring contest, calling Heather's name to get her attention. "Hey! What's going on with you? Wait, don't tell me." Softly Emeline murmured, "Hector."

The girls all knew about Hector. He was Heather's old boyfriend, back when she was caught up in the neighborhood gang lifestyle. Things hadn't ended well when she had found out he was a cheater. Turns out he had a girlfriend —with a child. Heather had been his dirty little side secret. When she walked away, he had not taken it well.

Heather's nostrils widened, her eyes creasing at the corners as if just hearing his name caused her immense pain. "I don't want to talk about him." She sat up and took a long swallow of her drink. Licking her lips, swirls of pastel colors dotted her tongue from the melted sprinkles. "If you guys are leaving, we need to talk about the company."

"We will—in a minute." Emeline was not letting this go. "Look, Heather, I may have been out of touch for a while, and for that I'm sorry, but I'm here now. Hopefully I won't get kidnapped by aliens again—so we should be good. Now what's going on with Hector? Is he bothering you?"

Dropping her head to her chest, defeated, she finally gave in, saying, "Fine. I'll tell you. I can see if I don't, you'll just nag the shit out of me." Looking up, she glared at Ami, who was pointing her finger at her.

"I knew something was going on with that asshole. That handsome face hides an evil inside. What's he done now? Come on—spill it, girl." Ami crossed her arms expectantly.

Heather drummed her fingers on the table. The tiny white scars from the gang tattoos she'd had removed were still visible just under the skin above her wrist. Using her index finger, she lightly traced the pattern over and over as she spoke. Her words were harsh as she explained he was having his *friends* dropping by her parents' house at all hours of the day and night. The excuse was always the same—he wanted to *help out* her family. Show her how he had changed. The real reason was to keep tabs on her. "It's been a nightmare. He won't leave me alone. Somehow, he found out I'm a hacker and wants me to work for him. You know damn well none of it would be legal. The *idiota* tried telling me it was finished with his latest baby mama and how much he still loves me—needs me. Bullshit! Like I would believe anything he had to say.

I've been sleeping in the lab at night because it's the only place I know he can't get to me. My poor parents are scared shitless. He's been harassing my cousins. I don't even know what to do anymore." Looking up, the tears forming at the corners of her eyes slowly made their way down her cheeks.

Emeline's heart broke for her friend. Ami was ready to take him out with an alien blaster, saying no one would know or care. He'd just disappear one day.

Crying out angrily, Heather told them to just let it alone. "If anything happens to Hector, his friends have been given orders to come for me and my parents. Thanks, but no thanks, Ami. Besides, you've got more important things to worry about than my problems with my old life. I can handle it."

Ami came around and pulled Heather into a tight hug, quietly telling her, "Chica—you will always come first, no matter what."

With a nod from Ami, Emeline told Heather to hang on a second, she'd be right back. She knew the perfect person to take care of this.

With perplexed looks passing between Heather, Fiona and Lorelei, Ami released Heather and returned to her seat at the table. Leaning back in her chair, she crossed her arms over her chest, asking, "So Fiona, love the smell in here. Is that a new candle scent? What is that—eau du burnt cookies?"

Fiona sniffed the air, causing both her and Ami to make a run for the oven. Ami opened it quickly as Fiona grabbed a dish towel and pulled the cookies out, dropping the pan on the counter.

Emeline came rushing into the room, stopping short when she saw that her cookies had been saved. Relieved to see only a few with darker brown edges, Emeline smiled warmly at Heather, telling her, "All done."

"What do you mean 'all done'? What did you do?" Heather demanded, her voice laced with fear.

Going over to the counter, Emeline grabbed a spatula and started transferring the cookies onto a cooling rack. "Oh, I called Liam. He said he'd take care of it." Seeing her confusion, she continued on slyly, "He's going to call his new contact he met the other day. Someone will be contacting you in the morning for all the details. Hector and his entire gang will be gone by the end of the week."

"Really?" A look of relief washed over Heather's face.

"Uh-huh. Oh, and Heather, I have a message for you from Liam. He said he'll meet you in the training room tomorrow. Something about needing to work with you on trusting your friends—I don't know. Anyway, something like that." Emeline grinned as a look of pure dread formed on her friend's face. Liam would be putting her through an intense fitness workout as he lectured her about trusting the people that loved you.

"So now that that's settled, we should probably talk about what's happening with the company." This brought them into a lengthy discussion about what roles each of them were willing to play in the continued running of the company.

Emeline wondered out loud if maybe they should consider selling when Lorelei insisted that she was going to Delicia with them and she wasn't taking no for an answer. Telling them this was her opportunity to study space outside our solar system and no one was taking that away from her. "Besides..." Lorelei leaned on the counter, a twinkle in her eyes, telling her friends, "Who else is going to get the real details about aliens? I owe it to my fellow sci-fi romance readers to be thorough in my research."

Rolling her eyes at her crazy friend, Heather spoke up, saying she was not inclined to leave the planet at this time. They all declined to translate her actual words, knowing it was something along the lines of no freakin' way only way more colorful. Heather agreed to run most of the day-to-day operations, while the girls went off on their adventure. Having alien communication devices made all the difference.

Emeline thought it was best to keep the lab in Boston for the foreseeable future but was thinking of moving the main lab to a new building on a secluded piece of Fiona's land. It was a bonus her parents' property abutted a large tract of preservation land, giving them lots of privacy. She wanted to leave her options open, but for now all she wanted to do was focus on blending her new life with her old one.

"I'm still planning on working with Loris and Nox on

increasing their force field capabilities, and Dr. Datrem and I have a few ideas we're considering." Emeline took a bite from one of the cooled cookies, savoring the rich chocolate gooiness as she licked her lips. *Seriously, that Mexican vanilla Mum gets makes all the difference. I've got to remember to bring a bottle with me to Delicia.*

Holding up the plate of cookies to Ami, she watched her friend take one of the extra crispy ones. Emeline always loved that you always knew what Ami was feeling. Her body language usually mimicked her emotions. Emeline watched as Ami dipped her cookie into her drink. A look of pure unadulterated joy spread across her face, prompting Emeline to follow her lead. Groaning from the taste of so many delicious flavors truly was, as Ami had put it, *orgasmic.*

Emeline and Ami giggled as Fiona, Heather and Lorelei quickly followed their lead. They stood at the island laughing and joking along with lots of teasing until finally the long day began to catch up with them. It could have been partially from the overindulgence of chocolate and booze, but soon all the women were lounging in their comfy clothes.

Emeline was the first to ask Ami about where her thoughts were on new projects she was considering.

Ami's hands made the shape of a small pistol as she excitedly told them, "I'm considering a small handheld blaster that our military can use to incapacitate the enemy as opposed to automatically killing them. Em, you saw how fast we were able to take out those agents in France. Imagine if we combined your force fields with my blaster." Her hands ended up on her hips as she lasered them with an intense look. Ami was passionate about her work and wanted to do whatever she could for her planet.

Emeline laughed at Ami's imitation but thought she was onto something. A force field that was like a shield around the soldiers—that was intriguing. "You guys, I think Ami is right. It's worth doing some investigating." Emeline's mind swirled at the possibilities that lay in front of them. They wanted to do so much but they were also hindered because of the UAP. "You realize that the UAP isn't going to authorize giving Earth alien weapons any time soon."

A look of resigned acceptance to her hands being tied briefly crossed Ami's face as she agreed with her friend. "I'm going to try anyway." Smiling inward, Ami murmured, "They won't be paying attention to me. They'll be more focused on the delegation. Besides, who knows when I'll be back on Earth again? I want to explore what's out there." Rubbing her hands together, Ami looked almost giddy, saying, "I can't wait to leave. We are going to see some amazing things."

Emeline watched as her mother got caught up in Ami and Lorelei's enthusiasm. It was the first time in a long time she looked excited about the future.

As the night wound down, Emeline remembered one thing she forgot to tell Lorelei. Standing at the sink, loading the dishwasher from her cookie mess, Emeline called over to her friend, a naughty glint in her eye, "Hey Lorelei, I forgot to tell you, that's a no on the two penises." Emeline laughed out loud at the brief look of disappointment that flashed across her friend's face. "Seriously, girl, you've really got to let that one go."

Lorelei shrugged her shoulders in agreement as Fiona reached over, giving her a motherly pat to her hand, saying, "It's probably best, sweetie. Did you see the size of those two Delicians?" Fiona visibly shivered, saying, "One would be more than enough, thank you. I couldn't imagine two of them."

Heather snickered at Fiona, "You think Nyx and Nox are big—wait until you meet General Tarek. He's *massivo!*" Her hands made an outline of a man so large, Fiona gasped, covering her mouth.

"No way."

Ami and Emeline laughed as they both said, "Yes way."

"But, Mum, he's the nicest, sweetest guy. He has a botany lab on his spaceship. Wait until you see it. Plus, he's also wicked handsome."

Ami could be heard grumbling how Tarek wasn't so sweet in the training room, at which Emeline nodded her head, wholeheartedly agreeing.

"You mean the botany lab you got kidnapped from?" Fiona's face paled to a ghostly white.

Emeline came around the island, squeezing her mum's shoulders in comfort. "Yes, it is, but you don't have to worry. That won't ever happen again—Tarek made sure of that. It's perfectly safe. I promise, you're going to love it. We'll have to bring some seeds with us. Tarek has agreed to let us use some space in his lab."

Yawning, Fiona covered her mouth trying to hide it, but that set off a chain reaction of yawns around the room. Seeing the tired faces around her, Fiona rubbed her daughter's back, telling them, "Before we all go to bed, there is just one last thing we need to discuss."

"Oh, Mum, can't it wait until tomorrow?" Emeline bent her head down into the crook of her mother's neck, always a clear indication that Emeline was tired.

"No. It's just something I want you to think about."

"Fine. What is it?"

Reaching up to rub between Emeline's shoulders, she said gently, "Where do you want the wedding—here or on the ship?"

"WHAT?" Emeline stood up quickly, nearly shouting at her mother.

"Your wedding to Nox. I'm sure you and Nox want to get married before we all leave." Fiona just looked at her daughter, her face neutral, tone matter-of-fact as she continued, "Em, darling, I know you and your sister have both planned your weddings down to the last detail since you were little." Holding up her hand to stop her daughter's protest, Fiona said, "Don't even try to fight me on this. I think it's important and I know you do too."

Getting into a staring contest with one's own mother was never a good idea, Emeline thought as Fiona returned her look...especially since Emeline secretly agreed with her. She did want to get married with all her friends and family surrounding her and Nox. She knew that he would agree to anything she wanted—well, within reason, especially when she told him about the honeymoon afterwards. Biting her lower lip, Emeline wondered if it was even possible to pull off a wedding before they had to leave for the UAP.

Looking up, her mind going a mile a minute, Emeline smiled at her friends' hopeful faces. Could she do it? Judging by the expectant faces looking at her, they were damn well going to try. "Okay."

"Okay?" Fiona pulled back, shocked. "Wait, that was too easy."

"Yup. Let's do it. Let's show the Delicians how humans throw a wedding."

Clapping her hands in childlike glee, Fiona grinned from ear to ear. "I better make some coffee. We've got some planning to do."

Nobody got much sleep that night, which was evidenced when Liam and the Delicians showed up the next morning expecting to be met with a house smelling like waffles as they'd been promised. Instead, they found five sleeping women stretched out all over the family room. Papers and martini glasses littered the coffee table, along with empty coffee cups and a plate with only cookie crumbs left.

Liam sniffed the contents of a glass he had picked up from the coffee table, the whiff of alcohol burning his nose. Pulling his head back quickly, he choked out, "Whoa, that's strong. I wonder what Lorelei called this one?"

"A Dirty Delician," was mumbled by Lorelei as she rolled over and went back to sleep.

"What did she say?" Nox asked as he picked up the glass, noticing the swirl of pastel colors floating in the bottom.

"Don't ask. You should be more worried about this." Picking up what looked like a very long list that lay just off of Emeline's hand, Liam's face split into a huge grin as he waved the paper at Nox. "Uh oh, Nox. Looks like the girls spent the night busy planning."

Grabbing the paper from Liam's hand, Nox saw that it was written in English. Thrusting it back at Liam, he demanded, "I can't read this. What does it say?"

Slapping him on the back, Liam chuckled with glee, saying, "Looks like you're getting married—brother!"

CHAPTER 32

Her wedding day had finally arrived. Studying her reflection in the oval mirror that was set into the corner of her old bedroom, Emeline hummed with excitement.

Fingering the unique feel of the alien material she had used in the design of her dress, she was beyond thrilled it had turned out better than she could have ever hoped. Adding both human and Delician styles was her small way of combining her new life with her old one.

Turning from side to side, the dress fit her perfectly. She had never felt more beautiful or sexy...confident that she was exactly where she was supposed to be—getting married in front of all the people she loved most in the world. *No, that's not right—it's "universe" now,* she thought with a merry laugh. These were memories she would treasure forever.

Emeline smiled, remembering all the craziness that occurred over the last few days. Once Tarek had given his approval for them to have the wedding at her mother's house, planning took over their lives. Tarek was honored when Nox and Emeline asked him and Ami to officiate their ceremony. Tarek would do the Delician portion with Ami doing a traditional American ceremony.

Belle came hurrying into the room, asking if Emeline realized what time it was. With hair several shades darker than Emeline's pale blond hair, Belle was petite like their mother. When their eyes met in the reflection of the mirror, misty smiles stared back at each other. Belle had returned from LA only to be blindsided with not only the news that first contact had been made but that her little sister was marrying an alien. Adding to that, Emeline was taking most of her family and friends to Delicia, leaving her behind. At this point in time, Belle's life was tied up in her work and leaving Earth wasn't doable for her.

Knowing that Belle could be extremely vocal, especially in times of stress, Emeline had to give her sister credit, she took the whole thing annoyingly in stride. Well, except for the part about taking Mum to Delicia with them. That was still an ongoing discussion.

Surprisingly, the person with the most calming influence on everyone over the past few days had been Nox. For some odd reason, he and Belle had become fast friends. Emeline thought it was weird but chalked it up to Nox's almost insatiable desire to learn as much as he could about Earth.

Beyond curious about Earth's entertainment, he had figured out early on that it only took asking the right question to get Belle to go into a detailed explanation on whatever topic he was curious about. It was heartwarming to see her sister getting along so well with her future husband. It made leaving slightly easier. However, when playing video games started to interfere in finishing their assigned tasks, Emeline had Fiona pull the plug. It drove both Nox and Belle crazy for a good twenty minutes before they finally figured out what Fiona had done.

Emeline had tried to appease Nox when he complained how he was finally beating her sister, telling him, "Don't worry, babe, I already downloaded them to bring with us." She winked, giving him a sexy grin, saying, "Although, I'm sure I can think of other things that might be more entertaining."

Watching her face blush in the mirror, she remembered how Nox had leaned his body into hers, catching her hand in his as he pressed it against his heart. His lips moved to her ear, his breath causing a spark to ripple across her skin as he told her, "So can I, Pulmina, so can I." As his lips had lightly grazed her neck, a soft sigh escaped her lips, causing her mother and sister to tell them to take it upstairs—so they did. *I am so happy.* She grinned sheepishly at her sister.

Belle gave Emeline a silly grin as if reading her mind. "Save that thought for later. Right now, we need to get you married." Bending down to adjust Emeline's dress, Belle gushed out, "Oh Em, you look so beautiful. Your dress came out amazing. That replicator thing is nuts. Can you get me one?"

"I knew you would love it. I can't get Mum off it. At least she'll be entertained on the ship." Emeline gave her sister a side glance—judging her reaction to her mention of the ship.

Belle's hand gently squeezed Emeline's shoulder. "Don't worry, Em. I'm not going to bite your head off. I know it's a good thing for Mum. It's just—I'll miss you guys." Her face scrunched up slightly before she straightened up, shaking off her gloomy thoughts. "It will be fine. We'll video chat every day. Besides, this is about what Mum needs, and she definitely needs to get out of here for a while. I just wish it wasn't so far away," she added wistfully.

Placing her hand over her sister's, soaking up as much of her familiar warmth as she could, Emeline smiled at her. Her relationship with her sister went beyond just being siblings. They were lifelong friends and allies. Belle's acceptance of this trip to Delicia was the last roadblock that Emeline had been facing. "Thank you, sis. This means so much to me. I'm going to miss you, but you can be damn sure we'll be talking every day. Hey, how about we cook together one night a week? I'll have the guys show you some Delician dishes. Maybe you can show them your zucchini bread recipe." Emeline smiled as Belle happily agreed.

"So...do you feel like a princess?" Belle asked, already knowing the answer.

"Yes." She barely was able to breathe out her answer she was so overcome with emotion. Mum had been right; she and Belle had planned every last detail of their weddings for years hoping to find the kind of love their parents had for one another. Emeline had found it with Nox. She knew her dad would have been over the moon for her.

Emeline smiled shyly at the fairy princess reflected back at her, her laughter tinkling in delight as her eyes took in the culmination of years of planning. She glowed from the inside out like how a full moon shined down on newly fallen snow—soft and breathtakingly beautiful.

Her dress fit perfectly over every curve. The multi-layered gown was a combination of Delician silk with an overlay of tulle covered in hundreds of tiny crystals. The material clung to her upper body, flaring out just above her hips before falling softly against her legs.

A band of Delician crystals about an inch wide trimmed along the sweetheart neckline. A wisp of lace covered the transparent straps that held the dress in place, creating a soft romantic cap sleeve accentuating her bare shoulders. The back of the dress was open to just above her hips, held together with two crisscrossed amethyst-covered straps. The pop of color was her way of incorporating Nox into her design.

She'd gone back and forth on what to do with her hair. A chance glimpse in a magazine of exotic hairstyles inspired her to get creative. With the help of YouTube and her sister, along with the copious amounts of hair that Emeline had, the result was worthy of its own video. Her hair was pulled to the side with a cascade of flowers, some real, some made from her own hair, interlaced with the same crystals that were on her dress. She had wanted to make sure her hair was off her face, proudly displaying her bond mark for Nox to see.

Of course, she wore a crown. *All princesses wore crowns!* Her veil was sheer and simple, hanging just below her hips. The effect was mesmerizing.

Fiona poked her head out from behind Emeline. Her eyes shone bright with tears as all three Cameron women stood side by side. "I love my girls." Fiona's happy face couldn't quite hide the small hint of sadness behind the smiles. "You look incredible, my darling girl. Your daddy would be so proud of you."

"We love you too, Mum." Emeline squeezed her mother to her side, trying desperately to hold back her tears. "I wish he was here."

"Me too, baby. Me too." Fiona choked back her emotions. Sadness and grief had its place, but not today. "Today is about happiness and love. Celebrating your love with Nox would have made your dad so happy."

Belle was the smart one and handed each of them tissues, telling her sister, "Cut it out, Em. We don't want to mess up that gorgeous face with puffy eyes. You know how blotchy you get when you cry." Belle's own hand dabbed at her own tears.

Smiling down at her sister, Emeline tried not to mess up the makeup job that Belle spent more than an hour on.

Fiona was not having any sadness, not today. Giving them both a quick squeeze, she gently chided them, saying, "Come on, girls, no crying. This is a happy day. Your dad would not have wanted to see any sad tears. He would rather you raised a glass of Guinness to him. You know how much he loved his Guinness. Besides, you know how proud he was of his family. His favorite thing in the whole world was to brag about his three awesome kids."

Giving them a watery smile, Emeline said softly, "I know. I just miss him."

"I know, darling, but he would want you to be happy. So, let's go find your brother and get you married." Fiona turned to leave when laughter could be heard through the window.

The three women peered out as a small group of Delicians were making their way across the lawn. They were dressed in similar outfits—long tight navy pants with sleeveless bright white shirts. Decorative golden arm bands gleamed in the late afternoon sun. Even from this distance, they were an impressive group of well-developed males.

Emeline beamed when she saw that Nox was among them. Her cheeks warmed as she felt his excitement and love through their bond. It had been a long lonely night without him. Her mother had insisted they spend last night apart, informing them that they had to keep some human traditions.

Gasp!

"Mum? You all right?" Emeline looked sharply at Fiona who was staring hard out the window.

"Who is that?"

Emeline followed her mother's gaze. Tarek was following slightly behind the rest of the group. Grinning from ear to ear, she replied, "Oh you mean Tarek? Impressive, isn't he?"

"If he's the humongous guy in the back, then yeah." Fiona became thoughtful for a moment before saying, "So that's the illustrious General Tarek. Heather was right—he's HUGE! And pretty."

"Pretty! Oh, god, Mum, please, please, please—don't tell him that. I'm begging you." Emeline was mortified at the thought of her mother telling Tarek he was pretty. She didn't think Tarek would be all that amused.

"Why not? Don't you just love the way the colors play off their skin in the sun? It looks like a prism." Fiona turned toward her daughter, a playful glint in her eye, knowing full well the effect her comments were having on Emeline. "They're all just so—big." Wagging her eyebrows at Emeline, she sighed wistfully, "It makes you wonder."

"Not going there." Emeline held up her hand, giving her mother a dirty look.

Fiona threw her head back, laughing at her daughter's discomfort.

Belle was gazing out at the males, only her eyes were focused on one particular Delician—one with a long braid.

Shaking her head as if to bring her mind back into focus, she quipped out, "All right, you two. That's enough. Mum, really? Mind out of the gutter."

"Can't help it. It's been a while, you know." Fiona blew out a long heavy sigh.

"Eww!" Both girls laughed as they let their mother know their thoughts on her sex life.

"Boy, you guys are no fun." Fiona turned away from the window and, taking Emeline's arm in hers, said, "Fine. I'll be good. Now let's get this show started."

Emeline allowed her mother and sister to lead her out of the bedroom. Even though she was sad that her dad couldn't be here, she was thrilled that Liam had eagerly stepped in. He had arranged for a huge tent to be erected close to the house. With a covered walkway from the house to the tent, they were assured their wedding celebration would have total privacy. The inside of the tent had been transformed with the help of a portable replicator and several tall, strong Delicians to reflect both Emeline and Nox's styles. Plenty of flowers and candles were scattered throughout the space. The ceiling was awash in twinkle lights that promised to give the illusion of the bright starry sky when night fell.

They had decided to have the ceremony just before dusk. Ami and the girls had created an arbor for them to stand under that was covered in flowers from both of their worlds. It was breathtaking how well the flowers blended together so beautifully...a perfect reflection of Emeline and Nox's bond.

Waiting on the stairs as Fiona and Belle went to get Liam, she scanned the wall that lined the hallway filled with pictures of her and her siblings. Nox had been fascinated at the *wall of shame,* as they all referred to it. Following each picture of Emeline as she grew and changed over the years, she fell even more in love when he told her what beautiful children they would make. She had been quick to remind him she wanted to wait a while before having kids —wanting to get acclimated to her new life before having children.

Liam came around the corner, yelling, "Em, you ready to… Wow, Em—you look amazing." He carefully pulled her in for a hug, mindful not to crush her dress.

"Thanks, big bro. You don't look so bad yourself." Emeline looked her brother up and down, impressed with his appearance. He was so handsome in his new Delician uniform. Reaching up, she traced the Celtic symbol Liam had incorporated into the design of his armband.

"Seriously, sis, you look like a princess. Nox is going to be blown away." Liam took her hand in his. "I'm not going to ask if you're sure about marrying him. The way you two look at each other, I can only hope to find that someday."

Emeline's face flushed at her brother's heartfelt words. 'Thank you, Liam. It really means a lot to hear you say that. And you're right…Nox is my future. I love him more than I can say."

Squeezing his hand, Belle stuck her head around the corner of the stairs, asking if they were ready.

"Yes."

Emeline turned to straighten out the small train at the back of her dress. The detachable train was lined in Irish lace interspersed with Delician crystals. The crystals mimicked the skin tone of the Delicians, creating an opalescent effect when she walked.

"Em, your dress is spectacular. Nox is going to freak, but where's your necklace? You're looking kind of naked there." Belle pointed to her neck that was bare without any jewelry.

Putting her hand to her neck, Emeline replied, "I know. I feel naked, like I'm missing something, but Nox told me not to wear any jewelry. Something to do with part of the Delician ceremony." Emeline shrugged her shoulders at their curious looks.

"Okay. Now you've got me curious. We better get going.

We don't want to keep your fiancé waiting." Belle grinned as she handed Emeline her bouquet of red roses.

Emeline had replicated the bouquet that was wrapped with an iridescent ribbon. She hoped that Nox noticed the way in which she tried to incorporate small touches of each culture into their wedding. Grabbing Liam's arm, she beamed up at her brother, telling him. "I'm ready. Let's do this."

Turning when the sounds of the traditional wedding march wafted through the room, all her childhood fantasies were coming true. It wasn't the dress, the flowers, or even the music. She was marrying her true love. Life didn't get any better than that.

Walking through the house out into the yard, a long white runner lined with flowers led the way to her beloved. The weather was beautiful but crisp. The sky was just at the beginning stages of turning from light pink to purple as the sun was beginning to set just above the trees.

Nox was waiting for her, his amethyst eyes intense as he watched her float down the aisle toward him. He was gorgeous in his black tuxedo with the sparkling white shirt. He had insisted on incorporating both their traditions into his attire as well. His hair was loose, blowing slightly in the soft breeze. His smile was radiant—meant only for her as she made her way towards him and their life together.

Ami was up first, taking them through the traditional American wedding vows. Even though they'd said their own private vows to one another the night they completed their bond, Emeline had wanted it all—from the *I dos* to the *you may now kiss the bride*. President Jenkins had even managed to obtain a secret marriage license for them. He said it was the least he could do after what had happened at the conference.

Emeline nearly lost it when Nox slid her mother's wedding ring from her dad onto her finger. Her eyes filled with happy tears as she glanced at her mother, who blew her a kiss when Ami handed her Hank's ring for Nox. A range of emotions filled her as she looked down at their intertwined hands, Hank and Fiona's wedding rings—a symbol of love, commitment and long-standing devotion was now theirs...glinting in the twilight.

When Ami said those magic words, "*You may now kiss the bride,*" Nox bent Emeline over his arm, locking her snuggly against his chest.

She lost herself in his kiss, forgetting everything but him. It took Tarek clearing his throat, making a comment that if they didn't end soon, he'd be doing the Delician part of the ceremony in the dark, to break them apart, a happy dazed look on their faces.

Nox helped Emeline stand, his arm tight around her as she swayed on her feet. "You take my breath away with your beauty. I love you, wife."

"I love you, husband." She giggled up at him, wondering how much more happiness she could possibly stand.

Tarek stepped forward; a large square white fabric-covered box held firmly in one hand. He stared at their clasped hands, perhaps a moment too long, before speaking, "Nox, Emeline—this is a special moment in the lives of all Delicians. As you know, finding one's bondmate has become rare. You have given our people hope for the future. On a personal note, I would like to extend my congratulations and happiness to you both on your marriage and bonding. Emeline, we did some digging and after a thorough search of our databases, ARI found many references of bondmating ceremonies. None were as elaborate as your human ceremony. However, they all, like yours, had one thing in common." He held up the box for everyone to see.

Handing it over to Nox, Tarek continued. "A gift created by the male bondmate that reflects his devotion and connection to his beloved."

Everyone held their breath as Nox turned towards Emeline, snapping open the box. Lying stark against a black backdrop was a unique golden pendant necklace. The center stone was large—at least five carats. The color was a deep ruby red cut into a triangle. It was set into a large gold circle, the remaining spaces filled with rows of sparkling white diamonds. The golden chain, the same color as the pendant, was flat, about an inch wide. It was surprisingly lightweight considering how thick it was. If you looked closely, there were symbols delicately engraved along the chain.

"Wow." Emeline was stunned at Nox's gift. "Did you design this?" Nox smiled, nodding his head. "This is amazing." She was overcome with emotion at this moment.

"Emeline, my beautiful bondmate, this stone was my mother's that has been passed down through her female line. It was found buried deep within the Delician moon Cyrund. The alloy in the chain is made from two metals that are mined on Delicia's second moon, Voltunic."

Leaning down, his breath caressed her neck, telling her, "I know she would be happy for us and pleased to have you wear this." Picking up the necklace, Nox slowly circled around her, placing the stone across her chest, its glorious red color shining vividly against the white of Emeline's skin.

Closing the clasp of the chain at the base of her neck, he turned her around. Holding the necklace gently in his hand, Nox appeared lost for a moment...deep in thought as his eyes focused on the stone.

Catching her eyes in his, Nox spoke from his heart, "If you look deep within this stone, you will see that it is made up of countless facets...some perfect, some with tiny flaws. It's those flaws together with the perfect ones that makes this stone unique and special...a one of a kind. Emeline Cameron, that is how I feel about you. You are unique and special—my one of a kind. Neither one of us is perfect but together we are complete."

Emeline's eyes filled as she saw the sincerity and love

smoldering in his eyes.

"Oh Nox, that was so beautiful. You are perfect to me." Looking down, she fingered the necklace. "I love how you blended our love together. Thank you." She leaned in, capturing his lips in a gentle, soulful kiss.

He pulled her flush against him, deepening their kiss. Their guests egged them on with hoots and hollers from the males and maybe more than a few tears from the women.

Finally breaking part, the newly bonded/married couple spent the next several hours eating, dancing, laughing, enjoying their happy celebration. Everyone had contributed to the food, most bringing their favorite dishes for everyone to try. Nyx had been insistent that Fiona try his vegetable gratin while Jagger had sent along his fish wrapped in leaves. Jagger was supposed to be there, but had to cancel at the last minute due to problems with the Hexians. Some of them were taking their sweet time returning to Hexia.

Leaning back into Nox's embrace, Emeline was curious as she watched her mother talking with Tarek. He was showing her a bottle of Capum, a Delician whiskey. Fiona was nodding in agreement as she moved over to the bar to grab two of her whiskey tasting glasses.

"Come on." Emeline pulled out of Nox's arms as she headed towards Fiona.

"Hello beautiful girl. Hasn't this been fun? Tarek was just giving me a taste of Delician whiskey. What was it called again—Capum?" Sticking her nose in the glass, Fiona breathed in the sharp fragrance of the liquid. "What a wonderful scent."

Turning to Tarek, she clinked her glass to his smiling up at him saying, "Slàinte"

"Slàinte," Tarek returned her toast, taking a sip of the smooth liquor.

Picking up the bottle, he started to ask Emeline and Nox if they would like a glass only to be interrupted by his wrist comm beeping. Jagger was calling with an urgent message.

Tarek held up his hand for silence. The music was quickly turned off as everyone stopped to listen.

Giving Jagger the go ahead, he filled them in on the latest incident with the Hexians. The *Maelstrom's* sensors had detected a particle trail coming up off of Earth from the quadrant that mined the Himalayan salt. It was a Hexian ship. "It has to be cloaked, which means you know who it is."

Tarek nodded his head in agreement, muttering, "Tarquin."

"Yeah, but the good thing is we might have damaged his ship." Jagger continued telling them that by calculating the trajectory of the particles that were emitted from the errant ship, he ordered several of his ships to fire their weapons at predetermined coordinates along projected routes. They did detect a slight energy burst, but then nothing. They were scanning the area for debris but so far, the results had been negative. "I'm not positive, but there's a distinct possibility we did some damage to the bastard's ship."

Jagger's frustration at the thought of Tarquin getting even one iota of Earth's resource could be heard over the comm unit. "I can't believe that skizoid got away—and I'm willing to bet my favorite sphere that he stole a shipment of Earth's salt. I'm sorry, Tarek. Let's hope we did enough damage that he'll eventually have to shut off his cloaking device. We'll be monitoring for any signs. I'll report back to you if we find anything."

Tarek looked up to find the room had gone silent. He was just as annoyed with Tarquin as Jagger was. Nothing would make him happier right now than to catch that— *asshole.* Tarek liked that human term. It was appropriate —Tarquin was an enormous pain in Tarek's ass. Jagger had nothing to be sorry about. "Not your fault, Jagger. He's a slick one. Good thinking on the shooting. Have Marsel do a continual sensor sweep."

Jagger grunted in agreement.

"Keep me informed. We'll be coming back on board in a few hours. I'll let you know when we leave. Tarek out."

Tarek turned to look at all the captivated faces that had been staring a hole in his back. He surprised them by announcing that this was still a celebration. There was no way he was going to allow Tarquin and the Hexians to ruin Emeline and Nox's special day. He ordered Liam to crank up the music. He wanted to hear some of Earth's rock and roll music.

Emeline moved to Tarek's side, giving him a huge hug, only briefly considering that she was hugging the biggest badass war-hardened general in all of the UAP. But Tarek was more than that to her. They were friends and had each other's backs. That meant a lot to the both of them.

Squeezing him tight, she could feel how tense he was at her touch. Giggling lightly, she felt him relax and chuckle with her. "Tarek, thank you for all you've done for us. None of this would have been possible without your help. You have been such a good friend to the both of us."

Tarek was visibly flustered at Emeline's sign of affection, unused to this type of public display, and gently patted her back. "My pleasure, Emeline. I just want you and Nox to have a happy day."

Taking pity on him, Fiona suggested Emeline take Nox out onto the dance floor for a while.

Dropping a quick kiss on Tarek's cheek before leaning in to kiss her mum, Emeline ran off to join Nox and her friends and family on the dance floor.

"How do you do it?" Fiona glanced up at Tarek, her face was flushed and not from the whiskey. Not giving him a chance to answer, she continued her thought, "I mean I raised those three and let me tell you—there was never a dull moment. They kept me and their father on our toes. But you..." She turned her dark blue eyes away from her three kids to gaze into his deep forest green ones. "I only had three to deal with, while you—you have what? Thousands of individuals that you're responsible for. That's quite a load to carry." Raking her eyes over his wide shoulders, she couldn't help herself from blurting out, "Good thing you have such strong shoulders." Her hand covered her mouth as she stifled a gasp.

Tarek's eyes widened at this tiny vibrant beautiful female that stood tall in front of him. She was stronger than most males that he knew. Being small in stature didn't mean you were weak in spirit. However, this was a first for him—the first time anyone had ever acknowledged the immense responsibilities he carried in his life.

His shoulders shook as he laughed at her words, telling her, "You are a rare female, Fiona Cameron. I have not met many who are as perceptive as you are." Leaning down, he whispered in her ear, "I find you intriguing."

Blushing as red as her hair, Fiona smiled up into his soulful eyes, murmuring back, "And you, Tarek, have forever altered our lives and I couldn't be happier."

EPILOGUE

Emeline dug her toes into the wet, gritty sand. A natural pedicure, her mother would always say whenever they were at the beach.

The tide was at its ebb—that point in between high and low when creatures that hid beneath the surface were left languishing in the wet sand. The air was filled with that familiar ocean scent of pungent brine punctuated with a light fishy smell. This particular beach was on a private island off the Carolinas that Leslie Merriman had arranged for them. The water in their little cove was clear and smooth as opposed to outside the breakwater where it was a gray green. Whitecaps raced across the sea, chasing one another to see who could reach shore first.

The day had turned out perfect. Emeline was thrilled to be able to spend time alone with her new husband—plus the added bonus that the weather had decided to cooperate. Usually this time of year, the air temperature was cooler but not today. It was hot—over 80 degrees—although the water was still a bit chilly for her taste.

Not so for Nox. She'd told him he was insane for jumping into the frigid water to do laps around their little cove. The sun beat down, glistening across Nox's shoulders as his powerful strokes cut through the waves with ease.

Sighing with happiness, Emeline found peace in the moment. They had been thrilled when Tarek had surprised her and Nox with a few days away. A quick honeymoon he'd said—before the human delegation came on board and they set course to the UAP. Emeline snorted, seeing her mother's hand in Tarek's sudden offer. No way he even heard of a honeymoon before. *Yep, Fiona is all over this. But hey, who am I to question a mother's love?*

Glancing up quickly, Emeline watched as two birds zoomed by overhead, recognizing one of the birds as a Jaeger—a falcon-like bird that came down from the Arctic to nest. Its contrasting colors of dark above and light below were a blur as it chased an unsuspecting gull that was lucky enough to snag a clam that lay exposed in the wet sand. The Jaeger were known for stealing food from other birds. They were similar to the Hexians in that way—taking what they wanted instead of working for it. Emeline had seen that first hand.

Shaking away her dark thoughts, she reminded herself that she had fought back and survived—with the help of her family and friends. Now she had a husband and a new adventure waiting for her.

Standing ankle deep in the cool waters, she tried not to ogle Nox as he pulled his magnificent body through the surf to come stand beside her. The sun reflected off his wet skin, reminding her of a sequined costume she'd once worn at a dance recital. She was ecstatic that Nox loved the sea as much as she did and looked forward to checking out the Delician beaches with him. He had promised when they returned to the lab to show her the different types of boats the Delicians used.

Looking out across the water, Emeline watched the sun twinkle on the waves like a blanket made of sparkling stars. Laughing to herself over the word "stars"—life sure had changed over the last few months. Who would have thought aliens would have found Earth and that she would have found the love of her life—her bondmate? Definitely not her.

A strong arm reached around, brushing against the ties to her bikini bottoms to settle in that spot just below her belly button. "I want you, Pulmina," he murmured into her ear as his other arm fell across her breasts, pulling her against his hard chest.

His cold body pressed tight against her hot skin startled

her briefly. It didn't take long for his body to heat up, matching hers. She knew what was coming and her body shuddered in anticipation. Nox, her bondmate, her lover, her husband—he could reduce her to a quivering mass of emotional goo just with a gentle touch or quick glance from his spectacular eyes.

Leaning back, she nestled her head under his chin. She could smell the sea on him...feel the heat from the sun coming off his body. She pushed her hips against his, wiggling her bottom against his groin. When he groaned, she smiled, knowing she had gotten the desired effect she was going for.

Turning her head slightly, she pressed her lips against his sun-kissed skin. Her tongue snaked out, tasting the salt on his skin. A giggle escaped her mouth.

"What's so funny?"

"I was just thinking how a substance as common as salt could have caused so much chaos."

Purring into his neck, her tongue slowly caressed his damp skin as she considered her next words. "Without any warning, life can change so quickly from one moment to the next. One minute you're going along and you think you know where your life is headed and then whoomph! Aliens are attacking your home, trying to take away your liberties and your way of life." Not to mention, she mused, that you could also find the one person in, well, in the entire universe that you had been searching for.

"Aliens attacking, huh? I'll show you how this alien likes to attack." Nox grabbed her waist, turning her quickly as he brought her flush against him. She smelled of sunscreen and the sea. His nose nuzzled into that sweet spot where her neck and shoulders met that was just begging him to taste. His wet tongue drew circles against her soft skin, eliciting a soft moan from his lovely wife. The sound of her arousal pushed his desire for her to another level.

Her nipples pebbled hard through her bikini top as she

rubbed them against his chest. His hand roamed up and down her body as she became restless in his embrace.

Nox didn't know the reason why he had gotten lucky enough to find his bondmate, but he wasn't about to question it. She was his. This sexy, beautiful, kind, intelligent woman from Earth was his forever.

He couldn't help noticing how her skin had started to take on the same colors as his own...wondering if she had noticed the different changes her body was beginning to show.

"I need you," he whispered, his voice husky with desire.

Hearing his words laced with want, Emeline felt her body respond, her own need matching his. She felt him hard against her belly, sending sparks of delight through her.

Pulling away, she grabbed his hand, her voice full of passion as she urged him along the dunes towards the house they were staying in. "Maybe we should take this inside." The house was owned by NASA. Leslie had been more than happy to help in finding a secluded place for them to have their honeymoon.

All of a sudden, Emeline found herself swept up into strong arms. "What are you doing?" she squeaked.

"I can't wait any longer. I need you—now."

He lowered her gently to the sand, not caring where they were. Pushing her legs apart, Nox settled himself between her thighs. He could feel the heat rolling off of them as he pressed himself against her hot, wet core...pushing his hips against hers, trying to get as close as he could. Their passion burned as hot as the sun beating down on his back. He knew she would be ready for him—her need equaled his own, but he didn't want to rush. *Breathe, Center, Focus,* he chuckled to himself.

Emeline gazed at him with a mixture of lust and confusion. "Do you find something funny at this particular moment?" she huffed, her breath blowing at some of her hair that had fallen against her face. It had not gone unnoticed the lavender highlights that now blended softly throughout her blond hair.

Looking down, Nox's eyes skimmed lovingly over her face—her eyes dark with desire, her breathing came in pants as he whispered across her skin, "No, my beautiful girl. I'm trying to slow down so I don't disgrace myself in the sand before you find your pleasure. I was trying out your mother's calming technique."

"Babe, I love that you are using her technique, but can we leave my mother out of this right now?" Growling her impatience, she cried out, "I don't want slow."

Reaching down, undoing the ties on her bikini bottoms, she lifted her butt, pulling them out from under her, then flung them off to the side.

Her focus solely on Nox, she brought her hand around to the front of his bathing suit, releasing him into her hand. "This is what I want." Emeline loved the feel of him—hard and smooth all at the same time. She could feel herself spiraling out of control the more she touched him.

Nox's concentration wavered as she stroked and caressed along his length. "This is going to be over before it starts if you don't stop that," he gasped, his hunger beginning to overtake him.

Entwining their fingers, he entered her in one swift motion. Always aware of her feelings, he stopped briefly, thinking to allow her time to adjust to his entry, but his Pulmina wasn't having any of that. *No, not my passionate bondmate.* She squeezed him, trapping him in her tight grasp.

They moved together as one as they found themselves soaring high above the clouds, their love propelling them faster and faster until that deep moment when they reached the apex of their peak at the same time. The energy swirl of their bond wrapped tightly, binding them together.

Floating back to reality, Nox kissed each of her eyes, her

eyelashes and brows, rubbing his nose along the side of hers...gently kissing her lips. His own body still hummed from his release. He could feel her soft hands trailing up and down his back, lovingly caressing him. Again, he wondered how he had gotten so lucky.

As Emeline's brain slowly emerged from its euphoric haze she and Nox had just shared, she became aware of the gritty sand lodged in places it was not meant to be in.

Slowly pushing on his chest, she moved away to lie at his side. She felt his lips blowing flecks of sand that had embedded themselves all along her skin. Her body began shivering again, amazed that just the caress of his breath against her skin could cause her hunger for him to ignite all over again.

Deciding it was time to take this party in for a long hot shower, Emeline rolled over, looking for her bikini. She had a special meal planned for him and it wasn't going to cook itself. She was looking forward to having Nox try some of the regional seafood this area was famous for.

Rising in one movement, she leaned down, tugging on his hand. "Come with me, my sexy alien. It's shower time." She winked at him as she turned to run up the path towards the house.

Now that Belle had agreed that their mother going to Delicia was a good thing, Emeline looked forward to the future. It would be fun exploring the universe with her mother.

And since General Tarek had ordered a fleet of Delician ships to patrol Earth's solar system in the event the Hexians or any other species tried to contact Earth, Emeline felt comfortable leaving Earth for the foreseeable future.

Heather would be holding down the fort here on Earth while they were all away. They would miss each other terribly, but had scheduled pot luck dinners at least once a month. Lifelong friendships such as theirs would always endure separations.

Using his long legs to shorten the distance between them, Nox leaned over and scooped her up in his strong arms as he continued to run towards a much-anticipated shower.

Emeline giggled happily rubbing her cheek against his. "I love you," she whispered against his lips as she brushed hers against his. Their breaths mimicked the way her soul felt to his...connected as one. Her life had been altered in such a way that she never thought possible, but then again, wasn't life supposed to be challenging, to make you feel alive? Now with her bondmate by her side and new opportunities that were opening up to her, there was no telling what the next chapter would bring.

As they came through the door, Emeline jumped down, hurrying towards the bedroom, yelling over her shoulder, "I'll get the shower going. I've got sand in places it shouldn't be." She winked at Nox, her face alight with laughter.

"I'll be right there. I'll be more than happy to help with any sand removal." He sent her a playful leer as he grabbed his comm off the table.

Emeline had no sooner gotten the water turned on when she heard Nox calling her name. "In here, babe." Seeing the look on his face, Emeline felt her stomach drop. "Oh god, Nox, what's happened." Fear raced across her face as she held her breath waiting for his answer.

"Ami is missing."

To be continued...

ACKNOWLEDGEMENT

There were so many people who supported me throughout this process of creating this exciting story.

My oldest daughter, Jillian, for her guidance, honesty and website building skills. You helped me to become a better writer. My patient and supportive husband, David, who at the very beginning of my process gave me a crucial piece of advice: It's your story. You can make your worlds be anything you want them to be. I don't think he realized what he had unleashed. My son-in-law, Stephen, your genre knowledge was key in helping with some of the finer points of my story. Joe, you are by far the smartest man I know. Thank you for letting me pick your brain on so many subjects. Kelly, my jeweler, your influence made this story better. Phill and Patti, my beta readers/daily brainstorming confidants, you are a constant source of motivation for me. Sharron, your insights were spot on and much appreciated. My youngest daughter, Eden, thank you for being my inspiration, daily sounding board and social media consultant.

Carolina De Los Santos, Calladia Design - your talent and imagination speak volumes. You brought to life the image that had been floating around in my head. Thank you for creating such an amazing cover.

My friends and family - encouragement promotes growth and inspires you to reach for the stars. I am blessed to have you all in my life.

CAST OF CHARACTERS

Humans

Emeline Cameron - Scientist, bondmate to Nox
Liam Cameron - Astronaut, brother to Emeline
Fiona Cameron - Mother to the three Cameron siblings
Isabelle Cameron - writer/actress sister to Emeline and Liam
Hank Cameron - deceased husband and father
Ami Jefferson - aerospace engineer, friend and colleague to the Camerons
Lorelei Windwalker - astrophysicist, friend and colleague to the Camerons
Heather Garcia - computer whiz, friend and colleague to the Camerons
Leslie Merriman - Head of NASA
Gregory Jenkins - President of the United States
Ivan Orlov - Russian UN Security Council member
Claude Lanoue - French UN Security Council member
Margaret Mower - UK UN Security Council member
Neha Dewan - Pakistan UN Security Council member
Ming Zhu - Chinese UN Security Council member

Aliens

Delicians

Nox - Scientist, Director of Scientific Development for the
Sandovar (Sando-var) - Senator, father to Nox
Elara (E-lara) - Scientist, mother to Nox, wife to Sandovar
Loris (Lor-is) - Scientist, assistant to Nox
General Tarek (Tar-ek) - Commander of the Delician mili-

tary and special liaison to the UAP

Jagger (Jag-er) - Captain of the Maelstrom

Nyx (Nye-X)- Commander of Tarek's elite solders/pilot

Ezio (Ez-e-o) – Pilot/elite specialist

Ramola (Ram-o-la) – Elite demolition and retrieval

Karola (Car-o-la) - chief weapons officer

Yilmaz (Yil-maz) - security chief for the Maelstrom

Marsel (Mar-cell) – chief science officer

Farzie (Far-zie) - communications officer

Paulo (Pau-lo) - chief engineering officer

Wayra (Way-ra) - navigation officer

Dr. Datrem (Day-trem) - chief medical officer

Dr. Senta (Sen-ta) - medical officer

Tulio (Tul-e-o) - medic

Violia (V-ol-e-a) - medic

Etha (E-tha) Violia's grandmother

Lilith (Lil-ith) Dr. Datrem's granddaughter

Hexians

Tarquin (Tar-quin) AKA Quin - leader of Hexia

Hagen (Hag-en) - second in command to Tarquin

ABOUT THE AUTHOR

N. W. Couillard

Growing up the middle child of seven in a military house-hold, NW would create stories as a way to entertain herself on long car rides. With five brothers, action adventures and science fiction were usually front and center. After obtaining a BS in computer science and traveling the world, NW settled down in New England with her husband and children. When she's not writing, you can find her in the kitchen creating new recipes or with her face in her Kindle.

Visit her website at: nwcouillard.com

Made in United States
Orlando, FL
16 April 2022

16907004R00420